Whisper of Iron Omnibus

Books 1-3

Matt Pivots

ROYAL GUARD

Whisper of Iron

A LitRPG Crafting Fantasy

Prologue

In the sprawling city of Fulgar, nestled in a verdant valley beneath towering mountains, Pomius watched as the sky lit up with bursts of lightning. He had seen many storms in his long life, but this one differed. The air crackled with energy, and he could feel the magic coursing through his veins.

Pomius was a human, one of the inhabitants of the planet of Prixa. He had lived in Fulgar his whole life and had seen many strange and wondrous things in that time. But lately, things had taken a dark turn.

For generations, the humans of Fulgar had coexisted peacefully with the Feka, a race of cat warriors who wielded creation magic as effortlessly as they did their weapons. But long ago, a massive battle had broken out between the Shadowalkers, monstrous werewolves and vicious canine creatures who lurked in the shadows in a faraway city, and the Feka and the humans had fled like cowards.

An agreement had come into place between the humans and Feka to keep the humans with magic a secret and guard the pass leading to their hidden city. Now, only a handful of Feka knew of the city's existence. The old warriors were gone, and the magical humans were forgotten except by a small batch of the highest-ranking felines. Non-magical humans were traded and bred as tribute to be owned by the Feka. The Feka were fierce, proud, and loyal. Pomius had always respected them. But now, tensions were running high.

The Shadowalkers hadn't forgotten. The alpha had lived through surprisingly many seasons and had vengeance in his evil heart. Rumors had been circulating for weeks that a newly united band of Shadowalker packs had emerged and were planning an attack on the Feka again. The Feka, it was said, could not survive an all-out attack from the monsters, and the Shadowalkers would launch a full-scale assault on Fulgar after their destruction of the capital Fekan city of Fayport. He wasn't sure if that was true, but there was too much to lose not to take the reports seriously, especially when they came from a feline with farsight powers.

The humans of Fulgar were not defenseless, of course. They had their magic, most notably, the power to wield fire and lightning with deadly precision against their enemies. But even with their formidable abilities, they knew they were no match for the combined forces of the Shadowalkers' many packs. There were just not enough mages and too many canine monsters.

That was why they had hatched a plan to save their city.

Pomius had been present at the council meeting when the plan had been proposed. A group of humans, led by a man named Marcus, had devised a daring idea: they would teleport someone from another planet to help them in their fight. Someone who could create, like the days of old. Someone who could add more magic to the world.

The old wizards had searched for many days and nights, scouring world after world. With their lightning powers, they could flash in and out of faraway atmospheres and gain vision of the world, searching for large quantities of mana within individuals. This was time-consuming, of course, and drained tons of mana. But it was the price that was demanded.

The man they had chosen was a young wizard named Noah, who hailed from a planet called Earth. According to Marcus, Noah could become one of the most powerful wizards in the universe and would be able to turn the tide of the battle in their favor. He had the perfect mixture of skills to create mighty mage armies and turn Prixa into a human powerhouse.

Pomius had been skeptical at first. Teleportation was risky, not to mention extremely costly. Space magic was the third element after air and fire, and extremely rare among mages. It would take all six teleportation mages almost three seasons to recover from such an event. And the idea of bringing a stranger to their world to fight their battles seemed foolhardy at best. But the more he thought about it, the more it made sense. They had nothing to lose and everything to gain. When he arrived, they would finalize their plans.

As the storm raged overhead, Pomius watched as the humans of Fulgar made their final preparations. They gathered in the town square in front of the scryer and waited for the moment when the Earthling would arrive.

Pomius didn't know what the future held, but he knew one thing for sure: the fate of their world hung in the balance, and only time would tell if they had made the right choice.

Chapter 1

Blacksmith Apprentice

I LIFTED MY HEADSET MIC AND YELLED DOWNSTAIRS, pausing my game. "Mom! Can I get some hot pockets for lunch?" I brushed the crumbs of Doritos off my chest and took another pull of my Mountain Dew.

No response. "Mom!" I yelled louder, standing up from my leather gaming chair with a *creak*. I pursed my lips, confused. To my left, my cat Dingo stared up at me. "What do you want, you fat cat?" I asked, shooing him away.

I walked down the hall and into the living room to find the TV on with Judge Judy telling a teenage girl that she owed a man custody of her child. I shook my head, chuckling. To my right, my mom was fast asleep on the couch. I walked over to the bin full of blankets and pulled one out, slipping it over my mother. She was probably just exhausted from her night shift at the hospital, and I didn't want to wake her.

I opened the freezer, popped two hot pockets into the microwave, and grabbed another drink. After the three or so minutes were up, I took them out and returned quietly to my room.

My cat had relocated to my window, meowing at the pigeons outside my Brooklyn apartment. The window was open, and a soft spring breeze filtered through the room. Our apartment didn't have reliable air conditioning, so summer was brutal in the city. For now, the air was pleasant, although it smelled like curry sauce from the open window across the alley.

The neighbor's pit bull saw the cat at the open window and began jumping at the window, going nuts. I hated that damn dog. Sometimes I would shoot at him with my slingshot when I didn't have much to do. I never tried to hit him, but the sound of the slingshot ammo hitting the brick usually shut him up for a few minutes. But I had run out of pellets long ago and needed to restock them.

It was a boring Sunday. My friends were out on spring break over the last week on their fancy family vacations. My mom didn't have much money, so my spring break was lots of time in the house while she worked her two jobs. I didn't have much to do, since my homework was already completed and projects were done. Video games were the only thing challenging enough to keep my interest most days while I waited for school to start again.

My various engineering projects were scattered around my bedroom: a catapult, two castles, and a bridge made of popsicle sticks. I was only sixteen but took advanced classes at the local community college.

I sat back down in my chair. Suddenly, there was a voice in my headset. It sounded like a computer-generated voice, like Alexa or Siri.

[YOU HAVE BEEN CHOSEN BY THE ASTRAL MAGE ON THE WORLD DESIGNATED AS PRIXA. PREPARE FOR DEPARTURE]

I looked down at the cat. "Did you hear that?" I asked him. He cocked his head at me, then jumped into my lap. I stroked him as I swiveled in my chair to get another look at the computer screen. Oddly enough, my game was still paused. *Huh.*

Then the voice spiked again.

[DEPARTING IN 3...2...1...]

I blinked awake on my back, the warm sun shining on my face. The grass was wet, and there was a horrible smell surrounding me. It was so bad that my eyes started watering. I groaned, rotated my head to the left, and saw the source of the smell: an exploded creature was all over me. Black blood and guts enveloped me in a semicircle like I was part of a satanic ritual without my knowledge. I was lying in a puddle, a few innards on my t-shirt, and my pants and shoes were soaked.

I cried out in a shrill voice and stood up quickly. My right foot slipped in the blood, hitting my head back on the ground with a loud *smack*. I let out an *oof*, the air leaving my lungs momentarily. *Please tell me that isn't Dingo around me.* My heart raced, and I felt the urge to vomit. I rolled to the side to puke but realized more gore was on this side. I gagged.

I closed my eyes tightly, unsure if this was real. Was I injured too? Nothing hurt that I could tell, but maybe I was in shock. I'd heard stories about people with metal rods in their backs after a car crash that didn't feel them because of shock from an accident. My hands ran over my disgusting clothes, moving pieces of animal out of the way as I searched for injuries.

Suddenly, the same voice was in my head. The female one from my headset.

[WELCOME TO PRIXA. WE HOPE YOU ENJOYED YOUR TRAVEL THROUGH THE OUTER PLANES. WE HAVE COMPLETED OUR INITIAL SCAN AND WILL BEGIN THE CLASS ASSIGNMENT PROCESS. PLEASE WAIT]

I pushed myself up again, careful not to slip on the muddy ground this time. "Umm, hello?" I said out loud, shaking my hands and getting more goo off. I had never seen a dead animal before, especially one this...nasty.

My eyes darted around my new environment as I dropped to a defensive crouch. Giant trees were densely populated with chattering birds amid a landscape dotted by colorful bushes and fragrant flowers. The atmosphere reeked of dampness as if it had just rained, and man, was it hot.

To my left, a giant vulture looked up at me with its beady eyes, standing in the dead animal gore with a piece of animal leg sticking out of its huge beak. I put my hands up and took a few steps back. I stumbled into a plant with bright purple blossoms as it started creeping up my leg. I quickly swatted the vines away, and the plant hissed while receding. The vulture also hissed, then returned to its meal with the crunch of bones.

Insects chirped, and camouflaged creatures rustled the leaves in the canopy. The soil beneath me was black with streaks of red. Spiders slid on silky strands from trees to elaborate webs they wove in the undergrowth, sometimes spanning seven feet across. They had brightly colored rear sections and looked super poisonous. Everything seemed to be observing me. I sniffed the murky air rising from the ground. It was vile smelling.

I stood as still as possible, trying not to gain any attention from the jungle creatures that were likely in the area. I couldn't remember how I got here or what the voice said. What was an outer plane? The last thing I remembered was being in my room, then blinking awake; there were no memories in between. Sweat was poured down my back; the folds of my overweight stomach were drenched. Dark stains appeared beneath my arms.

The voice spoke again, freaking me out. *Was this some telepathic creature communicating with me?*

[IT HAS BEEN DETERMINED THAT YOU POSSESS THE ABILITY TO USE MAGIC IN OUR WORLD. A

NEW CLASS WAS ASSIGNED. YOUR HIGHEST
ATTRIBUTE IS *INTELLIGENCE*, AND YOU WERE
AWARDED THE **BLACKSMITH APPRENTICE***
CLASS. YOU HAVE STARTED AT LEVEL 1. ALL
ATTRIBUTES HAVE BEEN ADJUSTED
ACCORDINGLY.]

Class? Magic? What in the world is going on? Why do I feel like I'm in a video game? Is this a dream? It all felt so real. I couldn't remember signing up for any VR experiments. I didn't even own any hardware that could do VR.

The high intelligence sounded right if this was a game or a dream. *But a support class? Really?* I certainly wasn't going to get a strength-based class, but a non-combat class didn't seem very threatening. I had always been the most intelligent guy in the room, almost to a fault. Other students in my class hated how little I needed to study to pass a test or how creative my projects came out. I could make anything to solve any problem. My future was to work for some corporate giant and patent my way to glory.

A burning startled me. I jerked my arm back, then looked down at it. Tattoos dotted my skin with various symbols and numbers. A red 15 and a blue 10 were visible.

[PLEASE CHOOSE YOUR NAME AND OUTFIT]

I looked down at the options. Three clothing items appeared from thin air and landed on the ground before me. *Prixa must have studied the history of humans,* I thought, as I explored my options: a toga, a loin cloth, or overalls. "I will choose the overalls. My name is Noah." My voice was shaky, the stress of the situation showing itself. At least I would be able to get out of these blood-soaked clothes.

My arm changed, reading 'Noah' at the top of the tattoo. The readout looked like a simpler version of a character sheet. *So red was health, and blue was mana? Was this world again tapping into my experiences?* I examined my tattoos more closely. There wasn't much information.

[NOAH]
[LV 1 - BLACKSMITH APPRENTICE]
[HEALTH 15]
[MANA 10]

I stripped down to my boxers and donned the overalls - simple brown pants, suspenders, and no shirt. *A shirt would have been nice. I wonder why I didn't get one.* I kept one eye on the vulture creature as I changed. The overalls looked ridiculous on my enormous frame, almost like I was a coal miner or something. I looked around for socks but didn't see any. That was a bummer since my feet were drenched in blood like the rest of my clothes were. I sighed and slipped the new boots from the mysterious entity onto my feet, which fit perfectly.

I took a deep breath. *What do I do now?* I needed a plan. *I was a blacksmith. Blacksmiths can make weapons and armor.* I looked around; the jungle was dense and suffocating around me. *Maybe this was some kind of puzzle game.*

I picked up a moss-covered rock but dropped it, unsure what to do with it. To my left was a half-dead log. I swung it around a few times, but it weighed a ton and wouldn't work as a weapon. I didn't get any prompts, and nothing magical seemed to happen. A huge insect ran out of the end of the log near my hand, and I threw it, recoiling and shrieking embarrassingly. A few birds flew out of the canopy at the sound.

I heard a screeching *hiss* sound and looked up. Three more giant vulture-looking birds had gathered on the tree branches, similar to the one on the forest floor ten feet away. They had the same enormous beaks and dark feathers, their heads tilting at me in unison.

A calm seemed to develop in the jungle, like before a golfer took his shot. They looked at each other and with a louder *hissss*, one dove at me.

I threw my arms above my head and tried to protect myself from the crazed bird. Talons flashed and gouged my forearm, the gash burning horribly. Blood exploded onto my cheek in a quick spurt, but the bird didn't let go. I was shocked at the deep cut as its claw sliced through the muscle. My left hand went limp. "Ah! Bastard!" I yelled, punching the bird with my other hand.

I turned from the gore and sprinted away, the bird still attached to my arm. Its talons were stuck in the sinew of my forearm. It continued shrieking, wings pounding me in the face. Suddenly, I tripped on a fallen log, landing on top of the crazed bird. I felt a *crunch* as its head gave way under my weight, and it went still.

I rolled over, looking at the creature. It was even more terrifying up close, even flattened. I took my right hand, which was shaking violently, and carefully removed the talons, then set the giant bird on the jungle floor.

Damn it! What do I do? I glanced frantically around me, seeing if there was anything I could use to defend myself. Seconds later, the blood and guts had disappeared from the bird's remains. All that was left was red-stained grass and a three-inch-long talon. There was no trace of anything else, almost like the forest floor had eaten the remains. I grabbed the talon and stood back up, another bird flapping its wings and soaring toward me through the trees. I dove to the side just in time for the vulture creature to miss me by an inch.

Suddenly, it was as if the talon in my hand *wanted* to turn into a dagger in my mind. I focused on letting it choose its shape, a feeling in the back of my mind leading the process. A few seconds later, I held a six-inch long white dagger. *How did I do that?* There was a sucking feeling coming from my arm, like someone was taking blood.

The giant vulture had retreated to the tree, and the last one swooped down at me. The jungle sounds were back again as if the creatures of this place were watching in anticipation. I swung at the bird and missed, only for the creature to leave another long, bloody gouge down my other arm, my right hand going numb now. I tucked the dagger in my pocket, turned, and finally took off running, batting plants out of the way with my non-working fingers. Another *hiss* and a bird swooped at my back, leaving another long, brutal cut. The gashes burned terribly, and I arched backward, screaming in pain. Blood exploded down my shirtless back, joining the sweat to moisten my skin further. I screamed again and ran faster, trying to leave the birds behind me.

Just ahead was a dense thicket of intertwining branches. I continued sprinting, my huge frame lumbering down the path and new boots pounding in the black dirt. I kept my eye on the winding path leading into the enormous trees and ignored the sound of fluttering wings. I stumbled on a fallen log, frantically maintaining my balance. I kept going, branches and leaves whipping my face. My left eye started watering after a stick made contact, blurring my vision considerably.

When I arrived at the jungle opening on the other side of the dense vegetation, I stopped, panting and wheezing with my hands on my head, desperately trying to regain my breath and ignore the pain. I quickly turned around to see if anything was still following me, but for now, nothing did. Blood was pouring out of my bird wounds in gushing pulses. There was a black tinge to it, which didn't seem good. I let out a meek cry, pain wracking my body.

I wiped the tears from my injured eye, but the dirt from my hands made things worse. *What the hell were those things? I was a 6-foot tall, 235-pound teenager with a long, scraggly beard and short curly hair...not some action hero.*

The pain was excruciating. Those two monster birds proved I was no hero. I was bloody and possibly dying because I couldn't handle two birds. If I was honest with myself, I looked like I belonged at a tabletop game convention, not running away from giant vulture creatures and using magical powers.

I had to do something about my wounds, but only if they weren't hunting me still, I thought desperately. One final look showed the birds retreating to their branches. Before they chased me down again, I hid behind a log, trembling and bleeding.

After a few seconds, I peeked above the log as my body screamed in agony, eyes darting around the trees. Three-inch-long ants crawled all over the log, a few walking on my hand as my blood dripped around them. I shook the ants off, afraid of getting bit. Nothing else moved except for my trembling body. The calm jungle sounds returned; the entertainment for the creatures was over for now. I just needed to make sure I didn't die.

Chapter 2

Creation

THERE WAS A SUCKING FEELING COMING FROM MY ARM near the red tattoo. I watched it tick down to [4/15] and stop. My injuries vanished, the skin healing where the bird gouges were. I gasped, amazed at the magic of the tattoo and the relief from the pain. A symbol of an anvil had imprinted itself right below my mana reading, which had decreased to [5/10].

[YOU HAVE UNLOCKED THE *CREATE* SKILL]

I jumped, forgetting a voice would announce things in my head. *Thank goodness, a skill to help me. Maybe this is a video game after all.*

My first twenty minutes in this world had been terrifying. I sat back, resting for a moment with my eyes closed. I felt exhausted. I certainly wasn't used to that kind of activity. Those injuries felt so *real*, even though they were gone now.

Satisfied that I wasn't going to die, I slowly stood up. *What else could I make?* I picked up a random stick on the ground but felt no pull to make anything with it. *Well, it must only work for some things here, then. Since the bird monster had been a living thing, what was left behind could be changed into other items?*

17

I needed to figure out if there was a way home or how to wake up. I didn't want to live in a world where monsters roamed free and I had little chance of survival. This game, if that's what it was, was way too realistic. I had no interest in playing something that resulted in feeling real pain unless the magic and class thing could outweigh it. *I don't know how to quit or get out, so I guess I'll continue for now.*

I dusted myself off, leaves and dirt all over my pants from hiding behind the log. With the abundance of plant life here, there had to be something I could use to craft some basic protection- armor or bracers. *Hell, even a shirt.*

I stumbled through the dense jungle, batting large insects out of my face. I scoured the jungle for materials, looking for anything I could use. If my dagger cost me five mana, and I had five left, I assumed I could create one more thing before I ran out. I began walking around and gently touching various non-poisonous-looking plants around the jungle.

I felt a pull in the back of my mind when I put my hand on some thick, fibrous vines surrounding a thick tree. The *feeling* was the same thing that had led me to craft the dagger, so I trusted the instinct. My eyes followed the tree from the base to the canopy as I found a spot to cut some vines off. The plant was around four inches thick, and I doubted my little dagger could cut through it.

My lips pursed in thought, unsure how to proceed. I knew I needed this material and wanted to move fast in case something attacked me out here. Out of options, I tried my dagger on the vine.

I made sawing motions back and forth but made very little progress. Sweat dripped down my face from the effort. A new idea struck me. I ran over to a moss-covered rock, grabbed it in my right hand, then returned to the tree. I placed the dagger on the vine and began hitting it with the rock.

It took a few hits, but I eventually sliced the vine. As soon as it cut through, the vine snapped around the tree, slapping me right in the shoulder. I yelled in pain, an angry welt forming like an experienced cowboy had just whipped me. A moment later, another sucking feeling from my arm, and my red tattoo took care of it, taking the pain away. My arm read HEALTH [3/15] now. *Crap, I can't keep getting hurt!* I dreaded what would happen when it reached zero. I didn't know the rules of this place, but if it was real, I certainly couldn't risk dying.

I gathered the vine that lay on the floor. Next, I looked for thick leaves to use as the padding. At this point, I didn't dare try my luck with hunting an animal for a pelt. Plus, I was unsure what lived in the jungle with me. If a couple of birds could take me down, then actual forest predators were probably much worse.

I spotted a plant that resembled a bird of paradise from Earth about 30 feet away and walked over to it. My crafting sense told me that this would work. I plucked a leaf and jumped back, pretty scarred from injury at this point. Nothing happened. My eyes continued darting around the area, looking for a threat. Satisfied that nothing would jump out of the bush and kill me, I gathered a few more leaves.

As soon as I held my third leaf, my crafting sense blared in my mind, telling me I held something that could be combined together. I held my breath, thinking about combining the items, and after a brief shock to my arm around the blue tattoo, a green vest appeared in my hand.

My eyes widened at the sight. *Holy crap. This is so cool. Maybe I can deal with the pain for this!* I donned the vest, sliding it over my head. There was even a little vine-colored strap at the sides. With my armor complete, at least for now, I set off down an animal path toward that clearing that I had seen earlier.

My main goal was to get out of this damn jungle before something else attacked me. I cautiously walked through the opening in the trees and into the clearing. I stopped in my tracks, gasping at what I saw.

The planet had three moons, one of which was massive. Two were smaller and pea-sized in the star-dotted sky. I hadn't been able to see them while I was in the jungle, but I could view them now with the canopy cleared around the settlement before me.

A dirt path led through the clearing with thirty-foot-tall drooping trees everywhere in a valley below me. Between the trees were farms of red plants growing about 15 feet high. And in the fields were humans working. They looked filthy and tired with long, sad faces. It smelled like manure here. Or more like a wet stink like we were in a swamp.

The humans were silent, working to the sounds of diggings and picking vegetables off the enormous stalks. The same black dirt from the jungle made up the farmland, tilled into rows similarly to how it was done on Earth. To the right, a few humans used a giant saw to cut a branch off a big tree, littering the ground with sawdust.

Behind the farms were tall, vine-covered walls made of a blackish stone, with turrets and towers peeking above the greenery. The defenses didn't look like they were in very good condition. I saw two large, muscular cat humanoids guarding the gates, visible through the path leading to the city. They stood about six feet tall and resembled white tigers with stripes crisscrossing their shaggy fur and had leather armor on their chest and legs with curved sabers hanging from their belts. Their facial expressions seemed to denote a high level of intelligence.

Rising above the thick wall was a colossal, circular, wooden tower with three levels holding the buildings, homes, and streets of the town's center. It reminded me of an intricate cat tower. I had no idea how it supported itself; the physics of the building beyond what I imagined was possible.

Suddenly, another feline creature, this time resembling a snow leopard, walked out of the rows of corn plants and stopped when it saw me. On its face and arms were spots instead of stripes. He wore similar armor as the guards. Protecting the creature's chest was gleaming silver armor. He made eye contact with me and scowled.

Chapter 3

The Feline City of Dunbar

"HUMAN! WHY ARE YOU NOT WORKING? GET BACK TO work before we have to get the farm manager! And where is your shirt? What's that you're wearing?" the large cat yelled at me. I looked wildly at the other human faces, but they all looked down away from my gaze, shuffling uncomfortably. The other humans wore similar overalls to mine, some choosing the toga style and the rest selecting the overalls. No one chose the loin cloth. *Damn voice.* I would have looked like an idiot if I had picked a loin cloth. The workers all wore grey shirts with a pitchfork symbol.

"I...sorry, I..." I stammered.

A boy looked around and made eye contact with me, then ran toward us when the cat humanoid yelled. He looked to be about 15 years old. He had tan skin and wore simple pants and a black shirt, the logo matching the one on my arm. "There you are! Sorry, sir, he is coming back from ingredient duty. He replaced our fallen adventurer for Romas" He winked at me behind the cat's back. *What in the world?*

"Uh, right. Ingredients." I said, playing along. If this world had humans as slaves, that would make the game even more challenging to advance.

"The vest he's wearing was from Romas to keep him from getting eaten in the jungle. It's the lowest level armor he had," the boy continued. *Damn, this kid is good.*

"Alright." the cat said, looking down at me with a scowl. "Take your findings to the smithy then. Can't have you sitting around staring off into space, now can I? Romas will have my head."

I looked at the boy, who came over and grabbed my hand, pulling me along before I could object. *This can't be happening.* I didn't know who this Romas was, but I hoped the situation would be better than it was in the farmland. These people looked miserable.

I need to get stronger. That's how it worked in the video games I played. The hero always goes through a long journey, finds the wizard responsible for the predicament in which he or she found themselves, and demands the issue fixed. But with my support class, the chances of that seemed slim. This still didn't appear to be a dream; everything felt real. *Well, let's see where this boy takes me.*

"Thank you, sir. We will be going now," the boy replied to the giant cat. We hurried back down the path through the farms, up through the gate, past the guards, and into the settlement.

"Keep your head down and follow me. Don't stop or talk to anyone. If we're stopped, then follow my lead. Try to stay focused!" the boy whispered, then scurried ahead, dodging through the busy cat-filled streets.

We were on the base level of the settlement and below the cat tower's first level. The streets were narrow and winding inside the gate, lined with shops and cafes decorated with cat-themed murals and sculptures. The buildings were constructed with an eye for detail, with arched doorways, ornate balconies, and intricate carvings adorning every surface.

I couldn't help but look above, where a grand palace dominated the first level of the cat tower and the city center, its walls made of smooth stone and decorated with golden cat warrior motifs that I could see from here. Towering spires and domes rose from the roof, and the windows were set with stained glass depictions of heroic cats from what I assumed was the city's history.

As we walked through the dirt streets, I encountered various cat species going about their daily business. Some were lounging on balconies, while others were darting through alleyways, chasing each other in playful games. I even saw what must have been part of the city's ruling council or government. They were a group of majestic-looking lion creatures who got head nods from the other cats as they walked down the street.

Large, fat cats held wares and trinkets at merchant stalls announcing sales to passersby. One even had a plant that resembled catnip. Another was sitting on a platform, moaning a soft meow-like sound to the music that played. I bumped into a tiger while I was looking around. "Hey, watch it, *human!*" He brushed off his outfit like I had left a stain on him.

The boy backtracked toward me and shot me a glare, grabbing my arm and pulling me forward. "Come on!" he hissed and kept us moving.

I smelled bread and baked goods wafting up to my nose as we walked past another stall, realizing how hungry I was after my sprint through the jungle. However, I didn't dare go over and speak to the merchants as I was dragged along.

Bright plant life was everywhere, dotting the sandy walkway. Up ahead, the settlement base was enormous, probably a half-mile in diameter. It was solid, like a tree trunk with a rough exterior. And the way the arms and platforms of the first level of the settlement jutted out above me made it look like a giant tree. The tower was rough and irregular, presumably so cats could grab hold and climb it. I saw all manner of feline species jumping vertically to climb various levels or onto flat transition pieces to change buildings.

To the left of the tower's base, we passed a lined field with a small set of bleachers. A group of kittens surrounded a warrior in the middle of the field. They held sticks and swung them at each other while the lion walked around, nodding his head and instructing the cats on their form. A few older cats lounged in the stands and viewed the activity with disinterest, some licking their paws or snoozing in the sunshine, curled up. Two cats darted out of tunnels or raised platforms and performed sneak attacks on straw dummies.

Cut into the base of the tower was a ramp, seemingly for humans to use to access the main level of the settlement. I followed the boy, passing people as they came and went. Humans carried things like serving trays, objects, and even baby cats. These people wore bright outfits with varying colors and symbols. *Various work types or ownership, maybe?* I thought. Like the farmhands, the humans kept their eyes down and avoided eye contact.

I started getting a pit in my stomach for what was to come. I didn't know this boy or where he was taking me. But I didn't seem to have a better alternative at the moment. *I can't survive on my own in the jungle. Hopefully, this will be a safe place to figure things out.*

I kept a brisk pace to keep up with him as we started up the fifty-foot-long incline, panting again. It appeared that everyone who lived here was in great cardio shape. When we finally reached the top of the ramp, the boy looked back at me with a disappointed look, but he didn't say anything about my subpar endurance. I started wheezing again, the hot jungle air making breathing tough.

From here, the paths were made of a beautiful red-streaked stone resembling granite. There were even more trees up here with various flowers and fruits. Water fountains dotted the level as cats bent over and drank from them during their passing. Seeing 6-foot-tall walking tigers and jaguars drinking like their feline counterparts on Earth was strange for me.

"This is the crafting district of the city," the boy whispered back to me, waiting patiently for me to catch my breath. "The dirt section we just came from below the first level is the lower class

24

section of the city, mainly where the no-classers live. You saw the farm hands, but the dock workers and fishermen live there too."

We kept walking through the stone paver streets, then started making turns down alleys. The alleyways were not as clean as the merchant's square outside, and humans were less frequent back here. Coal fires burned here and there, creating thick grey smoke that rose above the buildings to the next level. Around the next corner, two smaller cats wrestled, growling at each other.

"Wait here," the boy said as he ducked into a dimly lit building. I looked into the building's main window. It looked like a warehouse mixed with a pawn shop. Various weapons hung from shelves, armor glistened on dummies and racks, and jewelry was displayed in cases upon cases. A smokey smell wafted out of the building, and inside the door was a forge with red glowing ore releasing black fumes through the chimney on the roof.

Suddenly, the boy returned to me, holding his hand in a 'gimme' gesture. I jerked my head back, confused. "What?" I said.

"Your...vest thing. We need to throw it away before Romas sees it. I don't know where you got it, but I don't want him asking any *questions*."

I scoffed, but the boy continued holding his hand out. I shrugged my shoulders and took it off, handing it to him. He placed it on the side of the building, then walked into the shop. I followed behind him, ducking into the doorway.

"Who do we have here, Jasper?" a black panther asked from behind the counter with a sneer. He put down the piece of fur he was holding and got up off his oddly shaped chair.

Chapter 4

The Feka

"GOOD DAY TO YOU, SIR. I'VE FOUND KEPLER'S replacement. He was the best candidate in the bunch. The other humans were not as lively as this one." The boy bowed his head and backed away after he spoke. I raised my eyebrow at him. *At least we don't call them master.*

The seven-foot-tall cat walked closer to us. "The best candidate? Boy, this human is fat and looks out of shape. He's sweating just standing there. How is it possible that he was the best candidate?"

"He..." the boy stammered.

"Ah. Well, come in, come in. No going back now; there's work to do, boy. What do I call you?"

"Noah, sir," I replied, a bit tentatively. The huge panther looked like it could maul me at any moment.

"Fine." the large cat said gruffly. "Begin your cleaning duties immediately. We have our merchant's auction this evening, and many chores are left. The Spring Games are upon us in two more days, and we've been tasked with setting up the courses. Jasper, get this boy a shirt, for moon's sake." Without another word, he left the room, going through a back doorway.

At least this doesn't sound as bad as being a farmhand. I always wanted to be an engineer...maybe I could learn a thing or two here!

The boy hurried to the right toward a group of lockers, opened one, and grabbed a shirt out of it. "Here. Put this on. It's one of my extra shirts until I can have one made for you," Jasper said as he handed me a shirt. It looked a little small. I complied, slipping the tiny shirt over my head. The fit was terrible, showing off my large midsection and belly rolls.

I sighed. "I take it you can make the next one a bit...bigger?"

He laughed. "Yeah, I can tell them to use more material and match the dock worker sizes. I'm Jasper, as you heard. Pleased to meet you. Who the hell are you? And where did you come from?"

"I'm Noah. I am still determining exactly how I got here. A voice told me that I was traveling on some plane, and then they picked a blacksmith class for me, and now I'm here. What class do you have?"

Jasper raised his eyebrows almost comically high. "What do you mean by voice? And a class? I...work for Romas in the smithy? Is that what you mean?"

I stepped back a half pace, then replied slowly. "Wait...doesn't everyone get assigned a class? I figured this was some magical world where people all had magic powers or something."

Jasper looked at me like I was crazy. He grabbed my arm and pulled me to the back of the smithy where it looked like a worker quarter was set up. There were cots set up with a wash basin and toilet, I assumed for worker hygiene needs.

"Only the Feka get classes. And only they get magical ones. Humans don't get magic; we work for the masters. Servers, litter cleaners, farmers, we even raise their kittens for them if the females go to battle another colony. Sometimes the strongest humans get ingredient duty, but that's it." Jasper sighed. "That's

28

what happened to the guy you're replacing. He was really good with a bow and was sent out to hunt squamish squirrels. He never made it back from the jungle."

"Feka?" I asked. "Sorry, I don't really know much about...these parts of the world."

"Wait, so you came from a non-Fekan settlement? I didn't even know there were any!"

"Sure. Let's go with that."

He looked me over, unsure of my response. "Well, that's what the masters are called. It's their race. They get classes of either a dexterity-based skillset or a stealth-based skillset. You can tell which ones have it and how high of a level they are from their fur."

"How?" I replied.

"Well, the Feka that come in for daggers and cloaks usually have stripes. And the ones that fight have the spots. The more spots and stripes, the more kills or levels they have. It's pretty easy to tell," Jasper explained.

"So wait, humans are allowed to use weapons? When? It appears that people are..." I trailed off, not knowing how to finish that sentence. *I should verify my status with the Feka.* "...owned? By the Feka?"

"Yeah, we are. Each business here employs humans. We trade labor for protection, food, and shelter. It's dangerous out in the jungle, and we couldn't possibly fend for ourselves. Most of us are raised in the capital and sent out to the various goods-producing settlements."

I pursed my lips as tons of questions went through my head about how things worked here. *Are we servants? Slaves? Do I have rights working in the smithy? Do I make income? Can I spend money? Are there places for humans to buy stuff, interact, and that sort of thing?*

Jasper saw my facial expression and continued. "Well, there is a competition. Romas mentioned it. The Spring Games. It's mainly for the Feka, but humans compete in shooting competitions and other events. Anyone can join, and the winners get special treatment and special job status at the settlement." Jasper had a dreamy look in his eyes.

That surprised me a bit. *Maybe they allowed humans to participate to keep morale up?* Hope was a powerful weapon for lower class citizens, after all.

"The...Feka, who owns the blacksmith. He didn't have stripes or spots; he was all black. What's that all about?"

Jasper nodded. "He's different. He's a creator. Creators are basically a magic class instead of a warrior class; they make all the items for the Dunbar army to use and even normal, everyday items for the colony. You have to have a high intelligence for that. Romas is super smart."

I pursed my lips in thought. *That seemed to match my class. Did he have skills that I could learn? Could I make weapons like the ones I saw around me? Could he use the weapons or only create them?* I couldn't imagine becoming proficient in twenty different weapon classes. It was like my teacher said, 'If you are a jack of all trades, you are a master of none.'

"And ingredients?" I asked. "What's that mean? Why was I on ingredient duty?"

Jasper eyed me suspiciously. "They really must have sent you in from a super far settlement." He sighed, then mumbled about how I had probably never worked a day in my life. "The ingredients are what remain after a kill, certain plants, or ores from the caves. Romas can use those ingredients to make items. Sometimes you can plant ingredients on farms, like the bow trees or frumen plants at the front of the settlement. Or, Romas hires adventurers to kill things he needs to make better equipment."

That makes sense. So I was right; the talon remained after the vulture creature died. That was called an ingredient.

30

We heard a loud clang in the forge room at the front of the black-smith, followed by growling. "I better get to cleaning. You should too, Noah. Grab a broom from that locker over there, then spray the tables down we set up yesterday and get the dust off. I'll handle the fur cleanup and chairs. Let's meet up tonight after the merchant's auction. I want to hear more about your myste-rious past."

He left the room, leaving me standing there to process the conversation. But a knock sounded on the front door before I got too deep into thought. I heard some inaudible conversation between the smith and whoever it was, then heard the padding of paws approaching me.

"New human," Romas said to me. "You must report with the councilor here to complete your arrival paperwork." He motioned with his paw toward a regal-looking striped lion crea-ture, who looked down at me with interest.

"I didn't realize you would be lowering your standards, Romas. This one is a real *gem*." He turned to the panther and smiled, joking at my expense.

Romas growled in reply. "Yes, my idiot human assistant picked this one from the group of fresh humans from Fayport and the surrounding settlements." They talked about me like I wasn't standing right before them.

The lion laughed. "Well, it's good that the work here isn't very *taxing*. And you had better up your food storage, he looks like he will need twice the feed as the others." He smiled again, turning to me. "Come, boy. Let's get you checked in."

He turned and left the room, my cue to follow him. Stripes criss-crossed all of his exposed fur, which was mostly his arms and legs. It was strange seeing a striped lion. The councilman had jewels and beads adorning his mane, glittering in the sun as we walked toward the main palace structure further into the settlement.

As we walked, I had time to think. *Since arriving here, I landed in a half-eaten creature, got attacked by birds, made a leaf vest considered 'trash,' and became owned by a giant race of feline warriors. And humans apparently couldn't use magic, so there's that. My best bet is to play dumb until I figure this out.*

We left the dingy alley streets behind, walking into a more residential part of town. It was cleaner here, with trees and bushes dotting every viable space. Not all the inhabitants here were seven feet tall or walked on two legs. Smaller cats roamed the streets, almost resembling house cats from Earth. They were twice the size and didn't have spots or stripes. *Non-magic Feka, or children perhaps?*

The whole time we walked, I got stared at. As far as the humans here were concerned, I seemed to be on the larger side, my large frame almost matching my escort's, so I stood out.

I still didn't grab socks and my feet were sweating inside my boots, making a soft squishing sound as I walked. *Hopefully, I won't get a blister.* Mercifully, we arrived at the palace gates. Two white tigers guarding the ornate wooden doors bowed to the cat, allowing us entry.

My eyes widened inside the palace. It was gorgeous. Trees were planted everywhere, with light streaming in from all directions on various stained glass windows. Streams and bridges crisscrossed throughout the main floor, a soft gurgling filling the space. In the middle of the floor sat a manx with a feather pen, scribbling away on parchment.

The councilcat walked up to her, confident and aloof. "I have the last remaining human transported from Fayport. We need to speak with the magistrate immediately so I can close this..."

The cat at the desk looked up and held her paw up. "One moment, Lamas. Be a dear and *shush.*"

What the hell? I thought to myself, chuckling slightly. *This councilcat just got put in his place by the manx.*

He growled in response, hair standing up on his neck. He crossed her paws but stopped talking and waited. *Damn, lady. Nice work.* I applauded her.

Rule number one - always be nice to the secretary.

She finally stopped scribbling and looked up. A moment passed, then she finally spoke. "He will see you now."

Chapter 5

Night Ingredient Duty

THE COUNCILCAT HUFFED AND GRABBED MY ARM. "COME, boy. I have more pressing matters to attend to."

He dragged me back, claws digging slightly into my arm. We ducked around a few trees that formed a pathway, winding around until we reached a door with a half-moon on it. He knocked, then waited. "Yes!" came the response inside the room.

With his paw, the lion opened the door and gave me a 'go inside' motion. I complied, then he shut the door abruptly behind me. *Ok then.*

"Name?" A huge desk sprawled before me made of beautiful black wood. He was a large cat but looked more like a house cat than any other talking Feka I had seen. Striped, but in a way that a tabby cat was striped, not like a tiger. Another water fountain sat in the corner of the room, the sound of water running becoming a staple in here. I peered into the water and saw fish swimming around in there. My eyebrows rose, totally caught off guard so far. A growl from the magistrate snapped me out of my thoughts. "Name!"

"Uh...Noah, sir," I replied quickly.

"Noah...Noah..." He flipped parchment pages, one claw shooting out of his paw and digging into the parchment to turn them easier. "Ah, here you are. Noah. The Monarch herself transferred you, eh? What did you do?" A curious gleam shone in the cat's eye, burning into me.

I had no idea what to say. I didn't know who the monarch was or why she would even take an interest in me. There wasn't even a valid reason that I should be on that page at all, to be honest.

Unless the entity that teleported me here arranged for that. Makes sense that they could do that, and confirms that I was expected to come here. If they were powerful enough to communicate with me telepathically and bring me who knows how far through the universe, they could add my name to a document in an outlying settlement full of cats.

"You agree to the rules of Dunbar and all the consequences of breaking them?"

"...yes?"

"You agree that clan loyalty is above all else. You agree to follow the word of your Fekan employer without question?"

The magistrate sounded like he had given this speech hundreds of times today and barely looked up from his papers as he recited the rules. "Yes."

"You agree that you are prohibited from killing other humans without express permission from a Fekan employer?"

"Sure."

He looked up at that. With a slight frown, he continued. "Finally, you agree that Fekan property is off limits, and you will not steal anything that surrounds you during your work?"

"Yes."

He held out his paw. "Finger, please."

I frowned but held out my hand. He grabbed a quill, similar to the cat at the front of the palace, then pricked my hand. "Ow!" I yelled out. The cat made a face at my outburst but wrote my name in a book, the blood-red name shining in the lamplight.

"Welcome to Dunbar. Report back to Master Romas. Head straight there. Do not dally."

"Yes, sir," I said, turning and leaving this damn place. I closed the door, then walked down the winding tree hallway. My boots crunched on the dirt. Outside in the main hall of the palace, another Fekan worker waited for me. It nodded to me and began walking in front of me, I assumed to take me back to the blacksmith.

As I headed for the main door, I took one last look around the palace. The manx at the main desk looked at me with a toothy feline grin as I passed her. "Stay out of trouble, human. Maybe I'll see you later on."

What the hell was that supposed to mean? "Yes, ma'am."

I broke away from her glare and picked up the pace toward the door.

Sweeping the smithy was oddly calming, giving me time to think and scheme. It was nice to do something so earthlike, even if being a low-class citizen in a new world was a lot to adjust to. I needed to learn more about my skills, class, and this world. *If this is a game, I need to understand how to play before I die. And what would even happen if I die? Is this a permadeath situation? And if this blacksmith cat was some rare creator, did that mean I had a rare class too?* The way Jasper responded to my claims of having magic, I felt pretty special. When I passed the feline creatures in the streets, I noticed many of them with spots and stripes, and if what Jasper said was true, they had access to magic here.

Overall, it was a crazy day with a lot to unpack. *What would happen when I went to sleep? Would the VR pause and put me back in my bedroom?* Outside, another night was already falling.

Either day was very short here, or I didn't notice how much time had passed.

Once I was done wiping all the tables down, I helped Jasper get T-shaped carpeted stands out, apparently where the cats sat during the auction. The chairs also needed fur removed. *I need to create a tool for this,* I thought with a grimace. I wanted to pull Jasper aside to ask him more questions, but Romas kept us busy.

Once I arranged the remaining decor, I sat in the corner near the forge and pulled out the dagger I had made. It was a beautiful, bone-white dagger with a plain handle. I lacked basic combat training, so I had no idea how to use the thing. I had no muscles and was overweight by around 60 pounds. Plus, my hand-eye coordination was horrible.

A sudden roar made me jump out of my skin. "Human!! What did you steal??"

"Romas! Nothing! I...I made this!"

"Here for one day and already causing trouble! I bet you're some kind of criminal from Fayport, like the other vile humans here. You cannot create. Humans are non-magical scum! You were warned of the laws here at Dunbar when you visited the Magistrate!"

"Sir...I..." Terror began rising in my chest, my heart thudding in my throat.

Romas had a terrifying look in his eye. "I don't have time for criminals in my smithy. Your punishment for thievery is night-time ingredient duty. A *creator* like yourself should know how to use a dagger, right? Now out!"

"But sir, I..."

"Out!" he roared, showing his teeth. The black fur on the back of his neck was standing straight up.

I looked for support, but Jasper looked at the ground, avoiding my gaze much like the humans in the fields had. I was probably going to get the poor kid in all kinds of trouble for bringing me in here. I slowly stood up, and with one last look at the angry creature, I opened the door and went out into the night. I barely remembered where to go to get to the ramp.

I walked to the end of the block, sighing deeply. My start in this world was not what I hoped for after being chosen for some form of rare magical class. I had barely been able to use my abilities, had no idea what I could and couldn't do, and didn't know what materials were needed to make things. I was lucky enough to land in a blacksmith, and all I was allowed to do so far was sweep the damn floor. *Unless I was picked up by Jasper on purpose...*

I glanced up, sighing. Only two moons lit the sky; one had gone below the horizon. It was beautiful on this planet, that was certain. The cats of the city walked around the settlement, completely ignoring me. Merchants called out, attracting customers. Food and drink stalls dotted the walkways, smelling fantastic. I was starving.

I turned and looked back toward the smithy to the sound of music. Romas had moved to the front of the smithy building and greeted ritzy-looking cats as they entered. He saw me standing there, growled, and made a 'go away' motion with his paw. I turned and walked further into the settlement, my pulse quickening.

This late, very few humans passed me. It was relatively lively in the settlement, however, with the cat creatures matching the tendencies of Earth ones as nocturnal beasts.

"Hi!"

I jumped and turned around.

"Good to see you again, boy. So you're the newest blacksmith recruit, huh? What happened to Kepler? Let me guess...dead?"

I nodded my head. It was the manx from before. *Was she following me?*

"Father needs to stop killing the humans. I'm not going to let him waste another one. Where are you going this late? It's dangerous for a human to be out at night."

"Wait, Romas is your dad? I was banished on night ingredient duty because he thought I stole this dagger, madam. But I'll die if I go back into the jungle." I took it out and showed her the gleaming white knife. "I didn't steal it, though, and I certainly don't know how to use it. I'm not a very...skilled fighter. Especially in close combat with a knife."

"Of course, you aren't. Look at you." She paused, looking me over. "I can take you. Plump humans like yourself won't make it very far in the jungle. And stop calling me madam when there are no others around. I'm Deehana. People call me Dee. I could use some night ingredients and make sure you don't get killed."

Again with the fat thing. I appraised the cat, able to see her up close now. Deehana looked like a larger version of a lynx, with about 4-5 stripes on her face and pointed ears. Her piercing blue eyes bore into me, a common trait among the Feka. She wore leather armor with no sleeves, tight pants with straps for knives and daggers, and an 8-inch long small sword along her back. Truthfully, she looked terrifying.

"Don't you think your father will be upset if you come?" I asked, trying to avoid being followed around in a jungle by a tiger creature with daggers.

"Oh, he will be just fine. I can do what I want with you. I'm partly your boss, after all!" A menacing gleam crossed her face.

I recoiled by instinct just as Dee started laughing hysterically, which sounded like a high-pitched whiny growl. "Oh, relax, human. Do you want to survive or not? What's your name, anyway?"

"Noah."

"Nice to meet you. You smell different." She sniffed the air, looking at me suspiciously, but didn't say more. "Let me see that dagger again."

She took it into her paw and swung it around a few times in what I could only describe as quick, 'stabby' motions. A couple of swings got closer to my face than I was comfortable with. "And you want me to believe that you made this? It's a nice dagger. I don't see anything special about it; it feels like a dagger. Sure is pretty, though!"

I crossed my arms. "It's not stolen! I made it!"

Dee looked at me for a long time, not saying anything. Finally, she winked at me. "Sure you did. Only one way to find out, I suppose! Come now, keep up, fat human!" She jumped off the side of the tower and onto the ground, almost 30 feet away. I sighed. *Ramp it is, once I make it there.*

Chapter 6

Jungle Escort

I finally caught up with Dee at the bottom of the ramp, where she sat patiently licking her paw. "Took you long enough."

"I can't jump off 30-foot cliffs, Dee."

"Nope. That's why humans will always be no-classers. Let's go!" With that, she crouched and slithered off ahead.

Trees framed an eerie walkway as we left the settlement. The path was lit with flaming torches, ending about 100 feet from the spot I stumbled out from earlier that day. The huge moon provided most of the light, but it was relatively dark out, lights from the settlement behind us glowing softly. Laughter and music wafted over on the slight breeze, and tiny clouds dotted the sky.

Going into a jungle with a talking manx where I was attacked by vulture monsters earlier in the day seemed like a bad idea. But returning to an angry blacksmith owner seemed a worse option, so I walked behind Dee.

My heart was racing as I walked closer to the woods. I kept looking back, thinking of all my options. I couldn't run since I didn't even know where I would go. At least in the settlement, nothing was actively trying to kill me. If I ran away from Dee in the jungle, I was sure some horrible beast would kill me.

Once we got to the jungle opening, I took one last look back and went in, Dee leading the way. The joking vibe had vanished, a business-like demeanor showing in her body.

This is going to suck. Only two steps into the jungle, the darkness became suffocating. I peered into the forest, trying to keep up with Dee. About a half mile into the woods, I tripped on a rock and fell into a bush full of thorns. Looking ahead from the bush, I saw Dee jump effortlessly from branch to branch, zipping around like she was born for this.

"Dee! Wait up. I can't see much."

She looked back, a scowl on her face. "I know you humans have horrible vision in the dark, but at least try and avoid the first rock your big feet stumble upon."

I got up, ripping out a few thorns in the process. She continued. "I might be almost immune to poisons, but you certainly aren't. Please be careful. I don't want to take you back to father as an ingredient. Some of those bushes and thorns are poisonous."

"You're immune to poison? How?" I asked.

"Everyone in my class is as we grow stronger. It helps us navigate terrain like this and not worry about which plants will kill us."

I looked enviously at her. "Yeah, that seems useful for a jungle cat climbing trees. Or, you know, a defenseless human."

She grinned. "Oh, cheer up. You're with me. What could go wrong? Now stay there. I'm going to test the claims that you can create." And with that, she took off up the tree.

As I waited, I looked around the best I could. A few streaks of light came in from the moons, dancing around on the forest floor. Flowers opened when the moon's light hit them, then closed as the light vanished. There was a general sound of insects, but it was pretty quiet. A light rain began to fall, making a soft sound on the leaves above.

Dee had mentioned something about *night ingredients*, whatever those were. On Earth, a different set of creatures roamed the forest between day and night, so maybe that was what she meant. I became slightly more aware of my surroundings, standing there while creatures with night vision most likely stalked me.

I heard some rustling and a *hiss* as Dee struck at one of those vulture things, killing it and bringing a beak down to me. "Ok, *creator*. Let's see what you've got," she said sarcastically as she dropped the bird's beak at my feet.

I picked up the beak. It was red with black streaks and weighed about two pounds. My creation sense began blaring in my mind, letting me know that I held something that I could create with. I looked back, unsure. I wasn't some trained monkey and really didn't feel comfortable using my skills around this creature. "I really don't think I..."

She frowned as I hesitated, growling. "Now," she demanded, her commanding tone surprising me.

I closed my eyes and let the item speak to me as the talon had. I felt it pulling into a hook-shaped dagger, so I let it go, using my 'CREATE' skill again. Suction came from my mana tattoo again, and I looked down at my creation. It was another hook-shaped dagger, about four inches long, wickedly sharp, and gleamed a dark red color.

"Amazing! Let me see that!" I handed it over to her. "Oh wow! That's beautiful! I could use another hooked dagger!" She looked me over again, a gleam in her eyes. "We can't tell anyone about this. You could be super helpful to my father in the smithy. I don't know what the other Feka would do if they found out. The ingredient you would probably drop..." she trailed off, lost in thought.

I looked down at my arm; the red mark, which had slowly refilled throughout the day, had gone down to [12/16] as the wounds and poison were taken care of, and the blue mark was again [5/10]. *That skill costs five mana, then.* And I must have

45

lost a little health from the thorns. Now that I thought about it, my right knee had hurt a bit, and my arms had been bleeding freely from six thorn-sized holes. The damage was repaired now, just like the last time I got injured.

Also, I noted that my health max had increased by one to sixteen. That was a relief, as I could apparently grow my health somehow. Although how, I had no idea.

We sat there, deep in thought, not saying anything for a moment. "Where did you say you were from again?" Dee finally asked.

"I didn't," I replied.

She waited, making a 'go on' motion with her paw.

"Ok. I'm a high school student from a planet called Earth. I was training to be an engineer there." She made a confused face, so I continued. "The same thing as a blacksmith in your world. We make things to solve problems that other humans are having. I was playing a video game and then somehow transported here. I woke up on the ground covered in guts." I omitted the part about the bird attack for fear of her reaction.

"Then I was told I had a class, found a talon on the ground, and transformed it into this dagger, unlocking a skill to create things..."

She cut me off. "Wait, are you marked somehow, like we are?" She looked me over quickly, expecting to see something.

I nodded. "Yeah, I can see my stats on my arm."

She looked but shook her head. "No. Only you must be able to see them, unless you mentally allow them to be seen." She looked back up at me. "We can't tell anyone about this."

"Yeah, I figured that out too. I don't know much more about my markings, though."

"Don't worry, boy. I'll keep you alive. We have to be careful out here. We should probably head back after we grab a few ingredients for my father. But we need to be careful. I don't want to be the reason the first ever blessed human dies."

I turned to start walking back when I heard the bushes rustle in the distance, followed by a long howl. It was picked up by other animals howling; an eerie, bone-chilling sound filling the night air. I turned wide-eyed to Dee.

She looked at me, fear in her eyes. "Uh oh."

Chapter 7

Stalkers

"DAMN, A SHADOWALKER. WHY IS ONE SO CLOSE TO OUR settlement?" she panicked. Her eyes darted around, making a quick escape plan. "Run!"

She took off through the trees, running at a furious pace on all fours toward the settlement. My eyes skimmed the surrounding trees, and then I took off, running behind her as best as possible. To my left, I heard another howl, followed by another closer to the opening in the jungle. As I lumbered through the woods, branches whipped across my face and arms, leaving scratches and gouges. It sounded like there were more of them, howling to each other as they closed in on us.

Dee stopped running toward the opening in the jungle and sprinted back to me. "It's a Stalker pack! We can't make it back quickly enough! We need to find somewhere to hide, or they will surround us!" she hissed in a whisper.

She took off at a 90-degree angle under a branch. I jumped over it, only to be clipped in the forehead by another branch, dazing me momentarily. *I don't need a magical health bar to know it hurts like a bastard*, I thought. Through the foliage up ahead, briefly visible in the moonlight, I got a glimpse at one of the

49

beasts. It looked like a horrifying wolf, with dark brownish-red fur and teeth that were way too big for its body.

The wolf beast growled and stopped Dee in her tracks. Her hand flew to her waist as a dagger appeared in it as she threw a blade at the dog, then spun to the left, running in a new direction. The wolf yelped and fell back, the blade catching it in the shoulder. I took the opportunity to follow her, hearing pursuers all around me. For once I was glad of the heavy foliage and dense trees."This way!" she cried.

Dee went down a hill and ducked into a cave hidden behind some bushes, scurrying out of sight. I slid down the slope, diving into the cave opening. My left knee buckled, feeling like a hammer hit it. I grunted in pain as I rolled farther back into the hole of the cave. "Dee?" It was even darker than the jungle floor, with no visible light.

"Quick! Get under this." She draped a cloak over the two of us.

"What does it..."

"Shhh," she whispered. "It's a scent blocker. Now quiet, or they will hear us."

We waited, fear still gripping us. At the mouth of the cave, I heard panting and the sounds of animals walking around in the brush. Eventually, the sounds began receding. "I think they're gone," Dee said, getting up. "I should be able to hear them if they come back. It looks like we will have to camp here tonight. Come on; there should still be a few good ingredients here."

She started into the cave, leaving me at the entrance still wearing the cape. My health dipped further, to [9/16], as my wounds began closing and my knee bruising lessened. Once my wounds closed, I slowly stood up.

I found the wall to my right and slowly felt my way further into the cave as it opened up into a larger chamber from the small entrance. Dee was so quiet that I could barely hear her walking ahead. My fingers felt the wall turning right, so I followed. Up ahead, a tiny streaming light was coming from a hole in the cave, letting moonlight in.

I tried to think about how a 'scent-blocking cloak' would even be made. I sighed internally, wishing for a moment that I could ask Romas.

"Careful," Dee whispered, sounding closer than I thought she was. "We don't know what lives here." She looked down, scooping up a purple, glowing mushroom and putting it in her pocket.

We passed under the moonlit passage, still on high alert. I could see veins of silver and red in the walls, with a tingling in the back of my mind telling me that these were valuable. "Dee, what are these cave walls made of?"

"Hm? Oh, I don't know. They look like rocks to me. Father goes into caves like these to get ingredients."

Curious. Can I see ore veins through the rock? Is that part of my 'CREATE' skill too?

Dee stopped ahead. "Let's stop here for the night. There's a little light for your human eyes; this way, you won't be so afraid of the dark." A smile crossed her feline features.

"I am not afraid of the dark. Just... what's in the dark. On a planet I've never been to," I replied, weakly attempting to defend myself. "I'm going to look around a bit."

My eyes finally adjusted to the darkness as I headed into a side tunnel. I approached a wall with glowing silver veins near the surface and touched it with my hand. Then it was as though my hand went through jelly.

I pulled my hand back in shock and gasped. "What??" Dee whispered, crouching and looking around rapidly.

"Check this out!" I reached through the rock again.

[YOU HAVE UNLOCKED THE 'MINE' SKILL]

I jumped, the voice in my mind still startling me. My arm burned again, so I rolled up my sleeve and glanced down. I had a new pickaxe symbol below the anvil. I looked over at Dee. "I have a new skill!"

Dee shook her head in amazement. "Humans with magic...this will take some getting used to. What does your skill do?"

"Well," I said slowly. "I guess I can reach into these walls and grab ores. I have no idea what the ore does, though. Should I get some?"

"Of course! What are you waiting for!" she hissed back to me in an excited whisper.

With that, I reached in, thinking about how I wanted to grab the ore I saw. While I did, I felt a sucking coming from my tattoo, mainly the mana reading. I was reaching into the wall at eye height and could see the blue number. It slowly ticked down; 8... 7...

I quickly pulled my hand out with the ore. "The wall is taking my mana!"

Dee laughed and shook her head. "Your skill must be a mana per second usage. It's like when I go stealth. I can go almost invisible for mana per second. But using skills like that limits what you can do after, so it's key to use the skill as quickly as possible. I can't just wait in the wings in stealth while I stalk prey. I need to have already hunted them with other skills."

I thought about that. "How do I level my skills up? I don't have enough mana to do much at all!" I whispered back.

"Use the skills. Practice. The more you use skills and complete what your class wants you to do, the more advanced your level gets. I get experience from stalking and killing prey. Even escaping more serious threats gives me experience. But beating a human over the head with a stick won't get me anywhere."

I laughed. It felt good to laugh. "Ok. So let's mine some ore then!"

I spent about two hours testing my 'MINE' skill while Dee lounged in the cave. I told her to get a cat nap before I started, chuckling to myself. She didn't look as pleased with that one. Eventually, she curled up and fell asleep while I reached into the walls.

I grabbed five pieces of ore from various parts of the cave wall; two silver and three red pieces. I got faster at capturing ore, but the first few times took me a few seconds, wasting valuable mana. It took about an hour to recover five mana, meaning I could make about two mining attempts per hour. In between attempts, I studied the ore, finding out very little other than its appearance. The ore didn't have any pull in my mind to make an object like the talon or beak, which confused me. I also rested, feeling the day's weight and that I hadn't rested since I arrived. At some point, I dozed off for a bit.

The moonlight was much brighter when I woke up; the moon must have been entirely over the cave. Additional light began filtering in from various cracks in the cave walls. My eyes had fully adjusted to the low light conditions of the cave.

I continued my mining experiment while Dee was curled up and slept. Halfway through the fifth time of grabbing ore, my arm burned again, but I didn't jerk away this time. I finished getting the ore out, then looked down at my arm.

[NOAH]
[LV 2- BLACKSMITH APPRENTICE]
[HEALTH 18/21]
[MANA 11/15]

"Dee! I leveled up!" I shouted.

The sound echoed off the walls far into the cave. After the echo stopped, there was a brief silence, followed by an enormous roar. I had become too comfortable in the cave and forgot to whisper.

I looked at Dee. "Oops."

"Run!" Dee took off down the tunnel toward the entrance. I started running, following the cave walls more easily with the additional moonlight. Looking behind me, I saw what I had awoken; an enormous bear creature. Its eyes were bright red and terrifying. It rumbled down the cave toward us, gaining speed.

I ran through the twisting cave back toward the opening. Thankfully we hadn't gone too far into the cavern. The monster seemed happy just scaring us out of its home and receded into the darkness with one final roar.

We reached the front of the cave, panting and looking around. "Sorry about that, Dee. I got a bit excited." We heard another roar deeper inside the cave as the bear returned to its lair, the walls shaking.

In the jungle was another long, eerie howl. The same as before. "Oh, come on!" I groaned. This world was a death trap.

Dee looked at me with a sad expression but looked determined. "They must have heard the Mecho's roar. We can't return to the cave, or they will surround us. We're going to have to fight. I'm going into that tree to make my sneak attack and kill at least one. I have a scent blocker in my belt, so they won't know I'm there. I'm going to have to use you as bait."

"Bait? What!"

"Sorry, human. Once it's down to four Stalkers, I'll try to fight the rest of them. Use your dagger if you can." With that, she darted up the tree.

Well, this is most certainly how I die. I suddenly realized I didn't wake up in my room when I fell asleep. Certainly not promising, and pointing to my stay here as something permanent.

I grabbed my dagger, focusing on it. There was a new pull from the silver ore in my pocket- one I didn't feel before I leveled up. It wanted to *combine* with the dagger. But I could tell I'd need to focus on both pieces at once to combine them. I took one piece of the silver ore in one hand and the dagger in the other, hearing the sound of howls and animals trudging through the underbrush. I focused on combining them and felt a jolt of power. My arm felt numb, as my mana reading said [1/15].

[NEW MAGIC TYPE UNLOCKED - AIR]

Air magic? What?

Before I could think too much about the notification, a dark brown Stalker burst onto the hill above the cave and looked down at me. He looked around, raised his head, and let out a long, slow howl. It chilled my blood, putting fear into my heart. The fear of death. Four other Stalkers enter the area from all directions, making a circle.

"Look at what we have here. A little lost human out on a nighttime stroll," he said in a growling, low-pitched voice. The werewolf stood up on two legs and sauntered over to me. "We've been out here scouting the Feka for a week now. It sure makes me hungry. Might be time for a snack before we head back."

"We should probably bring him to the alpha to consume, back at the city," another werewolf said as he stood up, looking nervous.

"Quiet! The alpha doesn't have to know," he said with a gleam in his eye. He started inching toward me. I held the dagger before me, trying to look way more threatening than I felt.

Dee leaped from the tree like lightning, stabbing a stalker closest to the tree with a dagger and disappearing. The lead Stalker looked around, confused. "Come back here, feline scum!" he roared after her.

They circled the tree, jumping at its base, seemingly forgetting about me. I swung my dagger across the back leg of the nearest Stalker, and a lightning bolt arced from the dagger's tip. The dog yelped in pain as it fell to the ground, the others backing off. "What? What is this magic, human?" He couldn't move his back leg, having been paralyzed.

The three remaining wolves circled me, anger in their eyes. I stared right back at them. I swung my dagger, whiffing the nearest dog. It pounced and pinned me to the ground, jaws flashing.

Suddenly, another blur of motion, only this time it wasn't Dee. A gigantic, golden-colored jaguar with black spots tackled the dog, then raked its claws across its face. The cat stood up, drew its sword, and plunged it into the dog's neck, killing it easily. The other three Stalkers, including the one I'd wounded, ran into the woods, yelping away into the brush.

Dee reappeared, sighed, and looked at the jaguar cat. "Hey, brother."

Chapter 8

Wind Dagger

"Deehana, what in the world are you doing out here at night with one of stepfather's no-classers?"

"Typh, I can explain..."

"You're lucky I was on night scouting duty! You could have been killed!"

Dee looked down at the ground, ashamed. The jaguar looked at me, disgust crossing his spotted face. "Human. Come with me immediately back to the settlement. I have hereby overturned your coordinator's decision by the power of the Baron."

"Typh...father made him go!" Dee blurted out.

The cat looked at his sister for a long time. "Why in the world would stepfather put this human in the woods at night? He would have certainly been killed. Humans can barely function during the day, let alone when their horrible eyes can't see in the dark!"

Dee crossed her arms, standing taller. "He thought Noah, that's the boy's name, stole a dagger from him. He was preparing for the merchant's auction. You know how he gets before one of those. He roared at the human and sent him out for night ingredient duty as punishment."

Typh shook his head and, in a low voice, said, "He needs to stop killing the humans. He thinks they're all thieves, criminals, and rejects from Fayport, but it doesn't mean he can waste them. He's shorthanded in the smithy as it is."

"Typh, that's not even the craziest part. The human wasn't lying. He really can create!" she continued, excitement on her furry face.

The jaguar turned to me, thoroughly looking me over. He loomed over me at about seven feet tall, a terrifying sight to behold. My human instincts told me I was about to be attacked by a jungle cat. It took every ounce of determination to stand my ground in Typh's gaze.

"Humans do not create. They never have and never will. Hand me your dagger."

I had not seen the dagger since I combined it with the silver ore. I held it up, looking at it before I handed it to him. The dagger now had silver lightning bolt marks running down the blade and a golden hilt. It was beautiful.

[YOU HAVE UNLOCKED THE 'INSPECT' SKILL. THIS IS A PASSIVE SKILL AND REQUIRES NO MANA TO USE WHILE HOLDING AN OBJECT OF POWER THAT MATCHES YOUR SKILL.]
[DAGGER- UPGRADED (WIND)]

I looked up at Typh, who was holding out his paw expectantly. Dee saw the changes in the dagger and gasped but didn't say anything, following it with her eyes. I handed it to him, hilt side toward the cat. He took the weapon, turning it over in his hands.

"Human, what kind of trick is this? There is no information here. My 'INSPECT' skill tells me this is a dagger but gives me no other information."

I looked between the cats, afraid to speak. I gathered myself, took a breath, and explained. "I'm a Blacksmith Apprentice class. Dee called my class a Creator class. I don't know too much else at this point. My skill is very low level, and I haven't had much chance to practice since I was... *acquired*...by Romas"

I didn't give them much additional information. I wanted to keep most of my skills a secret. I didn't mind telling these creatures what they wanted to know since they could rip my head off at any moment. But I wouldn't give up too much.

He looked down at the weapon. "You will address me as sir, human. Do not disrespect the Feka, or you will be punished, no matter how my kid sister treats you," he growled back, giving Dee a sidelong glance. "And how do you explain this dagger, then?"

"Before the Stalkers attacked, I felt the pull to combine one piece of silver ore I mined in the cave and that dagger, *sir,*" I added, a little bit of human sarcasm in the last part. "When I did, I upgraded my original talon dagger. Now it shocks whoever I attack with a little mini lightning bolt thing."

"Then why can't we see that?" Dee asked, taking the weapon from her brother. "I can't inspect anything about it either! Hang on a second."

Dee took off up a nearby tree. A few moments later, she struggled in the canopy as she attacked a bird. Typh and I waited at the tree's base. She came back down, a small blue beak in her mouth. "Nope, it's just a stabby dagger. No lightning came out when I stabbed the bird with it."

They both looked at me, their gaze boring into me. "Guys, I don't know what to tell you," Typh growled, but I continued. "It's called a 'WIND DAGGER,' whatever that means. And when I stabbed the dog in the leg, it sent a shock through its muscle. The Stalker couldn't stand up again for a few seconds."

Typh looked around, the darkness fading as the planet's sun rose. "I will need to think about this. For now, tell no one. Deehana, keep the boy safe but don't tell anyone we are interested in him. I don't want anyone getting too close to this human. One whiff of him, and it's easy to tell that something is off. Keep him busy in the smithy. And keep him away from the Spring Games. We can't have him competing and getting any additional *interest.*"

The two of us nodded, agreeing with him. "Romas said he wanted me to help him prepare the course, so I don't think that will be an issue, sir," I responded.

"Typh, he gains levels from creating and mining. I think we should allow him to go into the caves with the adventurers," Dee said, looking back to her brother. "He could become useful to us!"

"Absolutely not. I don't trust any of those mercenary scum. I will have to take him. He will also need to create a better weapon. No offense, human, but you're pretty inept. I doubt you will stab any Shadowalkers, even with your new magic. We will need to train your pathetic body as well." A sly smirk crossed the cat's face for the first time since I'd met him.

Dee scoffed a meowing laugh. I looked at her, hurt in my expression, and she cleared her throat. "Sorry, but it's true. You should have a weapon that keeps you far away from the actual fighters."

I pondered that. Dee had a point. There was no way I was getting in the middle of giant wolves and jungle tigers fighting each other without getting torn to pieces.

"Don't forget the ingredients from the fight!" Dee said with a grin. My eyes widened, almost forgetting what was most likely high-level loot.

After I picked up a shining wolf tooth and a pelt, we took off toward the settlement.

The journey back through the jungle went smoothly. The commanding presence of Typh was undoubtedly helpful in scaring off any predators looking for an early morning snack. We entered the bustling settlement through the front gate, people bowing before us as we entered.

"Typh, sir, are you some kind of king?" I asked him as we walked, as he continued to get reverence and 'good morning, sir' from the cats we passed on the way to the ramp.

"I'm the male in charge of security at the settlement. Baron Gilbert is the mayor here."

Dee rolled her eyes at her brother, then beamed at him, a proud look showing. "There's a battle once a season between the male security chief and any interested males. The winner gains the title and the authority that comes with it. Typh has been the chief male at our settlement for three seasons now."

He paused, nodded once, then jumped to the next level at the base of the ramp. Dee continued before following him. "He doesn't like to boast. He's the best fighter our settlement has seen since the Baron. But the Baron gets his power from cloak and dagger, in my opinion. Not pure power."

She jumped up the walls, and I hurried up the ramp.

I continued through the streets with the two Feka, the city alive with preparations for the festival. Back at the blacksmith, it looked as though a bomb had gone off. Food and drinkware were everywhere, with T-shaped chairs strewn about. At the center of the smithy, a cleared circular area was made at some point in the night for dancing. Unless the cats didn't dance. Maybe it was for fighting. Or hell, perhaps even mating. I didn't know these creatures well enough yet to have any clue.

"Yikes. Have fun cleaning this all up! I'm going to get some sleep. Bye, Noah! Bye, brother!" Dee said, turning and leaving the building and bounding off further into the settlement.

Romas was curled up in the corner, purring loudly. Typh looked around, disgust on his face. "Merchants," he muttered under his breath, shaking his head. He turned to me. "You and Jasper have your work cut out to clean this place up. I'll return tonight once you've done your chores. We can speak then."

He turned to leave but then stopped, turned around, and went to the corner where Romas slept. Typh took a swinging kick at the sleeping cat, startling him awake. Romas jumped straight up, fur sticking into the air, hissing at Typh. Typh looked at him. "Don't you ever waste another no-classer again, you bastard," he growled, and with that, he turned and left into the morning light.

Romas looked after the leopard, sighed, and curled back up in the warm building, quickly falling back asleep.

Chapter 9

The Alpha

I TOOK A DEEP BREATH AND PICKED UP THE SMITHY. THE amount of fur everywhere was concerning. *Don't these cats ever clean themselves? Or is that another task for human workers to complete,* I thought to myself grimly.

I was completely exhausted. My need for sleep was continuously forgotten here. The Feka pushed us hard, and with my night activities, there was no time for rest.

It felt strange to go back to my janitorial duties when so much had happened. I had three skills now, of which I knew very little. It was nice to be able to experiment with my mining skill in the cave, but I still didn't know what I could do or what this ore was. All I wanted to do was make more items and start training, but a messy smithy and some kind of feline Olympics stood in the way. I also had to start thinking about what I wanted to make next.

Do I want a spear? Something I could throw? A sword? Or a bow? Being far away from these monsters and paralyzing them from a distance seemed helpful to the Feka, who could quickly dive in and out of combat. But the wolves appeared to use their numbers to circle the cats and make escape impossible. If I wanted to make a difference, I would need something to help prevent that. No matter what weapon I made, I would have to practice with it since I had no experience whatsoever with battle or killing.

I also needed some armor or something to protect myself. My base overalls and boots wouldn't hold up to the jaws of a wolf beast, and the vest I had made early on was a joke, apparently. It was easy to die in this world, and I was at the bottom of the food chain. I hadn't done a very good job of *blending in* yet and didn't want any additional attention. If I was going to continue sneaking around the settlement, I couldn't afford to have any disciplinary setbacks.

Suddenly, I was attacked into a huge hug. "You're alive! I can't believe it! How did you survive night duty?" It was Jasper, his head buried in my back.

I broke away from his grip. "Dee came with me. She met me at the top of the ramp on my way out of the city."

Jasper looked around. "Man, I wouldn't trust her. She's...tricky to read. You should have seen the way she treated our last few no-classers."

"Well, she saved me twice out there. Her attacks are so cool." I retold the story of the cave, the stalker attacks, and the intervention of Typh. Jasper looked on with awe, nodding along and gasping frequently. "But there was a moment where she...*used me* as bait, though. Is that what you mean by how she treated them?"

Jasper looked away, not responding. "I better not..."

I decided not to push him. "Ok." I rolled up my sleeve, looked around, ensured we were alone, and showed him my arm. This time, I allowed him access to my tattoos.

Jasper gasped as they became visible to him. He quickly examined the symbols on my arm. "What do they do?" he whispered, looking up at me.

"Well, the anvil symbol is the one that lets me create things. That's how I made the dagger. It costs five mana to use. That's the blue number. But then I upgraded it, and that cost ten mana, maybe? Anyway, the second one is a new skill called 'MINE.' It lets me stick my hand into rock walls and get the ore out. That one is about one mana per second to use." I took out the three remaining red pieces. "I got five pieces of ore from the cave. Two silver pieces of ore and three red."

Jasper examined the ore, taking one from my hand. "This is Tinderstone. I've seen Romas use this before. He makes items that heat the Fekan homes and power the forges. It catches on fire super easily. But I've never seen him use it to make a weapon."

He returned the ore to my hand, and I put them and the one silver ore under my bed. I didn't know if Romas would want to see later what we produced during our trip. I took out the silver-streaked Wind Dagger and continued, "The silver piece of ore just called me and wanted to combine with the dagger. Then I upgraded the first dagger that I made into this one."

His eyebrows shot up. "This is beautiful! I've never seen anything like it! And I've seen hundreds of daggers and swords made by Romas. So that's how you shocked that Stalker?"

"Yep. The Wind must mean something. You've never heard that term before?"

"No. What did Typh say when he saw it?"

"That's the weirdest part. Typh couldn't even tell that it was anything other than a dagger."

"Let me see that." I handed the dagger to Jasper. "Yeah, I don't feel anything either. Very strange. Why were those Shadowalkers around our settlement?"

The snoring stopped in front of the smithy, and Romas woke up. "We better get cleaning. I don't want another reason for Romas to try and kill me," I said and got to work.

Ambros led the other two Stalkers through the gates of Niridge, still limping from the strange human attack. That hurt more than a stab with a dagger should have. Where did he get that tool? Had he stolen it from the Fekan settlement? Is that why he was banished to the jungle?

The Stalkers were very tough to replace since they required years of training and had to consume very high-level kills before their bodies evolved into the werewolf state. The alpha was going to be unhappy about losing two. They had specific orders not to be found by anyone in the Fekan settlement. Their battle plans were supposed to be a surprise. But with the hiding abilities of the cats, the Shadowalkers needed to fully understand what troops to bring with them to make their attack work to its fullest.

A roar came from the top of the castle's tower as the scouts walked up the streets. "COME!"

The three wolves shrank back and looked at each other but continued through the Shadowalker city. Soon they were entering the castle halls, the castle residents staring at them with interest as they passed. The pack climbed the stairs, passing pictures of alphas throughout the centuries. The current alpha had been in power for a suspiciously long time. Ambrose knew it was from the sacrifices but didn't tell anyone else for fear of angering the alpha.

With their ability to strengthen their bodies beyond normal canines' average 12-15 season lifespan, it was understandable to live to 20 or even 30 seasons old. But the current alpha was around 40 seasons and could still defeat any beta challenges.

Undoubtedly, the walkers were enjoying prosperity in their city as they had never experienced before. And with the plans to expand into Feka territory, that could get even better. But the felines were tricky, and defeating the nearby settlement would be a complex task.

The pack got to the alpha quarter, slinking to the door. "Enter!" he roared. They shuffled into the room. "Report!"

The alpha was an enormous werewolf creature. He stood about eight feet tall with a slight hunch forward. His fur was black as night, with rippling muscles bulging from his arms and chest. He had a ragged, long face filled with scars from battle. Leather pants covered his muscular legs.

"Sire, we completed the survey of the Fekan settlement. Two towers exist on the corners of both front walls. They have increased their wall size since last season but have not made any other visible improvements. Our militia troops and Bullhead warriors should easily destroy the decrepit wall. Once inside the settlement, we can access their tower's upper levels with the main ramp to complete the attack. They will probably have archers so a blocking board will be needed."

The alpha nodded along, some of the anger receding. He looked over the three wolves. "Fine. Why do I smell so much fear? Where are the remaining numbers in your group?"

Ambros came forward, slinking further into the floor. "We caught the scent of a human alone in the woods. He must have wandered out of the nearby settlement. We were going to return him to you for consumption." He paused, the other two wolves looking back and forth, knowing this was a lie. The alpha noticed as well.

"Lies," the alpha growled. "You will be punished for thinking of stealing from me. Continue."

Ambros continued, not lying further about wanting Noah for himself. "We chased it but lost its scent. It must have been hiding from us somehow. A Mechos bear chased it back out, and we circled it. But a hunter class Feka emerged from a tree and assassinated one of our group. We didn't know she was there. She had a high-level scent blocker like the human and went into stealth. We chased her up a tree when the human attacked my rear leg with a dagger."

The alpha recoiled. "What do you mean, attacked?"

"He had a dagger that he swung at me. Somehow it paralyzed my leg, and I couldn't move. Then Cronus dodged his next swing and jumped on him when their head of security flanked us. He must have been in the area and heard the battle. He knocked Cronus out and killed him. We..." Ambrose paused, knowing he had to admit cowardice to the alpha.

"You what," the alpha said, slowly growling out the question, the sides of his lip quivering and showing a few blackened teeth.

"We...ran, sire. We fled." He backed away, talking faster. "He was a fully grown Feka and outclassed us in fighting ability..."

"SILENCE!" he roared. "They will know we are interested in the colony now. The attack will be moved up. Gather the troops. Sound the horns. It's time to move out!"

"Yes, Alpha. Right away." Ambrose turned and barked out orders to the nearby pack.

"And Ambrose..." the alpha said with murder in his eyes.

"Yes, sir?" Ambrose weakly replied, at this point, almost melted into the floor.

"Do not disappoint me in the upcoming battle. I'll be watching."

"Of course, sir." And with that, he fled down the stairs with the rest of his group. In the distance, orders were barked out all around the city, the sounds of an army grinding into motion. Horns sounded through the town, followed by long, eerie howls. The time had come.

END OF ACT I

Chapter 10

Slingshot

As night fell in the city, Jasper and I finally finished our chores. It took the whole day, two food breaks, and a quick nap, but the smithy looked good as new. As for food in the settlement, the cats ate everything raw and thought humans should do the same. They ended up just serving us a version of sushi mixed with corn, brought in by serving girls every few hours. It was terrific. Much better than the Dorito and Mountain Dew diet I used to be on. Every time Jasper ate, though, he made a face. Apparently, the kid wasn't a fan of sushi.

There was only one human establishment at the settlement from what I was told, and you had to gain access through your supervising Feka.

While I worked, I thought about what weapon I wanted to build. I wanted to go with a ranged item but needed to know what kind. As a kid growing up in New York City, I loved shooting my slingshot. But that was about as much experience as I had. Plus, a slingshot seemed...childish. I was surrounded by talking monster cats and didn't want to make a fool of myself. But I also didn't want to be useless.

"When did Typh say he was coming back?" asked Jasper in a whisper, stacking the last couple of bronze breastplates on the upper shelf.

"He said night, which should be soon. But with the Shad-owalkers scouting the city, I assume he will be preoccupied looking into why they were here."

"Makes sense," Jasper replied. "I don't remember the last time the Shadowalkers were here."

I looked around, dropping to a whisper of my own. "I want to test my level 2 'CREATE' skill, but I don't want to steal anything from Romas. I learned after the first time," I said, remembering my adventure in the jungle.

"I can help with that!" a figure slithered out of the shadows.

I jumped, but Jasper, who was used to Dee's shenanigans, said, "Dee, you shouldn't sneak up on people."

"Quiet boy! And that's madam to you. So...what did you decide to make, Noah?" Dee asked me.

Jasper grumbled in the background something about calling me by my name.

"Well, I wanted to make a ranged weapon, but I don't know how."

A smile crept across her face. "Good news, we grow bow trees here at Dunbar!"

"OK, but how do I get some wood? It's outside the settlement, and I can't steal it..."

Dee thought for a moment. "We can go late at night. About an hour or two before sunrise, the largest moon is at its lowest light. The settlement sleeps around then. Plus, father tends to get drunk after a successful auction. He will be fast asleep by then."

"Ok. I could use some rest anyway. Get me when it's time to go. Unless Typh comes, then we can wait."

I found my cot in the corner of the smithy and plopped down, beyond exhausted. I heard Jasper do the same next to me. Sleep came quickly to us, and we slept deeply before long.

I felt a paw at my side. "Hey. Wake up!" It was Dee, pawing at me.

I groaned and rolled over. Jasper was snoring in his cot next to me, still fast asleep. Further into the smithy, bottles of some kind littered the floor surrounding a sleeping Romas. As Dee thought, he had hit the bottle pretty hard in celebration.

"Let's go find some wood for that weapon of yours. Follow me." I followed Dee out into the night air, still not fully awake. It was raining and colder than it had been the previous day. "Remember, you're my no-classer. I could be taking you anywhere for any purpose. Make sure to act like it." A grin crossed her feline features.

We passed a few cats, none of them paying us any attention. This late at night, almost no one was moving around. As usual, Dee jumped down from the settlement level to the ground, glancing up and looking back at me. I went down the ramp.

Outside the walls, she turned toward one of the enormous looping trees. "This is a bow tree. We grow it here to supply the entire empire with wood for our longbows. Feka are very good with bows because of our high dexterity. They provide a boost to our archers. I don't know if I can get a full piece down. Humans use huge saws to get a piece for Romas to make one longbow. Plus, if we get pieces down it will wake the farmhands up..."

"I shouldn't need a huge piece. I don't want a longbow since I've never shot a bow. What I have in mind is a bit...different." A grin crossed my face.

"Have at it then, human," she replied, stepping aside and waving her paw.

I sized up the tree, thinking about what I wanted to make.

[YOU HAVE UNLOCKED THE 'DESIGN' SKILL.]

Suddenly, the world slowed to a crawl. I felt the same suction motion coming from my arm, like when mining the ore. This must be a mana-per-second skill. *I had better hurry,* I thought.

In front of me, plans came together, showing a simple slingshot. Above it, I could visualize two blank slots; the one on the left labeled 'Bow Tree Stick' and the other slot labeled 'Rodent Tail.' I stopped the skill, and the world returned to normal speed.

"What was that??" Dee exclaimed, looking at me wide-eyed. "Your eyes just went completely dark for a few moments!"

"I got a new skill! It lets me plan out my weapon build and helps me design things I need when the ingredient isn't telling me what it wants."

"Well, be careful. You can only have a set amount of skills for your level. Unlocking skills is great, but you will have to pick and choose pretty soon," Dee replied. "So you know what you need for your weapon?"

"Yeah. I need a twig from this tree and a rodent tail. I can get at least one ingredient!" I jumped up and grabbed a branch, leaves going everywhere. I snapped the front part off, the branch snapping back up and catching me in the face.

Dee burst into her growling laugh. "Human, you are something." She laughed as I wiped the blood from my cheek and rubbed my left eye.

"Let's just get the rodent tail," I said, trying not to be embarrassed. I picked up the branch and walked toward the ramp.

We wandered back through the empty settlement, Dee assuring me that mice were everywhere. Apparently, in Prixa, cats didn't chase mice. Humans were the ones who dealt with rodent problems. After walking through the streets briefly, Dee stopped, crouching low. She took off, becoming tough to see as she went into stealth mode. I took the hint and stopped as well. I heard a loud *squeak* up the path, a mouse having met its untimely demise.

Dee padded back to me, still on four legs, a tail bouncing in her mouth. "One rodent tail, as requested."

"Thank you," I said, grabbing the tail. I looked at my arm. [11/15]. My mana recovered slightly from my early 'DESIGN' spell as we searched for mice and returned from the grove. *I should be good if level 2 items cost ten mana.* Holding the rat's tail, I felt its pull to the stick in my pocket. A promising sign, indeed. I grabbed the stick from my pocket, holding the two items together. Then, as last time, I willed them together, merging them in my mind.

In my hand sat a wood slingshot. *It worked!* I inspected the item.

[BASIC SLINGSHOT]

My arm burned again as the mana got all used up. The slingshot was simple, but I hoped it would get the job done. I would have to train with this thing and ensure I wouldn't be useless in a fight. My aim used to be pretty terrible back on Earth. Hopefully, I would get a skill or something as I practiced with it.

"Having fun?" said a voice behind us. I jumped and turned around. It was Typh.

"Hey, brother. Noah figured out what weapon he wanted to make. I hope you don't mind that we...collected a stick from the tree farms."

He looked at me, appraising. "Let me see."

I handed him the slingshot. "And you think this will be able to wound a fully grown Shadowalker, do you?" A sarcastic grin crossed his feline features.

"Well, not on its own," I replied, crossing my arms. " I need ammunition for it. I plan to make something I can shoot from the silver ore like I found in the caves. If I can make pellets that shock the Shadowalkers, it gives your warriors more time to attack. Especially if they outnumber us as they did before."

Typh smiled, and his green eyes narrowed, showing his amusement. "Clever. Perhaps the fat human won't be so useless after all."

Chapter 11

Fish Processing

I snuck back into the smithy, Typh and Dee bidding me farewell after instructions to wait for Typh a little after first light. When I asked how I would get out of my daily chores, he told me he would handle Romas. Judging by how his peers treated him at the settlement, I was sure he could.

For the last remaining bit of the night, I couldn't sleep. I had some fantastic skills now and was excited to learn more about them. When I saw my reflection earlier in the day, I felt like I was already a bit slimmer. It could have been the overalls. But in this jungle heat, I sweated like an animal, and taking that damn ramp and getting in tons of steps was good cardio.

I planned on asking Typh as many questions as possible while training with him. I needed to get a good feel for what this world had in store, including the strengths and weaknesses of the terrifying Shadowalker creatures.

I wanted additional information on how I got here or even how I could get home. While this world was certainly exciting, if I was being honest with myself, I missed my fat, lazy life on Earth. Nothing was trying to kill me there. *Well, other than diabetes.*

I looked around, ensuring everyone was still sleeping, and pulled out my slingshot. I stroked the weapon, admiring my handiwork.

It was just as beautiful as the dagger I left under my cot. The wood was a dark amber color with specks of gold.

I was deeply disappointed that this world didn't have some kind of magical storage sacks or infinite inventory system like the video games I played. All I could do was carry stuff around in my overalls. *I will need to start making non-weapon stuff too. I wonder what I could use to make a belt...*

Suddenly the world slowed down to a crawl. Thinking about making something started my 'DESIGN' skill. *No! No!* I would have to be more careful about planning items. I cut the spell off right away, chuckling to myself. Finally, I tucked my slingshot away and fell asleep.

Morning came quickly, Jasper shaking me awake. My disappearance went unnoticed, which was a relief. We moved to the sinks to wash up for the day.

"Humans! That you?" Romas yelled from the front of the smithy. "Good. Clean my quarters. Then fetch me some cronny berries near the eastern farms to dye these leather bracers. Then prepare for the Baron's arrival. He will be picking up his high-level saber today. I must ensure that it's spotless in here. Then we must make the tree spikes for the games and get..."

A voice spoke up from the doorway. "That will be unnecessary. I have arranged for a no-classer trade for today. You there," Typh pointed at me, pretending he wasn't as acquainted with me as he was. "Take off your blacksmith attire and put on this dock worker attire. We will be heading to the cannery with the fishing workers. You will be replaced today by a smaller human who can certainly handle the day's sweeping duties of the smithy."

"Typh!" Romas growled, jumping off his T-shaped chair and standing up to full height. "You cannot move my humans around again. This fat one is mine, and as useless as he is, I want him here. He needs to get me iron for the games. And I have a million other things to get done today!"

"Romas, there will be no time for power struggles. I am taking this one. The dock requires a human of this size. A piece of equipment has broken down, and they are shorthanded at the processor," Typh replied, standing closer to Romas, eye to eye with him now.

The two looked at each other, both growling quietly. The fur stood up on Romas' neck. Typh showed his teeth in a snarl. I looked to Jasper, seeing if this was a regular occurrence here. He looked just as afraid as I felt. The tension in the air was palpable. Eventually, Romas backed down, knowing he was unmatched in a fight. "Fine. Take the large boy. I expect two humans in return. If we can't get the games set up in time, it will be you who I call out to the square for a brawl, Typhonious."

"We have an accord." He nodded at me. "Let's go."

I quickly changed shirts and followed Typh out the door, not looking back. I knew better than to publicly say anything to him with all these Fekan eyes on me. We turned left out of the smithy, a way I had yet to go.

His stride was very long, and I struggled to keep up. I was drenched in sweat when we got to the water, panting in the jungle heat. "Over there, human. They're waiting on you."

"Sir, I thought that whole 'dock' thing was a ruse to get me to training?"

"This is the start of your training. It's time to toughen up and strengthen those fat arms. Slingshot or not, there will come times when a Shadowalker will be within melee weapon distance. It's best if you don't die in those situations."

I looked at the fish processing device. It was an enormous flat weight held on ropes and little spikes at the bottom. It looked like a tenderizing hammer from Earth, only the size of a couch. The rope looped around the support beam at the top and led to the front human, who held it in his hands. Two others stood behind him, also holding the rope. All at least 6 feet tall, the men bulged with well-toned muscles. It looked like they were ready for a game of tug-of-war. They looked at me expectantly as I wandered over.

"Morning, gentlemen. What do we do, exactly?" I asked in my friendliest voice.

The workers looked back and forth, confused. "We...package. We package the fish."

My eyes darted side to side between the three of them. "No, like, what do we do? With the device here?"

The no-classers were just as uncertain as I was. "We pull the weight, smash the fish, and can the meat," he said slowly like I was a small child asking why the sky was blue. I felt like I was back in high school all over again, the jocks giving me a hard time.

"So you just pull the rope over that beam there? No pulleys or anything?" They nodded, looking back and forth with confusion on their faces. "Ok, fine. Let's get after it then, shall we?" I looked back to Typh, who smiled, turned, and walked away.

The night began to fall on the worst day since I arrived on this godforsaken planet. Fish juice, blood, and guts drenched me. It was in my eyes, ears, mouth, everywhere. And my clothes had been soaked through after the first twenty minutes, putting me in a perpetual state of sweaty grossness.

The Feka could catch an incredible amount of fish out of the gulf. Every time a fish got gutted and loaded onto what I called the 'smashing table,' we played a game of tug-o-war with the weight, lifting it and smashing it down, pulverizing the fish over and over until it was flat and chopped up with the bones crushed.

Then we would gather all the pieces, loading the meat into a giant bucket and putting it on a rope hook. Another worker on the above tower would pull the bucket up, I assumed, for further processing. When one fish finished, another was loaded onto the table. Over and over, all day long. Some fish were long, some fat, some big, and some small, but the smallest fish were still over three feet long. The biggest fish resemble marlins from Earth.

But they all got pulverized by the enormous weight. The bigger the fish, the more times we had to pull the weight until the lead no-classer stopped, tying off the rope, and deemed the fish adequately crushed.

My arms burned, and a numb sensation went down my forearms. I had bleeding blisters and rope splinters sticking out of my hands. The three others were sweaty and gross like me but showed no other signs of wear and tear.

It was funny; my health started decreasing as I further injured my hands, but it grew in value. It now read [18/24], telling me I could train my body and increase my overall health by working on physical tasks. It looked as though this was Typh's mission. I wondered if the cats had a way to tell their total health, mana, and even level. I only saw a way to tell their level by how many stripes or spots they had. I would have to ask Typh later. It was amusing, however, that I didn't unlock a skill for playing tug-o-war with a giant fish-smashing device. I was starting to think that everything I accomplished here got a skill.

I sat on the dock, waiting for Typh to return for me, as he instructed earlier in the day. The other three no-classers, whose names I never got, had already gone home. I ate a piece of fish that the dock's quartermaster handed to me. He shook his head the whole time, looking at my bleeding hands when I sat down. My health bar had healed the bleeding, removing another three points from the overall bar, but the cuts kept opening up when I ripped out new pieces of rope fragments.

I finally saw Typh walking down the nearest ramp. He stopped to talk to a different dockmaster tiger-looking cat, handing him what looked like money and winking at him. I shook my head. These sly cats were going to be the death of me.

He saw me and walked over. "Enjoy yourself, human?"

"Yes, sir. It was a fantastic day. I noticed there wasn't any kind of pulley system, so we were able to struggle even more than I would have initially imagined," I said in the most chipper voice I could muster, sarcasm laced in my voice. "The smashy canning device gave me a new appreciation for Romas and his chores."

"Do not speak of creators this way, human. Romas is a vital part of this settlement. But yes. You have a very cushy job at the blacksmith. But then again, Romas is a very *cushy* person." Typh smiled, letting me know he had made a joke. "Let's go back. Your sense of direction is probably just as horrible as most other humans. I don't want you wandering off. Follow me. We will have more training in a few days."

"What's on the schedule for tomorrow?" I asked, afraid of the answer.

"Tomorrow, you will be introduced to the Fekan Spring Games."

Chapter 12

The Spring Games

Romas woke us early, igniting us into motion for the day. I could see the stress of the day on his face. Jasper filled me in on the last few weeks in the smithy as he prepared for the games, telling me about the grueling deliveries and hot nights in the forge.

Apparently, I had missed an especially tough day high in the treetops yesterday. Jasper was tasked with installing objects in trees for the climbing event, and the workers taking my place when I left had transported sand from the beaches to the training fields for the sprints.

The city was abuzz, though. The Feka had set up a grand arena in the center of the settlement, and I was amazed at the level of detail that had gone into the setup. Flags and banners adorned the arena flying various symbols and work groups, and food and drink were being served to the spectators who had already started filing into the stadium. The event was highly anticipated by both humans and Feka, who would conduct feats of strength, agility, and power to demonstrate their prowess to one another.

I was actually excited to be a part of the event and eagerly set to work. Romas had given me a detailed list of the last items

81

needed, and I grabbed them from the various lockers, sweat pouring down my face.

After our mid-day lunch, we walked to the arena to deliver the weapons and armor. For the first time, I got smiles and nods from the passing Feka. I was amazed at the level of detail required for each piece. The Feka were very particular about their equipment and demanded the highest quality craftsmanship.

Romas worked long hours, forging and shaping each piece until it met the exact specifications of the event. I couldn't imagine what types of weapons they used for actual battle if this was the level of quality of their practice gear.

Walking through the village, I saw the Feka preparing for their events. They were stretching and warming up, their muscles bulging under their bare, armorless fur as they readied themselves for the challenges ahead. I was awed by their physical prowess and agility..

Romas had assigned me to the field setup crew for the games, and I jumped right in, joining Jasper and a few farm workers. We placed archery equipment in a line, the targets taking four of us to move around. A cougar-like judge walked around, barking out orders and instructing us to adjust the targets until they were in the right spot.

With that task done, a horn blew, and a regal-looking lion walked onto the stage. A hush came over the crowd as Romas waved his paw to us, signaling us to come over to him and off the fields. "People of Dunbar! I am excited to present another thrilling Spring Game!"

Cheers erupted from the Fekan crowds. The event felt like a mixture between an American football game and a gladiator match from ancient Roman times. It was fascinating. The lion spoke further, then roared, signaling the start of the festivities.

As the games began, I watched in awe as the Feka demonstrated their extraordinary abilities. They quickly ran, jumped, and climbed, displaying their strength and agility. The crowds cheered as each event unfolded, and I was swept up in the moment's excitement. Dee got third place in the stealth competition, a dark maze where you searched for your opponent. Typh won his strength event- quickly wrestling each other competitor to the ground and pinning them. The winner of the tree climb jumped around with such grace that I could barely keep up with their movements.

One event that caught my attention was the archery contest. The Feka had selected their prized human workers to compete against each other, with the winner receiving freedom from lower-class servant status and receiving their own paid job in the settlement and access to the human shops. This was a long-standing tradition among the Feka, and one that I was very interested in. Even though I couldn't compete this spring, I dreamed of joining the fun next year to try and gain freedom and begin blacksmithing in earnest.

Some of the entrants were horrible, and the Feka cheered for them anyway. Some laughed at a few attempts. But two competitors stood out and made it to the final round. One was a young man named Michael, who had been chosen by one of the influential councilor Feka that he worked for, and a woman named Carissa, who served one of the merchants. I had seen her walking around the first level of the settlement with service trays before.

I watched as Michael stepped up to the line, his bow drawn and ready to fire. The girl watched him intently, sizing up her opponent. With a nod from the judge, the contest began, and Michael let loose his arrow.

The arrow flew straight and true, hitting the target dead center. The crowd went nuts, cheering the boy on. The girl stepped up to the line, her bow drawn, and let loose her arrow. The crowd watched in anticipation as the arrow sailed through the air and hit the target - just a fraction of an inch away from Michael's arrow.

The judge declared him the winner, and the crowd erupted into cheers. The Feka who Michael worked for stepped forward, smiling and holding his paw out expectantly. The boy took his shirt off, revealing a muscular frame underneath, and held it out. The cat took the shirt and threw it into the dirt, putting on a ceremonial display for the crowd, who was still going crazy.

Finally, he handed him a hammer and a box of nails, which must have been a symbol for the job he would begin. I watched as he was led away, tears streaming down his face.

As the Spring Games drew to a close, I felt humbled by the incredible abilities of the Feka. Romas nodded to us, smiling. "Nice work this month, Jasper. And Noah, thanks for your help. After you two clean up the arena with the other no-classers, there are beers with your names on them."

I couldn't help but smile at that. Music began blaring in the settlement behind us as a band started playing. The party had begun.

Chapter 13

The Smell of Fear

THE FOLLOWING DAY, TYPH CAME WELL BEFORE DAWN FOR me before anyone else woke up. I groaned and rolled over, still groggy from the previous day's events. The Feka were tough bosses, but even the humans were allowed to let loose last night.

Of course, we were responsible for cleaning up everyone's mess. But it was worth it. Today, however, Romas was going to find his smithy shorthanded again. This concerned me, but I didn't tell Typh that. I was sure Typh would help keep me safe from Romas' wrath. Typh looked in good spirits. He did not partake in the festivities, citing the need to 'guard the settlement.'

We walked through the still-sleeping city at a brisk pace, not speaking. Typh appeared to want to leave the colony before too many Feka saw him, which was fine by me. Once we got to the jungle clearing, he turned to me. "Are you ready for what lies ahead?"

"Yes," I replied after thinking for a moment and taking a deep breath. The grogginess was leaving my head, a fierce determination returning. I was ready to continue developing my skills and begin training in earnest.

"Then we begin. Go in ahead of me. I will support you, but you must struggle to earn your powers. Deeper in the jungle, I will explain more about our culture, our enemies, and what I believe to be true here on Prixa. For now, take out your dagger and prepare yourself."

I nodded, gathered my strength, and took a look at my character tattoos. Small level symbols showed themselves next to the images.

[NOAH]
[LV 2- BLACKSMITH APPRENTICE]
[HEALTH 25/25]
[MANA 15/15]

 L1

 L1

 Passive

 L1

It was a calm, hot night in the jungle, moonlight filtered through the unmoving branches as a focused calm came over me. I ambled along, placing my feet very carefully. Typh observed me carefully as he walked behind me. We traveled farther into the jungle, and I heard him bend over and snap a branch off some bright blue plant. He began chewing on it. *It must be an ingre-*

dient. I need to get better at recognizing the essential items out here.

We journeyed deeper into the jungle. The last time I was here had been after a traumatic event, so I remembered almost everything. Deeper along the path to my left, I heard a slight rustling of leaves and a *squeak*. A three-foot-tall squirrel-rat creature with vicious-looking teeth sat on a branch and looked at me. I froze, not moving any farther forward. The squirrel cocked its head, assessing me. I held my dagger before me and tried to intimidate the monster squirrel. *Make my day, bitch.*

We stood there, sizing each other up. The squirrel started sniffing at the air, then suddenly, it turned and skittered up the tree. "Well done," Typh said, nodding gravely.

"Huh?" I questioned, looking back, confused.

"Many creatures in these woods can smell fear, myself included. Gaining power for most creatures is obtained by consuming other things. Sometimes it can be from plants, such as this Gee Bark." He held up the stick. "Other times, it is animals. When an animal smells fear from another, it most likely will attack, knowing it has found something weaker to prey on. Winning a battle against another results in greater power for the victor. When you have no fear, some creatures take that as a sign of being outmatched. This may have just been a squabbish female, but the principle was there."

"Squabbish?" I asked, cocking my head confused.

Typh blinked. "Yes, that's the creature's name."

I nodded. "But if it was that easy, why don't the Feka just kill everything they see in the jungle?"

"It is a risk to fight. If you die, it becomes harder for the *next* Feka to win against that creature. This is why we don't have massive battles very often. Significant conflicts result in many casualties, and the remaining warriors become stronger after consuming the fallen, ruining the balance of power in this world. One or two kills won't skew the balance of power, but an entire army could make for a much more powerful foe later on. In fact, I understand that the alpha for the Shadowalker colony kills his own, raising pups for strength and then sacrificing them. It has kept him alive and in power for so long, unable to be challenged."

"When you killed that Stalker a few days ago, you didn't consume it. Why not?"

"The Feka are a civilized group, unlike the disgraceful beasts in the Shadowalker city. We have found over the centuries that we can instead *create*. And with those creations, greater power is achieved. Just consuming meat or plants allows for small bodily gains. We started there as a species long ago. Eventually, we gained higher intelligence and awareness. We found that letting the ingredient *become something* is best. It often links to the Feka that killed it, which is how the most incredible power is achieved."

"That's how I created this dagger. The talon told me it would best serve me as a weapon like that, so I let it."

Typh nodded his head, continuing. "Correct. Now it will only serve you. If you had consumed the meat of the dead creature- if humans are even capable of such things- it would have resulted in much smaller bodily gains. Noticeable, and permanent, but nothing you could have continued using. The items we use are part of our power. So if we fall, it's our total power being consumed. A risky proposal."

I understood that, so I decided to change the subject. "How do you know your levels, skills, or anything else? It's been driving me crazy. I have tattoos on my arm telling me valuable information about my body, yet all I see on the Feka are stripes or spots."

Typh smiled. "Ah, a secret among us. When someone becomes blessed, the first thing they are taught is 'INSPECT.' This allows for inspection of the world, but they can also inspect *themselves*. I can think about my body and will know my stamina and health. I can think about my weapon and get information on it. Outwardly, you can only see stripes roughly translating into what you call 'levels.' Our skills also gain power as we use them for their specific purposes. You've noticed that your 'CREATE' skill has produced better weapons. Again, correlated to levels."

I chewed my lip, thinking about what I had experienced so far. Typh was right; ' CREATE' seemed to match my level, but it was the only skill I had used so far. I only used' MINE' and 'DESIGN' once, and it was probably some form of level 1. I wanted to know if increasing my mining ability would allow for less mana used per attempt. Or even finding more rare ore types. And 'INSPECT' was a passive skill, as Typh said.

That didn't explain the dagger situation, though. "Why couldn't you tell what level my dagger was? Any idea what happened there?"

Typh shook his head, frowning. "That is still a mystery, certainly. I have theories, but I will not share them at this time. Come. We must get to the cave. We need to work on your skills."

While tense, the rest of the walk resulted in no further action. Typh found his way to the small cave opening and pointed toward it. "In you go."

I looked in the hole, remembering the dark interior with trepidation. I slid down the side of the hill more carefully this time, mentally flinching as I recalled my banged-up knee. Once inside, Typh crushed something in a vial, creating an eerie purple glow. *The mushrooms that Dee picked up, I bet!* Seeing ingredients being used for items was so cool.

The light helped immensely, enhancing my vision somehow. It must have been the power of the mushroom. *Focus.* I entered further into the cave, this time able to see the paths more clearly and avoid stumbling over rocks.

"Show me this mining skill," Typh commanded.

I looked around, seeing the same silver and red ores as a ghostly trace behind the cave walls at varying depths. I went to the wall up and to the left since the silver ore appeared closest to the surface. I thought about mining the ore, activating my skill. The familiar *sucking* motion activated from my arm, taking mana per second. I stuck my hand into the wall, diving in, getting the silver, and pulling it out. I cut off the skill and looked back at Typh excitedly.

"Fascinating. Romas must have a skill like this that he keeps hidden from the clan. He's always told me that mining these ores is extremely expensive and charges a premium for red ore heating items for our homes. What a bastard."

I chuckled. "Yeah, nothing to it. That used..." I paused and looked down at my arm, "Four mana. It takes about an hour to regenerate five mana." Typh looked confused at that. "Oh, you must not have hours. Well, it takes a little while for my amount to come back. Either way, I can do more if you want?"

"No. I would like for you to make your slingshot pellets. It's time to find the monster and take it out. If I can get that ingredient, I can have Romas make me some armor. This leather armor I have now won't do against a pack of Whitetooths."

"What are Whitetooths?"

"That's the infantry branch of the Shadowalker army. They're muscular, have powerful bites, and can get through most defenses and armor. They come in mass and hunt in huge packs, scattering the Feka and encircling them so they can't escape."

"Ok. Hang on a second." I already felt the pull of the ore to its desire to make me some ammo for my slingshot. It was different than before- the silver ore did not want to combine with the slingshot but wanted to be a part of its use. I let the ore shape and five gleaming silver pellets sat in my hand. I looked at my arm, which now had six mana left.

"That should be plenty for what I have in mind. Prepare your-self, human. The battle begins."

And with that, Typh took a deep breath, went on all fours, and let out an ear-splitting *roar*. I covered my ears, but they were already ringing from the blast of noise.

It was a challenge to the occupant of the cave. It was a challenge to fight to the death.

Chapter 14

Battling a Mecho

THE WALLS SHOOK AS TYPH'S ROAR ECHOED OFF THE WALLS like an explosion. We waited in the purple darkness, my hair standing on my arms. Sweat poured down my back, and my heart thudded a frantic beat in my ears. *Was his roar some kind of fear or intimidation skill by how my body reacted to it? Or was I just that afraid?*

Then a roar trumpeted back up the cave. Loud, fierce, strong. Answering the challenge.

"Good. It is still here." Typh looked me over, his eyes scanning rapidly as I stood in my overalls and held my tiny dagger. I must have looked ridiculous next to a sleek, fully outfitted Jaguar. "Put that silly thing away. Take this vial of Poruslight. It will help your eyes when you're shooting." *So I was right. There was some magic vision enhancement with this mushroom light item.*

A rumbling sound was growing, the monster heading toward our position. "I need you for support in this battle. If you can help me defeat this beast, your time as a no-classer will be over. I do not know what we will do with you yet, but that can be discussed outside the cave. During the battle, your best chance for us will be to stun it with your magic when it's least expected.

Let's test your slingshot out and hopefully get you a skill. Now hurry - head into that side tunnel!" He pointed ahead.

I complied, slipping my dagger into my belt loop. I looked around in the dim light, seeing what he was talking about. There was a branching tunnel ahead where I could slide out of the direct conflict. I scrambled away, hearing the monster getting closer and closer. I assumed I could hit a colossal bear monster from close range, even with the dim lighting and my shaking, crack-addict-like hands.

This had to be the most afraid I had ever been. I had never been in mortal danger once in my life on Earth. Since coming here, that had changed multiple times. I took a quick look at a gleaming silver pellet, inspecting it.

[WIND PELLET SLINGSHOT AMMO X1]

Well, nothing surprising there. I loaded the pellet into my slingshot, putting the rest in my front right pocket for reloading. Sweat beaded and ran down my neck now. I shivered, but not from the cold dampness of the cave. My whole body was rigid, on high alert, waiting for the attack that was coming. All that we could hear was *boom boom boom* as the beast ran through the cavern tunnels. All around me, the ore veins showed themselves to me. Further back, a dim ray of moonlight filtered in.

I saw Typh, now about 20 feet away, getting himself prepared. First, he took a few deep breaths, cycling his shoulders up and down. Then he fell into a much more feline pose than I had seen him use before. He crouched like he was about to attack but had his head up and his shoulders raised. His weapon was strapped to his back, most likely useless in a fight like this. His eyes darted side to side, expecting the beast to come any moment, most likely seeing much better than I could in these conditions.

Then suddenly, one more ear-shattering roar and the Mecho burst free from the tunnel. It had a massive head with red eyes and a long snout. Its fur was reddish brown with streaks of grey and thick like a polar bear's. I doubted many creatures in this jungle could even hope to take it down, hence its age and graying fur.

Typh growled and pounced, powerful swipes with his sword dancing through the air in furious motions. His ears were pinned back, his teeth bared. The bear ran right into the attack, taking the claws to the face and grunting but continuing its charge. It took Typh down, and he went to the ground, the bear overtop of him, jaws wide. The bear was about twice the size of Typh, now dripping blood onto him from cuts on its face.

I broke free of my stupor and shot. I hit it right in the rear end- the most significant target facing me. A piercing white light snaked out from the impact site. The bear roared- this time an angrier-sounding version- and reared back, hitting its head on the cave ceiling. *Holy shit. This thing must be 12 feet tall.*

The bear glanced around, looking for the damage source. If I could have sunk into the wall to hide, I would have. Instead, I grabbed blindly into my pockets for another shot.

Typh took that chance to slash the Mecho in the lower leg with his claws and pulled down to make long, parallel gashes. The bear stumbled to the side, swiping at him so fast I barely saw his paw move. Typh barely dodged in time, rolling backward. He stood up gracefully and swiped his paw in one fluid motion.

The bear took Typh's strike to the side in stride and returned a bone-rattling shot to Typh's left arm with all the power of a twelve-foot-tall monster. He flew into the cave wall with a loud *thud*, unmoving.

I took the chance to fire at the bear again, this time hitting it in the arm. Bolts of lightning shot out again, this time with more lightning. The bear roared, its arm falling limp and unmoving. It turned toward me, its red eyes gleaming with murderous menace.

[YOU HAVE UNLOCKED THE 'SMALL PROJECTILE
WEAPON' PROFICIENCY LEVEL 1]

Not now, voice lady! I'm trying to concentrate! I panicked as my trembling hands shoved my slingshot into a pocket, and drew my dagger as I backpedaled in fear. The bear went to all fours and charged me, limping badly. I panicked. It closed the 20 feet in about three strides and was upon me in moments, even with its paralyzed leg. I fell backward as it bowled me over, all 1,000 pounds of the bear over me.

I stabbed the dagger into its left paw. Lightning again shot up its arm, causing it to collapse on top of me. I let out an *oof* as the air left my lungs, trying to scramble back but completely stuck under the beast. I couldn't move or breathe, gasping for breath. I pushed up on the bear's face, but I might have well pushed into a brick wall.

The mecho spasmed in place, trying to get its front legs working, which bought me a few seconds. Its head went wildly from side to side, grunting intensely. Slobber went all over my shirt and overalls, but its teeth stayed away from my face and arms. I went for a stab at its neck but missed with a glancing blow off the thick fur. The dagger slipped to the side, flying backward and tearing free of my grasp. I yelled and released a few inaudible curse words. *I'm officially screwed.*

The bear's first leg began moving as it forced itself up, the paralysis wearing off. It rose to full height, and its arm swung backward to pummel me into the cave floor. I got a full roar in my face as it looked down at me, showering me in spittle. I wiped the mess from my eyes as I scrambled backward. Suddenly a sword stuck through the beast from behind to the front, stopping it in its tracks.

A sword I had seen just days before. It was a high-level saber made for one man. Baron Gilbert. The Baron roared a defiant, victorious sound, declaring himself the alpha of the cave.

The bear made one last gurgling noise, looked around, then fell into the cave wall with an enormous *boom*. The Baron grabbed his saber from the bear, cleaning the blood off. Typh was still knocked out cold against the wall, but I could see him breathing. *Good, not dead.*

Typh was bleeding from his head and shoulder, the blood pooling on the ground around him. Gilbert looked around for any further threats but detected none.

The bear dissolved into the cave floor, leaving a huge fur mass ingredient on the cave floor. The Baron sheathed the sword and held his paw to me, looking me directly in the eye.

"I believe we have a lot to discuss."

Chapter 15

The Sound of Laughing

I GRABBED THE BARON'S PAW AND WAS HOISTED UP. "I heard of a mysterious human I didn't remember buying or transporting from Fayport. What's your name, boy?"

"Noah, sir." I looked at the cat. I remembered him being enormous from the Spring Games, but up close like this, he was even larger. In fact, he was the largest Feka I had seen thus far.

He was well-built and about a foot taller than even Typh. He had lion features but was spotted like Typh, marking him as a warrior class Feka. The decorated sheath hung on his belt with two crossing straps holding various vials, daggers, and utility tools. The straps looked worn but had golden thread and bronze-colored beads adorning the edges.

Baron Gilbert's eyes narrowed, looking me over. "You were about to get mauled by a Mecho, in a cave at night, with our settlement male. Care to explain why, human?"

Behind him, Typh woke up in a coughing fit. "I can explain, sir." He slowly got up, shaking his head from side to side.

"Well, look who decided to join the party!" The Baron had a mysterious grin now. "Bit off more than you could chew, eh Typhonious?"

"I was...training...the boy..." he said, grimacing in pain as he spoke, now holding his ribs. His light dimmed, so he took out another vial and crushed the contents, returning the cave to a purple glow.

"Training?" Gilbert took two strides toward the leopard, growling his words out. "Typh, tell me what's happening now, or I will take your security status immediately. You're lucky I caught your scent on my way out of town as I headed toward Fayport for the high senate meeting. I was *curious* why the scent of a human and a Feka would be heading this way and investigated. I found you knocked out and the boy about to be pummeled into the cave floor. You put the whole settlement at risk!" He looked furious. "I understand the need to take a no-classer to haul ingredients back from a kill, but this time of night? In a mecho cave?"

Typh took a deep breath, thinking through his response before speaking again. "I didn't mean training him to be a better blacksmith worker. I meant mentoring him. He is a creator. A *human* creator. I didn't believe it when I first heard it, but it's true. Not only that, his magic and items are like nothing we've seen. The items he makes are exceptionally efficient against canine beasts. He calls it Wind magic."

The Baron thought on this information, saying nothing for a few moments. Finally, he turned to me. He whispered so that Typh couldn't hear. "Let me see your markings, human. Allow me to see them."

My eyes widened, confused about how he knew of my arm markings. I rolled up my sleeve, thought about allowing him to see them, then displayed my character sheet tattoos. "Curious," he said. He muttered to himself about creators and thinkers, knowing more than Typh. *He may make a valuable knowledge source*, I thought. "We must bring him back to the smithy at once. And the Monarch needs to be informed immediately. When she finds out what she threw away..." He trailed off, deep in thought.

"Boy, you must create armor for yourself," the Baron continued. "Romas can lend you some material that should work for you." I looked in disbelief, doubting Romas would give up any of his precious materials to me. "And you've made a weapon? May I see it?"

I handed him my slingshot, somewhat embarrassed at my weapon choice. He turned it over in his paw, observing every inch of it. "The magic doesn't register with me. Curious. This matches everything I've heard from the Monarch. What ammunition have you created?"

I took out a pellet from my pocket. "I made these from the silver ore in the cave walls here. I can mine it with one of my skills. When I hit the Shadowalkers, lightning shoots out from the wound and stuns their limb for a few seconds."

"Have you made anything with the red ore yet?" he questioned.

"No, should I be? I thought it was basically just coals for heating things."

"If you could make items out of this silver ore, you should certainly try with all the ores. Who knows what you could make! What magics you could unlock past your Wind magic! Typh, you were right to train this boy. There are things about his race that he must know. He could either become a great ally for us or..." he trailed off, looking at me. "Let's say we will want him in touch with our leader immediately. She will know what to do. Typhonius, you are hereby bound to secrecy by the power of my Barony under the authority of the Monarch. Until our leader can come to the settlement, we will keep this between us."

Typh nodded with a grim expression.

The Baron turned to leave the cave, the conversation completed. Typh watched him go, a look on his face that I couldn't quite place. He looked back at me and pointed at the giant fur mass on the cave floor. "Pick that up and carry it back to the city. We will want to begin work on my armor immediately. Per our accord before the battle, you are no longer a no-classer serving the Feka, even if that battle result was...less than stellar. I will not put you in even standing with our kind until your release is official." He gave me a look of disdain, turned, and walked out of the cave after the Baron. I may have heard him muttering about my weight and lack of fighting prowess.

I scrambled toward the fur and picked it up before the purple light entirely left with Typh. The last thing I wanted was to be stuck in the cave with no lighting. The fur pelt weighed around 100 pounds, and I strained to get it on my shoulder. Unsteady, I moved toward the cave entrance.

We walked through the jungle, the sounds of insects filling the air. It was quiet and peaceful with moonlight filtering in through the canopy. The Feka made no sound as they walked down the path. Their ears constantly swiveled back and forth, on high alert for danger. I didn't speak as I followed along.

Watching Typh get mauled by a bear creature had hammered home how out of my league I was on Prixa. *If a 6-foot-tall leopard warrior could barely survive this place, how could I hope to? All I did was hide in the corner and shoot pellets.* I needed to create bigger, bolder items. I needed traps, utility devices, and armor; the list was long. But if the Shadowalkers were vulnerable to air magic, I would have to find a way to make more weapons.

But why couldn't the Feka tell my weapons had magic?

I peered at my arm, noticing some new tattoos had formed.

[NOAH]
[LV 3- BLACKSMITH APPRENTICE]

[HEALTH 26/32]
[MANA 14/21]

 L3

 L2

 Passive

 L1

I had gained a level during my fight, increased my health and mana, and got a small weapon class. All in all, a solid outing. Other than almost dying, of course.

I clomped loudly through the woods, the 100-pound fur ingredient weighing me down. I was panting and sweating profusely between carrying the fur and trying not to trip on logs. It was a long night, and I desperately wanted to lie in my cot. A smile crept across my face, however; I was a free man. Although I wasn't sure what that entailed. Romas would not be happy to give me up, even though I felt like I didn't do much for him. Or perhaps I would work with him, and now under him? I would love to start a business here. Maybe engineer some gadgets for these cats? I was excited to find out.

The cats were far ahead now, not looking behind as they gracefully walked up the path. Suddenly the insects stopped chirping, and a silent calm claimed the jungle. Typh and the Baron stopped in their tracks, hair suddenly standing upright. I looked around, confused.

In the distance, I heard the sound of laughing hyenas — tons of them. The sound echoed through the night, distant but loud. It was high-pitched and cackling. The laughter seemed to come from everywhere at once. I stopped walking, a chill creeping down my spine. Dogs barked, rough and deep. Then long, eerie howls erupted into the night air, being answered by hundreds of dogs.

Typh turned back to me, shouting, "Run! We must return to the settlement immediately! We are under attack!"

Five or six horns sounded, varying in sound but deep and blaring. I took off, the fur bouncing wildly on my shoulders as I exploded through the trees. My Fekan allies left me in the dust, making it to the gates and running through. I paused momentarily in the clearing near the settlement and assessed the situation. The humans assigned to night farming were screaming and running into the gates. Cresting the hill to the right was an army of Shadowalkers. I took off toward the gates, joining the mass of people streaming through them before they closed.

Chapter 16

Fire Magic and Pit Bulls

I FINALLY GOT THROUGH THE GATES AS THE LAST FEW humans squeezed in with me. There was a line of Feka checking us as we filtered by. They roughly grabbed shirts to check logos and looked in our eyes for any trace of red. "All humans, report to the worker bunker immediately! All humans, report to the worker bunkers immediately!" a large Feka shouted out repeatedly, pushing people toward the base of the ramp. Someone grabbed my pelt and looked it over roughly.

"It's for Typh! I was in the cave with him!" I yelled. The tiger looked back at me, nodded, and pushed me forward. I broke free from the throng and headed toward the ramp. I needed to get to the smithy, drop this ingredient off, and figure out what the hell was happening.

At the top of the ramp, the scene was just as chaotic. Cats with bows ran everywhere, jumping off the first level of the settlement and sprinting to their positions on the wall. I saw the gleaming bow tree wood sparkling on their backs with its gold specs as they ran past on all fours. I went to the wall and glanced at the attacking foe.

"Noah!" a voice called behind me. It was Dee.

"Dee! What's going on?" I yelled to her as she sprinted over.

She pursed her lips, her whiskers twitching slightly. "Looks like the friends we made in the woods told their boss to bring an army to us! Hope you're ready to fight some monsters!"

I looked over the wall. In the front of the army that crested the hill, a pack of bulky pitbull-looking monsters were barking enthusiastically. They wore spiked collars and had teeth that protruded up the sides of their faces, almost like piranhas. Their fur was grayish-black and streaked with red. Beady eyes glared at us, ready to attack at a moment's notice.

Behind them was a pack of around fifteen stalkers. They looked the same as I remembered; dark brown fur and a face like an elongated wolf. They were double the size of the Earth variety, some standing tall on two legs. They howled madly behind the pit bulls, edging them into a frantic frenzy. The laughing continued from the pack of hyenas to the left, and I saw them for the first time. They looked like the Earth equivalent, but smaller. The hyenas paced side to side on all four legs and looked around wildly, seemingly excited to join the chaos of battle. They wore creepy expressions on their faces, almost smiling in anticipation.

Finally, in the rear were creatures resembling the cave bear. They had enormous bodies and helmets on their heads. Their fur was brown and not as shaggy as the mecho's. They looked more like grizzly bears than polar bears. They stood silently, looking into the night, not making a sound.

All in all, a terrifying sight. The air was filled with a new smell of wet dog. It mixed with the musky swamp odor, creating a pretty unpleasant odor.

"I need to drop this pelt off at the smithy," I yelled as I turned away from the wall.

"I'll come with you. Let's go!" Dee replied, slithering between city occupants on all fours.

Cats and humans jostled me as I ran down the alleyways. The fur ingredient slowed me down, and a rash formed on my shoulder where it chaffed from running.

At the smithy, Romas was strapping on a gold-streaked leather chest plate. It had a similar threadwork to the Baron's straps and was no less embellished.

"Human! Where have you been? Get this strapped on me immediately, then head to the no-classer bunker. Everyone else is already on their way there!" Romas ordered, noticing me standing there."Deehana, to your position at once!"

"Yes, father," she said, giving me one last look, then scurrying off.

I held the pelt in front of me. "The Baron killed the mecho in the cave, sir, and wanted me to deliver this to you. It's the ingredient the monster left behind."

"Yes, yes. Throw it in that stack over there with the other armor ingredients." He pointed to the back corner, leather and fur remnants stacked in a pile. "I'll be able to pick it out for him after the battle."

"Right away, sir." I walked over and helped him with his breastplate, then dropped the fur in the corner as he instructed. I continued acting as his servant since an invasion was about to start. I would worry about the rest later when I had help from Typh and the Baron.

Once Romas finished adorning his armor, he grabbed a massive longsword and headed out into the night. The barking sounds were getting quieter now; something about to happen outside the walls. I looked around, ensuring no one was left in the smithy. I looked at my arm. My mana read [16/21]. *That should work.*

I grabbed some light fur from the stack, listening to it with my 'CREATE' skill. It looked like it came from the squirrel creature that almost attacked me during my jungle adventure with Typh. Suddenly, the pelt began molding to my upper body. I let it change, feeling the urge to protect myself visually in my mind. The material started creeping up my chest, then wrapped around my sides and over my back, completing at the shoulders. The armor sat there, tight on my body and fitting perfectly, keeping a gray hue and matching the fur's color. I inspected it, seeing the result of my creation.

[SIMPLE SQUAMISH ARMOR LV 1]

I was glad this was only a level 1 item because I needed more ammo for my slingshot. I reached under my bed and pulled out the last piece of silver ore but paused. The Baron had mentioned something about making ammo with the red ore. Curious, I swapped the ores in my hand, looking the red rocks over carefully. If this worked, I had eleven mana left and could make ammo from both ores, so I let the rock speak to me.

The ore lit a fire in my mind, a deep and burning heat. It didn't hurt; only let me know of its fiery power. I sat this way for a moment, enjoying the heating sensation. When the feeling faded, I looked down at my hand. Sitting there were five glowing red pellets.

[NEW MAGIC TYPE UNLOCKED - FIRE]

Fire magic? Things kept getting more interesting. Outside the blacksmith window, I heard the sound of yelling, possibly from a canine general or multiple generals. This part of the city was quiet, with all the humans hiding and the Fekan warriors assembled at the front of the settlement by now. The Feka were yelling battle cries and roaring on the walls, the howling picking up again.

I needed to hurry. I inspected the new pellets I had made.

[TINDER PELLET SLINGSHOT AMMO X5]

I quickly put them in my left pocket, the right pocket reserved for the air magic. What would these do if the air magic could stun the canine beasts? And the air was called Wind, the fire called Tinder. I would have to investigate what that meant later.

I grabbed my silver ore, repeating the previous process and making five Wind pellets. I had six total now, having used four in my two battles—eleven total shots against an army of Shadowalkers. I sighed deeply, feeling like my contributions wouldn't be enough, my mana now depleted.

I walked into the empty street wearing my new armor and looked around. I knew my best impact on the battle would be finding a place to hide and shoot at the Shadowalkers. If they saw me, I would be easy prey for them. My whole body was shaking, impacted by the sounds around the city's walls. It felt like my blood was cold, even though I was sweating again.

On this city level was a tower with a window facing the courtyard below. I jogged toward it, dodging in and out of alleyways. A horn sounded, and the giant bear monsters ran full-bore at the walls on all fours. When they impacted the wall, an explosive thud echoed into the night air, the wall shaking violently and stones flying into the air.

The Feka responded with growls and roars, shooting at them with their bows. The bears retreated, now riddled with arrows. When they got to the top of the hill, they turned and ran toward the walls again, slower this time. The crash on the wall was effective in two spots, exploding the stone and sending Feka jumping away. Large pieces of the decrepit wall tumbled down onto the ground and broke apart.

The hyenas ran in, fast and agile, toward the wall before the Feka on that part of the wall could recover. They grabbed chunks of rock and stood on their powerful rear legs, running away from the impact site. The other archers on the nearby battlements tried to take them down, but they were fast. By the time the last hyena was killed, all of the stones had been moved, and their jobs were completed. With two sections opened up, more howls filled the air, and the pit bulls ran toward the wall, ready to attack the city.

Chapter 17

The Battle of Dunbar

A LINE OF LIONS AND JAGUARS MET THE PIT BULLS HEAD-ON inside the walls, roaring and growling as the dogs barked. Jaws flashed, and claws swiped. Blood filled the streets, dogs yelping and retreating as they got clawed or stabbed with blade strikes. As I watched from the window, I saw the prowess of the Fekan combatants. They were each taking on five, six, sometimes even seven canines at once.

I was too far away to do much; my slingshot could only go 20 yards. I had a clear line of sight to the courtyard at the top of the ramp and figured the battle would eventually fall back to that position. In the towers surrounding the square was a killing ground where cutouts and holes hid the hunter class Feka. I saw the Baron waiting with Romas and a few high-level soldiers. There was another militia there, forming a defensive semicircle around them.

The archers had turned their attention to the advancing Stalkers, who waited until the pit bull fighters were out of the way in the makeshift holes in the wall. The Stalkers carried a large wooden board in front of them to shield themselves from arrows. Cats jumped from spot to spot on the wall, trying to get a vantage around the blockade, but couldn't get a good shot. The thudding of arrows on wood filled the night, directly contrasting the growling, yelping battle on the sandy streets inside the wall.

At the wall, the Stalkers stopped, sounding their eerie howls before dropping their board and running through the opening. The fifteen or so warriors, Typh included, saw this oncoming attack and knew they were outmatched. They turned and retreated, three Feka holding their retreat. The Stalkers were on them in moments, dodging clawed paws and returning strikes of their own.

The next wave came, the hyenas joining the fray. Their laughter rang out, hysterical in pitch now that the battle had fully begun. The enormous mass of canines ran through the walls quickly, as they were the fastest troops in the army. They didn't join the fight on the street but instead turned to access the archery towers. The cats shot wildly at the oncoming threat, dropping three or four at a time, but they were quickly overwhelmed. Hyena carcasses piled up everywhere.

The front line Feka put their bows away and pulled daggers as the remaining hyenas stormed the battlements. A line of brave archers stayed and made a line at the wall access to allow their fellows to retreat, but were surrounded and taken down, the laughing ever-present.

By now, the warrior Feka had climbed the tower and joined the ramp's defense. *Why was there no drawbridge mechanism on it?* Maybe this was the first battle here, and the Feka thought it was optional. I wasn't sure. The pit bulls reformed their lines carefully now that archers were no longer a concern for them. The Stalkers looked around as blood dripped off their face and teeth. They smiled, letting out victorious howls, riling up the other two troops into a second frenzy.

In response, the Baron jumped onto the tower wall, 30 feet above where the Shadowalkers stood. He let out an ear splitting roar.

One of the Stalkers came forward, speaking for the first time, his voice a low growling sound. "Baron Gilbert of Dunbar. Give yourself to us, and we will leave this city in peace. Your life is for the alpha to consume."

The Baron looked down in disgust at the creatures. "I think not, you vile beasts. You come into our settlement and make such demands? Your alpha has not even shown himself here."

The beta werewolf smiled again, his eyes narrowing. "He does not waste his time with petty things like this battle. We have gotten into your city and will finish what we started. Either come with us alive, or we consume your whole settlement."

"Then you better come and get us!" A horn sounded, the Feka cheering and roaring in the tower's courtyard. They took the same pose as Typh had in the cave- shoulders up, crouching on all fours, ready for battle.

This is it. When the Shadowalkers come up the ramp, I'll try and help somehow. Otherwise, I'll end up as food for these despicable creatures. I tasted blood in my mouth as I chewed my lip in nervousness. My view from the window was clear, but I would be stuck here if they saw me. There was only one way in, with the only other way through the window. For the Feka, that was doable. But for me, the 20-foot drop was a death sentence.

The Stalkers pointed and yelled, releasing the cannon-fodder hyenas up the ramp. The laughter echoed off the walls, loud and insane. In moments they burst through the opening, diving and lunging onto the warriors stationed in the square. For the most part, the hyenas were no match for the Feka. One or two paw swipes put the canine creatures down. The Feka turned, twisted, and moved, unable to be hit. It was beautiful to watch. Yelps, once again, filled the night air.

The pit bull creatures blasted through the ramp opening, joining in. The Feka were strong, but being surrounded by this many beasts at once, jaws flashing in every direction, became too much. They fell back a bit and scattered toward the hiding towers.

The pit bulls followed, their eyes wild from battle. The hunters came down from the holes like lightning, assassinating roughly twenty pit bulls and ten hyenas. The surprise of losing all those troops shocked the wolves as Dee and her fellow warriors retreated up the tower into other recesses.

The ten Stalkers made their way to the top of the ramp, ambling along on their two legs, watching the battle unfold. The hyena ranks had been cut in half, the pit bulls scattered, and about a quarter of them killed. They regrouped around their masters, the two sides taking a quick moment to regain their breath. Chests heaved, the sound of panting filling the air.

The Baron stepped forward, full of blood and a massive gouge on his left ear. He had a slight limp. "Do you concede, monster? Your numbers have been cut in half. Leave now and never return."

The beta male stepped forward. "Oh, I think not. That was a cute trick with your little kitties, but that won't work twice. And by my count, it's only fifteen of you against all of us." He looked side to side, howling. The howls were returned, the battle resuming.

The Feka resumed their twirling dance, the fight moving closer to me. *Here we go.* My heart was racing, the thumps loud in my ears. My palms were sweaty, and keeping hold of the slingshot was hard. I reached into my pocket, grabbing a silver pellet. I loaded up and shot, the familiar lightning taking a pit bull down to the ground. A Feka took advantage, spearing it in the head with his blade. He didn't seem to notice the pellet's effect.

I grabbed a red pellet, curious about what it would do. A Stalker and a Feka were close by, the Feka losing badly. The Stalker landed a blow to the side of the warrior's head, sending him to the ground and standing over him. I let fly, hitting the monster in the back. Flames engulfed him, spreading up the back of its fur. The wolf looked wildly around, fear in its eyes. I dove below the windowsill, afraid it would see me. I stayed that way for a moment, then peeked my head up. The wolf lay there, back charred, with a sword wound through its head. The Feka looked up at me and narrowed his eyes, looking confused. He nodded to me.

A pit bull lept at him, the moment passing and the jaguar returning to the battle. I scanned the action, looking for anyone else needing my help, and saw the Baron surrounded by three Stalkers. They lunged at him, no one making a move. His beautiful saber gleamed in the moonlight, warding off the creatures momentarily. The pit bull troops were still circling, nipping at legs, arms, whatever they could get to, but staying out of the larger creature's way. I took a shot at the Stalker to the left but missed, the pellet skimming off the ground and impacting the far tower wall harmlessly.

I took out another fire pellet, took aim, and shot again. This one hit the creature in the lower arm. It burst into flame as well, the other two looking around wildly. The two remaining Stalkers saw me there, slingshot in hand. "There! It's the human from the woods! Get him!"

Five pit bulls took off toward me, trying to find a way to where I hid. I heard the Stalkers yelling about retreat but was too preoccupied with figuring out my next move. I turned from the window, putting my slingshot away and taking out my dagger. I heard the scratching of paws running through the alleyways as they tried to find me.

I knew it wouldn't take long for them to find my scent.

Chapter 18

Attack in the Corn Storage Tower

AMBROSE LOOKED BACK AT THE FEKAN TOWER, CONFUSED at what he had just witnessed. The battle was going to plan- the Feka scattered, the archers eliminated from the walls, and their foremost warriors left. His battalions continued streaming out of the city, the alpha's instructions very clear. He was camped about half a day's trot to the south, waiting for the initial attack to finish. With him were the rest of the troops to complete the invasion of Dunbar.

Ambrose had made the retreat call when his Stalkers started catching fire. He thought about it, remembering the human in the woods and that strange lightning attack. This was different; the smell of the burning fur was still lodged in his nostrils. He wondered if it was another human with fire magic. Then again, he saw that human in the tower's window, now most likely eliminated by his Whitetooth troops. But if humans now had access to magic types, that was worrisome. He would need to tell the alpha immediately.

The Shadowalkers couldn't lose any more troops in the initial raid. The Cacklers and Whitetooth platoons were allowable losses, but Ambrose needed to keep his Stalker group together. They were the brains of the operation, directing the lesser-minded Shadowwalkers where they needed to go. Unfortunately, the hasty retreat didn't provide time to consume their kills. By now, the Feka must have gotten rid of the loot from their fallen comrades—a shame and so wasteful.

If there was enough to consume after the final battle, many of his melee troops could evolve and join the Stalker pack. To double his group would be fantastic. And if he could consume some of the higher-level Fekan warriors, or even some of those damn assassins, he could finally challenge the alpha. It was time for a change.

Ambrose looked around, nodding in satisfaction that Dunbar was ready for its final attack. The five Whitetooths he left in the city would eliminate any fire-wielding humans. It was a small sacrifice if the dogs successfully rooted them out. If there was one thing those mangy mutts were good at, it was finding a scent and attacking the prey.

I peered over the edge of the box, still hearing sniffing and scratching paws on stone as the pit bulls searched for my room. I was in a corn storage area, smelling musty from the farm equipment and food. I heard a low growl and saw the lead dog at the doorway, its eyes glowing in the moonlight. The other four joined the lead dog, salivating and snarling, ready to attack.

My heart was pounding. This was the worst danger I had been in yet on this damn planet. I was trapped and about to be surrounded. I quietly slipped my slingshot into my pocket and grabbed my dagger. It felt flimsy and useless against a pack of enormous dogs, even with its magical ability. I also doubted my Squamish armor could hold up against those jaws, but it was better than my t-shirt.

The main dog sniffed around and began barking at the others. The lead dog finally saw me, then ran and jumped toward me as I heard a roar and saw one of the rear dogs fall to the ground, a longsword sticking out of its side. I crossed my arms in front of me and got bowled over.

The dog snapped its jaws at me, growling madly and slobbering on my face. I smelled its rancid breath, disgusting from the battle. I freed my right hand, taking damage to my left arm but rammed my dagger into its rear end. The dog jolted forward over my head and into the corner from the shocking attack. My ear had been cut open somewhere during the struggle, bleeding freely, and my shoulders had gouges from where the dog sunk its black nails into me. Corn dust flew everywhere from the struggling, making me cough violently.

With another flurry of movement, Romas sliced the head off another dog. The rest of the pack scattered, trying to encircle the panther. The pit bull in the corner finally joined the other two, deeming Romas the more significant threat.

I put my dagger back on my belt and grabbed the slingshot, backing up against a wall and loading a silver pellet. The dogs lunged and snarled at Romas but were deflected by his sword. I aimed and shot at the dog closest to me, hitting it in the rear leg. It yelped, collapsing to the ground as lightning spread and paralyzed it.

Romas' eyes widened in shock, but he stabbed it in the head, the dog yelping but falling still. I grabbed another silver pellet, too afraid I would light something on fire in here if I used the red ore.

I watched the chaos of battle in front of me, but I couldn't get a good shot. I waited, watching patiently as the Feka and the two enormous dogs. I didn't want to waste what little ammo I had left. Finally, a dog lunged at Romas but was kicked back, dazed. I took my shot, hitting it in the ribs. It spasmed and fell still. *Wow, did I kill it?*

The final dog looked around, now outnumbered, and ran out the door where it came in, only to be clawed across the face by Typh. He must have heard the commotion and had come to investigate. The final dog yelped, its head bashed into the door frame, then fell still. A moment later, the five dogs dissolved and left fangs on the ground. Typh looked around, worry on his face. He looked terrible.

Romas cleaned the dark blood from his sword and sheathed it slowly. He pursed his lips, a thoughtful expression on his feline face. He started to speak but stopped, unsure what to say. This must have been a first for him.

"Romas, let me explain," I started, but he held up a paw.

"Typhonius, tell me what's going on immediately. Did you know about this boy and his powers?"

Typh paused, thinking through his response. Finally, he said, "I did."

Romas narrowed his eyes at me. "When I thought you had stolen that dagger..." He stopped, putting everything together and turning back to Typh. "Why didn't you come to me?"

Typh chuckled, a growling, guttural sound. "Romas. We know how you would have acted. All you would have cared about is how to monetize him."

"I almost killed this boy! I punished him!" Romas shouted. Outside the tower, I heard the sound of bells which apparently was the signal for humans to return to the courtyard. A murmur rose from the streets, everyone seeing the destruction for the first time. The same Feka who told the humans to go to the bunkers told everyone to begin wall repair. Romas and Typh heard the same.

"We better move. There is a lot to do to prepare for a return attack. I doubt that was the last we've seen of those monsters. And now that the settlement is without a proper wall..." Typh didn't finish that thought, worry plastered across his feline features.

Romas nodded. "We are going to have to prepare for a retreat to Fayport. We cannot lose any more of our kind, especially if it will strengthen the Shadowalkers." A sad expression tugged at his eyes.

"Agreed," Typh nodded. The two Feka didn't say anything for a while. Finally, he continued, "I made a deal with the human in the cave. He has been released from the work class."

Romas scoffed. "Well, he's a creator class. Of course, he won't be a no-classer! I don't know what to do with him right now, though. When the other Feka find out..." He trailed off, unsure. "Who else knows?" he finally asked.

"The Baron," Typh replied. "And my step-sister."

Romas chuckled. "Of course she does." He turned to me. "What other tricks do you have, human? Your lightning attack seems very useful against the Shadowalker troops. Anything else?"

I caught him up on where I was at with my powers, not hiding much. There was no reason for secrecy, especially if I could gain a master blacksmith mentor from the deal. If the Shadowalkers returned, the Feka would be hard-pressed to stop them a second time. He may lend me some of his ingredients to create with. My mana was slightly refilled, now showing [8/24], but I wasn't even close to being able to make anything else of value.

I needed to learn more about getting faster mana regeneration, more mana, and cheaper mana costs. I saw Romas make tons of weapons and armor in a day. There had to be a shortcut. But I doubted he would tell all his secrets around Typh, especially when I learned about his 'expensive mining costs' lie that I debunked by accident in the cave. Typh was a buyer of his goods, after all. Mysteries around creating these high-level items needed to remain, or people would spend less on what Romas created.

Then there was the magic itself. *Could Romas tell when I made the fire class items? He couldn't seem to tell when I made air magic. Was I the only person on this planet who could use these two branches of magic? I highly doubted that. Were there even more branches to unlock? If there was fire and air, maybe there was water and earth.*

There were secrets to unlock here on Prixa, and I needed to find someone who knew some answers. With that, we returned to the courtyard to prepare for another attack, the sun rising on a horrible night.

Chapter 19

Pulley Physics

It felt good to have my cards on the table. If I was going to make a difference here, I needed to be able to mine, train, and create. Ideas had been springing up in my mind throughout my time at Prixa, and it was time to use my engineering skills to solve some of the problems the Feka had. There were some glaring ones, that was for sure.

I followed Typh and Romas into the courtyard, and I could see the damage up close for the first time. The salty air from the gulf helped with the smell of death, but there was still an overpowering stink throughout the settlement. Fires went up to burn the fallen ingredients, the smoke black and rancid. I looked on in interest, a sadness forming in the pit of my stomach. *It looks like the Feka won't take ingredients from their fellow warriors.*

Fountains were damaged, leaving stone and water scattered in the streets as jets of water soared everywhere. Merchant stalls were blasted apart, and wood pieces were being picked up by the merchant no-classer crew in their bright yellow shirts. Another group of no-classers picked up arrows, now free of their targets.

And, of course, the wall. In the sunlight, it was clear that we weren't fixing the wall anytime soon. I scanned the workforce, looking for Jasper. He was near the battle site, picking up fangs and dog pelts with the two other younger human workers who replaced me when I went to the docks a few days ago.

Romas swooped down to make sure every ingredient was accounted for. He barked orders to Jasper, pointing and growling to get him moving faster. A moment later, Jasper made eye contact with me and waved. He looked confused when he realized I wasn't over there with him cleaning up the ingredients. I gave him a small smile, waved, and continued walking, catching up to Typh.

"Typh, can I have a moment?" I asked the jaguar.

Typh looked at me, distracted in thought. He paused, considering, then nodded. He ushered me into a side alley. "What is it, Noah?" I noticed he didn't call me human, or boy, like usual.

"It's time I helped at the settlement. Being a Creator isn't just about making weapons."

"What do you mean?" he asked, confused.

"Back where I came from, I was an engineer. Well, I was in training. You could call me an engineering apprentice. Engineers make devices to help with day-to-day chores, transport materials and people faster, all kinds of stuff."

Typh narrowed his eyes. "And these...engineers. Do they fight for your people? Do they make weapons?"

I chuckled. "Some do. In fact, engineers are responsible for the largest weapons that we have back on Earth. But most do not. Our people have created glorious castles, monuments, and even vehicles that can fly. I need to learn to do that, but I have skills here. And right now, we won't beat the Shadowalkers in a head-to-head fight. If they come back, they will win. They will track us down and kill us. We will need more time to retreat to your central city."

"And you think you can create something useful before they return?"

I nodded, a mischievous smile crossing my lips. "I think so. Or I would like to try. But I'm going to need some help."

I looked around the small room, faces of humans and Feka staring back at me. I gulped down the fear bubbling up from my gut. I wasn't too fond of public speaking, and it had been a while since I presented in front of this many people.

My palms were sweaty, and I felt my heart beating rapidly. When I told Typh my plan, he sprang into action, tracking down the three humans from the dock, Dee, Romas, and a few other humans I didn't know. They wore purple shirts with a logo I hadn't seen yet. It looked regal, with crossing birds and a lion roaring over a field of the crop I saw in the farms. A few other warrior class Feka were present, including the one I saved from the battle.

"Hello, everyone," I started, voice squeaking a bit. I cleared my throat, the room's occupants glancing at each other. "You're here today to help improve the city's defenses. And to learn a secret that has not become public knowledge yet." I paused to ensure I said this next part correctly. "I'm not from this world. I'm from a place called Earth, not Prixa. When I came here, I was assigned a Creator class. I can make things here on this planet." There was mumbling among the group, eyes darting around the room. The humans looked hopeful, the Feka unsure.

"On my planet, creators make magnificent structures. Defenses that even the most battle-hardened warriors can't get through. And moats. Moats were a fantastic idea. I really like moats. Anyway, the first thing we need here is something called a drawbridge. The way the pulleys work together helps reduce the overall weight of the bridge, enabling just a few humans to pull something extremely heavy. Since you have only one way up into the upper levels of the settlement, the wolves shouldn't be able to attack us if we pull the ramp up. So instead of having a moat around your city, you have

125

floating tree arms 30 feet up in the air. It should work the same way."

Everyone looked at each other like I was speaking another language. Romas spoke up first. "This seems impossible. You cannot make something weigh less."

"You can," I replied. "In my world, it's called *physics*. You're not making something weigh less...you're changing the force needed every time you add pulleys. For example, if you have one pulley and pull a 100-pound weight, it will feel like 100 pounds. But if you make that system three pulleys, the same weight only feels like 33 pounds."

"What's a pound?" Typh asked.

I wasn't getting anywhere explaining the physics here.

"Look, at the end of the day, they're dogs. Dogs can't climb like you Feka can. If we take away access to the upper part of your town, they will need to figure out a new way in, buying us some time. I can design this system if you can trust me." I looked around the room, seeing the uneasy faces of the Feka, the idea of trusting a human baffling to them.

"Which brings me to my next idea." I looked at the dock workers. "I want to transport the spikey fish destroyer to the upper levels and make them dog destroyers instead. Hopefully, we have some spares?"

The lead no-classer from the dock spoke up. "Yes...we have three in rotation. They weigh as much as four Feka, though. How do we get them up the hills? This all seems like a waste of time to us, Creator."

That was strange, being addressed by 'Creator' instead of 'no-classer' or even 'Noah.'

I nodded to him. "Getting them up here will be hard work, but these traps will be worth it." I grinned again, excited now. "It will take time to set all this up, so we must hurry. Romas, I'm going to need some help. I hope to show you the blueprints using my

'DESIGN' skill, and you can execute the creation. I don't have much mana and have no idea how much these items will cost, so all I can do is design them."

Romas scoffed at that. "Bah, creators do not make pulley toys. We make weapons and armor. I hope you know what you're doing, boy. The Shadowalkers will be back in a moon or so."

Trust me...I hope so too. "That's why we need to hurry. The first thing we'll make is a good ol' drawbridge."

I used my 'DESIGN' skill to create the pulley system and ropes needed for the drawbridge. The contraption needed three medium size pulleys mounted to the tower's underside and two bigger pulleys mounted inside the ramp's entrance. They connected to a wheel that turned horizontally through inter-locking teeth with the last pulley, which was clever. I saw iron and wood from the bow trees in my mind, with slots designating the amounts for each. *Was that me being clever or Prixa? I still needed to understand who was 'designing.'*

This time, another design called 'Advanced Drawbridge' showed in my mind and involved counterweights. We didn't have time for that, but seeing multiple iterations was excellent. I looked at my arm and realized 'DESIGN' had leveled up, which must have been a benefit from the increased level.

My mana went from [10/25] to [1/26], the advanced designing used mana much faster than before. *Is this the same for mining and inspecting? I also want to know what versions to use and when. If I tried to think of something small or simple, would it use level 1? If I was only mining silver ore, could I choose that? If I needed some unfound ore, I could do some advanced mining.*

I wasn't sure and hadn't had a chance to talk to Romas yet. I told him the amount of iron and bow wood material needed and described the pulleys to him, and he took it from there. He told me he made the pulleys for the dock and didn't need 'some human to tell him how to do his job,' then huffed off to the smithy. We had plenty of rope in the settlement, so that wasn't an issue. I didn't know where the hostility came from, as the city's survival was much more important to me. Regardless, I rolled my eyes and continued to the next assignment.

"You three." I pointed at the strong dock workers. "Eventually, I want to make carts for you people. How you haven't invented the wheel yet..." I trailed off, shaking my head. "Regardless, I don't have any mana to help you. All we can do is take shifts carrying those fish-crushing devices up here. Get as many dock workers as possible and get them hauling those weights. Then we will need to install them directly over the ramp."

Dee looked at me, stepping forward. "I can help with your mana. My father has a mana regeneration device. It's how he's made so many devices in a day. The drawback of it is the payment. The mana you use is taken from mana later on...so you will regenerate mana much faster, but your body can only take that for so long. He says you get 'mana poisoning' and do not regenerate mana for as long as the bracer is on. It's why he drinks at night. He works doubly hard during the day and sleeps just as hard at night. But since a battle is coming and your pulleys seem reasonable on his mana load, even though they are enormous, I bet he won't wear it to save some mana for his fighting skills."

My eyebrows raised at that. I knew there had to be a way to make things more quickly; the mana on this planet was abysmal compared to some video games I played on Earth. I had been here days and only made a choice few items and mined a few rocks. But since none of my skills needed mana to shoot my slingshot, I didn't care if I was out of mana. My proficiency with it was mana free and passive, and the pellets used mana to create, not to shoot. I needed to defend the city, then let the professionals do the actual combat. "Great. Can you grab it for me?"

Dee's face lit up. "Of course!" With that, she bounded off into the street.

The remaining Feka in the room shuffled their feet, the one I saved from the last battle speaking up. "What of us, human? What do you need of the warrior Feka? We cannot sit ideally by and wait while everyone else works."

"You three with me," I replied. "We will return to the caves after I get my bracer on. It's time we added a little fire magic to these dog crushers."

Chapter 20

Mana Smells Like Fish

Dee brought me the bracer, excitement plastered across her face. "Put it on!" She dropped it at my feet, backing up expectantly.

I picked up the bracer, the metal cool in my hands. It was a gleaming silver circlet with delicate patterns and runes dotting its surface. It had a smell that I couldn't place. I looked up at her, nervous. She grinned back at me, making a motion with her paw.

Before proceeding, I looked down at my wrist to see the changes in my character sheet.

[LV 4- BLACKSMITH APPRENTICE]

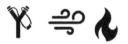

[HEALTH 38/41]
[MANA 3/26]

L4

L2

Passive

L3

I had made some sizeable gains. As my health increased, I began feeling better overall. I huffed and puffed less while walking up the ramps, could pick up heavier items, and ate more fish-corn mixture the Feka provided. My mana went up, but I couldn't regenerate fast enough to make anything valuable or use skills for very long. I took a deep breath and slipped the bracer on my left wrist, determined to make a difference on this planet. Suddenly, the voice spoke in my head, asking what I wanted to do.

[YOU HAVE ENABLED A '**MANA REGENERATION**' ITEM. WOULD YOU LIKE TO TAKE A {1 MANA/1 MINUTE BOOST FOR ONE (1) HOUR}, OR {20 MANA NOW, 1 MANA/3 MINUTE BOOST FOR ONE (1) HOUR}?]

She paused as I thought on that, then continued.

[REMINDER, USING THIS ITEM WILL RESULT IN MANA POISONING, RESULTING IN A EIGHT (8) HOUR LACK OF MANA REGENERATION]

Interesting! It gave me a choice. Was that again from my level 4 'CREATE' skill? Or even 'DESIGN?' Who knew? Either way, I had to decide if I wanted 60 mana over an hour, but I would get it slower or 20 right away, filling up my mana pool immediately. But that option only had 40 total instead of the full 60. I could see the use if you needed to make something in a pinch, but I was in a different situation.

Considering I still had to travel to the caves with the warrior Feka, I decided. "I will take one mana per minute." Dee glanced at me, startled that I seemed to speak randomly. I shrugged. "Guess we see what happens now."

I looked down at my arm, feeling a strange sensation from the bracer. It felt like someone injected warm fluid into my veins, almost like an IV drip. It was the opposite effect of the ore mining or design skill, the bracer becoming a warm, tingling sensation on my arm instead of a sucking feeling.

I estimated my current mana regeneration at around one mana every ten minutes. I could replenish my 26 in about four hours. Health regeneration left me entirely in the dark, as natural healing was all I could do when injured, and that took time. The three health missing was most likely from my scratched shoulders and ear. I was sure there was some health regeneration item, but I didn't worry. The health bar on my arm left a lot of information to be desired.

"Well? Is it working?" Dee asked, leaning forward and sniffing my arm. "Smells like it is!"

I looked sidelong at her. "Seriously? You can smell mana?"

"Well, kind of. You can smell food when it's sitting on a plate, but can't smell it anymore after you eat it. It's like you're wearing fish on your arm." I looked at her, confused. "Ok, well, not fish. Something not as smelly. It smells amazing." I continued staring, not sure what to say to that.

"Let's get going. Can you come with me to the caves? I should trust these three warriors, but I don't know them..." I asked, changing the subject.

"Of course! I thought you would never ask. We will meet you on ground level!" With that, she bounded off again, the group of them jumping down to the ground. I shook my head as she left. There were times here on Prixa when the cat creatures reminded me of home.

Ambrose slowed his run as he reached the encampment where the rest of the Shadowalker army hid. He had been careful to send Whitefangs around the perimeter to sniff around and ensure the Feka were not scouting them. The beta was still determining how this would go with the alpha. He hit the directives in battle but lost several Stalkers to the new magic.

A fox-looking creature sat in front of a map, waiting for Ambrose to report back so he could update his battle plans. His troops walked past him, panting slightly and barking at their friends in friendly greeting. A few sniffed butts in hello. *Miserable creatures,* Ambrose thought to himself. He saw the Jackals with their serving bags strapped to their backs, wandering the camp looking for troops to serve.

In the middle of the camp was the alpha's den. He went straight there, ignoring the calls of the red fox. He knew if he lingered, the alpha would know. He peeked his head into the tent, sniffing. "Sire, we have returned."

The alpha opened one eye, sleeping on his back on a black cot. Ambrose knew this was mostly for show; the alpha rarely slept for fear of being challenged. He rolled onto all fours and stood, shaking his head from side to side. The alpha stood up to his full height, almost hitting his head on the structure. "Report!" he growled, narrowing his eyes.

"The attack on the settlement went to plan. The walls were not very strong, and our Bullheads blasted through them without effort. However, we lost all but one of those creatures. We also lost about one-third of our troops inside the settlement but eliminated their archer troops and a few of their warrior class. A surprise attack by their hunters got more troops than I would have liked." Ambrose growled, thinking of the cowardly attack on his Whitefangs.

The alpha sniffed the air, leaning toward him. Ambrose couldn't help but lean away, fear bubbling in his gut. "Why do I smell such strange death on you? How many of your group have you lost, beta?"

"Unfortunately, we lost two of our Stalker group. It was that human boy again, and possibly others. They had access to fire magic and lit Gyros ablaze. His fur singed during battle, leaving him vulnerable to a Fekan attack. It appears the humans are helping the felines."

The alpha narrowed his eyes. Finally, he spoke in a low growl. "Have you eliminated this threat? Or can I expect more *surprises* in the settlement upon our final attack? Since when can humans use magic?" He practically screamed this last part, the walls shaking slightly.

"I sent five Whitefangs into the tower where the attacks came from. Even if the Feka got to them after, they would have eliminated the humans hiding there. We will be good to attack."

"We better be. You have performed well. I smell no lies or deceit on you. However, I do not smell any fresh meat to consume. Explain."

"Sorry, sire, we had to retreat before our losses from battle continued. The archer's bodies had to stay."

The alpha growled, loud and long, causing Ambrose to shrink back. "No matter. We will have plenty of warrior Feka to consume. And once we break into their bunkers, we will feed the humans to the pack. Possibly keep them for our use. We will become stronger than ever, preparing for our attack on Fayport. Get some rest, beta. We move out in at the largest moonrise."

I walked down the path, flanked by my posse of four 6-foot-tall cat warriors, feeling a bit like a boss. I had friends back home on Earth, of course, but none that could kill a 3-foot Squamish squirrel for me without even batting an eye. I was never 'cool'; the only attention I got from athletes was when they needed help with their math homework.

It was quiet in the jungle, and the effect of having four predator cats prowling around was evident. They moved in a line on the path, ears circling and eyes darting around the fauna, looking for danger. As we walked, I stared at my arm, obsessed with how quickly my mana was filling up.

By the time we got to the cave, I was already at [14/27]. The other benefit to having the bracer on was the increase in total mana, my body working hard to process the additional mana, almost like a cardio workout. Once we got to the cave entrance, I addressed the Feka. "You guys stay here. Make sure nothing comes in. I can yell if I need anything. Dee, you're with me."

"Woah, Noah. I know you're a Creator now, but calm down the orders." She smiled but mumbled about bossy humans and went into the cave. She took out a purple mushroom vial, bathing the light in the eerie purple glow. I followed the light into the cave.

Further in, I saw the same two ore veins behind the walls. I wanted the red ore for my plans with the settlement defense. "Do you need me for anything else? Because if not, I'm going to take a little nap."

I chuckled. "Nope. I just wanted you away from the other three. I can't have those warriors see this part." She nodded, curled up in a beam of sunlight, and closed her eyes.

I walked to the cave wall, picked my target, and stuck my hand in the wall. The IV drip feeling stopped, and the familiar sucking returned while I dug around the wall. I pulled out a piece of the red-streaked rock and put it in my pocket. [9/27]. Nice. I could get 2-3 more pieces of ore in this charge. My skill would level up by then, unlocking who knew what.

Over the next five minutes, I picked out three more pieces, only having to wait a few moments to fill up my bar enough for the final piece while the bracer did its work. I grabbed three red ores and one silver since I needed additional ammo. During the battle, I used my last Wind pellet to avoid having one ammo type.

I glanced at my arm, and sure enough, my mining skill had risen to level 3. My overall mana read [2/30], the mining and bracer continuously upping my mana pool. I hoped I would have a whole pool of mana by the time I returned to the settlement. I needed to make three dog-crushing devices, and if I was the only one who could use fire magic, I had to make them. Hopefully, it would cost one piece of ore per device. If it were more, I would be out of luck. I took a minute to look at the walls, not noticing any new ore.

Slightly disappointed, I woke Dee up, getting us moving. I emerged into the jungle, the moist air noticeably different than the stuffy cave air. By my calculation, I had about 30 mana left from the bracer. I smiled and nodded to the warriors, finished with my task. They nodded back and headed off into the jungle.

It was time for the next phase of my plan. I hoped there was enough time to install all of this stuff before the Shadowalkers returned. Romas should be done with the pulleys by now, but I didn't know how long the dock workers would take to bring the crushers up the hills. If there was anything I learned from engineering class, it was whatever could go wrong usually did. There was so much to do. I sighed, putting one foot in front of the other. We had to hurry back before the mana poisoning started.

Chapter 21

Drawbridge 101

THE TOWER WAS LIKE A BUZZING BEEHIVE WHEN WE returned. I looked at the Fekan structure again, admiring it. Surprisingly, the cats took my advice and focused entirely on the drawbridge idea, abandoning the walls. This shocked me since the Feka were very prideful creatures. I didn't know the engineering behind the floating arms of the various levels, but I assumed it was built just like a tree. Who knows, maybe it was an enormous tree at one point.

I had given my plans to Romas that morning. I don't think the city was to scale, but at least he could see where everything was going and how the pulleys would be hung.

Around the base of the ramp, humans with purple shirts dug up the base and corners of the ramp, freeing it from the ground. Over centuries, the front of the ramp had sunk into the soil, a challenge that even my pulleys wouldn't have overcome. I was glad they had thought of that, or I would have ripped my pulleys right off their mounts the first time we tried to pull the ramp up.

I chuckled to myself, wondering what else I had forgotten about. Sitting on the ground to the right of the ramp was one of the gigantic fish-smashing devices. I hoped the other two were on their way, but I could get started on installing the first one. I planned to hang them from various sections of the tower's underside. There were sections of the castle that stuck out over the base level. If I hung dog smashers on pulleys controlled from the first level, we could release them onto unsuspecting dogs below as they waited to enter the ramp's tunnel. It would only work once or twice for a sizable casualty event.

At the top of the ramp, Romas directed both Feka and a few humans. He saw me and waved, moving his paw in a 'come here' motion. I took off jogging, getting to the ramp, and looking up. "Looks good!" I called, giving a thumbs up.

Romas pointed at the underside of the tower, right over where I was standing. "I've finished the three medium pulleys," he said, looking slightly excited for once. I looked up, seeing them hanging up there in a vertical line. "They have been installed in the section you requested over the corners of the ramp. Are you sure, human? This looks strange. How do we install the rope?"

I took a deep breath and looked at the cat on the ladder, awaiting my instructions. "Ok, so you start at the top pulley. The rope goes to the bottom pulley from where we're pulling it over there." I pointed, the cat threading the rope through the first pulley but dropping the rope. His paws were not ideal for tasks like this. "It's ok. Swap out with a human. We have fingers for tasks like this."

The Feka looked around, their hair slightly raised and a low growl escaping their throats. It was just low enough that it was tough to hear, but I didn't miss it. "Sorry. You're doing great!" I tried to smile, but it was too late. *Ugh, contractor management is totally not my thing.*

The Feka got down from the ladder, switching with the lead no-classer from the docks. He grabbed the rope and climbed up, pulling the rope through the first pulley. "Ok, now go to the bottom one and loop it from top to bottom. Yep, just like that! You want the bottom pulley in a little sling."

I thought carefully about this next part. "Now pull the rope from the bottom pulley around the top of the middle one. That will lead to the ground, which connects to the corner." He did as I said; the rope dropped to the ground. "Ok, come down. I'll show you how this works."

I walked over to the bottom of the ladder. "Now pick me up," I told the dock worker, getting weird looks from everyone. He did so with a slight *oof*, picking me up in a bear hug. I may have lost some weight in my few weeks here, but I still had to weigh over 200 lbs. I got about a foot off the ground, then said, "Ok! That's enough." He put me down.

Glancing back to the top of the ramp, I saw a crowd of warriors and merchants gathered there, watching the show. *Now for the fun part.* I walked over to the 'weight' part of the rope and grabbed it. "Great, now go grab the part of the rope we're going to pull to activate the drawbridge." He did as I said, the Feka all leaning forward. "Now pull!" I yelled, hanging on.

With a yank, he pulled the rope, causing me to fly into the air. "Let me down! Careful!" I yelled, laughing and grinning, the Feka on the wall whooping and cheering. The dock worker looked absolutely amazed at what he just saw. He held the rope in his hands like he was holding a magic wand, then glanced up at the pulleys, waiting for them to jump off the tower and eat him.

"Well done, human! No-classer - what did it feel like? Was he lighter?" Romas yelled down, excitement all over his furry face.

The no-classer looked around, never having the authority to speak to the masters. "He was...very light. He felt like two bags of corn instead of ten!"

I laughed, knowing the math here. That was a stretch, but I was glad the worker felt the difference. My whole plan depended on it.

Once the other pulleys were installed and ropes attached to the corners of the ramp, we started to work on the large pulleys. The opening at the top of the ramp was around 20 feet high, so the rope came at almost a straight line from the top pulley to the first level. "Ok, install those lifting pulleys at the ramp's opening. We will install the winch, the wood thing you made with the arms, Romas, behind the big pulleys. One goes on each side of the walkway. Eventually, we can build a gatehouse. For now, we need to put these in here and here." I pointed.

The large spool connected to the winch just looked like the rod for a fly-fishing pole, the winch interlocking with the spool's teeth to turn the gigantic spool to reel in the rope. It was glorious. "We must ensure the two sides lift evenly, or the ramp will come up all crooked. As we rotate it with the arm, the rope will wind around the big spool."

The Feka got to work, installing the pulleys to my designation. While they worked on that, I went to the bottom level to check on my dog smashing device. On the upper level, two humans had finished cutting a small rectangular hole in the floor. They installed another pulley there, with rope hanging down. On their way to the other side of the ramp, a different section of the tower hung over the main level's dirt. They smiled at me and waved, hope in their eyes.

I approached the fish-smashing device, tying the rope to the top. "Anyone up there to try this thing out?" I yelled.

A few moments later, a head peeked down. It was the warrior from the cave trip. "We will pull this for you, human. Is it ready for trial?"

"It should be!" I double-checked my rope. The knot looked good. "Give it a pull!"

The rope went taunt, paused momentarily, then the weight began lifting. I heard growling and straining up on the first level of the tower. Eventually, the weight reached the top, hitting the underside of the first level. "Ok, now drop it!"

I scrambled out of the way, watching intently. The weight crashed down at breakneck speed, impacting the ground with a thunderous **boom.** The Feka put their head in the hole, looking down. "That was amazing! We would have certainly killed anything under there!" The three smiled, grabbed the rope, and tried to pull. The weight wouldn't budge.

I looked closer; the impact was so great that the teeth had lodged into the ground, making it nearly impossible to get out. *Oops.* "Uh, take a break, guys! Thanks for the first test!" I shook my head, thinking about how to solve this issue.

Before I could get too deep into troubleshooting mode, I was called to the top of the ramp. The system was installed and ready for its first test. *Hopefully, this test will go better than the dog-smasher.* I jogged back over to the pulley. A burning in my arm got my attention. *Oh no, the mana bracer!* I thought with slight panic. My mana now read [33/30], and my arm turned a shade of blue like the circulation was being cut off. I glanced around, deciding to combine the fish-smasher teeth with my red ore.

I grabbed a piece, ran back down to the fish-smasher, then held the side of the weight. The ore felt *confused* in my mind, not knowing what I wanted to do. I used 'DESIGN' and went through the process of making the teeth include the fire magic within their metal. I cut off my 'DESIGN' skill, and the ore now understood my goal. I felt the ore disappear from my hand, the weight turning red. I inspected the weight.

[FISH PROCESSING DEVICE - FIRE TAINTED]

In the distance, I heard the sounds of barking and laughing of the hyenas filtering through the trees. A few howls rang out, increasing in volume as more dogs joined the cries. I left the weight in the ground, abandoning the project for now, and took off as fast as possible toward the ramp. I hoped the ramp was ready because there wasn't any more time to test it.

Chapter 22

Hold the Line

HORNS SOUNDED IN THE SETTLEMENT AS THE FEKAN warriors saw the coming Shadowalker army. The bells rang again, alerting the humans to return to the bunkers. No one was in the fields since the workforce was put to use inside the settlement. "Wait!" I yelled up. "I need those dock workers! Don't let them go back to the bunker!" I wasn't sure if anyone had heard me.

The sun was setting on Dunbar and the winds were picking up. I felt a few splashes of rain on my face as I reached the base of the ramp and turned back to look around. A storm was brewing in the jungle; the waves beyond the settlement were gaining height. It hadn't rained as much during my few days here as I figured it would, being a jungle and all. The heat was manageable too. I wondered if it was some season where the temperature fell and the rain subsided. They had called that Olympic event the *Spring Games*, so that made sense.

"Human, faster! We need to get this ramp up!" one of the warriors yelled. I sped up the incline as fast as my legs could, shaking the whole thing now that it was hanging on the thick ropes. I blasted out onto the ramp landing, looking around at the once again chaotic scene unfolding. With the missing archers, there was no one in the towers. But that gave me an idea.

145

"Typh! Where is Typh?" I yelled to a few of the Feka, who shook their heads and ignored me. I scrambled around, looking for familiar faces but finding none.

"Noah! Noah over here!" I heard my name from the crowd. It was Dee. She pushed her way through and ran over to me.

"Not now, Dee. We need to get this ramp up before the army gets here."

"I heard you shouting for Typh. What do you need? I saw him on the upper levels gathering some merchants to help fight."

I tossed my hair out of my eyes, the rain starting to fall harder. "I wanted to see if the hunter class could use bows. Or even the Spring Game winners, can those humans help us and shoot bows?" I looked to the woods, seeing the first few canine troops coming through. I spoke faster. "If this ramp works, we will have free shots at the Shadowalkers before they can retreat out of range. They shouldn't have a way to get up here. Not yet anyway."

Dee nodded. "Well, we aren't going to be as good as the fallen archers. But we can certainly shoot pointy arrows at these disgusting beasts," she said with a grin. "I'll gather up the remaining archers and the hunters."

"Great. Thanks, Dee!" She bounded off toward the hunter towers. I sucked in a deep breath, yelling, "Everyone to the winch! Now!"

The three dock workers, who were held back from the bunkers as I asked, took up their position at one of the winches while me and three of the warrior Feka went to the other one. The whole army had broken through the treeline, way more dogs than before. The troop types varied as well. Last to come through the trees were the ten or so Stalkers, flanked by their alpha. I had never met the beast, but I could instantly tell who he was.

"Push!" I yelled, straining to get the wheel to move. We put our backs into the wheel, the rope getting taunt on the upper pulleys. Then, after a few of the longest few seconds I have ever experienced, the ramp came off the ground. "Let's go! Keep the momentum!" I yelled at the pulley team.

The pulleys strained on their mounts, the total weight of the ramp on two metal connections. I had no idea how the Feka connected those pulleys, but I hoped magic was involved some-how. Their settlement architecture had physics that I didn't understand, so I knew they could make some strong structures.

I hear howling in the distance, the frenzied barking starting and getting closer.

"Hurry!" It was Romas, of course not helping and only watching, eyes darting between us and the woodline. They must have seen the dogs almost at the walls. Behind me, two other giant Fekan warriors joined in. On the other hand, I saw a similar situation. *I've got to add more pulleys to reduce the weight more. Later, Noah! Focus!*

The wheels started turning smoothly, the rope coiling into the spools. "It's working!" a Feka cried behind me.

"Ok, Keep pushing! I need to make sure everything is holding together!!" I yelled. I stepped away from the winch, checking out the ramp's position. We had moved it about ten feet off the ground, one-third of the way up. I peered over the wall of the building's level, seeing what the army was doing.

As expected, the pit bulls ran back and forth under the ramp, barking madly. *If I only had my dog crushers,* I thought to myself. Behind the front-line troops, the Stalkers talked amongst themselves, pointing to the ramp and walls. The alpha sat back, observing the situation, a neutral expression on his face. He saw me, his eyes narrowing, his teeth bared. That wasn't a good sign.

Suddenly, the seven-foot-tall werewolves took off toward the settlement. If they could jump even slightly on their two legs, they could reach the ramp and pull it back down. The pit bull and hyena troops were no concern at the moment due to the height of the ramp off the ground, but they would swarm the walkway as soon as it was on the dirt. If that happened...well, we would all get torn to shreds.

"Keep going! The Stalkers are coming!" I yelled, fear in everyone's eyes. Getting their fear translated into momentum took a brief, terrifying moment. But the ramp rose, slowly but surely. "Romas, tell me when we're there!" I rushed.

Sweat poured down my face, mixing with the rain coming down harder now. The wind was whipping, the smell of the musty jungle taking over the air. I heard the *twang* of bows as the hunters started raining down on the troops below. A few yelps sounded, but not as many as I would have liked.

Finally, Romas stopped us. "You're there! Stop! Any higher, and you will hit the pulleys!" A ragged cheer went out from the human and Feka.

"What now?" A straining Feka asked behind me, holding the winch in place.

I looked between the two pulleys. "Ok, there is a spot that needs to be locked with a locking pin. Romas, where did you put it?" I glanced at the panther. He looked back at me with the '*I don't know what you're talking about*' look.

Below, the howling and barking was at a fever pitch. The frustrated dogs tried everything they could to access the cat tower without getting shot with arrows. "Romas! Damn it! I have to run to the shop for the pins! Hold it steady!." *Oops, maybe I didn't tell him.*

I activated my 'DESIGN' skill, knowing I had enough mana for this, but that mana poisoning would prevent me from gaining anything back. I would be useless after I made these rods. I thought about the long metal T-shaped pieces and what materials I needed. It ended up being two simple pieces of iron, but now I had the plans. I flew toward the blacksmith and yelled, "Hold the winch there! Don't let it go, or the ramp will drop!"

I didn't get a chance to glance back but heard the strain of the group holding a ton of ramp. I sprinted through the city, finally getting to my destination. I exploded through the door, and panic set in. Romas' collection of iron, steel, brass, and every other non-magic metal type was in the corner.

I dug through the bin, tossing metal everywhere. In the darkness, all the metal looked the same. Slag cut my hand and arm as I continued my frantic search. I finally found two pieces of iron, stopped my search, and combined them in my mind. After a moment, a long rod sat in my hand with a large cross piece at the top so it wouldn't slide through the teeth.

I repeated my search, finding two more pieces and creating the other winch pin. Turning and running out of the blacksmith, I returned to the winch. I heard even more barking and chaos below the drawbridge.

New Feka were replacing the exhausted warriors who were holding it in place. I shimmied around them, getting to the spot between the two teeth where I could slide in the locking pin. It went in with no problem. "Ok, let go!" The warriors looked at each other, unsure. "Guys, it's ok. Let go!" I shimmied back out from the winch and ran to the other, performing the same task.

I stepped back, looking at my handiwork. The Feka and dock-workers looked on in astonishment. The winch held the pulley in place without anyone touching it, the drawbridge fully up. It had worked.

Baron Gilbert came over, putting his paw on my shoulder. "That was great work, human. You say your world doesn't have magic? Well, I don't know what else you would call this. You've saved us all today." He had a fatherly smile on his face, beaming down at me, fur matted and drenched from the downpour.

The Shadowalkers had already been called back, retreating to the woods. Fangs and pelts littered the dirt below, hyenas and dogs meeting their end at the hunter's hands. The pack of stalkers went into the jungle next, a few turning back one last time to look at the settlement, then disappearing. Finally, the alpha, who had been watching the whole time, turned and started walking into the jungle. Before he did, he let out a long, slow howl. It prickled my skin and made my hair stand up. I covered my ears from the sound.

The warrior Feka jumped onto the tower's edge, roaring victoriously at the alpha. With that, the werewolf leader turned and retreated into the jungle.

END OF ACT II

Interlude

The alpha stopped short of their city, calling to his beta in a low, threatening growl. "Ambrose. To me."

The dog stopped in his tracks, about to head to his den and sleep. After days of trotting through this godforsaken jungle, he was so tired. And all for nothing, the Feka figuring out a way to close their settlement to them.

The alpha would only call him short of the gates for one reason; a challenge was about to be initiated. Pride kicked in, Ambrose standing tall on his two legs to face the alpha. "Yes, sire?"

"You have failed me for the last time. Face me, and prove you should be allowed to live."

"Of course, sire." The beta wolf trembled but strode forward, facing his death with dignity. The other Stalkers looked on, not saying anything. The city's noise filtered through the air, but outside the gates, all was still. The rest of the troops had already entered the town, their canine brains not advanced enough to know what was happening.

The Stalkers had seen this play out countless times before, each beta failing the alpha somehow and losing in a challenge, only to strengthen the alpha further. They made a semicircle, long wolfish faces grim.

The Shadowalkers had lost their third in command at the first battle of Dunbar; the human setting him on fire with his magical powers. After this battle, there would be a power struggle for the title of beta of the city. The alpha wanted it this way, most likely. Keeping his second-in-command combat-ready was his top priority. Even a group of three Stalkers could rarely defeat a fully trained Feka, so melee training was crucial.

The two werewolves circled each other, neither making a move. Ambrose realized he was overmatched, so he took the offensive. He dashed forward, claws and jaws flashing. He dove for the alpha's neck but was batted away. The alpha growled, red eyes flashing.

He landed a kick to Ambrose's side, sending him flying into the pack. They pushed him back into the circle. He stood up, wavering slightly, and dove at the alpha again. They each went for the neck, arms, and jaws flailing, but as their bodies slammed together, neither could bite the other as they wrestled.

Then the alpha shifted his hold, shoving Ambrose backward and pushing him to the ground. His powerful jaws clamped down, Ambrose struggling underneath him with a yelp. He tried to swing his arms to knock his opponent loose, but the alpha was too strong. After a few moments, the duel finished as Ambrose stopped moving. The alpha stood up, blood in his teeth from the bite.

He turned to the pack and howled, long and eerie. They joined in, the howl clearing birds from the jungle canopy. Then the alpha turned and dove into his meal, consuming his prey.

A few of the Stalkers turned and went into the city. The dogs at the bottom of the pecking order knew they had no chance of becoming beta and would get seriously hurt in the upcoming scrap. Those who wanted the position waited out of respect until they were inside the gates.

The four remaining Stalkers circled each other, dropping into a fighting stance while the alpha continued his meal. Unlike the alpha's challenge to the beta, this would not be to the death. But serious injuries were likely. Such was the cost of power. Such was the cost of living in Niridge.

One of the dogs lunged, and the fight was on.

Chapter 23

Gifts to the City

I WOKE UP THE NEXT DAY FEELING BETTER THAN I HAD since being here. There was something about solving a problem through engineering that I couldn't describe. The Feka thought what I did was *magic*. I had never thought of physics in this way before; that was the whole point of physics back on Earth. It wasn't magic, it was science.

But to these creatures, what I did was unheard of. I had stopped an army of vile dog beasts with several pulleys and some rope. *And about ten cat creatures who are much more muscular than I could ever dream of being,* I thought, chuckling to myself.

"Human, you are needed in the courtyard immediately," Romas called toward where Jasper and I slept. Jasper groaned, still tired from the evening's events. I had barely slept but felt rested. I rolled out of bed, donned my squirrel vest over my black shirt, and slipped my slingshot into my belt loop. My dagger was always on me now. *Never sure what would happen in this world.*

Romas cleared his throat, continuing. "Jasper, you too. We want the whole settlement present, no-classers included."

Jasper's head jolted up, his eyes blinking rapidly. He looked at me, confused. I shrugged my shoulders. "Better get moving," I said.

We washed up in the basin, Jasper lending me his comb. My hair was getting longer; the curly mess was almost in my eyes. My scraggly beard started to slowly fill in. *I need to make some hair-trimming devices. Do the cats use stuff like that?* I added that to my growing list of items to create.

With our grooming taken care of, we headed into the city. Most of the Feka were outside, chatting quietly. The trashed merchant stalls still needed to be repaired, but the wood was picked up off the streets. Humans filtered into the square wearing various colors and were flanked by their masters or owners. Baron Gilbert was standing on a broken fountain in the center of the court. He looked around expectantly. "Gather round, folks. I have a lot of special announcements this morning."

The rain and wind had stopped, and the air was muggy and hot. The sun was blazing today, heating up the moisture in the ground from the previous day's downpour. The musty smell of the jungle wafted through the air, overpowering the salty gulf.

Voices filled the air as the crowd pressed in, interested in what the Baron had to say, myself included. He adjusted his armor, waiting for quiet. Finally, he spoke.

"Yesterday, we were attacked by the Shadowalker empire for their second attack. They brought their entire army and had a force like we had never seen before. It was undoubtedly meant to destroy us, our consumption making them a dangerous threat to Fayport. But one man came through to defend us in our time of need. A human, no less."

The Baron paused for dramatic effect but looked at me and smiled before resuming. "His name is Noah. For those of you who have not met him, I recommend it. He was sent here from another world and chosen as a Creator." A few gasps from the merchant Feka, looks of surprise on their faces. Baron Gilbert raised a paw, calming the roused crowd before continuing again.

"It was he who created the system to raise the ramp. It was he who saved the city. He can make items that set our enemies on fire. He can make objects that shock and paralyze. I'm sure he has powers that have yet to be discovered. With Romas to guide him, we may be able to usher in a new era in our glorious empire!" A cheering roar escaped the throats of the Feka, the humans looking between themselves and smiling.

"First off, I would like to commence the Warrior Naming Ceremony." He looked around the crowd and nodded to a few feline warriors and a couple of hunters. He waved his paw to get them onto the stage. "You have made your people and your parents proud in the face of certain death. For as our ancestors say, 'It is not wise to stand in the face of death, but it is unwise not to either.' You were called up from the training fields as the members of this settlement fell in the first battle and stood with us in the face of certain defeat and did not flinch. You did not waiver. And for that, you obtain your leathers and weapons and will now be given your warrior names."

A cheer went up from the Fekan onlookers. The new warriors smiled and went up to the Baron one by one. The next part of the ritual was very private, and the announcements were over for a moment, quiet discussion returning to the group. A few of the merchants came to me and clapped me on the back and said various thanks to me. I smiled and nodded back, unsure what to say or do in something like this.

Finally, the Baron finished the last warrior and turned again to the crowd. He held up a paw, bringing a hush to the gathering.

"Secondly, we discuss our hero from yesterday. At this time, I officially release Noah from service to the Feka. He is a free man, but I hope he chooses to serve our cause, humble as it is. As a gift for his help in defense of our city, I bestow upon him this Stalker pelt, from his most important kill to date." He bent over and picked up a fur belt in his paws, similar to the Mecho's pelt I had carried through the woods after we killed it. "May he create something marvelous to defend himself from the vile creatures that roam this world."

I didn't know what to say. All eyes turned and looked at me, smiles on the faces surrounding the square. I took a step forward and bowed. "Baron Gilbert, I am honored to be a part of your settlement. I will put this pelt to use and continue assisting the Feka during my time here."

I walked over to him and took the pelt. It smelled terrible, having been recently on fire. I hoped that wouldn't affect what I could make with it. I did a quick inspection of the hide.

[Stalker Hide - Level 8 Ingredient]

I whistled appreciatively. *Man, a level 8 ingredient.* I had no clue if I could even use it yet. "Thank you, sir. I appreciate everyone trusting me with the pulley idea. Sometimes, it's tough to be sure if an idea will work when you create. So...yeah. Thanks for letting me try." I cleared my throat, unsure whether that was a good speech. The Feka nodded their heads, accepting what I said. Dee beamed at me and gave me a little wave of her paw. I caught Typh's eye, too, and he gave me a slight nod.

I continued. "I want to create a few more things to help your city and its workers. There are many things from my world that I can bring here through my creations. If you will let me, of course." I trailed off and looked at the Baron for approval.

"Of course, boy! Your ideas are always welcome here. If you have ideas for the lad here, come to me. I will filter through them and present them to our human creator based on merit to the city. For now, let's get back to work repairing our settlement. We have much to do. That wasn't the last we've seen of the Shadowalkers. They will be back, and we will be ready. Typh - send our fastest scout to the capital. We must replenish our warrior troops; archers being the main focus. I also need a meeting with the Monarch."

Typh nodded. "Right away, sir."

I rubbed my hands together, excitement crossing my face. My mana poisoning had worn off, but I was still only at [18/34]. When I made the rods, they only cost five mana, so I hoped that any 'everyday' items I made were cheap to create. I would have to use my skill to get the plans and ingredients needed.

Let's get to work, then! I had some skills to train.

Over the next few days, I checked a lot of issues in the settlement off my list. The first was the fish processing device. I created a crank system for it, incorporating the pulley system from the ramp. It was much easier to raise it and then have a release button to smash it down. And the rope splinters were removed.

Second, I created counterweights for the ramp. It took a full day of mining with Romas to get our needed materials. Iron was one of the primary ores he could see, and once he showed me where it was, the training unlocked the ore for me. I tried to return the favor and show him the silver ore, but it didn't work for him. I didn't know the secret behind that air magic. We could both see the red ore, since Romas used it as a heat source for the Feka.

Retrieving all that ore increased my 'MINING' skill to level 4 and increased my total mana by five. Romas wanted me to make all the weights, claiming I needed the training. He lounged on a bench with a beverage while I waited for my mana to recover. When I finished the fourth and final counterweight, I finally leveled up.

Third, I made a hair removal tool. It was silly, but I gifted it to Jasper. He swiped it over a Fekan chair, looking at it in awe. Just one swipe had taken a whole clump of fur off. It was a comb shape with little interlocking teeth, similar to the gadgets on Earth sold in stores to remove pet hair off couches. He wrapped me in a bear hug, then returned to work, humming to himself and ripping balls of fur off every surface he could find.

The last thing I wanted to make was a ballista for the towers. The cats may be unable to use air or fire magic, but that didn't stop me from making giant crossbows and piercing bolts. It took almost a full bow tree per weapon, but the massive crossbows were a huge success. They were level-four weapons and cost me twenty mana, so I used almost my whole mana pool when creating one.

One week later, the city had walls again, tower defense, and a working drawbridge. You only needed to release a pin, and the counterweights did the rest. It was magnificent. I looked around, though, wondering if it would be enough. When they returned, I was sure the Shadowalkers would have something up their sleeves.

Chapter 24

Ingredients Must be Earned

THE NEXT THING I WANTED TO MAKE WAS A SPEAR. A SPEAR could be used to ward off a pack of Shadowalkers and buy me some time until someone could come to my aid. I could only use the dagger up close and didn't want to be within biting distance of an angry pit bull. I didn't have any experience with weapons like this, but Typh probably did. I hoped he would be able to train me. *How hard could it be to point a sharp object at an animal? Cavemen did it for hundreds of years on Earth.*

The Stalker pelt was too high of a level for now, so I couldn't make anything with it. Romas declined when I asked him if he would make something for me. He said a Creator needs to construct their own armor. After experiencing how the Squamish armor molded perfectly to my body, I could see why.

I had used my 'DESIGN' skill for the spear, but I wanted to use earth magic this time. Unlocking a third magic type would increase my battle options. I figured poison or a different kind of lasting damage would be perfect against these beasts. But when I got the results back, I saw two '???' slots—one apparently for the rod and the other for some unknown ingredient. I hoped the bow tree could work for the handle, but no dice.

Romas had never made a spear before, so he was no help. "When a creator can't figure out what ingredients he needs, he goes into the jungle and finds them." He smirked, the trademark of his tutelage these days.

I rolled my eyes internally but nodded along. Romas continuously pushed me to do my work and grow my skills. Not wrong as a mentor, but also not super helpful. So I went to find Dee, and we made a field trip into the jungle.

The jungle was quiet as I walked with my Fekan entourage. The rain became more frequent, an on-and-off affair that left the air hot and humid. Plant life was also changing, with more flowers dotting the ground and hanging from the branches. Trees on this planet loved their flowers.

I had grown quite familiar with the jungle at this point. I knew most of the paths near the settlement, where the poisonous bushes were, and the worst spider infestations. Also, having the warriors and hunters with me was comforting as I wandered around here. I mainly went to and from the caves, but today I wanted to try going somewhere different to see what magic I could try and unlock.

My health has not grown much over the last week, but my mana was at [32/40] now after the previous ballista bolt was made. I had improved at choosing the level and type of item I wanted to make. Since none of the Feka could seem to use my magic items, I made regular ammunition, costing me five mana each time. I had gotten really good at mining iron, my skill improving to level 4 a few days ago.

We had also gotten the dog crushers installed under the first level of the settlement. That would be a pleasant little surprise for the Shadowalkers when they returned. It would be brutal to see a bunch of dogs crushed and set on fire, but such were the horrors of war.

The lead Feka, whose name I didn't catch, stopped and put his paw up. He looked to the right, up in the canopy.

I was nervous here. The surroundings were unfamiliar to me. The other Feka looked and crouched into defensive postures. The sun came out momentarily, the heat hitting me in waves. Sweat was beading on my forehead and pooling under my armor.

I looked around but didn't see anything. The Feka clicked his belt, a soft purple glow surrounding us. My eyesight felt sharper, picking out more detail in the canopy. A blur of motion to the left caught my attention, then another to the right. The forest went eerily silent, waiting. The last time this happened, vulture monsters had attacked me. I grabbed my dagger, waiting.

One of the hunters took off up the tree so fast I could barely keep up with his movements. Another Feka went up a separate tree in the same manner. Then the jungle erupted with a roar and cough of gorillas. The sounds came from everywhere at once- A loud threatening yell. The remaining Feka and Dee made a circle around me, swords out.

Swinging from a branch was a four-foot monkey beast. He had a silver chest with stripes of white fur criss crossing his entire body. Teeth protruded out of his mouth, similar to the White-fang dogs. He dove off the branch, landed gracefully on the ground, and swung at Dee.

She ducked, returning a kick to its shin. The beast let out an 'oof,' spun, and tried a two-handed power swing at her. He was too slow, Dee already shifting behind him. She took out two daggers and thrust them into the monster's calves. I watched in horror, unable to move, standing there with my dagger like an idiot. Behind me, the two warrior Feka fought an orangutan beast and a spider monkey swinging from the tree. He was throwing some projectiles at them, missing as the agile Feka dodged them.

I backed away from the battle, looking around for danger. To my left, Dee had killed her prey, stabbing it in the back of the head. It fell over with a *boom*, but she was gone before it even hit the ground. Behind me, another gorilla creature busted through the foliage, running at me with its arms over its head. It swung down as I dove to the side. As I rolled out of the way, my legs broke through a spider web, the sticky substance getting on my pants.

A spider shot out of a log onto my leg. I shrieked and kicked my leg as hard as possible, sending the spider flying. Meanwhile, the gorilla had come up from behind me, sending an uppercut to the side of my head while I was distracted. It knocked me to the side, spit flying out of my mouth as I fell to the ground in a heap. I lay there dazed and curled into the fetal position, arms over my head.

The gorilla stood over me, murder in its eyes. It was tackled to the ground by a warrior Feka, and the two struggled in the brush. I crab-walked on all fours back toward the path. The white tiger landed a claw strike to its face, knocking it out. The Feka looked back, anger all over his face. "Fight back, human! What are you doing?! Get up!"

I looked at him for a moment, gaining my composure. I nodded silently, rapid movements up and down with my head.

I stood, looking around me. Monkeys were dead all over the jungle floor. A smaller monkey began getting up, waking up from a fall from the canopy. I grabbed my dagger from the ground, ran over to it, and thrust my weapon into its back. The monkey arched, lightning shooting up its body. It let out a terrifying screech and spasmed there for a bit. I pulled the dagger out and staggered backward, watching in horror.

It stopped moving, falling to the ground. I slowly walked over and kicked it, ensuring it was dead. *My first official kill on Prixa in hand-to-hand combat!*

The jungle was quiet now, the attack through. Any remaining monkeys must have run off if the Feka didn't kill them all. After a few seconds, the animal dissolved and left a fur pelt. I picked it up with shaky hands and put it on my shoulder. I squeezed my eyes shut for a moment, feeling guilty.

The Fekan warriors and hunters slowly filtered back down through the trees showing various degrees of injury. They circled me, looks of disgust and anger on their faces. Dee looked down, shuffling her feet after she put her daggers back in her belt.

Finally, the lead warrior spoke, wiping blood from his eyes from a cut above his eyebrow. "Deehana, I cannot fight alongside this human. He is inept, untrained, unfit, and has no business out here with us. I am sorry. Ingredients must be earned. If he cannot accumulate them through his own kills, he will never be strong enough to create for us, or anyone else." He turned and walked away, the other three growling at me and following him.

She looked at him and began to speak but stopped. She looked at me apologetically, turned, and headed back toward the settlement.

Chapter 25

Tempered

We walked back to the settlement, an awkward silence hanging over the group. I had fought so poorly during that battle. But in my defense, I didn't have the right skills or weapons. *I am a creator class, damn it. No more excuses! If I want something, I make it.*

I stood tall, a grim determination on my face. I called ahead, "Dee. I need more combat training. Can you help me?"

The warriors ahead of me paused and exchanged a look, then kept walking forward. Dee turned around. "Of course! It would be my honor. When we get back, I will set something up in the training arena."

I smiled. This world would not hand me anything. It was unforgiving and brutal. But it also lent me skills to cope with that. I thought I was in a VR game or something when I arrived. *Hell, I still could be.* But if I really was here, transported to Prixa by some unknown means, I needed to do a better job of surviving on my own. There had been too many times that one of the Feka intercepted a threat just in time to save me.

When we broke into the clearing, I could tell something was up. Rhino beasts stood on two legs with twenty-foot-long halberds at the city's gates. Humans rushed here and there with bowls, gathering corn off the red-stalked plants. Most notably, the city noise was louder than usual...almost like a party.

The Fekans looked at each other, grinned, and dropped their ingredients on the ground. They ran into Dunbar, leaving me confused on the dirt path. I saw them stop and grab a couple of humans, pointing back at the fur pelts on the ground, most likely instructing them to deliver them to the smithy. I did the same...because why not.

I strolled into the settlement as the prior battle embarrassment started leaving my mind space, thrilled to see all the excitement. New breeds of Feka walked this way and that, mainly of the smaller variety. They looked wealthier than the Feka who occupied Dunbar, with more jewels and accents on their fur and far fewer stripes, if they had any at all. Before I could walk through the newly repaired gates, one of the rhinos stopped me, sticking out a giant foot. In a deep voice, he rumbled, "Human- report to the smithy immediately. The head of security will find you there and take you to the second level of the settlement." He stood back up, returning his gaze to the jungle.

I had never been to the second level. To my knowledge, there wasn't even a way for humans to access that part of the city. The ramp got us to level one, and word on the street was that hidden stairs somewhere took humans up to the wealthy part of town on the second level.

After I reached the first level, I went to the smithy. I walked around the smithy and found Jasper putting chairs out. "Where's Romas?" I asked.

"Nice to see you too," Jasper replied, frowning and looking up from his chair duties. "You know, it would be nice if you helped out around here." He avoided my glare and unstacked another chair.

"Jasper, come on. You know I don't work for Romas anymore. I'm trying to get stronger so I can help with the settlement. The Shadowalkers will be back; this time, I bet they will figure out a way to the upper parts of the city. When they do, I need to help fight back."

He stopped and finally met my stare. "Yeah? Well, I thought we were friends. I needed help around here and was hoping you could be the one to help. It was stupid. I'll let you go back to your tasks, *sir*." He did a mock bow and turned away from me.

"Jasper, stop, man!" I tried.

Suddenly, he bent over and picked something up off the ground during his bow. "Here, Noah, one of your *magical pellets* must have fallen out of your pocket while you were asleep..." he trailed off, a shocked look on his face.

"What?" I asked, alarmed.

Suddenly the room changed. A smell filled the air, something I couldn't put my finger on. It was sweet, but more like a flower and less like food. Jasper gasped, his pupils turning a reddish black. He looked into the air, not saying anything, almost like he was reading text. Then he answered, "Jasper!" and looked down at his arm. Tattoos appeared.

He blinked twice, looking at me, the pellet, then back at me again. "Noah..."

My mouth hung open, staring at the scene. I finally walked over, plucking the pellet from Jasper's hand. It was one of my fire pellets. "How in the world...what just happened? Show me your arm." He complied.

[JASPER]
[LV 1- TEMPER MAGE APPRENTICE]
[HEALTH 15]
[MANA 10]

"What's going on back there?" a voice from the front of the smithy yelled. It was Romas. "What the hell are you creating, Noah? It smells like mana back there!"

So that was the smell. These damn cats and their mana sense.

I turned to Jasper and whispered, "Not a word of this to anyone. I need to think." He nodded silently. I grabbed the pellet from him and shoved it into my pocket.

I walked toward the front of the smithy. "Romas! I was looking for you. I need to get to the second level. Any idea how I do that?" I tried my best not to sound like I was hiding something, but my voice failed me when it broke, making me sound like a prepubescent teen.

Romas stared at me, narrowing his eyes. "Who said you..."

"I'll take it from here, thank you," a voice from the door called out.

Romas slowly turned toward the door. "Why is it that whenever something seems *amiss*, you always show up, Typhonius?" Romas sneered at the cat.

"I don't know what you're talking about. Regardless, I must take Noah to the second level on orders of the Monarch. Come along, boy." He turned and walked out the door before Romas or I could respond.

I looked at Romas, a sweet smile on my face. "Catch you later!" He snarled back as I left the smithy.

What the hell was that? I wished I didn't have to see the Monarch, as exciting as that was. I needed to figure out how Jasper could unlock magic after touching one of my fire pellets. He had felt my air magic daggers before with no change. He even held my dagger before, and that had been crafted. *Why the sudden change?*

And if he could unlock magic, could other humans use magic as well? Could that explain why the Feka couldn't tell what my dagger or pellets did? Was this human-only magic? And even then, would only specific humans interact with specific magic types? All these years, humans were considered non-magical because they were touching the Fekan items. *Maybe I was special after all...*

We wandered down the alleys on the first level as I pondered all this, weaving between houses and stores. Finally, Typh went to the rear of a support pillar, touching three patterns on the walls in a specific sequence. I stayed silent as I watched. Suddenly a door swung inward, allowing us access to black stone stairs. They wound up in a spiral.

He looked at me, opened his mouth to speak, but closed it. He looked straight ahead and began climbing the stairs. From the first level, I only saw the ten-story high tubes as supports, and the hidden stairs surprised me. I had seen the Feka climbing to the upper levels less often than the ground level.

We finally reached the top of the stairs. I wheezed as the door swung out. Typh shook his head at me. "Aren't you in better shape yet?"

"I just climbed...150...stairs." I wheezed out. "That's a lot where I come from." I put my hands on my head, squeezing my eyes shut.

Typh let out a sigh and continued walking forward. Up ahead, a regal-looking lynx sauntered over. She looked me up and down, appraising, as the Feka liked to do. "So this is the one, Typhonius?"

"Yes, your highness," he replied, standing tall.

"He's fatter than I thought he would be. No matter. I will take him to the upper level. I require a word with him."

"Of course, Monarch." Typh looked at a nearby cougar-looking creature and nodded. The cat came over to me, rested his paw on my shoulder, and closed his eyes. The world lurched, feeling like my head was being pulled underwater.

I opened my eyes and panicked a bit. I turned and looked back, seeing the region from new heights. I was higher up than I was previously and surrounded by densely populated trees. I was on the third level of the settlement in what appeared to be an intricate garden. New types of trees surrounded me, paths twisting every which way. They had exotic flowers dotting their

171

branches, sometimes with fruits hanging off them. Fountains were placed in clearings between the trees along the paths, shooting blue-tinged water out of their nozzles.

In the distance, the gulf surrounded the rear part of the settlement, land nowhere to be found. Fishing vessels were everywhere, bobbing up and down in the waves. To the north, the jungle sprawled as far as my eyes could see. The trees were taller than the tower, larger than I thought possible.

A moment later, the Monarch appeared beside me out of thin air. She glanced around, making eye contact with me, then smiled. "I assume that's not your first time being teleported, is it, young human?"

This was going to be a delightful conversation.

Chapter 26

The Monarch

"NOAH, IS IT?" THE LYNX ASKED, CURLING UP ON THE LIP OF a nearby fountain. I edged forward cautiously, not sure what would come of this exchange.

"Yes, your highness."

She turned around and drank from the fountain, leaving a lingering silence. Finally, she turned back to me. "You have been blessed with magic in this world. Tell me everything."

I pursed my lips, unsure how to begin. "What has the Baron and the others told you about me?"

The Monarch held up her paw. "How about I share a secret with you, so you feel more comfortable sharing one in return?" I shrugged my shoulders, then nodded. "On Prixa, there are two other branches of magic that Feka and humans may share. One is time magic, and the other is space magic—or, as you call it, teleportation. I've seen what's happened to you. And I've seen glimpses of what's about to happen. I possess the ability of foresight. The latest version of the future was...not acceptable and had me extremely worried. Now I am here to evaluate the situation." She scoffed, a disgusting look crossing her features. "Apparently with a *human*, no less! Whatever has the world come to."

She jumped off the fountain and walked over to me. "Your turn."

I paused for a few moments, returning her piercing gaze. She had sparkling blue eyes and long whiskers. Spots dotted her entire face, scars crisscrossing her delicate lynx features. I took a breath. "I was contacted on Earth through a sound channel; they're called headphones. It told me that an astral mage had chosen me. Then I heard a countdown and ended up here. I was attacked by some vulture monsters upon arriving. That's how I made this dagger." I held it up for her review. "One of the vulture's talons was left after it... dissolved."

She grabbed it out of my hand faster than my eyes could process. "Curious. I sense no magic in this dagger, but I can see how it was made. It's quite lovely." She looked up at me, meeting my curious gaze. "This corresponds to my belief of how magic functions here on Prixa. Continue, no-classer."

I let the no-classer thing slide. My entrance into this world... where did I begin? "Well, I was taken in as a blacksmith no-classer when I arrived around your spring festival thingy but was sent to die in the woods when the master blacksmith thought I had stolen the dagger. I told him I made it, but he didn't believe me." I couldn't hide the spite in my voice after retelling these events. "I met his daughter, Dee, and she helped me." I held up the slingshot. "I gained a few skills and can now create all kinds of things, mine my materials, and assist the Feka with this weapon."

"Strange." She glanced up at me. "I've never seen a device like this. You can't *possibly* tell me that it can injure a Shadowalker?"

I nodded. "Yeah, but not standard ammunition. I made shots that had either fire or air magic, and when they hit the Shadowalkers, they were very efficient. I added the silver ore to my dagger too. That's how I was able to attack the Stalkers." I paused, thinking. I didn't say anything for a moment. An awkward silence hung in the air between us, signaling the end of my sharing for the moment.

A smile crept across her feline features. "Very well. This one is a valuable secret, and I expect one in return. Humans have been magical for ages but abandoned their non-magical kind generations ago. Now the only humans left that we know about aren't able to use magic. We have taken them on as a labor force to strengthen and protect our settlements. Your kind is feeble and would not survive the jungles. Their work pays the cost of our protection. But my lack of knowledge of half of Prixa's historical events tells me the human astral mages can block my sight. I do not know where the magic-using humans have gone. Now, across our empire, the Feka provide safe communities where humans can live and labor. A fact that I know displeases you." She looked knowingly at me. "We have not seen humans use magic before your...*appearance.*" She said the last word with a hint of disdain, almost like she was upset that I was here at all.

"I won't deny it," I replied. "In my world, class systems are a...touchy subject. But humans lord over other humans, so things are a bit different. It still didn't feel right to enter an indentured situation in a world I had never been in."

The Monarch nodded. "I understand. But this is a world full of power and struggle. The weak must provide for the strong, whether that's in the form of ingredients or workforce. Even the Feka without fighting skills aid the strong somehow. That even includes the Feka that I brought. They cater to me, and in return, I grant them wealth and status."

I understood. Even on Earth, there was a pyramid of power. This was nothing new; the weak always served the strong in some way. But a rigid class system was another thing together. That took the *choice* out of things.

She saw the thoughts going through my head and continued. "My greatest fear is that you will abandon our cause and join theirs. I do not know these humans. I do not know what they are capable of. But I also fear that the Shadowalkers will overwhelm the troops stationed here and become too strong for us to deal with. I need your help, and I hope you can find these humans and negotiate on our behalf one day."

Yikes. I was not good at politics. I had no experience with negotiations or alliances and didn't even play video games with these elements. I just liked to make stuff, not interact with two nations that could go to war at any moment, mainly when one of the races comprised giant lions and tigers.

I responded with some trepidation. "I will do my best. For now, the Shadowwalkers will return. I've been preparing the settlement, but I doubt it will be enough to stop them this time. So what are the next steps here? You should have seen the army they have!"

We sat there for a moment, not saying much, the burbling of the fountains providing the sounds up here on the third level of Dunbar. Birds tweeted softly above the various fruit trees. The Monarch looked away, troubled. Her whiskers twitched as she went deep into thought.

She finally spoke. "We may have to give up the settlement and retreat everyone to Fayport."

My head jerked back, surprised. "What? Why!"

"These beasts outmatch us. Not in fighting power, but brute force. They counter our dexterity with their strength. They counter our cunning with their numbers. We can only survive an attack for so long, even with your help. The only way to save our people is to abandon our post and retreat. I will not give any additional troops to this place, just to have them consumed."

I shook my head. "No way. There are strong warriors here. I saw it myself. And I can help! The Dunbar humans can access magic!" *Oops.*

Another silence broke out, this time the Monarch crept toward me. I gulped. She got right near my face, her catlike eyes narrowing. "What do you mean *they can access magic?*" she said slowly. "I told you what I've seen...but..."

"Before I came up here, the other boy who works at the blacksmith unlocked a new class. He held one of my fire magic items and got assigned a class, just like I did. If we let the humans here hold my items, I can see who opens similar classes. I believe they've had the possibility of magic all along; we didn't know because the Fekan weapons can't unlock their magic class. I can make items that do!"

"You want to empower the humans here with magic?" she asked, pursing her lips. I could tell this was not something she had ever considered.

"If you want to survive the attack against the Shadowalkers, we need an army. One that has the magic to help counter the Shadowalker troops. So far, my two branches of magic can do that. And I believe there might be two more branches of magic that I haven't even unlocked yet."

"What stops the mages from turning on us? Using their powers to take over the settlement?"

I glared at the Monarch, tilting my head to the side. "Your Highness, your people's prowess is without a doubt. Even with magic, humans don't compare with Feka as warriors, and magic doesn't make them less squishy. I have no idea how many people here will gain access to magic. But for the people that do, I will train them. We will forge an official alliance with the Feka. You have my word. But please, let me do this. Gather the humans, and let's see who we get." I smiled, trying to convey my sincerity to her.

The Monarch turned from me, looking up into the canopy. She paced for a moment, not replying to me. Her body jerked back and forth, her eyes darting around. Finally, she said, "I have looked ahead into this pact. I see death and destruction but cannot tell much more. There is a significant battle ahead of us. I see fire and lightning. Many lives will be lost on this day. Losing a battle of this scale will make the Shadowalkers too strong for even Fayport to handle. There is a great risk here, human. I stand by my previous decision to withhold additional Fekan troops."

She turned back to me, a blaze in her eyes. "You will not break your vow to me in this hallowed ground, human. Your kind blocks my sight when you are involved, so I do not trust them or their plans for you. I cannot protect my people from you if things evolve a certain way. For now, we have a mutual goal. Let us hope that will be enough to keep you honest."

I nodded sincerely. "Of course, Monarch."

She nodded, taking a deep breath. "Gather the humans. Let's see what we have to work with."

Chapter 27

Fireballs Away!

AFTER MY CONVERSATION WITH THE MONARCH, I WAS teleported back down to the second level. I glared at the cougar, asking why he couldn't transport me to the first level. He scowled back and disappeared away. I saw Typh waiting for me where I had disappeared from earlier. I sighed, walking over to the skyscraper's worth of stairs between me and the first level, and began climbing down, Typh following behind.

Silence lingered between us- Typh knowing better than to talk about what the Monarch and I spoke about in the secret garden. We finally reached the bottom, and the door swung inward toward us to let us out into the jungle heat. It was remarkable how much hotter it was down here; the air was moist and heavy on the tower's first level. The sun had almost set, a purple sunset over the treetops. The wind was still. I could see the two small moons already appearing, the larger one still beneath the horizon.

The leopard turned to me, addressing me for the first time. "I assume the Monarch gave you a task? Something I can help with?"

I nodded. I wasn't going to hold back secrets any longer. "She needs us to gather all the humans and bring them to the town

179

square on the first level. I can release magic in some of them. They can unlock their class when they hold my items, should they have one."

If Typh was surprised, he hid it well. "Very well. Is she sure she wants to go down this path? There will be no turning back after we do this."

"Yes. The Monarch looked ahead and saw the battle. She knows there is no other choice if we want to hold Dunbar from the Shadowwalkers. Also, I'll need to make something that can shoot fire. Maybe a wand?"

Typh looked at me, confused. "I do not know what a wand is. Head to the smithy first to see if you can make what you need. We won't have time to search the jungle and find the ingredients, so I hope Romas can help. I think our time before battle runs short. I will work on sending word to the no-classer coordinators to gather the humans at work day's end."

I thanked him and headed left toward the smithy. Thoughts ran wild in my head. While walking, I used my 'DESIGN' skill to plan my wand. The world slowed down, instructing me on what to do next. I needed a *'living tree branch'* and two *'tinderstone ore'* pieces. I had plenty of the tinderstone stockpiled from my mining activities but had no idea what a living tree branch was. I hoped Romas would.

I walked into the blacksmith and saw Jasper gathering cat hair with his fur removal device. He saw me and flashed me a huge smile. "You're back! Is it true? Did you go up to the second level? Was the Monarch there?"

I laughed. "Slow down, buddy. We have a lot of work to do. Where is Romas?" Jasper's face dropped a bit, thinking I was putting him off. "No! Hey, we can catch up about...everything...soon. Very soon. I have an important task to do. It is going to make life a lot more interesting around here."

Jasper perked up at that. His eyes darted around the room, and his voice dropped to a whisper. "Is it about my...*situation?*"

"Something like that." I winked at him. "Now, where's Romas? I need to find a *living tree branch*, whatever that means. I always thought all trees were living, but what the hell do I..."

"Oh, Romas has a bunch over here," Jasper said, interrupting my ranting, and turned and went toward the back of the smithy.

That was easy. "He does? What is it?"

Jasper opened a locker door with a golden tree symbol, the hinges creaking with the effort. He started pulling boxes out of the storage locker, sticks, twigs, and leaves flying everywhere. He sat on his haunches, looking over the materials. "Noah. We grow trees here. We have pretty much every tree-related material you could imagine. If you want fish or sticks, you come to Dunbar." He chuckled at himself. I just looked on, shaking my head. *That has to be the worst city slogan I've ever heard.*

I dug into the first box, inspecting sticks and leaves to see which matched the one I sought. It only took a few tries before I got one. The image of the rough grey stick in my hand clicked into place in my mind, locking into the open slot next to the tinder-stone. "I got it!" I exclaimed.

I returned to the locker Romas assigned me and grabbed two pieces of ore. As soon as I did, the ore leaped into the stick in my mind. I looked at Jasper, smiled, then concentrated. He smiled back, giving me a nod. I combined the items, looking down at what I had created.

It was about nine inches long, stark black, and had glowing red runes up and down its length. I inspected it hastily.

[FIREBALL WAND LEVEL 1]

Jasper whistled across from me. "Wow, look at that thing. That's beautiful. Can...can I touch it?" He looked at me with begging eyes. I nodded, handing the wand to him. While he inspected it, I looked at my arm to see what that cost me. My mana was at [26/41], the wand setting me back the standard ten mana. The other five mana had been from my 'DESIGN' skill.

"Noah! I just unlocked an 'INSPECT' skill! I can tell what this is! Wait...it says I get 150% damage while using it! I bet that's from my class!" The excitement on his face made me smile.

"Wait - I wonder if it uses mana when you shoot it. I wonder if I can shoot it! We need to test this before Typh returns with the other humans. I want to know what it can do before I show it to everyone." I grinned again, this time with a mischievous tint. "You want to go on a quick adventure?"

We didn't need to go far to test the wand out. The jungle was damp from the recent rainstorm, with moisture running down our clothes as we walked under the wet leaves. We ran down the ramp, avoiding everyone's glance. People had started to gather by now, a few Feka setting up a platform in the middle of the square.

Once we were a few steps into the woods, I stopped, Jasper stopping behind me. He looked around anxiously, eyes darting everywhere. "You've never been here, have you?" I asked.

He gave me a nervous smile. "Nope. Man, it's dark in here. It feels like I can't breathe. And everything is so tall!"

"Yeah, you get used to it. But come on. Let's try this thing out. Two humans in the jungle is risky. The animals here can smell us from a mile away, and without my Fekan entourage, I feel pretty vulnerable."

I looked around, spotting a moss-covered rock wall nearby. "Ok, shoot the wand at that wall. I assume that won't catch anything on fire, especially with it as damp as it is."

Jasper held the wand out, the tip wavering slightly. For a moment nothing happened. "Concentrate," I prompted. "Listen to the voice in the back of your mind. I know that sounds crazy but..."

182

He closed his eyes and a red glow formed at the wand's tip. I stepped back just in time as a fireball the size of a beach ball exploded out of the rod. A roar sounded as it ripped through the air, striking the wall. "Holy crap!" I exclaimed, eyes going wide.

Jasper opened his eyes, looking at the destruction he had caused. The wall was charred and black, and rock chips were blasted everywhere. He let out a *whoop* and jumped into the air, fist raised in triumph. A roar sounded further in the jungle, making our eyes widen in fear.

"We should head back to the settlement now," I said, backing up slowly. He nodded, and we walked briskly back into the clearing.

I smiled one last time at Jasper before we walked up the ramp to the circus above, beaming at him after the show in the jungle. "How much of your mana did that use?"

"That was five mana. I have half left. Man, that felt powerful! Thank you, Noah!"

"Don't thank me yet. You're going to have to show off what you can do. I'll have you blast a fireball into the jungle and show everyone, finishing the rest of your mana. It's time to build ourselves an army of human mages!"

No one gave us funny looks as we joined everyone else on the first level. I figured two humans returning from the jungle would cause some form of alarm, but there was much more attention to everyone being called to the square. This time, the Monarch and her people stood on the raised platform, inspecting the crowd. I assumed she was looking for me.

Finally, she locked eyes with me as we walked up and tilted her head in an *'Are you ready?'* look. I nodded back, anxiety bubbling up in my gut. I sure hoped this worked.

Chapter 28

The Patron of Humanity

"GATHER ROUND, HUMANS. GATHER ROUND!" A REGAL-looking gray panther yelled to the group gathered around the podium. The no-classer coordinators looked back and forth, unsure of what was happening. Eventually, they directed their humans toward the stage at the Monarch's request. Every color t-shirt was present since the event was mandatory by the head of the entire Fekan empire.

I got the feeling that you didn't cross the Monarch.

"Good. Thank you. We apologize for any interruptions in your house services, but the Monarch has an important announcement for all beings in the settlement, Fekan and human." He turned and bowed, facing the lynx. "Your Highness?"

She nodded slowly and stepped forward into the center of the platform. "Thank you, Layal. And thank you, honored Dunbar residents, for your cooperation. As you're aware, the Shadowalker threat grows in severity every day that passes us by. My scouts tell me they've begun their final preparations for another invasion of Dunbar. They've learned from their previous defeat and have made adjustments. I fear they will have no problem accessing our settlement this time. *All* of our settlement."

185

Worried looks passed between the Feka, memories of the previous encounter playing in their minds. Murmurs broke out as conversations started. The Monarch held up her paw, quieting the crowd.

"I won't lie to everyone. The alpha's army outmatches us. Their numbers exceed ours by six to one. While we remain the stronger fighting force, we can kill only so many Shadowalkers simultaneously. Eventually, they would overrun us. And I have yet to see the alpha fight in battle, his abilities uncertain." A look of sheer determination crossed her face, and she took a deep, steadying breath.

"With that, I will get to why we're all here." She glanced around. "According to my official records, we have 87 humans onsite. Well...88 if you count our mysterious guest here." She looked knowingly at me, all eyes of the gathering boring into my skull. I turned beet red, embarrassed by all the attention. "He has helped prepare the settlement defenses and, as the Baron alerted me, has been blessed with the first ever magical ability a human has ever seen here on Prixa. But that's not true."

More murmurs broke out, this time louder. Growls and yells asked the Monarch inaudible questions, hair standing up on some of the Feka as they reacted to this news. The Monarch's panther jumped forward and roared, startling the humans near the stage. The sounds died down, the Feka calming themselves.

The Monarch continued. "Thank you, Layal. Please, let me finish. I have always assumed that humans had access to magic at some point in history here. As of today, however, Noah here has proven it. He was able to unlock magic successfully in one of the human no-classers. Noah, please come up here and discuss this matter further." Confusion broke out in the square, the news a shock to everyone. During the chaos, the Monarch pointed next to her on the stage and moved aside, waiting for me.

I looked back and forth, seeing the massive crowd through fuzzy eyes, my vision clouding from the stagefright. I felt bile in the back of my throat and nausea like a hammer blow to the gut. If

186

this was what leadership was, I wasn't interested. *For now, I need to do this.*

I stepped forward, putting my hands on the platform. It was about five feet off the ground with no stairs. The Feka leaped up with no issue, but I had to hoist myself onto my elbows, then belly up and swing my legs around. The Feka looked disgusted at the showing. I got up and dusted myself off.

I cleared my throat and licked my lips, the dry mouth preventing me from speaking. "Hello." *My voice sounded weird. Why did my voice sound so weird?* I cleared my throat again. I locked eyes with Jasper, who gave me a big smile and a thumbs-up. *I like that kid.*

I took a breath, determined to force down the nausea I felt. "For those who do not know me, I'm Noah. I was chosen as a creator class when I arrived here. Most of you have seen the things I can make for the settlement. But what you haven't seen is *this.*" I pulled out the wand, holding it over my head.

More murmuring broke out in the crowd. I kept speaking over the noise. "Some of my fellow humans will hold this item and unlock magical powers. Some will not. But if you don't unlock access to fire magic..." I dug into my belt loop, pulled out my dagger, and held it up. "You can try to unlock air magic with this dagger."

The humans surged forward, crowding the platform. I saw the three tall dock workers surging to the front, heads above most no-classers. I held my hand up and recoiled a bit, shouting over the noise. "Wait! Guys, let's be orderly. Make a line. Everyone can get a chance."

———

The Monarch's attendants helped me restore order to the crowd, lining everyone up in a long, winding line around the square. I couldn't blame everyone for being excited. If I had lived my whole life as a no-classer, I would certainly push to unlock magical abilities. The weather was perfect today with no rain in sight, which was preferable since I was about to start unlocking electrical powers in people and didn't know how they would do around water or puddles.

I stood at the edge of the tower's first level, looking out into the jungle. Jasper stood beside me, ready to show off his new fireball skill. There was so much excitement in the air you could almost taste it. Finally, I nodded to Jasper once everyone was lined up and watching. He nodded, squared his shoulders, and held the wand toward the trees with eyes closed.

A second later, the roar of fire escaped the wand's tip, blasting out into the jungle. Fire erupted up the stalk of a large palm tree about thirty yards away. Gasps sounded around the crowd behind us, as fire magic was a new concept to Feka and humans alike. Jasper deflated a bit, the last of his mana burning up with the mighty fireball. The fire snuffed out, smoke replacing flame as the damp air protected the tree.

I leaned over and whispered to Jasper, "Wow, that went a lot farther than I thought it would!" and flashed him a smile. Louder, I addressed the crowd, making eye contact with one of the dock workers at the front of the line. "Ok, step on up! Let's see what you've got!"

The dock worker was at the front of the line. He took a confident step forward and grabbed the wand. A few moments passed, and nothing happened. He furrowed his brow, then closed his eyes. He shook his head, looking disappointed. "It's ok, try this," I said, grabbing the wand and giving him the dagger. As soon as I gave it over, I could feel the air electrify around the dockworker.

The smell of mana filled the air, and his head shot upwards, staring at the sky. He reminded me of Raiden from the old Mortal Kombat games as his eyes shone an icy blue. His veins turned blue up and down his arms like the blood was electrified. I beamed at him, pleased at unlocking my first air mage. I got a notification for the first time in a while.

[YOU HAVE UNLOCKED THE 'PATRON' SKILL]

Patron? Like guiding these people into mages? I thought, wondering what that skill did. I tried it out, reaching into my mind and activating the ability. Suddenly, about one-half of the no-classers had a red or yellow tint about them. I glanced at Jasper, who appeared as a glowing red beacon- much brighter than the dull no-classers standing around. Mana sucked out of my arm much more rapidly than when I mined ore, so I cut the skill off. That would be a helpful skill once I unlock more magic. I wondered if I could figure out what weapons would work best for someone eventually. *Maybe I could even guide their skill selection?* There were a ton of applications for the skill as it evolved.

"Ok, now take a swing at this training dummy over here," I said, pointing to the straw dummy that I had Typh find for us. The dock worker nodded, then stood in front of it. His arm returned and swiped across the straw, electrifying the entire thing and blasting it backward as static electricity filled the air.

The no-classers all whooped and hollered, hugging each other. I nodded silently to myself, excited for what was to come. The worker returned the dagger and stepped aside, shock and awe on his face. "Next!" I yelled.

The next human stepped up, holding their hands out expectantly. I placed the wand and dagger in their hands, but nothing happened. I didn't click my skill on, but I recalled the next glowing person was three people back. But they didn't have to know that I knew. Even though I knew the outcome, I would give everyone a fair shot at magic.

After everyone got tested, I ended up with 18 fire mages and 22 air mages. I didn't have any weapons or items for them to use and had my work cut out for me to outfit all of these people. Typh said he could assist with the "weakness training," as he called it. I assumed he meant melee or weapons training, but you could never tell with him. I remember back to my fish-smashing experience.

I noticed a similarity in each of the mage classes. The fire mages were smiling, outgoing types with small stature and big personalities. They congratulated each other with smiles and laughs, sometimes clasping arms. The air mages were strong, silent types. A lot had athletic builds and serious expressions. I could tell they would be using their skills in hand-to-hand situations. It was an interesting group.

I addressed the remaining people, giving them confidence that I would test them again once I unlocked the remaining two branches of water and earth mana. They looked downtrodden but hopeful. Their coordinators scooped up what remained of their workforce with scowls and returned to their various sections of town. By now, it was the middle of the night, and the Monarch released us to our sleeping areas.

For me, it was time for the fun part. Tomorrow, it was time to train my army.

Chapter 29

The Creation Stone

It was early morning at the settlement, and the sun was not up yet. The wind howled, but there was no rain. I turned in my cot to find Jasper's bed empty- the boy most likely starting his chores around the smithy. Even with his new status, he refused to let his work lapse. I had to applaud him. I got up and washed my face, hair, and beard, and prepared for the important day ahead.

The Monarch and her people departed last night, leaving us with a grave one-week timer until the Shadowalkers returned. The scouts told us their newly designed siege equipment would slow them down.

I donned my squirrel armor and put my weapons in my overall belt loops. After one final check that my hair was combed and I looked my best for my army, I walked out the door and into the settlement.

I approached one of the merchant stalls, the smell of bread and fish entering my nostrils. My stomach growled, hungry for a quick breakfast. The merchant Feka waved me over and prepared a steaming bowl for me. I thanked him and started walking away when he said, "Good luck today, creator." *Interesting.* I turned back, smiled, and nodded to him.

191

I walked around the settlement, checking on a few projects that were going on under my direction. An hour or so later, the group of mages had filtered into the square, and I walked over. The sun was now peeking over the horizon, starting another hot day in the jungle.

"OK! Gather around, everybody." The group of new mana users surrounded me, flanked by Typh, Dee, Romas, and Baron Gilbert, who looked on anxiously. A few curious Feka tried to look busy at their merchant stalls, but I could tell they were listening intently.

My little army had their various new shirts on. I found as many red shirts as possible for the fire mages and as many yellow shirts as possible for the air mages.

I had them approach me individually and show me their tattoos. There were Tinder Mages, the same as Jasper, for most of that red group. A few people were in a class called Ember Alchemists; their symbol was a bomb exploding. That was super cool. I didn't know what that meant or what they did, and I hoped my new Patron skill could help me. But if I had people specializing in traps and explosives, we would get along just fine. It also reduced the need for around five weapons if they didn't use wands or swords.

The air mages only had a few Wind Mages who, I assumed, I would outfit with air wands, but the majority were a class called Zephyrs. They had a symbol resembling a monk praying where my anvil was. I assumed that was a group of people that would excel in hand-to-hand combat. The people in this group were all muscular and athletic, with the dock workers included in the lot.

Eventually, I would get separate shirts for the two classes as well. It would help logistically on the battlefield. I assumed a Feka somewhere on the settlement made shirts for their primary job.

As far as the mages went, I needed to make them useful by expanding how much mana they had, which meant practicing their skills. A tingling knowledge in my mind told me they couldn't shoot fireballs and lightning bolts off into the sky, a passive ability of my Patron skill. We would need to go and get into some trouble to get them the aptitudes they required for the upcoming battle that loomed.

My task right now was to figure out how to outfit 50 people with whatever they needed for their classes. To my knowledge, there wasn't a way to use magic with just your bare hands. Looking at the Feka, their items boosted them unless they used their claws for hand-to-hand fights.

"You will be breaking up into your various subclasses today to begin training. The Zephyrs will be training with the Baron, who has graciously offered his time this morning. I don't know exactly how long it will take until the Shadowalkers return, but I doubt it will be very long. I have the difficult task of making enough magical items for everyone, so for now, you will need to grab a weapon from the smithy.

"The fire mages will go with Typh and Dee. You will spend half the day with some basic fighting lessons before you go into the jungle to get into some trouble. Bring back as many ingredients as you can. When you kill something personally, it responds better to an item I make for you." *How did I know that?* Random knowledge started filling my brain's blank spots as I leveled up, my recent tattoo showing me at level 6 now.

I continued. "The remaining Wind mages can go into a separate part of the jungle with the warrior Feka. They used to take me places and are a great asset to keeping you safe while you expand on your skills." The group of large, muscular humans nodded back at me. They had similar builds to the Zephyrs.

I looked at Romas, and he looked back at me expectantly. He nodded. "Romas will take everyone to the smithy now to be outfitted with non-magical weapons. Choose something that can keep you alive for now. If the weapon is something you like, I can combine it with the magic of your mana class and make it your weapon."

Smiles broke out across faces as everyone processed this. The days of servitude were behind them, but battle and death presented new stakes. "The first thing I'll be making is wands for our Tinder Mages since they need equipment the most right now. Any questions?"

Heads shook no. "Ok, good. Let's move!"

The group turned and followed Romas up the stone path. A girl in a red shirt held back and smiled at me. "Noah, I just wanted to thank you from the group of us." She fidgeted but kept eye contact with me. She was cute, with long auburn hair, blue eyes, and freckles across her cheeks. The girl was tall, about my height.

My cheeks burned. "Uh, yeah, don't mention it," I stammered. *Stupid.* "I'm excited to hang out with some fellow humans for once instead of these huge cats all day." I chuckled, and she laughed back a forced, awkward giggle.

"This is all really exciting. I'm nervous, but it will be better than cleaning litter all day, right?"

I beamed at her. "Definitely." The group had moved on a bit, leaving us behind them. "You better get up there."

She looked down at the ground. "Uh, yeah. Of course. Bye!" She turned and scurried away. My cheeks stayed red for another few minutes as I stared off after her.

A few hours later, the smithy had been picked clean. Most of the army grabbed small, light weapons. The Zephyrs didn't take any, which surprised me, but if my monk theory was correct, I doubted they would fight with them. Near the smithy door, Romas continued negotiating with the Baron about who was paying for all the weapons while I shook my head and laughed.

After the groups went off with their respective mentors, Romas pulled me aside. "You've proven yourself to me, boy. It's time you learned restricted knowledge of my kind. Come, Creator, to the next step of your training." He looked around the smithy and made sure no one was around, then he turned and walked to the rear wall of the building. I followed him, curious about where we were going.

The panther pressed on a piece of gray stone, stark against the black that made up the structure. I had never noticed this piece before, even though I had been here for a while. He turned the stone counterclockwise, the part clicking into place and swinging open to show a hidden stairwell.

Romas turned to me and pointed down the stairs. "After you, apprentice." A mischievous gleam flashed across his features. I looked back and forth between him and the stairs, unsure. "What, after all this time, you don't trust your master? Come, boy. It's time to learn the secrets of creation." He walked down without me.

I hesitated one more moment, but my curiosity overwhelmed my suspicion, propelling me down the stairs. My boots clomped noisily on the stone, echoing in the dark chamber. My eyes couldn't pierce the darkness, such as it was, but there was a flicker of lamplight at the bottom. I continued, feeling my way along until I finally reached the bottom.

The landing opened up into a vast stone chamber. Gaslights shone along the walls, the eerie purple of the mushroom lights. With this many vision-enhancing lights along the wall, I felt like I had cat eyes. Scattered along the floor were various devices, almost like a workshop back on Earth. There were vices, saws, and welders. Pulleys hung from the ceiling to support heavier metal items. Two walls had full forges, lit with blazing, smokeless coals of tinderstone.

And in the center of the room, an anvil. It had runes up and down its length, glowing various shades of blue. It seemed to blaze with magic, pulling at my soul to use. Romas saw me eyeing the anvil and smiled. "Beautiful, isn't it?"

I looked up, broken free of my reverie. "What is it? How does it feel so powerful?"

Romas walked over to the anvil, putting a hand on it. "This here is a Creation Stone. It's a secret that my master bound me to, and I now bind you to. Do you accept the oath of complete secrecy, held here to your full being by the magic in this room?"

I felt a chill overtake my entire body. It was like chains were wrapping themselves around my very soul. Romas looked at me expectantly, waiting for my response. I breathed in, lungs filling against the pressure. "I accept." The chains released, but I felt a mark on me. It was all so strange.

Romas nodded. "Now that that's over, let's get crafting, shall we? We have an army to outfit."

Chapter 30

Work Smarter

I LOOKED AROUND THE ROOM MORE CAREFULLY AND SAW symbols on the various workstations that matched my arm. A 'DESIGN' symbol on a design bench, papers, and ink quills scattered everywhere. To the right was an 'IDENTIFY' station with magnifying glasses, scales, hammers, and other odds and ends.

And, of course, the anvil. I was beyond excited. "What do we do first?" I asked Romas.

"You wanted to outfit your fire mages with wands, right? I saw you looking at the design bench. Since you already have the plans, you shouldn't need to use any other workbenches, but they can help with the other items you will need to design. But go ahead and put your hand on the tables." He grinned at me, pointing at them.

I wandered over, still in awe of the room. This smithy was much more than it appeared. A prompt appeared in my mind when I put my hand on the design bench.

[DESIGN TABLE - USE 75% LESS MANA WHEN USING A DESIGN SKILL. GET 2X EXPERIENCE WHEN A SUCCESSFUL DESIGN IS CREATED.]

My eyes widened, thinking through the implications of this. I usually burned through about five mana when designing an item in my head, and that was the simple stuff I've been doing so far. I assumed that more intricate designs would need much more time. Using the bench would mean I could save a bunch of mana every time. That was huge. And the experience boost would be essential too.

I walked over to the identification bench, wondering how this one would help me, since identifying skill was passive and didn't cost any mana. I touched it, and a similar prompt appeared.

[IDENTIFICATION STATION - IDENTIFY ITEMS UP TO TWO (2) TIMES YOUR SKILL]

Twice the level! That meant I could identify a level 12 item down here! At this point, I basically ran to the other tables to check them out. There was a magical saw that could reduce ingredients to smaller items and a welder-looking thing that could return combined items back into their components, which would be great for upgrading items. Romas said the saw took large pelts from one piece of armor to three or four gauntlets or a huge tree branch into manageable chunks that could be used around the city too.

He told me that many creations are different from the flashy items that sell best. Yes, everyone loved a new armor vest or longsword. But you only really needed a new weapon every five to six levels. What warriors needed most were belts, boots, sight enhancers, and much more of the "boring" stuff. And then the settlement itself needed things made for their houses, stores, and schools. It was a never-ending list.

Along another wall was the glowing forge. The tinderstone was made into heating items for the Fekan homes in this forge. I could make my ore into commodities, but Romas needed to learn about the silver ore and its capabilities. He could mold the ore into all kinds of things.

And finally, the anvil. I saved this one for last, shooting one more look at Romas. He smiled, a fatherly grin crossing his features. He waved a paw in a 'go ahead' movement.

I put my hand on the cold steel, my excitement through the roof. The prompt appeared.

[CREATION STONE - FIVE (5) USES PER DAY - CREATE A LEVEL 1 ITEM WITHOUT A MANA COST, AND EVERY ADDITIONAL LEVEL ITEM FOR 50% MANA COST]

I ripped my hand away and stared at my mentor. "Free items! Half mana? Are you kidding?"

Romas grinned and walked over. "Yes, this is how I make items here in the settlement. Without the stone, I would be much less efficient."

"What's the best way to use it?" I asked him.

Romas moved to a T-shaped chair near a workbench and continued his tutelage. "Well, I would first make many free items at once and save my mana for other things. Eventually, I started making my high-level items down here. The 50% discount on mana costs starts adding up quickly."

I nodded. "If I combined all of these tools down here with that mana bracer, I could make tons of items per day!"

Romas nodded. "Now you have gotten a glimpse into my day. The Baron's saber was a level 20 weapon with top-tier ingredients. It would have cost me 150 mana, and that was before I designed it and used mana for the ingredient preparations. With the stone and some work benches, I made it with no problem. Although it exhausted me mentally."

"Romas, what level are you? How much mana do you have?"

"Ah, I was wondering when you would ask me that. I am a level 25, stagnating there. My mana is slightly over 200." My eyes widened at that, thinking of everything I could do with two hundred mana.

He continued. "There are certain thresholds that you must break through. You are approaching your first one around level 10. At each major upgrade in our class, you must create something that pushes your limits and breaks you somehow. I thought the saber would do it for me, but it did not. The army supply should be enough to push you into the next class status. Or possibly your first major kill being used in a high-level weapon or armor. Remember, creation is about more than just making things. It's about how the ingredients were obtained, and the end item used."

That was a lot to take in. I looked at my arm, seeing an updated character sheet.

[NOAH]
[LV 6- BLACKSMITH APPRENTICE]

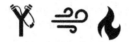

[HEALTH 48/48]
[MANA 43/43]

 L5

 L3

 Passive

 L3

 L1

I did some simple math. If I got half off the mana costs while using the stone for my level 2 creations, mainly the wands, and if I got five of those today, I could make five wands for twenty-five mana. That would give me enough to think through the design of an air wand and make that on my own.

I wanted to avoid using the bracer today since I wanted to see what the troops brought back from their training excursions in the woods. I wanted to make a weapon for one of the Zephyrs.

On the far wall was another storage locker, similar to the one upstairs. I went over to it, pulling the doors open. Along the left side were boxes of wood. I saw the needed gray sticks, pulled five out, and then went to the forges.

Romas stopped watching me and picked up a few items from the bench that he was sitting at. "I'll leave you to it, boy. I have other tasks to complete today. Return to the surface once you've used your five charges, and we will reunite with your armies. I doubt they will stay in the jungle for over half a day."

"OK. Thanks again, Romas," I said, turning back to him. I saw him hoist himself off the chair and head up the stairs, barely making a noise as his paws touched the stone.

I turned back to my task at hand. The red ore I needed for the wands made up a whole bin on the right side, but Romas had melted them down into long bars. I picked one up, feeling its weight in my hand. It was still warm and smelled like smoke.

This must have been four or five pieces melted together and purified. I had to be careful not to use too much and accidentally create a higher-level wand. My mages could only use a level 1 wand, or at least that was my assumption. I took the bar over to the saw, attempting to use it for the first time. When I placed the bar on the bench, options flowed through my mind. I could cut it down into two, three, or four pieces. I chose four. The saw spun momentarily, the rod magically cutting apart into four pieces.

This felt more like it, each piece more closely resembling what I would pull from the rock wall in the cave. I took the four tinder-stone rocks to the anvil, excitement building in my gut. Sweat came down my back and face from the heat of the forges and got in my eyes. I placed a gray living tree branch on the anvil and two pieces of tinderstone. I thought about the fire wand, pulling the two ingredients together mentally.

I watched as the runes on the anvil lit up, blazing a bright red, and glowed brightly. Then, sitting on the anvil was a wand, just like I had made before.

I quickly looked at my arm, checking my mana.

[37/43]

Six mana! Excellent! It must have cost one mana to use the saw and five to make the wand. *I even gained a mana point just from my work!* I scrambled back to the saw to grab my other two pieces and sat down to make the rest of my wands.

Once they were all completed, I set them in a neat pile by the stairs. As I projected, my mana was down by 25. I walked over to the workbench and thought through an air wand, similar to the fire wand. Of course, the silver ore came up as a component, but I was surprised when the rod material wasn't a 'living tree branch' but a 'water sapling.' That would be a problem, as I had no idea what that was or how to find it.

I found it ironic that the rod material for the fire wand was a living tree, and the material for a lightning rod was a water sapling. I supposed that was how things worked here on Prixa. At a dead end for now, I sighed, grabbed my wand bundle, and headed back up the stairs to meet up with my army. I was excited to see how they did on their first training day.

Chapter 31

Biokinesis

I WALKED OUT INTO THE CITY, HEAVY RAIN FALLING outside. Small rivers flowed between the paths, brown streams forming. The merchants had packed up, not interested in working through the downpour. The feline creatures on Prixa did not like the rain, that was for sure. I listened to the rain for a moment, closing my eyes.

My head jerked up out of my reverie to the sounds of shouting. I sprinted toward the edge of the first level to see what was going on. I hoped it wasn't the return of the Shadowalkers. We weren't ready for them yet. As I reached the edge walls, I saw that it was something else.

My relief didn't last, however. Two of the warrior class Feka were army-carrying injured mages over their shoulders. Their long strides left the humans in their wake, who ran behind them. To the left, near one of the fields, the Baron and his troops got off the benches they were sitting on and ran to meet the group. They had returned from their training already.

I turned away from the wall and ran to the ramp to the ground level, water drenching my clothes and dripping into my eyes. As I turned the corner, I slipped on a wet rock, hitting the back of my head on the pavers with an *oof.* I lay there, dazed momentarily, shaking the spots from my vision. A sucking feeling from my arm told me my health bar would take care of it, but I chastised myself. *I can't be seen stumbling around the settlement. I need to do better and be a leader here.*

I got up and wiped the mud off my hands onto my robes, looking around. *No one saw.* When I got to where they were just outside the wall a group was huddled around two people. "What happened?" I yelled with more panic in my voice than I would have liked. I pushed through the group to a gruesome sight.

A blond-haired boy lay there with half his face gouged, claw marks covering his ear and cheeks. One of the mages ran over with a rag and pressed it to his face to slow the bleeding. If he continued bleeding at this pace, he would undoubtedly die. I saw his health bar tattoo at [1/20], his magic unable to absorb any additional injuries. It also appeared that something was keeping the wounds from closing.

I looked over at the other body on the ground; this one was already gone. It was a younger boy with a blood-soaked shirt. The creature that attacked him left deep gouges right in his chest.

"What the hell happened out there?" I demanded, looking the first Feka in the eyes. *I haven't been in charge of these people for a day, and I've already lost one mage, potentially two.*

The white tiger stood tall, matching my piercing gaze with his own. "I told you when we were in the jungle together, human. Your kind are not warriors, even with your fledgling magic. We can only protect them to an extent while they try to use their magic and level. They all need physical and weapon training."

The Baron stood up from the ground, his inspection of the blond-haired boy complete. "That's enough, Percius. Thank you for volunteering to work with them on their weaknesses. Back to the settlement with you." The tiger's hair stood up, and a growl escaped his lips, only to get one in return from the Baron. The mages shuffled uncomfortably, watching the exchange.

Finally, the tiger turned and left the scene, the other warriors following him. Baron Gilbert continued, not affected by the interaction. "Noah, we have some first aid items, but I do not know if they work for humans. You may have to create something and quickly. This boy doesn't have long. I smell all kinds of poisonous mana coursing through his veins."

I frowned, not sure what to do. The Baron saw me hesitate and growled. "Go! Now! Create something!" That sparked me into action.

I raced up the ramp and headed straight to the smithy. Romas was chatting with a merchant when I blasted through the door. They both startled, leaping slightly off the ground in a feline startle response.

"Romas! I need help!" I shouted.

"Slow down, boy. What is it?" he responded, walking over to me.

"One of the new mages got killed in the jungle, and another was injured badly. I need a health regeneration item! But I am afraid any you have would only work on Feka."

He nodded gravely. "Yes. Mana is universal, but I fear that a health bracer made by a Feka would only work on a Feka, since we're talking about anatomy. Quickly, it would be best if you designed something. Then tell me the ingredients, and I will assist you."

I glanced down at my arm. "I don't have that much mana left! My wands took most of it, and I only have fourteen left."

"One problem at a time." Romas looked to the merchant standing there, watching the exchange. "Clide, you will have to excuse us. Please show yourself out."

The merchant looked back and forth between us, then nodded. "Good day to you, Romas."

After he left, we headed to the basement. If I was going to create something to help my mage, I would need to use the workbench to design it and hope it would only cost me ten mana. I ran over to the table, sitting down on the cat-shaped chairs.

I rested my hands on the table, thinking deeply about a healing bracer to regenerate the user's health more quickly. Instead of the slots of required ingredients showing themselves in my mind, I got an error.

[WATER MAGIC NEEDED TO UNLOCK ITEMS OF THIS NATURE]

Damn it. OK, so that isn't going to do it. What else can I do? If healing magic was considered water magic, that was fine. But there had to be a way to stop the bleeding.

"Well?" Romas inquired, standing near me.

"I got nothing. Healing magic is from a mana source I can't access yet."

The panther started pacing the room, thinking deeply. "That doesn't make sense. I have made a health bracer before and cannot access your mana types. But my healing items come from space magic. It takes health and the materials it needs from healthy body parts to help the damaged parts. But I'm not quite sure."

My eyes lit up. "Space magic?"

Romas nodded. "Yes. Why?"

I smiled excitedly. "The Monarch said our two species share space magic! That and time magic. Quick, please give me one of the bracers! I need to unlock that mana type!"

Romas looked at me momentarily, clearly confused by this, but then complied. He raced up the stairs, running faster than I had seen him move before. One minute later, he returned down the stairs, running over to me. "Here. My health bracer."

I grabbed the bracer, turning it over in my hands. As expected, a notice appeared. But not one that I expected.

[NEW SKILL UNLOCKED - BIOKINESIS]
[TOO MANY SKILLS ASSIGNED. REMOVE A
CURRENTLY ACTIVATED SKILL TO USE]
[SKILL SWAP OUTS REMAINING TODAY- 1]

What the hell was biokinesis? And I got a skill from holding the bracer, not a magic class?

"Romas, I got a skill from holding this thing. You're sure it's a healing bracer?"

He looked away. "Well, not really. I mean, it is, but not in the way that the injured creature is healed. This is what I had that might help."

I huffed, frustrated by this whole exchange. "I needed healing magic, not whatever the hell this is. Thanks anyway, Romas." I tossed the bracer down on the table and turned to run back up the stairs.

Behind me, Romas growled. "I thought..." His voice faded away as I reached the main floor of the smithy. Before I left, I ran to my locker, where the mana bracer was. Romas had let me keep it due to my low mana pool. I grabbed it, putting it in my pocket for now.

The rain was coming down much harder now. As I ran, I internalized which skills I had active. The only one I didn't need was 'MINE' since I would specifically go out and perform mining activities. The biokinesis clicked into the place where the mining slot was.

Down on the base level of the settlement, the mages still stood around the injured mage. The fire mages had all returned at this point, also gathering around the wounded human. The boy looked washed out like he had no time left.

I skidded to a stop in front of him and knelt. "Move aside!" The girl holding the rag on his face skittered backward from me. I placed my hand on his face, seeing what this new ability would do.

Suddenly, I felt his injuries. It was like a CAT scan, his face showing in a 3D view in my mind. Apparently, as part of my creator class, I could create other things than just weapons and armor. *Cool.*

I thought of creating skin to cover the claw wounds over the boy's face. My mana sucked out of my arm, forming three skin tags over the marks, sealing the injuries. Gasps sounded around me, the mages watching me work. The skin I made was bright white, like a scar from an old injury. My arm became numb, and my mana was utterly depleted. I glanced at his face; blood was still coming from his ear and the back of his head.

I didn't dare remove my hands from the boy for fear of losing my progress. "Someone put the bracer from my pocket on my arm! Quick!" Jasper ran over, fishing in my overall pockets for the metal bracer. He found it and took it out, slapping it on my forearm.

The choice appeared before me, the bracer asking me if I wanted mana upfront or mana over time. This time, I chose the twenty mana upfront. Instead of the IV drip feeling, it felt like a bucket of ice water was dumped on my head. I continued healing, filling the remaining gouges in the boy's face with skin.

Lastly, I saw the poison filtering through his system. I didn't know of a way to get that out. He would have to let his body fight it. The skill focused on growing things, not healing or poison removal.

I stood up, red, bloody mud all over my pants and hands. Sweat and rain poured down my face. I glanced at my arm, seeing [8/46]. I had gained almost four mana from all of this. My mana would start ticking up from the bracer, but I would have mana poisoning now. The air mages who returned with the injured boy grabbed him and retreated to their living quarters to watch over him as he healed.

No one spoke for some time; the rain was the only sound in the clearing. Finally, the Baron approached me and put a wet paw on my shoulder. "That was amazing, boy."

I looked at him, not sure how I felt. "Yeah. I hope that saves him. He has to beat the poison going through his body, but at least he won't bleed out. And now," I looked around at my mages. "I won't be able to create many more items today. I was able to make these five wands, but I'll need some time to recover from this before I can make any more." I took out the wands, showing them. "Hopefully, you all had a better training session than my mages." I looked hopefully at the Baron.

"Oh, we did." The Baron smiled. "For now, I must retire. I have other things to attend to. I will catch up with you at sundown this evening."

I nodded. "Thank you, Baron Gilbert." He turned and walked up the dirt path, the Zephyrs following, looking exhausted.

The fire mages all looked excited, but none moved or said anything.

Jasper finally moved toward me, breaking the silence. "Noah, we have to tell you what happened in the jungle. It was awesome."

Chapter 32

A Kick in the Nuts

"Jasper, what happened out there?" I asked, still down after how the day had gone so far. The sun was starting to set, the sky a bright pink color. The rain had stopped, leaving the air still and muggy, and insects were out in full force, landing on my arm and face. I had grown used to them, but windless days were the worst.

"Well, we went out into the jungle with Typh and Dee. They already had experience with you, so they were good people to train us. They knew you touched the cave wall and unlocked a mining skill."

I nodded. "Right. It's been how I've unlocked most of my skills so far. The only exception was my design skill and now this newest one, where a bracer unlocked my healing skill. But that's similar to how you guys unlocked your fireball and lightning skills when you touched the dagger and wand."

"Right! So Dee had the idea to return to where I blasted that tree with my fireball from yesterday when I showed off the wand. She said ingredients of a certain type usually group together. She gets her dexterity stuff high up in the trees, and Typh gets his warrior stuff in the caves by battling huge monsters. So we went over there, and the jungle floor was littered with debris and charred tree pieces."

I didn't know where this was headed, but I was tired, about thirty minutes away from mana poisoning, and was internally mourning the death of a guy in my army. I hurried Jasper up with a hand motion to get to the point.

"Uh, right," he stammered, the poor kid getting flustered. "Well, Jamie here picked up some of the coal pieces left from the blaze. In her mind, they were marked as 'affected by fire magic.' She's one of those bomb mages..."

The amber-haired girl cleared her throat. "Ember alchemists."

Jasper nodded. "Right, alchemists. She picked it up, concentrated, and lit it back on fire!"

Jamie smiled. "The skill was called 'Ignite Tinder.' Since the stick piece was already burned, it must have unlocked my skill. I had the other alchies grab some, so a couple of us have the skill. We could only find a few pieces that worked, but they were one-time use."

I grinned at her. "That's awesome! I thought I would have to make something to unlock other skills for you guys."

She shrugged her shoulders. "Well, we all have a wand proficiency and a 'Fireball' skill, no matter what class we got. But we tried reshooting the fireball without the wand and couldn't. Until..." She trailed off and looked at another boy, who cleared his throat and stood up.

He pulled a bright red mushroom out of his pocket and concentrated. It burst into a smoke cloud, instantly causing me to burst into a wheezing cough. My lungs burned, feeling like someone put a clamp on my windpipe and a blindfold on my eyes. Oddly enough, I was the only one coughing. I could barely even breathe or see the people around me.

Finally, the smoke cleared ten seconds later, the mages staring at me with grins. Further away, Dee and Typh glanced over in amusement. "You guys knew about this, didn't you!" I yelled their way, accusation in my voice.

They chuckled a meowing laugh, lounging on chairs nearby. "Yeah, it was quite a shock to us when it happened. Nasty little skill, that."

The boy spoke up. "Yeah, 'Smoke Bomb' that one is called! We were looking around the trees for more coal, and when I kicked one, it burst into smoke, and I got the notification. There were two more growing around the base, so I grabbed them. This time, the skill asked if I wanted to start the smoke bomb, but I declined. Unfortunately, when I gave one to another mage, they got the skill, but the mushroom went up in smoke again."

Dee spoke up from the chairs. "They didn't get us that time!"

Another mage spoke up. "We seem immune to the smoke, but Dee and Typh weren't." They all looked at each other and smiled, faces that told me they were proud to give the Feka a little kick in the nuts.

A mage handed me a water skin. I took a pull, my coughing subsiding. "Well...that seems...useful," I barked out, my voice raspy after the effects of the smoke. I took another pull of the water and cleared my throat again. "OK, the alchemists got an ignite skill and a smoke cloud. That's cool. Jasper, did the Tinder Mages get any additional skills?"

Jasper spoke up again. "Well, no. I let Lennie over there shoot a fireball at a separate tree to generate more coal and mushrooms for tomorrow, but there wasn't anything left. So, for now, only a couple of them have the ignite tinder, and the other two alchies have the smoke cloud. Once you touch the coal, that's it. It won't unlock the skill for anyone else. So weird. We didn't really see any creatures, and the rest was uneventful. Dee kept us out of the spider infestations, then we came back when we heard all the shouting."

I processed this for a moment. On Prixa, ingredients you get from creatures dying could be turned into reusable items. But elements like plants and ore could only be used once, whether that was to unlock a class or shoot as a pellet. And combining an element with an item could give it additional, permanent properties.

I thought about how that could help me. For now, the fact that six of the mages had wands now and four others had skills was a step in the right direction. I thanked the group and told them to head back to their living quarters to get some rest. I wanted to check on the air mages to see how their adventures went, but I had a couple of errands first.

I headed down the path toward the docks, the largest moon peeking above the horizon. The sun had set since I started my walk to the docks from the front of the settlement.

I had already checked in on the injured boy. He stayed in the farming barracks and had been put on a bed. He was blazing hot, his body fighting the poisons still. Some of the color had returned to his face, but the bright white skin tags were even more prominent, with his face turning a sweaty red. The other air mages had covered him with cold, wet rags, but I feared it wouldn't be enough. At this point, there wasn't anything else I could do.

I tried using my designing skill to get a poison removal device, but I got a similar error, saying that I still needed to unlock earth magic. Opening the final two elements would be extremely important for me to grow my army and get vital item access.

I was absolutely wiped and still needed to check in on the Zephyrs. Of all the new mages, they interested me the most. The mana bracer on my arm had worn through its charge, leaving me with [32/47] mana, unmoving for the next eight more hours as the mana poisoning set in. I used some already with my design ability but decided to save the rest for tomorrow. Before I headed to the docks, I had put it back in my locker at the smithy.

When I got to the dockworker's barracks, one of the large boys I had pulled the fish smasher stood to watch outside. *They still need to trust the Feka, it appears.*

He bowed his head at me. "Creator! Welcome." He looked up at me and moved aside from the door.

I shook my head with a slight chuckle. "No need to be so formal. What's your name, anyway?

He grinned. "Mathew."

I returned the smile, tired as it may have looked. "Nice to meet you. Are they all in there?"

He nodded. "Most are sleeping. Bates will speak with you. I assume you are here to speak about the day's events."

"Yeah. Which one is Bates? The huge one?"

He laughed. "Yes. We have him as our group leader. He has always watched out for us and was the logical choice."

I thanked him and walked into the hut. The smell of fish and guts was overwhelming, reminding me of my training here, which felt like weeks ago. The cabin was simple, with a few cots and hooks with clothes on them. There was one window, the moonlight coming in. The sound of waves mixed with some gentle snores.

I saw Bates in the corner of the hut. He stared up at the ceiling, not asleep yet. When he heard me cross the threshold, he looked over and rolled out of bed. He didn't have on any clothes other than a loincloth, but strode over to me and held his arm out in a welcoming gesture. I may have blushed a little; nakedness embarrassed me. *Finally, someone with the loin cloth option!*

He noticed, grabbed a pair of pants, and slipped them on quickly. I nodded to the door, a signal that I wanted to speak to him outside the hut. Bates followed behind, ducking his head to leave the building. He greeted Mathew guarding the door as I led the way toward the docks in a slow stroll.

"Sorry to bother you at night. I know you guys had a busy day and probably wanted some rest, but I wanted to catch up with you before the day ended to see how training went and plan what we need to do tomorrow."

He strolled casually, looking at the sky and not saying much for a while. "The Baron is an outstanding fighter. We trained in hand-to-hand combat all day. The other guys are wiped."

I nodded slowly, following his slow pace along the shoreline. "That's good. Did anyone get any classes or skills during the training?"

He stopped and pointed at his two new arm tattoos for me to see. There were two simple human postures; a fist with an explosion at the end and a kicking motion. "Nice! What do they do?"

"My Knockout Blow is a skill that, upon impact, can knock out the attacker, depending on their level. I unlocked it when I dodged a fellow mage's attack, then landed a counter punch in his face, knocking him out. Upon training, a few others also unlocked this skill, but not all of us are so easily hit." A sly smile crossed his face.

He continued. "The other skill is similar; we had to land our first successful kick, and the magic pushes the enemy back further. That one is called a 'Blowback Kick.' One of the other Zephyrs unlocked a blocking skill, but he was cunning and would need to share the details. Unlocking fighting skills throughout the day became a...competition.

I wasn't sure that's how I wanted this to go, but I couldn't say it surprised me. A bunch of big jocks fighting each other all day would undoubtedly lead to some friendly competition. At least I hoped that it stayed friendly. But we didn't have much time to waste on pride and puffery.

"I would really prefer that you guys shared skills as they unlocked. We need as much help as we can get before these Shadowalkers return. But I get it. I doubt you can unlock a fighting skill without actually landing the skill in a fight. These don't seem any different than the skills I have unlocked so far, which I get from performing an activity for the first time."

I stopped and turned back toward the hut. "Anything else? If not, we should head back. The Baron said he would look for me sometime tonight, so I have to return to the smithy."

Bates shook his head. "It was a good day. But we didn't go into the jungle. I want a chance with my team to go in there tomorrow. We will fare better than the other mages did today."

I chewed my lip, nervous. "Let me discuss with Baron Gilbert and see."

He looked like he was going to protest, then stopped. "Yes, sir."

We made it back to the hut, our conversation dying out. I still wasn't used to being called sir around here. "Get some rest. I will see you tomorrow." With that, I walked back up the hill to the blacksmith.

Chapter 33

Final Components

THE ALPHA STOOD UP AND SHOOK HIS FUR, THEN stretched. The moon had just risen, and the final day of preparations was completed. He had thought of everything this time. He would surely overrun the Fekan settlement with the troops at his disposal. Once they were wiped off the planet, he would consume their bodies and strengthen his strongest warriors.

Over the past two weeks, he had gone through two betas and four other Stalkers as they fought for supremacy, adding their strength to his own as he consumed them. The beta male was the most sought-after position in the pack, even with its risks. But now that the battle was here, he had stopped all other struggles with a pack-wide peace to prevent other casualties. Growing stronger was important, but additional losses could not be sustained.

As for his other troops, they were in the hundreds. Various canine breeds walked around the city in every direction, packing for the march to Dunbar. He found additional Mecho bears to attack the walls, foxes to scout around the city during battle, and a breed of wild dog that could run faster than any other Shadowalker in the pack. Their primary use was to hunt in an enormous pack and overwhelm the Feka.

The alpha looked over the siege weapon assortment they had created for the occasion. Long tree branches were strung together and would be carried by the Whitetooth troops. It would protect them from arrows and be used inside the walls to reach the upper levels. He also brought a sizeable mecho skin full of water in case any remaining humans could use their fire attacks on it. The hyenas were versed in what to do in that case.

He had one of the Mecho bears reserved to stand on its hind legs and pull the ramp down. He calculated it would be about twenty feet up, so they could stand on two legs and pull it down when he assembled his platform beneath the ramp.

Lastly, each of the stalkers had pouches filled with water on their backstraps. The idea here was to fling the bags into the battle, and if the humans used that shocking attack, it would backfire and electrocute them.

The alpha grinned a toothy, devilish smile. He had thought of all the major hurdles and was ready to invade. This time...there would be no retreat. He would keep pushing through the city until every last human and Feka was destroyed. He would consume the whole place, then turn his sights on Fayport. He would kill the Monarch.

With the Great Moon upon them for the season, his body shook with increased power. He would time the moon's arrival with his own at the Fekan settlement.

He howled, the sound picked up by hundreds of dogs. The hyenas laughed their chaotic cackles, battle lust evident in the sounds. It was time to move out.

Sweat poured down my face and back. My fifth fireball wand today, and the last one for the army, gleamed in the flickering torchlight as it sat on the anvil. Romas sat unmoving at the design table, looking at the surface for over an hour now. He was deep in thought, designing something or another.

The last few days had been eventful for my army, but we had lost another three air mages and two fire mages to severe injuries. No one was killed, luckily. But we were losing mages quicker than I would have liked. A few picked up random other skills and a few levels, but I was afraid we would be no match for whatever the Shadowalkers would throw at us. It was a full week since their last invasion, so I knew they were cooking up something good.

Between pumping wands and Zephyr gauntlets out at the anvil and training with Dee in our sparring sessions, I was starting to feel more and more prepared. My 'PATRON' skill leveled up again at some point last night, directly correlated with my mages and fighters leveling up. I was level 8 now, with my creation skill keeping pace with my overall level. As I neared level 10, I got excited about what kind of upgrade my skills would get. I remembered Romas mentioning something about that in the secret smithy.

My mana was slowly ratcheting up as well as I trained with it. I looked proudly at my tattoos, impressed with how far I had come.

[LV 8- BLACKSMITH APPRENTICE]

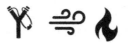

[HEALTH 60/60]
[MANA 21/55]

L8

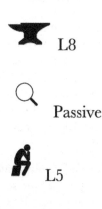

Passive

L5

L4

L1

[UNSELECTED SKILLS -  L6]

The army was looking good. Most of my mages were level 3 and the Zephrys were level 4.

So far, the most incredible thing was when an alchemist made a bomb. It was the cute auburn-haired girl. She found more combustible material, then could light a long vine on fire and it would act as a wick. The quick ignition would run up to the bomb and explode it. I decided she wasn't allowed to go in the jungle anymore, instead assigned to 'bomb duty' around the settlement. I had her planting them all over town to leave some nasty surprises for our eventual guests.

The bombs only cost her a few mana to create but would cost around five mana when she lit the wick aflame. I had to calculate that when the time came. A few other mages had the same ignition skill, but she was the only one with bomb-making capabilities. I told the other alchemists to keep at it when out in the jungle.

For some reason, the creatures of the woods left the fire mages alone for the most part, but ravenously attacked my air mages. No one seemed to know why. I had a feeling that many of the creatures in the jungle had some earth magic affiliation...but I couldn't prove that. The ingredients that were brought back didn't spark any upgrades for me.

The Zephrys also had some interesting characteristics. They could hold their own against many of the creatures of the woods. Baron Gilbert started bringing a few hunters with them to team everyone up. The Baron told me that the Zephrys were like a stone wall- able to defend against most attacks they faced, and the hunters would come in with their sneak attacks to finish off prey.

Keeping my front-line troops safe and armored was my next priority since outfitting my backline attack troops was done. I had a mound of pelts and claws near my locker, just waiting for me to make something with them. With my last wand created, I could get started on them next.

The alchemists were self-sufficient and didn't need my help at the moment. The air mages were still down half their troops and didn't seem motivated to fight, so I sent them with the other groups until their friends recovered from their injuries. Their morale was completely gone.

I set a place for them to fire lightning attacks at straw dummies, but it just didn't seem to get them any gains. Nothing was ever going to be like the real thing in the jungle or on a battlefield.

The warrior Feka was still pretty standoffish as well. I needed to bridge that divide before the Shadowalker army returned.

I stood up, gathering my bundle of wands in my arm. I glanced at Romas one last time, curious about what he could be designing. I shook my head and walked up the stairs.

Jasper was there, waiting for me. He knew about the workshop now. I had convinced Romas that it would be vital to have Jasper down here with us to give another hand, since he delivered my ingredients as needed. It took some convincing, but eventually, he agreed. Romas made me hold the soul-binding ceremony, citing the need for my soul to break if the secret got out, not his. I shuddered at the thought of that.

Jasper saw the bundle of wands and grinned, his smile reaching his ears. "Nice! Is that the last of them?"

"Yep," I replied, smiling back. I wiped my arm across my face, turning my sleeve a dirty brown. "I need to wash up. One day we can get Romas to design an air conditioner down there."

Jasper chuckled. "Let's wait until after the battle, eh? What's he making down there, anyway? He's been down there all morning!"

I shrugged. "Dunno. It must be something epic, though. He's been in a design state for over an hour." I filled the basin up with water. "Can you hand out the wands?"

"Sure!" Jasper said excitedly. I handed them over, and he took them out into the city.

I plunged my face into my hands, cold water washing over my filthy features. I thought through what else I had left to make. My mana stood at [21/55], so I could think through something the Zephyrs brought back. I wanted to make a boot for them that could use air mana to complement their gauntlets. I returned to the cellar to see if Romas had finished the table.

He was at the forge, melting down some large iron ore rocks. "Hey! Romas! You're finally done with the design table?"

He looked at me, a scowl crossing his face. "I'll have you know; that's how long master blacksmiths take at the table. I don't just make little toys for people to use."

I scoffed at him. "These *toys* will burn the Whitetooth troops to the ground!"

Romas mumbled insults to himself but concentrated on his task. I shook my head and walked to the design table, sitting on the still-warm seat. I thought about an air gauntlet that used the Squamish and monkey pelts that the Zephyrs brought me. The world slowed as my skill activated.

Two options were shown in my mind; a spiked attack gauntlet that would influence their damage upon a hit or an air gauntlet that would electrify on impact. They both used the gorilla pelts, not the Squamish fur, but one required fangs and the other the silver ore. I cut off the skill, looking around. Romas was gone, the forge coals still burning. My mana was at [9/55]; the design session was much more in-depth than usual. Even with the reduction in mana usage, I burned through eleven mana.

I got off the chair since I would have to wait until tomorrow to make anything else. Outside the smithy, there was a lot of commotion. I peeked my head into the courtyard to see what was happening.

The Baron was talking with a striped leopard, blood pouring from his shoulder. *One of the scouts,* I thought with a panic. Then he started pointing north into the jungle, and my heart stopped. It seemed my time for preparations was over.

Chapter 34

Battle Phase I

"ALL NON-ENLISTED HUMANS REPORT TO THE NO-CLASSER bunkers! All non-enlisted humans report to the no-classer bunkers!"

My stress level was through the roof, but I couldn't help chuckling as I passed the coordinator's cries, slightly different than the last time the city was attacked. I had made a sizeable impact on Dunbar, humans now aiding in defending the Fekan settlement.

The first few Shadowalkers began popping through the trees, and horns sounded all over Dunbar. I took off in a sprint, making sure my ramp came up. I stopped in the courtyard, looking around frantically. One of my locking pins was removed, but the other looked stuck, the weight of everything settling the rod into place.

There were two Feka already there, trying to pull out the pin. It was jammed in there good. I ran toward them, my boots slamming down the stone walkway and sweat pouring down my back from the hot air. When I arrived, two other Feka had joined the cause, all four pulling and straining on the pin.

"Guys! We practiced this! Just turn the wheel!" No one listened over the chaos. I pushed one of the Feka out of the way and got a dirty stare from him. "Move! Help me with this wheel!"

I took hold of the horizontal wheel and started pushing. "Two of you, push with me. You there, stay on the rod. Pull it when I say now!"

The Feka glanced at each other, then came and joined me. We pushed, the counterweights adding a thousand pounds to the struggle. Finally, I felt the wheel move slightly. "Now!"

He pulled the pin, and the wheel pushed against us. "Let go! Let go!" We let the wheel go, the force of the counterweights moving us backward like a rubberband. I ran over to the ramp and watched it slowly rise up. I let out a long sigh of relief. *One thing down.*

Next, I looked at the ballistas. Two hunters were assigned and had yet to arrive in the left tower, but the right building had a tiger carrying a few missiles and the other winding the heavy string with the cranks. *Good.*

Two warrior Feka took their position over the dog-smasher devices and checked the rope. It was still tied to the concrete, ready to be released at a moment's notice.

As for my mages, they joined the fray. The Tinder Mages took their positions in the lookout towers near the walls, wands held at the ready. My alchemists strode over to their bomb huts, created by a couple of Fekan builders to look like a merchant stall but would act as a place where they would hide and light their fuses.

The weeks' training had raised their mana, most leveling up to level two or three. The mages could shoot at least three fireballs, maybe even four, from their wands. And with fifteen of them in my army, that was a lot of firepower. But I instructed them to save their last bit of mana for emergencies. I assumed the Shadowalkers would bring ladders and ramps this time so my pulleys wouldn't thwart them again. I would be ready to light those bastards on fire.

My Zephyrs took position around the warrior Feka and the Baron in the courtyard's center. They would mesh well during battle, allowing the two groups to link their attacks. It took some discussion, but the Warriors deemed them the 'least likely' to be human cowards. I sighed deeply but caved.

Lastly, my Wind Mages stayed at the very back of the battle. They were mostly still levels 1 and 2 and looked around anxiously. I didn't have much confidence in their abilities, so I put them as last-ditch defense units.

With my preparations in order, I walked back to the edge to examine the attacking force. There were easily a thousand Shadowalkers, outnumbering us six to one. As I figured, the pit bull troops carried wood structures and ladders, and a couple of bears pushed a siege tower. Wood boards stood upright in front of the stalkers as well.

Foxes were skittering around the troops, too; their purpose was unknown to me. The Stalkers had grown in number with their pack numbering around twenty or so. I didn't recognize most of the faces since the main werewolf was missing among them.

I felt a paw on my shoulder and turned around. It was Baron Gilbert. "How are you holding up, boy?" he asked.

"As well as anyone can, I suppose. I hope all of our preparations are enough to stop them." I made eye contact with him, his piercing blue feline eyes boring into me. "My troops just aren't ready, and I haven't made enough items, and..."

He held his paw up. "Your service to our cause has made me proud. Without you, we would have no chance here today. I am forever in your debt." He bowed to me.

My head jerked back a bit in surprise. "Thank you. That means a lot." I cleared my throat, still awkward at this kind of stuff. A few of the warriors that surrounded us noticed and scuffled their feet uncomfortably. "Well, I had better get to my position."

He nodded. "May you find your marks today, Noah. Now, let us hunt!" And with that, he let out a ferocious roar that the other Feka picked up in the settlement. The sound carried far into the jungle, birds startling from the trees.

From deep in the wood, a slow howl answered the roar, picked up by hundreds of dogs.

The alpha paced back and forth, a battle of this size getting his heart drumming in his chest. He surveyed his troops and formations one last time, the beta waiting on his command. Satisfied, he nodded to the wolf with a toothy grin.

With a howl, the beta turned and started the plans in motion. Four enormous Mecho bears started pushing the tower with their heads, slowly rolling it out of the jungle. Hyenas followed behind, laughing and carrying water in pouches, sloshing side to side. To the sides, large blockades were held by a few Stalkers. The ground shook and trembled as siege towers began their descent, pushed with grunts and roars from the Mecho troops.

The Feka on the wall saw the colossal structure and started yelling back and forth, figuring out who to shoot first. They scrambled and knocked their arrows, the tips quivering in unsure movements. As the tower neared the walls, arrows began to fly, thudding against the wood surface. The cats jumped along the wall for a better vantage point, but the blockades protected the bears.

Suddenly, the archers stopped and backed off, jumping off the walls and leaving them wholly abandoned. *Strange,* the alpha thought. A quiet descended on the jungle, the only sounds were the grunting bears. A moment later, the siege tower pushed against the wall with a *thud,* the Mechos looking around confused as though they expected a tougher resistance. Then, with their job completed, they lumbered back up the hill.

The hyenas placed the blockades against the top of the walls, turning them into ramps with a grinding pull backward. They also scampered up the hill, swapping places with the melee troops.

A howl sounded again, and the Whitetooth troops took off at a full run toward the walls. Two hundred pit bull monsters charged ahead, no fear on their warped canine faces. Slobber poured from their mouths as they reached top speed toward the siege equipment, tongues hanging out like they were chasing a ball. There was still no resistance to be found from the settlement.

The first couple of dogs reached the siege tower, claws scratching against the wood surfaces. *Perhaps the felines never regained troops after our attack,* the alpha thought, watching intently and looking for traps.

Then, a loud roar came from the left tower directly behind the wall. But this wasn't a jungle cat roaring; this was the roar of a gigantic fireball. It flew right at the siege tower, now full of Whitetooths. It impacted the siege weapon with a *woosh*, rocking it to the side with force. The flames licked up the sides, dogs yelping and barking inside. Two dogs jumped out the side and hit the ground with a *thud*, unmoving. Another flew from the other tower, hitting the tower from the other side.

"Hyenas! Water! Now! Now!!" the beta barked out. The laughter ratcheted up, hyenas breaking out of the jungle with their sacks of water. They ran on their two legs, looking ridiculous with two legs and backs arched, holding the heavy sacks. The archers returned, shooting at them as they ran. *It was a trap. I will not let this settlement beat me again.*

The wood of the towers was thick and wet for this purpose with the Shadowalker builders choosing the greenest trees they could find. That helped, but the flames ate through the wood quickly. Finally, the hyenas arrived at the siege tower, throwing their water sacks at the fire. Some missed, but a few hit, putting out some of the fires with a sizzle.

Hyenas were getting picked off left and right by arrows. Fireball after fireball came from the towers flanking the wall, hitting the ramps, ground, whatever. Five, six, seven fireballs. Flames were everywhere, too much for the hyenas to put out. Dead troops littered the ground everywhere, Whitefangs jumping over their fallen brothers to continue before the remaining wood failed entirely.

A loud *twang* and enormous missiles rained into the mass of Whitetooths, taking out a whole row of them. Then another, a missile coming from the other side. The alpha saw two cats in there, turning an enormous wheel to reload the damn thing. "Beta! Take out those weapons! Now! Get your troops on that wall and let the army in the gate! We need to hurry; we're losing troops too fast!"

The beta howled and more troops were released into the fray. Another ballista rocketed in but only took out a few pit bulls in the rear, flying too far. It looked like the crank on the other weapon wasn't turning, inert for now.

Eventually, the fireballs stopped as my mages ran low on mana, and the melee troops reached the top of the burning structures. Hunters jumped up behind the wall at the top of the ramps, hacking and slashing at the Whitefangs. They had shed their bows and fought with claws and daggers, taking on the White-fangs in hand-to-hand combat. The alpha's troops had finally claimed the wall and could do what they did best - melee combat. The mages couldn't do much else, for fear of friendly fire. The ballista troops also abandoned their positions for fear of being trapped in the towers by the enemy.

"Stalkers! Now!" The beta yelled, and phase two of the battle began.

Chapter 35

The Calm Before the Storm

I YELLED A HALT TO THE FIRE MAGES, SATISFIED WITH THEIR initial destruction. The magic worked way better than I thought. The Shadowalker wood structures were charred and blackened. Per my plan, the mages retreated, leaving their towers and dashing along the wall's walkways. The Baron told me about a secret tunnel and stairwell connecting the walls to the first level. It was installed before the ramp could be raised, but it allowed wall troops that lost their position to retreat to the courtyard secretly. The mages used it now, disappearing from view.

Outside the walls, the Stalkers ran toward the ramps at full speed, unprotected from arrows. Since the pit bull troops were on the walls fighting the hunters in hand-to-hand combat, they didn't need to worry about air support from the Feka. There were a few hunters stationed in the towers on the corners of the walls shooting down into the mass of pit bulls and Stalkers.

I watched the hunters hold their ground, but the sound of battle surged as more and more enemy troops surged onto the walls. Foxes began slithering up the ramps and siege tower, almost invisible to my vision and blending in with their white fur. The hunters mostly ignored them, jaws flashing toward them from every direction now. The fox troops descended the stairs toward the gate to open it for the remaining Shadowalker troops.

235

The hunters pulled out all their tricks, keeping the pit bull troops at bay, but many began falling, with cuts and bruises all over their striped fur. "Typh! They're getting overrun! Do something!" I yelled to the leopard over the roar of battle 100 feet away.

"Back! Hunters, to me! Back!" Typh yelled over the sounds of barking and growling. The hunters jumped and flipped off the walls, not bothering with the stairs. This gave them a slight head start on the pit bulls.

The dogs looked over the walkway's edge, barking madly, battle adrenaline in their eyes. They sat on their haunches, staring up at us on the first level; phase one of their attack finished. A few began biting into the deceased Feka, tearing into them with their sharp fangs. I looked away, nauseated by the horror of it. Blood began dripping down the stone structure.

A howl from the alpha shook the whole place, calming the dogs into silence. Everyone simultaneously looked up from their tasks, surprised by the sudden, eerie silence. Even the jungle stilled.

The fox troops found the mechanism to the gate and began working on it with their little paws, the wheel taking four of them to work. The Feka ignored all of this, since the distance from the first level to the gate was much too great to do much; at least 200 yards away. Plus, with how short-handed the settlement defense was, we had to keep our troops all gathered on the first level for the next stage of the battle.

"Air mages!" I yelled. They walked over to the side of the level and pointed their wands.

Lightning began shooting out of the wand tips, zig-zagging in every direction. The lightning was uncontrollable, arcing to the first structure that it found in most cases. Faces dropped all around me as the attacks failed, and the stalkers watched on with grins on their wolfish faces.

I cut off the attacks and sent them back further into the settlement.

What remained of the hunter troops made it to the settlement and jumped the thirty feet to join us, panting and bleeding on the stone. A grinding sounded as the gates slowly opened, the metal scraping over the dirt path. Hyenas and pit bulls paced the gate, waiting for it to open like a dog on earth would before he was let outside.

I felt disappointed in myself for my lack of insight when improving the settlement. There needed to be a way to shoot at enemies from the first level who had claimed your walls. Or at least harass them in whatever ways possible. There was nothing you could do now other than watch an invading army prepare their second phase of the invasion. *Stupid. I need to think through everything more carefully next time. If there even is a next time,* I thought grimly.

I looked at the fighters, assessing their wounds. I found Dee among them, who smiled up at me, surviving the encounter. She seemed pretty ragged, though. I gave a thumbs-up back to her. Romas went around with his bracer, allowing them to biokineti-cally fix their gashes, and smaller felines gave water and bread to the battle-worn hunters.

I felt a warmth spreading across my chest- a symptom of leveling up. I glanced at my arm, delighted to see I was now level 9. My patron skill had leveled up throughout the battle as well. I wondered if that was from my army performing so well. My tattoos had changed slightly, adding an 'unused skills' section.

[LV 9- BLACKSMITH APPRENTICE]

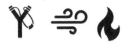

[HEALTH 65/70]
[MANA 34/60]

L9

Passive

L5

L5

L1

[UNSELECTED SKILLS - L5]

I wondered what came next from Patron and design. Creating higher-level items would be helpful later but was useless to me while I outfitted my troops. I hadn't tried designing at a higher level since most of my work came from the basement now on the design table. The mana usage was minimal, but I had yet to design something fantastical.

The mages emerged from a building further down, panting from running through the settlement and the stairs. I ran over with a smile on my face. "Nice work, everyone! That was amazing!" A few of them were holding their arms; a sign that they were completely out of mana.

The mages smiled and grasped shoulders and high-fived, pleased with themselves. Jasper spoke up first, coming forward. "Noah!

Those fireballs we shot were huge! Your wands are amazing!" The excitement in his voice made me happy. These humans had a new lease on life after many years of servitude to the cats.

"Yeah, I couldn't believe the impact on the wood structures! Really great stuff out there, everyone. Go rest up. We will need you when they try to put them up against the settlement. The first part was only the beginning."

We all looked over at the wall, the deconstruction beginning in earnest. Stalkers and Whitetooth troops eyed us, ensuring no one from our group tried attacking while staying out of arrow range. We didn't have enough archers to man the walls, with the hundreds of Shadowalkers pacing them now. Luckily, they didn't see the secret compartment accessing the city. Even if they did, there was a way to blockade it off.

The siege tower rolled through the gate, leaning slightly to the left. The bears were pushing hard, forcing it through the tight opening. Chunks of stone fell off as it blasted its way through, a piece hitting a hyena and killing it with a yelp.

I shook my head. The whole thing was unlike any battle I had ever seen. The logistics differed from Earthly human fighting. At least the battles I had learned about in school. *A lot of waiting in between phases of the fight. Or maybe this was how wars used to go,* I thought to myself.

I walked over to the alchemist's hut, knocking on the door quietly. "All ready in here?" I asked. The door swung over, and I made eye contact with Jamie.

"Yep!" she said, smiling back at me, causing my heart to flutter. *Control yourself, idiot. Werewolf beasts are about to try and eat everyone, and you're blushing like a middle school boy.*

I cleared my throat, gaining composure. "Great. When the Shadowalker troops get in range of the two sides of the courtyard with their ramps..."

"I know, blow the first charges. We've got it," Jamie stated, cutting me off with a smirk. The other alchemists rolled their eyes slightly, the plan very clear.

"OK, hot shots," I said with a chuckle, realizing a pun was made beside. "If you need help, the Tinder mages can assist. A few have mana left to light your fuses, even though it costs them way more mana than you guys."

They nodded.

"Good luck!" I said, closing the door behind me. I saw them peek their heads out of the cloth shade facing the courtyard.

Next, I walked to the Zephyrs, who got in line with the warrior Feka. The Baron was behind them, looking regal in his new armor. Romas had finally finished it for him, taking all day yesterday.

Nervous energy filled my gut. I looked around for something else to do but couldn't think of anything now. I walked back over to the edge of the first level and scanned the canine troops as they worked, trying to understand what was to come. I felt eyes boring into me and glanced over to see the alpha standing there. Troops flowed around the giant werewolf like a river, ignoring his presence as he stared up at me, hatred burning deep. He took two strides toward the tower, then stopped. His teeth were barred, his lip quivering, and the scruff of his neck stood straight up.

Then he turned and left the walls, walking back out into the moist heat of the jungle. Troops were forming up now, filling in their lines. The ramps from before waivered in the air as hyenas held them upright again, protecting the troops from attack. I had about ten to fifteen fireballs left and hoped that was enough to take the structures out. I had to try and keep them from accessing this level. Or at least slow their pace so we could handle the melee troops as they surged up here.

There were a few ladder-looking things, too, that I had just noticed. The foxes carried them behind the lines of troops. I wondered what they were for since they were only about ten feet high. Behind me, archers reassembled, this time ready to shoot all the arrows they possibly could into the mass of Shad-owalkers. The dog-smashing ropes were taken up and held, ready to drop onto the enemy once they worked below the level.

No one moved. No one spoke. My new friends and allies were behind me, taking up their positions. I had no hard feelings about the whole servitude thing. On Prixa, the strong controlled the weak. And humans were indeed more powerless, so they answered to these creatures. Now, with them needing our help, we stood side-by-side. It was time to prove that we indeed belonged.

This battle would be brutal. I did not doubt that. But this time, I was prepared. I had an army of mages with me, low-level as they were, who would blast these bastards into oblivion. And they were outfitted by my own creations. That was just amazing.

I had plenty of ammo for my slingshot, ready to do my part. We would make it out alive today. We had to. The howls sounded into the evening air, a sound I had grown much too familiar with these days.

No discussions. No negotiations. The final battle for Dunbar had begun.

Chapter 36

Bombs Away

Horns sounded throughout Dunbar as the second wave of the attack slowly meandered toward the tower. Now in the middle of the army, the siege tower began moving toward us again, a chunk falling off to the side. To the left and right, the ramps-made-blockades wobbled left and right, carried by hyenas again. I noticed additional bears and Stalkers strolling behind the structures in no particular hurry.

*Just a bit further...*I thought, waiting for the monsters to walk over the first set of bombs we had placed earlier in the day. We figured the troops would come at the settlement in lines and had installed them accordingly.

No one breathed, waiting for the charges to go off. I kept shooting nervous glimpses to the alchemist's hut, knowing I should stop giving up their location. The ramps moved closer to the tower, the action unfolding slowly. Finally, the Shadowalkers crossed over the charges.

... nothing happened. The Feka looked at each other nervously, waiting, but no one spoke. Barking and panting became more audible as the attacking army moved closer. *Now guys. Come on!* They continued forward toward the ramp and walls.

A thunderous *boooom* rocked the settlement, the wood from the right ramp flying everywhere and sending canine parts into the air. Then another, this time in front of the left barricade, blasting it backward on top of the Shadowalkers. *It worked!* The dogs scattered, confused by the chaos. My eyes darted around the scene, excitement boiling into a fever pitch. A final charge in the middle blew a wheel off the siege tower and blasted another chunk off the side, making it more unsteady than ever. The bears ran from the building, one hobbling on only three legs, blood pouring onto the dirt below.

"Arrows away!" a hunter yelled, and both Feka and humans alike began firing the dogs again as they ran below.

"Calm down, you mutts!" said the beta Shadowalker, screaming over the noise. Shouting and barking sounded from the rear lines, the generals trying to restore order to the troop formations. Pit bulls ran everywhere, terrified of the loud noises like an Earthly dog listening to 4th of July fireworks. I saw a bunch of dogs dart under the bottom of the settlement - right under my dog smashers. It was time to cause optimum chaos.

"Release the smashers!!" I screamed, making a signal with my hands.

The Feka released on both sides, the rope streaming down the opening in the floor. I ran over to the edge, looking down to see the effect. Since the hole would land below where we stood, I wouldn't see the exact carnage.

A *thud* sounded, followed quickly by another. Yelping cries filled the air, the smashers making contact. I hoped that made a dent in the masses of troops below us. The Feka started lifting the smashers back up. I had created a crank system for it, incorporating the pulley system from the ramp. It was much easier to raise it and then have a release button to smash it down. Dogs scattered again, many looking around wildly and shaking. Some whimpered in place, unable to move, as arrows quickly picked them off.

The enemy troop count had been greatly reduced, but not as much as I had hoped. Suddenly my arm burned, and I looked down. My creation skill had leveled up to seven, apparently empowered by the successful usage of my creations, which was awesome. However, my tricks had been almost fully utilized at this point. By now, what was left of the right ramp was picked back up, arrows pelting the troops there. The hyenas eventually abandoned it, helping the Shadowalkers with the only functioning platform. Foxes sprinted from the back lines, holding ladder-looking things. They disappeared under the tower.

"Mages!!" I screamed, and wands stuck out again over the side of the level. Lightning and fire shot out into the mass of canine monsters below, adding to the chaos.

Dogs still ran everywhere, order had yet to be returned to the melee army. I heard a creaking from the pulleys holding the ramp up, seeing them straining out of the corner of my eye. I sprinted over, looking everything over. Panic filled my mind, wondering if the ropes that held the drawbridge up were beginning to fail.

The wheels slowly moved in the wrong direction, the ramp lowering somehow. Two warriors dropped formation and sprinted, arriving at the pulleys and attempting to hold the wheels back. Their feet were being dragged in the dirt, the two losing whatever unseen battle raged at the ramp below. "Noah... what's wrong with these things?" a Fekan warrior shouted at me, eyes full of fear. He regripped the wheel and planted his feet but was still dragged along the stone floor.

"Wait a second..." I pondered out loud, realization dawning on me. I peered into the darkened rampway, skimming desperately for some cause of my pulley failures. I couldn't see anything. "Quick - someone throw me one of those purple light vials!" I yelled back toward the troops.

A grey cougar unsnapped one from his belt and tossed it over. I tried to catch it, but it sailed over my head and clinked noisily down the ramp. I swore, cursing the throw. On the third bounce, it exploded, purple light filling the tunnel instantly, almost like a flash grenade.

During that fleeting moment, I saw four sets of white bear paws on both sides of the ramp. *Uh oh.* The bears that pushed the siege tower must have climbed those little ladders that the foxes carried and were using all twelve feet of their stature to pull the ramps down. And since they were directly under the settlement, I could not attack them from here.

At the same time, the hyenas had finally connected the undamaged left ramp, surviving the arrows long enough to attach it to the first level. As always, they laughed hysterically as they worked. The ramp had a clever metal hooking mechanism on the front, the hyenas dragging it into the stone wall. I heard Typh behind me, shouting orders to the warriors to kick the structure off the wall, warriors scrambling into action.

"Form up! Form up!" Type yelled to his remaining troops. The hyenas threw the end onto the dirt below, pit bulls finally seeing a way to attack and galloping toward us. The Feka and Zephyrs lined up at the platform's top, waiting for the scrambling dogs.

Their nails didn't grip on the wood platform too well, almost like they were running up an icy surface. If the situation weren't so dire, I would have laughed.

Stalkers had taken the job of the mecho bears and were pushing the 40-foot-tall siege tower toward us, three wheels squealing in protest as the fourth wheel spot dragged in the dirt. The archers froze, not knowing how to triage where to shoot. "Shoot the Stalkers!" I yelled over the battle sounds; my voice drowned out by the barking and scraping of nails. Then the pit bulls were on us, diving headfirst into the line of Feka.

To my right, the rope on the right side of the drawbridge snapped, that part crashing down onto the top of the bears like a thunderclap. The bears stumbled back, dazed by the impact, but not killed. The two Feka holding the left side pulleys were thrown backward, the wheels spinning wildly out of control and sending the ramp into freefall. The two bears pulling the left side jumped off their makeshift ladders, learning from their brethren and avoiding the impact.

My eyes darted wildly around the battle, things going from bad to worse for us. Hyenas darted up the ramp, the laughter bouncing off the walls and echoing chaotically. "Alchemists! Now!" I screamed, spit flying, and my voice cracked in panic.

A charge went off at the base of the ramp, blasting dirt and debris out of the tunnel like a mine shaft explosion. Three hyenas were blasted apart and spit out the front of the landing, apparently in front of the charges when they went off. The blasts happened so fast that the dogs didn't even get a chance to yelp in pain. The Feka shrugged the guts off of them and kicked some other parts away.

I heard more paws thundering up the ramp, the blast only slowing the front troops down. I ran over, glanced down the tunnel, and saw hyenas stopping to rip into their fallen brothers. Other hyenas continued up the ramp and jumped over them, almost at the top. I felt nausea boil up again, feeling like puking at the sight.

The archers had abandoned shooting into the mass of Shadowalkers and donned their smaller blades, ready to engage in hand-to-hand combat once more.

The siege tower finally bumped into the surface, creating one final access to the battle.

The enemy had breached the first level of the settlement.

Chapter 37

Grim Determination

"FORM UP!" TYPH SHOUTED FROM THE BACK OF THE LINES as his troops engaged the oncoming horde of Shadowalkers. For now, only one or two were coming over the edge at a time, dispatched by the warrior Feka there. On the other hand, the central ramp was open for the enemy to use, and hyenas poured up the ramp and onto the landing.

The sun had gone down by now, and the wind was still and calm. The jungle was noisy, excited about the battle starting in earnest. The Feka, with their razor-sharp claws and fangs, stood tall and proud, their striped fur glistening in the moonlight. They let out a deafening roar, signaling the start of the battle. With their muscular bodies and sharp teeth, the werewolf troops responded with a howl that echoed across the jungle canopy.

The first wave of the attack came from the Feka, who charged toward the Shadowalker troops with a ferocity that seemed impossible to match. The hyenas and pit bulls, however, were not intimidated. They braced themselves and met the tigers head-on, clashing in a thunderous collision that shook the first level of Dunbar to its core. Cackling laughter continued echoing in the ramp tunnel and throughout the settlement.

A few more fireballs and lightning bolts rained down on the rear parts of the attacking force aimed at the siege tower. Troops poured from the building onto the level, looking like hellhounds leaving the flaming edifice as they ignored the fire. Eventually, the building leaned left, cracking and splintering as it fell apart. Dogs that had caught fire lay still, burned alive.

I waved a signal, and my mages departed the battle. There was no way I was going to leave them out here.

The sound of claws clashing against jaws filled the air as the two forces engaged in a fierce battle. The warrior Feka leaped and pounced, their claws slicing through the air as they attempted to tear the werewolves apart. The Shadowalkers, however, were quick and robust, evading the tigers' attacks and retaliating with powerful attacks of their own. I shot a few rounds of fire pellets but felt no dent in the charging army. It was a sea of canines coming from every available access to the level.

Blood spilled on both sides as the war raged on. The landing was littered with the bodies of hyenas and a few Fekan warriors, their lifeless forms serving as a testament to the brutality of the conflict. The hunters joined the warriors and fought with an unbreakable determination, driven by a sense of duty to protect the settlement from these monsters. Yet, neither side showed any signs of relenting.

I turned and retreated to the smithy, running from the melee battle to try and gain a better vantage point to affect the fight in some way. *Maybe I can shoot the generals instead,* I thought.

Battle sounds echoed through the alleyways as I ran, finally getting to the smithy. There was a silent calm back here, separated from the struggle yards away. I blasted through the door and up the stairs to the attic, already prepped for me to set up. The alchemists had abandoned their hut a while ago; their job was completed for now. Their instructions were to head to the bunkers and mix in with the other humans. The fire mages joined them, mostly out of mana and unable to help further. I feared what would happen if they fell in battle and were consumed by the Shadowalkers, so I instructed them to retreat as soon as the action moved closer to the courtyard.

I looked into the courtyard. The Zephyrs had joined the battle, punching and kicking as hyenas attacked. They looked majestic, seemingly unable to be hit by the small canines. As the battle raged on, the Feka began to gain the upper hand. They had managed to push the Shadowalkers back, holding the three entry points well, all hands on deck at this point. However, the Shadowalkers were not ones to give up easily. They rallied their forces and launched a counter-attack, the Stalkers now joining the battle. I shot at the werewolves, hitting one in the arm. He yelped as lightning sparked up into his ear, and he looked around for me. I shot a few more times, hitting the wall behind him and then the other sailing over his head. He bared his teeth and began running to my position, but I shot him in the chest, sending him sprawling backward. He spasmed and didn't get up.

There was no rest for the Fekan troops as Stalkers rushed the front lines. The Shadowalkers fought with a newfound ferocity as their leaders joined the fray, their eyes burning with a fierce determination to emerge victorious. They tore at the Feka as they circled them, claws and fangs ripping flesh and bone. In minutes, the front line Feka were reduced to a mere shadow of their former selves, the mighty warrior army now lying in ruins. I took down one more Stalker, hitting him in the back, the momentary pause becoming his demise as a Feka blasted him into the wall with a swipe of his paw.

Hunters were getting separated and encircled by pit bulls, barely holding on as they lunged and snapped at the feline troops. I shot a few rounds at the pit bulls, but if a dog went down, it was replaced with another. I saw Dee, backed into a corner and fighting for her life. *No!*

I left the smithy to try and run to her assistance. I would have a better chance at helping her from the corn storage tower window. I sprinted through the alleyways, the streets almost second nature to me now. Sweat poured down my back as my boots stomped on the streets, turning left and right in my mad dash to the building.

The laughing was at a fever pitch as mini-battles unfolded throughout the settlement. I exploded through the door and dove at the window. A pit bull was tearing at Dee's arm, blood streaming down her fur, as her other arm fought off a hyena. I shot a Wind pellet, then reloaded before seeing what it hit. Then another. And another. Dogs went down left and right, Dee looking back at me with a smile. Her arm was completely limp, but her working arm thrust her dagger into the neck of a nearby dog.

Out of nowhere, a Stalker lunged at her, jaws connecting with her shoulder. He shook his head side to side, Dee going limp in his jaws.

"No!" I screamed, shooting a pellet at him. I hit him in the leg, and he burst into flames, but he continued mashing his jaws on her as he fell to the ground. I pulled out my spare air wand and aimed at him.

I fired, blasting him right in the chest. He flew backward, dropping Dee, but she spasmed on the ground. I took off running through the settlement.

A Stalker looked up at me from the stone walkway to my left, a grin crossing his features as he consumed a fallen warrior. He licked his lips, slowly taunting me. I ignored him and continued dashing through the city to where Dee lay.

Battles ended all over the main level of the settlement; the Feka were overwhelmed and killed one by one.

I finally got to Dee and closed my eyes, tears streaming freely now. My whole body shook, the useless slingshot falling from my grasp. I grabbed her up in my arms and dashed back into the settlement. I ran, twisting through the streets, until I got to the smithy. I quickly grabbed the scent blocking cloak from my locker and draped it over us, then continued, heading to the corn tower to watch the rest of the fight. The Stalkers released a howl of triumph echoing across the platform. The Feka fought valiantly, and the back lines were all that remained.

Once we returned to the tower, I used my biokinesis skill on her to see what I could do, but there wasn't much. She was still breathing, but blood was everywhere. I closed her wounds with my mana, found a few blood vessels to reconstruct, and waited, sitting there in the quiet room.

I set Dee down, then walked to the window and saw the first level of Dunbar. It was now stained with blood from the fallen Feka, with only a handful of troops left. Dead Shadowalkers also littered the city, their numbers in the hundreds. Rain poured down now, puddles forming on the stones.

The Feka circled Baron Gilbert in a tight formation, a mixture of Zephyrs and warriors. I was proud of my air mages. They had fought brilliantly with the bit of training they had. Typh was among them, bloodied and battered from the constant attacks. Two of the dock workers stood tall, one of them dead on the ground nearby. Their knuckles were red, and their shirts bloodied. They pulled the dead Zephyr behind them, shielding him from the oncoming Shadowalkers. Typh grabbed the other three fallen humans, doing the same. About a hundred or so enemies remained and slowly walked toward them, making sure there was nowhere for them to escape. It was a pyrrhic victory for the Shadowalkers, that was for sure. Dee groaned slightly behind me, but didn't move much. *Alive, at least,* I thought.

"Steady," the Baron growled, showing no fear at the looming death approaching him. The warriors around him showed the same grim determination. Most hunters had retreated even further behind the Baron, joining a secondary defensive line with Typh and Layal, the Monarch's Marshall in charge of the empire's security. He had stayed back with us when she departed. The mages had completely retreated.

The alpha strolled into the courtyard, eyes red and leg muscles bulging as he walked over. He had blood all over him, apparently joining in battle at some point or maybe just consuming fallen warriors. I couldn't tell. I watched from the corn tower, utterly irrelevant in this battle. My devices had failed, and my troops could not break the Shadowalker equipment with their few wands. I needed to make more equipment, and I had failed.

I watched in awe as the full moon rose higher in the night sky, casting its pale light upon the alpha werewolf. As the werewolf's form shifted and transformed under the moon's light, I could see the immense power surging through the creature. The alpha werewolf's fur bristled, his muscles rippled, and his eyes blazed with a feral intensity. I could feel the raw energy emanating from the werewolf, and I was both captivated and terrified by it.

With a primal howl, the alpha werewolf charged toward the Baron and his group. I held my breath as I watched the werewolf unleash a devastating shockwave of force, sending the cat creatures flying in all directions. The sheer power of the attack was awe-inspiring, as if the werewolf had become a force of dark nature itself.

I could see the Zephyrs desperately trying to regroup and mount a counterattack, but the alpha werewolf was relentless. He moved with astonishing speed and agility, his claws slashing through the air with deadly precision. I could hardly believe my eyes as I watched the werewolf crush the circle of troops with almost supernatural strength. I had heard stories of werewolves, but seeing one in action was an entirely different experience.

Finally, as the moon descended from its peak, the alpha werewolf's superpower seemed to wane. He spun and jumped over an attack by the Baron and clamped down on his neck. I heard a loud *crack*, and he lay still.

He breathed heavily as he stood over the carnage that he had created. In mere moments, the Baron and the whole group surrounding him had been wiped out.

The alpha let out a thunderous howl that echoed across the platform. The other werewolves took up the call, their cries of triumph mingling with their leaders.

Chapter 38

Up in Smoke

THE ALPHA TOOK A BITE OUT OF A NEARBY FEKA, ALMOST hauntingly slow. Blood spurted out of the arm he bit into, his body growing slightly in size. Then, he strolled ahead toward the group of Feka. He was shocked to see humans fighting alongside the felines during the battle. So much so that he sent extra troops to break them down. He was very curious about what they would do when he consumed them. He smelled a type of unfamiliar mana in their aura.

Whitetooth after Whitetooth had tried to break them down, and in the end, only three fell. And to his shock, seeing them up close now, they had very little armor and no equipment to speak of, just a robe and their gauntleted hands. By the way they fought, it appeared they had unlocked some melee defense class. All of it was very interesting to him.

He had taken many more losses than anticipated. The fire mages had repeatedly gotten the better of him, assumedly trained by the original problem human he had heard so much about. If the Stalker pack had killed him all those weeks ago, he might have won this battle much more quickly. The alpha had his scent, though, and it was nowhere to be found. Either he had died during the fight or had fled. He assumed it was the second option, as humans always smelled like fear. Well, except for these strange humans with shining blue eyes before him.

The alpha needed to be careful. He couldn't lose too many troops, or the beta that he left back at the city would become more powerful than he. He was younger, faster, and hungrier but had a long way to go. He had to be fostered, but he was always a step behind the alpha himself. He had the loyalties of some of the newer members of the pack, though, which was never a good thing.

His troops stood behind him, not making any further moves, both sides waiting. His moonlight attack had left him winded, but the Fekan leader was destroyed.

He addressed the remaining group of warrior cats in his growling voice. "It appears the day is won. Your little kitties and humans put up a good fight, but we have emerged the victors. If you allow us to imprison all of you standing in the courtyard and bring you back to our settlement, we will not kill the rest of your people in hiding. Including the human mages, who, by the way, I can smell from here." He shot the Fekan standing before him a wicked smile, who looked away at that. The Fekan bunker would work to keep them out for a time, but it certainly did not mask the smell of fear within.

The alpha continued. "Come with us, and I will feed you to my up-and-coming packmates. Mainly the young ones who show the most promise. They will fight you, train on you, and beat you, until you eventually succumb to death, then consume your body. They will grow strong with your warrior souls."

The Feka shuffled a bit, no doubt aghast at the thought of death in that manner, but held firm. They all pressed slightly closer, bristling and growling in their fury. Their eyes narrowed, and their lips quivered at the thought of going down without a fight.

"You vile beasts," the lead male Feka, Layal, spat out, his white teeth gleaming in the moonlight. The wind was picking up, ruffling their fur side to side. "If you think for one moment our best warriors would willingly go with you, then you haven't been paying attention."

The Stalkers looked on in horror as the Fekan general leaped over his line of defenders, claws extended toward the alpha in a surprise attack. The alpha dodged with uncanny speed, and the two leaders clashed in a flurry of fur and teeth. Their massive bodies slammed into each other with incredible force, blood flying as claws made contact with hair. Their blows echoed across the platform, drowning out even the cries of the other combatants looking on and roaring or growling for their leader. Animalistic sounds filled the night sky as two alpha predators battled.

The two fought without pause for several long minutes, neither giving an inch. The alpha werewolf's claws eventually tore through the Feka's majestic armor like tissue paper, drawing blood with every strike. He moved at an increasingly faster pace, drawing additional energy somehow. The Fekan leader, however, was equally ferocious, his massive jaws snapping shut just inches away from the werewolf's throat, then his saber gleaming with deadly intent as it hummed through the air.

The battle was at a stalemate, with neither side able to gain the upper hand. With a fierce snarl, the alpha leaped back from the tiger leader, then charged towards him again with incredible speed. The Feka, caught off guard, braced himself for the werewolf's attack. However, the werewolf's movements were too quick for him to follow. With a sudden twist, the alpha werewolf landed behind the tiger leader, then sank his claws deep into the tiger's flesh.

The Fekan warrior let out a deafening roar of pain, his body writhing in agony as the werewolf's claws tore through his flesh. The massive tiger leader released a pained gasp, then collapsed to the ground, knocked out and bleeding freely. Seeing their leader fall, the other Feka released a chorus of mournful cries and pressed closer together in a tighter defensive formation. The werewolves barked and howled triumphantly, celebrating their victory in the moonlit sky. "Grab them and take them to the city!" the alpha yelled to his beta.

The alpha looked back at the line of defenders and shook off his claws, sending their brethren's blood into the first warrior in the line. He snarled and leaned forward.

As the alpha werewolf celebrated their victory, a jet of fire blasted out of the shadows toward the Shadowalkers, eviscerating a few Stalkers behind him. Then a sudden crackle of electricity filled the air. A lightning bolt streaked toward the alpha werewolf, narrowly missing his head and striking the ground behind him. The werewolves immediately acted, their instincts telling them they were under attack. They scanned the area for the lightning source but saw nothing but the smoldering grass where the bolt had struck.

Then, from out of the shadows, a human with a wicked smile appeared. With a fierce snarl, the alpha werewolf charged toward the newcomer, his claws bared. The other Stalkers followed with their teeth and claws at the ready. Water poured over them from out of nowhere as they focused on the human in front of them.

It was a different human than he had seen from the woods. He wore yellow robes with red trim around the exterior, his eyes a blazing blue under the hood over his head. The human let out a crazed laugh and raised a wand brimming with crackling electricity. He sneered at the werewolves.

"Take this, you vile creatures!" He fired another lightning bolt at the alpha werewolf. This time, the bolt struck true, sending the alpha crashing to the ground, spasming out of control. The water on the alpha enhanced its potency, completely paralyzing the monster. The Stalkers pulled up, afraid to get near the crackling electricity.

Suddenly, a burst of flame erupted around the Stalkers. It made a perfect ring around the five of them, preventing them from moving further. Steam hissed into the air as the water from earlier quickly evaporated. The werewolves snarled and growled but stood in the middle of the fire, confused and restless. The flames parted, and two mages walked through, wearing bright red robes with blue trim. They held out their hands and chanted, a glow forming at the tip of their wands.

A roar of energy like a freight train blasted the Stalkers with a fan of flames, pushing them back into the flame circle and instantly killing them. Smoke rose from the center of the action, the smell of burnt hair wafting into the noses of the onlookers. With the threat taken care of, the mages cut off their flame circle spell and stepped back to the lightning mage, who looked on with a crazed expression.

The Feka watched in horror at the power of these humans, who seemingly appeared out of nowhere. There were only a few of them, but they took out the generals of the Shadowalker army with just a few spells. The pit bull and hyena troops broke down, seeing their leaders ignite in flames. They turned and sprinted down the ramp, yelping into the night air.

———

I walked into the courtyard, still holding a limp Dee in my arms. I set her down by the other wounded as I looked between the carnage and the mages with dread, then at the Feka. They looked back at me, unmoving and not saying anything, but gave me anxious expressions.

The dead werewolves dissolved in puffs of smoke, leaving various charred ingredients behind in the courtyard. One of the fire mages calmly walked over to the pile of fur, claws, and teeth, picked everything up, and loaded it into a purple velvet sachel. He took the alpha's head and tossed it to the lightning mage, who caught it like they were tossing a beach ball back and forth. The fire mage turned and returned to his friends, showing no emotion. One last mage came out of the shadows, this one wearing a black robe with stars and runes on it.

The black-robed mage stepped up to the group and addressed the awestruck Feka. "Tell your Monarch to deliver your

259

remaining human mages to us and that, with our work here, our alliance is hereby concluded." He turned to me. "You are now the property of the Overlord. Come with us."

What the hell? Property of the Overlord?

Before I could do anything, he grasped me by the wrist, closed his eyes, and began chanting. The three other mages grabbed hold of the chanting mage, and the five of us blinked out of existence, leaving a vacant spot where we had stood seconds before.

Epilogue

I GASPED, THE FEELING LIKE I WAS UNDERWATER PASSING me by, as I blinked my eyes and cleared the fog from my brain.

I broke out of my astonishment and looked around. "Follow me," the mage in the black robes commanded. The other three set off behind him, heading into the city. I immediately felt the electricity in the air. Countless lightning bolts illuminated the sky above, and flames danced from building to building. As I walked through the bustling streets, I couldn't help but feel a sense of awe at the power on display. After being surrounded by cats for so long, seeing humans walking around a settlement felt...strange.

Fire mages were hard at work, using their powers to forge weapons and cook food, while lightning mages zipped about, delivering messages and powering the city's machinery. Everywhere I looked, there were signs of magic at work. It seemed like there were non-magic-using humans, but they were well-built and seemed to be some warrior class instead.

The buildings were impressive, made of sturdy stone and metal but adorned with intricate designs that seemed to shift and change with the light. Some structures were adorned with glowing runes that pulsed with energy, while others were

261

topped with spires that reached the sky. Color scheme systems separated the various mages and classes, with robe trim matching some groups walking around the city.

I continued to explore the city as I followed the four hooded figures, taking in the sights and sounds around me. The mages here were clearly skilled in their respective elements, but many had also mastered multiple disciplines, and their powers combined in dazzling displays of magical prowess. I even saw some mages summoning elemental creatures that roamed the city alongside their masters.

Despite the feeling of chaos and danger of living in a city filled with such powerful mages, there was a sense of order here. The mages appeared to have established guilds and institutions, many wearing bracers on their arms that I assumed regulated their powers somehow. I didn't know how I knew that, but I felt it in the back of my mind.

And yet, even with these safeguards in place, the city still crackled with the raw energy of its inhabitants, a reminder of the immense power that could be wielded by those who used the elements and equipment here.

I couldn't help but feel a sense of excitement at what lay ahead, even after the horrible events that had just unfolded. Who knew what kind of magic and adventure awaited me in this city of lightning and fire mages? But what did the alliance ending have to do with the Feka? Were they just primitive beasts to these people?

I had lost a lot of good friends in the last few hours, including Baron Gilbert, who was extremely kind to me when I thought about it. I was taken against my will to this random place, once again unsure of my position.

We stopped before a giant white building with tall four-story columns framing the entrance. The five of us waited there momentarily, and my eyes darted back and forth, uncertain. It was much cooler here, and I noticed snow-capped mountains in the background for the first time. I had to admit; it was nice not to sweat. Finally, an elderly man came out the front door, a long white beard blowing in the slight breeze. He looked me up and down, appraising me.

"Welcome, Noah, to Fulgar- the human city of fire and lightning. We've been waiting for you."

END OF BOOK 1

Thank you so much for reading Whisper of Iron. If you enjoyed - please leave a review on Amazon and Goodreads. Reviews mean the world to authors!

Whisper of Iron Book 2

A LitRPG Crafting Fantasy

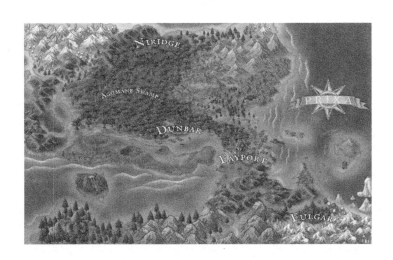

Book 1 Recap

Noah's journey began when he arrived at Prixa and was assigned the class of blacksmith apprentice. He made a dagger from a vulture talon then encountered the Feka, a race of cat warriors, and a boy named Jasper. Jasper took him into the settlement and assigned him to Romas, the master blacksmith. However, Noah soon found himself in trouble when Romas accused him of stealing a dagger. As punishment, he ventured into the jungle at night, where he met Dee. She was a hunter class of Feka and became a valuable ally to Noah as they explored the jungle together.

Noah unlocked a mining skill in a cave after he and Dee faced dangerous werewolves known as the Shadowalkers. They managed to survive and returned to the blacksmith's workshop. There, Noah met Typh, Dee's brother and the head of security in their settlement. Typh recognized Noah's potential after he learned about his access to magic and helped him develop his skills. The two faced a formidable bear creature together but were rescued by the Baron of the settlement. He discovered Noah's secret.

The Shadowalkers launched an attack on Dunbar but were initially repelled. Noah devised a defensive strategy and built a drawbridge, effectively thwarting the werewolves' second assault. As a result, Noah was released from servitude and gained newfound respect.

To his surprise, Noah discovered a unique ability. When humans held the equipment he had forged and matched the item's mana affinity, they could unlock their latent magical powers. This discovery led him to train the settlement's human mages and prepare for a final confrontation with the Shadowalkers.

Despite their efforts, the werewolves proved to be a formidable foe. Under the full moon's power, the Shadowalkers' alpha killed the Baron, creating chaos and uncertainty. In a sudden turn of events, an unknown group of human mages with incredible fire and lightning magic arrived on the scene. Exhausted by the battle and overwhelmed by the mages' power, the Shadowalker generals and the alpha were defeated. The human mages kidnapped Noah taking him to the city of Fulgar, and severed their Human alliance with the Monarch of the Feka.

Chapter 1

Black Onesies

I HAD ARRIVED SOMETIME DURING THE NIGHT AFTER THE mages had saved us from the Shadowalker attack, and the teleportation mage had gotten us out of the demolished Fekan city of Dunbar.

Well, more like kidnapped me. When I arrived, I was taken into the grand palace at the city's center, then sent directly to my room to rest without stopping and talking to anyone. I had no idea who these people were, but they seemed to know me.

An elderly man with a long, white beard had escorted me to my room, then I heard a lock click on my door after I entered.

Sleep didn't come to me as I played the day's events in my mind again. I had done everything possible to save Dee and hoped it was enough. I had so many questions, mainly about the status of my friends.

I tossed and turned but couldn't fall asleep. It was dark in the room, the only light coming from a tiny torch and some brief flashes of lightning. I saw a few twinkling stars through the small window near the ceiling. It looked like one of those horizontal windows people sometimes have in their showers back on Earth.

Once morning came, the door unlocked, and I was given a meal of potatoes and something that looked like Spam. It was horrible. I had gotten used to Dunbar's fresh fish and corn mixture, and this was like being served prison food. The juice was a hot beverage reminding me of coffee, and at least that was good. Much to my mother's dismay, I had just started drinking coffee about a year ago and enjoyed it.

After breakfast, I tried the door. It opened, and I walked into the hallway and looked around at the gleaming halls. They were constructed from gray granite filled with red and yellow streaks. Flickering torches lined the long hallway, and I saw guards standing at attention near my room. They saw me but glanced away quickly.

A skinny man in a blue onesie rushed up to me, a worried look on his face. "Excuse me! You cannot be out yet. We are not ready for you! You must wait until everyone's breakfast is over!"

I looked at the man, appraising his ridiculous outfit. I tried going with *friendly*. "Good morning. Can you tell me how much longer it will be? Or what I'm even doing here?"

He glanced away. "No, I cannot. For now, please return to your room."

I didn't move at first, and the guards shifted in their stances. I held up my hands and backed away. "Alright, relax, everyone. I'm going." I turned and went back into my room.

The door shut behind me and clicked again, locking me in. *Am I a prisoner? What the hell? From one servant situation to another?*

I looked around my room, seeing it better in the morning light. It was simply furnished, with a bed, a dresser filled with the same onesie the man outside wore only black, and a washing area and toilet. My boots sat to the left of the dresser. I left the onesies in the drawer and kept my overalls on even though they were stained red from the battle, uninterested in such a ridiculous outfit.

I decided to try to sleep again and lay back on the bed, staring at the white ceiling.

A knock came on the door, jarring me awake. I groaned and rolled over. "Noah, you must be in the hallway in five minutes." It was the same voice as before.

I pursed my lips. "Alright," I answered back through the door.

I got up, slid my boots on, and walked to the wash basin. The reflection staring back at me from the mirror looked horrible. I still had blood smeared on my left cheek and bags under my eyes.

I had come a long way from the overweight kid from Earth. I was now a skilled blacksmith apprentice with unique creation abilities and magic powers. I even had a little definition in my arms. I wouldn't go so far as to call it muscles, but still. As I looked out into the mirror, I couldn't help but feel a sense of hesitation and uncertainty.

I washed my face and used my fingers to comb the mess of hair on my head, then walked outside my room.

Three other humans stood at attention outside their doors, all wearing black onesies. No one looked at me, only straight ahead. The man in the blue hurried over to me. "No. You need to wear your new outfit. This one is...*unfit.*"

I looked back at him. "I would really feel more comfortable wearing it for now, if that's okay."

He paused, unsure. His green eyes narrowed at me. I couldn't help but look at a long burn mark along the left side of his face. "Fine. We will bring you down like this since you're just arriving and didn't have time to change. Yes. That's good. That's good." He started mumbling to himself as he turned and walked down the hall, waving a hand over his head to signal us along.

273

The other people near me turned and started walking down the hallway, passing me. I saw one girl dart her eyes at me with a slight smile, then continue looking straight ahead.

I followed in the back, curious about where we were going. We took a few turns down other hallways, picking up more people standing outside their doors. They had other colored onesies, and I started getting the same servant vibes as the Fekan cities. *Strange.*

The group of us followed the blue onesie man to the front of the palace, everyone's boots stomping on the polished stone. Finally, we all stopped in front of the large double doors as he walked up onto a small stage and turned to address us.

"Assignments today. Yellow team, you will be in the northeast quadrant to assist in road duty. Supervisor is Lucas. Green team, you are on western wood gathering. Supervisor is Haley. Blue team, you are at the water well repair project. Supervisor is Nicholas."

He continued through the group of colored outfits, finally getting to mine. "Black team, you are in Karak Hold. Supervisor is Craig."

I didn't know what that meant, but the other people in the black onesies walked through the doors, and I followed them. A man in a black robe greeted us on the street. His head darted back and forth, and he mentally counted how many of us there were. Finally, he spoke. "Let's go, crew."

Craig looked like a stern, no-nonsense man. He was burly with a grizzled appearance, a long beard, and a face that was etched with the marks of years of hard labor. He led our group with authority, setting a brisk pace as we walked through the city.

The streets were crowded in the early light as people began going about their day. No one paid us much attention as we walked. The snow-capped mountains gleamed white in the city's background as the sun peeked over the hills. I saw the magical city around me a bit clearer, looking slightly different than when

I got transported here last night. Mages walked around, but the lightning had stopped. However, the mages I saw still pulsed with dangerous energy. Many eyed me warily as I walked past. Each mage wore a metallic bracer on their arm, the item's runes glowing softly. I assumed they were some sort of limiter, but had no idea.

We took a road that led out of the city and walked for another ten minutes or so once we cleared a set of city gates. Up ahead, a square wooden frame led into a dark tunnel with a steel sign that read 'Karak Hold Iron Mine.' Inside, torches flickered merrily.

Once inside the mine's entrance, the crew picked up pickaxes as Craig barked orders, assigning them to their respective tasks. Some were to extract the iron ore from the mine walls, while others were responsible for hauling the heavy carts filled with ore to the surface.

He pulled me aside, looking around to ensure the workers had gone to their jobs and no one was paying attention. "I have an extraordinary task for you, boy. I heard you can pull special ore from the walls without using equipment?" His eyes gleamed in the torches like a man who saw a treasure chest.

I didn't know how he knew that, but I played along. "I can get a few pieces of ore, yes."

He smiled a predatory smile. "Yes, I've been briefed on your skillset. Once we get some ore from the walls, we will return to the forges to watch you make us some creations. I'm okay as long as it's non-iron. Now plumb the depths of Karak Hold and find me some specialty ores!"

With that, he shoved me hard in the back and farther into the mine.

Chapter 2

Capes Up!

THE CAVE HAD A MAIN TUNNEL LINED WITH TORCHES THAT cast an eerie flickering glow off the wet rock. I heard the pounding of pickaxes echoing off the tunnels from various directions, now noticing side tunnels that branched off in several directions.

I stopped in my tracks, realizing that I hadn't reassigned my mining skill to my character sheet. It was still in the 'unselected' section of my skills. Since I felt like battles were over for a while, I swapped out my 'Biokinesis' skill for now.

[LV 9-BLACKSMITH APPRENTICE]

HEALTH [60/60]
MANA [55/55]

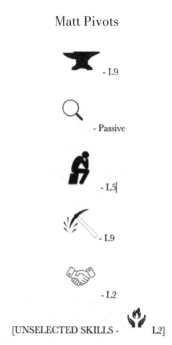

- L9

- Passive

- L5|

- L9

- L2

[UNSELECTED SKILLS - L2]

I hadn't noticed, but there was a new hourglass tattoo, most likely my time and space mana that I had unlocked. All of my stats had recovered overnight. I noticed my healing skill had risen to level 2, probably from my work on Dee during the battle. *Maybe she survived, so I got a level!* I thought with a glimmer of hope in my heart.

With the mining skill reassigned, the walls turned opaque in my mind as various ores showed themselves. I gasped, seeing the new colors shimmering in the walls. I had no idea what region of Prixa we were in, but there was a completely different ore structure here. In fact, I didn't even see the silver or red ores here. *Further into the mines?*

I saw lots of iron ore, but left that for the other crew members to gather with the manual methods. My task was straightforward. I was supposed to gather other ores. Craig wanted me to get any non-iron ore, but I needed to find out what my options were.

They must have been watching me somehow. Maybe that's how they knew to come to Dunbar for the battle! I thought anxiously. I would have trouble hiding anything if they knew what I could do.

I turned down a random side tunnel, checking out the ore over here. Banging sounded from up ahead as the girl I saw in the hallway worked. She stopped working and looked at me, a curious look on her face. Behind her was an orange ore that I had never seen before. It reminded me of the color of copper. I wondered what I could use it for.

"Hey! What's up, new guy?" the girl said, smiling at me. I barely heard her over the noise in the mine. "You're the one they watched in the town square, right?"

What the hell? "No idea. They...transported me here yesterday. I slept in those prison cells disguised as rooms, and now I'm here. Trying to get ore for the bossman." I paused. "I'm Noah. And you are...?"

She smiled. "Mara." She held out her hand. "Nice to meet you officially."

I shook it politely. "So, are we all locked away at night? Or was it just me?"

She grimaced. "Yeah, there is a curfew. They don't want us wandering around the city. We get one night a week with a few extra hours on the town to blow off some steam. Other than that, you need to earn your unlocked door. Like our shining hall monitor, Doug." She rolled her eyes a bit.

Oh, the tool bag in the blue onesie. Got it. "What, like a promotion?"

She nodded. "Something like that."

Suddenly I heard a siren sound, then shouting from the tunnels behind me. Two mages in red robes ran past, followed by two men with sabers. I looked at Mara, and we took off toward the main tunnel to investigate. I reached for my dagger but realized it wasn't where it usually was in my pocket. *Oh no, they must have taken it when I got here!* I was totally unarmed, which wasn't a good feeling.

Flying creatures poured out of the tunnels further into the cave and dive-bombed the workers and mages.

"Employees! To the walls! Capes up!" Craig yelled, gesturing to the walls. He had run up the tunnel and passed me to address the situation.

We watched as the workers partnered up and began unzipping something that looked like a hood on the onesie. Once both people unzipped their partner's hood, they threw it over their heads and went into a fetal position in the dirt.

Even knowing where they were and watching the whole thing, I couldn't see them anymore. They blended in so well with the dark tunnels that they were basically invisible. The bat creatures continued diving at the warriors, who now held massive tower shields to defend themselves.

"Fire in the hole! Everyone back! Fire in the hole!" Craig shouted.

The two mages in the red robes extended their hands, and flames exploded in a fan shape toward the bats. They began dropping left and right on the ground on and around the workers huddled there. Screeching erupted from the creatures as they burst into flames, becoming little mini-fireballs. The onesies apparently had minor protective properties, shielding the workers from the flaming creatures. I doubted they could stop a bite, though.

The bats that hadn't been scorched retreated back down the tunnels, screeching and hissing like their obliterated buddies. I felt a pull on my arm as Mara pulled me back down the side tunnel.

"That was too close," she muttered. "I can't believe how many there were this time."

I looked at her with a questioning expression. "Are attacks from those things common?"

Mara sighed, looking at me. "We get attacked pretty regularly. Mainly from the bats, but some of the rodents can attack in mass as well. The damn rats are the worst - they can teleport in and out of the rocks and surround us quickly. It makes the mages' job much tougher since they can't just flame throw all of them. But they all hate fire, so we always have our trusty fire mages with us. And these ridiculous outfits. But they won't let us take anything to defend ourselves. They're afraid of..." She trailed off, looking uncertain. "Never mind. Let's just get back to it."

Mara seemed to relax, and she pulled me into the tunnel to return to work. As we made our way deeper into the side tunnel toward her pickaxe, I couldn't help but feel a bit uneasy. The unexpected attack made me wonder what else was lurking in these dark caverns.

Mara returned to chipping away at the iron ore with her pickaxe as I walked toward the wall where the coppery ore was located. I tried to focus on the task at hand, but my mind kept drifting back to the attack.

Suddenly, Mara spoke up. "So, what do you think of Fulgar so far?"

I looked over at her, surprised by the sudden change in topic. "Uh, it's...different. I mean, I haven't seen much outside my prison room and the mine yet."

Mara chuckled. "Yeah, I know what you mean. You will get used to it. They keep working for most of the day, and we don't get much free time. Once the lunch horn sounds, we swap with the gray team and get our ore smelted down in the forges."

I reached into the wall and pulled some orange ore out. I heard her gasp slightly and I turned and smiled. We fell silent again for a few minutes before Mara spoke up again. "Noah, can I ask you something?"

"Sure, what is it?"

"Can you really do those things we all heard about?"

I looked at her with a curious expression. She continued, a bit flustered. "I mean, we aren't supposed to know. But someone on the Blue team overheard one of the mages talking and heard about what you did over in your old city, how you rescued those servants. Turned all those people into mages, like the people here." She had a wistful expression on her face.

I sighed. "I didn't end up rescuing anyone. I was able to unlock magic, but that was it. I could barely train people, and the ones I did failed. We lost in a battle against these werewolf monsters. Almost the whole settlement got wiped out before the mages from this place saved us."

She looked at the cave walls. "Can...can you make more items? Can I unlock magic?"

I looked at her. "It's why they brought me here, if I had to guess." I didn't say anything else as Craig rounded the corner.

"New guy! What have you produced so far?" He stormed over with his hand out. I glanced again at Mara, but she was already hammering into the wall with her pickaxe like we never spoke.

"I see some ore here. Here's the first piece that I grabbed. There wasn't anything of interest further up the tunnel. I'll start getting some now. I can only get around three or four an hour, though..." I lied with an unsure expression on my face. I wanted to ensure I hedged my actual production so I wouldn't come up short.

"That will do. Get what you can, then rest and recharge your mana. My supervisor briefed me on your mana situation before we entered the caves. We have around five more hours left in the shift, so I expect a quota of twenty pieces of specialty ore to be mined today. That means anything you see that's non-iron ore."

I sighed, then nodded, and headed to the walls.

Chapter 3

Forged

I FINALLY PULLED MY TWENTIETH PIECE OF ORANGE colored ore, identified earlier as 'Temperite,' out of the wall to fill my day's quota. I was flanked by the other mining crew members about a half mile farther into the caves. Our trusty fire mages looked on, chatting to each other softly.

I glanced at my arm and saw my mana read [21/55]. I did the quick math in my head. We finished our five-hour shift, and I started with a full 55 mana charge. It took around three mana to mine the ore pieces on average, depending on the depth I had to go into the walls. That was somewhere approximately 65 mana. So that meant my mana regeneration was around six per hour. *Not bad.* I had taken my time, getting ore at a controlled pace and resting between. All in all, it wasn't too bad of a gig.

I didn't know the plan after the mining shift was completed, so I was glad to have some mana in reserve. Craig had been coming over every thirty minutes to get the ore and stow it away in his duffle bag. Each time his eyes gleamed with a hunger that I couldn't quite understand. *Does he get a bigger cut for this ore?*

A horn sounded toward the front of the caves, and my coworkers looked up from their tasks. They slung their pickaxes over their shoulders, gathered the remaining iron pieces they had mined, and placed them roughly into the mining cart. With a nod to the cartman, they walked up the incline toward the entrance. The sounds of wheels grinding on dirt followed behind us.

We had no other attacks during the shift, which was nice. I was unarmed, as was the rest of the team, so there was a feeling of helplessness that came with this assignment.

Sunlight streamed into the cave opening, and we broke the threshold into the afternoon light. It was a gorgeous day, but much cooler than I anticipated. The cave was around 65F and much warmer than the air around me now. And after a few weeks in the jungle, my body had acclimated to a moist heat, not this dry mountain cold. I shivered slightly as the air hit my exposed arms but looked around at my unaffected team. I saw my breath in a fine mist as I breathed. *Figures. I either look ridiculous sweating like an animal in the jungle, or shivering like a wuss in the mountains. Great.*

I emerged from the dimly lit cave, shielding my eyes from the bright sunlight that assaulted my senses. I didn't realize how dark it was in the caves, the torches providing most of the lighting.

Fulgar was nestled amidst the snow-capped peaks of the mountains, its tall spires and gleaming buildings standing out against the stark white landscape. It looked small and compact in the distance from our ten-minute walk to the mines, putting us farther away than I thought. The buildings had been constructed with precision and care, their intricate designs and beautiful architecture was a testament to the skill of the mages who created them. They were crafted from various materials, including stone, metal, and wood, and were adorned with all manner of carvings and decorations. The runes that I had seen last night shone on the sides of buildings, but I had no idea what they were for.

As I walked through the city's bustling lunchtime activities, I felt the chill of the mountain wind biting at my skin. The people of Fulgar moved about their daily business, bundled up in heavy furs and thick cloaks to ward off the cold. They looked at me with interest, their eyes widening as I passed like they knew who I was somehow. A few fire elementals trailed behind a group of red-robed mages and air mages soared overhead. *Incredible,* I thought.

I continued following my crew through the streets, trying to figure out where we were going. Finally, we stopped at what appeared to be a restaurant. The large wood sign outside read "The Iron Hearth" in bold letters, with a picture of a pickaxe and shovel crossed underneath it.

Inside the building, I could see the reason for the name. An enormous fireplace of gleaming iron sat in the back wall, a floating white fireball blasting out heat. A few men were seated at the tables wearing blue onesies, laughing and joking, and I could hear a lively tune playing on a wooden flute player in the corner of the room.

Mara waved me over to the counter and patted the seat beside her, signaling me to come over. As I made my way to the counter, a woman with bright red hair and a friendly smile greeted me. "What can I get you, loves?" she asked warmly.

Mara ordered us a bowl of stew and a chunk of bread. She nodded, then hurried down the line to the rest of the mining crew. "You're going to like the food here. It's much better than the palace food." She paused, sarcasm lacing her voice. "They keep us fed well during the day to keep our spirits up."

"Sure smells good in here. I'm starving," I replied, looking around at the other crews eating. I saw three of the seven teams present from this morning, the others most likely still out at their jobs.

The barkeep returned and handed us a steaming wooden bowl and spoon. We went to a table near the fireplace and sat down, savoring the warmth that enveloped us. The stew was thick and savory, with chunks of meat and vegetables that melted in my mouth. The bread was warm and crusty, with a soft center.

Mara and I didn't talk much. As I ate, I listened to the chatter around me. The miners spoke about their day's work, complaining about the cold and the long hours. I didn't feel like I fit in with them, being an outsider to the city, but I listened and nodded along. It was still odd for me to be surrounded by humans...weird as that was to admit to myself.

Craig approached our table, the crew grumbling slightly. "Let's go, everyone. Forge time." He threw three bronze coins on the table with a pickaxe adorning the front, then turned and walked to the door. I looked at the currency with interest, curious about how this all worked.

As I headed out the door, the cold air again hit me. The crew walked nonchalantly before me, my eyes still taking in the city's sights. After four turns on the various streets, we pulled up to a four-story warehouse billowing out smoke from the chimneys. It was a brick building with long panes of glass windows.

Craig opened the twenty-foot-tall door and ushered us inside, a bored look on his face. When he saw me, he stuck his hand out. "Find me inside once the crew starts their work. I will instruct you on your next task." I nodded.

I stepped into the massive building and was hit with a wave of heat and the overwhelming stench of slag. The pinging of metal being hammered and steam hissing filled my ears as I saw the towering ceiling. The forge was at least four stories high, with catwalks and ladders crisscrossing the entire interior, allowing workers to move from one area to another. Iron supports spanned the whole building, allowing for an open warehouse floor plan.

At the center of the room stood four gigantic furnaces, each large enough to accommodate an elephant. The fires inside them burned with an intense orange glow. Molten metal bubbled and hissed within. Teams of workers in heavy protective gear moved around the furnaces, pouring molten metal into molds or hammering it into shape on anvils.

The walls were blackened with soot, and the floor was slick with spilled water and metal shavings. It starkly contrasted with the pristine and orderly blacksmithing area I was used to working in back in the hidden smithy in Dunbar. Despite the chaos and heat, the workers' movements were purposeful and efficient. Everyone seemed to know their role and worked together to ensure the metal was processed quickly and efficiently.

The crew spread out and went to their stations as workers in gray onesies passed us, assumedly the team we were replacing. They had tired, sooty faces and filthy clothes. I walked around the forge and observed for a few minutes before Craig signaled me over.

He handed me a couple of wolf pelts and the duffel bag filled with ore from earlier in the day. "Alright, *creator*. Let's see what you can make with this!" Mages filtered in behind him, forming a tight circle around me.

Chapter 4

Leather Armor of Binding Fire

I GLANCED AROUND AT THE TIGHT CIRCLE OF EAGER FACES around me, not all that pleased with the looks on their faces. I sighed and looked down at the ingredients in front of me. I put down the stack of pelts and lifted one over my shoulder, inspecting it simultaneously.

[Whitetooth Pelt - Level 3 ingredient]

Okay, if I make something with this, it will cost me around 15 mana. There goes the rest of my mana...

Next, I dug out a piece of the temperite ore and waited. I felt a slight tug from my crafting sense, but not enough to make anything happen. *If this is a level three ingredient, that means...*

I took out two more pieces, but nothing changed in my mind. I looked up at the mages who were eyeing me suspiciously. "Well?" Craig asked, eyebrows rising steadily.

"Hang on. I must be missing something. Give me a minute."

I started my 'DESIGN' skill, and the world slowed to a crawl. I thought about making a piece of armor using these two pieces, and the skill filled in the rest. I was attempting to make a 'FIRE-PROOF LEATHER ARMOR' out of my items, which sounded awesome. Since the pelt was a level three item, I needed three different ingredients, two of which showed images of the items I already had; a Pelt and 3x Temperite. The last piece was just one piece of 'SINEW.'

I broke the skill off, and the world resumed to normal speed. My mana had gone to [16/55]; the design skill took five mana. I looked at Craig. "I need sinew to finish this build. Probably an ingredient from the bat kills or a rat, anything. Maybe a tail. Any ideas?"

He looked at one of the mages in the black robes and nodded to him. The mage nodded back, then blinked out of existence. I jumped, surprised by the quick teleportation. We waited a few seconds, the tight circle of mages still surrounding me.

With a *pop*, he returned, holding a couple of rat tails in his hand. "We've been stockpiling resources of all kinds from kills throughout the years while we waited for a Creator to return to us. Here."

A creator to return? So the people of Fulgar don't have anyone to make things like this? So that's why they're manually mining and smelting ore down with the work crews. So equipment that the mages use...was that passed down through generations from the previous Creator?

Now that I thought of it, there were certainly mages walking around the city. But I had only seen a few handful of air mages and these five or so fire mages. Then the black-robed teleportation mages. It only made for a few dozen total.

I held out my hand and accepted the tails, and my crafting sense blared in my mind, happy with these three ingredients. I smiled back at them. "Yep, that did it. Okay...here we go!"

I closed my eyes and concentrated, combining the five ingredients in my mind. I felt the sucking from my arm as mana flooded out of my tattoos and into the materials. I felt the pelt leap onto my body and spread out, slowly covering my chest, back, and arms. Straps formed along the sides. I heard gasps from the circle of mages, evidence that what I had crafted was spectacular.

I inspected the piece.

[LEATHER ARMOR OF BINDING FIRE]

Sweet name! I thought, pleased with myself.

I opened my eyes and looked down at my creation, then over at Craig and the mages. Their eyes were wide with shock and awe. The leather gleamed with a coppery orange, glowing slightly. I felt the forge's heat dissipate entirely around me, like I had stepped into an air-conditioned room.

The mage in the black robe strode ahead and put his hand on the armor, his eyes scanning it. "Incredible," was all he muttered. The other mages came over and put their hands on it, and I felt like they were all petting me. It was super awkward, but I stood there, allowing them to inspect me and the armor.

Craig finally broke the silence. "How many of these can you produce?"

"That used the rest of my mana from the day. The next one I could make would be around four hours from now with my current mana regeneration." I added an hour, once again hedging.

He nodded, looking slightly disappointed. He turned to the mage in the black robe. "Take him to the Overlord. It's time the two of them met." I felt a hand on my arm, and we blinked out of the forge.

I gasped as I appeared in a flash of light in the Overlord's office and took a breath to steady myself. The room was grand, with high ceilings and walls lined with ornate tapestries. The air smelled of rich leather and polished wood. The Overlord sat behind a large desk, his eyes trained on me as soon as I appeared.

"Welcome, Noah," he said, his voice deep and commanding. "I've been observing you, and I must say, I'm extremely impressed."

I frowned. "Observing me?" I didn't like where this was going, but I already had a feeling that Fulgar was watching me from the moment I arrived.

"I mean your skills as a Creator," he said, leaning back in his chair. "You've created some of the most unique items we've seen in a long time. Level 3 armor? That's quite a feat. And the devices you built in Dunbar..."

Yep. Watching me all right. I shifted uncomfortably, not used to being praised like this. I shrugged, not responding.

"Modest. I like that," he said with a small smile. "But I have a proposition for you, Noah. We've been without any new magical items for the past thirty years. The only magical pieces we have left have been passed down or held by the mages. We need new items, and I believe you're the Creator we've been waiting for."

I raised an eyebrow. "And what exactly do you want me to create?" I was curious about where he was going with this and what I was being offered.

"Whatever you desire," he said, his voice smooth. "But I have a list of things that would greatly benefit our city. Items that would help our people unlock their full potential and secure our place in Prixa. It would grow your skills, while, at the same time, help my people out. A win-win proposition for you."

So he wants me to unlock more mages with the items I create. Got it. I shifted in my seat, my eyes scanning the room. The room was dimly lit, with only a few torches flickering on the walls. The Overlord's desk was made of dark wood, surrounded by shelves of books and scrolls. The mage in the black observed silently from the corner of the office.

"I'm not sure I'm comfortable creating weapons and items for you," I said hesitantly. "I don't know what your intentions are with them. We just met and all..."

The Overlord chuckled. "I intend to secure the safety and prosperity of Fulgar, of course. You have my word on that. I believe I already demonstrated my...*willingness* to assist your Fekan friends, have I not?"

"Yes..." I said, unconvinced.

"I will want to strengthen our alliance. Make sure the Shadowalker threat does not return. We must ensure both of our races can withstand their forces."

I sighed, feeling like I didn't have a choice. "Fine," I said. "What do you want me to create first?"

He leaned forward, a gleam in his eye. "I have just the thing in mind," he said. "Maybe some kind of equipment that will greatly aid our miners in their work. Or maybe some better tools for your assigned crew. What do you say? No weapons for the first batch of creations so we can...get to know each other." Something shone behind those piercing eyes, and I doubted I would have long to make non-weapon creations. But it bought me time to think of something else.

I nodded, feeling the weight of responsibility settling on my shoulders. "I'll do it," I said. "But I want to ensure my work is going towards something good. I don't want to create more mages or weapons that will hurt others. Enough people have already died from my interactions with this world."

The Overlord smiled, his eyes twinkling. "I understand your concerns, Noah," he said. "Rest assured; your work will be used for the betterment of Fulgar and its people. Return to your work in the forges. We have a lot of work to do. As a show of good faith, keep your armor."

He nodded to the black-robed mage, who strode over and grabbed my arm.

"We will meet again soon, Creator." The Overlord smiled toothily and looked down at the papers on his desk.

We teleported out and returned to the forges, the heat hitting me in the face once more before the armor negated it.

I left the Overlord's office feeling uneasy. I didn't know what to make of him or his intentions. But I knew I had to keep creating, hone my skills, and discover my capabilities. And maybe I could find a way to use my creations for good, to help the people of Prixa rather than hurt them.

But I knew one thing for sure - that man controlled my position and freedoms, but I had a bad feeling about helping him too much. This would be a fine line to walk, working with them to level and learn while figuring out how to escape without becoming more of a prisoner.

Chapter 5

Keg Pop

DURING THE FOUR HOURS I SAID I NEEDED TO WAIT FOR MY mana to regenerate, I helped out in the smelter. Without my mana, I was no different than the other workers. I volunteered to do the smelter job because of my new armor. I didn't feel any of the heat radiating off the three-story oven.

I used tongs, placed iron ore into huge pots, and then pushed them into the oven. Over and over until my four hours were up. As soon as it was, Craig pulled me over into a similar mage ring, where he handed me a pelt and the bag again.

"No, the Overlord said..."

Craig shook his head. "I know what he said. Make one more armor vest today and start on tools tomorrow. As you've seen, the vest can go to another worker to shield them from the heat. Then you can have another smelter employee helping you. The vest is a great tool for us in here!"

I looked at the group of high-powered mages surrounding me. Like before, I didn't have a choice. At the end of the day, it wasn't a vest. It was high-level armor, and I wanted it to stay in the right hands. But if it would be used for a worker here, that could help. And if it unlocked their fire abilities...

295

"Okay. Fine."

I wiped the sweat from my face, the air around me sizzling with heat and smoke. I turned to the side and let out a long deep, barking cough. To my left, three mages in their red robes watched me work. They seemed immune to the fire and heat, with no sign of discomfort on their faces.

I turned back to the project at hand. The loud train horn sounded in the forges, signaling the end of the work shift. Outside the two-story windows, snow began to fall as sunset approached. My face and clothes, as with my team members, were caked with black soot. My armor, though, looked like new. A few boys clapped each other on the back and started walking toward the door, happy that the day was over.

"Hey, new guy! Are you coming to the Workman's Friend for mid-week later with us? Celebrate your first day on the job?" one of the younger guys yelled over his shoulder at me. Mara looked up from her forge locker and smiled, then continued slowly putting her tools away.

I knew I needed to socialize, let off some steam, and get to know the crew, so I agreed. "Uh, sure? I don't know where that is, though," I yelled back.

The boy laughed. "We're going to get cleaned up first back at the rooms, man. Can't get those girls from Yellow to talk to us looking like this, now can we?"

He had a happy aura about him, and I was instantly drawn to him. I smiled. "No, I suppose we can't."

"We will come to scoop you up. We have until midnight tonight for midweek employee entertainment until the curfew kicks in."

I shrugged. "Okay! Sounds great."

They turned and continued walking out the doors and into the snowy road. A larger boy joined up with them and started telling a story and waving his hands while the other boys laughed. Mara came over to me with an appraising look. "You know your way back to the rooms?"

I nodded. "Hard to miss the giant palace that we all stay in," I said with a slight chuckle.

She smirked. "No, I meant the room itself. Not the palace."

"Oh. Actually, we did take a lot of turns in the hallways. I wouldn't mind an escort."

"Come on, then. We won't want to miss keg pop!" She smiled toothily at me, then grabbed my hand and pulled it out the door. I blushed a little at the contact.

Outside, the sun was setting into the mountainscape behind the city, a beautiful red blossoming in the sky. Breath misted before me as my gaze returned to the palace before us. We continued walking, making small talk. I was excited to spend time with my coworkers at the...bar? Restaurant? Well, wherever we were going. I had never drunk beer before and was slightly nervous about that. I assumed that was what came out of said keg when it popped.

The day's events played in my head as we walked. I had now made two pieces of high-level armor...one of which I wore. I had met the Overlord, who seemed friendly enough. But I had seen enough movies to know a snake when I saw one. I appreciated the opportunity to upgrade my skills through creation - something that I never got to do while I was in the servant class at Dunbar. But even if I was indirectly making weapons...I shuddered at the thought.

I wondered what would happen to my armor when I took it off in my room. *Would it be taken? Would they leave it for me to wear in the forge?* I doubted they would take it, as then they would lose my trust. I could *almost* see my armor helping people in the forges. *Almost.*

For now, I would keep mining my ore and making equipment. I planned on designing a better mining pickaxe. One that could help my coworkers get to the iron ore faster and with less manual labor. I could also create more fire-resistant tools for them using the temperite ore. I thought about going a different direction in the mine tomorrow to see what other ores there were. If Dunbar had red and silver, I wondered if this place also had a couple.

I would make as much helpful gear as possible for as long as I was allowed before the Overlord required me to make weapons. Hopefully, that was at least a week or so. That way, I could get my bearings.

We entered the palace as two guards eyed us wearily. They nodded to us, then returned to their bored expressions. I followed Mara up the stairs and into the winding hallways until we reached our rooms. "I assume the guys will be ready in about thirty minutes. Don't take too long getting yourself prettied up!"

I laughed. "Oh, I need much longer than that to get pretty." I cursed at myself. *Idiot.*

If that was a stupid joke, Mara didn't show it. She just smiled and turned to go into her room. I went into mine and found my way to the wash basin after taking off my disgusting clothes and armor and putting them in the corner. As I noticed in the forge, my armor had no soot on it at all. In fact, it displayed absolutely no sign of wear from the work.

I turned the knob to start the hot water and looked into the mirror. This city, just like Dunbar, had running water, but the water that came out here was heated. The cats hadn't figured that out yet.

My face wasn't even recognizable from all the soot. *Maybe I wasn't kidding about needing more than thirty minutes.*

We walked for a few blocks and finally arrived at the bar. It was a small, dingy place with a wooden sign swinging above the door. Inside, it was packed with people wearing their colors and clean onesies. The air was thick with the smell of alcohol and smoke as a cool breeze followed us into the establishment.

The bartender greeted the group with a friendly nod and an empty mug. "Welcome to The Workman's Friend! Keg pop should be any minute," he said, smiling. I was handed a mug and followed my crew to the corner of the bar.

A group of men stood in the corner, playing music on a fiddle and a banjo. Their lively tunes filled the air, and I found myself tapping my foot to the beat. It reminded me of something you would hear in the deep south.

After two songs, someone jumped onto the bar, and the music slowed and stopped. The large man had a long, brown beard, and a jolly expression. The bar quieted down as all eyes looked at him. "Welcome to the mid-week celebration!"

The workers cheered in unison, raising their empty mugs. "Tonight, we have a special brew...made by our own Gastus in the back. Gastus, come out and wave and such!" the man commanded, his deep rumbling voice ringing out in mock sternness. Another gentleman stuck his head out of the kitchen, gave a cursory wave, shook his head in disdain at the barkeep, and shuffled back into the kitchen. The crowd of people roared with appreciation.

"What, no keg pop of your own beer? What a party pooper." The crowd roared again in laughter. I appreciated the barkeep's showmanship.

"With that, I give you...first keg!" The music started again as he popped the tap in, pumping it a few times and starting the stream of beer into the mugs nearby. I couldn't help but smile as people surged to the front of the line.

While I waited, a thought occurred to me. Curious, I snapped on my 'PATRON' skill. I didn't see a single person light up in red or yellow. *Interesting.* I also looked at my team and saw no color there, either. I quickly snapped the skill off and held my head as it pulsed viciously. My mana was slowly refilling since the forge and was back down to [4/55]. *Ouch. That used a ton of mana with all of these people here.* I finally got my mug filled and returned to my team's table.

I digested the lack of information my skill gave me. *So this town was focused on fire, air, and teleportation. They must have a way to find those with the talent for those magics, or maybe that was the 'promotion' that Mara was talking about. If the crews worked hard, they got the chance to try and unlock their magic. But that would mean the humans in Dunbar had never been to Fulgar though. Maybe they were second-generation humans outside of Fulgar? I wished I had more magic elements opened so I could see more potential. I didn't have earth or water magic unlocked, so the people in this room could be affiliated with those.*

"You look deep in thought!" Mara said, gazing at me, the music shifting to a slower song.

"Oh. Yeah. It's just a lot to adjust to. There wasn't this kind of place back at Dunbar." I didn't say much else and downed my beer. It was delicious. The cold liquid was a relief to my parched throat. I sat there quietly, watching the band and appreciating the music. Eventually, I downed another mug of beer and then another. Before I knew it, I was feeling the effects of the alcohol. Conversations evolved around me, many of which I was uninvolved in.

My head was spinning, and my tongue was loosened. I tried to blend in with the crew by making small talk. The younger boy, who invited me during the shift, involved me where he could out of pity. I looked around and saw my coworkers nodding politely but not listening to me. Most were already deep in conversation or telling private jokes where I wasn't there to understand the humor. Even Mara had gone off to another table, her hands flailing animatedly as she told a story to the girls sitting there. I watched a few boys from my crew waltz over to the girls' table, just to be rebuffed and ridiculed by the table I found myself at. A couple of boys tried to pull the girls up to dance, but they got rejected.

I felt a wave of loneliness wash over me, and suddenly I missed Dunbar and the Feka even more. I missed Dee and Jasper. I also missed my mom and my apartment back home for the first time in a while. I had been so busy with life-threatening emergencies that I had not really even sat down to feel anything about my previous life. But it all came back to me in a drunken rush. A tear formed in my eye, and I wiped it away quickly before anyone could notice.

This place still felt so...*off*. Tonight's celebration seemed to be a way to keep the beaten down working-class tame and happy. To forget about the long hours in the dangerous conditions. But maybe I was being too tough on things here. I wasn't very trusting at this point.

I finished my last drink, mumbled something about being tired, and waved to the group. I don't know if anyone even noticed my departure. I stumbled back to my room alone, the sounds of the bar fading away behind me. A few guards watched me walk toward the palace but didn't say anything.

After a few wrong turns through the winding hallways of the palace, I finally found my way back to my room. As I sank into the bed, I thought drunkenly about the future and what it held.

Could I use my skills for good to make a real difference? Or would I be stuck making magical items for an unknown purpose here, contributing to the already unequal society of Fulgar? Or even strengthening a city of humans with dangerous goals that affected the Feka?

Only time would tell. I needed to find out the plan for me and my equipment.

A few minutes later, I heard my door lock with a *click*.

Chapter 6

Power Struggle

DEE'S EYES FLUTTERED OPEN, AND SHE GROANED IN PAIN AS she tried to move her body. She felt stiff and weak, and her entire body ached. She tried to sit up, but a sharp pain shot through her chest caused her to gasp and lie back down. She inspected herself and was shocked to see her health still [14/265] and her stamina down to [2/105]. This had to be the lowest she had ever been. Well, except for that Leeper attack from a few years ago.

She looked around and realized she was in a makeshift hospital. The walls were made of white fabric, and several beds with injured Fekan warriors were lying in them. The room smelled of antiseptic and herbs, and a strange humming sound was in the air.

Dee tried to remember how she got there, but her memories were blurry. She remembered the battle, the pain, and the fear, but everything else was missing. She moved her gown back a bit and saw fiery red bite marks lining her shoulder near her neck. She shuddered slightly. *So that's why my health won't refill.* The hunter class Feka were immune from plant and insect poison, but not infections and other serious illnesses. Injuries like these bites often prevented health from regenerating as the body fought the inflictions.

The tent flap to her room, if you could call it that, opened, and her father walked in. He looked tired and worried, and Dee could see the lines of stress on his face. But when he saw her, a tired smile formed. "Dee, you're awake!" he exclaimed, rushing to her side. "How do you feel?"

"Hey, Father. I feel...I don't know," Dee replied weakly. "What happened? Where are we?"

"We're in the infirmary that Jasper and I constructed," Romas said. "You were injured in the battle, and we brought you and the others here. You lost a lot of blood and are fighting a nasty bite infection, but the doc said Noah reconstructed your busted veins using his strange bio skill. It was risky, but it worked and I'm glad he did it. You're lucky to be alive. I'm not sure of the long-term effects, though..."

Dee smiled, a warm glow filling her heart at the thought of Noah saving her during the battle. "How is he?" she asked, her voice barely above a whisper.

"No idea," Romas said, a frown crossing his furry features. "He got taken by some powerful humans at the end of the battle. The mages killed the alpha and routed the Shadowalkers. They mentioned something about an alliance being fulfilled. We are all still in the dark about the whole thing. The Monarch hasn't been here yet to address us."

Dee gasped, shocked by the news. "Seriously?"

Romas nodded. "Things have changed since Noah left, Dee. The Baron is dead, and a new Baron has taken over. Some aristocrat from the capital. He's locked down the city, blaming the human race for the attack that happened."

Dee's eyes widened in shock. "Locked down the city? But why?"

"He's paranoid," Romas said, his voice bitter. "Baron Tobias believes that humans are the enemy and that they will betray us again. He's afraid they'll use their powers to harm us, especially after seeing how powerful those mages were. The mages we trained and equipped at our settlement were low-level and still tremendously impacted the battle. He even confiscated all the weapons and tools that Noah made for them. He locks them away in a heavily guarded chest."

"That's not fair," Dee protested weakly. "Noah is different. He helped us. He saved our lives. Multiple times!"

"I know, Dee," Romas said, his eyes softening. "But not everyone sees it that way. The new Baron isn't much of a warrior and is a proud Feka who won't listen to reason. He wasn't here for all that. We have to be careful, or we'll end up in even more trouble."

Dee felt a wave of despair wash over her. She expected things would be different if they could turn away the Shadowalker threat and defend Dunbar. The humans were fun to hunt with and had incredible skills that meshed well with the Feka. She had hoped that they would be able to live in peace and freedom, growing the settlement further than their kind could do on their own.

But it seemed like their troubles were far from over. She just hoped that the new alpha of those monsters was less of a threat than the old one.

———

Annos was a massive werewolf, towering over the young challenger that awaited him in the woods. His fur was a deep shade of midnight black, with scars littered across his muscular frame. One, in particular, ran diagonally across his left cheek, giving him a menacing appearance.

The young werewolf stood no chance against the seasoned alpha from the distant pack. They clashed outside the city's walls, snarling and snapping at each other, claws and teeth baring. The alpha's strength and experience quickly became evident, and he soon had the young werewolf pinned to the ground with his powerful jaws around his neck, defeated. With a fierce howl, he announced his victory, and the other werewolves of the pack joined in, their howls echoing through the woods.

He tossed the dead body to his beta like it weighed nothing. The beta would preserve it for Annos to consume later in his den. His power had grown exponentially with each alpha challenge, and this should be the last one. No one else would dare challenge him, and he would officially take over as Shadowalker alpha tonight. The moon's power wore off, and he felt a pang of exhaustion but did not show it in front of his pack.

The alpha turned his attention to his next goal, satisfied with his victory. He sought allies to help him take down the Feka once and for all, something the old alpha had failed to do. He would set off into the woods with a small group of his most trusted pack members, using his heightened senses to search for potential allies. He knew exactly who and what to look for.

As they entered the Shadowalker city, the eyes of the residents darted to their group curiously. Many canine beasts had blood on their fur or scars from the previous battle. The city was completely silent as he strode on his two legs through the town square, flanked by his beta and highest-ranking warriors. He finally stopped and looked around. Dogs had emerged from all over the city to see the victor emerge from the days of power struggles. Twenty or thirty various species of Shadowalker, all out of their dens, stopped what they were doing. Now, they all felt it. They felt the power radiating from this beast—the head of their pack.

New blood had filtered in from all over the northern parts of Prixa, filling in dens where the fallen Shadowalkers used to live. The old alpha was a terrifying beast and had kept out many of the potential city inhabitants. But now that he was slain, the city filled to the brim.

Strung up from the vacant alpha's den was the body of the dead Fekan Baron. Somehow, the hyena beasts had snuck it out in the chaos of battle and preserved it before the humans' surprise attack had ruined their plans. Annos looked at it, licked his lips, and looked back. It was unspoken among the Shadowalkers that only the new alpha would consume the powerful body once a champion emerged.

He squared his shoulders and looked around, addressing the silent city for the first time since arriving. He growled his challenge. "Anyone else?" was all he uttered, waiting.

No one moved. No one dared to breathe for fear of the alpha's glare falling upon them.

Satisfied, the alpha leapt and yanked the body down, starting to devour him and growing in power with each bite.

As the alpha consumed the Baron's body, his muscles bulged, and his eyes glowed with a newfound intensity. With his power now at its peak, he let out a deafening howl, signaling to his pack that they would be unstoppable.

The Feka had no idea what was coming for them.

Chapter 7

Beneficiation

As I descended into the mines, I contemplated the task ahead. The miners and forge workers needed something to make their jobs easier, something that would help them get the job done faster and more efficiently. And I was the Creator that would have to come up with it. But that didn't mean I would make whatever I wanted. I decided to ask the crew for their thoughts.

I looked around at my coworkers, who were already hard at work, chipping away at the walls and hauling out the rusty brown iron ore chunks. It was warmer down here than usual, but the workers didn't mind.

I approached Craig, who was closely monitoring everyone to ensure work continued as the beer made its way through everyone's system. "What do you need me to do today, Craig?" I asked.

"I need you to get twenty pieces of ore, same as yesterday," Craig replied, disinterested.

"Got it," I said. "I want to make something to help the workers. Can you give me some ideas on what they might need?"

Craig continued staring straight ahead but stroked his chin, thinking. "Well, they could use something to help them extract the ore from the walls quicker. If I could increase my quota for the Overlord..." His eyes got that look again, dreamy and hopeful. "And maybe something to help them haul it out of the mine. The incline from the ore seams to the opening is pretty steep, and it takes forever for my guys to push it to the top. And it's treacherous to bring the carts back down the slope."

I nodded. "Okay, I'll see what I can come up with." Instantly, a conveyor came to mind. I doubted the people of this world had ever seen something like that. *Easy enough. But without rubber...how would I make that?*

As I made my way through the tunnels, I noticed that a few of my fellow miners were struggling with their tools. Some had rusted, while others were broken or too dull to work efficiently. I wondered about the purity of the iron coming out of the smelter.

I wandered over to a group of workers chipping away at the walls with their pickaxes. We had started a little slow this morning after yesterday's celebration; the boys and I were groggy from our hangovers. "Morning, fellas," I said to my crewmates. "I'm looking at designing something to help you guys out around here. Any ideas?"

They looked at each other, then down at their tools. Finally, one spoke up. "Can you make something to extract the ore like you do? You know, *without* banging on the walls and blasting them apart?" The crew chuckled, and I smiled in return.

"I'll see what I can do, but I doubt that," I said. "Any other ideas?"

A few other workers had noticed the stoppage in work and had wandered over. A younger boy, whom I hadn't really talked to, spoke up, holding his pickaxe in the air. "If you could do something about these damn things rusting and breaking, that would be great. The boss blames us for a broken tool and takes the cost of a new one out of our pay!"

Mumbled agreements broke out. "And maybe some better lighting in here?" More agreement. I thought back to the purple vials from Dunbar and their eerie vision-enhancing light. I

310

hadn't seen any of the mushrooms up here, but maybe they existed farther into the caves.

"Anything else?" The guys looked back and forth but shook their heads no.

I had some ideas. I would need to fire up my design skill after lunch since I still had all my ore to gather for the shift. Apparently, solving production issues for the crew didn't get me out of my quota.

"Thanks, guys. I better get to it."

With that, everyone got back to it. There were a couple of ways we could go here. First thing first, I needed to take the iron ore and make a processing plant. This way, the rock and garbage would be discarded, and the carts would be filled with legit ore.

I had noticed the iron produced from the smelter looking...blotchy. I wondered if this was why much of the equipment was rusting so quickly. The end iron would be better if I could get a more pure product up and out of the mines. And then maybe we could even make steel. But with the ore grade coming out now, and with very little processing, we had no chance of that.

I was excited to see what my skills would do here. But I knew it would take almost all of my mana if I wanted to design something of this scale. I needed Craig to lay off on the ore quota for a day. He needed to work with me here. Short-term production would need to decrease slightly to increase output in the long run.

With resolve, I walked up the slope to find him. After checking a few of the tunnels, I saw him pointing and yelling at one of the crew. I waited until he was done, then walked over.

"Craig, I have an idea. But it will take me a while to design and probably use all of my mana. I need to skip today's ore production, but I promise it will be worth it," I said in my best salesman voice.

He eyed me with a stern expression. "No."

My head jerked back. "No? What do you mean, no?"

"No," he repeated. "You're just trying to get out of working today, and I have a quota to fill. So no. Nope. Nuh-uh. Not gonna happen. Need me to be any clearer?"

My eyes clouded, rage finally blasting out of me after days of holding it in. I had enough. "Listen, *Craig*. You are going to *let me* do what I need to. This is going to help you and your crew get *more ore*. *Understand?* I don't mind working in this shit hole. But I will make it better for everyone down here, including you. Understand??"

The banging stopped around me, workers hearing my outburst and looking over, shocked looks on their faces.

I breathed heavily, surprised at how close I stood to the large, older man. His eyes were wide, dumbfounded at my outburst. I doubted he had ever been spoken to that way. He stayed silent, unsure of what to say. Finally, he responded, speaking in a low whisper. "You get one day. *One.* Consider this a loan. If your plans don't work, I will keep you here 24/7 until you repay your lost ore quota, times three. Dismissed."

He looked straight ahead, trying to regain any semblance of control over the situation. I took the small victory and retreated to the front of the mine. Once I got away from the noise, I turned down a side tunnel and sat on the dirt, crossing my legs and sitting comfortably in almost a meditation position. *Yikes, no pressure. I better get to it, then.*

Since coming to Prixa, I had leveled up my skills, but I needed to figure out what the increase in skills meant. Back in Dunbar, Typh had said that the Feka could inspect themselves and their skills and get additional information. I had the voice lady in my head when I got new skills or had options to choose from, but it had been a while since I heard from her.

I wondered about my inspection skill, and if I could do anything with it, and to my shock, information sounded out in my mind.

[YOUR LEVEL 9 CHARACTER ALLOWS INSPECTION
INFORMATION FOR SKILLS LEVEL 5 OR HIGHER]

Oh, sweet! I wonder what my level 5 mining skill allows me to do.
I pulled up my mining skill in my mind, inspecting it.

[MINING - LEVEL 5 - ORES UNLOCKED - 6 -
SUBSKILLS UNLOCKED - 3 - SUBSKILLS - ORE
EXTRACTION | ORE CRUSHING | ORE
BENEFICIATION - MANA REDUCTION FOR MINING
OPERATIONS - 5%]

*Wow. What the hell were those subskills? What in the world was
beneficiation?* I did the same with my design skill, curious about
what I had unlocked.

[DESIGN - LEVEL 5 - INGREDIENT SKILL LEVEL 5 -
DESIGN SLOTS PER CREATION - 3 - DEVICE SIZE
UNLOCKED - SIMPLE | SMALL - MANA PER SECOND
OF DESIGNING - 0.055 - MANA TYPES UNLOCKED -
AIR | FIRE | SPACE]

I wondered what classified as a medium device size and how to
tell. Maybe I would get an error when I tried to make something
too big, like when I tried to make an earth-based spear back on
Dunbar.

Also, I had an idea. I had space mana unlocked. So if I was
constantly being watched, either with some form of scrying or
spell, I would have to make a scrying blocker just like I had worn
a scent-blocking cloak back in the caves with Dee. This way, I
could...*get into some trouble* without fear of anyone seeing. Or
have private conversations in my room without my lips being
read.

I kept inspecting my skills, going to my primary skill next.

[CREATE - LEVEL 9 - MANA COST = 5 x DESIGN
LEVEL]

That was it? I was surprised by the lack of information, but that skill was more of a feeling. It told me when I had the items required to make something. Even though inspecting this stuff didn't take any mana, I was starting to get a headache, although I wasn't sure why. I didn't have any other skills above level 5, anyway.

I still wondered what would happen when I broke the level 10 barrier and what I needed to do to get there. Experience here didn't tally up like some video games from Earth. It was more of a *do something extraordinary or new, get a level* thing. Which was fine, but what the hell did I need to do next?

I assumed that creating an iron ore processing plant would go a long way toward leveling me up.

With that, I closed my eyes and started designing.

Chapter 8

Hematite Ore

I fired up my 'DESIGN' skill and felt it pull from my newly acquired mining knowledge about crushers to figure out what I needed here, the world slowing to a crawl as was usual during designing. It was cool that my skills worked together. I didn't know that was going to happen.

First, I designed a crusher that would be used to break apart the iron rocks into a fine powder. I thought of a simple cone crusher and trusted the skill to guide me here. The design broke into three parts; the cone shell on the outside, called the crushing chamber, the inner mainshaft to squeeze and break the rocks as they tumbled down the cone, and the gear and pinion to rotate the mainshaft around the shell. It looked like we would have to manually wind the gears to operate the crusher, which was fine. Electricity wasn't a thing here, and motors didn't exist. Well, unless the air mages could power stuff. But I wasn't taking any chances.

Satisfied with the crusher design, I clicked the skill off but was shocked to see my mana down to [33/55] already. *Ouch.*

I also looked at the ingredients for each part of my crusher and wasn't pleased with the results.

[SIMPLE MANUAL CONE CRUSHER - CRUSHING CHAMBER 10X IRON | INNER MAINSHAFT 5X TUNGSTEN / 5X STEEL | GEAR AND PINION 5X STEEL / 5X IRON]

Great. Where the hell was I going to get steel from in a place where that didn't exist? That was another thing I would have to create. And tungsten? I hadn't mined that yet. But the fact that it showed up, maybe I had seen it down here, I just didn't know it yet.

Curious, I used my design skill and considered what ingredients steel would need. The forges operated by melting the iron in the rocks into hot slag, combining it, and letting it cool in various shapes to make tools. My basic understanding of steelmaking was either the addition of oxygen through blowing into pig iron or to add coal. Or maybe both? I couldn't remember. *Let's see what my design skill thinks.* The world slowed again, but I got my result quickly this time.

[STEEL - 9X IRON | 2X TINDERSTONE]

Interesting. It seems easy enough, but how will I get the tinderstone? I'm not in Dunbar anymore...

Satisfied that I had a way to get the parts for the crusher, I designed a chute leading to a beneficiation machine that used magnetic separation in a rolling magnetic pulley to separate the iron from the tailings.

The parts and ingredients showed up, and their three boxes were clear in my mind again.

[SMALL IRON BENEFICIATION MACHINE - MACHINE FRAMEWORK- INLET SLURRY BOX - 1X BUCKET WATER / 5X IRON | OUTLET CONCENTRATE BOX - 5X IRON | OUTLET TAILINGS BOX - 5X IRON]

[SMALL IRON BENEFICIATION MACHINE SEPARATOR DRUM - 10X STEEL / 3X MAGNETITE ORE / IRON ROD, MUST BE ADDED AFTER CREATION OF FRAMEWORK IS COMPLETE]

So the 'DESIGN' skill broke the machine into two parts, a 'MACHINE FRAMEWORK' and a magnetic drum. I had a few mana left, and wanted to see if my mining skill could project what the finished product would be.

[YOUR 'MINING' SKILL PROJECTS THAT YOUR CURRENT LOCATION'S HEMATITE ORE DEPOSIT WILL RESULT IN 65% IRON | 35% TAILINGS FROM YOUR SELECTED CRUSHING EQUIPMENT. FINISHED PRODUCT AFTER BENEFICIATION ESTIMATED AT 90-92% IRON. THIS PRODUCT CAN BE PROCESSED AT A 1.65/1 RATIO AT YOUR LOCAL BLAST FURNACE TO PRODUCE STEEL]

[THE LOCAL IRON DEPOSIT IS 89% HEMATITE AND 11% MAGNETITE]

Man! A 90% pure iron. Craig would be thrilled at that, I thought with a grin. *So if the mine had been operational for a while, I wonder if Craig and his team had mined some magnetite already. They would be able to tell the difference.*

I continued inspecting various parts of my designs and thinking of questions to things I didn't understand. My mining skill told me that magnetite was a black iron ore, whereas hematite was red from what I had seen so far. Then, when I wondered what the hell a slurry was, my mining skill filled in the details again.

It sounded like the beneficiation was something where water floated the fine grain ore, called a slurry, to the magnetic wheel, and anything that wasn't magnetic would fall into the tailings bin. Anything magnetic would be carried on the wheel to a separate box called the 'concentrate box.' *Simple enough!*

I cut the skill off, exhausted and totally out of mana. My arm hung limply at my side, a pulsing numbness radiating from the tattoos. I felt thrilled with the process and wished I could be in Romas' basement using the design table. Using all 55 mana felt horrible, and I was utterly useless until my mana began refilling.

Either way, I was excited to put out a better iron product *and* open up the ability for the city to make steel.

I crawled further down the tunnel and sat on the cold dirt with my back against the wall, eyes growing heavier by the minute. Between the hangover and the rapid reduction in mana, my body was completely spent.

As the white noise of the workplace surrounded me, I felt my eyelids droop.

"Noah. Noah!" I heard shouting coming from the front of the tunnel. It was Mara, eyes wide and running over to me. I jerked awake and stood up like a kid caught in the middle of something naughty.

"Hey, what's up?" I said, a bit groggily.

"Don't *what's up* me! Craig is looking for you and looks red hot mad. You've disappeared during almost the entire shift!"

I grimaced. I certainly hadn't meant to fall asleep, but with the gentle breeze from the mine's natural ventilation and the absolute darkness, sleep had come easily to me. I had also had a hell of a few weeks and probably needed the rest.

"Sorry," I said, trying to look ashamed. "I designed a processing system for the mine to increase production, which totally zapped me. How much longer is the shift?"

She huffed. "Lunch horn has already sounded! Come on, I'll pretend we were mining together. Here, take some of this iron." She shoved some ore in my onesie pockets, and my face reddened slightly at her hands in my pants.

She noticed and rolled her eyes. "Oh, grow up. What, a girl's never had her hands in your pants before?" Now her expression shifted to a smirk.

I began stuttering a response like an idiot, but she saved me the trouble. "Come on. Let's head up and hand in our production for the day." She grabbed my hand and pulled me up the dark tunnel toward the main walkway as the crew passed us. I got a few curious glances from the older boys, assumptions flowing freely through their minds.

At the top of the tunnel, Craig's darting eyes found mine, a scowl crossing his features. "You! To me, now," he said with a 'come here' gesture. I separated from Mara and walked over to him. He grabbed me roughly by the shoulder and pulled me aside as the last of the crew stepped up the path toward the city.

"Well? Did you get done what you needed to?" he asked, eyes wild with excitement.

I handed him the iron ore. "Yes, but it drained my entire mana supply and exhausted me. I should be partially restocked with mana in about four more hours and able to create, but I have the blueprints ready for the processing devices now."

He eyed me curiously. In a low whisper, he asked, "What did you design?"

I hesitated but told him about the two machines and their costs. He nodded as I told him about the crushers and the magnetic slurry device separating iron from rock. "This will increase the purity of our iron product *and* make each cart carry much more ore. Amazing," Craig said. "I hope it works. So you can just...make these things?"

I nodded. "Once I get enough materials. But I am going to need to make steel. Your planet doesn't seem to have that or know what that is, so I'll manually create it for the first batch. It will take me a few days to make everything I need."

Craig narrowed his eyes at me, not believing the delay in the project timeline. "What else?"

"I also need something called magnetite ore. It will be iron, but a much darker color, not the red of the regular iron. Have you seen any? It would probably stick to the iron carts."

He nodded. "Yes, we scrape that iron off the carts once a week. It doesn't dump out as easily. It sells for a premium. We store it separately."

I continued, "Well, I will need three pieces of that ore. Also, I need 35 iron, an ore I haven't found yet, and a ton of steel. Not counting the iron I need to make the actual steel. It will be labor intensive for me to make the steel and an iron rod for my drum. Once I have it all and recover all my mana, I can make the machines. We can start using them immediately".

He didn't say anything for a while, weighing my response. Finally, he responded. "I'll have to submit this to the Overlord, but I'm sure he is as curious as I am to see what you're cooking up for us. The production value that a 35-40% increase will yield..." He trailed off, again with the 'treasure eyes' as I had come to call them. "And this...*steel* is worth it?"

"Yes. Steel is amazing. It's a far superior product to iron. Especially at the grade we've been smelting."

I wanted to make sure no one had any false assumptions. "Remember, Craig, it's not more iron. It's just a higher concentrated product, with less waste filling the carts, and the ability to make steel," I corrected him. "Also, a quick side note...I will need something called tinderstone. Is that something you can get for me? I need it for the steel production."

"Yes, yes. I'll have a porter go get the ore...he will be back with it within the hour. He can bring the magnetic iron ore that you need as well."

Porter? I thought. *Like, teleporter? Interesting. Where are they going to get the ore from?*

"Once you get everything, just make your things, and we will go from there. You have three additional days. Your work at the forges is suspended for you to get whatever rest you require, and my mages will deliver your ingredients as you request. Write them out with the scribe at the front of the facility; he will get you what you need. I hope you realize, however, that this means you will be under lock and key in the mines when they're delivered. You will need to produce the equipment there and only there. This is an enormous expense for us."

I knew this was coming. "Of course. I will make the steel and subsequent crusher in the mines themselves."

He nodded. "Very well. Let's get you what you need!"

Chapter 9

Crushin' Time

I HEADED DEEPER INTO THE MINE, THE FIVE PIECES OF tungsten clanking around in my pocket. The blue-hue ore was much deeper in the cave walls, and I almost had to submerge my entire body into the rock wall to reach it. I didn't want to go entirely into the rock, which was terrifying, so I had to be careful when mining.

Back here, there were very few crew members near me. A bored-looking mage stood at the front of the tunnel, watching and protecting me. He tossed a stone in the air, catching it in his hand.

A low growl sounded out, sounding almost like two rocks grinding together. The mage sprung into action, a small fireball shining over his head as he looked wildly in every direction. I cut off my mining skill and began backing out of the wall. The growling got closer, and I finished pulling my hand out just in time to duck a swing from what looked like a rock monster. The tungsten flew from my hand, joining the rubble on the floor. The cave wall burst into small pieces of rock as the monster's granite hand made contact.

"Noah, out of the way!" the mage yelled, but I wasn't sure where to go.

I dove backward, finally getting a look at the creature. It had shining red eyes, almost like lava, a pitch-black body, and stood around four feet tall. I turned and started running up the tunnel, but a rock arm hit me in the legs, sweeping them out from under me.

I hit the ground with an *oof* as panic started to set in. The creature raised its arms over its head to strike down on me, but a fire lance caught it in the chest, knocking it back. I stood up, shaking my head from side to side. A firewall spread before me, but the monster walked right through it, glowing red.

The mage started shouting back down the tunnel, and another lance shot out, again knocking the creature back but not damaging it. I went to the tunnel beside the mage, eyes darting around for a plan.

Craig was running toward us, pickaxe in hand. "Come on! Back this way!" he yelled, charging down the tunnel faster than I thought he could move. We raced past him, and a grinding noise behind me sounded out as the creature stalked toward us.

Craig stood defensively, allowing the rock monster to come at him. A rock hand swung at him, which he expertly ducked, then swung his pickaxe up at the creature. He connected, the left arm breaking off and flying into the tunnel. With a grinding roar, the beast swung its right arm and connected with Craig's side. He cried out but spun and connected with the monster's chest, sending rock fragments everywhere.

He breathed in ragged breaths, holding his side. The creature must have broken his ribs.

"Craig! You okay? That was awesome!" I yelled, impressed with the fighting prowess of the older man.

He grimaced. "Yeah...I'll be...okay. Let's get you...back." A gold nugget remained where the rock monster was. Craig eagerly picked it up and slid it into his pocket.

We started walking up the tunnel, but I stopped, turned, and ran back to grab my tungsten. It would have been a shame to forget my ore.

I breathed in and closed my eyes, focusing on the mana flowing through me. I felt it gathering in my arm, ready to be released through my tattoo. I held the iron and tinderstone ore with a steady hand, ready to combine them into steel.

The tinderstone had been delivered to me moments earlier by one of the mages in black, known as the Porters. I took a nap, noticing that when I fell asleep in the mine, my mana increased to around eight per hour instead of my usual six. I had [28/58] now, my mana growing slightly over the last two day's hard work. After that, I was escorted to the forges and into an office-looking room to perform my steelmaking operations.

I activated my 'CREATE' skill, and the mana flowed out of me in a rush. I felt the energy coursing through my veins as I directed it toward the ingredients in my hand. The iron and tinderstone started to glow, and I carefully brought them together, watching as they melded into a molten mixture.

The heat was intense, but I couldn't look away. I needed to be sure that the steel was perfect and that no impurities would weaken it. Satisfied, I cut off the skills and looked down at my arm. [18/59]. *Damn. I had hoped steel would be level one material and cost only five mana, but the steel costs two ingredients, so that makes sense.*

I also noticed my design skill had leveled up to level 6. I didn't know precisely when that happened, but it was awesome.

The result of my work was three gleaming bars of steel, solid and unyielding. I felt the drain on my mana reserves and the weariness from using my skills. Gasps sounded from the room as the mages looked at the steel bar. The Porter strode forward, holding out his hand.

I placed one of the bars in his palm and observed him as he closed his eyes, focusing on the steel. His eyes snapped open, and he turned to the closest fire mage, whispering something in his ear. The mage's eyes widened, and the others got giddy. *I guess they're happy with it! Although, I wouldn't say I liked the look in his eyes...*

The Porter finally addressed me. "This is excellent. I see the uses of this product, and your claims of it being far superior to our iron products are verified. I have inspected the material and give my blessing for your path toward producing it in our forges."

I looked at him with a sideways glance. "Thanks, I guess. Yeah, this is what my world uses more than any other building material. It's just a better version of iron, that's all. Once I make one more batch of steel, we can go into the mines and make the crusher parts up. I should have enough tungsten now. "

The Porter dug into his velvet bag and handed me two more pieces of tinderstone and nine more pieces of iron, and I went through the process again with the steel. The mages all nodded to each other, grins showing under their hooded faces. Craig was beaming like a proud father as he looked on.

Although, if I was honest, I was tired of being watched like some zoo animal doing party tricks for his master. *What could I make if I had steel available for use in my ingredients? What would these people make?* I didn't plan to stick around long to find out. For now, we forged ahead.

We had separated for lunch for my mana to recover again, and I ate alone in the inn lost in my thoughts. The shifts had already swapped for the afternoon, and the barkeeps eyed me with disdain as I dirtied what I assumed was supposed to be an already cleaned plate. I also had pretty cold food, the cooks not bothering to reheat my lunch.

I followed Craig and the other mages down into the mines with the ingredients for my crusher in tow after my break. I could feel their eyes on me, watching my every move to ensure I didn't run off with the new materials. *Like I had any chance of doing that.*

Once we arrived at the spot I designated for processing ore, I began setting up my materials. Earlier, with the help of some of the crew, I had laid out the foundation for the crusher, using large rocks to create a flat surface. Then I took out the materials I needed for the three crusher ingredients.

This whole process was very similar to how things worked when I created the ballista and counterweight back on Dunbar. You had to make the device parts with the ingredients first, then combine them all into the whole. It was very time-consuming, and I hoped my skills would be upgraded to make this easier and less mana intensive. Luckily, my crafting skill was more like video game crafting than real life crafting. I didn't need to weld or screw things together.

I laid the ten iron ore ingredients on the middle of the pad that I made, unsure of what to do next. My skill nudged me to direct the mana into the mass of iron and think of the 'Crushing Chamber' part. I did this, raising my hand toward the pad.

Gasps again sounded around me as the ore swirled and hardened into a six-foot-tall structure. It was a shiny chrome color and an access door facing us with a ladder attached. I smiled, happy with what I saw.

Next up was the actual mainshaft - the part that would spin around and crush the ore as it went down the cone-shaped device. I took the five pieces of tungsten and steel, using the ladder, and loaded them one by one into the crusher. I didn't know how heavy the crusher would be, but all that weight would be challenging to load into the middle of this thing, so I decided this was best.

Standing on the ladder, I repeated the process, directing mana to the middle of the structure. It forged together into a large bell shape, open at the top and expanding toward the bottom until very little space existed between the side of the crusher and the mainshaft. It sat on a round table with a shaft sticking out, waiting for the final piece to be created; the gear and pinion.

Sweat was flowing down my face freely at this point. I had eleven mana left, just enough for the final piece to finish off the crusher. The last part had two ingredients: steel and iron. I assumed that meant a ten mana cost.

I climbed down and wiped my brow as one of the mages hurried over, dropping the steel and iron at the device's base. I sighed, catching my breath as I looked from the pile to the mages. They were like children waiting for an amusement park ride that was about to open for the first time.

When I picked up the final pieces, my creation skill blared in my mind, telling me I was about to complete the equipment. I pushed through the fatigue and continued to assemble the crusher. I pointed my hand again and watched as the gear and pinion attached to the crusher shaft to create a mechanism for operation.

Finally, I stepped back and sighed, surveying my handiwork. The crusher looked solid and sturdy. The mages around me *whooped* and clasped each other on the back.

"Let's try it!" Craig said, gesturing to the pile of iron rocks nearby.

I looked at the mages, who looked back at me expectantly. *Apparently they mean me, the guy who just made all this for them. Cool, fellas, thanks.*

I walked over, took a fifty-pound rock, and loaded it into the crusher, feeling a rush of excitement as I took up a position near the wheel. I grunted as I pushed the wheel, feeling the resistance at first, but then a loud crack sounded as the rock traveled down the chute. I was amazed that I could turn this by myself, to be honest. I thought the crusher would take a few people to operate.

Or maybe I've gotten that much stronger! I thought with a smile.

I continued spinning the wheel, the machine sounding fierce in its rock-destroying power. When I didn't hear any more crushing sounds, I stopped turning the wheel and walked over to the storage bin at the bottom. I pulled it out and looked inside. The rocks were crushed into a fine powder precisely as I had designed.

Craig nodded in approval, a huge smile crossing his face. "Looks like it works! Now what?"

"Next, we redo all of this again tomorrow to make a machine to take the iron out of this dust! For now, your miners should be approved to crush their iron findings. We can make a pile over there, and I can load it into the next machine once I make it!"

I grinned in satisfaction, feeling a sense of pride in my creation. While I still had a bad feeling about helping these people, I couldn't help but get excited about solving a problem.

An alarm horn sounded down the tunnel, followed by shouts of concern and 'capes up,' and the red mages ran off. It was easy to forget that I was in a dark cave with hostile creatures sometimes.

Chapter 10

Blood in the Swamp

THE OVERLORD SUMMONED ME THE FOLLOWING MORNING to discuss my progress in the mines. I held out my arm, accepting my teleportation ride to his office. When we arrived, the Overlord was looking out into the city from his balcony, his presence commanding and formidable.

He turned to me with a smile. "Ah, Noah. There you are! Good to see you again, boy!"

"Overlord," I greeted him.

"I wanted to discuss the progress of our mining operations you've been working on. The Porter here tells me things are going well!"

His piercing eyes bore into me. I nodded in agreement. "Yes, it seems my skills can do more than just pull ore from the walls. We should be able to get much better mining results," I said proudly.

He smiled and clasped his hands together. "See! What a wonderful use of your skills. What else?"

I continued. "Next up, I've been working on a design for a machine that could magnetically separate the iron ore from the rock it's embedded in. By harnessing the power of magnets, we can streamline the extraction process, reducing manual labor and increasing productivity. It would revolutionize our mining operations."

The Overlord's expression shifted from curiosity to intrigue. "A fascinating concept indeed, Noah. Such innovation has the potential to reshape our entire industry. How far along are you in developing this machine?"

"A few more days," I replied, not going into details.

The Overlord's eyes gleamed with a hint of admiration. "Your ingenuity and resourcefulness continue to impress me, Noah. Your vision for the future of Fulgar aligns with my own ambitions. I shall support you in this endeavor, providing the necessary resources and expertise to bring your magnetic separation machine to fruition. And for this, a pay increase would come your way. Keep this up, and you may even see yourself promoted into the upper work class ranks!"

I smiled politely, and bid him farewell. I knew he was just telling me what I wanted to hear. The system at Fulgar kept the work class down. If you weren't a mage, you didn't have a life. I wanted more freedom, and I had earned that at Dunbar. I missed that place and really wanted to go back.

Annos and his pack of Stalkers crept through the murky swamps, their senses sharp and on high alert. Annos and his elite warriors had been traveling through the swamps for days, their sharp noses following the faint scent trail of the Saurites. The scent was difficult to track, often disappearing or becoming muddled by the thick vegetation and water. But Annos was determined, and his group was relentless in their pursuit. He had come all this way with one goal; to follow his nose and track down the smell of earth magic.

The swamps were a maze of murky water, tangled vines, and thick vegetation. It was rugged terrain to navigate through, especially for someone unfamiliar with the area. The air was thick with humidity, and the scent of decaying vegetation mixed with the earthy smell of the mud. Mosquitoes and other insects buzzed around constantly, making it challenging to avoid getting bitten.

They followed the scent trail deeper into the swamp, crossing through murky water and traversing over slippery mud. They could hear the sounds of the Saurites, the soft thudding of their feet as they moved through the earth. Annos knew they were close.

As they trekked through the swamp, their muddy bodies stunk of dead soil and rotting plants. The Stalkers walked on two legs to try and stay above the filth, but a slip or a fall submerged them right back in the mud. Annos stopped and raised his nose, finally getting a whiff of the target scent. He looked at his party and waved his paw to the left. "This way," he growled in a barely audible whisper.

The new alpha was a wolf of very few words. When he did speak, it was either to give out disciplinary actions or directions. The party followed without question, turning toward the drooping trees. As his eyes darted around his surroundings, he realized that the Saurites were using the earth to create a network of tunnels that crisscrossed beneath the swamp. Annos could see the potential in this. With their ability to burrow into the earth, the Saurites could sneak into Dunbar undetected and launch surprise attacks from below.

Up ahead, the Stalkers suddenly came across a group of lizard-like creatures. The lizards blended in with the treeline and were huddled together around a small fire, cooking what looked like a fish-like creature over the flames. They had not heard the party of wolves approach yet.

The Saurites were reptilian creatures with tough, scaly skin resembling tree bark. They had long, slender bodies adapted for moving through the dense vegetation of the swamps. Their tails were powerful and muscular, and their legs were equipped with sharp claws, allowing them to climb trees and move with incredible agility.

Their heads were elongated and triangular, with sharp teeth perfect for tearing apart their prey. Their yellow-slitted eyes were large and luminous, allowing them to see in the dim light of the swamp. They had long, forked tongues that flicked out to sense their surroundings, and they communicated through a series of hisses, clicks, and chirps.

From what the alpha could tell, their coloration varied depending on their environment, with some individuals having mottled brown and green skin that blended in with the trees and undergrowth, while the ones he had seen back in his home village had vividly colored scales in shades of blue, orange, and red.

Despite their fearsome appearance, the Saurites were a peaceful race. They were deeply connected to the earth and its natural cycles and were skilled in herbalism. They lived in small, tight-knit communities and fiercely protected their own kind. Annos remembered stumbling upon them as a young pup during one of his first scouting missions. They showed him no aggression back then, but he remembered them hissing fiercely when he approached. They shook their backs, which made a threatening rattling sound.

From what he heard the village leader say, the Saurites were formidable opponents in battle. Their thick hides provided excellent protection against physical attacks, and they could burrow in and out of the ground with extreme speed. However, they were vulnerable to fire, which could quickly overwhelm them and cause their flesh to blister and burn.

Annos stepped forward, his pack of Stalkers flanking him on either side. The Saurites shot their heads around and immediately tensed up, forked tongues darting in and out quickly, with claws at the ready and hisses sounding from their throats. But Annos held up a hand, a gesture of peace.

"Greetings, Saurites," he said in a deep, commanding voice. "I am Annos, Alpha of the Shadowalker pack. We come seeking an alliance."

The Saurites eyed him warily, their small, beady eyes flickering back and forth between Annos and his pack. No one moved. Suddenly, under their feet, the ground began shaking. Then, out of the dark earth popped a giant lizardman, a more imposing creature than the rest.

The pack jumped back and got into a defensive posture, growling and caught off guard by the sudden appearance of the Saurite leader. *They will be perfect*, Annos thought to himself.

The Saurite leader looked down at Annos, sizing him up. "What do you want, werewolf?" I am Gornak, leader of the Saurites," the creature said in a gravelly, hissing voice. "What do you seek from us?"

"We seek your aid in the coming war against the Fekan scum in the nearby cities," Annos replied. "Our packs are strong, but we cannot take on the Feka alone. They have aligned themselves with human mages who can shoot fire and lightning. We need allies. I will finish what the alpha of our pack before me could not."

Gornak snorted, his nostrils flaring. "We have heard of these felines. There was a time when they hunted our young for a food source. We had to move away from that place and settled here. But why should we help you?" he asked. "What do we gain from this alliance? I do not wish to go to war."

Annos took a step forward, his eyes locking onto Gornak's. "We can offer you something that the Feka cannot," he said. "We can offer you the one thing you desire above all else. Fire resistance."

Gornak's eyes widened in surprise. "Explain, wolf," he said.

Annos smiled, a fierce glint in his eyes. "They have fire mages in their city," he said. "You could consume them, and perhaps their flesh will decrease your fire weakness. But with this threat removed from your people, you will be unstoppable. The light-

335

ning mages would be useful to me, and I would keep them. We would split the corpses from battle in half to provide a consumption source for your warriors."

Gornak considered this momentarily, his eyes flickering back and forth between Annos and his pack.

Finally, after what felt like an eternity, the Saurite leader spoke. "Very well," he said. "We will join your alliance. But there are conditions. We will not be subservient to your pack. We will fight alongside you as equals."

Annos nodded his head in agreement. "Agreed," he said. "Together, we will bring down the Feka and their allies and restore balance to this land." The stalkers howled, and the Saurites hissed as they beat their chests in a primal lust for battle. The Saurites would assist the Shadowalkers in their mission against the Feka using their skills to burrow beneath the walls of Dunbar and launch devastating sneak attacks. In return, the Shadowalkers would provide protection and aid to the Saurites in recovering the land they had lost to the Feka.

He took a knife from his pocket, sliced his paw, and handed the blade to the lizardman hilt first. Gornak paused, considering one more time before grabbing the dagger. He cut his scaly hand, purple blood oozing out.

And with that, the two leaders shook hands, sealing their alliance in blood.

Chapter 11

The Overlord's Favorite

I walked toward the palace around sunset, another day behind me. The largest moon followed me, about three-quarters full. After spending most of the last day and a half in the mines helping the gray team load ore into my crusher while waiting for mana to recharge between ore gathering missions, my shoulders ached, and my body was exhausted. When I left the mine, there was a pile of crushed ore with hundreds of pounds ready for part two of my little experiment. A mage stayed behind when the end-of-day siren sounded, I assumed to guard the cache of the ore.

My mana was about halfway refilled by now, but I looked forward to sleeping through the rest of the recharge. I almost felt like the recharge process slowed down when my body was exhausted, but I couldn't prove that. The mana still slowly ticked up, one at a time. I neared the familiar streets around the center of the city, and I ran into my crew. They were leaving the forges, covered head to toe in soot as usual.

Curious, I tried to design something I had been thinking about lately. The world slowed to a crawl as I thought through my options on what I needed. Finally, the results showed up.

[ANTI-SCRYING DEVICE - 5X SKITTEREN CARCASS |
2X STEEL | 1X LUNAR MOSS]

Before, when I saw an ingredient I didn't know, I just asked
Romas. Now, with my higher level inspection, as long as the
ingredient wasn't a high level, I hoped that I could tell what it
was. I identified the skitteren carcass first, seeing what the hell
that was.

[SKITTEREN CARCASS - LEVEL 1-2 - FOUND AFTER
KILLING A SKITTEREN RODENT - MAIN HABITAT -
UNDERGROUND AREAS IN YOUR LOCAL REGION]

*Sweet! Those must be the rats that Mara mentioned sometimes
attack the miners! Apparently killing one could result in space
magic devices.*

Next, I checked out what lunar moss was or where I could
find it.

[LUNAR MOSS - LEVEL 4 - A MOSS THAT FORMS
UNDER THE LIGHT OF THE LARGEST MOON OF
PRIXA WHEN IT'S AT ITS FULLEST. FOUND ON 9.3%
OF TREES IN YOUR LOCAL REGION ONLY
ATTAINABLE FIVE DAYS PER CYCLE]

Damn. So I not only needed to kill five rats somehow, unarmed,
but I also had to sneak out in the middle of a full moon and
gather moss that only grew on 1/10th of the trees in the whole
region. *That's just fantastic.* I sighed, but a plan started to come
together. If I could make an anti-scrying device, then hide what I
did in the mines, I could finally start working toward my goal of
getting out of here. Make some weapons, and store them deep in
the caves where no one else went.

Maybe I could even explore deeper into the caves. But without
weapons, I didn't dare go back there. After the rock monster
attack, I kept a wary eye out and didn't go far without armed
guards nearby.

John, the oldest boy, noticed me standing in the street and called out to me, breaking me out of my thoughts. "Look who it is! The favorite son of the Overlord has graced us with his presence! Not a surprise...he's just staring off into space." The boys around him laughed.

"Hey, John," I replied. "How was the shift?"

He shrugged and continued closing the gap toward me. "Meh. One more day closer to payday tomorrow, eh? Where did they take you this time? To an ice cave?" I stopped walking, but he continued toward me. "The forest to find some water nymphs?" He got closer, now in an aggressive way. His voice dropped to a whisper. "Or did you just go drink beer with the boss? We all seemed to notice Craig missing today."

I frowned, not knowing where the aggression was coming from. The boys surrounded me, and my heartbeat picked up a bit. "I went back to the mines with the gray team. I started on my processing machines," I said, eyes starting to dart from boy to boy.

"I see." He inched closer, now looming over me, which was quite the feat, as I still had 210 pounds on my 6'1 frame. "And we should all *thank* you, right? Our savior? Coming to our rescue and helping us work harder for the bossman? Let me guess, you have unlocked room privilege already, right?"

A deep voice rang out from behind me. It was Craig. "That's quite enough, John. To your rooms, boys. Now. Supper is in an hour in the main dining hall. Clean yourselves up and report at six bells."

I grimaced. This was the *last* thing I needed. If the boys thought I was a boss' pet before, this certainly wouldn't help. John sneered at me and backed off, his hands coming up placatingly. "No problem, boss. We'll see you in a bit." He winked at me and left with the crew.

I shook my head. *Yep. Definitely made friends with the cats much easier than these guys.* Craig turned his glance to me. "Don't worry about them. You're interrupting the status quo, which never goes unnoticed."

I nodded but didn't say anything. Craig put his hand on my shoulder. "Let's get you back to the rooms. You need to eat." We continued up the road of the snowy city.

The six bells sounded from outside my room, and I pulled my boots on and walked out into the hall, following the winding maze down into the lower part of the palace. Workers streamed out of their rooms, and I blended into the group of random crews.

I was looking forward to a hot meal and some rest. I entered the main dining hall, and the smell of roasted meats and freshly baked bread filled my nose. It was always crowded here, with workers from different teams and different levels of experience all coming together to eat and relax.

I saw Mara's hand waving at a table near the back of the cafeteria and walked over to her. She was sitting with some of the girls from the mid-week celebration. To my right, I saw the crew boys sitting around the table. John saw me again and perked up in fake excitement. "Hey, guys! It's him! He's here again! Someone get me a pen. I want him to write me a signed letter that we can hang up in the mines! That way, we can remember him fondly when he's not there!"

The boys laughed, and my face reddened. "What's your problem, John?" I asked, trying to keep my voice calm.

"My problem is that you're a lazy, good-for-nothing brat who thinks he's better than the rest of us," John spat back. "You're always getting out of work and trying to make us look bad. And now, you've made some piece of shit thing that will probably increase our workload even more! Well, tonight, we're going to teach you a lesson."

340

Before I could react, John jumped out of his chair and lunged at me, and we were grappling on the floor. His friends joined in, and soon fists and feet flew around me. I tried to fight back, but I was outnumbered and outmatched. I could feel the pain radiating through my body as the blows rained down on me, my body curling up into a fetal position.

Cries of alarm sounded around the cafeteria as people circled around us and watched, some cheering us on and others, like Mara, yelling for them to stop.

Finally, another miner stepped in and pulled John off me. It was the boy who tried to give me some ideas for my creation the day before. The boys laughed and jeered as they walked away, leaving me battered and bruised on the ground. Mara was at my side as well.

The commotion had caught the attention of the bosses and supervisors. They came over and broke everything up and sent everyone back to their tables. John and his friends were sent to their rooms for the night and apparently were not allowed breakfast the next day. I assumed to keep us separated and give everyone time to cool off. One of the bosses came over to check on me.

"Are you okay, Noah?" he asked with genuine concern.

My arm suddenly started repairing my bruises and cuts as the health bar tattoo siphoned the injuries away. *Crap- I don't want anyone to see that,* I thought, quickly getting to my feet.

I nodded, still feeling shaky. "Yeah, I'll be okay. Thanks," I said quickly.

He patted me on the back and turned to the rest of the crew. "Alright, that's enough. Let's all go back to our rooms and get some rest. We have a month's end shift tomorrow. Half of you aren't even close to quota, and it could be a long day." Groans sounded out, and most people in the cafeteria stood and returned to their rooms. The other half went back to eating.

"Let me get you some food. Head to our table," Mara said, turning and quickly hurrying away toward the dinner lines.

I started limping toward Mara's table, even though I didn't need to. I decided to look injured for the room, so they didn't know about my health bar. I felt a sense of deep despair wash over me. *Why did they hate me so much? What had I done to deserve this?* I just wanted to improve things for everyone, but no one appreciated my efforts. *Well, except Craig,* I thought with a snicker.

The food that had seemed so appetizing just moments ago now made me feel sick to my stomach. I couldn't even bring myself to look at it, let alone eat it. "Hey! Mara!" I called out to her. "Don't worry about it. I'm not hungry. I'm just going to head to bed."

She frowned and returned to me. "Let me come with you," she replied.

"Nah, I'm good. Go ahead and eat. I'll see you tomorrow morning. Let's get breakfast together, okay?"

Mara tilted her head but didn't say anything. She nodded and hugged me. I hugged her back and walked toward the rooms as she turned and returned to her table.

As I walked away, I could hear the crews laughing and joking as if nothing had happened. But for me, everything had changed. I wondered if I would ever be able to find a place where I truly belonged here on Prixa.

No, I thought to myself. *I did have a place where I belonged. Fulgar would never let me control my own destiny. The Overlord would always have the final say in everything I do here. I'm going to go back to Dunbar no matter how long it takes to get free.*

I looked out the window at the moon. It was almost full.

Chapter 12

Benny

I WOKE UP DETERMINED NOT TO LET THOSE OLDER BOYS GET to me. I was a threat because I was different, and any time you get the attention of the higher-ups, there will always be problems. It used to happen to me in school, too.

I'll tell you what it didn't get, though, was female attention. Mara seems interested...

I shook my head. I didn't have the energy to chase after a girl, even if she was super cute. She had beautiful blond hair that she usually had up in a ponytail and freckles dotting the skin under her piercing green eyes. But no. There was just too much going on right now to worry about that kind of thing. Plus, I had never had a girlfriend before so I wouldn't know the first thing about that.

I heard a knock at my door and hoisted myself out of bed. I threw on my overalls, which were my pajamas these days and opened the door. My face instantly reddened as I saw Mara looking back at me. She smirked at me, looking me up and down and getting entertainment from my overalls with no shirt. "Did I wake you, princess? Wait...is that the style of clothes in that city you lived in?"

343

Speak of the devil. I coughed, trying to hide my expression in my hand. "Uh, no, just wasn't really moving too fast this morning. And yeah. But there were usually shirts involved. So, yeah."

Mara smiled, enjoying my embarrassment. "Can I come in for a minute? We should have about ten minutes until the first bell for breakfast."

I nodded and stood aside, signaling for her to come in. I closed the door behind her as she sat on the edge of my bed. "How are you feeling this morning?"

I shrugged. "Not bad. A little sore."

"Yeah, looks like you don't have any bruises, so that's good?"

I nodded but didn't say anything else. A long silence broke out between us, neither knowing what to say next. Finally, Mara broke the silence. "You know, most of us on the crew are good people. John and those guys...he's just older and expected to have moved up out of crew level by now. It makes him..."

"A dick?" I said, filling in the sentence.

She laughed. "Yeah. Exactly. John gets threatened by people. The last guy that transferred in got promoted a few weeks later, right under his nose. When you came in..." She left the sentence trailing, but I understood.

"It's not like I've been given much of a choice so far. I'm lucky I've been able to pick my projects. Since I've been here, I've been under lock and key or constant supervision. But even that has been a battle with Craig and the Overlord."

Mara's eyes widened. "Wait, you met him?"

"Yeah. He has this... predatory look about him. It's hard to explain. He told me things, but I felt something underneath everything he said." I cut it off at that, knowing he could probably be listening to me right now.

"Maybe we should change the subject," she said, clearing her throat.

The night before, I had designed a simple lock pick. It cost 3x iron. It was a simple thing, and I wanted to try it out tonight. The full moon was coming, and I needed a way to leave the room.

"Hey, do you think me and you can meet up after the shift?" I looked side to side, and leaned close to her ear, dropping to a whisper. If the Overlord was watching, I wanted him thinking I was asking her something...well, something a teenager would ask another teenager sitting on a bed together.

She took a sharp intake of breath when I leaned in. I whispered, "Can you smuggle me up three iron pieces? I need it for something. Put it where the pickaxes are stored."

I moved my head back, looking at her face. She looked down, disappointment all over her face. Finally, she responded. "Oh, uh, yeah sure. I can."

"Thanks," I said, confused at her expression. *Wait...did she think...*

The moment passed, and her face returned to the normal Mara smile. "Come on, let's get some food. You must be starving. And don't worry; I'll protect you this morning." She flexed her skinny arms and scrunched her face up. I laughed a belly laugh, then smiled back at her.

"Hang on, let me get my work uniform on," I said, motioning for her to turn around.

She complied, facing the opposite wall. As I changed, I sighed and said, "Hey, Mara? Thanks."

"For what?" she asked, back still turned to me.

"You've been the only cool person here so far. Well, you and that other boy who helped me. What's his name?"

"Tyler," she responded. "And don't mention it. You're different from the other boys in the crew. I don't know what it is, but I like that."

I didn't respond but felt my heart flutter like crazy. First, the moment before on the bed, and now that. I rested my hand on her shoulder, then, with a smile, nodded my head to the door. With that, we walked out into the hallway with the mass of people heading to the cafeteria.

———

The lunch bell sounded as I slipped the last piece of steel into the mage's velvet bag. Craig had separated me from the group again since he had heard what had transpired at the cafeteria. He spoke about all working together, but the nods were half-hearted. His threats to John and the other boys at the morning crew meeting seemed to fall on deaf ears as they looked at me with malice.

Craig explained that I was working on a device to increase production and lessen the mining output needed, which I wasn't sure was true. But I went along with it, trying to regain the team's good graces.

My crew was far behind their target production, and seemed to blame me for that. They were technically shorthanded by one person, so that made sense. Of course I knew the circumstances, but they didn't.

During some small talk by the forges, I had asked about the way crew move-ups worked. Apparently, the people that hit their quotas got a promotion and a raise in pay. Promotions meant no curfew, no locked rooms, and better meals, which made everyone work hard during the month. But from what the gray crew member said, the quotas were so high that people rarely hit their numbers.

I sat in the inn alone again, only this time, I was served hot food. I didn't mind eating by myself, so that was fine. My mana read [32/60] since I had to make nine more pieces of steel. With the extra one from yesterday, I had enough for my last piece of equipment...the beneficiation machine. I was really excited to see that in action. The thought of dumping non-iron waste and only keeping the iron ore got me super pumped.

I was still stuck at level nine and didn't know how to break through the first wall. I could feel my body ready to evolve, but I didn't know what to do. I wished that Romas was here to guide me. Hopefully this last machine would do it.

The math was on my side for finishing my machine up today. I would regenerate twelve mana over two hours and needed forty to construct it. I also wanted to find a way to tie the two machines together with a chute or conveyor. But this way, the crushed ore would filter directly into the 'Benny,' as I called it now.

I was excited to see the results of the machine and planned to inspect the finished product to see what we got. If the raw rock ore took a $9/2$ ore to tinderstone ratio for me to create steel, this new ore would cost much less. My mining skill said $1.65{:}1$, which was more like $3/2$ instead. Almost 3x less material to produce the same steel.

I surveyed the space near the crusher. There was room under the giant rock smasher to swap the box out for a chute that could feed Benny, but I would worry about that later when I had some extra mana to spend. For now, I would manually take the 40 pounds of crushed rock and dump it into the inlet.

But with the plan ready, I started my work. With the help of the mages, I put the fifteen iron ore on the ground and a bucket of water in the middle of it all. I could create the inlet box, the outlet box, and the tailings box all at once, and they would automatically create a frame for the device, similar to how the crusher formed up on its own accord.

I took a few steadying breaths and closed my eyes, my gut churning in nervousness. As usual, the mages all formed up around me, most leaning forward in excitement. I pointed my hand at the ore and began concentrating on the first design- the machine framework.

I watched as a frame sprung up next to the crusher, then a large box near the front. The bins in the back formed next, one under where I assumed the giant magnetic wheel would go and one at the front of the device. A wooden scraper formed on top of the box, apparently for scraping the iron off the wheel and into the bin.

I gasped and cut the create skill off, sweat pouring down my face. My arm throbbed as the mana left me again. The mages rushed over and looked over the device, talking excitedly to each other. I used the back of my arm to wipe the sweat away and started toward the steel, but Craig waved me back. "We've got it. Where do you want your ore, the steel bars, and the rod?"

My eyebrows raised in shock. "Uh, right in the middle there. You can see where the wheel is going to sit."

I took a quick hiatus, waiting for my mana to refill the rest of the way. It was at [7/60] and only needed another thirty minutes. In the meantime, Craig called a couple of gray crew over to load the inlet bin with some of the crushed ore from the pile. As they worked, the boys eyed me suspiciously. *Great. More people seeing me sitting around, not doing any manual labor.*

I gave myself one extra mana, but once I reached sixteen, I stood up and walked over, a hush coming over the mages. I didn't wait, pointed my hand, and concentrated on the separator drum. A two-foot diameter drum sprung up and was around five feet wide. The rod shot out the end and formed a wheel that I could either manually turn or eventually connect to the crusher wheel with rope to rotate both machines simultaneously.

The mages cheered again, and one walked over to the wheel and threw some crushed ore on it. About half of it stuck to the wheel, the other half falling into the bottom of the trash bin. The mage's eyes widened, and a huge smile was plastered over his face.

"Very impressive!" Craig said, walking over and inspecting Benny like everyone else.

I walked over to the wheel. It looked like a giant ship wheel with hand holds spread around the diameter. "Alright, hands away, I will start it up!"

The mages backed up a bit and watched. As I turned the giant drum, the water churned, and ore started sucking toward the center. Black specks lined the separator drum as I made a few more revolutions. A few more turns of the wheel and the wooden scraper pulled the iron off and into the concentrate bin at the front.

Holy shit, it worked. It actually worked!

Chapter 13

Change in Plans

I stopped turning Benny's wheel and walked over to the concentrate bin at the front of the machine. I dug out some of the black ore and inspected it hastily, excited to see what I was able to accomplish.

[IRON ORE CONCENTRATE - LEVEL 3 INGREDIENT - 92% IRON OXIDE 8% VARIOUS SILICA]

Nice. I also pulled up my tattoos to see if I leveled up, although I doubted I had. I felt absolutely no different.

[NOAH]
[LV 9- BLACKSMITH APPRENTICE]

HEALTH 60/60
MANA 1/60

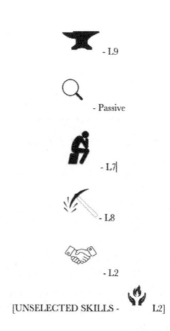

- L9

- Passive

- L7

- L8

- L2

[UNSELECTED SKILLS - L2]

I let out a mumbled curse word. I hadn't leveled up yet, even though I was almost positive that I would after this little project was completed. However, my mining skill had gone up two whole levels, and design had gone up one to level seven. *At least I got some respect from the system from this one!*

'CREATE' also looked stuck at level nine, even after I created all that damn steel. I needed to figure out how to push ahead to the next tier of this class and fast. I didn't want to keep wasting experience.

The mages started getting a bit antsy, and I looked at them questioningly. Finally, the Porter came over, breaking the silence. "Noah, please put the ore back and move away from the equipment."

I scoffed at him. "Seriously?"

The mages stared at me behind their hoods, unmoving. "Fine," I retorted, throwing the ore on the ground. The mages all groaned in unison as the ore mixed with the dirt.

Craig approached me and held his hands out, palms toward me, placatingly. "Sorry, just can't have you near the finished product. Protocol and all. But here. You've certainly earned your month's salary and then some."

He dug into his pocket and fished out two gold coins, both adorning the pickaxe symbol I had seen earlier from the inn. I accepted them and instantly inspected one of the coins. The voice lady filled me in a bit, which was nice.

[GOLD RUBICK - CURRENCY OF THE FULGARIANS - WORTH 4X SILVER RUBICK | WORTH 10X BRONZE RUBICK]

I had no idea if this was a lot of money or how much things cost in the settlement. Lunch had been paid for by the crew boss all week, although I had seen him pay with a few bronze coins, and I had yet to explore the city much.

But if lunch for a crew of ten people was a few bronze coins, then I was pretty wealthy already. Unless the town paid for lunch, and Craig was just tipping the barkeeps. I believed that explanation much more.

Either way, getting paid for my work was nice, especially since I had just produced a far superior product to the iron rocks that came directly out of the walls. Craig looked at me expectantly, but a frown crossed his brow when I didn't jump out of my boots with praise. "Noah, this is over four times the pay of your other crewmates for the month. Say thank you."

I shrugged and nodded. "Yeah, thanks. Sorry, I don't know the currency here yet."

He slapped me on the shoulder. "Well, that will make for a fun off day, eh? Go take some of the boys out on the town. I'm sure they will appreciate it." He winked and walked away, humming to himself.

His undertone was clear.

I spent the rest of the shift near Benny, helping with loading and operation. I was officially named the *Benny Equipment Operator* and just stood there turning the damn wheel for the next three hours as my mana slowly recovered. The mages watched me closely to ensure I didn't go near their concentrate bin. I could only imagine how much that iron was worth.

Every fifteen minutes, one of the mages would signal me to stop turning the wheel, then dump the bin into their velvet ingredient bag.

The siren sounded, and the gray team trudged up the tunnel, smiles on their faces. I stayed behind and observed as their crew leader, a man named Todd, dug two silver coins out of his pocket and put them into the palm of each worker.

Todd was a happy man, smiling broadly at each crewmate and asking them about their day off plans, often letting out booming laughs or jokes. I didn't see any women on this shift. Each of them passed me and gave me a nod, none showing my own crew's hostility.

So this really was a big payday for me! Nice. Now I have to figure out what to do with it!

I pretended to walk over to the stack of pickaxes to pick up the ore that Mara was supposed to leave for me. When I picked up a pickaxe, I couldn't help but inspect it.

[BASIC IRON PICKAXE - LEVEL 1 - CONDITION 33%]

This one looked alright, and it was at 33%. I picked up another one that looked rusty and checked its condition.

[BASIC IRON PICKAXE - LEVEL 1 - CONDITION 13% -
RUST INFILTRATION - CONDITION DEGRADE AT
1.44X NORMAL RATE]

Yikes. I need to upgrade these bad boys to steel pickaxes tomorrow. Let the crew come to work at the start of the new week with brand-spanking new equipment!

Focus, Noah! Under the second tool were three rocks, just like I needed. I looked back at Todd, who was paying the last crew member. I quickly picked the ore up and put it in my hands, then concentrated on creating a lock pick. I felt it change in my hand and slid it up my sleeve, not stopping to look at it for now.

Excited about my plan, I started walking up the tunnel and into the night when the Porter stopped me. "You. With me to see the Overlord."

Shit. Shit!

I sighed and held my arm out that didn't have the lock pick hidden away. The Porter grabbed it quickly, and the world lurched. I gasped when we landed in his office, the feeling after teleporting still causing me to lose my breath.

A gentle breeze filtered in from the open balcony window, the three moons lighting the office from the starry sky. Music played in the city below as people shouted and laughed. It seemed like some of the crews had gotten an early start on the night's activity.

The Porter retreated to the corner and sat on a plush couch, making himself comfortable. The Overlord sat behind his large wooden desk, his piercing gaze fixed upon me as I entered. His presence alone commanded respect, but his smug expression rubbed me the wrong way.

"Ah, Noah, there you are," the Overlord greeted with a sinister smile. "I must say, I'm impressed with your ingenuity. The crusher and beneficiation machines you created have exceeded my expectations."

I nodded, choosing my words politically. "Well, I'm glad I could meet your standards."

The Overlord chuckled, his voice laced with a hint of arrogance. "Indeed. But I must inform you, Noah, that we must increase our steel production. As you probably figured out, steel is not a commodity here on Prixa. I want to become the leader in steel weapon exports for our allies."

His words hit me like a punch to the gut. Anger surged through my veins, and I couldn't hold back any longer. "I didn't sign up for this! I didn't come here to be your personal blacksmith, creating weapons for a war I want no part in!"

The Overlord's smile faded slightly, replaced by a cold, calculating gaze. "You have no choice, Noah. You are here because I brought you here. Your skills as a Creator are invaluable to our cause. The fate of Fulgar, and your fellow humans, rests on your shoulders. You've gotten well paid for your work. I'd suggest enjoying the rewards of your labor."

I frowned, unable to contain my frustration any longer. I had no idea who this guy had aligned with and what he was planning. And even if he told me, I wouldn't trust him.

The Overlord leaned back in his chair, his eyes narrowing. "Remember your place, Noah. I already know you don't trust me from your *attitude. I've also seen how you're warming up to Mara.* I can take away everything you hold dear with a snap of my fingers. And I don't mean with a return trip back to Earth."

My breath caught in my throat, realizing his power over me. *So he was watching. Damn it.* I took a deep breath, trying to regain my composure. "Fine, I'll continue to create for you. But don't expect my loyalty or enthusiasm. I'm only doing this to survive."

The Overlord's gaze intensified, a hint of amusement dancing in his eyes. "Survival is a powerful motivator, Noah. Remember that. Go enjoy the coins you've earned."

With those chilling words, the Overlord dismissed me.

I turned on my heel and walked out the door, ignoring the Porter as he called after me. Anger burned inside me as I left the office. The weight of my circumstances pressed upon me, the realization that I was trapped in this world, forced to serve the whims of a power-hungry ruler. *Unless I did something about it.*

As I walked through the palace halls without knowing where I was going, the anger slowly turned into determination. I would continue to create but do it on my own terms. I would find a way to reclaim my freedom, to make a difference in this world without being a pawn in someone else's game. The almost full moon shone in the palace windows. It was time to act. It was time to try out my lock pick.

With renewed resolve, I headed back to my room. *No, my prison cell.* The road ahead was uncertain, but I knew I had to stay true to myself to hold on to my dreams amidst the chaos. And perhaps, while forging steel for the Overlord's army, I would also find a way to forge my own path.

END OF ACT I

Interlude

As the sun cast its warm, golden glow upon the humid settlement of Dunbar, Dee stepped out of the smithy and onto the street of the first level, taking in the bittersweet sight before her. The city that once thrived with hope and laughter now wore a cloak of sorrow. Gone were the vibrant tapestries adorning the walls with various house symbols and workmanships, replaced by solemn banners bearing the Baron's new emblem. The streets that once bustled with activity now seemed deserted, save for the heavy presence of guards monitoring the human population. Even the once boisterous merchants had taken to other means of sales.

Dee walked through the winding alleyways, her heart heavy with the weight of recent events. The air crackled with tension, the atmosphere thick with unease. The young Fekan warriors that had come with the new Baron patrolled the streets, their eyes scanning every corner, their weapons held with a sense of vigilance. It starkly contrasted the harmony that once existed between their species not so many days ago. The battle, with its countless Fekan losses, had changed everything.

She jumped down to the lower level and walked outside the gates, the dirt path stretching before her, leading to the lush green expanse of the jungle. She could see the humans toiling in the fields, their sweat glistening under the sun as they tended to the stalked plants. Their faces carried the weariness of oppression, yet their determination was palpable. Despite the hardships, they remained steadfast, working tirelessly to sustain their community. They knew Noah would return. The pride of humanity. The savior of the human race. He would come back for them and unlock the magic in everyone and finish the job he started.

The new Baron didn't know, but there were small shrines to Noah everywhere she went. A stick painted red here and a leaf painted yellow there. They were the smallest things, but they kept these people going.

As Dee made her way along the path, the echoes of sorrow followed her. Noah's creations to safeguard the settlement were dismantled, a sign of the shifting power dynamics. The absence of those protective structures only deepened the vulnerability that hung in the air.

She couldn't help but feel a pang of guilt. She had survived when many had not. And replacing the fallen was a new band of young Fekan warriors brought in with this new regime, their hatred of the human race and its potential dangers made known. She pushed her thoughts aside, focusing on the task at hand. Her father still had a smithy to run and items to create.

Soon, Dee reached the meeting point a short distance into the jungle, where the fire mages waited. They stood tall and formidable now, their fiery auras contrasting against the serene backdrop of the jungle. Wands were strapped to their sides, and thin leather armor glowed brightly on their chests. The alchemists had all manner of bombs and grenades strapped to leather bands that criss-crossed their chests. They exchanged brief greetings, the weight of the shared responsibility reflected in everyone's eyes.

With a nod, the group ventured deeper into the wilderness, everyone's senses attuned to the rhythm of the jungle. The foliage enveloped them, embracing the group in its vibrant embrace. The chirping birds and rustling leaves filled the air, momentarily easing the burden on their shoulders.

As they moved, there was the briefest sense of unity. In the heart of the jungle, the group encountered various challenges. Dangerous creatures lurked in the shadows, testing their mettle. But they stood strong, the combined strength and skill serving as a testament to the power of unity. Together, they leveled up their skills.

Yet even as Dee reveled in these brief moments of joy, a sense of urgency lingered in the back of her mind. The people of Dunbar knew the road ahead would be treacherous but they were determined to face it head-on. With each step through the dense foliage, with each pulse of magic coursing through their veins, they vowed to protect their shared home. The city of Dunbar might have been cloaked in sadness and guarded by warriors, but they refused to let despair consume them.

When the group returned, the Baron and his cronies waited with his large leather storage chest. One by one, the group dropped their ingredients and findings into the crate, along with their armor and wands. The warriors searched the humans to ensure nothing was hidden, for doing so was penalized by death. Typh, Dee's brother, was one of the warriors in the Baron's entourage, but the look that adorned his face differed from the others. It was his duty, but he did not enjoy it. He had been stripped of his ranks from the backlash he gave the new head of the settlement and forced to perform as a stooge of the regime.

In the privacy of her home, away from prying eyes, Dee shared her thoughts and fears with her father and brother. Romas spoke of his worries for the humans and his disdain for the new Baron who blamed them unjustly. He longed for justice and the restoration of balance. The wooden sign of an anvil hung outside the smithy symbolizing resilience in the face of adversity.

His anvil symbolized Noah.

For he would return.

Chapter 14

Basic Oxygen Steelmaking

ANOTHER DAY IN THE FORGE AWAITED ME. LIGHT FILTERED into my room, and I rolled out of bed. Rubbing the sleep from my eyes, I swung my legs over the edge of the bed and planted my feet firmly on the floor. I had a smile on my face, however. My lock pick had worked perfectly. I tried it as soon as I entered the room, then actually *locked* the door from the inside. I figured if I could lock the door with the tool, I could undoubtedly *unlock* it when the time came.

When I inspected the tool, I was surprised.

[BASIC LOCKPICK - APPROVED FOR LEVEL 1-2 DOOR
LOCKS - CONDITION 76%]

So I could get around four attempts out of it. That was good to know.

Since then, it had taken me two days to finish my last creation - the forge ladle. It was an enormous device that required 30x steel and 50x iron by the time the thick metal was formed. It had taken me almost all day to make the steel alone. They kept me out of the mines, which was fine for now. But tonight was the full moon, so I needed to act.

I continued scheming how to return to Dunbar but was under constant surveillance. My plan, as it stood now, was to get this forge operational and then get back into the mines. Then I had to get this moss and kill a few of those rat creatures, and then I could make a shield from prying eyes...and then...

And then what? Run from level who-knows-what mages who have power that you can't even fathom yet? With an all-seeing Overlord watching your every move?

I shook my head. One problem at a time. I slipped on my gray onesie; my black ones had been swapped out for now while I worked in the forge full-time. I was about to mass-create high-level steel weapons for an unknown benefactor. The Overlord never told me who this *ally* was, but I could only imagine it wasn't someone I would condone. If it were my Fekan friends, I'm sure he would have told me.

After a quick breakfast at the table with the gray team, I made my way to the forge, the familiar scent of smoke from fireballs and molten metal filling the air. The sound of hammers striking anvils reverberated through the workshop. The heat hit me in the face, but my armor kept my body comfortable.

Today's task was to focus on the steelmaking process and test what I finished late last night. The ladle sat there, ready for its trial run. The band of supervisory mages looked on as usual. As I approached the blast furnace, its intense heat radiated toward me, enveloping me in its fiery embrace. The iron concentrate, carefully measured and prepared, had been poured into the furnace before I arrived, where it underwent the transformation into pig iron.

So far, even the new iron product was far superior to the unrefined iron thanks to Benny's effect on its iron concentration levels. As the pig iron melted and flowed, it accumulated in the ladle, slowly moving like lava rolling down a hill. I climbed the ladder on the side of the ladle to access the top.

I added the crushed tinderstone, a crucial ingredient that would facilitate the removal of undesired carbon and impurities from the pig iron. Above me, from a platform, stood an air mage, ready to force air into the lance. It was basically a 30-foot-long steel straw with a leather mouthpiece that would introduce oxygen into the mixture. I was told that the air mage could produce high speed winds with his spell, so I wanted him blowing that into the mixture.

Probably the worst job in the forge, I thought glumly. Who knows what vicious fumes that dude would be sucking in as he worked. *I should teach the workers about the steelworker's unions from Earth next,* I thought with a chuckle.

The blown oxygen, combined with the tinderstone and high grade iron ore, formed a reaction known as basic oxygen steel-making. This process caused the undesired elements to bind with the oxygen and escape as carbon dioxide gas, leaving behind a purer form of steel. The tinderstone, which I had always assumed resembled coal from Earth, bound other forms of waste and fell out as slag.

As my mining skill leveled up, so too did my knowledge about all of this. It was awesome, if I was being honest.

After I poured the tinderstone in, the blower started, forming bubbles in the concoction. The ladle almost looked like a witch's cauldron, bubbling away happily and releasing steam into the air. With careful precision, I poured the liquid steel into molds using the giant gear wheel on the side to turn the bucket over. Each mold was carefully crafted to shape the blades of the weapons we would forge. The molten metal filled the molds, taking on the desired form, its fiery glow a testament to the power within. I was one of the few who could get close to this thing without melting, so with ultra thick leather gloves and my fireproof armor, I worked.

It was really interesting seeing the manual methods of making something on Prixa, instead of my magical *smash two things together video game style* way of doing it. But without an endless supply of mana, this was a great option for making things. Plus, I could scale operations with manual laborers doing this. I would need to be able to manufacture items that stemmed from initial ingredient lists for armor, weapons, and wands.

As the steel cooled and solidified in the molds, the blades began to take shape, their edges and sturdy frames coming to life before my eyes. I inspected each one, checking its shape to ensure I didn't need more steel in a mold before pushing it out of the way and moving a new mold under the ladle.

It was time-consuming work. Minutes turned into hours as I immersed myself in the rhythmic dance of creation. The heat of the forge and the sound of hammers striking metal became my world. I blocked out images of what I was making and who it would hurt. Those thoughts made me upset. But with every mold filled, I felt one step closer to breaking through my level 10 barrier. But I felt *something* was still missing.

The lunch bell sounded, and I looked up in shock. I had a little less than half of the ladle to go, which I estimated to be around five or six more molds, and knew I couldn't stop and waste this precious material. One mage shook his head 'no' at me, confirming my suspicions. I sighed, wiped my brow, and continued working.

As the day drew to a close, I surveyed the fruits of my labor, a collection of blades waiting to be honed and perfected by the Fulgarian blacksmith crew. The ladle, now emptied of its molten contents, stood as symbols of the transformative power of fire and steel.

I walked over to Craig, and he smiled at me. "There he is! Our village...what did you call it? Engine-air?"

"Engineer," I corrected him. "Hey, Craig."

"The Overlord is going to be ecstatic about this production. Eleven new steel blades! One of the mages inspected it and said its quality was unmatched. You will make unbreakable weapons that even the deadliest creatures will fear!"

I took a long, tired breath. "Yeah, that's all well and good. Can I ask a favor?" I needed to return to the mines tomorrow and stop working in the forge.

Craig eyed me suspiciously. "Possibly. Shoot."

"I want to try and combine steel and the pickaxes down in the mines, then test them out on the walls. Can I be assigned to the black team again tomorrow? I would also need a couple of pieces of steel to bring."

Craig nodded enthusiastically. "Yes, of course! Anything to increase our iron production!" His eyes gleamed at me, and he almost licked his lips. "I don't see that as a problem. I'll coordinate with Todd to get the gray team to start forge prep for you. They will have everything ready for you tomorrow after lunch, and we can do all of this again! But think about how to make the molding process more efficient. You only have half the day, not the full day!"

Typical boss, I thought smugly. *Never happy.*

"Okay, thanks," I replied, a plan forming in my mind.

"Also, you will be returning to your twenty-ore-per-day quota soon, so be prepared for that. We will need a few more leather vests for the workers, and then some gloves maybe. You should be able to whip those up, no problem. Get some food. And some rest. You look horrible. We will get back at it tomorrow!" With that, he turned and started barking orders to one of the forge workers as he walked away, almost buzzing with happiness.

I shook my head. This was getting ridiculous. I was still being treated like a prisoner even though I had made fireproof vests, a brand new method to mine iron ore, and created weapons that would outlast their iron ones by 10x. If I helped this damn city any further, who knows what leg up I would give them.

I walked out into the town, its snowy street quiet while people finished their shifts. I was starving but didn't want to eat yet. I had a plan to go over with Mara for tomorrow's mining trip and would need to casually bump into her at dinner to pitch it to her.

Then...I had a room to escape from. Fortunately I had led them to believe that the initial usage of the ladle would cost mana as I 'adjusted' it. I had worked hard but still had all of my mana.

Chapter 15

Lunar Moss

I LAY IN MY BED IN MY ROOM, ACTING LIKE I WAS GOING TO sleep and awaiting the opportune moment to execute my plan. Time seemed to crawl with agonizing slowness. The solitude weighed heavily upon me, and the chamber's silence echoed in my ears. I took a deep breath, attempting to calm the restlessness that stirred within me. I didn't know what, exactly, I waited for. I just knew I couldn't go outside my room right after the door locked. I thought through the plan over and over as I waited. The goal was set, and my heart pounded with excitement. I glanced at the lock pick hidden in my hand, a newfound tool that held the potential to unlock freedom.

I contemplated the choices that had led me to this point—the risks I was willing to take, the sacrifices I was prepared to make. Fear coiled within me, threatening to keep me in bed, safe yet unhappy. I yearned for the taste of freedom, to break free from the chains that bound me within these walls. The Overlord spoke of promotions, but I knew that was never going to happen.

My gaze shifted to the small desk nestled against the wall, strewn with parchment and quills. It was a testament to the mundane tasks I had occupied myself with in my idle moments. Yet, as I glanced at the unfinished sketches and designs, my mind yearned for a different purpose—one that would grant me freedom from this gilded cage.

As the moonlight shifted and cast elongated shadows across the room, a surge of resolve surged through me. The time had come. It was now or never. I rose from the bed, crossing the room to the door. With a steady hand, I held the lock pick like a surgical instrument and lifted the folds of my clothing away from my hand. My hand started to shake as I bent in front of the keyhole.

Steadying my shaking hand, I inserted the slender piece of metal into the keyhole and gently manipulated the tumblers. A soft click resonated as I applied subtle pressure and listened intently, signaling success. The voice lady made me basically jump through the ceiling of my room.

[YOU HAVE UNLOCKED THE 'THIEVERY' SKILL]

Jesus, voice lady. Not while I'm in the middle of something like that!

Silently, I turned the doorknob and eased the door open, inch by inch. The corridor outside was dimly lit, and the air was heavy with the scent of wax and incense. The door creaked slightly, and my heart skipped a beat as I spotted a pair of guards patrolling nearby. I pressed my back against the wall, my senses heightened and waited for them to pass.

Timing was crucial. I swiftly moved from one shadowy alcove to another, utilizing every nook and cranny as I navigated the labyrinthine palace corridors. The soft sounds of my boots were masked by the echoes of distant conversations and the occasional clatter of armor. A quick glance at my arm showed that my 'PATRON' skill had been automatically removed, most likely as the one I used the least. I felt lighter on my feet, probably from the new skill.

As I emerged into the main thoroughfare, I could hear the distant sound of marching boots. A group of guards marched past, their voices muffled by the distance. I ducked behind a marble statue, my heart pounding in my chest. I held my breath, my body tense, until they vanished around a corner.

Finally, at the bottom of the stairs, I turned down the hallway and stared down the palace's main floor. In the morning, before our shift, I never noticed just how big and open it was. *Crap, how do I get across without someone seeing me?*

Suddenly I had an idea. I slipped my boots off so that I just had my socks on. No one was around, so I made a run for it. I ran like a pack of Stalkers was chasing me. My socks made no noise, and I slid across the floor and into the night, very Tom Cruise-like.

Breathing heavily, I slipped my boots back on before my feet froze in the wet snow. The streets outside were eerily quiet, the cobblestones illuminated by the pale glow of the moons, the largest one huge in the night sky. All three were in the sky. I moved swiftly, sticking to the shadows, my newfound skill aiding me in avoiding detection. I darted behind crates and barrels, my senses sharp, ready to react at the slightest hint of danger.

As I ventured deeper into the city, I passed houses cloaked in darkness, their inhabitants asleep and oblivious to the covert mission unfolding right outside their homes. The cool night air brushed against my skin, a gentle reminder of the risks and rewards ahead. With each successful evasion of the patrolling guards, my confidence grew. The shadows became my allies, concealing my movements as I neared where the long road to the mine was located, anticipation coiling within me. I passed it, but a thought occurred to me. *If this works, I could come into the mine to get what I need alone. Not even have to involve any of the crew!*

My steps quickened, fueled by determination and the unwavering belief that I could triumph against all odds. The escape from my room was just the beginning, a small victory emboldening my spirit. The night was mine, and I would navigate its shadows with purpose and resolve.

Finally, I made it to the gates. They were open, but it was guarded by two men in uniforms. Unsure of what to do next, I watched the two guards there. I needed a distraction...something that would make the guards leave their post to check. Out of ideas, I ran to the alley next to the gate and started *meowing*.

Yes. Like a cat.

"What the hell was that?" I heard one of them say as boots started clomping toward my position. I quickly ducked around the house I stood near and circumvented them, running out the gates, shoes off again with tied laces so they hung down around my neck. I kind of felt like a ninja running around in socks and not making any sounds.

With the city behind me and the moon guiding me, I ventured into the wilderness, searching for this lunar moss. I had slipped my boots back on by now to avoid my feet freezing right off my body. The scraggly mountain trees surrounded me, casting elongated shadows that danced beneath the moon's gentle glow. Snow crunched, but it was eerily quiet, a vast difference from when I walked through the jungle. Out here, in the snowy foothills looking up to these giant mountains, nothing moved. Nothing even seemed to breathe.

I followed a winding path further away from the city, my eyes scanning the trees and undergrowth for any sign of the coveted moss. Every rustle and whisper of the wind carried the promise of discovery, urging me to continue my quest. The full moon seemed to have some sort of power, making trees dance and leaves open and stretch toward it.

I heard something take off under a bush somewhere, my heart racing into my throat. My eyes darted around, not finding any danger, and I continued walking. The city was a small backdrop now as I walked on.

As I traversed the clearing, I noticed a peculiar phenomenon—an ethereal glow emanating from a cluster of trees in the distance. A soft, silvery light bathed the area, drawing me closer with an irresistible allure. With cautious steps, I approached the source of the luminescence.

And there it was, nestled amidst the branches of an ancient tree —a beautiful web of lunar moss. Its pale tendrils stretched towards the moon as if reaching for the celestial energy that imbued it with its magical properties. I marveled at the sight, realizing that this humble moss was probably one of the highest level ingredients I had found yet.

Carefully, I extended my hand, mindful not to disturb the delicate balance of the area. The moss was surprisingly resilient yet delicate, its feathery strands responding to my touch. As I plucked a small portion, a surge of energy coursed through my veins as if the moon's blessing had been bestowed upon me.

[YOU HAVE UNLOCKED ASTRAL MAGIC]

Nice! So that must be the final mana type for space and time. Can I make teleportation items now? I would have to mess around with that later.

A little moon tattoo showed up next to my other mana types. I put some moss inside my boxer waistband, and some more in my boot. I tried to put it in places people wouldn't think to look, should I be captured on my re-entry into the city.

With the lunar moss safely secured, I retraced my steps toward the city, allowing the moonlight to guide me back. I quickened my pace, anticipation fueling my efforts.

"Well, well, well. What do we have here?"

I jumped out of my skin and turned around, dropping into a defensive posture.

It was the Overlord, standing there in the snow.

Chapter 16

Trust is Earned

"Ah, Noah," the Overlord's voice dripped with an unsettling mix of amusement and disdain. "Attempting to leave without bidding me farewell? How hopelessly thoughtless of you."

I stammered, my tongue betraying my attempts to form coherent words. "I... I didn't mean any harm, my lord. I simply... needed some fresh air." *That, and something to stop you from spying on me all the damn time!* I thought with a grimace.

A sardonic smile played upon the Overlord's lips as he closed the distance between us. "Fresh air, you say? And what were you doing out there in the prairie? Looking for *herbs*, perhaps?" A knowing look crossed his features, but he didn't say more.

My heart pounded in my chest, the weight of the lunar moss pressing against my boxer waistband like an incriminating secret. I hoped he thought I was unsuccessful in my search. I attempted to keep my composure, but the realization that my escape had been thwarted weighed heavily upon me. It took every ounce of restraint not to reach toward the moss or show signs that I had some.

Before I could respond, the Overlord snapped his fingers, and two Porters emerged out of nowhere, surrounding me in an iron grip. Panic surged through my veins as they bound my hands tightly, their cold fingers digging into my flesh.

With a cruel chuckle, the Overlord gestured toward the guards; his voice laced with authority. "Take him to the dungeons, our coldest and darkest cell. Let him ponder the consequences of his actions."

We blinked out of existence, reforming in a dark chamber. I was led through the twisting corridors of the prison, my mind racing with futile attempts to find an escape route. But the guards' grip was unyielding, and my every movement was met with a swift reprimand. *At least they didn't search me,* I thought grimly.

Finally, they thrust me into a frigid, dimly lit cell. I huddled in the corner, seeking whatever meager warmth I could muster. The icy air pierced through my overalls, sending shivers down my spine as the mountain air whistled through gaps in the stone.

Alone in the darkness, the weight of my success, however small, brought me some hope. I clung to it, my fingers brushing against the moss' delicate strands, reminding me of the freedom I desperately sought. The lunar moss remained nestled against my skin, a small comfort amidst the despair. It warmed my spirit somehow. A warmth spread through my body like an IV drip, fighting off the cold.

Time stretched endlessly as I awaited my fate, the cold seeping into my bones, matching the chill that had settled within my spirit. Until then, I would endure the solitude and continue planning how to get out of this place. If I ever got out of this prison cell.

Morning broke two weeks later, casting a dim light into the desolate cell as the heavy door creaked open. Startled, I rubbed my tired eyes and looked up to find the Overlord standing at the entrance, his gaze fixed upon me.

"Rise and shine, Noah," he said with a dismissive wave of his hand. "I trust you've had ample time to reflect on your foolishness. Although, I must admit, your departure from the city was...impressive."

I struggled to my feet, my body stiff and sore from the cold nights on the unforgiving stone floor. My voice was laced with a mixture of defiance and resignation as I replied, "I have learned that attempting to defy you comes with dire consequences, my lord."

The Overlord's eyes narrowed, his voice dripping with veiled menace. "Indeed, you would do well to remember that. But I am a generous ruler, Noah, and I believe in second chances. You have become extremely valuable to me, and for that, I will be merciful."

A glimmer of hope stirred within me, but I remained cautious, knowing well the fickle nature of his benevolence. "What do you expect from me, my lord?" I asked, my voice tinged with skepticism.

He leaned closer, his eyes boring into mine. "Your loyalty, Noah. I am willing to give you a chance to redeem yourself. Serve me faithfully, use your skills to further my ambitions, and perhaps, just perhaps, your days of confinement will be a distant memory."

I weighed his words carefully, my mind racing with conflicting emotions. The desire for freedom warred with the knowledge that defying him would only lead to further suffering. "What must I do?" I asked, my voice resigned. I would continue playing this game to escape and return to the mines for phase two of my plan.

A cruel smile played upon the Overlord's lips. "Continue your work in the mines, Noah. Use your talents to increase our steel production and craft weapons for our allies. I need more ore from the cave walls as well. The vests you make show lots of promise for us. You have already proven your worth, and perhaps I will consider granting you a measure of freedom. You've earned that much."

I nodded, swallowing my pride and accepting the terms. "I will do as you ask, my lord."

"Very well," he said, turning to leave. Without looking at me, he added, "Remember, Noah, your fate lies in your own hands. Prove your loyalty; perhaps you will someday earn the trust you so desperately seek."

With those final words, the Overlord departed, the Porters grabbing my arm to transport me out of prison. When we reemerged outside of my room, I was released from my physical confinement, but the weight of this interaction weighed heavily on me.

If I were to survive the treacherous game I found myself in, I would need to finalize my plan quickly. Outside the palace windows, the sun seemed to be cresting over the mountains, meaning my shift would start soon. I needed to keep my little *operation* a secret, get my ass moving, and change into my work attire.

Today was going to be a long day.

Just as I reached the palace entrance, Craig's booming voice called out from behind me, his concern evident in his tone. "Noah! You look terrible! We were told you were working on a special project for the Overlord, but what happened to you?"

I turned to face him, my expression a mix of weariness and resignation. The events of the imprisonment and my encounter with the Overlord were still fresh in my mind. I shrugged in response, unable to find the words to explain. "Just working hard without much sleep, is all."

Craig's concern deepened, lines furrowing his forehead. "Well, whatever it is, we've got work to do. Time for the shift, my boy! I have your steel here. I didn't forget what was next on the list!"

He patted his pocket. "Let's see what you can do with these pick-axes, eh?"

Nodding silently, I followed him as we made our way to the entrance of the mines. The usual hustle and bustle surrounded us, the clanging of tools and the murmur of conversations filling the air. We descended into the cave's depths, the dimly lit tunnels welcoming us into their cold embrace.

My thoughts were a jumbled mess as we began our work, the rhythmic sound of pickaxes hitting rock echoing through the cavernous space. I was absolutely exhausted. And after my punishment I decided to put my phase two escape plan on the back burner for at least a day. I was positive I would be under the watchful eyes of the scryers all day, and I didn't want to raise any suspicions. Mara eyed me as she walked into the mine, and I shook my head 'no' at her.

Craig's voice broke through my thoughts, cutting through the haze of my contemplation. "Noah, snap out of it! We've got quotas to meet. Grab that pickaxe over there."

I nodded, shaking my head to clear the cobwebs that seemed to form in my brain. When I was in prison, my mana had barely been refilled. I thought it was odd, but maybe there was a mana blocker or something. When I used my new 'Thievery' skill while sneaking around the city, it slowly drained my mana. I wasn't sure how much mana per second it cost, but from when I left my room to when I grabbed the moss, I had used around 22 mana.

Overnight, I only got ten back. Still, I had plenty of mana to do a few pickaxes and assumed it would cost the normal ten mana for upgrading a piece of equipment. I looked at my arm quickly.

[NOAH]
[LV 9- BLACKSMITH APPRENTICE]

Matt Pivots

HEALTH [60/60]
MANA [55/55]

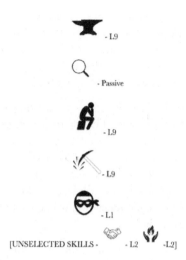

[UNSELECTED SKILLS - - L2 -L2]

I was still missing a bunch of health, most likely from the freezing cold of the prison, but I had no idea. I had watched it tick slowly down while in my cell. My mana had not regenerated at all while I was locked away.

They had fed me enough to survive. Maybe the Overlord was trying to soften me up with a different picture of surviving. He didn't understand that it only increased my resolve. But if my health bar had been keeping my body from freezing during the worst of the cold at night, that explained the IV drip feeling that I experienced. *Guess it wasn't the lunar moss after all.* I also noticed that three of my skills were up against the level 10 barrier. I really needed to level up.

I trudged over to the wall where the pickaxes sat, gathered the single piece of steel and one of the rusty pickaxes, and carefully combined them using my 'Create' skill. As the transformation unfolded, the familiar weight of the pickaxe in my hand shifted, becoming more solid and sturdy. The once-rusty surface was now replaced by a gleaming, polished steel head glistening in the dim light of the mine.

Running my fingers along the new pickaxe, I marveled at its improved attributes. The steel pickaxe felt substantial, balanced perfectly for efficient strikes against the unyielding rocks of the mine. Its sharp edge promised to make quick work of the stubborn ores, reducing the strain on the crew. I inspected it.

[STEEL PICKAXE - LEVEL 3 - CONDITION 100%]

The enhanced durability of the steel pickaxe meant that it would endure the demanding conditions of the mine far longer than its predecessor. No longer would the crew have to worry about the pickaxe chipping or breaking under the strain of repeated blows against the walls. Plus, the new creation started at a condition of 100%.

Craig let out a *whoop*, clasped me on the shoulder, and then took the pickaxe from my hands. He walked over to the wall and swung it into the rock. Pieces of ore and stone exploded into the tunnel, a bit of dust almost hitting me square in the forehead as I raised my arms to protect my face. He turned and smiled at me like a little kid with a new toy.

"More! Do all of them!"

I sighed.

Chapter 17

Sneaky, Sneaky

ANNOS STOOD TALL AT THE HEAD OF HIS SHADOWALKER army as they made their way through the dense undergrowth of the jungle. Behind them, a formidable army of lizard Saurites slithered and scurried, their eyes fixed on the prize—the Fekan city of Dunbar.

As they approached the city's outskirts, Annos signaled for a momentary halt. The second in command of the Saurites, a powerful and imposing figure known as Grendar, stepped forward, his scaled body gleaming in the dappled sunlight. Their leader stayed back in the city to guard the lizard families and non-warrior class. Annos didn't quite understand why he wouldn't want to be involved in the battle but let it slide.

"Grendar," Annos spoke, his voice laced with authority. "We have come to fulfill our alliance, to bring down the walls of Dunbar and secure victory."

Grendar nodded in acknowledgment, his eyes glinting in the sun. "Alpha Annos, we Saurites are ready to strengthen your cause. The time for the Fekan dominance ends today. We have many fallen Saurites that we seek to avenge in battle. Our scouts have returned, and things are looking promising."

Annos studied Grendar for a moment, assessing his resolve. "I appreciate your support, Grendar. Together, we shall reshape the destiny of these lands. Tell me, how do you plan to assist in the siege?"

Grendar's reptilian features twisted into a wry smile. "Our ability to burrow through the earth will be our greatest advantage. The Feka have built towering walls but have overlooked the ground beneath their feet. We shall undermine their defenses, strike from unexpected angles, and create chaos within their ranks."

A feral grin crept across Annos' face, his eyes reflecting the fire of determination. "Excellent. But remember, Grendar; we do not seek the eradication of their city. We shall coordinate our efforts, strike at their weak points, and ensure that the Feka fall before our might. Once we have secured our victory, we shall take over the city and use it for its exports and position on the gulf."

Grendar's gaze met Annos', the intensity of their shared purpose evident. "Agreed, Alpha Annos. We shall show them the price of their arrogance and offer them a quick death. But remember - we split the bodies among our people. You may keep the city, but we need the consumption power and the return of our hunting ground."

With their pact sealed, Annos and Grendar exchanged a nod of mutual understanding. They were united by a common goal—to overthrow the Fekan dominance and establish a new order. Together, they would unleash a force that would shake the foundations of Prixa, leaving a lasting mark on the history of these lands.

As the combined forces of the Stalkers and Saurites resumed their march toward the city, their determination resonated through the air. The echoes of their conversation faded into the jungle, leaving behind only the sound of footsteps and the rustling of leaves—a prelude to the impending battle. The destiny of Dunbar hung in the balance, and the clash of powers was inevitable. The lizards faded into the ground and took off in another direction.

A few moments later, a Fekan scout saw the werewolves from his tree and took off toward the city.

———————

Dee was jogging through the upper level of Dunbar, training her heart and regaining her stamina after her injury. Her stamina pool still only filled 25% of the total amount, filling a few percent higher with every long run.

As she reached the courtyard on the first level of the settlement, Dee spotted a scout waving his hands wildly to one of her fellow hunters. She ran over to see what was happening. Apparently, he had noticed an approaching army. He stood there, breathless and wide-eyed, his words tumbling frantically.

"They're coming! The enemy is marching towards us! A different pack of Shadowalkers from last time!"

Dee's resolve hardened, and she wasted no time. Her heart pounded in her chest as she raced through the bustling streets of Dunbar. She had to reach the walls, rally the defenders, and prepare for the imminent attack. Her eyes scanned the faces of the Feka, filled with determination and fear. Bells sounded behind her, the same alarm bells from a few weeks ago.

"To the walls! Prepare your bows! We may not have a draw-bridge, but we will defend Dunbar with our lives!" she yelled as she ran. Her heart rang out in pain, but she pushed through it.

The archers, well-trained and disciplined, swiftly took their positions. Their numbers had been refreshed as the Monarch sent reinforcements over the last few weeks. They notched arrows onto their bows, their eyes scanning the horizon for any sign of movement. Sounds were coming from the jungle, but no sign of activity yet.

A bitter reminder of the new Baron's foolishness loomed large. The absence of the drawbridge and the dismantled crossbow contraptions had left the defenders vulnerable. Undeterred, Dee turned her attention to the warriors gathered near the gates. She looked on as a white tiger, who had replaced Typh as male security head, spoke to his warrior Feka.

"Warriors of Dunbar! The time has come to defend our home, our people! Prepare yourselves for battle! Stand tall, fight honorably, and let the enemy know we will not yield!"

The warriors, their expressions resolute, roared and drew their weapons, forming a formidable line. Their swords gleamed in the fading light, reflecting their unwavering determination. They were ready to face whatever came their way.

As the tension thickened in the air, the distant sound of marching paws grew louder. The enemy was approaching, their intentions clear. Dee breathed in and out, steeling herself for the onslaught that awaited them. She ran up to the wall to look into the jungle, waiting to see what came through the tree line.

A group of around fifteen Stalkers came out of the trees first, their long wolf snouts the same as she remembered. They walked on their two legs, intelligent eyes observing the settlement. They began howling, and a new breed of melee troops emerged from the trees.

Hundreds of sleek, hairless dogs emerged from the woods. These creatures possessed powerful limbs adorned with razor-sharp claws that dug into the ground as they propelled themselves forward with remarkable agility. Their eyes, sharp and intelligent, gleamed with fierce determination. These hounds were a much different canine variety than the dumb Whitetooth beasts from before. The dogs in front of her looked to be able to outrun even an adult Feka.

Not good, she thought.

When the last dog cleared the trees, four hundred dogs stood before the settlement. *Not too bad!* Dee thought. They could handle a few hundred Shadowalkers and their Stalker masters.

The enemy stood there, unmoving. They didn't howl like they usually did. They just stared back at the Fekan city. They were still out of range of the archers, but Dee had no idea what they were waiting for.

The ground under the city began shaking. A slight tremor at first, but the shaking grew in severity until her whole body shook on the bouncing ground. The Feka looked at each other, unsure of what was happening. The Stalkers looked on, smiles suddenly creasing their long faces. "Steady!" Typh yelled, pacing behind the troops, their ears swiveling wildly as they looked around in panic at the unknown threat.

Suddenly, the ground exploded, and at least forty enormous lizards exploded out of the ground behind the line of Fekan warriors.

Inside the settlement.

Chapter 18

Like a Boss

I GRABBED THE NEXT TWO STEEL BARS FROM CRAIG AND walked over to the wall to get another pickaxe. My mana was at [41/60] from the ten mana I spent on the first pickaxe. I still felt exhausted, like I wasn't getting much mana regeneration in my post-prison state.

A sudden commotion erupted in the distance, and the air filled with the shrill screeches of cave bats. "Capes up! Capes up!" Craig yelled. The mages, ever vigilant in their duty, took off down the tunnels to protect the mine workers from the menacing creatures, forgetting about me for a moment.

Instinct took over, and without a moment's hesitation, I snatched the newly forged steel pickaxe behind me and the spare steel bars, my new 'Thievery' skill aiding my instinct to steal and run. "Noah! Get back here!" Craig shouted after me as I took off as fast as my feet could carry me.

I dashed down the tunnel, my boots pounding against the rocky ground. The passage was dimly lit, the flickering torches casting eerie shadows along the walls. I navigated the winding tunnels, the echo of the bat screeches growing quieter with each step. The sound of battle echoed off the walls, smoke filling the air around me.

I had told Mara my plan to make a device to block the mages from seeing what I was doing, and she wanted to help. We planned to meet further in the tunnel if a battle ever broke out. She wanted to go with me when I tried to put my escape plan into motion. I hoped she would keep to the plan. I waited, then finally heard her.

"Mara!" I yelled, seeing if she was nearby. "Mara?"

"Noah!" she answered back.

I saw her run past the tunnel I had run into. "Mara, wait! This way!" I screamed. She ran back, looking side to side, then saw me. She ran up to me, her eyes wild.

"This plan is just as crazy as I imagined it would be!" she said as we ran, an angry look on her face.

"Hey, it's working so far. Let's go!"

Our footsteps echoed as we stomped down the tunnels. No one chased us as we ran, preoccupied by the bat attack. The cave seemed endless, branching off in various directions like the intricate veins of a complex system. Yet, we pressed on, following an instinctual pull deeper into the heart of the underground realm. I started getting nervous that I would get lost down here.

The darkness enveloped us, and I finally pulled up to a stop. There was barely any light down here, so we couldn't go much further without bumping into rocks or a wall.

Occasional water droplets fell from the ceiling as a symphony of echoes reverberated through the caverns from the fighting further in. The scent of earth and dampness filled the air, intermingled with the musty odor of bat guano.

Off in the distance, an eerie purple glow filled the tunnel. "Wait here," I said, striking off toward the light.

"Where are you..."

I turned back to her. "It will be alright! That purple light is a mushroom that helps our vision. I'll be right back."

She scoffed. "Hey, Noah? Umm...your *pants* are glowing."

"Huh?" I said, confused. *The lunar moss!* I had completely forgotten about its storage in my pants. I took it out for the first time since grabbing it. It glowed merrily, casting moonlight in the dark cavern.

Mara gasped and came closer. "You are full of surprises, aren't you?" She had a smirk on her face, but I could tell she was impressed.

I smiled, then gave her the moss. "Hang on to this. I'll be right back. Let me grab some of those mushrooms."

She took the moss reverently, stroking the soft strands, and I turned to walk down the tunnel. When I got to the mushrooms, I picked one. I had never eaten any ingredients, but my create skill told me these were safe.

Experimentally, I popped one into my mouth. The cave instantly went into what I can only describe as a mix of 'Predator' mode, like the movie from Earth, and night vision goggles. Only instead of green, it was purple. I yelped, surprised by the change. Mara's form pulsed in the distance with red heat. "What?" she cried out, jumping. Suddenly, the voice lady told me what I already knew.

[NIGHT VISION ENABLED - TIME REMAINING - 5 MINUTES]

The mushrooms were scattered everywhere back here, and I picked a couple more, throwing them in my pocket. My Predator vision saw little heat masses gathering near the far wall as I turned around. I ran back to Mara, yelling. "Mara! Rats!"

She looked around, but I could tell she still couldn't see very well. I reached where she was and stood in front of her, waiting. There were more little heat masses now, ten or so, gathering just out of sight.

Suddenly, I heard *pop pop pop* as they started teleporting into existence. My heart pounded in my chest as the Skitteren appeared, their teleporting abilities allowing them to appear and vanish instantly. With a firm grip on the steel pickaxe, I swung at them, determined to hit these little bastards.

But the Skitteren were agile, darting around me with uncanny speed. Their sharp claws and fangs gleamed menacingly in the dimly lit tunnel, and their haunting screeches filled the air. I dodged their attacks, narrowly evading their slashing claws as I continued my assault.

Mara had retreated up the tunnel to my left but was chased by a few rats. One of the Skitteren managed to sink its fangs into her arm. Her pained cry cut through the air, fueling my determination to protect her from the little creatures.

My pickaxe hummed as I swung it, golfing one and blasting it into the tunnel wall, unmoving. Time seemed to blur as we engaged in a fierce dance of combat. I dodged their attacks, countering with calculated strikes of my own. The weight of the steel pickaxe felt natural in my hands, its powerful swing delivering blows that reverberated through the Skitteren's exoskeletons. One bit my neck as I screamed and threw it by the leg off of me.

Their teleporting abilities proved a formidable challenge, but I refused to let them gain the upper hand. I anticipated their movements, sensing the faint disturbances in the air that signaled their impending teleportation. The purple night vision helped. Before they teleported, their shapes started blurring, giving me a warning as the spell completed. With each disappearance, I readied myself, adjusting my stance and preparing to strike when they reappeared.

I looked back down the tunnel, and Mara had fallen to the floor, hands protectively over her head as three swarmed her. I dashed over and soccer kicked one, blasting it down the tunnel, then swung my pickaxe and managed to sever the head of one on Mara's chest. Its lifeless body collapsed to the ground.

392

"Damn, Noah! Not so close to my head with that thing!" she yelled from the ground.

"Sorry!" I said back. When I turned, the Skitterens had mainly vanished, a calm returning to the cave. I breathed in and out, my chest heaving.

"Are you okay?" I asked, holding out my hand. Mara nodded, wounded but alive, and I pulled her up. We exchanged glances, a mixture of relief and triumph passing between us.

A powerful presence filled the air as I stood there, catching my breath from the intense battle. The ground beneath me suddenly rumbled, and the rat boss materialized before my eyes. It was a towering creature with gnarled fur and glowing, evil eyes that pierced through the tunnel's darkness.

The rat boss's body was massive and muscular, adorned with sharp, jagged spines that protruded from its back. Its snarling snout revealed rows of razor-sharp teeth, and its long, sinewy tail twitched with anticipation. It emitted a low, guttural growl reverberating through the chamber, sending shivers down my spine.

"Mara! Run!" I screamed.

Suddenly, my eyesight returned to normal as my vision enhancement wore out. *Shit!* I thought as panic set in.

Mara turned and took off down the tunnel, taking the only light source we had now with her, but stopped when I didn't follow her. "Come on!" she yelled.

I turned back to the rat boss, squaring my shoulders. "Make my day, bitch!" I said, like all those weeks ago when I faced a meager squeamish squirrel with Typh. I hurriedly popped another mushroom in my mouth, and my vision enhancement spiked again, turning me into the Predator again.

[NIGHT VISION ENABLED - TIME REMAINING - 2.5
MINUTES - EFFECT 50%]

Crap, less duration now that I just ate one! With my heart pounding in my chest, I tightened my grip on the steel pickaxe. I could feel the weight of the moment, the magnitude of the challenge that lay before me. The rat boss lunged forward, its claws slashing through the air, and I braced myself for the fight of my life. But he went with a swatting motion as he dove toward Mara.

The rat beast is probably drawn to the lunar moss, I realized with fear gripping my heart. I swung at it and missed, and he tried to go around me and down the tunnel toward her. "Not so fast, big fella!" I yelled at it, the rat's head swiveling toward me and charging.

The melee training from Dee kicked in, and those days of sparring took over. Ducking and weaving, I evaded the rat boss's initial assault, narrowly avoiding its deadly strikes. Its immense size and agility made it a formidable opponent, but I refused to back down. I spun, returning a swing of my own. The rat blocked it with a spark from its claws.

The clash of steel against fur filled the chamber, echoing through the tunnels like a battle cry. I struck with all my might, pouring every ounce of strength into each blow. The rat boss retaliated with ferocious attacks, its claws swiping and teeth snapping dangerously close until one finally connected with my shoulder. I cried out in pain, but it was not a debilitating wound. The rat turned again and tried charging past me up the tunnel. I heard a scream as the orange heat blob that was Mara screamed out.

I connected with its leg from behind, and it screeched out a loud, piercing yell. I saw an opening. I jumped back from a wild blow from the ground and delivered a final, decisive strike, aiming for the rat boss's furry neck. The pickaxe connected with a resounding impact, severing its head from its body. The rat boss staggered momentarily, its life force fading, before collapsing to the ground.

Silence enveloped the chamber as the weight of the victory settled upon me. Sweat dripped from my brow, mingling with the dust and grime that coated my skin. My vision faded and returned to normal; the chamber bathed in the eerie moonlight of the moss.

The rat dissolved into the rock floor, leaving a long tail. I hurriedly picked it up, inspecting it.

[RAT BOSS TAIL - LEVEL 5]

Nice! I wonder if I can make an upgraded bow or something with this! I felt a fire lighting in my chest and realized something.

I had just leveled up.

Chapter 19

Journeyman

I CAUGHT MY BREATH AND FELT A SURGE OF ENERGY emanating from within. It was as if the very essence of my being was awakening, unlocking new potential. A soft glow enveloped me, accompanied by a faint tingling sensation. I felt a surge of power coursing through my veins, widening channels I didn't know existed. At that moment, memories and experiences flooded my mind. Everything I had crafted, every enemy defeated, every failure and every challenge overcome shaped me into the person I had become. The victories and defeats, the moments of triumph and moments of despair all contributed to my growth as an adventurer here on Prixa. And I felt it molding my skills.

I felt like the total of what I had done shaped what my level 10 skills would be. As the glow dissipated, I became acutely aware of the changes that had taken place. My senses felt sharper; my reflexes honed to a keen edge. It was like a veil had been lifted, revealing a world of possibilities and potential.

But it wasn't just physical attributes that had improved. My mind felt clearer, and my thoughts were more focused. I could tell that my skills had changed somehow, as the world looked different. My mind felt different.

Once the changes stopped flowing through me, the voice lady informed me about all of the changes.

[YOU HAVE LEVELED UP TO **BLACKSMITH JOURNEYMAN** - ADDITIONAL MANA AND HEALTH HAVE BEEN AWARDED]

[YOUR **CREATE** AND **MINE** SKILLS HAVE MERGED AND BEEN UPGRADED TO THE **MANUFACTURE** SKILL]

[YOUR **DESIGN** SKILL HAS BEEN UPGRADED TO THE **ENGINEER** SKILL]

[YOU HAVE UNLOCKED ANOTHER SKILL SLOT FOR A TOTAL OF SIX (6). UNUSED SKILLS HAVE BEEN AUTOMATICALLY ASSIGNED]

[YOU HAVE UNLOCKED A **PICKAXE** AFFINITY AND HAVE BONDED WITH YOUR WEAPON. ONLY ONE BONDED WEAPON CAN BE CHOSEN AT A TIME]

The tattoos burned my arm, morphing and shifting as new symbols appeared, replacing the old.

[NOAH]
[LV 10- BLACKSMITH JOURNEYMAN]

[HEALTH 46/85]

[MANA 63/95]

- L1

- L1

- Passive

- L1

- L2

- L2

Holy crap. Journeyman? What! Ore veins popped into view all over the cave, colors that I hadn't seen before. Some shallow and some deep. I could see even more of the ores now.

"Yes!" I cried, relief boiling over. Before I could inspect my new skills, Mara ran over, putting her hand on my back and checking me for injuries.

"Noah! Are you alright? That thing...what...and you..."

I looked up from my tattoos and over at her. She looked like she would speak again, but her voice failed her. She looked at the ground and started crying into her hands, the shock of the situation taking over. I pulled her into a big hug. We stayed that way for a few long moments. She looked up at me with unblinking tear-filled eyes. My heart, upgraded as it was now, beat rapidly in my chest. We looked at each other, neither one pulling away.

I just fought a rat boss and killed it. It was time to stop being a wuss. I leaned in and kissed her. Her head jerked back at first, and then she leaned into it. This was only the second girl I had ever kissed, but I let instinct take over. I had changed a ton since the overweight kid from Earth. And it felt amazing.

We pulled away slightly. "Sorry I dragged you into this. Are you sure you want to come with me? I may have started all kinds of trouble."

She nodded, and her cute smile shined at me in the moss-lit darkness. Our foreheads pressed together...

Wait! I thought. *The moss! I have everything for the scrying blocker now!* My head jerked back, and I looked around.

Mara saw my face, and her expression dropped. "What?" she asked, a self-conscious look on her face. Then her head jerked up, her eyes darting around, assuming more danger was coming our way.

"Oh! Nothing! I have to make something! Immediately! I have to make sure they can't find us until I get a plan together."

She nodded and backed up, the moment passing for now. I ran to the cave wall and started picking rat carcasses up. When I grabbed the fifth one, I walked back to Mara. "I need the moss back, if you don't mind," I said with my hand out.

She complied, putting it in my palm. Finally, I grabbed the two steel bars from my pocket, my hands a jumbled mass of ingredients. I concentrated, then combined the skills in my mind, wondering what the new skill did or if anything would change how I crafted things. All I knew was that the feeling was still there in my mind.

The ingredients glowed and molded together, flowing outwards into a long line. Mara gasped and backed up. The process finished, and in my hand sat a black leather belt. Embedded within the leather were intricately woven threads of enchanted silver, remnants of the lunar moss. I could tell that the threads possessed properties that disrupted scrying attempts. The silver lines formed an intricate pattern resembling ancient protective symbols, giving the belt a mysterious appearance.

I heard shouting up the tunnel. We had been spotted. I had made the belt too late. I quickly slipped it on anyway, then inspected it.

[SHADOWVALE'S SASH - SPECIAL ITEM - ANTI-SCRYING BELT]

Suddenly, I had another idea. I checked my mana. At [48/95], the fifteen mana was removed from the level three belt. I ran to a cave wall, reaching in and grabbing some temperstone ore. As I did, the ore from the wall *sucked* into my hand like I had an ore vacuum or something. One, two, three, then four pieces of the ore spit out of the cave wall and onto the ground. *Man, I'm super excited to see what these upgrades did.* For now, I needed to focus.

I picked up three pieces of the ore in one hand and held the pickaxe in my other, thinking about combining the two as the shouting got louder. Mara took off behind me to where the rat ingredient was and tried to duck into a side tunnel. She tripped, and I heard a loud *smack* as her knee hit something. Curse words sounded out.

The pickaxe glowed red hot, the head looking like burning coals. It stayed that way, casting an eerie red glow in the tunnel. I looked up and saw the first mage turn into our tunnel. "There he is! This way!" he yelled to the others.

I stood there, not backing down. Six mages turned down the tunnels. One even had a fire elemental with him. The air crackled with the energy of their fiery spells, but I stood firm, prepared to meet their assault head-on. The Porter addressed me. "Noah. By order of the Overlord, you are hereby apprehended for stealing from the city of Fulgar. Come with us peacefully, and no one will get hurt." He said that last part while looking behind me.

I laughed. "Yeah, that's a good one." I didn't say anything else.

They looked amongst themselves for a moment. "We take him alive!" the mage yelled to the others. One of the mages released a fireball at me, but I sidestepped it quickly. The other mage pointed his hand, sending the fire elemental in.

It floated down the hill and took a swipe at me. I let it connect with my armor so it would get close to me and heard a *hissing* sound, almost like it was being extinguished. I swung the new pickaxe, connecting with the elemental's arm. The beast was sucked into the pickaxe, completely gone from where it stood moments before.

I heard gasps from the mages and was actually stunned myself. I hastily inspected the pickaxe to see what in the world I had made.

[INFERNO'S EDGE (BONDED) - LEVEL 3 STEEL PICKAXE - TEMPERSTONE TAINTED - SPECIAL ITEM - ABSORB FIRE SPELLS UP TO YOUR LEVEL ONCE PER DAY]

I still needed to figure out the benefits of a bonded weapon. But I felt the bond. I could feel the weapon differently when I fought the rat boss. The mages looked on, unsure of what to do next. I could tell they didn't want to blast me with fire magic for fear of killing me and upsetting the Overlord. And now, they didn't know what my new pickaxe did. Finally, a mage walked closer to me, a manic smile forming under his hooded face. I recognized him. His fingers began glowing in the same way that they did all those nights ago in Dunbar. He was casting the fire circle spell so that I couldn't escape.

There was a loud *POP* as two huge figures appeared, looking around quickly. The mage's head jerked back in surprise, breaking his concentration and ruining the spell.

The Monarch had arrived.

Chapter 20

Zippy

THE MONARCH LOOKED UP AT THE SHOCKED MAGES AND strode forward. She addressed the starry-robed mage with a paw out. "You there. Porter. Tell your master that this human has an official alliance with the Feka and that further aggressive action toward him is an act of war on the Fekan Empire."

The black-robed mage walked toward her, scowling. "How have you found us, feline? You speak of acts of war, yet here you are, intruding on our settlement in a restricted area. I would watch your tongue."

Behind me, the cougar growled as his hair stood up. The mage brought up a good point, however. *How did they find us?*

"I will be taking the boy. He was still my property before you helped yourself to him. It was so *kind* of you to deliver him to us."

A knowing look crossed her feline features, and he frowned. "He stays with the Overlord. We earned him back with our involvement in the siege of your outlying settlement. Mages!"

Glowing wands shot out, and I heard a sigh from the Monarch. Daggers materialized in her paws, and she darted ahead faster than my eyes could see in the low light. A ring of fire formed around me, lighting the cavern and trapping me in place.

I knew my upper body would be safe from the blaze if I darted through it, but I wasn't sure what would happen to my head and legs. They weren't protected. I heard muffled screams and yelling as fighting broke out down the tunnel. Mara screamed behind me.

I stepped back and jumped through the fire without any more time to waste. I swung the pickaxe as I jumped, fanning some of the flames out of the way, but I felt the extreme heat scorching my legs and face. I let out an agonizing yell as I landed and lay there on the cold dirt.

"Idiot boy!" I heard over the commotion. My health bar was getting sucked into my head and legs horrifyingly fast. "Konna, now! Now!" I heard from up the tunnel. Suddenly, I couldn't breathe. It was like the air was sucked out of the tunnel. Paws picked me up and, seconds later, we blinked out of existence.

I heard a sizzling sound from my legs as we landed in a snowy landscape. I took a moment to take in my surroundings. The air was crisp and cold, filled with the scent of freshly fallen snow. Towering mountains loomed around us, their majestic peaks disappearing into the swirling clouds above. The landscape was blanketed in a pristine white, untouched and serene.

I lay there, afraid to look at my health bar. The snow beneath my boots and under my legs offered a soothing relief to my burns as if nature itself understood my pain. I could feel the coolness seeping through my skin, gently numbing the lingering ache. Eventually, the health bar turned idle, not absorbing any other injuries.

The scene was breathtakingly beautiful, almost ethereal. The mountains stood tall like ancient sentinels, their rocky faces adorned with jagged edges and veils of ice. Cascades of frozen waterfalls sparkled in the distance, their icy tendrils glimmering off the sun's rays. The landscape seemed untouched as if it had been preserved in its natural state for centuries.

"Are you alright, boy?" the Monarch asked, striding over to me. Her fur was singed in a few spots, and her left arm was hanging limp. Above us, the sky was a canvas of gray, pregnant with snow clouds. Fat snowflakes danced and twirled in the air, descending gently upon us like delicate whispers from the heavens. The silence was palpable, broken only by the whispers of the wind as it swept through the mountain passes.

"Yes, your highness," I said with a pained groan. I turned my gaze towards the Monarch, who stood over me, surveying my injuries with a mix of wonder and determination in her eyes. Her regal presence harmonized with the grandeur of the surroundings as if the mountains themselves recognized her authority. "What the hell happened back there? How did you survive all those mages? I saw what they did to the Shadowalkers. They're so powerful, and..."

The Monarch held up her hand, smiling. "Silly me, I thought I could take them on, but got a fire lance to the arm. I didn't want to use Konna if I didn't have to, but we didn't end up having much choice. His space magic skill can make a vacuum, which is a perfect counter to fire magic. It snuffed that fire right out, allowing us to escape. If you would have just *waited* a moment, we could have gotten you out too once we put the circle out."

I laughed. "Well, could have told me."

Beside us, the cougar remained vigilant, its emerald eyes scanning the surroundings. I sat up and saw Mara lying still on the ground beside me.

"Mara!" I yelled, attempting to stand.

The Monarch pressed me back to the ground with her paw, shaking her head. "Easy, boy. Your human friend is okay. They threw a fire lance at her too, but Konna threw a spatial shield in the way. The concussive force still knocked her out, but she will be fine."

I nodded, still in shock at these developments. *Damn, Konna is powerful,* I thought. Finally, I asked, "How did you find us? Where are we?"

The Monarch looked curiously at the belt I was wearing. "I was finally able to scry you. In the depths of the mine, you stepped out of the cloud that constantly shields Fulgar from prying eyes. When I looked in on your condition, I saw your plight. I decided that we needed to act and get our Creator back. I hope you don't mind our intrusion." A slight smirk crossed her lynx features, knowing that she had just saved me from what was most likely a horrible fate.

"I am in your debt, Monarch. I was drawing up an escape plan, but it...stopped around the escape part."

She laughed her meowing laugh at me. "Yes, it would appear as such. Some things never change."

I smiled at her, the well-deserved insult landing. "But where are we?" I looked at my arm to check on my health. It was surprisingly low, showing [15/85]. I would have certainly died jumping through those powerful flames if I didn't have my fire armor. *Idiot.*

She looked back at the cougar. "Unfortunately, we only had enough mana to get us into Fulgar and out. But with the little battle that took place, it would appear that this is as far as we could get. We will need to camp here tonight. I need rest to recover from the battle, and with the additional human girl to transport, Konna was forced to put us somewhere in the nearby mountains. He's a very experienced spatial warrior, but he does not have the mana depths the human mages have for teleportation after a battle."

I looked at her like she was nuts. "Monarch, you guys may have fur, but Mara and I don't. All I have is this *fire-resistant* armor and overalls. We will freeze out here!"

A knowing gleam formed in her eyes. "Then it's best if you use your new tool then, eh boy?"

My head jerked back, realizing what she was talking about. I crab-walked back to my pickaxe and picked it up, still sitting on the ground. It pulsed a fiery red, like embers in a fire. The pickaxe seemed to vibrate with magical energy, and as I held it in my hands, I could feel a strange connection forming, a bond between myself and this fiery being trapped inside.

With a flicker of anticipation, I released the being, and the fire elemental emerged from the pickaxe. A tiny thing, no more than a few inches tall, danced and flickered with an effervescent glow. Its form was ephemeral, resembling a miniature humanoid composed of dancing flames. As it materialized, it emitted a high-pitched squeak filled with excitement. The pickaxe seemed to reduce it to a much smaller version of the original elemental. While still a dark red, the pickaxe returned to metallic steel.

I watched in awe as the creature fluttered around me, its warmth comforting and exhilarating. It possessed a playful nature, darting and twirling in the air with boundless energy. The sight of this newfound familiar ignited a sense of wonder, and I couldn't help but smile.

I turned my gaze toward the Monarch, who observed the scene with amusement. Curious, her eyes sparkled as she watched the fiery creature flit about, casting a soft glow upon the surrounding snow. The Monarch's regal composure seemed momentarily softened by the enchanting display before us.

"Well, well!" she said. "Seems like you've got a new pet to care for!" She laughed again.

Behind us, a groan sounded as Mara woke up. She rubbed her head, clearly in discomfort. The fire elemental, sensing Mara waking up, zipped through the air toward her, its vibrant flames leaving trails of warmth. It circled around her head with an air of mischief. She screamed and shooed it away, scrambling up.

I laughed. "Mara, relax! It's okay. He seems friendly. She? Well, it. It seems friendly. Maybe I'll call him...Zippy."

Her chest was heaving as her eyes darted around her environment, then at me, then back at the fire elemental. "Noah, what part of this is okay? Who are *they?*" She pointed to the Feka and backed up a few steps.

I remembered the first time that I saw the talking cat creatures. It certainly was a shock. "They're friends. They saved us. Relax! It's going to be alright."

She seemed to calm down at that. "Well," I continued, "Other than needing to camp in the freezing cold. That might suck. But hey, Zippy, you want to help us get a fire going?"

He squeaked, *zipping* off into the nearby trees. I turned and smiled back at Mara. "Guess that's a yes!"

In the distance, a large pine tree burst into flames.

Chapter 21

Astral Mage

As we ventured deeper into the mountains in search for a campsite, our weary bodies sought refuge from the biting cold. The Monarch was planning to get us back to Fayport, which excited me. I had never been there and wanted to see it. She was also worried about potential threats to Dunbar, but wanted to know if the danger was verified.

While we walked, I inspected my new skills to see what information I could get, but it was brief since they were only level 1. The voice lady tried her best but didn't have much to tell me.

[MANUFACTURE - LEVEL 1 - SUBSKILLS UNLOCKED - ENHANCED ITEM CREATION - SPECIALIZATION NOT YET CHOSEN]

[ENGINEER - LEVEL 1 - SUBSKILLS UNLOCKED - MACHINERY AFFINITY - SPECIALIZATION NOT YET CHOSEN]

All in all, the skills sounded terrific. I was excited to see what specializations did and even what my level 1 subskills did. Building some cool machines and making enhanced items sounded particularly exciting. So far, my pickaxe was excellent, and the belt was a specialty item. I was off to a good start.

Eventually, we stumbled upon a cavern nestled within the rugged terrain. The cave yawned before us, its entrance framed by jagged rocks and draped with icicles that glistened like crystal daggers.

As we stepped inside, the atmosphere transformed. The air was thick with an earthy scent, carrying a hint of dampness. The cave walls were rough and uneven, and noise from a waterfall deep within the cavern echoed off the walls. We were safe from the wind in here, but not the cold. I saw no ore in the front of the cave but wondered what was inside.

Konna, in the best condition of the group of us, went into the wilderness to gather some firewood. We huddled together near the cave's center, where a shallow recess in the ground created a natural seating area. The fire elemental danced around us with its mischievous nature, casting its warm glow upon the cavern walls. Sensing our need for warmth, it eagerly awaited something to light aflame. Nobody spoke, our visible breath escaping our lips as we breathed in the cold air and shivered on the ground.

The cougar finally returned with his bundle of logs and sticks and dropped them into the middle of the opening, then curled up in the corner of the cave to sleep. Zippy raced over and eagerly lit the kindling, and soon a merry fire danced in front of us.

As the fire crackled and popped, the cave filled with a gentle warmth. Mara, ever inquisitive, turned to me with a questioning look. Her voice sounded hopeful as she posed her question. However, it wasn't the one I thought, since we still needed to breach the subject of the kiss.

"Noah, do you plan on helping me turn into a mage?" she asked, her voice laced with anticipation. *Well, that was blunt!*

I regarded Mara with a thoughtful expression, considering her words. "Well, that's up to you," I began, "I have an ability that can scan people and see if they can access magic. I already scanned you once before..."

She narrowed her eyes at me, looking insulted. "No!" I continued, trying to explain. "I scanned the whole bar at keg pop, you included. No one lit up with mana. But I can try again?"

Her eyes lit up as she nodded, and she scooted closer to me, waiting for my assessment. I closed my eyes and activated my 'PATRON' skill, seeking the subtle energies that lay dormant within Mara's being. As color bloomed before me, I was taken aback by what I discovered. Once empty of any mana according to my skill, Mara's aura now looked radiant white—pure and vibrant. I concentrated harder, wondering why the sudden change. But it was pure white—no doubt about it.

She frowned, seeing the confusion on my face. "What? Do I have the ability to unlock magic?" she asked, her shoulders slumping.

I opened my eyes and cut the skill off. I met Mara's gaze, my own eyes widening in amazement. "Mara, I can see your affinity," I said, my voice filled with awe. "You have a bright white aura! I think it's because I can see that mana type now!"

Mara's face lit up with surprise, and the Monarch cracked one eye open from her cat nap. "What does this mean?" Mara asked, her voice tinged with excitement.

"I dunno," I said with a shrug. "I haven't been at this for very long. My skill doesn't seem to know either..."

Suddenly, an idea hit me like a train. That lunar moss had felt really powerful. And when she held it, I remembered it curling around her hand. So far, only skills and such could be unlocked by holding ingredients, as I had seen from my experiences and my mages back in Dunbar. But you needed *items* to open classes.

I stood up and started slipping my new anti-scrying belt out of my overalls. Mara's head jerked back, surprised by the act. Her face turned a beet red. I noticed, chuckled awkwardly, and finished taking the belt off. "Don't worry. I'm not trying anything." It was a stupid joke, and we both laughed awkwardly. I could feel the Monarch roll her eyes at me, but she was fully awake now and watching us. I handed the belt to Mara.

She stood up, eye to eye with me now. She reached out, her fingers closing around the smooth surface of the belt, and anticipation pulsed through the air. The cave lit up like a Christmas tree as soon as it entered her hand.

White mana, radiant and ethereal, began to fill the cave, permeating every nook and cranny with its luminous essence. The air crackled with magical energy, and the very fabric of reality seemed to shift and tremble in response to the momentous event unfolding before us. My patron skill seemed to...smile? It was hard to explain, but my skill instantly leveled up to level 3. I could suddenly tell that unlocking a mage like this was a big deal.

A surge of power coursed through Mara, her body embracing the transformation with grace and confidence. She radiated an aura of serene command as if the very stars had celebrated her with their blessings. The cavern walls seemed to fade into the background, leaving only her luminous presence as the focal point of our attention.

Mara stood tall, her aura shimmering with newfound strength and purpose. Her hair turned white, and her now silver eyes gleamed at me. As she clasped the belt around her waist, a dazzling array of astral symbols materialized on the belt's surface, pulsating with radiant energy.

Sensing the monumental shift in the atmosphere, Zippy twirled and whirled with an added vigor, its flames dancing in joyous celebration. Its warm glow intensified, casting elongated shadows upon the cave walls, which seemed to bend and twist in response to the awakening magic. Konna and the Monarch had jolted up at the display and watched in awe.

Mara said her name out loud and looked at her arm. Then she looked at me and gave me that same *Mara grin* I liked so much. I grinned right back. "Holy shit."

"Right?" She was breathless as she stared back at me.

"Can I see your arm?" I asked her.

She held her arm to me, and I grasped it, looking over the tattoos.

[MARA]
[LV 1 - ASTRAL MAGE APPRENTICE]

[HEALTH 10/10]

[MANA 20/20]

 - L1

"Woah! You already have a skill! And that mana type..." I said, checking my arm. I had the same tattoo, next to my air, fire, earth, and space mana tattoos.

"Yeah, some voice in my head told me it was the 'Anti-Scrying' skill. I must have gotten it from the belt." She handed it back to me. "Guess I don't need this anymore if I have the skill!"

I took the belt back, putting it back around my waist. The Monarch stood up, peering curiously at the belt. "Fascinating. Child...this is an enormous blessing. Astral mages like us are few and far between. We almost as rare as your friend here." She jerked her head at me.

"We?" she asked, looking up at the Monarch.

She nodded. "Yes. I am in your class of mage as well, only the Fekan variety. While I don't have the Anti-Scrying skill, I can see possible futures." She didn't go into any further detail.

"Want to try it out?" I asked her, instantly interested in checking how Dee was doing. I had no idea how she was and hadn't asked the Monarch yet. In fact, I was curious how all of my friends and mages were doing. "Can you see far away things with your ability?"

Mara looked nervous. "I dunno, I think it's more of blocking enemies from seeing things. I don't have much mana though."

The Monarch walked over to her, placing her hand on her shoulder. She closed her eyes, and I smelled mana filling up the cave. Konna's eyes widened. "I will peer into the city with your help and teach you how to cast your mental sight to other locations. Human astral mages should be able to perform both skills, once I teach you. Come with me, child."

Mara grinned. "Sure. Let's see what we can do."

I was happy to hear how my friends were doing back in Dunbar. I was still really worried about Dee, and had no idea how my mages were faring. I hoped they continued growing their skills in my absence.

They sat facing each other in a lotus position, and Mara put her hands in the Monarch's paws. As Mara's eyes glazed over with a distant focus, her body went still, consumed by the power of her anti-scrying skill. The Monarch said, "Feel our connection and join me just above our bodies in the astral plane. Good child... Now follow me. It will take our combined effort to pierce their shield."

I watched her intently, sensing the weight of anticipation in the air. Suddenly, Mara's voice broke the silence, trembling with urgency.

"Monarch! What are we seeing?" she yelled, still frozen. The Monarch's body spasmed slightly, her face pursing together even harder.

"Pry their lock on Dunbar, child! Focus! We must move their mages aside to see the city! Something is wrong!"

I had no idea what they were talking about.

Mara's voice was laced with concern, "I can see Dunbar. It's like holding the planet in my hands. I found the city. It's surrounded by...some sort of cloud? A fog?"

"Yes!" the Monarch said. "Move it aside, and I will peer in with my skill!"

She focused harder. Suddenly, the Monarch spoke up again. "There is a battle there. The Feka are overwhelmed...there is an enemy!"

I gasped, as did the cougar beside me. I leaned in closer, my heart pounding in my chest as I listened to her words. The flickering flames from the fire elemental seemed to waver in response as if mirroring the turmoil I felt inside.

She continued. "Shadowalkers are rushing through the gates. Lizard men with long staff-looking weapons are fighting my kind. They're inside the walls," the Monarch continued, her voice filled with a mix of horror and determination. "It appears as though they have coordinated their attacks. They're allied, I think? The Feka are being pushed back. So many dead already..."

Her words painted a grim picture, and I couldn't help but clench my fists in frustration. The fate of Dunbar, the city we had come to know and love, hung precariously in the balance.

"Are there humans fighting? Anyone shooting them with fire or lightning?" I asked, confused.

417

The Monarch's voice quivered with desperation as she described the scene unfolding before her eyes. "No. I only see the Feka."

Mara's eyes snapped open, and she gasped. She grabbed her arm and grimaced. The Monarch's eyes also opened, terror there shining back at me. I pulled Mara close to me, the awkwardness forgotten. I could tell that she used all of her mana. She rested her head on my chest, breathing deeply.

A surge of determination coursed through me, and a fire kindled within my core. I couldn't stand idle while my friends in Dunbar faced such dire circumstances. The flickering flames of the fire elemental mirrored my resolve, their warmth urging me forward.

"We need to get back."

Chapter 22

Warhammer

THE MONARCH TURNED TO KONNA. "HOW MUCH MANA DO you need to get us back to the settlement?"

He spoke for the first time. "I have only gotten a quarter of my mana back, your highness. I will need tonight and at least half the day." It was already nightfall, and I knew we couldn't wait for morning to head out. With the way the werewolves fought, they were much stronger when the largest moon was out.

She growled. "That's not good enough. If memory serves, we are at least a two-day run from Dunbar. And that's at my speed. Our human friends couldn't hope to keep a pace like that." She looked at me with disappointment, her judgment of my race written all over her face.

A silence broke out between us while we thought. Finally, I spoke up. "Konna, could we get to the settlement? Just the two of us?"

He pursed his lips, then nodded. "Yes. We could make it. But that would strand the Monarch here for at least a full day."

I glanced at the Monarch. "I have an idea. But I need to get back to Dunbar for it. I can't tell you why because I was bound to secrecy."

419

She nodded, knowing what, or *where,* I was referring to needing to go. "I will guard your astral princess." She smirked. My face turned bright red, and I shuffled my feet.

Mara rolled her eyes, then embraced me. We locked eyes, and my heart fluttered again. She leaned in and whispered to me, "I'll be fine. Thank you, Noah. For everything." Then, quickly, she planted a kiss on my lips.

I savored the feeling and backed away, nodding to the cougar. With a squeak, the fire elemental entered the pickaxe, apparently coming along for the ride. With no time to spare, Konna grabbed my arm, and we blinked out of existence before I could change my mind.

I gasped, landing roughly on the rear of Dunbar's first level. It felt good to be back. My heart pounded in sync with the loud sounds of battle that filled the air. The scent of wet dog and swamp mixed with the metallic tang of blood filled the air, the heat pressing back down on me. This time, my armor cooled me slightly.

I turned to the majestic cougar, gratitude shining in my eyes. "Thank you," I whispered, my voice filled with sincerity. "Can you get my mages from the human bunker and send them to me? I don't know where their wands have been hidden, but maybe you can find them. It's time to cause a little chaos." With a nod of understanding, the cougar vanished into the shadows, its presence becoming one with the night.

Time was of the essence, and without hesitation, I set off toward the city's heart, my boots pounding against the cobblestone streets. The elemental shot out of the pickaxe, apparently coming and going when he wanted now, and followed, buzzing around the city in curiosity. The flickering flames from the little creature cast eerie shadows upon the crafting section of the settlement. It sounded like fighting was still down on the dirt level of the city, with growls and howls mixing with barking and...some new sound, perhaps from the lizard men.

Their sounds carried a primal quality, a unique blend of hisses, snarls, and guttural growls that reverberated through the air.

Their hisses were sharp and piercing, akin to the ominous warning of a coiled serpent.

The echoes of clashes and battle cries echoed through the narrow alleyways; each sound a testament to the ferocity of the conflict that engulfed Dunbar once more. No one was in the street up here, and I assumed it was all hands on deck below. Hopefully, my drawbridge still functioned.

I finally got to the smithy and burst through the door. Without wasting a moment, I darted towards the back of the workshop, where a few unique stones concealed the entrance to the secret basement. My hands trembled with anticipation as I fumbled for the hidden latch, feeling the rough texture of the stones beneath my fingertips. The latch gave way with a twist, and the entrance creaked open, revealing a descending staircase bathed in dim, flickering purple light.

An idea began to take shape within the recesses of my mind. Fueled by my engineering skill, the design table came to life before me. Its mental interface flickered to existence, ready to bring my vision to reality. I had a basic idea of what I wanted, but my skill took over, and I started designing.

Blueprints and schematics materialized, rotating and floating in the air as I examined them from all angles. My eyes danced across the mental controls, manipulating the virtual tools with precision and purpose. It was time to create something extraordinary—an iron breastplate with protection and attacking abilities. I wanted to combine my ability to make armor with my ability to shoot fire pellets.

The design process unfolded before me, reacting to my mind. My machinery affinity guided my choices, influencing the mechanisms and components I incorporated into the suit. With each modification, I ensured a blend of practicality and resilience. I chose how thick various parts were since I saw the cost of the parts I decided in real-time, allowing me to keep the costs within my realm of creation and not need some ingredients I had never heard of before. I could have made a suit out of steel, but the material costs weren't obtainable.

The suit took on a sleek aesthetic that looked like it could take a hit. Its surface gleamed with a metallic sheen in my mind. As I navigated through the design table's interface, I incorporated rotating joints with an option to boost them through friction reduction air magic, increasing my strength and agility. I could even add thrusters to the back from my air mana, allowing for swift aerial maneuvers and short bursts of high-speed move-ment. For now, however, I needed to keep this thing low-cost. I saved that design as "Iron Flying Suit."

I removed the air options for now; absolutely sure I wouldn't be able to afford the mana and material costs. Finally, I added flamethrowers to the base iron suit and arms by combining my fire wands. Well, fireball launchers. I didn't know any other spells than that. I put a tank in the back to store tinderstone ore, which was an option. My skill told me that the nozzles in the arms would convert the tinderstone into fireballs automatically for me and act more like fire cannons.

As I completed the design, the holographic blueprints converged into a single template, ready to be implemented in the physical world. It looked super cool. The world sped up again, and I gasped for air. I felt my 'ENGINEER' skill level up to 2. The workbench faded away as I cut the skill off, and a prompt showed me the cost of building this thing.

[IRON SUIT - IF **CREATE PROTOTYPE** SUBSKILL OF **MANUFACTURE** SKILL ACTIVATED - ONE TIME COST OF 20 IRON | 2X FIRE WAND | 10X TINDERSTONE ORE - COST 75 MANA - BUILD WILL LAST FOR ONE HOUR]

[IRON SUIT - IF **MANUFACTURED FOR GENERAL USE** - COST OF 60 IRON | 30X TINDERSTONE ORE | 5X STEEL - COST 200 MANA]

I listened to the prompts, unsure of what the hell just happened. Before, I would just create something. But now, my new manufacturing skill had subskills I could utilize, depending on who would use the product. The first one sounded like I could use fewer materials and make the suit for testing. One-hour durability sucked, but that was what I needed anyway.

I assumed the second option was for when I wanted to outfit fellow mages with this thing or when I built equipment or machines later. For now, I looked at my arm and checked my mana. I had recovered some from the belt and the fight in the cave but had spent about ten mana engineering the suit and was at [29/95]. *Crap. Not enough.* I raced up the stairs and dug into my locker, shocked to see the mana bracer. I slapped it on and chose the mana upfront option, but with my new levels, I got 40 mana shot into my veins and 20 over an hour, increasing from the 20 and 20 from the last time I used it. Mana poisoning would be worth it; after I was done with all of this, I would rest. Then, I rummaged around in the tree locker and grabbed some living tree branches for the wands.

I sprinted back downstairs to the forge and dug for iron bars. Each iron bar usually represented four iron in my prompts, so I needed to find five. I grabbed a few tinderstone bars, again representing the materials I needed for two wands and the tinderstone tank. I placed my hand on the anvil, making the two wands for five mana each. Next, I could make the suit for half price, which was 38 mana.

I closed my eyes and concentrated. The ore jumped off the anvil and onto my chest, fanning to cover me—a joint formed, then the arms. Finally, the tank sprung into life on my back.

With the iron part done, two nozzles emerged from the arms of my suit, glowing an ominous red color. Finally, the tinderstone bars broke apart, and I felt the tank get heavier, making clanking sounds as it was filled.

I took a deep breath, my chest wheezing as I adjusted to the weight of the suit. There wasn't a mirror down here, but there was one up in the living quarters of the smithy. I walked up the stairs, careful not to bang the new tank on the tight stairwell, and emerged into the main level. In the back of my mind, a one-hour timer ticked down ominously.

"Noah!" a voice yelled. I jumped, my heart racing. I looked up and saw the smiling face of Jasper. He started running over, but his eyes shot open. "What the hell is that thing you're wearing?" he yelled.

I laughed, turning to the mirror. I looked incredible. The tank looked straight out of a 1950s submarine movie but was more slender than I thought it would be. The armor was metallic, reddish, and the glowing three-inch nozzle tips looked menacing. Actually, I looked closer to the Warhammer 40k flamethrower characters, only without the massive guns.

I grinned at him. "Let's go burn up some lizards."

Chapter 23

Spray and Pray

THE OVERLORD PACED HIS OFFICE AS HE PEERED INTENTLY into the depths of his scryer mage's projection, his eyes fixed upon the unfolding chaos within the besieged city of Dunbar. Somehow the creator had escaped, but for the first time in his life, he couldn't see how Noah had slipped through his fingers. His scryers had never been blocked before. *They* did the blocking. Now he couldn't find the Monarch or the girl that went with them either. Perhaps they were out in the prairie somewhere. *No matter,* he thought. They will be too late to do anything about the battle's outcome.

The old scryer before him had one of the last pieces of sight power from the old days of creation. The sight blockage must have had something to do with his little stroll out in the wilderness. Noah must have created something new. *I should have searched him before I put him in the dungeon,* he thought bitterly.

At least the new alpha was holding up his end of the bargain. He had gathered an army of what appeared to be lizardmen; their staff attacks were mildly effective against the Fekan warriors. The new alpha didn't have many fox creators in his pack, so he must have gone with the earthen warriors to subvert the walls of Dunbar instead of using the siege equipment he saw from the

425

Matt Pivots

previous alpha's attack on the city. A clever move. It was a quick way to attack without waiting on bulky siege equipment.

And his steel production would begin in earnest, outfitting the warriors of Fulgar with weapons that had never been seen before in this world. He already had around one hundred blades. His blacksmiths just needed to finish them.

They would finally be able to stand their ground against the monsters of Prixa. Overall, not a bad outcome. He just knew this boy from Earth was trouble and could get in the way of his plans.

The new Baron was nowhere to be found either, most likely too ashamed of his actions to watch this all unfold. He had been paid well for his treason against his kind, but that probably didn't make it any easier. The fight would go smoothly with the human mage threat locked up in the bunkers.

The gates of Dunbar swung open from the inside, revealing the formidable Saurite lizardmen who had emerged from the very ground within the city's confines. The front lines continued fighting while the back line dealt with the gate for their canine allies. Their scaly forms moved with an unsettling grace as they clashed against the warrior Feka, their swords clashing against the lizards' staffs in a symphony of iron and wood. After the initial shock attack, the Feka recovered, forming a defensive formation against the troops. Still, half of the warriors had been slain, their bodies littering the dirt of the lower settlement.

The assassin group of Feka had yet to show themselves, most likely saving their attacks for when the Shadowalker generals entered the fight toward the end. Archers had been trying to pepper the back lines of the lizardmen, but they held up crude wooden shields and warded off most of the attacks.

The archers turned their attention to the sleek hairless dogs who sprinted toward the now-open gates. These hairless dogs had long, slender tails and moved like water flowing down the hill. They zigged and zagged, making for impossible targets for the archers to hit.

426

Another clever move. The Overlord was impressed with this new alpha.

But then, a figure emerged from the chaos. It was blurry to their scrying sight, blocked somehow in a dense fog. The figure stood firmly on the wall of the first level of Dunbar above the fighting below, its presence an unexpected twist in the battle's narrative. The war seemed to pause momentarily as the Feka saw whatever stood there, shocked looks on their furry faces.

Suddenly, pellets shot forth from the upper level, streaking through the air toward the back line of the Saurites. As the shots made impact, a few lizardmen were consumed by searing flames, their scaled bodies engulfed in a blaze ate at their scaled bodies. However, the Overlord observed a lack of precision in the attack, with the wild shots missing their targets more often than not. Fires bloomed from sections of wall and dirt, creating an eerie landscape of flame. A few more lizards and two or three dog creatures had caught flames, unmoving on the ground.

Yet, the battle was not confined solely to the figure's entrance. Those wretched fire mage humans of Dunbar inexplicably emerged from the city's depths, somehow escaping the prison and joining the fray with their mastery of flames. Fireballs roared through the air, crashing into the back ranks of the lizardmen and out into the dog pack. The Shadowalker melee troops that had run through the walls had been caught in some of the fire, and the hairless dogs burned up as well. But the Stalker generals had hung back, unsure what to do now. The alpha looked on in anger, his carefully designed plan now literally up in smoke.

The warrior Feka had retreated from the fight, scrambling up to join them on the upper levels of the settlement, while most of the lizards had fled underground to escape the flames.

The sky flickered with bursts of fiery brilliance, illuminating the ferocity of the struggle below. The air seemed to shimmer with the heat and intensity of the magical flames, casting an eerie glow upon the battlefield. The lizards, surrounded and unable to match this new threat, retreated outside the walls below ground.

As the battle finished, the Overlord cursed, sending books flying angrily into the wall. His scryer's eyes shot open in fear at the outburst, the spell fizzling out. He didn't need mages to tell him who the shrouded figure was.

It appeared he had been thwarted again by a teenage boy.

The enemy scampered away, dogs through the woods, and lizards through the ground. My head was absolutely killing me after using this damn suit. Each shot required one mana, most likely to convert the tinderstone into a fire pellet. The shots came out way too fast and were all over the place. I ran through my mana in about three seconds, then I was irrelevant until the bracer replaced a mana. I don't know what would have happened if the battle hadn't shocked the enemy and sent them retreating away. At least my mages had helped. Regardless, it was a great start. I was glad I could make prototypes before spending massive mana on something that wouldn't work too well.

I unclasped the heavy suit from the front and slid it off, the metal making a loud banging noise as it hit the stone pavers below me. I had a numb feeling that started spreading across my body from the lack of mana, but the bracer still had a while left before it stopped and the mana poisoning kicked in for the day.

As the battle subsided and the dust settled, I found myself standing amidst the survivors, the Fekan warriors looking at me with both shock and awe through the smoke. The human mages, their faces marked with soot and determination, knelt before me in a display of reverence. The city was quiet around me, the only sounds coming from the birds in the trees. A wave of awkwardness washed over me, uncertain how to respond to their unexpected adulation.

I cleared my throat. "Guys, you can stand," I said to the crowd of people kneeling in front of me. They looked confused, and slowly stood up. "This was a team effort. You guys were awesome out there."

Ever the exuberant presence, Dee rushed towards me out of her hunter hiding spot, her eyes wide with excitement. "Noah! You're back!" she exclaimed, her voice filled with relief and joy. She leapt up to the upper level and embraced me in a hug.

I offered a faint smile, glad to see a familiar face amidst the chaos. "Dee! You're okay!" I replied, my voice tinged with gratitude and exhaustion. "It's good to see you too."

But as her excitement and the gravity of the situation converged, I could no longer ignore the pressing question that hung in the air. I turned to face the assembled warriors and mages, my expression filled with genuine concern. "Why were the mages locked up?" I asked, my voice firm. "Where's Typh?"

The Fekan warriors exchanged glances, their expressions mixed. Some warriors wore expressions of anger, with hatred boiling over on their faces. Others wore expressions of guilt. One of them, a seasoned veteran with scars etched upon his weathered face, stepped forward. I had never seen this white tiger before.

"We...we thought the mages were responsible for the troubles that befell our land," he admitted, his voice tinged with remorse. "Fear clouded our judgment, and we locked them away for our own protection under the direction of this settlement's new Baron. Typh, after his continued insurrection, has been moved to Fayport to serve the warriors there."

A pang of empathy shot through me, understanding their misguided actions. The fear and uncertainty that had gripped their hearts in the face of the unknown had led them down a path of mistrust. I couldn't imagine what it had looked like when four humans decimated a pack of werewolves, then took me with them. Sketchy wouldn't even do it justice.

I took a deep breath, letting my empathy guide my words. "The mages are not our enemies," I declared, my voice stern yet compassionate. "We must unite our strengths to face the threats looming over us. Something is happening, and I think the Feka are in grave danger. I have returned to the settlement with a warning for the Baron. I need to speak to him." *Man, I was improving at this whole 'addressing big crowds' thing!*

Suddenly, a thought hit me like a ton of bricks. Without saying a word, I took off toward the ramp, leaving my iron suit behind. "Noah, where are you going?" I heard Jasper yell after me.

I sped down the ramp and onto the dirt path below, excited. My eyes darted around wildly, smoke and burnt earth making it hard to discern anything down here. Finally, I saw what I was looking for.

I raced over, a clawed hand sitting there in the moonlight. I took a deep breath and picked it up.

[YOU HAVE UNLOCKED EARTH MAGIC]

END OF ACT II

Interlude II

The Baron sat nervously in his opulent chamber within the Fekan palace, his mind clouded with fear and uncertainty. The recent turn of events had left him shaken, and the weight of the impending consequences bore down upon him. The victorious cries of the Feka outside only amplified his anxiety. He was a traitor.

"The Overlord will be furious," the Baron muttered to himself, his voice barely above a growling whisper. "How did those humans manage to escape?"

He had been ready to leave by the secret escape passage, but the smoke and flames had caught his attention. He couldn't understand what fire contraption the human had worn that caused so much damage.

As he pondered the unsettling questions, a sudden disturbance shattered the silence of his chamber. The air crackled with energy, and before him stood a Porter; the same one that visited him a few moons ago. The Baron's heart skipped a beat, for he knew the Porter only appeared in such a manner when delivering grave news from the Overlord himself.

"The Overlord is... upset," the Porter said, his voice barely audible. "He demands immediate action. You are to arrange for the elimination of this human, Noah. He has become too powerful and has gained the support of formidable mages. The Overlord sees him as an enormous threat to his plans that must be eradicated."

The Baron's blood ran cold, and his breath caught in his throat. Thoughts raced through his mind, colliding like shards of glass. He couldn't help but wonder how the tides had turned so drastically against him and his people. The humans, even with their magical powers, were weak. And yet somehow they had managed to gain enough power and influence to escape their confinement during battle and turn the battle against him. The weight of the Overlord's words pressed upon him, threatening to crush his very spirit.

Fear etched itself onto the Baron's face as he looked into the Porter's eyes, his voice trembling as he growled out his answer. "I... I understand," he managed to say, his words laced with terror. "I will do as the Overlord commands. The human...Noah, he will be dealt with swiftly."

The Porter nodded, his eyes narrow and unforgiving. "And the mages?"

"Locked away with help from my warriors," he responded.

With a wave of his hand, the Porter vanished from the chamber as quickly as he had appeared, leaving the Baron alone with only the sounds of a fountain gurgling nearby.

As the reality of the situation settled upon him, the Baron's mind raced, contemplating the dark path ahead. He knew the stakes were high and the consequences of failure dire. The Overlord's wrath was a force that brooked no resistance, and the thought of crossing him sent shivers down the Baron's spine.

His thoughts were abruptly interrupted as a soft knock resounded through the chamber, and he jumped halfway to the ceiling, his feline startle reflex propelling him into the air. "What?" he yelled angrily.

The door creaked open, revealing a figure cloaked in shadows. It was his trusted spymaster, whose loyalties were firmly aligned with the Overlord.

"I was told to see you, my lord?" the figure spoke with a voice dripping with treachery, its tone conveying a twisted pleasure in the Baron's predicament.

The Baron swallowed hard; his mouth parched as he struggled to form his words. "I...I have received the Overlord's command," he managed to say, his voice trembling. "Noah, the human, must be eliminated."

A sinister smile curled upon the lips of the figure, their eyes gleaming with a twisted delight. "Ah, the Overlord's wrath is swift and merciless," they hissed. "Fear not, sire. I have a proposition that may aid you in this task. Fortunately none of the Feka or humans here know of your loyalty to the Overlord."

The Baron's gaze locked with the figure's, a glimmer of hope flickering within his eyes. "'Tell me," he implored, his voice barely above a whisper. "What must we do?"

The figure leaned closer, their words a hushed whisper. After the plan was laid out, the figure's malevolent grin widened, a wicked pact silently forged between them. The Baron nodded. "Let it be done."

Hundreds of miles away, Mara opened her eyes, gasping for breath.

Chapter 24

Do Better

THE BELLS SOUNDED THROUGHOUT DUNBAR AS I STOOD there, surrounded by humans who had emerged from the safety of the bunkers, their eyes filled with awe and gratitude. They knelt before me like the fire mages had, their expressions reflecting the weight of their newfound hope. It was a sight that unnerved me. I quickly got everyone to their feet.

My intentions had always been simple—to survive this place, grow stronger, and try to find a way back to Earth. Yet, in the chaos and despair that had gripped Dunbar, my actions had garnered a level of admiration that made me uncomfortable. I had never sought this role of savior and didn't believe that I deserved the reverence they presented me.

I noticed the new Baron emerging from the palace, a crooked smile playing on his lips. I had not met this Feka before, and he did not look to be a warrior in any way. Jewels adorned almost every inch of his fur, and he wore simple leather armor with a sword strapped to his belt. He approached me with false sincerity, putting on a show for the watching crowd.

"Thank you, Noah," the Baron spoke with gratitude, his deep growling voice strained. The heads of the humans swiveled around to see him, fear in their eyes. *Odd,* I thought. "Your strength and leadership have saved us all. Thank the moons you have returned in time."

My gaze narrowed, skepticism coloring my thoughts. I couldn't believe the Baron would lock the mages away, fear of humans or not. They were a powerful counter to the Shadowalkers, and not using them had put his people in grave danger.

But, for the sake of unity and the greater good, I chose to engage him in conversation, concealing my distrust beneath a veneer of civility. "Well, you're lucky that the battle didn't reach the upper levels or the palace walls where you watched the battle. I'm not sure you would have survived if that happened." *Oops. Maybe a bit harsher than I wanted.*

The Baron's smile strained further. "Indeed, I was ready to fight alongside my people, but I am no warrior like the previous Baron in charge here," he replied smoothly. I caught a few Fekan hunters exchanging skeptical glances. "But your presence, Noah, turned the tide in our favor. Your skills and determination have given us a chance to reclaim our freedom. Perhaps I was wrong about you and your fellow humans."

"Well, not all humans. The city that I was taken to attacked your Monarch. She told them it would be an act of war, but they did it anyway." Looks of shock crossed many Fekan faces. There was a pause—a pregnant silence that hung in the air. I knew there was much left unsaid between us. But I had to tread carefully, playing the diplomatic role in this delicate dance of power. I was never good at finding the right thing to say, but I was learning quickly.

Still standing beside me, Dee shot daggers at the Baron with her eyes. *Something was going on here,* I thought. But it was late, I was exhausted, and my bracer had run out. My whole arm was numb, and I couldn't wait to sleep.

"Maybe we can speak privately tomorrow once things have settled down around here?" I asked.

The Baron nodded enthusiastically. "For now, all human mages place your weapons in the crate, as per protocol. I will need to think about your place here in the city."

"What!" I exclaimed. "Why? They just saved the city!"

He smiled, shaking his head. "Noah, I have my people's safety to consider. Your mages are getting quite powerful, as they just displayed for everyone. We just lost many of our warriors. It is a precaution that I must take for now."

Then, without further conversation, he turned to walk back toward the palace. A few warrior Feka flanked him, armor gleaming in the moonlight. A snow leopard marched forward, addressing the crowd of humans. "Okay, everyone. All humans assigned to night duty, begin cleanup. Everyone else, drop your weapons here and return back to your living quarters."

He waved his paws, and the crowd slowly dispersed, hushed murmurs breaking out. As people walked past me, I received a lot of smiles and nods. Some looked over at my iron suit with curiosity, but didn't say anything. The device would probably be around for another couple of minutes before it...disappeared? Exploded? I didn't know what would happen at the end of the one hour.

Romas came over to me and looked back over his shoulder. He put his paw on my arm, smiled, then said, "Welcome back, boy! I assume you have a hell of a story to tell me?"

I nodded. I couldn't wait to tell him about my creations, the work to create steel, and even my newest revelation of unlocking earth magic. "It's been a long few days. But I need to find someone. He..."

Suddenly, a figure emerged from an alleyway nearby and waved. He nodded at me from behind Romas' back and returned to the shadows. I looked at Romas and Dee, holding up a finger. "Hang on. I'll see you back at the smithy. Just give me a couple of minutes. I have to do something in private." They looked at each other, confused, shrugged, then headed toward the blacksmith. Everyone looked utterly wiped from the stress of the battle.

I waited a moment, the settlement's upper level clearing out. Finally, I walked into the shadows of the alleyway. Leaning against the stone was an exhausted-looking Konna. He spoke in a hushed, growling whisper. "Pretty amazing, human. That was quite the device you made."

I smiled at him. "Yeah, I just wanted to try something. It worked okay, but I have a lot of tweaks to make."

He nodded. "Before you say anything else, just know that it is within the power of those I saved you from to be watching. Even with the help of your belt, or your princess, we cannot truly hide our intentions from our enemies." He looked around and then made a funny motion with his paw. *My princess,* I thought, chuckling to myself. "Just know, I will take care of it. I estimate I can go tomorrow night, then return sometime the next day or two."

"Will they be okay?" I said, following his lead and keeping the conversation broad.

"Yes," he said but didn't say anything else. I nodded. As I turned to leave, he continued, "But human...there is something afoot here. This settlement was much too easy to take by our enemies. I wish that I had not been in Fayport for the past few moons. Had I been here the whole time..." He trailed off, but I got his meaning.

"I will be careful," I replied. Konna held out a paw, and I grasped it, then turned back to the smithy as he faded back into the shadows again.

Outside the gates, the pack of Shadowalkers continued trotting through the jungle, flanked by the lizardmen. Finally, a reasonable distance from that cursed town, the leader of the Saurite lizardmen seethed with frustration as he called Annos to a halt.

The once confident and imposing figure now bore the weight of failure upon his scaly shoulders. He would have to go back to Gornak with shame. He had been blessed with this chance to show his leadership and had failed his people.

"You said it would be easy!" Grendar hissed, his voice laced with anger and accusation. "You promised that the Feka would crumble before our combined might. Yet, here we stand, defeated and humiliated."

Annos' eyes flickered with resentment. "Don't place the blame solely on me," he retorted, his voice growled out. "Your Saurites failed to deliver the decisive blows we needed. Your warriors lacked the ferocity we expected. After your sneak attack, the Feka defended against your lizards and their sticks!"

The wolf seemed to grow before him, basking in the moonlight. Grendar had to be careful. This beast could rip him limb from limb. However, he was not weak...nor were his people. Nostrils flared with anger, his tail lashing back and forth in agitation as his forked tongue shot out in a *hiss*. "Do not dare to question the prowess of my warriors," he spat out, baring his fangs menacingly. "Your deal with the Overlord brought upon our failure. His plans cannot be trusted, as we told you before. They let the fire mages loose on purpose!"

Amid their heated exchange, a voice cut through the cacophony, silencing the bickering leaders. A human with black robes emerged from the shadows, silencing the debate. "Fools! It was neither of those things." The newcomer looked up at the two leaders, shorter than them by almost a foot. But he did not back down and showed no fear of being surrounded by beasts on all sides.

He continued, narrowing his eyes. "The human Creator found a way to escape our city of Fulgar and release the mages. It was he who brought upon the failure of your advances. But fear not; I have set things in motion to secure his departure from this world."

439

The alpha turned on the human, rising to full height. His fur stood up, displeased at being spoken to in this manner. He growled, blackened teeth showing as his lip quivered in the darkness. "Why should we trust you, *human scum?* Your Overlord has proven inefficient time and time again."

The lizardman nodded along with the alpha. The black-robed human strode forward, standing chest-to-chest with the werewolf. "Ever since the human, Noah, landed near the Feka, our plan has backfired in bringing him here. Because of his alliance with them, he is no longer useful to the Overlord and must be wiped off the planet, along with his mages and feline friends. Otherwise, we are in the same grave danger as your race, *Shadowalker.*" The mage basically spit the last part out. "The Overlord assumes that the original accord he struck with you still applies?"

The alpha nodded. It was a very nice deal indeed. After their defeat, ownership over the Fekan territories would make him wealthy beyond belief. The Saurites could have the swamp, and with his ownership over the jungles, he wouldn't have to worry about his pack going without food. The beasts of the jungle would be his, and his alone. He did not need to see the humans on the other side of the world again. They could go their separate ways. And if he found an ally to counter the fire mages here, they could also counter the ones at Fulgar, should they get any *ideas.*

"Good. We will handle our business with the cursed human. The Overlord requires you to do better than these..." he trailed off, looking at the lizardman in disgust. "...reptiles. We need an ally who can ward off fire attacks. Creatures who can defend us against their primary weapon. We must stop our enemies before they grow stronger."

The two leaders glanced at each other, their hatred momentarily set aside as they contemplated the Fulgarian's words. They knew the human spoke the truth—their fractured alliance would only play into the hands of their adversaries. Annos still needed the lizards and would keep his word to them when this was over.

They were undoubtedly handy and proved that in the last battle.

Taking a deep breath, the alpha reluctantly nodded, his pride begrudgingly giving way to reason. "Fine, human. Tell your master that we will continue our search for allies," he conceded, his voice tinged with a hint of humility. "We must find a way to work together once more, to strengthen our forces and reclaim what was lost."

"We will recover our strength and be ready when called upon," the lizardman said. He nodded to his warriors and they broke away from the group.

The human nodded, satisfied. "Look to the skies. There may be those, long ago forgotten, that can help. But they require...large sacrifices. Your journey for power must be worth the cost."

The alpha looked among them, most of his pack already far into the jungle now, with only a few choice Stalkers hanging back. The lizards looked on with unchanging expressions across their faces. "Power is all that matters here."

And with that, the human nodded and blinked out of existence.

Chapter 25

The First Cut's the Deepest

I LAY IN MY COT, THE HEAT OF THE SMITHY COMFORTING after being gone for what felt like ages. Jasper snored beside me, but it had been a fun night of storytelling. I was exhausted, but I couldn't help but tell my old friends what had happened. I only got into whatever detail the Overlord already knew since I was sure he could keep tabs on me without focusing on me. I hoped Mara could make it here soon...not only to have her with me but to see how she'd be able to help.

I hadn't had much time to think about the whole Mara situation. I was really into her, and I assumed she returned the feeling. But everywhere I went, danger seemed to follow. I didn't mean to get her wrapped up in all of this, but unlocking a rare magic class in her...well, she didn't have a choice now.

I again looked at my character sheet, basking in my five mana tattoos. My arm was really starting to fill up.

[NOAH]
[Lv 11 - BLACKSMITH JOURNEYMAN]

Matt Pivots

[HEALTH 90/90]
[MANA 8/100] [MANA POISON - DURATION 1.22HR]

- L1

- L1

- Passive

- L1

- L2

- L2

[UNSELECTED SKILLS - NONE]

Thankfully, my mana poisoning was almost over. I felt horrible, with a pounding headache and a dead arm. Looking over my sheet, though, I was delighted. Notably, my manufacture and engineer skills leveled up, along with my patron skill. Using the mages in battle satisfied conditions to level it up. And, of course, an incredible fireball-shooting iron suit leveled my other two.

The most exciting development was my earth mana. I had no idea what I wanted to try first with it, but I always wanted a spear. But now that I had my enhanced pickaxe, I didn't know what I wanted to do. I identified my manufacturing and engineering skills to see if I had any more information about them now that I had leveled them up.

[MANUFACTURE - LEVEL 2 - SUBSKILLS UNLOCKED - ENHANCED ITEM CREATION | CREATE PROTOTYPE - SPECIALIZATION NOT YET CHOSEN]

[ENGINEER - LEVEL 2 - SUBSKILLS UNLOCKED - MACHINERY AFFINITY - SPECIALIZATION NOT YET CHOSEN]

Nothing new there other than my prototype skill. I would head to the design table and explore the earth mana later on, once I had some mana. The fire element was resting in Jasper's cot with him, its soft glow lighting the cramped living space as they cuddled. I wasn't jealous when Zippy had taken to Jasper right when they met. *Okay, maybe I was a bit.* Still, I could never get mad at that kid.

Speaking of my fire mages, they looked incredible. They had all gotten at least three or four levels since I had gone, and their confidence was tremendous. I would have to use my patron skill and see where I could help them or what equipment they needed. The list was long. I felt very uneasy at their treatment by the Baron, but I understood his concern. It would be one hell of a fight if we turned on them.

Eventually, the warmth of the building helped me fall into a deep sleep.

———

The sounds of raised voices drifted into my ears, jolting me awake from a much-needed rest. With a groggy mind and heavy eyelids, I rose from my slumber and stumbled toward the commotion.

Rubbing my eyes to clear away the remnants of sleep, I peered through the slightly ajar door, my gaze falling upon Romas engaged in a heated argument with the Baron. Their faces were flushed with anger, their words laced with frustration. Despite the exhaustion that still clung to my bones, I knew I couldn't retreat back to the comfort of my cot. Conflict seemed to follow me wherever I went, like an unwelcome shadow.

As I approached, Romas caught sight of me, his eyes momentarily diverting from the Baron. He gestured for me to join them, a mix of weariness and determination etched upon his face. With a resigned nod, I stepped forward, prepared to face whatever dispute had ignited their tempers.

The Baron's voice carried a note of authority as he argued his point, his words echoing off the surrounding walls. Romas, however, stood his ground, his voice resonating with the firmness of someone who had weathered countless trials. Their disagreement revolved around resources and aid allocation after the recent battles and what to do with me.

"If you guys are going to talk about me behind my back, at least do it somewhere that I can't hear the conversation," I said, and both Feka glanced back at me. I smiled at them. "Morning, fellas. How are we doing today?"

"Noah, I was just about to wake you," the Baron said. "We need to continue our discussion." The Baron flashed me that strained, crooked smile again.

Romas bristled. "I think he is needed in here today. We need to begin work on reinforcing our town and returning it to how it was *before*."

I held up a placating hand. "I can hear him out, Romas. I'll be right back. I'll meet you back here in a bit, okay?"

He pursed his lips, then nodded, retreating toward the back of the smithy. Jasper had woken up and was looking on from the back room, but when I looked at him, he cleared his throat and followed Romas, Zippy following closely behind and leaving me for the Tinder Mage. I shook my head.

I almost grabbed my pickaxe, which was lying by my cot, but figured I would be right back. Plus, after his show of taking the mages' wands, I didn't want to start something with him already.

The Baron nodded, then led the way out of Romas' smithy. I followed closely behind, my curiosity piqued by his sudden change in demeanor. We traversed the streets of Dunbar, passing familiar faces and weary survivors, until we arrived at the imposing gates of the palace.

The grand entrance loomed before us. I had only been in the palace once in my time here when I was checked in on my first day. It looked the same as I remembered, with abundant plant life on the first floor. My boots crunched on the dirt floor as we stepped inside, the air heavy and hot as what I assumed to be summer was upon the settlement. My eyes scanned the enormous main floor of the palace, seeking out Dee in her usual seat behind the welcome desk. She was scribbling away on parchment when we entered, then stopped and looked at us.

However, as our gazes met, I sensed a shift in her demeanor. There was a flicker of suspicion in her eyes, a guardedness that sent a shiver down my spine. I offered a polite greeting to ease any lingering tension, but her response was curt and distant. Something was amiss, sending a ripple of unease through my core. The way she watched us walking...

The Baron proceeded without delay, his purposeful strides leading us deeper into the palace. I trailed behind, my mind spinning with questions and apprehension. "What is it you need to talk about?" I asked, slowing up before we entered one of the hallways branching off the main area.

The Baron turned. "Not here, boy. Let's go," he snapped.

The Baron's refusal to engage in conversation within the central area only heightened my sense of unease. I continued, following him down the hall. The Baron was looking around anxiously now, ears swiveling.

"Baron," I stopped again, mustering the courage to speak up, my voice tinged with caution. "Is there a specific reason we need to go somewhere private? What do you need to discuss?"

He glanced back at me, his expression serious and guarded. "Noah, there are matters that require utmost discretion," he replied, his voice lowered to a hushed tone. "It is imperative that our conversation remains confidential."

His words only served to deepen my intrigue. Up ahead, he waved a paw to me, opened a door, then hastily went inside the room. I pursed my lips, but no one was around me in the long hallway. *I'm being silly,* I thought. *I just saved his city. I'm sure I'm just tired.* I looked around one more time, then followed him.

As I stepped into the dimly lit chamber, a sense of foreboding washed over me. The door slammed behind me with a resounding thud, and before I could fully grasp the situation, I found myself under attack.

A figure emerged from the shadows, swift and deadly. The assailant moved with grace and precision, their every strike calculated to incapacitate. I instinctively leaped back, narrowly evading a flurry of blows aimed at my vulnerable form. I had no weapon or armor, having just woken up. The Baron rushed around us, opened the door, and escaped into the hall, most likely to separate himself from this betrayal.

My heart raced, adrenaline coursing through my veins as I sought to defend myself. The attacker moved with an eerie silence, their face obscured by a cloak, their intentions veiled in darkness. They were very skilled, moving much quicker than I could see.

A spin and a knife found its way into my shoulder. I let out a scream, the sound loud and echoing in the chamber. "Noah, watch out!" Dee's cry filled the air as she emerged from the hallway. She threw a knife at the enemy, who dodged it and stepped back from me. Dee raced in to close the gap between them while I backed up further, holding my throbbing shoulder.

Her combat skills, honed through years of training, were on full display as she engaged the attacker, her graceful strikes parrying their blows with deft precision. I watched in awe as she expertly maneuvered, countering the assailant's every move.

I quickly looked at my shoulder. Blood was pouring from my wound, black-tinged and clearly poisoned. The clash of steel filled the chamber, the sound reverberating off the stone walls. The assailant proved formidable and kicked Dee's chest, sending her sprawling into the oak desk and sending papers everywhere. With us both in the rear part of the chamber, the assassin escaped into the hallway.

Dee got up, a cough wracking from her lungs. "Coward!" she yelled, then continued coughing. She held her chest where I had repaired her heart damage from the last battle.

"Dee! Are you okay?" I said, scrambling over to her. My health was at [76/90], but it was ticking down and had a skull and crossbones symbol next to it. *Not good,* I thought with a panic. Taking a moment to catch my breath, I hugged her on the ground, a look of admiration in my eyes.

"Thank you," I whispered. "I owe you my life."

She stood up, legs shaky. She looked around, making sure no one else came into the room. "Consider us square." She smiled, then coughed again. "That damn Baron. I knew he was trouble."

I shook my head. "I think that assassin poisoned me. I need to figure out how to stop the bleeding and eliminate the poison, or I won't make it much longer. We better get back to the smithy."

We returned to the empty hallway and sprinted toward the palace door before someone else tried to take us out.

Chapter 26

Shadowvein

ROMAS PUSHED THE BRANCH, ENSURING IT BENT WITH THE correct weight for the archer's order. It burst back, making a *snap* sound. He nodded, smiling, and added it to the stack. Lost in his work, he was momentarily oblivious to the world beyond the smoky confines of his smithy.

He had been tasked with making new bows for the archers since the ones they had didn't seem to penetrate the lizard's hard scales. He wanted to increase the draw weight and create improved piercing arrows if they returned. It would take practice, but the archers would be much more effective.

The door creaked open, and Romas glanced up, setting aside his tools to greet the visitor. A Feka he had never seen before—an unfamiliar face that immediately raised his guard. Sensing something amiss, his muscles tensed.

"Can I help you?" Romas' voice carried a hint of caution, a subtle wariness that underscored his words. He studied the stranger, seeking any sign of their intent or purpose. It was a smaller feline, wearing a mask over its jaw and a hood over its face. The cat strolled in and picked one of the bows up from the pile. "Excuse me, what is it you need?" he said, annoyed now. A moment or two went by, the figure just staring at him.

Out of the corner of his eye, he saw movement. Before Romas could respond, shadows erupted from the corners of the room, figures materializing with swift precision. A gasp escaped Romas' lips as hands, strong and forceful, seized hold of him. Panic surged within him, his heart pounding against his chest like a captive bird desperate for freedom.

"Jasper!" Romas called out; his voice tinged with urgency before they put a gag in his mouth. As his eyes scanned the surroundings, he saw more figures emerging from the shadows. They went to the back of the smithy, clearly in search of his human assistant.

"Yeah?" He heard a crash and muffled yells from the back of the building. Resistance flared within Romas, and stubborn defiance surged through his veins. He fought against the grasp of his captors, muscles straining against their iron grip. But their numbers overwhelmed him, their strength overpowering his every effort.

As his captors dragged him away, Romas cast a final gaze toward his unfinished work—those bows meant to bring protection and hope to those who wielded them. The irony was not lost on him, the bitter taste of unfinished business mingling with his uncertain fate.

Dee and I quickened our pace, a sense of urgency propelling us forward as we returned to the smithy. The streets were shrouded in eerie silence in the early morning haze, the city not awake yet. With the poison coursing through my veins and drawing my health, my chest rose and fell rapidly in quick, gasping breaths. The summer heat of the jungle certainly didn't help.

My heart raced, a foreboding knot forming in the pit of my stomach. Something was amiss, and the sight that greeted us as we arrived at the smithy only intensified our concerns. Tools were scattered haphazardly across the floor, disarray sharply contrasting with Romas' usual meticulousness.

Dee's voice broke the silence, her words laden with confusion. "This is strange," she remarked, eyes scanning the chaotic scene. "My father never leaves his tools out like this. It's unlike him."

I nodded in agreement, my mind racing with possibilities. *Had something happened to Romas? Was he in danger?* The absence of his presence only fueled my growing unease. With each passing moment, the weight of uncertainty settled upon us, amplifying our sense of urgency.

"See if you can find him, and I'll work on designing a poison remedy. At least if I can figure out the ingredients, maybe we can find them in the jungle or something. I won't have enough mana to make anything." I looked at my arm, panic setting in at the [63/90] showing on the health bar. In only the time it took to get from the palace to the smithy, I had lost another thirteen health. *Shit, shit, shit.* "Meet near the gate in a few minutes."

Dee nodded and darted out into the street again. "I'll see you in a few!" she said over her shoulder.

"Jasper?" I yelled, walking back toward the smithy's basement.

No response.

I swung the door open and dashed into the basement, pain radiating from the cut on my arm. A quick look at the injury showed black lines, like spider webs, branching from the cut.

I raced to the design table and set my hand on it. The world slowed down, which I forgot about as a benefit of using the design table. This would actually help my health stabilize while I made a plan. I planned to activate my engineer skill, but I felt another skill take over- my Biokinesis skill. Initially, I was going to design an antidote or something, but with this skill, I could analyze my problem and find a quicker solution.

The skill threw the name 'SHADOWVEIN' up on my mind hologram. When I investigated, it gave more information.

[*Shadowvein is a sinister toxin that possesses a dark, malevolent nature. When it infects the body, it takes hold of the veins, causing them to turn a deep, inky black color. This peculiar manifestation gives the poison its name, as the affected veins resemble shadowy tendrils]*

[The insidious nature of Shadowvein lies in its rapid spread and ability to disrupt the body's circulatory system. As the poison progresses, it progressively impairs the body's ability to pump blood, leading to severe circulatory dysfunction. The once-efficient network of veins becomes compromised, hindering the flow of oxygen and vital nutrients throughout the body]

As I grappled with the dire effects of the Shadowvein poison, I pushed my skill to figure out a cure. Something that I could find in the local jungle. My earth mana activated as well, helping to develop an antidote. The task at hand required discovering two vital ingredients.

The first ingredient was called a *Jungle Orchid*, apparently known for its remarkable healing properties and ability to deter most poisons in my region. It looked like an orchid from Earth would, its purple flower soft and delicate, and hung down from branches of a particularly large tree. This dainty flower possessed unique compounds that could counteract the effects of the poison and rejuvenate the circulatory system. I remembered seeing this flower high up in the trees, so I would need Dee to come with me. Hopefully, she could climb and get one for me. I would need to keep some on hand if poison was used again. Most of the Feka in Dee's class were immune to poisons, but the humans here weren't.

If I could find and consume the flower, the poison would be slowly eliminated from the body. The problem was, my skill said it wouldn't do anything to fix the damage that the toxin was causing. And I doubted my health bar would be able to either, judging by the losing battle I felt from my health tattoo.

The second ingredient just showed question marks, then I got an error that said I had run out of mana, the design table fading and the world returned to normal. *Great,* I thought warily. I guess I need to stop the poison for now and will have to deal with the second ingredient once I get some mana back.

With at least a basic plan, I cut off the skill and raced up the stairs to find Dee. I ran into the street and headed toward the courtyard toward the ramp when I saw the Baron standing on the second level of the palace, flanked by around ten warriors. He looked down at me and pointed, anger in his eyes. "There!" he yelled. "There is the traitor! He attacked me in my chambers! Guards! Guards!"

The warriors took off running. They were around 200 feet away, but with their speed, it wouldn't be long until they closed in on me. I cursed and ran as fast as I could, making my way to the docks.

"Help!" I said, the attackers closing fast, turning down the narrow streets faster than me. Up ahead, one of the Zephrs saw me. He yelled into the dock huts, and six figures emerged and ran toward me.

Chapter 27

The Jungle Orchid

THE SIX ZEPHYRS LOOKED ME UP AND DOWN AND SAW MY horrible state, with blackened blood drenching my arm now. Without hesitation, they formed a defensive semi-circle behind me, their collective presence a shield against the looming threat.

"Run, Creator!" one of them shouted, their voice carrying a commanding tone. "We will fend them off!"

Gratitude welled within me as I realized their sacrifice and willingness to protect me. But I couldn't allow them to bear the burden alone. I couldn't abandon them to face danger while I sought safety. But I also knew that I was no help to anyone dead. Reason prevailed, and I reluctantly stepped away, watching as the wind picked up around me from their presence. Their hair tousled as they took defensive postures, blue eyes shining.

The warriors closed in and swords emerged in paws. Coordinated attacks from the warriors began, fast and furious. True to their monk training, the Zephyrs unleashed a flurry of agile strikes and evasive maneuvers. Their movements were a harmonious blend of grace and precision, their bodies flowing like the wind itself. They had come a long way in the short few weeks since I had left this place. The warrior Feka almost looked like they were trying to fight in a hurricane, their movements slow and clumsy.

With disciplined focus, the Zephyrs countered each attack, deflecting blades and delivering swift, targeted strikes of their own. Their hands became deadly weapons, their kicks and punches imbued with the power of the element they commanded. They danced through the chaos, their bodies a testament to their honed martial prowess. Feka flew backward or became immobilized as skills were used.

Each Zephyr fought with unwavering determination, but despite their skill, the warriors proved formidable opponents, matching the Zephyrs blow for blow. The clash of weapons and the crackling of elemental energies filled the air, creating a symphony of battle.

I watched the fierce engagement, my heart torn between gratitude for their sacrifice and the gnawing urgency of my predicament. Clearly, I couldn't delay any longer. The poison coursing through my veins gnawed at my strength, my health ticking down with every passing moment. I was now at [49/95] and getting lightheaded from the lack of blood flow, which seemed to accelerate. Plus, I knew they only had a limited mana pool, and when it ran out...well, I hoped they could survive this attack. I didn't want anyone else dying for me.

Summoning what remained of my resolve, I turned away, my legs carrying me further down the docks. The sound of clashing blades and the distant calls of battle faded behind me as I focused on my escape.

As I ran, my breath ragged and my steps faltering, I fought against the encroaching darkness that threatened to consume me. I sprinted desperately through the back alleyways and towards the cover of the jungle when a sudden movement caught my eye—another enemy, this time three warrior Feka, leaped out from the buildings with lethal intent. Panic surged through me.

"Die, human scum!" he yelled, fury on his face. The one closest to me held his blade over his head in a killing blow.

Time seemed to slow as Dee materialized beside him, her daggers gleaming with deadly precision. Her sneak attack landed in his thick neck, killing the warrior instantly. The other two swung at her, but she darted away, scrambling out of view and turning her stealth back on. They screamed at her as they saw their comrade fall. After using that finishing move, I knew she would be vulnerable to attack for a while.

The remaining Feka turned to me and saw me standing there, bleeding and alone on the cobblestones. Suddenly, they froze and began backing up. Behind me, Typh had arrived. He stood there, hand on his sword but not drawing it yet, his deep, growling voice sounding out. "By order of the Monarch, you must immediately halt this insolence. This human is an ally of the kingdom, and any action against him is an act of civil war."

The two glanced at each other, and one spoke up. "You would stand with these vile humans, Typhoneous? They cannot be trusted. Oh, *how the mighty have fallen.* We have the authority to kill this human. Move!" They ran forward in an attack.

Typh pushed me out of the way, probably harder than he meant to, and sent me flying into a nearby building. He drew his sword and was upon the treacherous Feka. I landed in a crash, hitting my head on the stone. I felt even more health draining from my tattoo. *Damn it!* I had to be more careful. I stood up, unsteady.

Blade clashed against blade, a symphony of battle erupting between the warriors and Typh.

"This way!" Dee shouted at me, suddenly reappearing and waving her paw. I ran, eyes beginning to blur. We finally made it to the gates, which were thankfully open. With the way everything was unfolding, I figured the Baron would have locked them.

We dashed out into the dirt path leading to the jungle, the humans at the farms just entering the fields for the day's work. I heard exclamations toward me but paid them no attention.

Gasping for breath at the entrance to the jungle, we had finally managed to escape the immediate danger, but the poison's grip on my body continued to tighten. I could feel its presence, an ominous blackness slowly spreading through my chest now, a grim reminder of the urgent need for a cure. Dee's eyes, filled with terror at my predicament, mirrored my own inner turmoil.

"We need to move fast," she urged, her voice laced with urgency. Every passing second felt like an eternity as my heart hammered away, trying to pump blood through now useless veins. I took a heavy breath, then into the foliage we dashed, our chests heaving with the strain of the last few minutes catching up to us. After a few minutes of jogging through the trees, I had to stop. "Hang on," I said, gasping. I could barely breathe, and my heart rate had to be in the 150s. We stood there, unspeaking momentarily, the sounds of nature all around us. "And thanks...for back there..."

"No problem," she replied, also having a really tough time, which was strange to see. "I couldn't find...Romas...but I ran into...Typh. He'd just returned... I told him something...was up." She gasped out.

I stood up straighter, hands on my head now. "We need to find... Jungle Orchid... Are you okay?" I asked, concern all over my face.

"Yeah, I'll be fine...just not used to this much cardio yet after my...injury." She closed her eyes in a grimace. Something didn't seem right with her. "Let's keep going," she said.

Together, we ventured deeper into the dense jungle, its thick foliage enveloping us in a realm of green and shadow. The air was heavy with humidity, adding to my breathing struggle, but there was no time to succumb to weariness. I forced my aching body forward, fueled by sheer willpower and the flickering flame of hope.

We navigated through tangled undergrowth and over increasingly more treacherous terrain, our senses heightened to the subtlest signs of the rare flower we sought. Dee's eyes scanned the surroundings with unwavering focus, helping me search. We knew of the tree we needed, but it was tough to find it when needed. We stayed clear of the spider infestations, not interested in introducing a new poison to my system. No creatures attacked so far, thankfully.

Carefully, we traveled.

Finally, just as doubt began to creep into my heart and my health got into single digits, a glint of vibrant color caught my eye. I stopped in my tracks, my breath catching as I gazed upon the delicate petals of the elusive flower we sought. It stood before us, a beacon of life amidst the backdrop of verdant chaos —a crimson blossom with ethereal beauty. There were about ten of them, all around 100 feet up in the canopy.

Hope mingled with trepidation within me as we stood before the towering tree. The flower, perched high above in the leafy canopy, seemed out of reach. Dee's eyes shimmered with determination as she assessed the daunting challenge before her.

Dee began her ascent with a steely resolve, her graceful form moving with grace and agility. She maneuvered through the intricate network of branches, her fingers finding purchase on the rough bark, her body defying gravity. I watched from below, nervous she was going to fall. From that height, I wasn't sure if even she could land on her feet.

After what felt like an eternity, Dee reached her destination—a precarious perch nestled among the highest branches. With a careful hand, she plucked the large flower, cradling it in her palm as if safeguarding a priceless treasure. Relief washed over me. "How many do you need?" she yelled down.

I looked at my arm. [6/90]. "Just grab the one closest to you! Hurry!"

She nodded, then began scrambling down the tree. With a practiced ease, Dee started her descent; her movements imbued with the same grace that had characterized her ascent. She navigated the tree's branches as if it were an extension of her own body, her connection with nature palpable.

She slipped on a smaller branch, and with a *crack*, the branch she held snapped. "Dee!" I yelled, but she recovered on the next limb.

She flashed me a smile. "I meant to do that."

I groaned. "Just hurry, please." I lifted my shirt and looked at my chest; black lines spread rapidly toward my heart, branching and ominous. *Definitely not good.*

Dee's feet found solid ground once more, and she ran the flower over with an outstretched hand. I grabbed it from her quickly and popped the flower into my mouth. I hurriedly looked at my arm. The poison tattoo vanished, and I watched for a few seconds. The health tattoo seemed to stabilize...at [2/95].

I closed my eyes and panicked a bit. At this point, the slightest injury could take me down to zero. And then, I had no idea what would happen. My head was pounding, and I felt the last of the poison leave my system, but my heart could barely beat fast enough to pump blood through the ruined veins. My eyes fluttered, and I passed out.

Chapter 28

The Fogs of War

MARA'S HEART RACED WITHIN HER CHEST AS SHE PACED restlessly in the ice cave, her thoughts consumed by one burning question: Where was that damn teleporting cougar? Every passing second felt like an eternity, and the weight of her worry pressed heavily upon her. Impatience gnawed at her, urging her to be by Noah's side to warn him of the imminent danger that loomed over his life.

Beside her, the Monarch, calm and composed, attempted to calm her mounting anxiety. Her voice, a steady anchor amidst the turbulence of her thoughts, tried to provide a sense of comfort and reason. Yet, Mara found it difficult to find solace in her words when her mind was clouded with concerns for Noah's safety.

Lost in her contemplations, Mara allowed her thoughts to drift back to Noah—the enigmatic young man who had captured her attention in ways she struggled to comprehend. He was larger than most of the boys in Fulgar but had a strength hidden behind those brown eyes. He was unlike anyone she had ever met, his presence radiating a unique aura that drew her in like a moth to a flame.

There was a certain authenticity about Noah, a genuine kindness and unwavering determination that set him apart. He possessed a quiet strength hidden beneath layers of resilience that Mara found both intriguing and comforting. She felt a sense of belonging in his presence, a connection that defied explanation.

Memories flooded her mind as she mulled over her feelings. The night at the keg pop, where she kept trying to *play it cool* by sitting at the girl's table. How she constantly took forever to put her tools back after shift so she could walk back to the rooms with him. But most of the time, he didn't notice her. It started making her doubt that he would ever become interested.

Until the night in the caves. When he told her about his plan, she agreed to go with him. *Silly girl,* she thought. *Following a boy deep into a monster-filled cave just to get him to notice you.* But she couldn't help her heart fluttering at the thought of that first kiss.

She had never let a boy get close to her before. Most of her crewmates that made passes at her had given up long ago. But with each passing day, her fondness for Noah grew, weaving an intricate tapestry of emotions that she struggled to untangle. And now, after she finally got what she wanted from the relationship, she wouldn't let him die.

The sound of footsteps entering the cave pulled Mara from her introspection, snapping her attention back to the present. Hope flared within her chest as the cougar emerged, its eyes gleaming with knowing. Without hesitation, Mara approached the majestic creature, ready to embark on the journey back to Dunbar and Noah.

"Can we go back? What happened? Where is he? Is he okay?" Mara's words tumbled over each other as a full day's worth of worry vomited out of her mouth.

The cougar, ever silent, held up his hand. He grimaced. "Things are bad. We must go. However, you will need to guide me. The enemy humans will have made it hard for me to find Dunbar."

Mara's chest tightened, panic setting in. She held out her hand and grasped the cougar's arm, ready to go. "I'm ready. My mana has recovered."

The Monarch did the same. Then, with a mumbled spell, they blinked out of existence.

Mara breathed in sharply, still not used to the jarring feeling of appearing after teleportation. She looked at her arm. Her mana read [15/25], using ten to allow them the vision to Dunbar. It was like they were flying over the world, and when they got close to the city, they had to dust off a spot right outside the gates to land.

On the ground, she was immediately smacked with how hot it was wherever they were. The humid air pressed down on her like she was underwater, a breeze barely helping. The air smelled different here too, not like the dry mountain air. They stood outside a stone defensive wall, the gates directly in front of them. They were closed, with two colossal cat creatures guarding them.

The Monarch, unfazed by the teleportation, looked around majestically. She looked to Konna, thanked him, and whispered orders in his ear. With a nod, he disappeared to the right, sprinting on all fours. Finally, she addressed Mara. "My sight is intercepted again here. The mages of Fulgar have doubled their efforts to block my eye. We must find Noah. He could be in substantial danger."

"I'll use my skill again."

The Monarch nodded and walked over to her. She placed her hand on Mara and concentrated. Together, they pierced the vale, fighting off the distant mages for a moment. Visions of an assassin, poison, and the jungle flowed to the Monarch before Mara was battled out of the way, the scrying mages clouding her vision again.

Mara gasped and opened her eyes, the pupils returning from silver back to green. "Should we try again? Did you see anything?" Her chest felt a warmth all of a sudden. She shivered, unsure what that was.

"No, child. Save your mana and your strength. I saw deception, poison, and Noah somewhere in the jungle. He is in grave danger. You must find him. I need to get into my town and discover what is happening here. The stink of the Fulgarians is everywhere here." She walked up to the Feka guarding the gates. "You there- unlock this gate immediately."

The two looked back and forth, unsure, then did as she asked. With a scraping noise, the gate swung open. The two walked into the city. "Good luck, child," the Monarch said and turned to enter the gates.

Mara took a deep breath and looked at the dense foliage a quarter mile away. Mara's heart skipped a beat as she absorbed the weight of the Monarch's words. Time seemed to stand still for a fleeting moment, the gravity of the situation pressing heavily upon her. Noah's life hung in the balance, teetering on the edge of an abyss. Without hesitating, she walked toward the entrance to the forest.

When she got inside, the darkness instantly closed in around her. It was almost like another world in here. Sunlight barely made it through the towering trees, with their competing lush green leaves intertwined and reaching to the sky.

The stink was more pungent here, the swampy odor reaching her nostrils and making her face scrunch up. Beneath her feet, the ground was a carpet of vibrant foliage, a mosaic of ferns, moss, and wildflowers. The verdant undergrowth sprawled in every direction, teeming with life and abundant colors. Delicate flowers peeked through the dense foliage here and there, their petals offering a burst of vibrant hues against the backdrop of lush greens.

With unwavering resolve, Mara embarked on the path through the jungle, her senses attuned to the subtle signs that would lead her to Noah. The air was thick with humidity, clinging to her skin like a heavy shroud. The clamor of chirping insects and the distant roar of unseen wildlife enveloped her, creating an eerie backdrop to her walk. Mara's senses sharpened, her instincts guiding her through the depths of the jungle.

The ground was undulated with gentle slopes and hidden crevices, a terrain that tested Mara's balance and agility. Roots snaked across the forest floor, forming natural pathways that led deeper into the heart of the jungle. She thought about calling out for Noah but was afraid of the jungle creatures that must live here. It looked like the only way to find him was to use her skills. She was unarmed and had no combat training whatsoever.

She brought up her skills again.

[MARA]
[LV 2 - ASTRAL MAGE APPRENTICE]

[HEALTH 15/15]

[MANA 17/30]

 - L2

 - L1

Her anti-scrying skill had leveled up, as had her overall class which must have just happened during her last partnering with the Monarch cat. At this point, she couldn't wait and save her mana. She needed to search for him faster and couldn't just follow this path further into the jungle. She didn't even know if she was going the right way.

She concentrated and took the world in her hands in her mind. She felt the mana sucking out of her arm and knew she had to hurry. Something was stationary on the jungle floor around what felt like a quarter mile further away. A barrier to her scrying surrounded the area. But not like the fog surrounding the city behind her. It was more like an impenetrable shell. She knew that she couldn't move this aside even if she tried.

But she didn't need to. She knew what it was. She cut off the skill and ran as fast as she could.

Chapter 29

Some Light Healing

Dee looked up at the tree again, planning what she would do now. Noah had been knocked out for a while now, and she feared what could come for them. She stayed brave, keeping fear out of her pounding heart, for she knew that the creatures of the wood could sense her dread.

Dee's body ached with exhaustion as she started climbing the towering tree again, her movements slow and deliberate. Her repaired heart thudded unevenly within her chest, a constant reminder of the lingering damage. Yet, an unwavering determination propelled her forward, her gaze fixed upon the unconscious form of Noah, lying vulnerable amidst the wilderness.

When she almost fell last time, she played it off as no big deal. But secretly, it was. Her eyes blurred, and her claws were unsteady. A fall from this height would undoubtedly kill her.

As Dee reached the uppermost branches, her weary limbs protested, but she pushed through the pain. She knew that every moment counted, that Noah's life hung in the balance. With steady hands, she plucked another orchid from its delicate perch, its petals a vibrant burst of color against the lush green foliage.

There was no way that she was getting two flowers. They were just too far apart. Just getting to this one was even more challenging than the first. Carefully, she retreated to the branches that stuck out from the tree and began climbing down.

Her stamina was now at [14/125], so she had to hurry. When that gave out, she couldn't walk a straight line, let alone climb a 100-foot tree with widely spaced branches. With the orchid safely secured in a leather strap crossing her back, she emerged from the canopy, her limbs trembling with the strain of her descent. Her breathing came in ragged gasps, and her vision swam with dizziness.

Dee's breath caught in her throat as a figure stumbled into the clearing, interrupting her progress. Startled and going very still, she turned her gaze toward the newcomer, her eyes widening with surprise and curiosity. The stranger's disheveled appearance and urgent demeanor made her seem unthreatening.

"Who are you?" Dee's voice trembled slightly as she addressed the intruder, her eyes narrowing as she assessed the person before her.

The figure, clad in a dirty one-piece clothing item, steadied themselves and met Dee's gaze with a determined, weary expression. "My name is Mara," the stranger replied, her voice tinged with urgency. "I'm looking for Noah. I need to save him."

"Hang right there; I'm coming down." [8/125] now. She needed to hurry. The girl walked the rest of the way toward Noah. "That's far enough!" Dee exclaimed, scaring the girl into an unmoving statue.

Dee finished the rest of the climb down without incident. Once on the ground, she gave the new human a once-over. She nodded, thinking the girl was telling the truth. "He's been badly poisoned. I grabbed a flower for him from that tree there. It seemed to help stop the poison, but I don't know how to get him to eat another one if he's unconscious."

Mara's eyes turned a shining silver, causing Dee to jump back a step. Mara held up her hands in a placating manner. "May I?" was all she said.

Intrigued yet cautious, Dee offered Mara the flower, placing it into Mara's outstretched hand. Her fingers gingerly brushed against the delicate petals, their vibrancy a stark contrast to the gravity of the situation. Suddenly, the smell of mana filled the clearing. Mara held the flower in her hand, magically floating there momentarily before absorbing it into her palm.

She raised her hand toward the sky and slammed it into Noah's chest with a burst of white light. Dee let out a scared yell, moving toward him, but then stopped and watched. Mara's eyes returned to normal, and she gasped for breath, hand to chest.

"What the hell was that?" Dee exclaimed.

Mara's chest rose and fell in ragged gasps. "I got a skill with the flower. I was able to focus the antidote... I hope anyway."

As moments ticked by, Dee's gaze remained fixed on Noah, her breath held in anticipation. She watched, searching for even the slightest glimmer of hope, for any sign the girl had helped Noah.

And then, like a whisper of life, a subtle change coursed through Noah's being. A soft flush of color gradually returned to his cheeks, while his breaths became less labored, as if infused with renewed vigor. Dee's heart swelled with relief. Dee had never seen healing done in this manner before. The only healing she had seen had been through the bracer that Romas carried around, and as she now personally knew, it had mediocre results at best.

His blacked arm and neck returned to normal color, the healing power of the spell chasing away the blacked veins. It looked to be a slow process, as though Noah's body was now winning the battle, but was still fighting. Turning her gaze toward Mara, Dee's eyes reflected a mix of awe and gratitude. "Thank you," she whispered.

473

Mara offered a weary yet relieved smile, her eyes shimmering with hope. "He unlocked my skills a few days ago. I'm still learning."

Dee smiled and chuckled slightly. "Yes, he seems to enjoy doing that to his fellow humans." She looked into the canopy. "Come on. It's getting late. We have to get him back. He's going to need to rest. I may need a few minutes to replenish my stamina."

Mara nodded but asked, "How will we get him back? No offense, but you look like crap, and I'm only 110 pounds."

Suddenly, a coughing fit sounded out from the ground. Noah's eyes fluttered open, and he smiled. "Oh hey!" he coughed out. "Mara, you made it! Welcome...to the hottest place...on this damn planet." He coughed more.

Mara and Dee both rolled their eyes at him.

Dee and Mara carefully supported Noah's weakened form as they returned to Dunbar. Every step was deliberate, their eyes scanning the surroundings for signs of danger. The dense foliage of the jungle seemed to close in around them, and they brushed away the occasional vines and leaves that reached out to impede their progress. A couple of birds perched on trees, carefully watching them, but made no moves toward them. Nobody spoke, afraid of alerting the wildlife to their presence.

The rain started coming down, slow at first, but increasing to a downpour. Beads of sweat mixed with the water on their brows, as they trudged through the thick undergrowth, fur and hair matted down. Insects buzzed around them, drawn by the warmth and moisture of the jungle. But despite the discomfort, they pressed on, driven by their shared determination to bring Noah back to safety.

They swatted away the persistent branches that brushed against their legs, mindful of the potential dangers lurking in the underbrush. Noah trudged on with their help, slowly regaining his health over the walk. Finally, they made it back to the clearing.

Dee and Noah exchanged a concerned glance as the echoes of heated voices reached their ears. The source of the commotion came from within the gates of Dunbar. With cautious steps, they approached the gate, their senses tuned to the discordant voices growing louder as they drew near. Noah could walk on his own by now, still looking like he got hit by a truck. He wobbled but insisted that he walk under his own power.

As they neared the open gates, an intense argument filtered over to them, and the distinct tones of the Baron and the Monarch became discernible. The Baron's voice rang out with authority and frustration, his words carrying a weight that hinted at deep-seated concerns. On the other hand, the Monarch's voice held a regal tone mixed with a hint of exasperation, her arguments fueled by conviction and a desire to maintain order.

"That doesn't sound good," Noah muttered, as they walked up the dirt path.

Chapter 30

Civil War

As I stepped through the gate, a wave of weakness washed over me, reminding me of the taxing journey I had just endured. The effects of the poison still lingered within me, but I could feel my body gradually recovering, the battle within me coming to an end. Though weakened, my determination remained unyielding, pushing me forward toward my next objective. I needed to take out this Baron somehow. My arm read [MANA - 13/95] and [HEALTH 9/90], so it was finally regenerating. But with a meager nine health, I was a few hits away from zero. I needed to be careful. And without much mana, I couldn't do much of anything.

My eyes scanned the surroundings, the familiar sights of Dunbar greeting me. But the bustling activity that once characterized this place had been replaced by an eerie quietness, as if the very air held its breath, awaiting the resolution of the conflicts that seemed to grip this once vibrant town. Warrior and hunter Feka were everywhere, fully armed, as if they could tell trouble was brewing.

My mind raced with thoughts of the weapons I needed to retrieve. The pickaxe, although something I had only used once against the rat boss, was something I could use in defense. And where was Zippy? I hadn't seen him before all of this craziness since the morning.

And then there was the slingshot, a simple yet reliable weapon that had served me well on numerous occasions. But I didn't have ammo for it anyway. I wondered if it was still tucked away somewhere within the smithy.

Up ahead, the Monarch stood on the lower level, addressing the city's residents above. I approached the duo cautiously, mindful of the tension in the air. The Monarch's gaze met mine, and a flicker of relief crossed her face. She gestured for me to join her, and I quickly closed the distance, my weariness momentarily forgotten.

"Don't go any further, human scum!" the Baron shouted down at me from the upper level, flanked by his young warrior Feka.

"What's going on?" I asked, my voice wavering slightly.

The Monarch asked me to join her at her side, and I walked over, Mara and Dee beside me.

"So it's true then, Monarch? You would stand here next to the traitorous human that would attempt to murder your civil servant?"

The Monarch scoffed. "Prove that he did, and I will exile this boy to the jungle immediately."

The Baron shifted, then replied, "I had no witness, but it's true. The fact that you would take a human's word over mine is all we Feka need to hear. First, the Monarch sends this man to attempt to murder me. Next, she will release the human mages on our town!"

The merchants nodded to themselves, murmurs breaking out. He continued, gaining momentum now. "And then, when our bodies are charred and ruined, just like the Shadowalkers, they will take the town. It's what humans do. They are a threat to our very way of life and must be put down!"

The Monarch strode forward, sensing that she was losing this political battle to her Baron. "That is quite enough, Tobias! Quite enough. Noah, you may address the city residents with your account of what happened in the chamber."

Taking a deep breath, I stepped forward, standing before the Feka who had gathered in the vicinity. Their eyes were filled with curiosity, concern, and skepticism. I knew this was my chance to address them, share my side of the story, and shed light on the events that had transpired.

Clearing my throat, I spoke, my voice steady and determined. "Your Baron is not telling the truth, and I need to address the dark shadows that have clouded your town. The events that unfolded were not mere coincidences or misunderstandings but a deliberate attempt to silence and eliminate me." I showed my blacked arm.

A murmur rippled through the crowd, their attention fully captured as they leaned in, eager to hear my account of the events. I continued, my words flowing with urgency.

"The Baron conspired against me. He sought to have me killed, to eliminate the threat I posed to his plans. But why? What did I do to deserve such betrayal?"

The tension in the air was palpable as I recounted the encounters with the Baron, the evidence that pointed to his treachery. I shared the moments when I narrowly escaped his assassin, the attempts on my life that I had managed to thwart. Each word I spoke carried the weight of truth, resonating with those who listened. I trusted in my belt to prevent the prying eyes of Fulgar from finding us.

"I am not an enemy of Dunbar. I want to be a protector, to fight alongside you people. But that man tried to kill me. So, yeah." I trailed off, my speech ending. The faces of the Feka looked at me with mixed expressions.

The Monarch took a step forward, waving her paw. "Guards, remove this man from my city. His false claims against the boy here are unfounded."

No one moved. "That is quite the tall tale. See?" He waved his paws around. "These humans have vile tongues that can spew venom. They infect us until, suddenly, they eliminate us. We must take them down! Guards, take the Monarch. Your regime ends here, in this place, before your human pets kill us all!"

Tension rippled through the crowd as the Baron's words hung in the air. The atmosphere was filled with disbelief, anger, and defiance. The Fekan warriors, who had previously stood by the Monarch's side, hesitated momentarily, torn between their loyalty and the sudden shift in the allegiance of their direct report.

The young warriors from the upper level leapt down to the ground below with determination, their movements fluid and synchronized. It was as though they had been waiting for this. Their intent was clear—to restrain the Monarch and subdue any resistance.

But before they could reach her, there was a *pop* noise as the cougar appeared, then a wave of Feka, led by Typh and other trusted allies, ran through the open gates, forming a protective shield around their leader.

Typh roared his challenge, and the young Feka faltered for a moment. The Fekan warriors, torn between duty and honor, shared uneasy glances. Some faltered, their resolve shaken by the weight of their choices, while others stood firm, their loyalty to the Monarch unwavering.

Amidst the rushing warriors, the Monarch remained composed, her gaze steady as she addressed her loyal followers. Her voice carried authority, filled with conviction and determination. "Stand firm, my loyal Feka. Our path is one of truth and justice. Lies and manipulation will not sway us. We shall overcome this challenge and restore Dunbar to its rightful state."

She looked at me and Mara. "You two, go with Konna immediately. You must retreat from this place. This battle is between Feka. You must not interfere."

With that, Konna led us away and through the gates. I looked back at the clash of felines that was about to unfold.

The Overlord's frustration boiled over as he barked orders at his scryers, their faces reflecting their fear at his overwhelming mana presence. He paced back and forth in his throne room, his mind consumed with the shell blocking his vision, preventing him from witnessing the events unfolding in Dunbar except at a high city level.

The Porter, who had just returned from his mission, approached the Overlord with urgency in his eyes. He relayed the news that the Monarch had arrived and was mounting an attack on the Baron. The Overlord's interest was piqued, a glimmer of anticipation flickering in his eyes.

"Tell me more," the Overlord commanded, his voice silky and deadly. The Porter recounted the details he had witnessed, describing the return of Noah and the upheaval of half the Fekan warriors against the Monarch for siding with the humans. At least the useless Baron had been able to lock up much of Noah's loyal resistance, including the blacksmith and his little mage helper.

"So the boy was not eliminated? How?!?!" the Overlord raged, his mana threatening to boil over.

"He possesses a powerful scrying blocker, and we could not find him after he escaped into the jungle. Our involvement in the events at the settlement needed to stay a secret, my lord."

The Monarch's involvement meant the stakes had been raised, and his plans needed to adapt accordingly. He pondered the significance of her actions, considering the potential outcomes and the impact they could have on his own machinations.

If the Feka eliminated each other, all the better. The weaker the city was, the easier it would be to take. His words to the Baron had always been empty, and he was planning to renege on his deal when the city was taken. His deal with the Shadowalkers had always been the real one. They would crush Fayport like a vice, with the beasts attacking them from the jungles in the north and his forces, newly outfitted with powerful steel weapons, from the pass to the south.

What first enraged him now enthralled him. The boy was weakened, his forces locked up, and the Feka fighting amongst themselves. If the alpha had allied with the water monsters he had heard about, they would eliminate all the remaining Fekan resistance.

For whoever won this battle in Dunbar would lose to him in the end. It was time for a new age on Prixa—one where the humans found their place at the top.

Chapter 31

The Fourth Battle of Dunbar

THE CLASH OF WEAPONS FILLED THE AIR AS THE BARON's forces surged forward, their determination etched upon their faces. The Monarch stood tall, her eyes scanning the battlefield, her mind focused and sharp. She knew that this battle would shape the realm's fate and was ready to face it head-on.

This was not a pleasant outcome, and certainly not one she foresaw. Her foresight powers told her that a bright future was ahead at Dunbar. But first, death and betrayal.

A group of armored warriors lunged toward her, their swords raised high. They were all far too eager to fight for this Baron and risked too much to gain in his power should he emerge victorious. But the Monarch, attuned to the ebb and flow of battle, effortlessly sidestepped their strikes. With a swift counterattack, she incapacitated them one by one, each movement calculated and executed flawlessly.

She was not the best warrior on the battlefield, far from it. Time seemed to slow around her as her visions granted her split-second insights. She anticipated the swords flying towards her and expertly deflected them with a well-timed wrist flick. She dodged the swinging maces of the lion Feka, weaving through the chaos with grace and agility. It was time to remind these people who their leader was. Sometimes, the price of ultimate power was large.

She cursed herself and cut a young Fekan warrior on the leg. She thought about the traitor that watched from the top of the walls. Oh, how she couldn't wait to cut his smug head from his body. He stank of human, and had undoubtedly been bought by the same people that took Noah from her. How easily they hid this from her sight. Those humans were able to hide things from her so easily. She could not rely on her vision to make decisions anymore.

She was outnumbered in this fight, but her strength and the old warriors surrounding her would prevail. Typh leapt in and cut more Feka down as she ducked another blow. As the battle raged on, the Monarch's foresight continued to guide her, granting her insights into the shifting tides of the conflict. She anticipated the enemy's moves, exploiting their weaknesses and young eagerness against them. Her presence on the battle-field was both commanding and inspirational, instilling fear in the hearts of her adversaries and bolstering the morale of her allies.

In the final moments of the battle, as the Baron's forces crum-bled, the Monarch stood tall, her chest heaving with exhaustion but her spirit unyielding. She surveyed the battlefield, her eyes lingering on the fallen, a solemn reminder of the sacrifices made in the name of peace. The victory was hard-won, but the price had been paid.

She looked up at the Baron, but he was gone.

I wasn't afraid to fight, but I knew I was no match for the battle that was unfolding behind me. But what I could do was make a trap—something he wouldn't see coming. I knew the Baron was a coward. He'd run in the end.

"Mara- you healed me with a skill, right? What was that?"

She nodded, "Antidote skill," she said, breathing heavily as we ran, trying to keep up with Konna. I knew where we were going- he was taking us to the rear of the settlement to the road that connected Dunbar to Fayport. I sprinted through the outskirts of Dunbar, my heart pounding in my chest.

The plan was set, and I had to act swiftly. The Baron, sensing his impending defeat, would try to escape through the road leading to Fayport. I didn't plan to allow that to happen.

In my overall pocket was the lizard claw. I had an idea for it back when I was in the smithy, but when the Baron came and got me, I hadn't had a chance to use it. It was time to change that.

With the cougar and Mara by my side, we raced along the path; my mind focused on constructing an earth-based trap that would ensnare the Baron and halt his escape. Maybe my affinity with the earth allowed me to manipulate the terrain to my advantage. I could feel the energy of the soil beneath my feet, its power surging through me.

This settlement viewed civil war differently than humans did. The sounds of metal weapons, growling, and roaring reached our ears. The battle was fully engaged, most likely with the Fekan non-warrior class watching. Power struggles happened in the animal kingdom, and the winner deserved the right to be the leader.

As we approached a narrow stretch of the road, I signaled for the cougar to halt and took a moment to survey the surroundings. My mind formed a plan. I looked at my lizard claw and remembered the lizardmen and their skillset. I didn't necessarily need a weapon or a trap to defeat the Baron.

I looked at Mara with one of those grins. "This is either going to be awesome...or horrible."

The Baron's heart pounded in his chest as he sprinted through the streets, his mind clouded with desperation and fear. He could hear the distant cries of the Fekan merchants, their accusatory voices echoing through the air. "Coward!" they shouted, their disdain trailing behind him like a haunting specter.

He knew he had lost the battle, the taste of defeat bitter on his tongue. His once loyal warriors had faltered, overwhelmed by the resilience and determination of the Monarch's forces. Panic gripped him, and his only thought was to escape, to flee back to Fayport before news of his failure reached the city's walls. Maybe he could sway a few key friends to support him before they found out about the loss.

With each stride, his mind raced, calculating his options. He knew that his chances of survival dwindled with each passing moment. He knew the Overlord wouldn't protect him. The idea of the Overlord offering him sanctuary within the walls of Fulgar was laughable. Getting to Fayport first was a slim hope, but he clung to it like a drowning man grasping a lifeline.

As he sprinted, the sounds of his labored breath filled his ears, his muscles burning with exertion. He glanced over his shoulder, paranoia gnawing at him. Had he been followed? Were the Monarch's forces hot on his heels, closing in with every passing second? The battle brought all the troops that wretched cougar had gathered up for the lynx Monarch.

But no wall was around the back of the settlement, protected on one side from the gulf. The front of the settlement was walled off from the monsters of the jungle but not from anything back here. The warriors of Dunbar patrolled these woods to get rid of problem creatures and keep the road safe for travel. Not all Feka were warriors, after all, including himself.

His paws made a soft *thud thud thud* on the muddy dirt, his speed carrying him away from the city.

Then, disaster. A hidden figure blasted out of the dirt and tackled him to the ground, followed by that cougar.

They held him down, then tied him up with vines they pulled from behind the trees. They rolled on the ground as he tried to escape, but the human was surprisingly strong, and the vines tied into place instantly. It was like the boy had an iron grip.

"Baron," the boy said, smiling at him in victory. "Your reign of tyranny ends here. You will answer for your crimes."

Chapter 32

The Transfer of Power

I STOOD BESIDE MY ALLIES, MY EYES FIXED ON THE captured Baron who was strung up in vines, his once haughty demeanor reduced to a pitiful figure. The weight of his crimes hung heavy in the air, suffocating any remnants of sympathy I might have harbored.

As the Monarch addressed the remaining warriors and the gathered onlookers, her voice rang out with authority and resolve. She listed the Baron's atrocities, each accusation a damning testament to his betrayal.

The Baron's face contorted in fear, his eyes darting around, searching for any shred of salvation. But there was none to be found. The weight of his actions bore down upon him, stripping away his facade of power and leaving behind the hollow shell of a man consumed by his own ambitions.

Most of his young warriors had been slain in the battle, and the few injured were imprisoned below the city. Romas and Jasper had been freed, and the fire and air mages unlocked from the bunkers. They had been fed lies about an attack, and when they asked to help, the warriors hadn't said anything. Without their wands, they didn't put up much of a fight and were corralled like sheep.

Three of my Zephyrs had been killed by this animal. I had left them to die for me, which was a heavy burden. The three remaining monks looked up, their blue eyes shining brightly at them as their anger flared at the sight of him up there. They had fought bravely against fully trained warriors, and once their mana gave out, they didn't stand much chance. I wasn't even sure how the few survived, unless they had an escape skill that I didn't know about.

It was night, the Monarch giving people a chance to rest and gather their fallen friends and family. A separate event would be held to honor them. For now, the Baron's trial had begun.

My gaze remained fixed upon the Baron, my anger burning. The memories of his attempts on my life, the pain and suffering he had inflicted upon others—I could not forget, nor could I forgive. I clenched my fists, my knuckles turning white, as I fought to contain the surge of emotions swirling within me.

When I made the earth stealth device, Mara thought I was insane. Going underground, even for a moment, would suffocate me. But when I used my design skill, I had all my skills to thank. With my mining skill, I could go underground and replace mana for air. With my stealth skill, a hiding device was applicable to me. And of course, my creation skill shaped the claw into my ring that I wore.

It would be an excellent tool to make for stealth mages. I could now give the ring to people, a green halo showing in only three people here at Dunbar upon quick examination using my 'PATRON' skill. I thought back to all the earth mages I bet I could unlock at Fulgar. But with the weakened state of the city, with over half of the warrior Feka killed, there would be a scramble to fortify this place. I still had very low mana and health since my regeneration wasn't fixed. I needed rest so badly I could taste it. My arm had been fully healed, and the only black that remained was a scar from the original cut that, almost like frostbite, didn't seem to change back.

But that was okay. It was a reminder of what happened here. Trouble followed me like a stink on this world, and if I kept walking around like a little lamb, I would definitely get killed one day. My luck would eventually run out, or people like Typh and Dee, or even Mara, wouldn't be there to rescue me.

Speaking of Mara, I looked at her with a smile. She looked as ragged as I did. She returned the smile and scooched closer to me, holding my hand.

The Monarch's voice pierced through my thoughts, drawing my attention back to her words. She recited the charges with unwavering conviction, her voice resonating with a sense of justice and the weight of her responsibility as a ruler. The crowd fell silent, their eyes fixed upon the disgraced Baron, awaiting his fate.

"Baron Tobias of Fayport, you are convicted in front of this congregation for high treason, attempted murder, and kidnapping. I hereby sentence you to death by beheading for your combined crimes against the Monarchy and the city of Dunbar."

Suddenly, the crowd erupted into roars and insults from the Feka at their traitorous Baron, their voices loud and growling. The Monarch's gaze swept over the gathered warriors, her eyes filled with a steely resolve. She raised her hand, quieting the crowd again.

I couldn't help but feel a sense of satisfaction and vindication, knowing that justice would be served.

Until she spoke the next part.

"I hereby name Noah, Human, the new reigning Baron of Dunbar, by the power of the Monarchy and..."

Her words were lost in the roar of yells from the Feka who surged forward toward her. She continued speaking, but I couldn't hear her. I felt bile climbing into my throat, my eyes blurring. *What the hell did she just say?*

Typh jumped up next to the strung-up Baron and roared, silencing the crowd slightly. Murmurs continued across the group, but the humans all shared excited glances.

My heart pounded in my chest as I stood before the Monarch, the weight of her words sinking in. The Fekan cats around me were filled with outrage, their eyes fixed on me with disbelief and anger. The Barony of Dunbar had been bestowed upon me —a responsibility I never sought nor anticipated. The crowd quieted, and her words sent a shiver down my spine.

The Monarch's voice resonated in the air, her words piercing through the heavy tension in the courtyard. "Noah, you must deliver the sentence to your predecessor. Please complete the transfer of power."

Fear clenched in my gut, and my hands trembled uncontrollably. *How could I be expected to carry out such a grisly task?* The eyes of the predator cats all bore into me, watching me for signs of weakness. I took a deep, steadying breath, dropped Mara's hand, and walked to the vines. Even the Baron had a look of smugness return to his face.

Typh, who had been by my side throughout this wild journey, approached me with my pickaxe. His eyes met mine, and he gave me a slight nod as if silently assuring me that I had the strength to do this.

I swallowed hard to steady my trembling hand as I gripped the pickaxe tightly. The bonded weapon glowed with its red fire, the elemental inside. I could feel its support beaming back at me, ready to finalize this act.

I mustered all the courage I could find. My legs felt weak as I ascended the platform where the old Baron was restrained, his fate hanging in the balance. The eyes of the Fekan were unblinking as they watched, their disbelief and resentment palpable. *I hope the Monarch knows what she's doing.*

As I walked, I glanced at the Monarch, her eyes blazed at me without expression, regal in her appearance. With each step I took, I could feel the weight of her trust upon me, urging me forward and pushing me to embrace my new responsibility.

Standing before the treacherous cat, I raised the pickaxe above my head and stopped trembling. The fear left me. All that remained was determination.

As I swung the weapon down, a resounding thud echoed through the air, marking the end of the old Baron's reign. The steel weapon cut through the creature like a hot knife through butter. My heart thudded wildly in my chest as I looked down at what I had done. The humans cheered, celebrating the end of tyranny. The Feka were silent as they watched, unsure what this would mean. This act marked the end of a Feka-dominated city.

This act began a Feka and human alliance forged in steel and justice.

My right arm burned, and new tattoos began forming on my arm. Suddenly, voice lady addressed me.

[YOU HAVE UNLOCKED THE **CITY MANAGEMENT** CODEX]

Chapter 33

Moats, Moats, Moats

As I walked through the bustling streets of Dunbar, excitement and trepidation filled me. It had been a week since I had assumed the role of Baron, and the weight of responsibility sat heavily on my shoulders. The once-familiar faces of the Fekan merchants now greeted me with wary gazes and lingering animosity. I understood their skepticism and the need to continue earning their trust. After all, I was still an outsider, and not even from the standpoint of being a human. I was as much of an outsider as you could be.

And now, I was thrust into a position of power. I kept hoping that the Monarch knew what she was doing, but I figured I would trust someone who could get visions of the future. Also, the Baron had dropped a surprisingly low level ingredient. The Monarch said that she would keep it for when I was ready, whatever that meant. She didn't even allow me to inspect it.

As my first act as Baron of Dunbar, and player of many city-building games back when I was on Earth, I went to work on building up city production and defenses. This world did not hold back when it came to city attacks, so I wanted to ensure we had a defensible position. And with really only threats from the north able to come at us, I had one direction to fortify. But with good defense also came a good offense.

495

The caves that contained the iron I needed for my army were located through treacherous jungle paths, so we needed to work on a road. I had a few workers start on it, flanked by the warriors that had stood by us during the civil war. They were loyal, and I was sure they could adequately protect my workforce. I estimated it would take three weeks to finish clearing out the jungle and grade a road, but getting iron in and out of there was a really long haul. That could be a significant problem for us. *It might be time to invent zip lines,* I thought with a smile. *Maybe I could put that rat boss tail to use...*

Romas and I had worked tirelessly to establish a steel production facility in the meantime. This was a crucial step in bolstering Dunbar's resources and providing something to export to Fayport and to build weapons with. I didn't want to fall behind Fulgar and their steel production I so *graciously* set up for them.

My 'MANUFACTURE' skill was incredible, as I could assemble large machinery with a one-time mana and ingredient cost to allow non-magical workers to generate items. In only one week, I assembled the whole forge to pump out steel for our new manual laborers once iron flowed into the city. Romas was delighted with the improved infrastructure and happy to leave his magical basement. However, the anvil and all the other creator-only items were kept down there.

Also, with their mastery of the flame, the fire mages were diligently stoking the fires of a newly constructed forge, similar to my experience in Fulgar. They could keep white-hot fireballs going in there, which would be able to melt metals in record time. They also didn't need fire vests to be immune to the tremendous heat inside the forges.

I couldn't help but feel a sense of giddiness and awe as I observed the changes that had happened in such a short time. I waved to Zippy as he flew past, who had now officially bonded with Jasper. It didn't really take him long to abandon me for the boy.

I wasn't bitter or anything. Pets, am I right?

My three new earth mages had gotten to work on a moat around the front of the city that faced the jungle with another draw-bridge to access the gates. I couldn't help myself. When I told the council that we needed one, I got sighs of exasperation, but every great castle deserved a moat. The earth mages could move dirt so quickly that it made sense, but their mana pools were microscopic.

It took days to dig out fifteen or twenty feet of the moat. But I kept them going, knowing that I didn't want Shadowalker bears able to ramrod the walls anymore and didn't know if lizards could use their tunnel skills through the moat. Using their skills, they would level up and gain more mana.

Amidst the flurry of activity, I consciously tried to engage with Dunbar's people and bridge the gap between Feka and Human. It was not easy, for trust is not quickly earned or mended. Yet, I persisted, listening attentively to their grievances, fears, and hopes. I approached the Fekan merchants, who eyed me suspiciously, extending a friendly greeting and a genuine desire to understand their concerns. They enjoyed having new human customers, as many of the restrictions on our workforce were lifted. But they still seemed to get higher prices on goods, which pissed me off. But baby steps and all that.

I made it a point to start hosting town hall meetings in the square just like Baron Gilbert used to do, where I encouraged open dialogue, allowing the citizens to voice their opinions and offer suggestions for the betterment of our community. My first meeting felt like a success. I knew that the Fekan council's insights were invaluable, for they were the lifeblood of Dunbar, the ones who knew its inner workings intimately. With each conversation, I realized that effective communication and empathy was the key to fostering unity and cooperation. I grew up quickly, and thoughts swirled in my head about what to do next.

My City Management Codex that the voice lady provided was awesome too. I glanced at the Dunbar flag on my right arm with pride. When I inspected it, information sounded off in my mind.

[DUNBAR - BARONY]
[RANK - OUTLYING TOWNSHIP]
[MAIN EXPORT - FISH | WOOD | IRON/STEEL]
[MAIN IMPORT - CLOTHING | ALE | STONE]
[LIEGE - FEKAN MONARCH]
[EMPIRE CAPITAL- FAYPORT]

All in all, I was thrilled with the way things had progressed. Nightmares about chopping the head off the previous Baron had started receding, and I moved forward into my role. My thoughts drifted to my home on Earth more and more, however. I missed my mother and had no idea what was happening with her or how she was dealing with my disappearance. I even thought about Dingo, the fat bastard. *Who would keep the damn pit bull from barking at him now that I was gone?*

"Ready to get something to eat, Baron Noah?" a sweet voice called out behind me as arms wrapped around my waist.

"Ah, my darling," I said in my best uppity citizen voice, pretending to adjust my monocle. "Grab your finest attire. I will be taking you to the Soiree this evening."

Mara rolled her eyes at me and embraced me in a kiss. "Yeah, since Dunbar is the cultural hotspot of Prixa. Also, you know that voice is super annoying."

I smiled. "Well, that's the only Baron voice I know. You try if you think you can do better." I dropped into a mock whisper. "You know, word around town is you're my astral princess, after all. You have to practice your haughty princess voice too."

She snickered, then punched me lightly in the arm.

We turned and walked toward the palace, the summer sun setting on another day in the hot jungle.

Epilogue

The alpha, flanked by his most trusted Stalker warriors, scaled the mountain's treacherous slopes, their breath forming icy plumes in the frigid air. The biting cold pierced their fur and chilled them to the bone, but their determination pushed them forward. The world around them was a stark winter wonderland, a blanket of snow covering every surface, glistening under the pale sunlight.

They had trotted for over two weeks as far north as they knew to go. Soaring high above the jungle were snowy peaks of towering mountains. Word from the Overlord was that water beasts lived there, and could be the key to bringing down Dunbar once and for all. But the creatures there were old and wise, and could block their scrying attempts. So it was up to the alpha to see for himself.

As they ascended higher, the winds howled with a ferocity that threatened to knock them off their paws. Each step became a struggle against the elements, testing their resilience and strength. But their purpose burned bright within them, igniting a fire that kept them going despite the harsh conditions.

Eventually, they stumbled upon a cave nestled in the heart of the mountain. It beckoned them with an enigmatic allure, its dark depths promising shelter from the biting cold. With cautious steps, the pack entered the cavern, their senses heightened, alert to hidden dangers.

Inside the cave, the air was damp and heavy, carrying a faint scent of ancient mana that their noses eagerly picked up. The soft glow of luminescent fungi illuminated the surroundings, casting an ethereal light upon the walls. And there, in the heart of the chamber, they beheld a magnificent sight—a water dragon.

The dragon's scales shimmered like liquid silver, reflecting the hues of the fungi. Its eyes, deep pools of ancient wisdom, regarded the Stalkers and the alpha with curiosity. The sheer size and power of the creature were awe-inspiring, a testament to the wonders that existed beyond the realm of ordinary beings.

With reverence and respect, the alpha approached the water dragon, his voice steady yet humble. He spoke of their cause, the invasion of Dunbar, and the need for allies in their struggle. He explained the dire circumstances they faced and the importance of victory for the survival of their pack. He mentioned the Overlord and his promise to engage his side of the battle when the invasion of Fayport commenced.

The water dragon listened intently, its gaze unwavering, its wisdom unfathomable. A deep rumble resonated within the cavern as the alpha finished his plea. The dragon's voice echoed, carrying a weight that matched its immense presence.

"I have watched your kind toil against these felines for generations. You seek my aid, young alpha, but such assistance comes at a price. A task of great significance must be fulfilled to balance the scales of our accord," the water dragon declared, its voice a harmonious combination of cascading waterfalls and gentle whispers of the wind.

The Stalkers and the alpha exchanged glances, acknowledging the gravity of the dragon's words. They knew that a favor from such a powerful entity could never be granted without sacrifice. With unwavering determination, the alpha stepped forward, meeting the dragon's gaze squarely.

"Tell me, mighty dragon, what is the task you demand of us? What price must we pay for your aid?" the alpha asked, his growling voice echoing in the cave.

The water dragon's eyes shimmered with an otherworldly light as it spoke, its words resonating deep within the hearts of those present. "In exchange for my aid, you must give my dragons all the kills from the battle, including the human spoils. Your kind will get nothing to consume."

The alpha stood there, his eyes widening at the dragon's demand. The Stalkers around him bristled at the dragon's words. The consumption of the fallen was the main perk of winning the battle against the Feka. Without those spoils, his kind would not evolve. The alpha hesitated, grappling with the magnitude of the dragon's condition.

But as he pondered, a realization washed over him. It wasn't about his personal desires or ambitions; it was about the survival and prosperity of their pack. His predecessor lost his way and failed them for this reason. The alpha knew that the dragon's assistance would be invaluable in their fight against Dunbar, and without them, his kind could not break through the mages and their fire attacks.

Taking a deep breath, the alpha straightened his posture and met the dragon's gaze once more. "I accept your condition," he declared, his voice steady and resolute. "You will receive all the spoils from war, and together, we will forge an alliance that will shake the foundations of Dunbar."

As his words echoed through the cavern, the air seemed to crackle with a shimmering intensity. The water dragon nodded approvingly, acknowledging the alpha's determination and selflessness. With a graceful motion, it extended its massive wings, causing a gust of wind to swirl around the chamber.

It stood to its full height and walked to the edge of the cave, over-looking the mountain range. With a deep breath, the dragon roared, shaking the ground and causing the werewolves to cover their sensitive ears. The earth shook, rocks trembling all around them.

From off in the distance, another roar bugled. Then another. Then from all around the mountain, dragons emerged from the caverns. The echoes of their roars reverberated through the land, a harbinger of the impending storm set to extinguish the fires of the city of Dunbar.

THE END

Whisper of Iron 3

A LitRPG Crafting Fantasy

Recap

Book 1 Recap

Noah's journey began when he arrived at Prixa and was assigned the class of blacksmith apprentice. He made a dagger from a vulture talon then encountered the Feka, a race of cat warriors, and a boy named Jasper. Jasper took him into the settlement and assigned him to Romas, the master blacksmith. However, Noah soon found himself in trouble when Romas accused him of stealing a dagger. As punishment, he ventured into the jungle at night, where he met Dee. She was a hunter class of Feka and became a valuable ally to Noah as they explored the jungle together.

Noah unlocked a mining skill in a cave after he and Dee faced dangerous werewolves known as the Shadowalkers. They managed to survive and returned to the blacksmith's workshop. There, Noah met Typh, Dee's brother and the head of security in their settlement. Typh recognized Noah's potential after he learned about his access to magic and helped him develop his skills. The two faced a formidable bear creature together but were rescued by the Baron of the settlement. He discovered Noah's secret of having magic and being a Creator.

The Shadowalkers launched an attack on Dunbar but were initially repelled. Noah devised a defensive strategy and built a drawbridge, effectively thwarting the werewolves' second assault. As a result, Noah was released from servitude and gained newfound respect.

To his surprise, Noah discovered a unique ability. When humans held the equipment he had forged and matched the item's mana affinity, they could unlock their latent magical powers. This discovery led him to train the settlement's human mages and prepare for a final confrontation with the Shadowalkers.

Despite their efforts, the werewolves proved to be a formidable foe. Under the full moon's power, the Shadowalkers' alpha killed the Baron, creating chaos and uncertainty. In a sudden turn of events, an unknown group of human mages with incredible fire and lightning magic arrived on the scene. Exhausted by the battle and overwhelmed by the mages' power, the Shadowalker generals and the alpha were defeated. The human mages kidnapped Noah taking him to the city of Fulgar and severed their Human alliance with the Monarch of the Feka.

Book 2 Recap

Noah began the story trapped in a room in a mysterious place, later learned to be Fulgar - the magical city of human mages of fire and lightning. He was assigned to mine duty by the city's Overlord to find rare and magical ores to create new tools for them so they could see what his powers could do.

During an attack in the mines, Noah met Mara and saw how dangerous the work in the mines was and how poor the conditions were. His boss, Craig, fought bats with the fire mages while his crewmates hid in their special onesies.

Once he had met his ore quota, he began working in the forges making fire-resistant armor, amazing those who watched him. He met the Overlord who talked him through his first few projects that he had in mind. Noah got a weird vibe from him and said that he wouldn't build weapons anymore. The Overlord agreed and sent him back to work.

The mid-week celebration arrived, and Noah got to see life outside of work shifts in Fulgar. He felt distant from his crew, however, and surprisingly missed the Feka back in Dunbar.

Back in Dunbar, Dee finally woke up and felt horrible from her battle injuries. Noah may have saved her, but at a huge cost. In Niridge, the Shadowwalkers anticipate a new alpha werewolf. Annos, a wolf from the eastern packs, churned through his challenges and defeated the final challenger to take the crown.

Back in the mines, Noah created the plans for an ore processing device. His goal was to learn how to create steel and show his value to the new city to unlock additional privileges. He designed an ore crusher and a beneficiation machine to process the iron into a more concentrated product for easier smelting.

When he finally created the crusher and beneficiation, nicknamed 'Benny', machines, the mages were amazed at his powers. But the crewmates in his shift weren't so pleased. The oldest boy, jealous of the attention Noah received and afraid he will lose out on the promotion to Noah, beat him up with his friends.

Noah finished his work in the forges to finally create steel, but was dismayed when the Overlord and the fire mages treated him no differently, keeping him a prisoner by locking him in his room every night. He decided it was time to plan his escape, by designing a secret device to block the scrying abilities of the Fulgarian mages. In Dunbar things went from bad to worse. The newly assigned Baron was not interested in magical humans and banned most magic inside of the city, including demolishing Noah's defenses and thinking that Fekan strength of arms was sufficient to protect the city .

At the full moon, Noah escaped his room and headed into the mountain prairie in search of a rare ingredient called Lunar Moss. When he touched, it he unlocked Astral Magic, something he didn't even know existed. But the Overlord caught him and threw him in a dungeon cell for attempting to escape.

As Noah was released from prison and returned to service, Dunbar was attacked once again...this time with lizardmen who could use a form of sneak attack. They burrowed under the walls and let the Shadowalkers in, causing massive casualties in the warrior Feka.

Noah used a bat attack in the mines to escape deeper into the caves and stole a pickaxe for defense. Mara met up with him in the caves to help him escape. They were attacked by teleporting rodents where Noah made his stand and finally defeated a high level boss, thanks to all his training. He broke through the level ten barrier and became a Blacksmith Journeyman. The fire mages found him and Mara and attacked, but were repelled when the Monarch appeared to save him. With her scrying, she was able to see him outside the city's protection deep in the mine and teleported to him with Konna to rescue him.

Mara unlocked her astral affinity when she held Noah's anti-scrying belt and matched the Monarch's class, much to everyone's amazement. They scried Dunbar and saw the attack, sending Noah and the teleporting cougar Konna there to help in the city's defense.

Noah hastily made a fire shooting suit in the smithy and repelled the lizards. The humans of Dunbar were relieved that Noah returned, but the Baron was upset. He saw Noah as a huge threat, and his treachery revealed that he was allied with the very Overlord that kidnapped Noah.

The Baron invited Noah into his chambers where he tried to assassinate the Creator, but failed when Dee came to the rescue. But the fight took a lot out of her and badly poisoned Noah. They escaped the palace to search the jungle for an antidote but were confronted with the new Fekan warriors, loyal to the Baron. Typh came to the rescue with the Feka who were loyal to the Monarch and had seen what Noah had done to save their city, causing a civil war to break out.

Mara and the Monarch returned with Konna. Mara rushed into the jungle to find Noah and save him as the Monarch challenged the Baron. Dee found the flower needed to stop the poison, but not repair the wounds caused. Mara found them and saved Noah with a new healing skill to fight dark wounds.

They returned from the jungle to a battle raging. The Monarch demanded they stay out of it, but hinted that there is something Noah can do to help. He made a trap at the rear of the settlement, knowing the Baron was a coward and that he would flee. He trapped the Baron and took him to the victorious Monarch for judgment.

But in a surprise turn of events, the Monarch named Noah head of the city and demanded that he complete the transfer of power by beheading the Baron. Noah did so and received a new codex on his arm to show him his new city.

In the mountains to the far north, Annos found water dragons and made a pact with them to attack Dunbar. He realized that water magic was the key to defeating the fire mages and taking the city once and for all.

The second book ended with dragons trumpeting in the mountains, ready to attack.

Prologue

THIRTY YEARS AGO

Eldric hummed to himself as he strolled through the bustling outpost of Fulgar, the air humming with the air and fire enchantments he had woven into its very fabric. He cradled an object that pulsed with immense power in his weathered hands—his newest creation. It had cost over 450 mana, and he was absolutely wiped.

Two years had passed since the battle of Fayport. The Feka had held back the werewolf beasts as the humans fled. They had retreated through the mountain pass, further south than any settlement he knew of. They landed on this flat spot in the terrain, and now he called the outpost *Fulgar*. It had an excellent defensive position, with the snow capped mountain surrounding every side. They would be safe here.

He asked that the Monarch keep their existence a secret. After seeing those massive werewolves in action, he dreaded what would happen if they consumed some of his mages. They were ferocious enough without the power to wield fire or lightning- or possibly have immunity to it. He wasn't sure what would happen if they took his people. But he knew he didn't want to see it transpire.

They continued their alliance, but without the protection of the cat warriors, Eldric was afraid for his people's safety. The world was full of monsters, and his people only had a few mages mixed among them. But he would ensure they continued unlocking as many as they could. The Monarch said they would meet again soon to discuss the future. He waited with bated breath.

He looked down at his arm tattoos, the symbols staring back up at him. He needed to unlock more than just fire and lightning mana, but didn't know how. He had been a Creator ever since he had killed that Shadowalker and picked up its ingredient.

As he navigated the busy streets, his eyes fell upon a young boy they called Pomius, standing and watching the other boys kick a ball around with their feet in the dirt. Eldric clicked on his 'PATRON' skill and observed the blooming magical users.

Colors, stats, and potential weapon affinities shone about each boy's head as he took in the information. But over Pomius' head...nothing. He cut off the skill quickly, still low on mana from creating the scrying mirror he was about to deliver to the head mage.

Curiosity sparked within Eldric, and he approached the boy and pulled him aside. "Good morning, Pomius, my lad."

The boy's eyes darted to his, breaking him out of his trance. "Good morning, Creator, sir."

He smiled at the boy. "Pomius, have you ever felt the call of magic? The choosing ceremony comes soon, and you still don't show up in my mind's eye as a potential magic user. I can't fathom why. Something is off about you."

Pomius looked up at Eldric with wide eyes as he leaned forward. "Yes, sir," he replied, his voice filled with a determined edge. "I feel something... something powerful within me."

Eldric pursed his lips as he observed the young boy, sensing the raw energy radiating from him that had yet to choose any of the four magic affinities he knew of. He nodded slowly, his mind contemplating the implications of what he saw. "I know something is there, but I can't figure out what it is. I will continue thinking on this."

Pomius smiled. "Yes, I can see it."

Eldric tilted his head and narrowed his eyes at the boy. "What do you mean, you can *see* it?"

Pomius looked at him with a neutral expression; his gaze fixed on the pulsing object held within Eldric's hands. "Will you teach me, Eldric? Will you guide me on this path?"

Eldric looked to his scrying mirror, then around the streets quickly. He pulled the boy into an alleyway. Casting one more glance around, he thrust the object into the boy's hands. Pomius' eyes widened in shock, but nothing happened.

"Curious..." Eldric said, then took the mirror back. "I will have to think about unlocking you, child. For now, run along and play."

Pomius nodded, then shrugged and walked back to join the boys playing.

As he watched the boy leave, Eldric couldn't help but feel a sense of unease. The raw power within Pomius excited and unsettled him, for he knew that the young boy's destiny was intertwined with forces far more significant than either of them could imagine.

A bell sounded, and the crews started walking out to their various tasks around the outpost. Mining, wood gathering, and food growing, to name a few. All these things needed to be done, and with or without magic, it didn't matter. Everyone needed to pitch in. However, magic users had risen to the head of the work camps, which was to be expected. With great power and all of that.

With a sigh, Eldric walked toward the central housing to deliver his package. After that, he would return to his blacksmith and start on something new.

Something he had yet to try.

Chapter 1

Steam Release Valve

As I walked down the newly graded gravel road in the forest outside of my city of Dunbar, my eyes fixed on the path ahead, and I couldn't help but feel excited. The swampy jungle loomed on either side, its emerald canopy casting a dappled shade over the forest floor. The air was thick with humidity, and the chorus of unseen creatures filled the air with loud chirps and calls. Vultures perched on the tree limbs, staring at me with their beady eyes. I wasn't afraid of them anymore, and they knew it.

Beside me, a steel cable ran parallel to the road, disappearing into the cave ahead. I had used my rat boss tail, a very high-level ingredient, and combined it with around twenty handmade steel ingots. When I finished, I ended up with a steel spool and stretched it to the cave on my new road by attaching it to trees along the side. This cable served as a track for the cave-turned-iron mine, enabling me to transport my carts filled with iron ore.

Over the last few days I had designed a steam engine. I had plenty of firepower here at Dunbar, and would make the most of it. My design was simple- I took an iron cart, which cost me around twenty iron to make, and suspended it below two pulleys that straddled the cable. Then, I designed a compartment on the back of the cart. Water was stored in a tank with a simple

519

combustion chamber below it. The mages could cast a fireball inside the chamber and close the heavy door. The water boiled, and a steam pipe led to the piston that powered the pulley wheels along on the cable.

My new engineering skill had kicked in to help me develop the whole machine instead of the separate elements I had to combine before my upgraded skills. And with my prototype subskill in my manufacturing ability, I could make a trial machine for about 25% of the total material cost for a one-hour trial.

When I tested the first version yesterday, it almost killed Jasper and me. I hadn't made the steam pipe large enough, and the pressure became enormous. Luckily, it zipped about thirty feet away, sending us into a whooping cheer, but then the wheels got stuck on the cable fasteners before it viciously exploded.

My second prototype was tested later that day, and the production version of it darted by me now. This time, I added a steam release valve to prevent an explosion when it got too much pressure and larger wheels to get over the cable clamps. I smiled as I watched it merrily chug along the cable and back toward the settlement, with Jasper and a few other mages running after it. The cart went around fifteen miles per hour if I had to guess, and went to and from the settlement in around six minutes.

"Noah! Look!" Jasper yelled, clapping me on the shoulder, and continued running.

I smiled and kept walking. It was probably the third trip that the cart made, but it never grew old.

I finally arrived at the entrance of the iron mine that I named Mecho's Cave Iron Mine in memory of the giant bear that had been killed down here months ago with Typh and Baron Gilbert. The mine walls glistened with a metallic sheen that reflected the torch lights and the sound of steel pickaxes echoed through the tunnels as workers tirelessly chipped away at the walls, revealing veins of ore hidden within.

I glanced at the rough drawings adorning the mine walls, displaying the intricate network of ore veins I had drawn out after surveying the entire front of the cave with my mining skill activated.

A tunnel forked left into the separate section I dedicated to extracting tinderstone, another common mineral with potent fire properties. The ore reminded me of coal from Earth. Purple mushroom lanterns illuminated that tunnel, casting flickering shadows on the walls. I was too afraid to use torches with fire around the tinderstone and limited their use to the tunnels focused on iron ore. I remembered hearing about coal mine fatalities on Earth, and while I didn't know all the details, I knew coal and fire didn't mix and stuck with the mushroom lanterns.

A crude wooden sign at the front of the tunnel read 'No Fire Mages' with a rough drawing of Jasper's face. I chuckled again as I looked at it.

But my purpose here was twofold. Alongside my pursuit of making steel for the settlement, I also had a pressing need to find a way to stop the Fulgarian scrying mages that plagued our city. I knew they could spy on us and even teleport into the city.

I couldn't have that. My warriors were already stressed enough, and I didn't need them jumping at their own shadows while patrolling the streets. There was barely any trust between the Feka and the humans who now coexisted under my leadership as it was after I had been named Baron.

Inevitably, a fight had broken out two days ago. Tempers flared, and emotions boiled over, shattering the fragile peace we had worked hard to establish. I watched in horror as a human farm worker, caught amid the chaos, suffered a grievous injury. Blood stained the ground outside the path leading into the jungle, a stark reminder of the consequences of our failure to quell the rising tension.

In that moment, as I knelt beside the injured human, I felt the weight of responsibility settle upon my shoulders. I had to find a way to bridge the divide and bring understanding and harmony back to our community. I just wish I knew what it was.

Maybe I could figure out a way to put humans and Feka together in a group that had a shared goal. That way, they had to work together and see the strength we had when we combined forces.

My first task as Baron was to stop the scrying with some kind of creation, which could be a perfect opportunity for that. Plus, I felt like I had to prove that I was more than just some kid with magical powers.

I knew I needed to create a larger, more powerful device to counteract the scrying magic than the belt that I made. Mara told me about the impenetrable shield around me when I wore it, and I wanted to create a new device to shield the whole city.

To do so, I required specific rare ingredients. A local flower called Voidbloom, rumored to possess the ability to nullify magical energies, could be found hidden in the deepest parts of caves like this. Or so my skills told me. I imagined they were similar to the glowing mushrooms.

When I designed the scrying shield, I figured lunar moss would be an ingredient, like the stuff I found back at Fulgar. But that was said to bloom only during the full moon in a different climate, making it a challenge to obtain. There was only jungle around me, and I had no faith in finding the moss here. So my skill shifted one of the ingredients of the device to Voidbloom.

Another ingredient was called Moonlit Silver. It was a rare alloy that could only be forged during the moon's light by combining silver and steel. Its unique properties could disrupt magical energies, rendering scrying spells ineffective. I needed to find the silver vein and figured the only way would be to explore. I hoped it would be one of the many shades of ore that I saw behind the cave walls, some extremely deep now that my mining skill had leveled up. I checked with Romas to see if I could take the ore that unlocked my air magic and smelt it down somehow since it was a silvery shade, but that didn't get us anywhere.

The last thing I needed was camomile leaves. That sounded like something I could find in the jungle. From what I knew about the flower, I thought it looked like a daisy and sent a few warriors into the wilderness to search for it. I had no idea what the flower had to do with scrying, but I intended to eat some and see if it had a limited stealth effect, similar to when I ate the glowing mushrooms and got enhanced vision.

I also needed Mara to cast her spell on the device to finish it off, a new requirement I had yet to encounter. I thought back to the device and its ingredients.

[ANTI-SCRYING DEVICE - CITY LEVEL - 3X VOID-BLOOM | 10X MOONLIT SILVER | 10X SILVERSTONE | 5X CAMOMILE FLOWER PETALS | ANTI-SCRYING SPELL]

There was another sighting of a Fulgarian spy reported by a scout, and the urgency to find a solution to the scrying dilemma and increase patrols grew more pronounced. It was a race against time, for with every passing day, fear increased, and the threat of conflict loomed closer. Plus, the Overlord could probably see right into my city and scout the new defenses I had planned, and I didn't know to whom he would feed that information. I had too many enemies as it was.

Even if I did create a way to keep eyes off my city, I still needed to have archers on the palace roof at all times, and increased patrols on the walls. This way, if anyone teleported in, I would get them.

Then, of course, I had to fortify the city from the inevitable Shadowalker and lizardman invasion, increase trade and prosperity, start a steel forge from scratch, and grow my army from the pitiful thing that remained after the civil war.

I sighed and turned down one of the tunnels, my bonded pickaxe gleaming on my shoulder.

Chapter 2

The Council of Dunbar

As I VENTURED DEEPER INTO THE MINE, THE SOUND OF steel pickaxes faded behind me, mingling with the faint echoes of my footsteps. The air grew heavier, tinged with the scent of earth and minerals. The walls surrounding me glistened with a kaleidoscope of colors, the hidden ores waiting to be uncovered. There were too many at this point for me to even be able to tell. I almost needed a way to filter these little dots of minuscule ore out.

I brought up my character sheet, pleased with the last week of work here in my city.

[NOAH]
[Lv 13 - BLACKSMITH JOURNEYMAN]

[BONDED]

[HEALTH 105/105]
[MANA 82/125]

-L3

-L3

-Passive

-L2

-L6

-L2

[UNSELECTED SKILLS - NONE]

I inspected my 'MANUFACTURE' skill, bringing up the interface in my mind.

[MANUFACTURE - LEVEL 3 - SUBSKILLS UNLOCKED
- ENHANCED ITEM CREATION | CREATE
PROTOTYPE | ORE EXTRACTION - SPECIALIZATION
NOT YET CHOSEN]

I thought about filtering out any ore the size of a dot or smaller and looked around, pleased to see the rainbow colors diminish to a reasonable level. It appeared that I could, in fact, filter my skill and what it showed me.

My eyes scanned the rock formations, searching for a silver-colored ore. Not finding any, I reached out, pressing my hand against the cool surface of the wall, allowing my senses to guide me. As my fingertips made contact with the rock, a surge of energy coursed through me, connecting me to the very essence of the earth.

Harnessing my skill, I focused my concentration. The ores near me in the walls responded, obediently suctioning into my palm as if drawn by an invisible force. They clung to my hand, their weight shifting and merging within my grasp. I turned and shot them out onto the cave floor, looking over the rocks that had emerged.

Tinderstone, silverstone, and some of the tungsten I used in Fulgar sat there. I quickly threw them in the leather fanny pack around my waist and continued.

I was careful not to go too deep into the mine, and after a while, I returned to the main area. I hadn't gotten anything new, but I was happy about the tungsten. That was a valuable ore known for its strength, and I could make some cool stuff with that. I used about 15 mana to get three groups of ores, all variations of the same two or three.

I retraced my steps, ascending the path that led me back to Dunbar. The weight of the leather pouch bounced against my hip. As I walked, my thoughts shifted from the mining exploration to the upcoming inaugural council meeting. It was a crucial gathering where the leaders of the Feka and my chosen human representatives would convene to discuss the pressing matters plaguing our city.

The new road, which still shocked me that we had it done so quickly, stretched out before me, winding its way through the outskirts of the forest. Shafts of sunlight pierced through the thick canopy overhead, casting fleeting shadows on the path. The sounds of nature enveloped me and allowed me some quiet time to think about what I wanted to say and how I wanted to run the meeting.

I crossed over the moat by using the makeshift drawbridge, which hadn't been completed yet, then I passed the farms and bow trees on my way in, nodding at the workers as I walked. They all smiled, and many addressed me with a "Baron!" or "Baron Noah."

Entering the city gates, I navigated through the familiar streets, passing no-classed shops and homes, but the reception from the Feka was a bit colder.

I walked up the ramp into the first level of the settlement, eyeing the drawbridge and counterweights to make sure they were fully repaired. The scent of freshly baked bread wafted from the bakery, mingling with the aromas of herbs and spices that drifted from the market stalls. I received nods and smiles from the humans in here as well, still wearing their assigned work class shirts.

Reaching the palace, I stopped and took a moment to compose myself, steeling my resolve for the challenges waiting for me.

I opened the door and went inside. Mara saw me and ran over, hugging me in a friendly embrace.

"How did it go?" she asked, knowing what I was looking for.

"Not great. I only got the same three ores. I'm going to have to go deeper. I hope there is some in there somewhere. Otherwise, every day that goes by that I don't find any..."

I trailed off, and she frowned. "We will be fine. You have everyone on high alert. They can't pull the same crap they did last time."

I nodded, unconvinced. "I'm going to get changed out of my mining stuff and meet you in the council chambers."

Her smile widened. "Are you ready? Big day!" she said, as she moved my hair behind my ear with her hand.

"Yeah. It's time we do this. I need to assign people to their roles here. We need to thank overqualified people by giving them more responsibility." I pursed my lips but didn't say more.

"Okay, well, I'll see you in there!" She kissed me, turned, and walked away.

She wore a short sun dress with small, green stripes around the midsection, and her feet were in leather strap sandals. Her hair, as usual, was pulled up in a ponytail. She looked stunning.

I didn't know how she would react to being pulled from Fulgar, the place she had known her whole life. But she continued to reassure me that the heat was where she belonged and that she was sick of wearing onesies. And with the way she sauntered off, with the dress hugging her athletic curves, I couldn't agree more. The breeze fluttered the bottom of the dress slightly, revealing her upper leg...

She looked over her shoulder and saw me watching and smirked at me. I blushed, coughed into my hand, and hurried off to change.

Inside the grand council chambers of the palace, the room hummed with hushed conversations and restless energy. The Feka and my human representatives gathered around a large, ornate table, waiting for the meeting to commence. Jamie and Mara spoke together, laughing at something, and Jasper and Kyle, leader of the Zephyrs, spoke together with their voices down. The strange T-shaped chairs the cats used didn't seem to fit my human council members either, and they swung their feet awkwardly as they waited for the meeting to start.

I walked to my seat at the head of the table, my mind racing as I carefully considered the words I would speak and the actions I would propose. The injured farmhand from the recent altercation weighed heavily on my thoughts, a reminder of the stakes involved. It was crucial to find common ground and mend the fractures threatening to tear us apart.

I thought I had just the way.

I cleared my throat, and the room became absolutely silent. I looked down at the parchment, where I prepared an outline of what to say for the meeting. My palms were sweating as I fidgeted with the piece of paper, clearing my throat again. "Honored council. Thank you for joining me today for our first-ever council of Dunbar."

The humans around the table cheered, and I couldn't help but look up and smile. The Feka frowned and looked at each other, surely expecting a different etiquette from high-ranking members of the town's society.

I continued. "Our city is off to a great start, but I fear we must move quicker. The Shadowalker threat is looming. I am certain their attacks are not done yet. The Overlord and the city of Fulgar aligned themselves with an unknown entity, and possibly even the alpha himself. He spies us on from afar with his mages and can teleport his people in and out. He is ahead of us on steel production and has undoubtedly made weapons of this higher tier. These threats cannot be left unchallenged."

I looked down at my parchment, moving to my next point. "I have the list of ingredients for an anti-scrying device that I plan to make for our city and Fayport, but I have to find them first. I will take a group deep into the caves to search for them. Assignments will be posted outside the palace walls detailing the members of the exploration party."

A warrior cat stood out of his chair, the first council member to address me since the start of the meeting. "Baron, I'm sure you will not leave the Feka out of this mission, correct? It would be wrong for your kind to...venture somewhere without us."

Typh looked at him and shook his head. "Feeling a bit jumpy still, Nyo? Afraid they're planning something? Speak your truth here in this place!"

He growled back. "Typhonius, I'm just saying that we don't want any humans *plotting* in the dark depths of the mines. They are still weak in combat..."

Typh growled at him and stood, hair on the back of his neck rising. I raised my hand in a peace gesture. "I want each of us to guard our minds against conjuring plots and schemes in the darkness. We need to focus on our future and building it rather than what some groups may be doing in the shadows. We will deal with actions, not what might happen. I was planning on a mixed group of mages and warriors, yes, Nyo."

He sat back down at that, as did Typh. "As for the trust, we need to work through this, guys. I know there have been a lot of changes in the last week or so. But we must trust our Monarch's decision." I purposefully went with *our* Monarch.

They both nodded. "Now, the last item of business here is the assignment of my advisors." The room grew a bit stiff again. I continued. "I need people assigned to various parts of running the city based on their skill set. These people will meet with me every few days to go through the most important updates and projects as they see fit. I will listen and will not run those meetings. If you are not chosen, it is not because I think that you do not have a seat at this table."

The Feka leaned forward, hungry to see who I had in mind. The humans at the table also looked anxiously between them, fidgeting in the large chairs. I had told Mara my plans the night before, and she liked the idea of assigning leaders to the various tasks in the city. She said it would increase cooperation.

To be honest, I only had the idea to do this based on a video game back on Earth that I used to play, where you assigned people these exact roles based on their highest attribute level and loyalty to you.

I wasn't ashamed of where the knowledge came from, but I had to laugh a bit.

"First is my Steward. Romas, that's you."

He smiled and pounded his paws on the table with a loud *bang bang*. "Good choice, boy!" He paused, frowning. "What in the moons is a Steward?"

I laughed, and small chuckles broke out. "The Steward is responsible for the trade and production of the city. You were an obvious choice, and I will put you in charge of my mining, smelting, and trade operations to free me up a bit."

He nodded, and I continued. "Next up is my Marshall. This person is in charge of the army, recruitment, and training of both human and Fekan warriors. Typh, you were the obvious choice here."

Roars of appreciation sounded from the Feka, and they hit their chests and rose from their chairs, bowing their head to Typh. I hadn't seen this gesture before but noted it for later use.

"Thank you, Baron Noah. I will not let you down," Typh said, nodding gravely to me.

"Lastly, my Chancellor. This person is in charge of the diplomatic relations between us and Fayport and finding new allies. I have plans to see who else can help us out there, and Mara, you're my choice here."

She smiled and stood, taking on a regal air about her. "Baron Noah, I will do whatever you require." She sat back down and winked at me. Jasper snickered at me, and I heard a few snorts of derision around the table.

I nodded, then clapped my hands together. "Okay, with that done, I will go through the rest of my short-term city plans, and how the new positions will interact for the good of the city."

With that, I dove into the extensive list of items I had prepared on my scrolls.

Chapter 3

The Road Ahead

ANNOS, THE FORMIDABLE ALPHA OF THE SHADOWALKERS, stood atop a rocky precipice overlooking the lush valleys that led to the swamps, finally returning from his grueling trip. His eyes, gleaming intensely, surveyed the city of Niridge bustling before him. His beta had done well while he was away.

The recent meeting with the water dragons had bolstered his determination, igniting a fire within him to carry out his final assault on Dunbar. The cursed city had thwarted his people far too many times, and with their new alliance it certainly wouldn't stand again.

The time for subtlety and patience was quickly coming to an end. The Shadowalkers had played the waiting game, gathering intelligence with help from their allies in Fulgar and building their forces. Canine troops from across the upper reaches of the Western Hemisphere had accumulated while he was away, drawn to the promise of a new life. Now, he would prepare for his final attack on Dunbar, the city he needed to set up for his assault on the Fekan capital.

Turning his attention to his trusted warriors, a select few Stalker generals who had journeyed with him to the realm of the water dragons, Annos began issuing orders. They looked weary from the long trip on the road but would never dare complain before him. The trip had been quiet, with no problems from the various mountain beasts, and not many words had passed between them.

His voice, calm and authoritative, rallied his pack to action. He outlined the next steps in their grand design; his words laced with menace. They broke off and got to work.

As he entered the city gates, his presence sent ripples of excitement through the Shadowalker community. Annos was a strong alpha, with the potential to be even stronger than the previous alpha. His fighting reputation had garnered him the loyalty of the generals who shared his vision of vengeance against the Feka and humans of Dunbar.

In the depths of his lair, Annos began the meticulous preparations for the assault with his beta. Later, he reassembled his warriors. They gathered around him, their eyes gleaming with anticipation. Most had heard what had happened in the cold mountain cave. They knew now the price their leader was willing to pay for their pack and the defeat of Dunbar.

"My brethren," Annos spoke with a voice as smooth as a whisper in the night. He stood up to his full height, straightening his back and raising his head high. "Our time rapidly approaches. After their civil war, the Feka have limited numbers, and their mages will have no chance against our dragon cohorts. But first, we must gather intelligence on their defenses. Their human creator has made improvements and will try to stop us from accessing the city. Our lizard allies will need new ways to subvert their walls."

He shared his plan with them, outlining the need for careful surveillance of Dunbar. With their ability to navigate the skies undetected, the water dragons would play a pivotal role in this operation. Annos had requested them to observe the city from high elevations before he left their caves, ensuring they remained unseen, like silent sentinels looming over the city. The dragons agreed.

As his warriors departed on their assigned tasks, Annos delved into his vast array of maps, scrolls, and ancient tomes with the skulk of foxes, the knowledge keepers of the pack. He studied the layout of Dunbar from previous attacks, analyzing its vulnerabilities and identifying the critical points of weakness. His mind worked like a master strategist, calculating every move, every potential obstacle they might encounter. This time, he would not rely on the word of a human and his intrigue to get the job done. He would crush the felines with brute strength.

In the shadows of Niridge, Annos's lair became a hive of activity. The scent of anticipation hung heavy in the air as the Shadowalkers made their final preparations, ready to unleash their fury upon Dunbar.

The moon was barely a sliver full, and it would take three whole nights to walk through the swamps with his pack, even with the help from the lizardmen. He only had around seven nights to finalize his preparations. In seven days, he would meet with the dragon and lizard leaders, their scheduled scouting missions completed.

He already met with the Overlord's representative. It was a quick meeting and the human told Annos all information he could gather through his spy mages.

It was a good plan. It was up to Annos to finish the job.

The Overlord sat behind his imposing wooden desk, his dark eyes gleaming in the flickering torchlight. Before him stood his trusted Porter, a figure clad in a black, starry robe that allowed him to blend seamlessly into the shadows as he teleported in and out of the hostile territory. The Porter had returned from a recent mission to Dunbar, bringing back valuable information.

"Report," the Overlord commanded, his silky voice tinted with his menacing demeanor.

The Porter bowed respectfully before beginning their account, clearing his throat. "My lord, I regret to inform you that I could not enter the city walls of Dunbar. They have bolstered their patrols, making infiltration nearly impossible. They are on high alert since they know of our...interference with this previous Barony. However, I did manage to observe their activities from a safe distance."

The Overlord leaned forward, his fingers intertwining as he listened intently. "Tell me, what did you see?"

The Porter's voice took on a cautious tone as they relayed the details. "The humans of Dunbar have been diligently fortifying their city. They are digging something called a moat, a water barrier impeding any direct approach from the lizardmen. Additionally, they are constructing a road leading into the jungle, a cable stretching the distance. It appears they are focused on securing their resources from the cave. I believe they are going to make their own steel production."

A flicker of interest danced in the Overlord's eyes as he absorbed the information. The significance of Noah's actions was not lost on him. The moat indicated a heightened level of preparedness, indicating they were aware of potential threats. The road to the mines hinted at a commitment to their mining operations. He was aware of the iron and tinderstone resources there, his people secretly teleporting the fire resource out for decades.

"Their actions reveal a growing sense of vigilance," the Overlord mused, his voice laced with calculated thought. "The humans of Dunbar are not to be underestimated. We must inform the Shadowalkers accordingly."

The Porter nodded, their gaze fixed upon the Overlord with unwavering loyalty. "Indeed, my lord. They are aware of the dangers that surround them. Their preparations suggest a united front, a determination to defend their resources and maintain dominance. But they will be unaware of the threat from the mountains. The Monarch has no way of knowing about this alliance."

A faint smile tugged at the corner of the Overlord's lips. "Very well."

The humans of Dunbar had grown formidable, but the Overlord was not one to back down from a challenge.

As the meeting concluded, the Overlord rose from his desk, a shadow of determination enveloping him. "Prepare our forces. Gather the spies, the assassins, and the strategists. We shall recalibrate our approach, for the road to victory may be treacherous but not insurmountable."

With a nod of agreement, the Porter bowed again, their commitment to the Overlord's cause unwavering. He moved to leave the office, but the Overlord stopped him with one more question.

"And this girl, Mara," the Overlord questioned, his voice tinged with curiosity. "Tell me more about her. How advanced are her Astral powers?"

The Porter paused for a moment, collecting their thoughts before responding. "My lord, the girl possesses some degree of Astral power but is not yet considered strong. Her abilities are still developing, and she lacks the mastery and control to make her a formidable adversary. She cannot see far, nor fight us away for long. Our coverage of the city keeps her blind and dampened."

The Overlord's mind began to weave possibilities, envisioning the potential uses of Mara's nascent powers by the enemy. Although she might not pose an immediate threat, her untapped potential intrigued him. Perhaps he could take her after the battle was won. The ingredient that she would drop might be exactly what he was looking for.

"Keep a close watch on her," the Overlord instructed, his voice laced with a calculated tone. "Monitor her growth, and should her powers show signs of advancement, report back to me immediately."

The Porter nodded, their expression a mask of dutiful obedience. "As you wish, my lord," he acknowledged and bowed deeply again. He blinked out of existence, and the Overlord turned to the myriad of plans that unfolded before him.

Mara was an unfortunate roadblock, but not one that would stop him or his allies. And a road into the jungle and a little water wouldn't stop him either. This time, he would best this teenager from Earth, then turn his sights on the true prize. The place where he would set up for the next stage of his domination of Prixa.

Fayport.

Chapter 4

Preparations

I WALKED BRISKLY THROUGH THE CORRIDORS OF DUNBAR'S palace, the parchment in my hand bearing the names of those chosen to accompany me on the scouting mission in the mines. I felt anticipation surging through me as I walked through the darkened hallways. It was night, and a steady rain fell from puffy, dark clouds outside. The council meeting had ended around an hour ago, and the members of the table assigned their short-term work duties to move the city's growth along.

I didn't know how long we would be away and had much to prepare for. Reaching the grand chamber, I unrolled the parchment and began pinning it to the wall near where Dee normally sat at the entrance during the day, each name designated alongside their assigned role. She wasn't there, having gone home after the meeting.

I had already sent a messenger to everyone's home to get the parchment delivered, but I wanted an official notice pinned to the palace door. It would be good for the city to see that it was a mixed group heading out on the mission.

On Prixa, mana was a game of 'rock, paper, scissors' when it came to the efficiency of the attacks. One worked better on some than others. And then, the way the Feka worked, hunters and warriors had their own rules. I wanted to confirm I had each mana type with me since I had no idea what we would face.

I didn't want to have all fire mages with me and face a water creature, for instance. I even made sure I had a skilled warrior with me.

Was it overboard? Maybe. But I wanted to make sure I wasn't caught off guard. I also called it a 'Scouting Party' in case spies from Fulgar were here or could watch somehow. I still needed to trust that I had a city full of loyal residents. I still wore my anti-scrying belt everywhere I went, but I knew that had a small area of influence.

The note read:

> Mine Scouting Party
> Noah - Miner
> Dee - Hunter
> Nyo - Warrior
> Jasper - Fire Mage
> Jamie - Alchemy
> Kyle - Air Mage
> Liza - Earth Mage
>   Meet at the city gates at first light. Be
> prepared to be gone for up to three (3) days.
>   Signed,
>   Baron Noah

I looked over the list one last time, satisfied. With the preparations set in motion, I made my way toward the smithy; my thoughts consumed by the impending mission and the pressing need for the silver ore. I needed to see Romas to check on something in the back of my mind since arriving.

Entering the smithy, the rhythmic clang of metal upon metal filled the air. Sparks danced before my eyes as Romas worked diligently on one of my mining carts, most likely manually crafting it while he waited for his mana to regenerate.

I stood there, waiting. I knew better than to interrupt Romas when he was in the middle of a project, Baron or not. Finally, the iron cart cooled enough for him to look up and nod to me. "Yes, boy?"

I smirked. "What, not calling me Baron yet like everyone else?"

He made a growling huff sound and frowned. "Eh, those others can call you whatever they want, but I'm still your master blacksmith. Our craft dates back generations, and there is no more noble relationship than..."

Before he went into a long speech, I held my hand up and cut him off. "Yeah, yeah. Call me whatever. I'm here because I wanted to try and make something with the Stalker pelt that Baron Gilbert gave me."

Romas frowned, his whiskers twitching slightly. "Yes, I stored it *you know where*. But I doubt you can make anything with it. The pelt is a treasure, but its level surpasses your current expertise. Its raw energy requires a more skilled hand to unlock its full potential."

Disappointment washed over me. I respected Romas' expertise and his knowledge of the intricacies involved in harnessing the essence of such a high-level material. I wanted to make something with it, but knew better than to waste it.

"You sure?"

He nodded. "A level 8 ingredient, to be used to its fullest potential, needs to be part of a very intricate build. Even using five slots wouldn't result in the best equipment." He looked around and dropped to a whisper. "I have eight slots now that I'm level 26, but it's a full day of design and build-out. And that's using the tables and the anvil. If you made something with it at your level, which you might be able to do, whatever you made wouldn't be worthy of the level of that ingredient."

"Okay. I hoped to make a slightly higher-level armor before getting into the mines. I don't know what I'll face down there."

"I get that, but sometimes the best armor comes from a journey into a hostile place and using what you find. Take the most common elements of the armor you've already made, and be ready to build in the field. That's my advice, anyway. But you can grab anything from the pile over there." Romas waved his paw to the corner of the smithy.

I looked at the fur pelts from the random ingredients the forest had provided. I sighed. He was right. There was no reason to burn 30 mana on something when I planned a trip like this.

"I'm good. Need anything else for the mines or the new carts?"

Romas shook his head. "All set. I'm making the carts manually for now, since you had the designs. I want to make sure we don't *miss* anything." He smirked, thinking about how my first cart blew up.

I rolled my eyes and told him I would see him soon. I had my 'Armor of Binding Fire' on, a level three armor, and most likely better than anything I would build here. It had excellent properties against fire magic, as did my pickaxe. But I had nothing protecting me against the other mana types.

I walked over to my locker and grabbed the mana bracer and other odds and ends. Some sinew, a few living tree branches, stuff like that. I threw it all in my fanny pack that I strapped to my back.

I didn't know how dangerous the creatures would be if we even saw any. But if I was going to get in a fight down there, I wanted to be ready to come back with some shiny new armor. And, of course, some random cave flowers and silver.

Next, I went through the bustling corridors of the city's crafting sector. My heart fluttered with anticipation as I sought out Mara. She was staying with a few of the other female mages in a house that didn't have anyone living in it. It had been a vacant home originally owned by a few fallen Fekan warriors, and I had repurposed it.

As I reached Mara's quarters, I knocked gently on the door, a smile tugging at the corners of my lips. The door swung open to female voices chatting quietly, revealing her radiant presence. Her eyes sparkled with mischief, mirroring the warmth in her smile as she greeted me. The two other mages looked on and smirked, then took their plates of food to the other room. One was Jamie, the alchemist I had invited tomorrow. Hopefully, that wouldn't cause any...*issues.*

"Baron Noah," she said, her voice carrying a hint of playfulness as she curtsied. "To what do I owe the pleasure of this visit?"

She gave me a peck on the cheek and offered me entry into the home. I walked past her, looking around. The space was sparsely furnished, with the girls having just moved in a few days ago. A few plants were along the back wall, with a rug in the center. A small wooden table had cushions around it, apparently where they ate.

I leaned in, my voice a low whisper. "I came to ask you a favor before I went into the mines tomorrow."

Mara's curiosity piqued as she tilted her head, a playful glint in her eyes. "Oh, and what might that be?" She walked in closer to me, wrapping her arms around me.

I smiled at her. "Not that kind of favor."

She playfully pouted. "No? Okay, what then?"

"I need you to scout the continent for me," I said, my voice filled with excitement. "I need your Astral powers to survey the land around us to see if there are any other cities or civilizations we don't know about yet here, especially near the mountains and around Fulgar. I have to figure out who the Overlord talked about when discussing allies. He has a plan for all of this, and I can't figure out what it is."

Mara's expression showed a touch of hesitation. "Noah, you know my powers are still developing. I can try, but I won't be able to look for long."

"I get it," I said, drawing closer to her. "You should have a few days while I'm out in the mine with my group. No need to try and make contact with them yet. Just see what you find."

She pursed her lips, then nodded. "Okay. Let me see what I can do. Be careful tomorrow." Her gaze turned serious, the worry evident on her beautiful features.

I reluctantly stepped back after a final gentle kiss, the closeness between us lingering in the air. "I will. I'm sure I have way too big of an entourage and will pack too many supplies. But I'll be careful." I winked at her playfully, my tone light-hearted as I spoke. "Until we meet again, Chancellor Mara."

I turned and headed out the door to return to the smithy and get some rest. I wanted full stat bars for tomorrow.

Chapter 5

Telepathy

I STOOD AT THE FRONT OF THE SETTLEMENT IN THE EARLY morning light, my eyes scanning the surroundings as I waited for my crew to assemble. I planned out my path in the cave, wondering where I hadn't gone yet. These thoughts mingled with the nagging thought that perhaps I had brought too many supplies for our scouting mission. Seeing the numerous packs, weapons, and food stores piled up beside me made me doubt my judgment.

Jasper walked out the gates first. He eyed me, the packs next to me, then sent a smirk my way. "I hope you're planning on bringing a mule with us. Is our mission to conquer the mines? Maybe setting up a trading post?" Jasper's voice dripped with playful sarcasm, earning a chuckle from the other crew members walking behind him.

I couldn't help but laugh, shaking my head at the absurdity of it all. "Well, Jasper, you know me. I like to be prepared for any eventuality. Who knows? We might stumble upon a hidden treasure trove or start our own village!" I retorted, unable to suppress a grin.

"That's just what you need. Another city to run!" Dee jabbed at me, walking out onto the path behind us. She wore her hunter gear, the leather armor well-oiled.

The jests and banter continued as the rest of the crew joined us, each carrying their own array of supplies. Laughter and camaraderie filled the air, easing the tension that had begun to build within me. I realized how nervous I was about this venture. The thought of the rat boss fight lingered in the back of my mind. I didn't want to take the caves lightly.

Nyo, the only Feka warrior to join the mission, walked out the gates and eyed us suspiciously. I smiled at him and wished him good morning. I mentally counted the members of our group, and my eyes landed on Jamie. She was the last to arrive, the fiery redheaded mage's presence captivating as always. A tinge of guilt washed over me as I realized my mind had momentarily drifted into thoughts that were...less focused on the mission at hand.

"Hey, Jamie!" I greeted her with a warm smile, trying to regain my composure. "Glad you could join us! Hopefully, we can get you some cool alchemy ingredients from this expedition."

Jamie returned the smile, her eyes gleaming with warmth. "Of course! I'm excited to be part of this journey. I've prepared a few concoctions that might just surprise you. Some drinkable potions and such!"

"Sweet. Excited to see what you've got. Is that everyone?"

Shaking off the distracting thoughts, I focused on the group, ensuring everyone was ready and accounted for. With one last glance at the piled-up supplies, I couldn't help but chuckle inwardly. Perhaps I had indeed gone a bit overboard. But, in the end, it was better to be safe than sorry.

I nodded to the group. "Let's go, squad."

Kyle, the silent Zephyr monk, grabbed a few packs without me even asking as his muscles bulged in his bare chest, and a few others grabbed a bag as well. Nyo shook his head and began toward the jungle, not bothering to take anything. I rolled my eyes at the stubborn cat.Our group followed into the jungle, everyone weighed down by my packs.

Mara watched from the upper level of the settlement as Noah's group strode away into the jungle, a pang of jealousy in her heart, both at the fact that she wasn't asked to go, and that her cute roommate was a team member.

Her gaze lingered on Noah, his determination and leadership shining through his eyes as his hands waved in excitement while he spoke. The playful banter and laughter didn't help Mara's mood.

She shook her head, scolding herself. *Silly girl. Noah likes you. Nothing is going to happen.*

But no matter what she did, she couldn't shake her envy. She sighed and moved on to her next task. Noah wanted her to find out who else was on this continent, or even this planet, that could help them.

Unfortunately, she could barely escape Dunbar whenever she tried to use her powers over the last few days. The mages in Fulgar had boxed her into an 'anti-scrying cage' of sorts, and she used almost all of her mana to get out of it. She looked at her arm, unchanged over the past week or so, other than the anti-scrying skill leveling up to three. Now, each time she attempted to break free of the city, she burned around five mana before she cut the skill off. She had tried this morning and was already missing some mana.

[MARA]
[LV 3 - ASTRAL MAGE APPRENTICE]

[HEALTH 20/20]

[MANA 21/33]

 -L3

 - L1

 - L1

The first skill, her anti-scrying, kept up with her current level, most likely from the work with the Monarch and her attempts at breaking out of the cage. Her second, the scrying skill, had not leveled up at all. Lastly, her antidote skill baffled her a bit. She

550

seemed to heal Noah back in the jungle when he was poisoned, but it was his veins she was fixing, not the poison itself. So it was more about the battle with the dark magic of the poison than helping someone with a spider bite. At least, that's what it seemed.

She needed the Monarch's help. The regal cat would be able to guide her through this. But she had returned to Fayport to run the capital, leaving Mara to her own devices. She didn't know what the Overlord's fascination was with taking Dunbar, but she was undoubtedly caught in the middle of something big.

Speaking of big, Mara's eyes were suddenly drawn to the sky as a flicker of movement caught her attention. Something large and majestic soared high overhead, its form obscured by the distance. Intrigued, she attempted to activate her scrying abilities, hoping to gain a closer look, but an invisible barrier prevented her from peering beyond its veil.

Frustration gnawed at her as she strained to see through the obstruction. The blockage she got from the Fulgarian mages kept her from going laterally across the continent, but upward? There shouldn't be anything stopping her, she supposed.

What could be blocking her scrying abilities? Who or what was this mysterious presence flying over Dunbar?

Just as her mind raced with questions, a sage voice resonated in her thoughts, its ethereal presence unsettling her. The voice seemed to surround her. It was everywhere at once, impossible to shut out even if she tried.

[CHILD OF THE ASTRAL PLANE. YOU MUST LEAVE THIS PLACE. IT WILL BE TAKEN SOON. THEY ARE COMING.]

The voice echoed with a sense of urgency, shaking her very core.

A shiver ran down her spine as she absorbed the weight of those words. *Who could be after them? Why would someone seek her out specifically?*

Her mind raced, considering the possibilities. *Was it something to do with her new magic class?* She could barely make out the creature as it circled in the wind. It looked like an enormous bird, but it couldn't be if it flew that high up.

Mara's curiosity and concern overwhelmed her, urging her to reach out to the mysterious creature soaring above. She used her mind and projected her thoughts upward.

[WHO ARE YOU? WHY DO YOU INTEND TO ATTACK DUNBAR?]

Suddenly, the female voice interrupted her conversation, informing her that she had unlocked a new skill.

[YOU HAVE UNLOCKED THE 'TELEPATHY' SKILL]

She jumped, startled by the skill being unlocked. Her arm burned as another tattoo imprinted itself below the other three skills.

To her surprise, the creature responded, its voice full of sincerity.

[I CANNOT SAY. BUT I IMPLORE YOU, CHILD, LEAVE DUNBAR. I CARE NOT FOR YOUR CITYS INHABITANTS, BUT I CANNOT SEE AN ASTRAL MAGE INJURED. THAT IS ALL I CAN SAY]

She saw the beast turn and fly off, heading north.

[WAIT!!]

She tried calling it, but there was no response. Mana continued trickling out of her arm as she pushed her thoughts outward, but she couldn't get an answer. Confusion and fear bubbled up in her gut. *Why would this creature, capable of telepathically speaking with her, warn her to leave the city? What hidden dangers lay in wait for her within the walls of Dunbar?*

Mara's mind raced, torn between her loyalty to her new city and her instinct to protect herself. She shook her head rapidly. Her mana was now at [12/33]. She panicked a bit, trying to send a thought out to Noah. She wanted to warn him before he went too deep into the cave. As she directed her thoughts, it felt like they bounced off a wall. She was still prevented from using any astral skills. Perhaps the creature had helped by forming the mental connection first.

She huffed in frustration again. With renewed resolve, Mara turned her gaze toward the gulf south of the town, her mind already calculating the next steps.

She needed to find a way to escape her scrying cage and find answers. Noah couldn't come back to a captured city.

Not on her watch.

Chapter 6

Spelunking

We stepped into the dark recesses of the mine, our footsteps echoing against the stone walls. The familiar mine scent lingered in the air as we traversed the front section. None of the miners were here to start their shift. The flickering glow of torchlight danced upon the rough-hewn walls, casting eerie shadows that seemed to come alive.

As we ventured further, the mine transformed into something more akin to the cave it used to be before our mining operation took hold. The rocky terrain shifted beneath our feet, the ground unevenly filled with boulders and crevasses. Stalactites and stalagmites jutted out from above and below, forming a natural obstacle course for us to maneuver through.

The large cat ducked and squeezed into some of the tighter gaps, complaining under his breath.

"You know," Jasper said, "You didn't have to come."

Nyo growled at Jasper. "I wouldn't miss a chance to see what you humans are up to."

"I'm here too, you know," Dee retorted, huffing slightly.

I shook my head and lit my mushroom lantern. I had made a few before the trip and had extra vials packed away in one of the backpacks. We continued further in as the air grew colder. The dripping water echoed throughout the cavern, making me wonder if a stream was nearby. Then again, the land above us was pretty swampy. It was no wonder water was finding its way down here.

My mining sense showed the various ore veins, but nothing new so far. "So, what are we looking for exactly?" Jamie asked from the back of the group. Her voice echoed off the walls.

"I need a specific ore type for my newest machine," I replied.

The cave seemed to stretch on endlessly, its depths unfathomable. Faint rays of light shone from the ceiling, a crack somewhere leading to the surface. We moved cautiously, our senses heightened, alert to any sign of danger or hidden treasures. The stomping of our footsteps reverberated through the cavern.

We had to be close to where Typh and I battled the Mecho. I remembered the battle like it was yesterday. The way the bear rumbled down the cave tunnel at us, the glow in its eyes, and its enormous height when it stood on its rear legs.

After a while, we reached a fork in the tunnel and chose to go left. Before we went too far, I held us up. I hefted my pickaxe and scratched an X into the wall, showing which way we had come from. We continued walking, on high alert in the purple light.

Up ahead, a chamber opened. The sound of water increased, a small waterfall flowing into a cave pond. "Give me a second, guys. I'm going to check the walls."

I heard the group put the bags down with a sigh of relief. We had only been walking for a couple of hours, but the rough terrain tired us out. The group sat on the packs and began talking quietly, but Kyle stood apart, glancing around.

There was more silverstone here, so I hoped we were getting closer. My mana was fully charged, but I only came here to mine if it was the silver ore. Since I didn't know how deep it would end up being, I saved my mana. "No dice. We need to keep moving further in. This isn't the right ore here."

I heard a few groans from the crew but didn't know what they expected. I knew we would need to search for a while before we found the silver. Suddenly, the peaceful gurgle of the cave waterfall was shattered by an eerie sound that echoed through the corridors. It began as a low, guttural growl that sent a chill down my spine. More growls came from all around the cavern.

Suddenly, a horde of four-foot creatures materialized from the shadows ahead of us, their monstrous forms illuminated by the flickering mushroom lantern. They were grotesque, a twisted mixture of rat and lizard. Their sinewy bodies were mottled, scaly skin, adorned with razor-sharp spikes gleaming with a pale luminescence. It was like they had their own glowing mushrooms growing from their backs. They reminded me of those deep-water fish that had lights over their faces.

Their faces were nightmarish, with elongated snouts lined with rows of jagged teeth, dripping with acidic saliva that sizzled upon contact with the cave floor. Their eyes burned with a primal hunger as they slunk toward our group. I hoped they didn't have the teleportation powers like the rats in the caves near Fulgar.

"Jasper! Fireball!" I yelled, my voice echoing off the cave walls.

His hand shot out, wand tip glowing brightly. With a roar, a fireball shot out toward the creatures. Three dodged to the side and climbed the walls, quick and agile. He hit one, and the monster burst into flames. *Shit, they can climb the walls? What the hell are these things?* I thought.

Nyo raised his sword before him, growling fiercely, teeth showing as his lip quivered. More creatures came out of the tunnel to the right. Acid dripped from their mouths as they roared.

I saw Jamie pull a bomb from her pocket and launch it toward the creatures to the right. They scampered away, the attack rolling to the right and exploding, sending shards of rock flying into the air.

"Jamie! Careful, I don't want the damn cave ceiling to come down! Form up!" I shouted, my ears ringing.

She looked bashfully at me. "Sorry!" She backed up, fear in her eyes. She was going to be useless in this fight and knew it.

Reacting swiftly, our crew formed a defensive formation, with the melee fighters to the front of our group, our weapons and spells at the ready. I pulled my pickaxe loose, the steel gleaming in the dim light. Kyle took a defensive posture to the right, and I felt the wind pick up around us.

The first wave of monsters lunged forward, catapulting off the cave walls at us. Acidic claws sliced through the air, their aim directed at the two Feka. They parried, dodged, and counterattacked with equal enthusiasm, showing the cave beasts who the predators really were. I heard the claws get sheared off with a swipe from Nyo's sword, and Dee took a hit to the side, only to cut off the creature's arm with her dagger. The other blade found its way into the beast's neck, killing it.

A powerful gust of wind erupted from Kyle, knocking the creatures further away but having minimal effect. A dodge and a counter from Nyo and his blade found purchase in the scaly hide of the monsters.

Acidic projectiles were launched from the monsters to the right, hissing and sizzling as they made contact with the cave floor, barely missing Jamie and me. One hit the air mage, and he yelled and held his arm.

We dove to the side, Liza putting up a rock wall between us and the ranged monsters. Dee and Nyo fought side by side, twisting and turning as the melee monsters dove in and out. Their green-tinted teeth flashed at them. Dee was immune to poison and was a good one to fight these things.

I saw an opening when one dove at Dee's leg and missed, swinging my pickaxe down on it. I sheared the leg right off, the monster hissing back at me. Nyo finished it off, taking its disgusting head from its body. Jasper shot another fireball at the ranged monsters, causing the walls to catch on fire now. Two of them were dead on the ground, smoke billowing toward us.

The tide of the battle slowly turned in our favor as we exploited their weaknesses, Dee and Nyo much too strong for the creatures and the fire eating away at them. The three remaining creatures scampered off into the darkness, their pale light fading away as they ran.

We stood around, breaths coming in ragged gasps. The smoke began choking us as we all started coughing viciously, and I yelled to Kyle to clear the air. He grimaced, holding his right arm, but complied. The smoke cleared with a gust of targeted air, and the fires were snuffed out. Liza took down her rock wall, returning the cave to how it was. She held her arm, clearly using a lot of mana with the defensive spell.

We took a moment to catch our breath, bodies battered and tired. Jamie dug into her bag, finding a bandage for the burn on Kyle's arm.

Finally, Jasper spoke. "Well, that's one way to start our trip. Noah, which one of these packs has food in it?"

Chapter 7

A Fekan History

We sat around the fire Jasper had started, the aftermath of the battle evident. Acid burns showed on almost everyone except Dee, slowly regenerating from our health bars. The trickling water of the cave embraced us as we took a moment to catch our breath, sitting amidst the fallen monsters and remnants of the fight.

"Damn, that was intense," I muttered, thinking through the battle in my mind. I still wasn't sure how far we needed to go, and if these were the monsters at the start of our mission, I wasn't sure we could handle the ones further back.

Jasper chuckled and slung an arm around my shoulder. "Yeah, but nothing our little squad can't handle!" He flashed me one of his trademarked smiles, and I returned the grin. Despite our exhaustion, it did feel nice to come out victorious from the battle.

I took a deep breath and looked around at my companions. Their tired faces mirrored my own, etched with the signs of the fierce struggle we had just endured. It was time to regroup and assess our next steps.

"Alright, guys," I began, my voice tinged with more weariness than I would have liked. I rubbed my eyes and took a deep breath. "We need to figure out our next move. We've fought worse in the jungles, but I'm not sure what else is down here. Or how far we will have to go."

I leaned forward, resting my hands on my knees, and spoke up. "The best bet is to push forward. I'll grab the ingredients from the monsters and see what I can make. Maybe I can assemble a few acid-resistant vests for us in case we run into those things again. And Liza, it's time you had a proper wand."

The crew murmured their agreement and returned to their dinner, the earth mage grinning at me in excitement. I walked over to one of the claws on the cave floor and inspected it, its jagged nails still glistening with residual acid.

[VITRIC CRAWLER CLAW - LEVEL 2 INGREDIENT]

Not bad, I thought. I went to design some armor with it, and the world slowed down. A simple armor vest cost me a claw and some leather. I had both. If I wanted to make a weapon, I could make a dagger with the claw itself or an earth wand that could cast a spell called 'ACID ARROW,' which sounded useful. It reminded me of a spell from a video game on Earth.

I cut my design skill off, my mana ticking back a few. The engineering skill used the same mana as my old design skill when I was in the field. The main difference in the upgraded skill was the options I could pull up for the same ingredients and the HUD when using a workbench.

I walked over to my pack, pulled out a few leather pieces, and concentrated. The claw and leather wrapped around my chest, forming a protective vest. The group had stopped talking and were observing me now as their gazes bore into me in the torchlight.

When I was done, I shrugged the vest off and tossed it into the semi-circle. I heard a few 'oohs' and 'ahhs' as the crew inspected the item but turned my attention back to my creations. I wanted to make the wand for Liza next. She would love to have an offensive skill, and I had plenty of mana."

Snagging the living tree branch and another claw from the ground, I concentrated again, forming the wand in my hand. I opened my eyes and saw Liza standing there, hand out expectantly.

I snickered. "Yes, can I help you?" I jokingly said.

She rolled her eyes. "Let's see it, then!" Her hand stayed extended.

I slipped the wand into her hand, and the smell of mana filled the cave as a skill was most likely added to her arsenal. She turned, pointed the wand at the cave wall opposite us, and shot a sickly green arrow at it. It exploded into the rock, green goo flying everywhere.

"Nice!" I yelled, surprised by the strength of the attack. "Guess you're leveling up from moving swamp dirt around, eh?"

She returned a smile and thanked me before returning to her jerky and bread dinner, cradling the wand in her arms before slipping it into her belt.

I continued gathering the last two claws, since the three in the fire were eviscerated, and saw Nyo eating slightly apart from the group and sat down next to him. The cat looked up from his dried fish, grunted at me, and then kept eating.

"You fought well back there," I said, trying to break the silence. He nodded, then kept eating. I pursed my lips, trying to bridge the gap between us. "Hey Nyo, tell me something. Why Dunbar?"

He stopped eating and bunched his eyebrows up, confused, but didn't respond. I continued. "Like, why are the Shadowwalkers so interested in attacking the Feka? And why Dunbar? Why don't they go around the swampy jungle to the eastern coast, march down it, and attack Fayport that way?"

Nyo looked me square in the face, weighing his response. The group had stopped chatting, listening intently for his answer. He let out a heavy sigh. "My elders fought in a war with the original alpha. He was just a Stalker back then, but he was ruthless. Many years ago, before the outpost of Dunbar stood, the Shadowalkers launched a devastating invasion on our capital, Fayport. It was a bloody affair, a clash between our two races that tore through the streets and left scars that still haunt us to this day. There was no real winner or loser, only death. Even the human mages took part from what I'm told before they retreated to their mountain refuge."

My brows furrowed in empathy as I absorbed the weight of Nyo's words. That must have been what the mages at Fulgar fought in before they went into the mountains. The Monarch had mentioned something similar when I first spoke with her. "I had no idea," I murmured, my voice laced with genuine concern. "But why target Fayport? What was the purpose behind that attack?"

Nyo sighed again, his gaze meeting mine. "The reasons behind the invasion were complex, rooted in ancient rivalries and a thirst for power. Our kind sought to expand our territory to assert dominance over the realm. Fayport stood as the heart of our civilization, a symbol of our strength and heritage. By conquering it, the werewolves sought to gain control over the entirety of the hunting grounds. The swamps and jungle contain all the food in our known region."

I nodded, understanding. The battle for territory was fierce in the predator world when there was a limited food source. "But why target Dunbar now?" I asked, curious. "The outpost was created to prevent another invasion of Fayport, right?"

"Indeed, Dunbar was established as a safeguard by the current Monarch, a bulwark against future invasions. She was assigned there as a Baron at the time. But eventually, the Shadowalkers' desire for vengeance and their hunger for power continued to fester. A new alpha won power, and he saw Dunbar as an obstacle, a thorn in his side, preventing them from reclaiming what they believed was rightfully theirs. Then he invaded, which you know about." He had a look in his eyes, almost like I was the cause of all the Fekan problems.

The cave was silent, the group taking in the cat's words. Nyo's gaze met mine, and his voice filled with determination. "Noah, we must not let history repeat itself. We cannot allow the Shadowalkers to take Dunbar. They would use it as a rallying point for their forces if they did. I do not want to see another invasion of Fayport."

With a firm nod, I looked Nyo in the eyes, our gazes locked in unwavering solidarity. "We won't let history repeat itself. We'll fight alongside each other, Feka and humans, united against the Shadowalkers. Together, we'll ensure the safety of Dunbar and the greater Fekan civilization. I gave our Monarch my word; you also have it here."

He stood up, pounding his fist to his chest, bowing his head. I stood up and held out my arm.

He clasped it firmly.

Chapter 8

Rock Town

We slowly made our way deeper into the cave as our torches cast long shadows that danced along the walls. I continued marking the walls with an 'X' every time we made a turn. I had to admit, though, it felt as if the very stone walls were closing in, the weight of the cave pressing upon us. There were more tight fits as we walked, Nyo having the most trouble maneuvering the tunnels.

I had my mining skill on high alert for a change in ores but didn't see any changes. As we went further, I saw more tungsten, however. There was also more of the orange-hued temperite.

Suddenly, a shrill screech shattered the silence, echoing through the claustrophobic space. My heart skipped a beat as I realized the source of the sound. Cave bats, like the ones from Fulgar, with leathery wings and beady eyes, swarmed from the crevices above, their movements erratic and disorienting. I could hear the 'capes up' call in my mind and almost laughed out loud.

"Jasper! Jamie! They hate fire! Everyone else, back up! Swords will be no use against them!"

The air became a flurry of wings, their black silhouettes darting through the flickering torchlight. Their high-pitched squeaks filled the air, creating a racket that drowned out all other sounds.

Jasper surged ahead to fire at them, but he was swarmed, screaming and holding his face. Bites and claw marks raked all over him.

Shit, I thought. The bats swooped and dived with alarming speed; their razor-sharp fangs bared as they aimed for any exposed skin. I swatted at them frantically, the air around me thick with their fluttering wings. There were more than I remembered seeing in the other cave.

Some of my companions managed to strike the bats down with the blunt parts of their weapons, and I saw an acid arrow take flight, exploding a few feet away and dragging three bats out of the air. But their numbers seemed never-ending. For every bat that fell, two more took its place.

Their proximity made it difficult to see, the torchlight casting flickering shadows that played tricks on my vision. I could hear the occasional yelp or grunt of pain as the bats managed to land a successful attack on my comrades.

I heard a *clink clink clink* as something rolled down the tunnel as Jaime yelled, "Eyes shut!"

Then an enormous *BOOM* shook the cave, followed by a blinding flash of light. I had shielded my eyes, momentarily disoriented by the sudden burst of brightness even with my eyes closed. As my vision cleared, I realized that Jamie had thrown a flash grenade.

The bats, caught off guard by the blinding burst, were thrown into disarray. Their wings flapped wildly as they collided with one another, disoriented and confused. The once-ferocious swarm faltered, their screeches turning into panicked squeaks as they tried to escape the blinding light. A bunch of them knocked themselves unconscious against the cave walls.

"Back!" I yelled, and the group retreated backward. Jasper, still squinting his eyes, shot a fireball into the cave roof, and a group of bats were taken down. The rest screeched off into the darkness, the beating of wings the only sound now.

Breathing heavily, I glanced at Jamie with awe. "Jamie, that was incredible! I didn't know you could make flash grenades!"

Jamie grinned, her eyes gleaming with pride and mischief. "Just doing my part! I told you I had some cool tricks up my sleeve." She looked immune to the grenade's effects, just like when they set off the smoke bomb.

People walked up and clasped her on the back as I took stock of the bats on the ground. There were a bunch of burnt-up corpses that wouldn't give us any ingredients, but a few had knocked themselves out on the cave wall. Dee helped finish any off that were still alive, and I put the wings into my bag for use later. They were just level one sinew ingredients, but at least we got something out of the fight.

No one was severely injured; a few bites and scratches throughout the crew. Kyle got the worst of it, once again affected more than everyone else by the earth-based creatures. He looked a bit pale, and his bites were bright red. I offered him the vest, but he didn't take it.

I had the group stop to see if there was something I could make to heal the acid damage he had taken, but I was given an error once again, stating that I needed water mana to create any healing devices. I looked at his arm and saw his health bar was almost half gone. It seemed his body didn't cope well with the scratches from the bats or the acid from the spitting creatures.

The number of attacks so far was worrisome. Luckily, we hadn't faced anything too strong yet. We had to keep moving, and after a brief rest I pushed us onward. I figured we would travel for another hour or so before stopping and making camp.

From further down the cave, Jamie called out to me. "Noah! Come take a look at this!"

But that plan was thrown out the window when the narrow passage abruptly gave way to an awe-inspiring sight. The cavern before us stretched out, vast and expansive, like a cathedral carved out of stone. The air grew cooler, carrying a faint scent of dampness and earth.

My eyes widened as they settled upon a rocky wall-like formation that dominated the cavern's center. In front of the wall was a group of towering figures, their icy-blue skin glistening under the flickering torches that lined the wall behind them. A small stream crossed the front, almost like a moat. In front of the water were violet flowers of all sizes. They seemed to absorb the light near them, leaving behind a chill in their wake. *Voidbloom*, I thought with a grin.

The trolls stood tall, their massive frames reaching a height of eight feet or more, their muscular limbs bulging. They held long spears, each with bat wings dangling off the sides. I signaled to my companions, gesturing for them to halt. We froze in our tracks, concealed in the shadows to the side of the tunnel, observing the trolls from a safe distance. We looked down at them, the path to the rock wall down a hill. Their attention seemed fixed on the rocky formation, unaware of our presence.

"By the moons," Nyo whispered. "Look at those things!"

Inside the little settlement, buildings were carved into the rock. Fires blazed occasionally but no smoke could be seen, somehow venting to the surface. To the left, I saw another hole leading into a dark cavern as smaller trolls with pickaxes came and went from the opening. Others pushed a cart in front of them.

I focused my mining sense to see what was in there, and silver and gold ore lit up my mind. *Holy crap. There it is! And a gold ore too!*

Carefully, I relayed what I had seen to the group, keeping my voice hushed to avoid alerting the trolls. Whispers of excitement rippled through our group. The two things I needed, both in one place. Getting them, however, was a different problem.

Jasper leaned in closer, his voice barely above a whisper. "Noah, those trolls are massive! What the hell do we do? I'm assuming they're water-based, just from the looks of them. Jamie and I will probably be useless. And it looks like there are around a hundred of them total!"

I looked over the little settlement, a plan forming in my mind. I didn't necessarily need to get in their little mine to get the silver. But I had no idea how far my skill could pull ore. If I wasn't close enough, it wouldn't work. And while I saw the ore, it was hard to tell its depth with my skill from this distance.

The stealth tattoo stared back at me from my arm. I needed to strategize and find a way to slip past unnoticed. But I couldn't risk them seeing me without any help. Carefully, I outlined a plan to divert attention to the other side of the cave using another one of Jamie's bombs. In this low light, I assumed the trolls didn't have very good vision. If we made sounds, they might chase them around. I also didn't know what kind of intelligence they possessed.

Nyo was the first to speak. "While the diversion is in play, we can move swiftly and silently. We must tread lightly and be mindful of our surroundings. Any misstep could alert the trolls to our presence. We will watch your back while you attempt to get the ore."

Suddenly, horns started going off in the settlement, and the trolls guarding the gates ran into the little town, closing a makeshift stone gate behind them. I heard yelling as a troll, running toward the city from behind us, screamed and pointed at our group.

"So much for the plan," I muttered.

Chapter 9

A Little Dinghy Ride

As Mara made her way toward the secret stairs leading from the second level of Dunbar to the first, her thoughts were consumed by the recent encounter with the creature from the sky. The memory of the sage voice warning her of the impending danger weighed heavily on her mind, causing a knot of unease in the pit of her stomach.

She had always heard folk stories about dragons and giant, flying beasts. *Could that be what it was?* She had thought dragons were mythical, but then again, she had seen many things since leaving the mines of Fulgar.

Her footfalls echoed softly against the stone steps as she descended. Near the bottom, the air grew heavier with warmer jungle air. She opened the door and glanced around, ensuring no one was watching. The door opened to a stone wall, so people rarely knew to look back there, but the protocol said to check.

The gentle sounds of laughter and conversation drifted to her ears, intermingled with the rhythmic clatter of tools and the occasional melodic hum of a craftsman at work. Noah had assigned people to various tasks and now the streets were filled with vibrant life that thrived within the crafters' quarters.

Taking a deep breath, Mara turned right down a nearby alleyway and began her descent toward the docks. It was around breakfast time, and the murmur of conversations and the clinking of glasses in the taverns behind her were replaced by the rhythmic lapping of water against the docks. The salty tang of the sea filled the air, mingling with the sounds of seagulls soaring overhead, calling out to each other. She smiled at them, the ridiculous creatures that they were.

As she walked, she thought more about the telepathic conversation. The encounter had left her with a deep sense of vulnerability, a reminder of the unpredictable forces that lurked beyond the safety of the city walls. She couldn't recall a time when an enemy force invaded Fulgar. But they were blocked by mountains on all sides, so perhaps no one knew they were there.

Mara turned one more left, the path leading down a rocky cliff. As her feet touched the dock's wooden planks, she paused momentarily, absorbing the tranquil surroundings. The soft creaking of the boats rocked gently by the water's embrace filled the air, a soothing lullaby that seemed to ease her troubled thoughts. The occasional clattering of fishing equipment being prepared by the dockworkers.

The dock workers were already hard at work, three of them deep in concentration, using that ridiculous looking spiky thing to smash the fish the Feka caught on the gulf.

The muscular workers immediately dropped the rope and knelt down when they saw her. "Princess!" they all shouted in unison, bowing their heads. The smashing device slammed down on the fish, sending guts all over them. They shared side-eyed looks of embarrassment.

Mara rolled her eyes and laughed. Much to Noah's delight, this whole *Astral princess* thing had taken off around the settlement. "Stand up, boys. No need for all of that."

They stood up, shaking some of the fish guts off. Kyle, the leader of the dock workers, was with Noah, so a new boy stepped forward, speaking slowly. "What can we do for you this morning, Princess?"

She took a breath. "I need a boat ride. Probably not too far, but I need to leave the settlement's shores for a little while." She didn't go into much more detail for now.

The boy nodded, then looked her in the eyes. Mara didn't deny feeling a bit...flustered by these tanned, extremely muscular shirtless boys. "We would, Princess, but the Feka are the only ones allowed to use the boats. But...you're also our Princess, so..."

He seemed to be having an internal war. Years of being subservient to the cats showed its toll.

Mara pushed on. "Have any of you sailed one of those things before?" She nodded to one of the small sailboats tied to the dock.

The boy nodded. "Me and Jack have our air powers, although we are low-level. Like some of my fellows, I have found more use with productive powers than combat. I can take you out for a time." Suddenly, he looked anxious. "But I must warn you; the water could be rough with the moons where they are."

She smiled. "That would be excellent. Let's go!"

Excitement coursed through her as they boarded the small vessel. Mara had never been on a boat before. The dock worker looked anxiously from side to side, most likely afraid of getting in trouble. A few Feka had passed them, looking on with disappointing glances, but didn't say much. She had a status here; even the cats knew better than to say something to her.

To her surprise, she felt the wind pick up around her as the boy's arms outstretched toward the sail. It poofed out, taking in the air and propelling forward. The boat glided smoothly across the water, driven by the dockworker's powers. Mara watched in awe as the wind responded to his command, filling the sails and carrying them further away from the familiar shores of Dunbar and into the wavy gulf. The boat's gentle rocking beneath her feet increased to a side-to-side sway.

As they sailed out, the shores gradually became smaller, blending into the horizon. Mara could see a tall, rocky cliff on the other side of the body of water. Mara's heart raced with anticipation, hoping that her astral powers would have a greater range beyond the reach of the city's protective anti-scrying measures. It was a rare opportunity for her to tap into her abilities without restriction.

"Can we get to the other side of the gulf? If I could get higher up, that would be best," she asked him.

He grimaced. "That's pretty far away still, and the middle of the gulf gets rocky. I've only been out here a few times to fill in during Fekan holidays to fish."

Mara nodded. "I'll take that risk. I won't be able to concentrate bobbing up and down in this damn thing," she yelled over the noise of the wind as her ponytail whipped behind her.

After around three hours of blasting through the waves in the dinghy, they finally reached the other side. Without the air mage propelling the ship, Mara assumed it would have taken forever to cross the large body of water, and she was thankful that it didn't take much longer.

The air mage looked exhausted but jumped out of the boat and dragged it to the sandy shore. They anchored in a secluded spot below the tall cliffs.

"I'm going to head up there. Do you want to stay with the boat?" Mara asked.

"I will escort you, Princess. We can't be sure what lives on this island, and you mentioned concentrating. If you need to do something that distracts your awareness, you will need someone to watch your back."

She smiled. "Thank you. What was your name?"

"Greg, Princess," he said, holding his hand out.

"Okay, Greg. You can stop calling me Princess and start calling me Mara, for starters." He looked at his feet bashfully. "Second, I don't know how to get to the top. Do you see any way to access the plateau there?"

They walked along the shore for a while, the sound of the waves picking up behind them as the heat of the day continued increasing. Finally, they reached a point where a ledge was only 60 feet up, with footholds to climb. "This looks like our best bet. Let's climb here."

She jumped up, holding on to the nearest rock before hoisting herself up. From below, she felt a slight push of air on her backside. She laughed out loud. "Greg, I should be good for now, thank you."

He coughed and cleared his throat. "Sorry, Prin...I mean, Mara. Just trying to help."

Mara's palms grew slick with sweat as she climbed the rocky wall, her fingers grasping the rough edges for stability. The heat of the ascent intensified, making each step feel more demanding than the last. Despite her best efforts, her footing faltered a few times, causing her heart to leap into her throat.

But in those moments of near-slippage, Greg was there to lend his assistance. With another surge of controlled air, he bolstered her, providing the necessary support to keep her from plummeting down the treacherous slope.

Mara didn't give him a hard time anymore.

Their determination propelled them onward, even as fatigue gnawed at their muscles. At long last, they reached the top of the rocky wall, their perseverance paying off. Mara's eyes widened in awe as she beheld the breathtaking vista that unfolded before her.

She could see for miles from their elevated vantage point in every direction. The land stretched out, and even though they appeared to be on an island, they could see the distant outline of what she assumed to be Fayport, the Fekan capital, a mere speck on the horizon but a testament to the city's immensity.

To the southwest, she could see smoke billowing from what appeared to be a mountainous volcano. And to the north, the jungle trees consumed most of the landscape, but she saw the three-tiered cat tower of Dunbar. Greg pulled himself up, completing the climb as well. He gasped as he took in the sight as well.

"This place is beautiful," Mara whispered. As they stood together, the wind ruffling their hair and the distant echoes of nature filling the air, Mara felt a newfound clarity. She felt back to...normal? She didn't know how to describe it. But her powers weren't constricted here.

"Alright, Greg. Watch my back. I'm going to sit over there. I'm not sure how long I will be like that. But I'm going to explore a bit."

He nodded, but she could tell wasn't comfortable up here. His eyes darted back and forth, looking for danger. But the plateau was only occupied by them, and there weren't any living beings as far as they could tell.

Mara walked to a flat spot of ground and sat down lotus style. She looked down at her arm one last time, seeing her blue mana tattoo still recovering from the telepathy usage at [27/33]. The skill used around one mana per second, so she had a little less than 30 seconds to explore the continent.

Closing her eyes, Mara focused her thoughts, visualizing the ethereal plane that connected her to the fabric of the universe. She allowed her astral senses to extend beyond her physical form, just like the Monarch had taught her, reaching out into the vast expanse before her.

A sense of freedom enveloped her. The cage of anti-scrying measures that had confined her powers within the city's limits dissolved, allowing her astral senses to expand unfettered.

She took the world in her hands and began exploring.

Chapter 10

Rock Beats Scissors

THE LONE SCOUT TROLL STOOD BEFORE US, A FORMIDABLE figure towering over even Nyo. Its muscular frame was draped in tattered animal hides that hung loosely from its massive frame, once vibrant in color but now dulled by time and wear. They looked to be the bat wing skins. The troll's skin had a sickly bluish hue, similar to the frozen glaciers I had seen in the distance at Fulgar. A tangled mane of unkempt hair framed its face, while beady eyes, filled with a glint of primal savagery, stared us down.

As Nyo and Dee drew their weapons, I couldn't help but notice the pungent stench that emanated from the troll. The odor, a combination of unwashed fur, decaying flesh, and an earthy musk, assaulted my senses.

With a swift movement, the troll lunged toward us, its massive club swinging through the air. In the tight tunnel, there was little room to move. With a fierce roar, Nyo swung his sword to meet the club and blocked the strike, their clash resounding with a thunderous crash of iron against wood. But the force made him stagger back, sword clattering to the ground as it was pounded out of his hand.

Before he could recover, the troll swung again, burying the spiked object in his furry arm, its brute force smashing into Nyo and sending him sprawling backward, crashing hard into the unforgiving wall.

The troll was picking up speed now, a berserk look in his eyes. Dee stepped back, cautious now. She had no chance against that club. She darted around the troll with remarkable speed, narrowly evading its heavy strikes. The rest of us backed up, and I saw wands at the ready, but no way to shoot at it without possibly hitting Dee.

With deft footwork and fluid movements, she launched her own counterattacks, striking at the troll's vulnerable spots. Yet, despite her best efforts, the troll's raw strength pushed her back, her petite frame struggling against the brute force of the towering creature.

I felt the telltale sign of the air picking up, and Kyle, still injured, raced to the front of the group. "Kyle! No! Liza, you need to hit it!"

Kyle didn't listen, shouldering us aside and standing before the enormous troll. Behind me, I heard a new horn sounding and looked back. The gate swung open now, and more trolls began pouring out of the little settlement.

Shit! I thought, looking around for a plan.

Jasper looked and saw the same thing, curse words flowing freely from his mouth. He blasted a fireball at them, the ball rocketing down to them. But to our dismay, the fireball *sizzled* on impact, making no dent in them at all. He held his arm, his mana most likely low from casting spells in both battles. I heard Jasper shout more curse words as I turned my attention back to the scout troll.

Kyle had engaged the scout troll and somehow had the strength to withstand the club strikes with his gauntlet. He used that hurricane skill where it looked like the troll was fighting in slow motion. Seeing my comrades' peril, I knew I had to do something. I had one rodent claw in my pouch and kicked on my engineering skill, the world slowing to a crawl.

Inside my mental HUD, I thought about the situation in a panic. Dee could dodge this huge monster, but there was no way her dagger would make much of an impact in a direct fight. Nyo was knocked out against the tunnel wall. The fire skills appeared to be irrelevant, which made sense against water creatures. Liza had her wand, but with her limited mana pool, she probably only had one or two arrows, not seven. And with the other trolls running out of the settlement toward us, we were running out of options.

I had to hurry, though. When I used the design skill in the field, my mana depleted pretty rapidly. I mentally pulled up the earth ring that allowed me a tunneling stealth skill but I couldn't do anything extra with that. I could make another wand, but the cost of me using it was huge for each shot.

In my testing with Jasper, I found that I could use all of the items I created, just like I found out at the battle of Dunbar, where Dee almost died. The night I shot a lightning bolt and never noticed how much mana it used. When Jasper and I tested his wand, I found that he used around four mana now to shoot a fireball, where it cost me twenty.

The same thing applied here. If I made another acid arrow wand with the monsters from the cavern, it would cost twenty mana per shot for me to use it. That, mixed with what I was burning now and the cost of making the wand, made that not an option.

To my surprise, the tungsten showed up as an earth-based ore. When I pulled it up in my mind, I started to see a pattern. Suddenly, a realization hit me like a freight train. *Each of the ores represented one of the branches of mana!* The HUD explained when I pulled up a new information panel with help from my inspection skill.

[ORE MANA STRUCTURE CODEX]
[SILVERSTONE - AIR | WIND]

[?? - AIR | ZEPHYR]
[TINDERSTONE - FIRE | TINDER]
[TEMPERITE - FIRE | TEMPER]
[?? - FIRE | ALCHEMIST]
[WATER MANA NOT YET UNLOCKED]
[TUNGSTEN - EARTH | LUTU]
[?? - EARTH | SLAIT]
[PURE SILVER - SPACE | ASTRAL]
[?? - TIME | ??]

Wow, this is so cool. I nerded out on the ore list briefly, taking it all in. It all made so much sense. I didn't realize some of the names of the mage classes, but now seeing it all in front of me, it clicked. Also, Prixa was boring in its ore names, taking them directly from the type of magic they represented.

I was surprised that I still needed to unlock the Zephyr or Alchemist ore. I also didn't have any temper mages yet. *Okay, Noah. Focus.*

I thought about making some kind of bomb to rain down on the trolls. The ingredients were simple.

[ACID BOMB - VITRIC CRAWLER CLAW | 5X
TUNGSTEN |COST - 20 MANA]

I quickly cut the skill off and rummaged through my pack to get the five blue-hued rocks out. "Liza! Shoot the troll! Jamie, here!" I yelled as I combined the materials. She ran over, looking at my hands. The ingredients combined formed a sickly green egg-looking thing. It pulsed with a dark green hue.

Jamie let out a loud gasp. "Gimme!" she said and snatched it out of my hands. I saw her eyes glaze over for a minute while she inspected it, then frowned. The battle between the scout troll and my crew continued to rage behind me, Liza looking desperately for an opening. "Noah, I can't use this! It's earth-based! Liza!" she called to the earth mage, watching both the oncoming trolls and the scout.

Her head darted around to us. "What?"

Jamie tossed her the grenade, and I gasped in horror, hoping she didn't drop it and blast us all with acid. But she caught it, her eyes glazing as she inspected it. Her eyes shot open, and she smiled. "Nice!" was all she said.

Suddenly, Liza seized the moment and hurled the acid bomb at the oncoming trolls. The bomb arced through the air, trailing a faint vapor of acidic energy before it made contact with the ground at the base of the hill where the trolls stood. She threw it a little short of the trolls, and it rolled ominously.

I watched in anticipation, but nothing happened yet. The trolls continued running and reached the location of the bomb. Then, Liza made a hand movement, and the bomb exploded in a green blast, throwing the nearby trolls in all directions. The explosion was deafening, accompanied by a blinding flash of light and a fierce wave of searing acid. The air filled with a pungent scent of burning flesh and a hiss of pain as the corrosive substance splattered over the trolls, consuming their icy forms with a voracious hunger.

Four of the trolls were instantly engulfed in the acidic onslaught, their bodies melting away with agonized cries. The raw power of the acid bomb proved devastating, reducing them to mere puddles of steaming blue liquid that mingled with the remnants of their icy skin. The others looked dazed and held their body parts that got hit by the acid, stunned at the device's power. Yells and screeches sounded from the settlement's walls as the other trolls looked on in horror at their brethren.

The remaining three trolls were not spared, although they managed to evade the full impact of the explosion. Nevertheless, they suffered severe injuries as the acidic residue clung to their flesh, eating away at their defenses and leaving them vulnerable.

As the trolls writhed in pain, their once imposing forms diminished and weakened, Dee dropped into stealth and used the distraction to get behind the scout troll and stab it in the calf. It turned around on her, and I seized the opportunity to swing my pickaxe at its back, impaling the beast. Its back arched in pain, and Dee finished it off, landing her other dagger in its long, blue neck.

The troll toppled over, Dee nimbly dancing off before it hit the ground. She looked tiny on its enormous frame. Down below, the three remaining trolls were still on the ground, their regeneration desperately attempting to defeat the acid. It bought us a little time to figure out our next move.

I saw more trolls up on the walls watching the whole thing unfold, but they didn't appear to be warriors. My crew stared back, taking the scene in.

Finally, Jasper broke the silence. "Noah...you are getting pretty scary with some of the stuff you can make."

Chapter 11

The Tree

MARA SOARED UP INTO THE CELESTIAL SKY, THE PLANET IN her hands. She felt the pull of mana streaming into this being from her physical body, and the clock had started. She knew she needed to hurry, but things were so peaceful up here.

She looked to the north, checking for the Shadowalker beasts. There was no fog here, and she peered down behind their spikey, log walls. The sight before her revealed a race preparing for war...an unsettling revelation that tugged at her heart.

The Shadowalkers moved with precision and purpose, their forms agile and stealthy as they worked diligently to construct massive walls of vibrant green wood. It was an unexpected sight to see foxes, known for their cunning and adaptability, working together as architects and builders; their skills harnessed for a common purpose.

The green wooden walls seemed imposing and formidable as they stretched high into the air, most likely to be used as a fire barrier.

Her heart weighed heavy with the implications of their preparations. Their invasion had to be soon if the flying creature was to be believed. Evidently, the situation had escalated, and another conflict loomed large on the horizon. Mara knew that the future of Dunbar and its inhabitants hung in the balance. But, from what Noah told her, the canine creatures had been trying to invade the outpost city since he arrived here. So this was really nothing new. Plus, she didn't feel the pull of the flying creature from earlier, so it was nowhere to be found. Unless it was blocking her again.

She moved on, heading east. Here, she saw a smaller settlement but couldn't see many details. The tree canopy blocked her view since the little town was small. She saw a few lizards moving about but nothing more.

Onward she went but found nothing else near Dunbar of interest. She was too afraid to go south near Fulgar, fearing that the mages there would discover her escape from their scrying cage. She still didn't know what type of powers the Overlord possessed.

With her mana still half full, she grew curious about what type of creatures lived on the other side of the world. She flew higher and over the ocean, continuing east. As Mara soared over the sea, her astral senses attuned to the pull of the distant mana. The powerful presence tugged at her like a magnetic force, drawing her ever closer, yet she knew that her mana was rapidly depleting.

The journey was a race against time, and she could sense the strain on her astral self with every passing moment. The vast expanse of the ocean seemed unyielding, a seemingly endless stretch that never ended. She saw a storm with waves as high as Dunbar was tall.

But the pull was relentless, a siren's call that beckoned her forward. Mara pressed on as she allowed her intuition to guide her forward on the trail of mana. The presence she was drawn to felt immense, unlike anything she had encountered before.

As she soared above the rolling waves, her awareness expanded, and she felt a connection with the world, matching the one she felt when she soared with the Monarch. The mana seemed to whisper secrets, ancient knowledge that transcended time and space. Her mana usage slowed, almost as if the source aided her travel. But even with this assistance, she drained her pool. Determined to reach her destination, she pushed herself further, driven by the anticipation of what lay ahead.

With her mana reserves near exhaustion, Mara reached the destination of the potent mana presence. Before her stood a towering ancient tree with its branches reaching high into the sky like the fingers of an otherworldly being. The tree's energy resonated with the mana, intertwining in a delicate dance of power and life. Behind it stood an ancient temple structure.

As Mara's astral self hovered before the ancient tree, she was confronted by the unexpected sight of a mage sitting cross-legged on the ground. Startled, the mage's eyes snapped open, and his gaze locked onto hers with an intensity that belied his calm demeanor. She felt like an intruder in the presence of something beyond her understanding, yet she could not resist the pull of its aura.

[Child!] he addressed her, his telepathic voice carrying a weight of age and wisdom that resonated within her astral consciousness. It sounded in her mind from all around. Her mana usage stopped, suddenly supplemented by this man.

Mara blinked, taken aback by the mage's ability to see her. Nonetheless, she sensed a genuine warmth in the mage's tone, a sense of familiarity that she couldn't quite place.

[I am Mara,] she replied telepathically to the mage. [Who are you?]

The mage's eyes seemed to hold the knowledge of eons as he regarded her. [Names matter little in the grand scheme of things, young one,] he replied cryptically. [I am but a guardian of this ancient tree, a keeper of its secrets and the knowledge it holds.]

Mara's intrigue heightened. The presence of such a venerable guardian amidst the mana-rich aura of the ancient tree filled her with a sense of reverence.

[Why have you come here?] the mage asked, his penetrating gaze seemingly peering into the very essence of her being.

[I was drawn here by the mana presence,] Mara explained. [It called to me, and I followed. I was exploring near my settlement and wanted to see what I could find to the east.]

The guardian nodded knowingly. [Ah, the call of mana,] he mused. [It is a language that few truly understand. You have an affinity for the Astral realm, and the tree sensed that connection within you.]

[But where am I? I can only see you and the tree, although I know I'm across the ocean from where my physical body sits.]

He smiled. [You are near the Trial Moon Sect. You may know of these people.] He had a knowing look in his eyes.

Mara shook her ghostly head. [I've never heard of them. Trial Moon?]

The mage stood up, dusting his knees, even though he was only a spiritual projection. [Your Zephyrs could be their third generation descendants, but these are their people.]

Mara's eyes widened, and she gasped. [Really?!] Her mind raced with the possibilities.

The mage continued. [I have watched your power bloom from afar. The day in the caves where you touched the lunar moss... that moss grows above my head.]

Mara looked up, and sure enough, the strands blew in the slight breeze. He continued. [The astral realm grants me glimpses into the unfolding tapestry of fate. Your journey and the war have caught the attention of those seeking to safeguard this world's balance. Especially against a specific enemy.]

[And who is coming for us?] she asked, her heart quickening in her ghostly chest. [I saw a creature flying above our city. He warned me of some sort of danger.]

[The Shadowalkers,] the guardian answered solemnly. [Their pursuit of Dunbar has become more aggressive, and if they succeed in their ambitions, the consequences will extend far beyond your outpost.]

Mara didn't know much about the wolf creatures other than their constant need to consume animals to survive and grow their strength. *Could they get new powers if they could consume the humans of Dunbar? Could they invade the Fekan capital? What then?* She didn't know if the Monarch could withstand such an attack.

[What can we do?] she pleaded, feeling a sense of dread weighing upon her.

[Rest for now,] the mage advised, his voice gentle but firm. [Recharge your mana and regain your strength. Once you are ready, seek out the Head of the Trial Moon Sect. He holds knowledge and resources that can aid you in your plight. For now, I must release my mana channel on you. I grow tired and have run out of mana.]

[Thank you for your guidance,] she said. [May I know your name?]

The guardian smiled faintly. [In the annals of time, I was known as Alarion,] he replied, voice growing fainter in her mind. [But in this realm, titles matter little. I am but a guardian of the Trial Moon Sect, a humble keeper of the ancient tree and its knowledge. I am pitted against those in my realm who strive to absorb mana into the void. To take all mana and remove it from this very world. Your friend Noah's of a world such as this. Remember, Mara, the path you tread is one of great significance,] Alarion emphasized. [The choices you make will ripple through the fabric of fate. Embrace your role as a seeker of knowledge and wielder of mana, for your journey has only just begun.]

Suddenly, she felt like a pair of scissors cut something tying her to the man, and she was sucked back to her body, unable to control herself.

Back on the island, Mara gasped for breath as she returned to her body. Her arm went completely numb, and she passed out.

END OF ACT I

Interlude I

ELDRIC GAZED AT THE TEENAGE BOY BEFORE HIM, ONCE again trying to understand the strange aura displaying itself when he used his 'Patron' skill. The usual vibrancy of the red or yellow mana, even the five scrying mages with their strange white aura, surrounding his students was absent; instead, an enigmatic darkness clung to him like a shroud. He wouldn't call it *black* per se, but it just didn't have a color. Eldric sensed something unique, even extraordinary, about the boy's potential. But something dangerous also fought him every time he neared him.

He had sent for the boy earlier, and he had stepped into the smithy. The choosing ceremony had been completed, and the 15-year-old boys and girls with the correct mana affinity were already unlocked for the year. Thirteen new mages...a new record. But with Pomius? Nothing, once again. He was sixteen now and hadn't unlocked his type in either choosing.

"Pomius," Eldric called gently, motioning for the boy to approach. "Come closer. Let's get another look at you."

So far, holding fire and air mana tools that unlocked the mages had resulted in no change to his aura. And he knew from the alleyway a few years back that the scrying mirrors wouldn't do anything. "You have an extraordinary aura, my boy," Eldric remarked, his eyes reflecting his curiosity. "It is unlike anything I have seen before. Tell me, do you feel any connection to the magic in you?"

Pomius looked down, unsure of how to respond. The truth was that he had always felt an odd disconnect with the mana that surrounded them. While the other apprentices reveled in their ability to wield the power of fire and lightning, Pomius felt as if he was an outsider, unable to tap into its potential.

"I don't know," Pomius admitted, his voice barely above a whisper. "The magic... it feels strange to me. Like I need to feed it."

Eldric pursed his lips, understanding that there was something more to Pomius' aura than met the eye. It was as if the boy's essence resonated with an energy that stood in stark contrast to the creation magic—the antithesis of the very fabric that he himself wielded.

Pomius looked up, his eyes searching Eldric's face for answers. "What does it mean, Master Creator? Why am I different?"

Eldric placed a reassuring hand on Pomius' shoulder. "You are different because I believe you possess a form of magic beyond what humans should be capable of—a power that comes from the realm of shadow we do not understand."

Pomius frowned. "It feels like I need to...feed it magic. Like it will consume me."

Eldric's eyes softened with compassion as he sensed the turmoil in the young apprentice. "You have potential. If we can understand your magic, perhaps we can better understand our enemies who consume power. But such power must be nurtured and guided, lest it consume you," he said gently. "There is one last thing I could try..."

Eldric trailed off and went to the back. He held a small, mysterious object wrapped in thick leather when he emerged. He set it down on the table but backed away from it.

"Pomius," he said, his voice grave, "I believe this item might hold the essence of what I'll call void magic. I recovered it from a high-level general of the Shadowalker army at the battle of Fayport many years ago." Eldric paused, taking a deep breath. "When I held it, the object attempted to consume my energy. The werewolves utilize this magic when they consume the fallen. It's how they grow in power. They kill, then take the strength of the dead to evolve. Something, or *someone*, made their magic into a powerful object. Perhaps it's from one of their alphas. I've kept it hidden away since."

The boy walked over, curious. He looked to Eldric, who nodded. Pomius pulled the string, and the leather fell away, revealing a small necklace with two fangs on the silver chain. Eldric recoiled as if struck when it opened.

Pomius looked at the necklace with trepidation. Void magic—the very name sent shivers down his spine. The twin fangs pulsed with dark energy.

"I sense that this device may be linked to your abilities," Eldric continued, studying the young boy's reaction. "It could be the key to understanding and harnessing the power you possess. Go ahead, lad. Just be careful."

As Eldric watched Pomius eagerly pick up the necklace, he felt a rush of mana surge through the smithy. Not the fragrant smell of mana being unlocked, but the smell of death and decay. He could feel the raw power contained within the small necklace, pulsating like a heartbeat, absorbing all the mana around.

Eldric's heart pounded as he witnessed the void power engulfing Pomius, its dark allure taking hold of the young mage. The moment was fraught with danger, and he sensed the urgency to intervene before it was too late.

But Pomius seemed distant; his eyes glazed over as if possessed by an unseen force. He spoke his name out loud, proving that he had unlocked a mage class, tapping into the power beyond the realms of creation.

"Yes, my master!" he yelled, then looked at his arm and smiled, veins turning black as the void spread throughout him.

As Eldric tried to reach out to the boy, a change swept over Pomius. The glaze in his eyes sharpened into a dark, greedy look, and Eldric could sense the dangerous shift in his demeanor.

"No, Pomius, you cannot let the void consume you!" Eldric pleaded, stepping back cautiously as he felt the raw power emanating from the boy. He thought of the Shadowalkers and their vicious appearance. He wondered if the boy was going to morph into a monster.

He needed to do something. "You are stronger than this!"

But the allure of the void had taken hold, and Pomius seemed lost to its dark embrace. A reckless desire for power seemed to consume him, and he reached out, his hand trembling as if attempting to draw the magic from Eldric himself. His arm blackened further as a thin wisp of blue streamed from Eldric's arm, and he gasped in agony.

Fear gripped Eldric's heart as he realized the gravity of the situation. The void was a realm of unpredictable chaos, and if Pomius allowed it to overtake him, the consequences would be dire.

"Pomius, listen to me!" Eldric implored, his voice firm. "You must find control within yourself. Embrace your magic, and let it guide you back from the edge of darkness."

Eldric immediately regretted this decision. He thought void magic would just be about shadows and rotting, not about obliteration.

As the void's allure continued to tug at Pomius' soul, his eyes turned a dark, bottomless black. Black veins crept up his neck. Eldric knew that he had to act swiftly to undo this. The boy would become a huge liability to them.

Drawing upon the power of his Patron skill, he desperately tried something he had never done before and extended his hand toward Pomius, invoking a reversal of the magic that had consumed him.

The female voice in his mind told him that he unlocked a subskill, and he pushed ahead. A surge of opposing energies crackled in the air as Eldric's creation magic clashed with the void's power within Pomius. The young apprentice's body trembled under the strain of the conflicting forces, and his mana was rapidly drained, leaving him weakened and vulnerable.

"N-No!" Pomius screamed, his voice filled with agony as he fought against the reversal of the void's magic. His eyes burned with defiance and desperation, but Eldric's resolve did not waver.

With the last reserves of mana, Eldric mustered his strength to channel the reversal spell to its fullest. He was willing to endure the burden if it meant saving Pomius from the dark path he had inadvertently stepped upon.

The void's magic finally began to recede from Pomius, returning to the realm from which it came. As the last traces of the dark aura dissipated, the young apprentice collapsed to his knees, his breath labored and his body trembling with exhaustion.

Eldric inspected his 'Patron' skill, which now had the 'UNDO AFFINITY' subskill. It cost 50 mana, doubled for space and time affinity, and four times for counter mana like he had just battled.

Eldric grabbed the cursed necklace and walked to the forge without hesitation, his steps heavy with determination. He tossed the device into the roaring flames, watching as the inferno consumed the dark artifact.

As the device burned in the red hot coals, Eldric breathed a massive sigh of relief. Just handling the necklace for those brief seconds had taken away the rest of his mana. He collapsed to his knees, breathing in sharply as smoke filled the small smithy.

He turned back to Pomius, who was standing now, a dark look in his eyes. "You bastard!!" the teenager screamed.

But before Eldric could react, a sudden, desperate rage over-came Pomius. In a moment of madness, he grabbed a dagger from the wall and lunged at Eldric.

Eldric's eyes widened in shock as he barely managed to evade the attack, the blade grazing his arm. The pain seared through him, but he knew the young mage was not controlling his actions.

"Pomius, no!" Eldric cried, trying to get up. Pomius kicked the smithy in the chest, sending him sprawling backward into the stone structure, knocking him out with a sickening *thud*.

He walked over and plunged the dagger into Eldric's neck, then leapt to the forge and grabbed the amulet, feeling the small amount of the tainted mana flood into him. He unlocked his class again before the item disintegrated into ash.

His tattoos reappeared, burning onto his skin.

[Pomius]
[Level 1 - Void Mage Apprentice]
[Health 20/20]
[Mana -2/-2]

Pomius fell to his knees in a wordless cry before the voice shook his mind again.

[Rise, my servant. Take your loot and return to your room without anyone seeing you. You have much to learn and farther to progress in your weakened state before you will be the tool to reshape this world.]

[Yes, my master,] Pomius replied as he rose. Sitting there on the ground where the Creator's body dissolved was a colorless, pulsating gem. He grabbed it before quietly exiting the Creator's room.

Chapter 12

Party Interface

I FELT CHANGES IN MY ARM AS MY SKILLS LEVELED UP. Now that the dust had settled a bit from the battle, I took stock of what was happening around me.

Dee was panting, dark spots forming on her fur as she bled from her spiky club wounds. Nyo shook the cobwebs from his head and shakily stood, dusting himself off proudly and looking at the dead troll. The rest of my crew looked haggard, chests rising and falling after the intense battle.

Liza, feeling powerful, had a big smile on her face as she held her arm. "That bomb was amazing!" She looked at Jamie. "That's the kind of stuff you use?"

Jamie nodded. "Yeah, but fire only. My mana type said it was a counter to your bomb, so even holding it made the thing almost explode in my hand!"

I took that fact in momentarily, and I checked out my arm as I did. With a curious frown, I examined my tattoos.

[NOAH]
[Lv 14 - BLACKSMITH JOURNEYMAN]

[BONDED]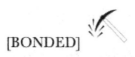

[HEALTH 110/110]
[MANA 93/135]

-L6

-L6

-Passive

-L2

-L9

-L2

[UNSELECTED SKILLS - NONE]

Patron had leveled up to level 8 during my time in the cave, I was now level 14, and my engineering and manufacturing skills were level 4. My mana had now grown to almost half what Romas told me he had at level 25. My heart quickened with excitement as I inspected my 'Patron' skill. I discovered that I had unlocked a subskill called 'Party Interface.'

With a thoughtful nod, I focused on activating the newly discovered subskill. Suddenly, a translucent interface appeared before my eyes, overlaying the world around me. My crew members' names and images popped up, accompanied by a health and mana bar floating above their heads. Their level was also displayed beneath their pictures. I smiled, enjoying the video game vibes in front of me.

The difference is these aren't just some characters in a game you're playing. You can't save before a big battle and reload if things don't go how you want. These are actual, living people under those stats.

I sobered at the thought. Still, the Party Interface would allow me to monitor my group's well-being during battles, making it easier to strategize and support one another. I couldn't help but smile at how this newfound tool would strengthen our teamwork.

Suddenly, a prompt got my attention.

[DISPLAY PARTY INTERFACE FOR MEMBERS OF THE PARTY? COST IS 0.55 MANA PER MINUTE PER PARTY MEMBER. YES | NO]

I pondered this. So if my party had six members, that would take 3.3 per minute of mana. I could click it on during battles since that would be very useful for people to see. But I couldn't fathom using the skill during large battles. *Could I select who was in my party during those events?* I wanted to know what would happen to the skill once it reached level 10.

For now, I selected *yes* to give my crew access to the interface. I wanted them to see it before I randomly clicked it on during our next fight. We still had to go down into the troll town, and I didn't know what awaited us there. We had just killed seven of their buddies, so I didn't expect a particularly warm welcome.

"Hey, guys," I called out to the crew, excitement bubbling in my voice. "Check this out! We've got a nifty upgrade here." I clicked on the skill, then gestured to the floating bars above our heads.

Liza's eyes lit up with interest. "This could be useful during battles," she said, contemplating the implications of the Party Interface.

Dee gave me a nod of approval. "Nice upgrade, Noah! It'll definitely help us coordinate better. I didn't know you had this skill!"

Jasper, ever smiling, couldn't resist a quip. "Finally, some health bars to keep track of who's slacking!" he teased, earning a few chuckles from the group. Nyo was missing almost half his health, and Kyle grimaced as he saw his at around 30% full. A bunch of my crew had no mana left at all.

I clicked the skill off. "I'll only keep it on during battle since it uses a good bit of mana to keep going. A five-minute fight will use, like, 17 mana just for that alone. I know my mana pool is growing, but as we saw in the last battle, I need to keep mana in reserves for *emergencies.*"

They all nodded at that. Below us, in what I still called Rock Town, the trolls had opened the gates, and an enormous troll strolled out, arms crossed and waiting for us. Hopefully, another fight wouldn't break out. My crew couldn't withstand another attack.

I sighed. "Guess we better go say hi."

Hurbnurr stood in front of the crude walls, and his ice-blue eyes fixated on the group of newcomers descending the hill toward his town. He had never seen creatures quite like them before. The display of power they had just unleashed, wiping out a group of trolls without breaking a sweat, commanded his attention and respect.

He had fought the earth-based creatures in the caves for centuries, and the tunnel that led up and out into the jungles had them interacting with animals of the land. Water battled earth down here in a continuous struggle.

But he had never seen these fragile little beasts walking toward him. They resembled weaker versions of the gorilla monsters from the trees near the cave entrance but walked upright and held sticks at the ready.

Hurbnurr scratched his head. *Were these little sticks the things that made that massive explosion? No, it couldn't be.*

As the crew of creatures approached, Hurbnurr's massive form loomed over them, his fur-lined armor glistening with frost. Now that he saw them up close, he also noticed two cats in the group. What a ridiculous little army.

He regarded them with curiosity, his sharp claws flexing at his sides. More warriors waited behind the walls, but he couldn't risk losing more of his force. He knew the cats from an interaction last season. One of their hunters had fought a few scout trolls. They had left one of the trolls dead and two injured. The trolls had eventually killed the cat, and the ingredient was delicious. He wished he could kill this group.

They stopped about fifteen paces ahead of the town, the lead creature stopping to look at the cursed flowers. He picked one up, then cried out in pain, dropping it. Hurbnurr shook his head. He had no idea why the creature was trying to pick such a dangerous item. Then, he pulled some kind of tool out of his pack, plucked a few of the flowers, then put them away in a different bag made of a shiny material.

He was five heads shorter than Hurbnurr, but somehow he weighed the same. He wore armor with an orange glow and wore a small pack around his waist that jingled as he walked. A pickaxe was slung behind his back, also gleaming a slight orange. He turned his attention on the trolls and walked over to them, the rest of his group staying behind and watching him carefully.

"What are you?!" Hurbnurr's deep voice rumbled, echoing through the icy caverns around them. "You come to our land, attacking with no warning."

The creature raised his hands in a peaceful gesture, his expression calm and respectful. "We are humans," he replied, "and we apologize for the misunderstanding. We didn't know this was your territory. We were simply defending ourselves. Your scout troll attacked us, and we saw others running toward us."

Hurbnurr regarded Noah momentarily, his icy gaze seeming to size him up. "Humans," he repeated, a hint of skepticism in his voice. "You wield strange magic, like no troll or creature we see. I know you, though." He pointed to the Feka. "You no welcome here, hunting cats. Who are you, and why you here?"

"We are from Dunbar, a settlement on the other side of the cave," the creature Noah explained. "We came seeking silver ore to aid in the defense of our home. Our settlement is constantly threatened by Shadowalkers and enemy humans, and we need the resources to protect ourselves."

Hurbnurr seemed to ponder Noah's words for a moment, his massive brow furrowing in thought. "Silver ore, you say?" he mused. "It my favorite rock, and I no give away."

The troll leader paused again, then continued. "You humans dangerous. Do you fight amongst yourselves? The battles must be fun."

Noah laughed, surprising Hurbnurr. "They certainly can be big." The human paused and seemed to ponder his response as Hurbnurr waited patiently. "We don't seek to take without giving," Noah said, his tone earnest. "If you allow us to mine the silver ore, we will provide you with other resources and materials that might be useful to your town. Perhaps we can even establish trade between our settlements, a mutually beneficial arrangement."

Behind him, the others in his crew bristled at that. Hurbnurr smiled, pleased with this little creature's bravery. Hurbnurr considered Noah's proposition, his icy gaze locked on the human before him. "A...trade?" he grumbled. "You give me things for my silver rocks?"

Noah smiled, sensing an opportunity to bridge the gap between their two communities. "We have skilled craftsmen who can create fine weapons and armor from various materials. Better than your iron," he offered. "We can also provide food and other provisions from our settlement. Your town will benefit from the alliance, and together, we can stand stronger against the mean wolves that endanger these lands."

The ice troll leader remained stoic, contemplating the potential benefits of the alliance. The prospect of gaining new resources and weapons seemed to sway his decision.

"Very well," Hurbnurr finally replied, his voice resonating with authority. "You show strength in battle, and I think you say truth. We will allow you to take the silver rocks, but if you lied, my warriors bang you on the head with clubs."

Noah nodded respectfully. "You have my word," he said, a sense of relief washing over him. "We are grateful for your under-standing and willingness to cooperate. You will be pleased with the steel weapons we can bring."

Hurbnurr nodded. "Come. All of you. Leave your weapons outside of walls, especially those magic sticks."

The human bristled at that. "We will not attack in the settle-ment. But we would feel more comfortable keeping our weapons."

The troll thought about it, then nodded. "Okay. Let's go."

As I was led to the silver mine by the watchful eyes of the troll warriors, I couldn't help but notice the glimmer of silver intertwined with the buildings in the settlement. I also saw silver necklaces around most of the...lady trolls? It was hard to tell, but there was a slight size difference. They had longer hair and were about a foot shorter than the club wielding variety.

Some of the trolls also wielded iron weapons, and I saw streaks of silver in them. It appeared that the silver was keeping the rust out of the items somehow, as I knew from experience that the iron weapons and pickaxes rusted very fast down here. The sight ignited a spark of inspiration and reminded me of something I had learned when playing video games.

Silver had properties that made it effective against werewolves.

The thought struck me, and I couldn't help but see the potential. Once I finished the anti-scrying device, I wondered if I could use the silver from the mine to forge weapons that would aid in our defense against the Shadowalkers. The alliance we had formed with Hurbnurr and his trolls was a step toward ensuring our safety, but we needed every advantage we could get. The trade proposal held even more promise; if I could access a silver mine, even through trade, that would be huge for my town.

As we reached the entrance of the silver mine, the air inside was cool and tinged with the metallic scent of precious ores. The mine's walls sparkled with the glint of silver, and I couldn't help but marvel at the abundance of the valuable resource. My heart quickened with anticipation at the thought of what we could achieve with this newfound treasure.

The trolls tried to take us deeper into the mine, but I stopped them. The workers chipped away at the walls, revealing veins of silver that shimmered under the dim light of their lanterns but stopped in confusion as we stepped into the tunnel.

I walked toward the walls and held my hand against the cool stone. I drew upon the power of my mining skill and, with focused concentration, I channeled the skill's energy, and to the astonishment of the trolls and my own crew, the silver ore began to flow from the wall and onto the ground in a shimmering cascade. My new version of the mining skill worked faster and more efficiently but took mana a lot quicker.

Gasps of surprise and wonder escaped the lips of the trolls as they witnessed the ore seemingly moving of its own accord. Their eyes widened, and they exchanged astonished glances with each other. The display of my mining skill had caught them completely off guard, and I could sense a newfound respect in their gazes.

The silver ore pooled at my feet, forming a small heap of glistening treasure. There were at least eight pieces of silver ore here. I needed ten to have enough for both anti-scrying devices. My mining sense showed the walls blank now, all the silver from the wall now present at my feet. I bent over, picked up the ore, and threw it into my fanny pack.

The trolls, still taken aback, regarded me with awe that I still hadn't gotten used to. Their mouths hung open as their pickaxes hung limply from their sides. I could tell that I had mined more silver in these few seconds than they could mine in a month.

I felt my mana tick down, under half now, the skill taking a lot of mana when it got this much ore at once. I nodded to the group of trolls. "Almost done. Just need one more wall, then we will be on our way."

The trolls looked amongst themselves, then walked near me, forming a semi-circle that reminded me of the fire mages in Fulgar. I started getting a bad feeling. One of the warrior trolls spoke up, holding his club in both hands.

"Maybe we no let you go," he said, a menacing glint in his eyes. "Maybe we keep you here, and you take out silver rocks from all walls, and we no work no more."

Chapter 13

The Power of Water

THE FIVE ENORMOUS BLUE DRAGONS SAT IN THE CLEARING, pruning themselves in the hot sun. They had killed three massive pig-looking creatures and brought them back to Niridge to feast on them. The alpha looked on, anger beginning to form in the pit of his stomach.

Since arriving, the dragons had eaten at least fifty animals from the nearby forest. Creatures that his pack needed. He shook his head, clearing the negative thoughts. Once he had control of Dunbar, his hunting territory would more than double.

Preparations for the battle had gone well. The walls he made should hold up to the fire, but if not, the dragons would be responsible for putting them out. He made a few makeshift bridges to get over the water he had heard about, easily broken apart and tied back together.

But he hoped the ice dragons would make short work of the water barrier and he wouldn't need the bridges.

As for his army; he had around six hundred melee troops, all sourced from the surrounding hills and mountains. The pack had grown exponentially since he had taken over. But that was a lot of hungry mouths to feed.

The lizards were ready with around a hundred warriors, this time with silver spikes coming out of their clubs. They called it *steel* and told him that the Overlord provided the weapons. They looked like enormous clubs that the troll beasts from the underworld wielded.

And then there were the dragons. He almost regretted involving them in the upcoming battle but knew he couldn't get through the defenses of the Fekan outpost. And if he couldn't even get through this city, how did he ever fathom that he would get through their capital?

Stories told of the battle almost forty seasons ago when the two races clashed. It had rendered both races decimated. Annos wasn't even a pup yet.

The previous alpha would have been successful if not for that damned human. He had interfered time and time again. Even when Annos had attacked, he had arranged for the city to be in a pitiful state. But again, the human interfered. This time, he would tip the scales so far in his favor that he couldn't possibly lose.

He looked at the dragons again, sunbathing on rocks nearby. It wasn't quite as hot this far north as it was further into the jungles of the Fekan lands, but he thought the dragons wouldn't like the temperatures here, being used to the cold, snowy mountain passes. But they looked like they were enjoying the temperatures very much.

Their head dragon stomped over to him, leaving his four brethren behind. He was about four times the size of Annos and towered over him. "When will we meet to finalize our plans to move? My kin grows restless. Our alliance has an expiration, wolf."

Annos held up his hand. "I will finish preparations tonight. We should be almost ready now."

The dragon appraised the wolf, then slowly nodded. "We will be ready."

Taking a deep breath, Annos walked to the courtyard and addressed the assembled warriors, his voice deep and commanding. The canines in the town stopped, no one making a sound as they listened to their leader. "Brothers and sisters of the night, honored lizard guests, both dragon and Saurite, tonight marks the beginning of a new era," he proclaimed, his words echoing through the rocky terrain. "We have come together to take what is rightfully ours—Dunbar!"

A chorus of low growls and hisses erupted from the ranks. The alpha held up his paw. "We will march with the full strength of our army," Annos continued, his eyes narrowing as he outlined the plan. "We will move swiftly and without hesitation. This time, the Fekan scum will fall before our might! This time, we will not fail!"

More roars and hisses. A blue, icy plume shot from one of the dragons into the air. The moonlight played on his silver-flecked fur as he spoke, and his powerful form radiated with confidence. The half-moon's power filled him. His pack, the dragons, and the lizards listened intently, battle lust on their faces.

"The journey will be long," Annos cautioned. "In three to four nights, we shall reach our destination, and there we will make camp, preparing for the final push. Ready yourselves, my brethren," he declared, raising his head high. "In the morning, we shall depart. And when the night falls at our journey's end, the outpost of Dunbar will tremble before our might!"

With those words, a wave of enthusiasm swept through the ranks. The alliance of creatures growled and hissed in response, unified in their determination to claim victory.

Annos watched as the war machine sprung into motion. Walls were unpacked and strapped together, the foxes swarming the structures like ants. Dogs strapped bags onto each other, carrying their provisions after weeks of preparation. Lizardmen sparred with their new sticks, sparks flying as the metal connected.

He picked the dragons for a reason. He had thought deeply during his journey back from the mountains. Almost twenty nights on the freezing paths gave him a lot of time to ponder things of the world. When he thought about it, he came to a simple realization.

Water was the king mana type here.

Air was inconsistent. It came in gusts and had power, but it was only temporary. Air only pushed water into larger waves and added to its power.

Fire could destroy nature and burn trees and vegetation, but it could be extinguished in far too many different ways. It was no match for water.

Mountains could rise from the earth, be shaped into weapons, and grow to enormous size. But even the hardest stone could be ground to sand or eroded with a stream. The earth could absorb a little water, but you could overrun it with too much water.

Water was the ultimate destroyer. Rivers carved through the earth, ice could be as deadly as a pointed stone spear. Waves eroded the beach and shores. Water was relentless.

And as the preparations unfolded, the dragons watched, unmoving. They did not need preparations.

Mara slowly opened her eyes, the sun setting low in the sky. She bolted up with fear, unsure how long she had been out. Her head felt heavy, but as her vision cleared, she saw Greg sitting beside her, his watchful gaze fixed on the surrounding landscape.

"You're awake!" Greg's voice shouted from the cliffside. "Woah, take it easy. Lay back."

Mara nodded, wincing slightly at the throbbing pain in her head. "Yeah, I think so. What happened?"

"You passed out after you were done using your skill," Greg explained, his eyes never leaving hers. "I found you here, unconscious. You've been out for a few hours."

Mara rubbed her temples, trying to shake off the lingering dizziness. "I must have overused my mana," she mumbled.

As she sat up, her mind returned to the vision she had seen—the man across the ocean. The memory was vivid in her mind, and she couldn't shake the sense of urgency she felt now. She had to get back to them.

"Greg," she said in a grave voice, "I saw something important. Monks, on the other side of the ocean. They spoke about the Trial Moon Sect. I need to find them. He warned me of something coming...something that would change the power structure of Prixa. They may have information that could help us."

Greg's brow furrowed, his eyes reflecting the weight of her words. "The Trial Moon Sect? I've never heard of that."

Mara shrugged. "I saw the size of the waves in the ocean. I can only imagine how big they get when there is a full moon. It would be impossible to travel across the ocean in a boat. But between that and the flying creature that spoke to me...Greg, something bad is about to happen."

Greg studied her for a moment, a kindness in his eyes. It looked like he didn't believe her. "Alright," he said finally, a resolute tone in his voice. "We'll find a way to get there. We need to get back to Dunbar. You may even want to tell the Monarch about this."

They carefully climbed down the rocky face of the cliff, Greg going first. He had found an easier path down the hill while Mara was out, figuring that was the best use of his time while he waited for her to wake. He was correct, as it took much less time to go down to the shore.

They found their boat, untouched and still tied up, and boarded. With a bit of air from Greg's outstretched hand, they were on their way. The setting sun cast a warm golden glow over the water, painting the horizon in hues of orange and pink. The waves were calm at sunset, and Greg said they could make good time. Mara just hoped he had enough mana to get them across the water. They would be stuck on the water without much wind until the winds picked up otherwise. And night was rapidly approaching.

As the boat gently rocked with the waves, Mara's mind was filled with thoughts of the mage and the Trial Moon Sect. She couldn't believe that the man was strong enough to support her mana usage from the tree. And the tree itself. It called to her still, almost like a lighthouse calls to a ship's captain.

Lost in her thoughts, Mara gazed over the gulf, watching the sun dip lower on the horizon. Sensing her contemplation, Greg remained silent, giving her the space to process everything that had happened.

The weight of responsibility rested on Mara's shoulders, recalling the man's warning that she played a large part in the upcoming struggle. Finally, Mara spoke. "I don't know how to get there, but maybe we can use your air powers and not go on the water at all?"

Greg looked back at her, hair fluttering in the wind. He shrugged, then looked forward again, not responding.

Mara sighed. *Noah would be able to think of something,* she thought, as she settled back in the boat.

Chapter 14

Negotiations with Trolls

"Hurbnurr!" I yelled up at the giant troll, clenching my fists at my side as sweat started beading up on my brow. "I thought we had a deal!"

He shrugged, clearly about to be of no help to us. "We kill your friends and keep you. Then you mine for us. Maybe you go home once all the silver is mined. It no take you long, magic rock man!"

He smiled toothily at me, the yellow, sharp teeth gleaming at me in the torchlight. Nyo and Dee were growling, and I heard Jasper muttering about how this was a bad idea.

They closed in and my group surrounded me with wands and weapons ready. In these close quarters, I didn't like our chances. The low light didn't help, and I had left my large bags at the front of the settlement.

I hoped I could convince him to let us go. The silver we needed to forge the anti-scrying devices was so close, but it was up to me to negotiate our way out of the silver mine with it. But we didn't have any other earth items to use on these guys other than Liza's wand.

Jamie pulled out a bottle of water from her sack and tossed it to me, winking at me. I caught the bottle, unsure, until Liza pulled her wand out. The trolls gasped and jumped back. Liza made a waive of the wand that was way over the top, but I got what they were doing.

I shook the bottle, making it look like she did something. The trolls growled and jumped back.

"Hurbnurr," I began, trying to keep my voice steady despite the tension of the situation, "we truly appreciate you letting us into your mine and the alliance we've formed. The silver is critical to my settlement's defense. I would hate to have to use this again."

I held the bottle up, the water glistening in the soft light.

The troll leader regarded me sternly, his icy blue eyes sizing me up as they darted between me and the bottle. The trolls around him fidgeted.

I tried one last ditch effort, knowing we were outmatched. "Okay. You take half of this silver that I mine. And I will give you my tungsten. It is a very hard metal. Good for making unbreakable tools. And I will give you more presents when we return again. And you let us go."

Hurbnurr frowned. "We maybe kill you and take it. Then we get all the things you own. We no scared of shiny water bombs."

I raised the bottle, and the trolls made a strained sound again. I smiled, calling his bluff, and held my hand up in a peaceful gesture. "Yes, but then you can't get more things. I want to keep trading with you. Get silver for my people's things from far away. You can't get that if you kill us. No one will know about our trade."

The trolls looked back and forth between us, unsure of what to do. My group stayed still, trying not to upset the trolls in any way. The troll leader crossed his massive arms over his chest, contemplating my words. For a tense moment, it seemed like the decision hung in the balance.

Finally, Hurbnurr let out a deep rumble, a sign that he had decided. "Fine," he grumbled, "Take silver rocks you need. Put bomb away!"

I complied, making a show of putting the water bottle in my pack as my crew breathed a collective sigh of relief.

It took around an hour to finish getting the ore I needed. The trolls began to gather the silver ore into bags, setting some aside for themselves, and I felt the incredible feeling you get when you finished a quest. Now we would have the resources we needed to forge both anti-scrying devices.

As we prepared to leave the town with the precious silver, I returned to Hurbnurr, feeling a newfound camaraderie with the trolls. "I will be back for our trade," I said sincerely. I stuck out my hand. He grasped it, shaking it fiercely as his yellow nails dug into my forearm. "We will return with more things to trade once I've made these devices. Hopefully, the way will be clear."

He nodded, and we headed back up the hill, this time with even more weight to carry. No one complained, however. We were just happy to have made it out of there alive.

Once we had everything, we ventured away from their town into the caverns, returning the way we came. About an hour into our return journey, I looked around at the team to assess how everyone was doing. Kyle stared off into space, Jasper yawned loudly, and Liza slouched against a wall.

The battle with the trolls and the last few hours had taken a toll on our group. Some were nursing wounds from the fight, while others struggled to keep up with the pace. The bags of ore clinked on Kyle's shoulder as he walked in the front of our procession. That dude was constantly grinding, and I could appreciate it. I wondered if he had some kind of mental toughness skill, because he never complained.

Matt Pivots

"We need to find a suitable spot to rest," I said, my voice betraying my own fatigue. "We need to make camp. I have no idea what time it is down here, but we've been at it for a long time. It's been a hell of a day."

The group agreed, and we began searching for a safe and sheltered area within the cavern. Most of the spots in the cave had rocks and crevices, and there weren't many good spots to house all of us at once. We stopped at a place in the cave where the walls loomed high above us, and the air felt damp and cool. I wondered if anyone would volunteer to be the first watch, but I had a sinking feeling that it would fall to me.

Finally, we found a relatively flat and sheltered alcove. We cleared away some loose rocks and debris, creating a makeshift campsite. Liza used her earth magic to create a lean-to of sorts, then Jasper cast a small fireball, providing us with a little warmth in the damp conditions.

He told us he would only keep it going for a moment or two, but it helped ease the chill a bit. How it was cold down here, I had no idea. Back at the troll town, there was ice in some spots. I didn't know if that was from the trolls or the depth, but there was no way we were that deep down here.

We ate some of the food rations and then the crew mumbled their goodnights, grabbing sleeping bags from the packs. As the others settled down to rest, Dee and I took the first watch. Jasper had warmed up some large rocks using his fireball, and they cast some heat on our backs as we sat on the dirt. I had the purple mushroom lantern on, casting its eerie glow on the wall Liza built.

"Well that was fun," Dee said, stretching her tired muscles and wincing slightly as she did so. "I never thought I'd find myself fighting trolls in a silver mine. Your adventures never cease to amaze."

I chuckled softly, nodding in agreement. "Thanks for coming with me. I have to admit, you were incredible back there. You fought like the Dee I remember!"

Dee looked down at the praise, her green cat eyes twinkling. But something else crossed her expression. "Thank you, Noah. I'm glad I'm finally back to normal. Or almost."

I rested my hand on her furry shoulder and embraced her for a hug. She hugged me back. "I never thanked you for helping me in the forest. You saved my life. I didn't think...I..." I stumbled, not able to get the words out.

She nodded. "Don't mention it. You've done the same for me."

We didn't say anything for a moment. "When I healed you, I screwed something up, didn't I?"

"You saved me. That's all I know. Not only did you fight off that Stalker, but you closed me up and hid me from those beasts. You did the best you could."

It felt better to hear her say that. Silence settled between us briefly, broken only by Nyo's intermittent snoring. I still felt something was permanently wrong with her, but I didn't want to dwell on it. Instead, I changed the subject.

"So, Dee," I began casually, "do you think we'll run into any more surprises on the rest of our little quest?"

She grinned mischievously, playing along. "Well, who knows? Maybe we'll stumble upon a hidden treasure chest filled with magical artifacts or a secret passageway to a forgotten realm."

I chuckled. "Yeah, that would certainly make for another fun adventure. I think I'm good for now, though. Rock Town was enough."

As we continued talking, I felt at ease in Dee's presence. She was a skilled fighter and a kind and genuine Feka. Our conversation flowed effortlessly, and I was grateful for the opportunity to talk to her one on one, just like in the old days. Our conversation didn't get bleak again.

I asked her if she thought the Monarch would expand the human mage group into Fayport. The working human class in the capital had not been exposed to my magic yet. I didn't even know if the humans there knew about my mages. It had been a whirlwind few weeks since I was kidnapped to Fulgar, and I doubted she had mentioned it.

Plus, I still thought there were trust issues there, to be honest.

As the night wore on, the second watch took over, and we settled down to get some rest. The cavern remained peaceful and quiet, the only sounds being the occasional water drip and my companions' soft breathing.

I closed my eyes and fell into a deep sleep.

Chapter 15

Home Sweet Home

I woke up feeling like I was forgetting something important. I sat up and rubbed my eyes as Jamie, who must have been on watch, looked back at me. She flashed me a smile, and I smiled back.

Suddenly, I gasped and jolted to my feet, scaring the whole party awake. The Fekan members hissed, jumping gracefully to their feet, and looked around for danger. "Sorry, guys! I didn't mean to...hey, did anyone loot that scout troll?!" I blurted out, my voice echoing off the cave walls.

Nyo's annoyed voice came from nearby. "I picked it up, Noah."

I walked over to him quickly. "Quick! Hand it to me! What did he drop?"

Nyo shrugged, his expression calm. "It was just a troll eye, and I thought it might be useful later. But here, take it." He dug it out of a hanging belt pocket.

He handed me the troll eye, and as I grasped it, a surge of energy coursed through my body. I felt the newfound power flowing into my core, and this time, unlike the other times I had unlocked mana, I felt something else. I felt...complete.

Matt Pivots

[YOU HAVE UNLOCKED WATER MAGIC]

My heart pounded with excitement. A broad smile spread across my face, and I couldn't help but cry out in exhilaration. "Yes! That's it! I have all four now!"

The actualization hit me like a wave crashing against the shore. I now possessed the four elemental magics—earth, fire, air, and water. With each element under my command, I could harness their powers and unleash a force to be reckoned with.

My companions cheered and clapped, talking excitedly about what we could do now. I glanced around at my companions, gratitude filling my heart. "Thank you, all of you," I said, my voice filled with sincerity. "Thanks for coming with me down here. Without you guys I would have been squished into the dirt from a troll club."

They all smiled. "But what do you think? Time to head back?"

The group all agreed, and we started packing up the camp. I looked at my arm, checking my tattoos as my arm burned the new one on.

[NOAH]
[Lv 15 - BLACKSMITH JOURNEYMAN]

[BONDED]

[HEALTH 115/115]
[MANA 140/140]

-L4

-L4

-Passive

-L2

-L8

-L2

[UNSELECTED SKILLS - NONE]

. . .

I had leveled up, besides. What a fantastic outcome for this trip. I had silver materials for my anti-scrying device, a new mana type to play with, and even leveled up a few times. Things were really starting to look up.

The journey back went relatively smooth, with only one small battle to contend with—the dreaded acid shooters. But this time, we were prepared.

Liza swiftly used her earth magic to create a sturdy wall, shielding us from the acid projectiles. Behind the protective barrier, Jasper, our skilled marksman, readied his weapon, ready to take down the acid shooters from a safe distance.

"Get ready, everyone!" I called out, my voice echoing in the cave. "Jasper, all you!"

Jasper nodded, his focus unwavering as he took aim at the acid shooters. With a steady hand, he fired precise shots, taking down the attackers in the back that shot at us from a distance. The acid creatures tried in vain to reach us, but their projectiles harmlessly splattered against the earth wall.

I was sad that Jasper eviscerated the creatures when he used his fireball since I couldn't loot them this way. But my crew's safety was more important.

As the last of the acid shooters fell, we emerged from behind the earth wall, victorious and unharmed. Jasper grinned, his pride evident in his eyes. "Not bad, huh?"

I had turned on my party view and saw his mana was at [5/40], so he had used almost all of it, shooting the fireballs at the creatures. Liza was at [9/25] since the wall had a mana per second cost. Other than that, we were unaffected by them.

"Not bad at all," I replied with a chuckle. "Nice shooting, Jasper." It was nice to have the counter-element on the team.

We retraced our steps through the winding tunnels and caverns, paying attention to where the X's were marked. I almost expected a quest completion notification as we finally reached the mine entrance.

My team was tired from hauling all the materials back, and as they warned me, I had seriously overpacked. We still had a whole pack of food left and tons of other items that we never even had to use. But better safe than sorry.

The workers in the mines stopped pounding on the walls and cheered as we came through the tunnel. I still had no idea what time it was or how long we had been gone, but I saw light at the entrance to the mine, meaning it was daytime.

We walked up the slope passing two of my steam engine carts as the workers loaded them with iron. I had forgotten that Romas was tasked with making a few more of the little things and was excited to see them sitting there. We kept going, and once we got to the front of the mine, we had to shield our eyes.

The heat hit the crew like a truck, and while I didn't necessarily feel it thanks to my armor, they all groaned. But we were on too much of a high from the quest's success and walked the now-graded road back to Dunbar.

I could feel the weight of the journey lifting off my shoulders. Our settlement's familiar sights and sounds brought comfort and ease, making me appreciate our home even more.

"Leave the bags here!" I called out to the crew, my voice eager and grateful. With a sigh of relief, they dropped their belongings, clearly happy to be home. "Thank you all for your hard work. You've done Dunbar proud."

My companions bid me farewell one by one, each offering a nod of appreciation or a warm smile. I reminded them about our upcoming council meeting in a few days, and they all said they would be there.

I bent down and took out some silver from the bag. It was a level 3 ingredient. I remembered that I had to make the box's ingredient under the moon's light, so I prepared myself for that. I pulled up the ingredients for the anti-scrying device again to refresh my memory on the costs.

[ANTI-SCRYING DEVICE - CITY LEVEL - 3X
VOIDBLOOM | 10X MOONLIT SILVER | 10X
SILVERSTONE | 5X CAMOMILE FLOWER PETALS |
ANTI-SCRYING SPELL]

I went to find Typh to see if his warriors had found the flowers from the jungle while I was gone. It didn't take long before I spotted him, training a few of the air mages in hand-to-hand combat. I walked over toward him, and when he saw me he dropped to all fours and rushed over.

"Baron Noah, your astral princess has been waiting for your return. She said she must speak with you immediately. It's urgent," Typh said.

"Nice to see you too," I said in mock hurt. Typh straightened at that. "Kidding. Where is she?"

"She was down by the docks last I heard with Greg, the Zephyr."

With a nod of gratitude, I hurried towards the docks. The bustling streets of Dunbar greeted me as I made my way up the ramp and through the settlement. People went about their daily routines and said hello to me as I walked.

Finally, I saw her. She still had a gentle glow about her. She was facing the water, looking out over the water as she lay back in the sand. "Hey!" I said, cresting the hill.

Mara looked back and saw me approaching, but she didn't smile like I figured she would. Something was wrong. She stood up quickly, brushed herself off, and jogged over.

"Noah, you're back!" she said, her voice urgent. "I've been trying to reach you. Something has happened."

Chapter 16

Anti-Scrying

SEEING THE PANIC IN MARA'S EYES, I KNEW WE COULDN'T afford to waste any time. She started talking about a dragon, and I immediately stopped her, placing a reassuring hand on her shoulder.

"Mara, wait," I said, my voice hushed. "We can't risk anyone overhearing this. Let's meet under the moonlight in a few hours after completing the anti-scrying device."

I was still exhausted from the trip but knew we needed to prioritize securing our communications. "Okay, sorry," Mara replied, her voice tense. "It's just really important to move quickly. A ton happened while you were gone. I'll gather the council members over the next few hours. We'll meet at the usual spot when you're done, and I can tell everyone at once."

I nodded. "Okay." An awkward pause passed between us. "Hey, I missed you!"

She leaned in for a kiss. "I missed you too. I can't wait to hear about your trip."

"I'll make sure the device is ready as soon as possible. Be safe until then." With that, we parted ways. I hurried to the smithy, my mind racing about what could have happened while I was gone. Crafting the anti-scrying device was now more crucial than ever.

I set to work, gathering the silverstone from the forge in the basement. The warriors had left the flower petals with Romas during my stay in the mines, and I had them in my overall pockets. I had no idea what to do with the voidbloom, however. That stuff was nasty. It tugged at me through all the layers of protection that I could think of.

When I picked it up in the troll cave, I felt it sucking away at my very essence. It was not a feeling I liked very much. It took away ten health and five mana after I picked the three I needed. Just...gone. My stats had recovered since then, but still. It was terrifying to see happen.

For now, I had everything that I needed. With Mara meeting me under the moon's light, she could cast her spell to finalize the object. Until the sun went down, I didn't have anything else I could do with this.

I went over to the engineering table and pulled up my mental HUD, checking on the status of my city. I learned that while my arm tattoos displayed only a few basic pieces of information, my city stats window showed a lot more.

[DUNBAR - BARONY]
[RANK - OUTLYING TOWNSHIP]
[MAIN EXPORT - FISH | WOOD | IRON/STEEL]
[MAIN IMPORT - CLOTHING | ALE | STONE]
[LIEGE - FEKAN MONARCH]

[EMPIRE CAPITAL- FAYPORT]

Using the engineering table to design and view my city used minimal mana, but I still had to make a huge build later on that would cost almost all of my mana. I assumed the *moonlit silver* part meant I had to use the silver in the moonlight, so I couldn't use the anvil. I had 135 mana available, so I mentally selected the 'MAIN EXPORT' section, and pulled up more details. Using the table slowly pulled from my mana pool, so I had a little time to check out how my city had evolved over the last few days.

[MAIN EXPORT - FISH | WOOD | IRON/STEEL]
FISH - ACTIVE BOATS | 5
WOOD - BOW TREE | READY FOR HARVEST - 35%
MATURING 65%
IRON - HEMATITE 86% MAGNETITE 9%
GEOTHITE 5%
SECONDARY EXPORTS - CORN (FIELDS) |
TINDERSTONE (MINE)]

It wasn't a ton of information about the actual production of my mines, but I wasn't surprised. My skills were still only level 4. I pulled up the 'LIEGE' tab and was interested to see that my council was listed there as well.

[LIEGE - FEKAN MONARCH]

[COUNCIL OF DUNBAR
MARSHALL - TYPHONIUS
STEWARD - ROMAS
CHANCELLOR - MARA POWANIS]

Super cool. Apparently, Powanis was Mara's last name. I don't think I had ever asked her, to be honest. I closed out the hud and went up to join everyone and get a bite to eat. My arm now read 129 mana, so I was ready to rock and roll. It was about to be showtime.

629

As the moonlight from the largest moon of Prixa bathed Dunbar in its gentle glow, I made my way to the meeting spot. The council members were already assembled, waiting to hear what both groups had to say once we could talk with confidence that we were, in fact, alone again.

"Okay guys, we can talk once I'm done with this. Let's get into it!" I said, excitement beaming from me. I plopped down the silver first, which had a ghostly glow as it soaked up the moonlight. Next was the silverstone, followed by the delicate flower petals.

Last was the voidbloom. I could feel the creepy mushroom things through the leather, through the bag, and through the gloves that I wore. They pulled on me like the wind pulls at a flame.

"Noah, you want me to take it out and place it on the ground?" Mara asked. "I don't feel it like you do."

I had told her about the voidbloom on the walk over here. "No. I feel like it has to be me. What kind of creator would I be if I couldn't even handle my own ingredients?"

I heard a few nervous chuckles, but no one really laughed. I took a deep breath and unstrapped my bag. I plunged my hands in, grabbing the leather package. The pull got much stronger, a siphon pulling away at my core again. I grimaced, and a quick look at my arm saw my mana and health ticking down at an alarming pace.

I worked even faster, unwrapping the leather from the mushrooms, and now the only protection I had from them was the tongs. "Aghhh!" I cried out and threw them onto the ground. The health and mana were freely flowing from me now, a red and blue stream flowing into them. This hadn't happened in the mine, and I wondered if it was something to do with the moon's power.

I held out my hand, concentrating on the creation of the device. Mana flowed out, combining everything together. I had never made anything this large before, and 100 mana was a ton. A box began to form, mana still exploding out of me. Everyone watching was gasping and crying out, trying to stop me. But there was no stopping now.

A box formed, and as the moonlight touched its black surface, the device seemed to absorb the light as if craving its energy. I looked at my arm and was at [7/140], and my health was [79/115]. Holy crap, it was taking my health and mana at an insane pace!

"Mara! Craft your spell! Agh!" I cried out again, the void box growing in strength. The other mages around the group began crying out, the unfinished box now affecting them. Mana was flowing out of them, oranges and yellows mixing with the silvery energy that I gave off.

Mara rushed forward, white light coming off her as well, but not as fast as the rest of us. As she said, void mana didn't seem to bother her mana type as much. Her hand glowed, and she rested them on the box as she cast her spell. Moonlight blasted down and rocked the box back and forth.

We all gasped, and then it was over. The clearing was absolutely silent, with even the jungle creatures not sure what the hell just happened. I stepped back, admiring my creation. The device hummed with power, its mana pulsating in a controlled glow now. I was far too afraid to even look at my arm. I identified the box to see what it did.

[OMNISECURE ORB - ANTI-SCRYING DEVICE - UNIQUE - MANA ABSORPTION RATE 96.6% - SCRYING NULLIFICATION RADIUS - 100 METERS]

Man, that thing was fantastic. *So I didn't need to charge it or put mana into the box for it to work?* One hundred meters was a little small, but if I put it directly in the center of Dunbar, that would be good enough.

631

"Now, let's see what this baby can do," I said with a grin, eager to put the device to the test. We walked back toward the settlement, the device now safe to hold. Once we were outside Dunbar's walls, I felt the mana within it surge. A gray fog I hadn't seen before began to be sucked into the object, slowly at first, then faster and faster.

I stopped, looking at it in awe. "Mara, is this the fog you were talking about?"

She nodded her head vigorously. "Yeah! This is what kept my magic boxed in, unable to get out and use my scrying skill!"

I smiled, "Well, it looks like that's over!" I took the box into the city and onto the first level, shocked that the fog was being sucked in like it was. At this point, it almost looked like someone had lit a smoke machine up in the bottom of Dunbar. Finally, the smoke stopped, and the device went still.

Finally, I broke the silence. "Well, I guess we can start our council meeting now!"

Chapter 17

Freedom of Speech

THE COUNCIL OF DUNBAR WAS GATHERED IN THE GRAND hall of the palace, the members speaking quietly to each other. I sat at the head of the table, Mara to my left. We came straight here after the box had finished sucking in the scrying fog surrounding the city.

I cleared my throat, and all eyes turned to me. I stood out of my chair, addressing the Feka and humans present. "Honored council. I want to get into the findings of my quest in the caves, but first, Mara has something urgent she wants to tell everyone about. Mara?"

I sat, and she stood out of her chair. Mara began, her voice clear and resolute. "Greg, one of the air mages down at the docks, took me in a boat across the gulf. He propelled it with some air magic to an island across the way. I was able to escape my anti-scrying cage, the mist you guys saw from the box when I went high up on that hill. I started by going north to see the Shadowalkers. They were constructing walls that looked like they could hold up to fireballs much better. But they're planning something, and another attack looks likely very soon."

She paused, then took a deep breath. "I didn't want to go south for fear of the Overlord seeing me. And I had a little mana left, so I tried looking east. While traveling across the ocean, I encountered a weird pull of mana. It led me to a place called the Trial Moon Sect."

The Feka looked at each other, unsure. "I have never heard of this place," Typh said. Romas growled in agreement, furry head nodding up and down. I leaned forward, eager to hear more.

Mara continued, "I was drawn there by a tree. It pulsed with energy...fueled me somehow. Actually, it felt the opposite of when I touched the void magic box. The void took mana, where this tree gave it. Then, under the tree, I found a man sitting cross-legged. He spoke to me. Told me what was coming and how much danger we were in. He was some kind of guardian of the tree and the mana that it possessed."

She recounted her interaction with the man, explaining how he spoke of the Shadowalkers and their plans to attack Dunbar. "He urged me to find the Head of the Sect, saying they would assist us in our war," Mara concluded.

The room was silent as everyone digested this information. Romas started speaking, but Mara interrupted him. "Oh, and I saw a huge creature flying overhead. It spoke to me telepathically, warning me that they were coming, whoever that was, and that the city will be taken soon. He wanted me to flee since I am an Astral mage. I won't, of course. But yeah, any idea what that's all about?"

Typh stood, addressing us. "There are rumors of dragon beasts in the mountain passes far north of here. Perhaps they have decided to become involved in our struggle with the Shadowalkers. I doubt it, though. They are a fickle, ancient race. Why would one come here to warn us?"

No one said anything for a moment. "What do you think, Mara?" I asked.

She pursed her lips. "It felt like the creature was scouting us. Almost like it was...surprised I was here. I think they're part of the attack. It definitely didn't want to warn us as much as me."

The Feka scoffed at that, as clearly, this was a bad sign for us. Romas stood now. "We must report this to the Monarch immediately. If dragons are helping the Shadowalkers, we don't stand a chance. They will sweep through Dunbar like a hot blade through silk."

Mara turned to me, a pleading look in her eyes. "I can't help but feel that there's more to the Trial Moon Sect than what I saw. There was something powerful there, Noah. Something that could help us in the fight against the Shadowalkers."

I nodded, understanding her concerns. "It's possible. But it sounds like no one has ever crossed the ocean before. Well, at least by boat." I turned to Typh. "Have we scouted the jungle much? I want to make sure we don't miss anything if the Shadowalkers decide to try anything."

Typh nodded. "We have our sentries out in the trees. A few hunter class Feka. They will alert us if they see anything."

Mara spoke up. "I just don't want to overlook anything that could give us an advantage. If there's even a chance that the Trial Moon Sect can aid us, we should investigate further."

"You're right," I said, reassuringly touching her shoulder. "We won't dismiss any opportunity that could help us. Let's gather more information. But proceed with caution. We don't know these people or their intentions. I feel like you're pretty exposed when you leave your body."

She nodded. "Yeah, I know. I'll try scrying again and see if I can find more about the Trial Moon Sect."

I clapped my hands together. "Well, all of that is pretty concerning. Hopefully, we can get more information about what the Shadowalkers are doing and when they plan on attacking us. At least our little adventure was a success!"

As the council members listened intently, I began to recount the events of our expedition into the caves. I provided a detailed account of our encounter with the ice trolls, explaining how we had negotiated a trade agreement that allowed us access to the valuable silver mine.

"I also unlocked water mana, so I need to head into the smithy and make a new item for a classing ceremony. My under-standing is that I can build a healing item, and then we can have healers in our army. We also got our first look at what a water enemy can do. It was pretty tough to fight them."

I told them about the acid monsters and the battle we got in, Typh and Romas asking questions here and there. I continued, "We've secured a beneficial arrangement with the ice trolls. They have agreed to let us mine the silver in exchange for a portion of the ore and other goods. It's a promising opportunity for Dunbar's economy. Silver seems rare here, and I can see all kinds of uses for it, especially against Shadowalkers. In my culture, werewolves are susceptible to silver. Maybe that's true here too."

The council members exchanged approving nods.

I continued, "The caves also seem to lead out somewhere deep into the jungle. We haven't explored the entirety of the passages, but it could potentially provide an alternative route for us to travel and gather resources. If I can extend the road that far, we could have a direct line to them. But with the Shadowalker terri-tory close by, we would need to do something about them first."

Mara chimed in, "Maybe we could send scouting parties to explore the jungle routes and assess their viability. With the anti-scrying devices we have, we can ensure they remain unde-tected by the enemy."

My eyebrows shot up. "Yeah, that's a great idea! They would need my belt, though. The box is only good in the city limits."

As the council deliberated on our next steps, we weighed the advantages of the silver trade and the potential jungle passages against the imminent threat of the Shadowalker invasion.

The council meeting continued well into the evening, with each member contributing their insights and expertise. We discussed various strategies for fortifying our defenses, training and unlocking the no-classers, and coordinating our resources effectively. If dragons were really involved, I would need a way to defend against air attacks.

Ultimately, we agreed to send scouting parties to explore the jungle routes after Mara scouted with her scrying power. She would have to save her mana and wait to travel across the ocean until we knew where the troll cave came out and how to get there. We also needed to know where our Shadowalker enemies were and if there were dragons among them. We also needed to know how quickly we should expect their attack.

I left the council chambers and walked back to my room, Mara next to me. We made small talk but didn't chat much more about strategy; both of us were clearly exhausted from the long meeting. I was looking forward to a good night's rest. And, maybe a little excitement with Mara before we went to bed.

But tomorrow, I had some water items to make and a town to fortify against dragons.

Chapter 18

Air Defense

I HURRIEDLY MADE MY WAY THROUGH THE PAVED STREETS of the first level of Dunbar, dodging past residents and market stalls. I decided that I wanted to start design work on anti-air devices as my first order of business. The Feka all gave me nods as I walked past, unaware of the impending attacks.

I finally arrived at the building, its wooden anvil sign swinging overhead with a comforting familiarity. I pushed through the door, the scent of hot metal and burning coals hitting me immediately. Romas was not back from the palace yet, and neither was Jasper, so the place was dead quiet.

Descending the wooden stairs into the basement, I felt the air grow colder. I lit the purple torches and headed to the design table at the back of the room. Touching the smooth surface of the table activated my Engineer skill, illuminating a mental heads-up display before my eyes.

I thought back to our last council meeting, where we'd discussed the potential threats. If the Shadowalkers allied with water dragons, that would mean they would plan to take my fire mages out. I already had a moat in place to slow down the lizards. Also, Mara said they had fire-resistant boards they were working on, so I would have to do something about that too.

"A tesla coil," I murmured to myself. It seemed a far-fetched idea initially, but its capability to produce high-voltage and shoot it out in any direction could be a formidable defense against aerial threats, especially if they were water-based creatures. I knew that shooting bolts of electricity through the air was dangerous, though, and I needed it to be high enough that it wouldn't arc down and hurt someone in the city. I also wondered if I needed to shoot it at something.

But we'd have a fighting chance if I could design it to target them with my air mages. I grinned in my mental space and began planning.

I began pulling materials virtually from the shelves, watching them hover in my display. I figured the structure could be made of iron and made the main shape. I also needed a resistor for the top, which I had never designed before.

The design started coming before me. The iron base formed a solid stand to ensure stability. On the base the wire wound tightly, made of interlocking patterns of silverstone. At its pinnacle, a donut-shaped structure also made of conductive material acted as the central reservoir of energy.

I could already imagine the brilliant arcs of electricity dancing from the top, repelling any airborne threats that dared approach.

Another idea occurred as I mentally adjusted the flow of energy from the air mages through the silverstone coil, optimizing the output for maximum range and potency. A single beam may not be enough if more than one dragon approaches. I added secondary coils around the main structure, producing multiple arcs simultaneously, targeting different enemies, or converging at a single powerful strike.

When I computed the costs, I almost threw up. I adjusted the plans and the costs displayed before me. Still horrendously high, but more doable.

[TESLA COIL - IF **CREATE PROTOTYPE** SUBSKILL OF **MANUFACTURE** SKILL ACTIVATED - ONE TIME

COST OF 5X SILVERSTONE (WIRE) | 10X
SILVERSTONE (HEAD) | 20X IRON ORE (MAINFRAME)
- COST 55 MANA - BUILD WILL LAST FOR ONE
HOUR]

[TESLA COIL - IF **MANUFACTURED FOR GENERAL
USE** - ONE TIME COST OF 15X SILVERSTONE (WIRE)
| 30X SILVERSTONE (HEAD) | 50X IRON ORE
(MAINFRAME) - COST 125 MANA]

I couldn't believe how expensive this thing was going to be. But I had the height at over 50ft, and even if I mounted it from the first level of Dunbar, it still wouldn't be high enough to clear the trees. I didn't know where the dragons would attack from, but I assumed from the rear of the settlement, where we didn't have any defenses. Flying over the gulf would be their best approach.

I tapered it down to 10 ft high just to make a scale model for the prototype. I saved the 50ft design and cut off the skill. My HUD disappeared as I got up from the table, slightly more depressed than when I sat down. I did some mental calculations of more wands, even higher-leveled wands, but nothing else came to mind to combat the dragons. Even if I could somehow design much more powerful wands, my mages couldn't use them. I just didn't have much time.

I looked at the *mini* Tesla coil's expenses and mentally jotted everything down. I had only saved ten mana.

[MINI TESLA COIL - IF **CREATE PROTOTYPE**
SUBSKILL OF **MANUFACTURE** SKILL ACTIVATED -
ONE TIME COST OF 3X SILVERSTONE (WIRE) | 5X
SILVERSTONE (HEAD) | 10X IRON ORE (MAINFRAME)
- COST 45 MANA - BUILD WILL LAST FOR ONE
HOUR]

My mana had drained down to [121/140], which was enough to make myself a prototype and see how this thing worked. Now, all I needed to do was gather the materials and bring this thing to life. *I can't wait to tell them about it!*

I headed down to the beach to find the mages in the dockworker's hut. "Hey, guys! You won't believe what I'm working on!"

As I approached, the Zephrys paused their work, turning their attention to me. It was evident from their weary faces and soiled robes that they'd been tirelessly preparing for the invasion.

Kyle, his cascade of silver-blonde hair blowing in the wind, smiled wryly. "Another of your ingenious inventions, Creator?"

I grinned, thinking about how cool the Tesla coil design was. "More than just an invention," I replied, excitement bubbling in my chest. "I'm designing something called a Tesla coil."

The other mages exchanged curious glances. Greg raised an eyebrow. "A what now?"

"A Tesla coil," I reiterated, trying to think of a simpler way to explain it. "Imagine a tower that releases lightning bolts, targeting and repelling any airborne threats. It uses the air mage's lightning skill for energy, silverstone for conductivity, and iron as its base. The lightning energy travels up the coils and shoots out the top, shot out by the ball of conductive energy I mount there. It should be able to amplify the attack high into the air if everyone pours the spell into it at the same time. I could even make a rechargeable battery..." I mumbled the last part, lost in thought.

Kyle's eyes widened in surprise. "That sounds... incredible. And extremely ambitious. But how can we help?"

"I need a vast quantity of silverstone ore, so I'll have to head back into the mines," I explained. "For now, we have enough to make the prototype. Also, if you and the air mages could help direct and amplify the arcs once the coil is operational, we could increase its range and precision. But I haven't thought all that through. I can make a miniature one for testing purposes. I plan to have it done tonight."

They looked at each other. "Once the coil is functional, we'll lend our powers to guide the electrical discharges," Kyle said. "The other air mages are in the jungles right now, but we will tell them when they return. I'll plan on meeting you at the entrance to the jungle at moonrise."

I nodded, agreeing to the time to test this thing out. "Why are the others in the jungle?" I inquired, genuinely curious. It was rare for the air mages to get out of the city these days, as much as it pained me to see it.

Kyle shrugged, "Even though they're scared of the jungle, they know it's filled with creatures that provide valuable experience when defeated. By grinding there, our mages can increase their levels. With you back, they felt more confident."

I thought back to when we lost a mage on the first day of them working in the jungle. To my knowledge, they hadn't gone back out since. "It will be awesome for them to improve their skills. When I show them my air defense idea, they should be excited."

"Once they've gained the necessary experience, with the Tesla coil and the combined power of our mages, we'll give the Shadowalkers a fight they'll never forget," Greg said, pounding his fist into his palm.

I nodded, smiling back. But this time, I wasn't so sure.

Chapter 19

Prototypes

I GRABBED SOME FOOD FROM THE PALACE'S KITCHEN, THEN found myself back in the basement of the smithy, gathering the required elements. Another problem with the anvil was that, while incredible to get half off crafting, it didn't save me when I wanted to build tall structures. For that, I had to make it in the field.

For this test, though, I was building a mini Tesla coil, so I piled the materials around the anvil. I looked down, thoughtful. I didn't know how to hold all of this stuff.

Nearby, I saw a shield that one of the Fekan warriors used and put on top of the anvil, then stacked the iron and silverstone. Satisfied, I began concentrating. The 45 mana cost would be halved if I used the magical anvil.

The Fekan shield, a beautifully crafted piece of curved metal adorned with bright paint, proved to be more useful than just for defense. With its broad surface, it provided a makeshift workspace for my materials.

Closing my eyes, I took a deep breath, feeling the flow of energy in the room. Slowly, I channeled my mana, focusing on the image of the tower and its respective parts. The heads-up display

I had become accustomed to using in the smithy's basement flashed before me, illustrating each step in the crafting process.

My manufacturing skill kicked in, and the device sprung up to life before my eyes. I felt the unique effects of the anvil kicking in, easing the burden on my mana reserves. The frame shot up first, almost reaching the ceiling. Next, the silverstone hung in midair, stretching into a thin wire.

Next, I carefully shaped the mini Tesla coil, adjusting its components for maximum efficiency in this scaled-down model. Finally, the last piece slid into place, and once the cap slammed into place, I stepped back, exhausted but satisfied.

Before me stood a gleaming, intricate piece of engineering magic: a mini Tesla coil, about five feet tall and pulsing with static power. I quickly inspected the thing, excited to see what I had done.

[TESLA COIL - PROTOTYPE - AIR MAGIC AMPLIFIER
LEVEL 4 - TEST TIME REMAINING 59 MINUTES]

I whistled. A level 4 magic amplifier sounded awesome, but I had never seen that classification before. I almost felt like I was starting to bend Prixa's magic classifications a bit. I chuckled to myself about that.

A test run was needed to check its performance. I placed a hand on its base, then picked up an air wand I'd made for the occasion.

With a low hum, the coil sprang to life. Tiny arcs of electricity danced from its tip, painting a mesmerizing light display in the dim basement. I smiled and cheered, setting the wand down. I had a sudden idea and ran upstairs to get a bucket of water.

I set it down, then again infused the coil with the lightning spell. A concentrated beam blasted straight into the bucket of water, and inside the bucket, the water glowed with electricity. The bright arcs of electricity lit up the dark corners of the smithy as they played over the water's surface. I stared, captivated, as the water in the bucket seemed to dance and shimmer with electric energy. Tiny bubbles formed rapidly, indicating the intense heat being generated.

This was intriguing. The electrical conductivity of water had always been a known phenomenon, but witnessing it firsthand in such a controlled environment gave me new insights. The water wasn't merely conducting the electricity; it was acting as an amplifier, increasing the intensity of the electrical display. If the water could enhance the power of the coil, perhaps there were other elements and mediums we could use to our advantage. Like...the moat, for instance. I needed to install one of these near the moat, set it off, and if anyone fell in the water or tried to ford it, they would get zapped.

I pondered on this. With Tesla coils positioned strategically around the settlement, I could almost make an electric fence to keep the dragons out. Furthermore, the water could serve as a conductor, spreading the coil's effect over a wider area than anticipated.

Say a dragon released a water attack, and I shot it with the coil. Would I make their attack actually more deadly? If the electric bolt hit the dragons, would the attack amplify, injuring them even faster? How could I direct it?

But there were challenges too. *How would we prevent our own citizens from accidentally coming into contact with these electrified water traps?* Maintaining the Tesla coils in such environments would be a task in itself. The air mages would be in charge of keeping them charged unless I could figure out storage, like a battery. That would have to be the next thing I would make, but I had never designed one before.

Lost in my thoughts, I hardly noticed Romas coming into the basement. I had so many plans to draft, people to speak to, and simulations to run.

"Would you look at that!" he exclaimed, clapping his paws together. "Sometimes I wonder what's in that head of yours, boy."

"I'm just trying to think ahead," I said with a modest shrug. "Every little edge we can get against the Shadowalkers could make a difference."

Romas approached the mini Tesla coil, studying it with an expert eye. He reached out a furry hand, hovering it just above the device, feeling the static electricity prickle his fur. "This is impressive, Noah."

I smiled. "It's fun making this stuff. But I still have no idea how to use it in a real-world battle. I still don't even fully understand what's coming for us."

He laughed heartily, his deep voice echoing in the basement. "Well, I might be good with a hammer and anvil, but this... magic and technology combined? It's beyond my expertise. I'm glad Dunbar has you. You'll figure it out, I'm sure. Now I need the anvil, so away with you."

He made a shooing motion with his paws, and I picked up the heavy Tesla coil, cutting the spell off. It banged against the ceiling, and I uttered a few curse words.

"Romas, a little help?" I yelled behind me, but his eyes had glazed over at the crafting table, so he wouldn't respond until he was done with whatever he was building.

"Jasper? Anyone?" I yelled.

No response.

With a sigh, I picked up the heavy base again and began slowly stomping up the stairs with my creation. It banged off the walls, and I had to set it down a few times to get a better grip, but I was happy I at least had the strength to lift this thing. It had to be over 200 pounds.

After fighting with the turn for a while, I finally got it clear of the basement, twisting it and turning it until I could pivot it around the corner. I thought of the *Friends* episode where Ross was taking the couch up the stairs, and I laughed.

"Noah, what the hell is that thing?" Mara asked, walking into the smithy.

"This," I said with a manic smile, "is how I protect the city from water dragons. Or at least I hope."

I inspected it again, noticing I only had 34 minutes remaining in my trial. I burned over twenty minutes just taking the damn thing up the stairs.

"We gotta hurry. Gather the air mages. It's time to test it!"

Chapter 20

Testing, Testing

"Alright," I began, addressing the gathered group as the sun fell behind the horizon. "The plan is to test the capabilities of this coil, especially when paired with water. If my calculations are correct, we could potentially use this against the water dragons." I paused, glancing at the bucket. "I need your expertise to guide and amplify its power."

The air mages all smiled, excited to see what we could do. "We are with you, Noah. Show us what needs to be done," Samuel said. He was the latest addition to the air mages. He had come from Fayport as someone who the Monarch thought had a shot at helping us. Fekan soldiers were coming in slowly from the capital as well as the Monarch learned of the impending attack.

I nodded, explaining the coil's intricacies, energy flow, and potential areas where their elemental magic could assist. "Where's Mara? Didn't she want to see this too?"

No one said anything, shrugging to each other. I shook my head. She was probably off trying to figure out how to get back to those monk people after her scouting trip up north was completed.

"Nevermind." The sky overhead darkened, an impending storm mirroring the tension on the ground. "Let's get testing. I'm not about to try out a Tesla coil in a rainstorm. Let's start with one air mage. You should be able to produce a more powerful bolt than I did."

A mage named Alan stood up and walked toward me. "I will do this."

I clicked on my party skill, showing the health and mana over everyone's head with my Patron ability, and sat back to watch. Liza had created a shelter for us to watch from. We figured being surrounded by dirt in a little makeshift cave would be safest.

Alan positioned himself beside the coil, taking a moment to steady his breathing. His hands extended, and I could feel the tingling sensation of his power even through the earth bunker. The hair on the back of my arm stood up.

"Alright, Alan," I instructed. "Focus your energy into the base there. Remember, we want to see how the coil amplifies and redirects the energy you provide."

He nodded, eyes closed in concentration. A gentle whirlwind started to encircle him, picking up leaves and dust. The air seemed to thrum with electricity as Alun began to channel his energy into the mini Tesla coil.

The coil responded immediately. The soft hum grew louder, almost resonating with his power. Then, with a sharp crack, a concentrated bolt of energy shot from the coil into the bucket of water. The display was even more impressive than before: brilliant tendrils of electricity danced atop the water, casting an eerie glow in the dim light.

The mages erupted in applause and cheers. Romas gave a hearty roar of approval, the noise startling us in the tight bunker. I rushed out and looked at the bucket. It still crackled with energy. If one mage could produce such an effect, imagine what a team of them could accomplish when combined with the coil's power.

The timer had 5 minutes left on it, so I retreated to the bunker again to try a duel mage test. This time, the lightning shot out much quicker, not taking even a few moments to charge up when both air mages put energy into the coil.

I smiled as we walked back into town, ready to make the full-scale model. If I had time, I would make two of them and have them make a line that would act almost as a fence.

Mara sat in the palace, the anti-scrying box humming merrily next to her. She felt incredible with that thing near her as if weights had been removed from her. She didn't realize how much the anti-scrying had impacted her, almost like a poison.

Her 'SCRYING' skill had also leveled up since completing the box, and she had more mana to work with now. She had no idea if it was enough to get across the ocean and find the leader of the monk people, but she had to try. She had a really bad feeling that something was about to happen, and wanted to get allies for the town.

She took a deep breath, steadied herself, then projected her being into the Astral plane.

Mara's surroundings blurred, the colors of the physical realm melting away to be replaced by the muted, ethereal hues of the Astral plane. The transition was always a bit jarring, a rush of sensation followed by the weightlessness of the astral form. Her consciousness hovered, unbound by physical constraints, a shimmering figure in this limitless expanse.

Navigating the Astral plane was unlike walking or flying. It was more like willing oneself to be in a particular location, a pure thought-driven motion. Mara closed her ethereal eyes, the vivid image of the Trial Moon sect's temple in her mind. The temple, as she remembered it, stood tall atop a hill, above that enormous tree. It was where she hoped to find the leader of the monk people.

She began to 'move,' pushing herself through the landscape, then over the ocean. She saw Fayport, the souls that made up the city. From the middle shone a bright aura, most likely the cougar or the Monarch. Something else was in the distance, but she couldn't make out what it was. It was a darker energy, almost sinister.

Mara's recent leveling up had made her more attuned to the energies around her, more in control of her astral projection. She didn't dottle, though, and kept moving. She still had a limited mana pool, after all.

As she traversed this otherworldly plane, Mara felt the familiar pull of far-off energies over the ocean. The tree, the vibrational signature of the sect, the calming, disciplined energy of the monks. Guided by this, she made her way across the vast ocean.

However, strange, shadowy figures existed out here. Figures she didn't notice last time. She ignored them for now, far off as they were, but she still looked on worryingly.

After what felt like hours but might've been mere minutes, the astral silhouette of the Trial Moon sect's temple loomed before her. She cautiously approached it, keenly aware that powerful entities might guard such a place even in the Astral realm. She felt she had about 1/3 of her mana left, but the tree took over, just like last time. It tapped into her spirit, providing energy to survive in this place above the physical plane.

The powerful Astral mage stood at the entrance to the town, his eyes glowing with the soft luminescence of the astral light. Recognizing it as the mage from last time, Mara greeted him with a deep bow. His physical body sat under the tree, meditating.

[I have returned to seek the leader of the Trial Moon sect,] she began, her voice echoing in the strange acoustics of the Astral plane. [Our town is in danger, and I need allies.]

The mage nodded sagely, a hint of sadness in his silver eyes. [It is good to see you again, child,] he said in an echoey voice. [I saw you coming. That was a clever little device your leader created to stop the interference. Come, for the battle has already begun. We cannot delay.]

Mara was taken aback. [What do you mean, *has already begun?*]

[Come. We must head to the temple. They are waiting for you there.]

He turned and zoomed away, urging her to follow. She did, floating behind him toward a large structure that sat on a hill.

Up ahead, a tall figure stood and looked in her general direction, eyes closed. He was draped in robes that shimmered with celestial patterns that seemed to bend and shift. He motioned for her to enter the temple, still with eyes closed. He was not ethereal but in his physical body interacting with her. Mara noticed the temple's walls pulsating with a soft, rhythmic glow, like the heartbeat of the temple itself.

She passed through the temple walls now that she was allowed entry, seeing the monks inside. They sat in a circle in the lotus position, eyes closed and humming an eerie song. It resonated with her mind, soothing her and empowering her like the tree had.

The abbot walked through the doors and sat on a bench nearby, glancing at her. "My brothers will power your form until you're ready to leave. For we have much to discuss."

Chapter 21

Reflections

I SAT IN THE PALACE'S COMMON AREA, RESTING WITH MY depleted mana slowly ticking up after dropping my mana pool down to single digits. I knew I needed to get to creating a water item, but there was always something that had a higher priority. A fire crackled nearby in a hearth as the sound of fountains gurgling calmed my mind. I found myself thinking about my success over the past week.

I had struck a deal with trolls, found a way to create an anti-scrying device that had a city-wide effect, and built a prototype Tesla coil that I hoped would shock water dragons into oblivion. I leaned back in my plush chair and smiled.

"Pleased with yourself or something?" Romas asked, curling up and sitting by the roaring fire nearby.

I looked over at the large Feka, his fur flickering with the warm orange hues of the firelight. His eyes bore into mine, filled with amusement and perhaps a hint of pride.

"Just reflecting on the journey, Romas," I replied with a wry grin, "From where we started to where we are now – it's been one hell of a ride. I've really had to grow up quickly in this place. I don't feel anything like who I was when I first got here."

657

Romas did his meowing laugh, the sound deep and rumbling, "That's one way to put it. I've been a Creator for decades, and never have I seen trolls negotiate or the creation of a device that shields an entire city. And now, electric coils that could very well fry our enemies? It's been quite the adventure."

I nodded in agreement. "Sometimes, I have to pinch myself to make sure I'm not dreaming. The challenges we've faced and continue to face...it's all been so crazy. But with every victory, I feel like I grow up a little more. Romas, we need to end these threats once and for all. We need to be able to grow this city, trade freely, and not worry that these werewolves are coming for us every chance they get."

The Feka nodded as the door creaked open and Mara entered, looking around, then fixing her eyes on us.

"Mara!" I shouted, getting up from the chair. "Where have you been? I was worried sick!"

She brushed a stray lock of her blonde hair behind her ear, her silvery eyes holding a hint of mischief. "I've been working, my dear Baron. Not all of us have the luxury of sitting by the fire." She shot a playful smirk at Romas, who responded with a grin of his own.

"Work?" I echoed, trying to suppress my relief. "What kind of work?"

She strode closer, the ambient glow from the fire casting a soft light on her face. "Well, while you've been making friends with trolls and zapping water with your fancy coil," she began, "I've been gathering information and rallying some other allies."

I tilted my head, curious. "Who?"

She pointed across the ocean, her smile growing larger.

"You got those monks on our side?"

She nodded, leaning against the back of a chair. "We discussed what's going on here at length. The Shadowalkers' aggression doesn't sit well with them. And after that dragon spoke to me..."

"That's incredible, Mara. With them on our side, our chances got much better. We need as much magic as we can get."

Mara winked. "Told you I was working. Although they still have no idea how they will help from across the ocean. Now, care to fill me in on all your electric adventures?"

We spent the next hours updating each other, discussing strategy, and plotting our next moves. With every ally we gained and every innovation we made, the city got stronger.

Eventually, I bid everyone goodnight. Tomorrow was a big day, and I had an electric dragon zapper to work on with Romas.

I woke up early the next day and found Romas already working in the main area of the forge. He was gathering up a bunch of silverstone that had come in from the mines.

The rhythmic clang of metal echoed through the expansive forge, announcing the start of another day. The orange glow of dawn mixed with the fire's luminance, casting long shadows on the stone walls. The Feka's massive form was a silhouette against the flames, his movements methodical and efficient.

Approaching him, I remarked, "You're up early."

Romas didn't look up from his work immediately, instead focusing on placing a hefty chunk of silverstone onto a cart. "Sleep is for those with time to squander," he rumbled, wiping the sweat from his brow. "Besides, with the amount of silverstone we need for the coil's full design, there's no time to waste."

Nodding, I surveyed the impressive stash. "The miners have outdone themselves. I wasn't expecting this amount for at least another day."

"The urgency of our situation has lit a fire under them," Romas said with a smirk.

Matt Pivots

It appeared word of the Shadowalker and dragon invasion had made it to everyone's ears. "I'll make sure they're compensated well for their efforts," I stated.

Romas grunted in agreement. "Good. It's not just about the money, though, even though that is something new around here for the no-classers. It's about showing them that their efforts are noticed and appreciated. A simple 'thank you' can go a long way."

"You never say thank you," I said, a smirk forming.

"Well, I'm not a Baron, now am I? Now get to it, lad."

I shook my head, then took up some silverstone and began working on drawing the ore out into long wire with Romas. With the two coils costing 125 mana each and my mana pool only at [140/140], I needed to find another way of lessening the mana load on me.

I had checked late last night at the design table if manually making any of the components would reduce the cost and was happily surprised when the answer was yes. The silverstone wire could be made manually, and the 15x turned into 100ft when I redid the calculations. The 125 mana cost was reduced to 90, which meant with the mana bracer, I could finish both towers today.

But these were going to be big ass towers. I had the entire Fekan warrior population on standby to install the things on the walls.

Romas said he couldn't make the air magic items since his race couldn't utilize that mana, nor could he assemble the item without the plans. So, he was just an assistant today, manually spooling wire. It grated on him a bit, I could tell.

"Romas," I began, "once we've fortified the city and – hopefully – fended off the Shadowalkers, I think Dunbar could benefit from a dedicated training academy. Not just for warriors but for craftsmen, mages, and miners. A place to hone skills, share knowledge, and train the next generation. Maybe I could even teach engineering!"

The Fekan blacksmith paused, considering my words, then nodded. "A fine idea," he finally said. "A city is only as strong as its people. And with the way things are, we need every edge we can get. And with the way you solve problems, even in wartime, we could use a few more mages with that training."

I smiled. I always loved it when a plan was in motion. We sat there in silence as the fire continued softening up the ore. The blueprints for the larger Tesla coils were intricate, requiring precision in both design and execution. Every piece of silver-stone, every component, mattered. But with Romas at my side and the raw materials now at hand, I felt more confident than ever.

Mara walked in, holding two bags that smelled incredible, most likely breakfast for us. I heard Jasper wake up in the back of the smithy, the smell most likely waking the kid.

"Morning, you two." Mara greeted us with a wide grin as she set down the bags on a nearby wooden table. The delightful aroma wafted out, immediately drawing us in. "Thought you might be burning some calories here, so I brought reinforcements."

Romas took a momentary break from his work, his large nostrils flaring as he inhaled deeply. "Mara, if I weren't so committed to my craft, I'd consider switching professions to whatever magical culinary arts this used."

She laughed. "Not magic, just a visit to Madame Eliza's down the street. But I'm sure she'll take the compliment." She winked at the panther, who rolled his eyes and shook his whiskers.

I hurried over, peeking into the bags. Freshly baked rolls, some with sweet fruit jam oozing out of them, and others stuffed with seasoned meats and melted cheese. There were also some flaky pastries dusted with powdered sugar. My stomach growled in response, reminding me I hadn't eaten since yesterday afternoon.

Jasper, with tousled hair and sleep-laden eyes, stumbled in, guided solely by the scent of the food. The usually energetic boy brightened up instantly upon seeing the feast. "Did you get the cinnamon ones?" he asked with hope in his voice.

Mara handed him one of the pastries with a smile. "Of course. But eat over the table; you know how messy these can get."

Jasper nodded, eagerly taking a bite and releasing a muffled sound of delight. "I'll be careful, mom," he joked, bits of muffin flying out of his mouth when he spoke.

"Dude!" I yelled, brushing crumbs off me.

Chapter 22

Bastion

Romas stood next to me, a gigantic wire spool next to him. I looked at the crowd around me, as they waited to hear my instructions. "Today, we will be installing two anti-air devices- one on the top of the palace, and one on the main wall. This device, called a Tesla coils back on my world, will serve as a crucial line of defense against airborne threats, including water dragons."

A murmur of excitement and curiosity rippled through the crowd. Eyes widened, questions were whispered, and more than one skeptical eyebrow was raised. I couldn't blame them; what we were proposing was unprecedented. A combination of magic and engineering, unlike anything Dunbar had ever seen.

Romas gestured toward the spool. "For those of you Feka that don't believe this will work, trust me when I say...Noah has outdone himself this time. This wire," he held up the silverstone wire, "is specially designed to conduct magical energy, specifically air magic. It will connect the magic of the air mages and amplify their power toward a water source, also known as a dragon."

I smiled at the master blacksmith. I continued, "We'll work in teams to complete this. One team will be responsible for setting up and securing the first coil base on the city wall and the other to the palace roof, while the other half will lay down the wiring on the frame and connect it to the energy source the air mages will use. Safety is paramount, so please listen carefully to the team leaders' instructions."

Mara stepped forward, a scroll in her hands. "I've written down the names of the teams and your respective leaders. Team A will be led by Romas, and Team B will be led by me, after Noah has made the base for the towers. Please gather around your team leader once we call out your name."

As she read out the names, people assembled around Romas and Mara, eager to get started but also visibly anxious. I understood their concern; this was new territory for all of us. Yet, as I looked around at Romas, Mara, Jasper, and the rest of the assembled crowd, I felt a surge of confidence.

"Alright, guys, we need twenty pieces of the silverstone ore for the core of the coil. Ten more pieces of iron for the framework. Let's get them up here, carefully. Once again, safety first," I instructed as my team started hauling the ores from the pile near the wall to our designated work area.

"Then, I'll form the base where the mages will work from in an attack. Then we will have to coil the wire around the structure to connect the batter to the head there," I continued, yelling over the noise of the scraping rocks. "Lastly, we run the wire to the roof and continue it around the palace coil and finish the wire at that discharge head."

The team moved with focus and efficiency. A few stronger members lifted the heavier chunks while others worked together in pairs to balance the load. When all the pieces were finally in place, I looked around at the faces of my team—flushed from the physical exertion but eager to proceed.

A silence broke out as all eyes looked at me. As I raised my hand, my focus narrowed, settling on the pile of materials before me. I felt a thrum of energy, a tether connecting me to each piece of iron and silverstone, created according to the designs I had magically drawn up. With a thought, they began to move, levitating into the air and swirling around each other. It was as if time itself had slowed, every twist and turn of the materials locked in a graceful dance, a ballet of metal and magic.

My Engineer skill guided me, mental schematics overlaying reality in my mental heads-up display. My hand moved almost of its own accord, directing the flow of materials.

The swirling mass of components began to take form, guided by the blueprint in my mind. The iron pieces locked into place, forming the robust framework of the Tesla coil. Meanwhile, the silverstone embedded itself into the core and head of the coil, a radiant heart within a body of iron. As the final piece slid into its designated position, I clenched my fist, willing the whole structure to lock together.

There was a moment of complete silence, as if the world itself was holding its breath.

It stood there, all fifteen feet of it, gleaming in the daylight—a sentinel overlooking Dunbar. Cheers broke out all across Dunbar as Feka and humans alike hugged in celebration.

I lowered my hand, feeling exhaustion and exhilaration wash over me as 90 mana left my body in a rush. My eyes met those of Romas, Mara, and the rest of the team. They all beamed back at me.

"Okay, A-team, focus on getting this wire coiled on, then we can test it out! B-team, let's get the other coil built!" I snapped the mana bracer on my arm.

Everyone nodded, and Romas nodded, pride all over his furry features. I could tell he had never seen such a thing before. Even when we made the drawbridge, the pieces were there the whole time; it just needed a little mechanical advantage. We headed toward the palace and up onto the roof.

But now, he had seen my manufacturing skill in full effect.

Dunbar was ready. And whatever the Shadowalkers threw at us, we would be more than just prepared. We'd be waiting.

"Is everyone clear on the last steps? We'll activate the coil in a controlled sequence, monitoring for any energy spikes or fluctuations. This is uncharted territory, so let's proceed with caution."

We had worked through the whole day, the teams coiling wire nonstop for hours now after building the second coil on the roof. The sun began to set as Liza formed her earth bunker for us to observe from, the towers gloriously staring down at me.

Wire ran from the mage battery to the wall then to the palace roof, swaying lightly in the breeze. After a few last-minute checks, we were ready. I didn't think we would have any issue with the Tesla coil, but it was better to be safely tucked away in a grounded bunker.

The moment had arrived. My heart pounded in my chest, and I looked at my team, then over at Romas and Mara.

"On my count. Three... two... one... activate!"

The air mages channeled their energy into the large battery input of the wall coil and the silverstone core began to hum, softly at first, then louder. Arcs of electricity danced from the first coil as it charged, reaching skyward as if challenging the heavens. For a moment, I held my breath as I looked at the arrow that we were going to shoot through the field to simulate a water dragon.

And then I felt it. My hair stood on end as electricity surged through me, the coil's heads nearing peak capacity. The second coil on the palace roof started shooting sparks into the sky as it also charged up. I nodded to the archer, who nodded back. She aimed from the dirt path in front of us and fired the soaked arrow high into the air above the city and the device.

As the arrow soared through the air, its wet tail trailing behind it, my eyes flicked to the Tesla coils. My hand, tingling with the electric charge that still pulsed through me, twitched subtly. The air mages intensified their focus, the hum of the coil rising to a near-roar.

With a deafening crack, bolts of electricity leaped from the forcefield, lancing out to meet the water-soaked arrow in mid-air. The result was spectacular—a dazzling burst of light and steam, the arrow disintegrated in a flash, leaving only a trail of dissipating energy behind.

The gathering erupted into cheers, the pent-up tension of the moment released in a wave of jubilation and awe. The mages who had been channeling their energy into the coil sagged a little, the drain evident, but their faces alight with triumph. They pumped their fists from the first level, shouting down to us. Even Romas, who had seen countless battles and skirmishes, let out a deep, appreciative rumble, his eyes sparkling with excitement.

I turned to the Fekan archer, who was staring wide-eyed at the space where her arrow had been just moments before.

"Good shot," I called out over the cheering.

She chuckled nervously, "Holy cow, Noah. That thing is powerful!"

I nodded. "Just wait until the dragons come. It will be spectacular!"

As the applause and cheers rang out again, I caught Mara's eyes across the crowd. She smiled at me, her eyes shining not just with pride, but also a deep, unspoken love. And as I stood there amidst the people I cared for, in the city I was sworn to protect, a sense of completeness washed over me. I had come a long way from the confused, lost boy who stumbled upon this city, bleeding from vulture wounds.

I felt warmth spreading across my body as I leveled up, most likely from creating these monstrosities. But I also felt a tingle on my right forearm, causing me some confusion as it came from my city arm. I rolled up my sleeve to reveal the tattoo representing my flag of Dunbar. I looked down at my right arm, where the city codex was located, and smiled as my city tattoo changed. It now read:

[RANK - FORTIFIED BASTION]

Chapter 23

Human Toys

THE ALPHA WAITED OUTSIDE OF DUNBAR, WAITING FOR HIS scouts to arrive back. Night was about to fall, which meant their attack would begin. He asked the dragons to hold back from flying overhead since that mage of theirs noticed them last time. He wanted this attack to be a surprise in the night.

The Alpha paced restlessly in the shadows beyond Dunbar's walls, his keen eyes scanning the horizon for the return of his scouts. His fur bristled with impatience, the inky night closing in. It would be the perfect cloak for their assault, provided they executed it before the city had time to bolster its defenses. The water dragons lurked further back, hidden from sight but close enough to be summoned immediately.

His ears perked up at the sound of approaching footsteps, and he turned just in time to see several shadowy figures emerge from the darkness. His scouts had returned.

"What news do you bring?" he growled, his voice tinged with barely restrained urgency.

The lead scout, a wiry Stalker with piercing yellow eyes, approached cautiously. "The humans have been busy, Alpha. They've built something... unnatural. A tower that emanates magic that made our hair stand on end."

A low growl emanated from the alpha's throat. This was unexpected and unwelcome news. He had been counting on the element of surprise, and any new form of defense would complicate matters.

"What about that mage? The one who sensed our dragons last time?" the alpha pressed, his eyes narrowing.

"She was there, consulting with another human near the new device," the scout replied.

The alpha pondered this new information, his mind racing through potential strategies and outcomes. *So they know we're here, then,* he thought.

He had been looking forward to a straightforward assault, a swift strike under the cover of darkness. But now...

"Tell the dragons to hold their positions," he commanded, a note of irritation in his voice. "And send word to the lizards to prepare for a ground assault. We will need to adapt our tactics."

As his scouts melted back into the shadows to carry out his orders, the alpha couldn't shake off a sense of unease. Dunbar had been a thorn in his side for too long, a stubborn enclave of human resistance in territory he considered rightfully his. And now, with this new development, the city had become an even more infuriating enigma.

The alpha cast one last glance toward the walls of Dunbar, a growl rumbling deep within his chest. Whatever this new device was, whatever tricks the humans had up their sleeves, he was determined to rip it all apart, stone by stone, bolt by bolt.

But as he turned away, preparing to rally his troops for the night's assault, a troubling thought entered his mind, one he couldn't easily dismiss.

What if the boy was ready for them again?

He heard an angry growl and turned to see the head dragon approaching him. "No one tells us anything, wolf. What's the problem? My brothers grow anxious."

The alpha met the dragon's gaze, recognizing the need for tact. Dragons were proud creatures, not used to taking commands, especially not from wolves. The sinuous beast before him was much larger than any werewolf in his pack, its scales shimmering with a dangerous iridescence, eyes like shining glaciers.

"Your impatience is understood," the alpha began carefully, "but there's been a development. The humans have erected a new defense, and we are not sure what it is or what it does. We need to reassess our approach."

The dragon snorted, a puff of smoke escaping its nostrils. "Since when do humans' toys concern us? We are dragons; we fear no contraptions they construct."

"Underestimating the enemy is a sure way to defeat," the alpha retorted. "Our pack would know, unfortunately. The creator human is clever. He utilizes magic not from this world."

The dragon's eyes narrowed, its massive form looming over the alpha. "We attack. No questions. We are not afraid of these felines and humans," it declared, the authority in its voice leaving no room for negotiation.

The alpha met the dragon's gaze, aware that pushing too hard against the creature's pride could strain their uneasy alliance to a breaking point. Dragons were known for their fierce independence and did not take well to being directed.

"Very well," the alpha finally said, restraining the growl that threatened to escape his throat. "But heed this: underestimate the enemy, and we risk more than just wounded pride. These are desperate people. Desperation makes for dangerous foes."

The dragon let out a snort, plumes of snow swirling around its snout. "Dangerous or not, they will feel the wrath of dragons. I will rally my brothers; be ready to unleash your pack when you see us in the sky."

As the dragon turned to depart, immense wings unfurling in preparation for flight, the alpha felt anticipation coiling up in his gut. The dragon's determination could be both an asset and a liability. Yet, there was no turning back now; the lines had been drawn.

He watched as the dragon lifted off, its form quickly disappearing into the gathering darkness. It was a signal for the rest of the pack and for the other creatures lurking in the shadows, awaiting the onset of battle.

The lead Saurite slithered over. "Are you ssssure about this?"

The alpha paused, eyes following the dragons, then nodded. "We have no choice. This is a battle we must win."

Turning back toward the walls of Dunbar, the alpha felt his fur bristle with a mixture of excitement and unease. The stakes were high, higher than they'd ever been. But come what may, the Shadowalkers and their dragon allies would descend upon the city tonight. And when the dawn broke, they would see themselves standing on the walls as new owners of the entire jungle.

As the final traces of the dragon's silhouette vanished into the twilight, the alpha let out a low, guttural call, summoning his pack to him. One by one, shadowy figures emerged from the dark recesses of the forest, their eyes glowing with a predatory light. Lizards, large and covered in chitinous scales, joined them, hissing softly as they awaited orders. Their new steel weapons glistened in the moonlight.

"The dragons will lead the assault from the sky," the alpha announced, his voice carrying with a low growl. "We will follow on the ground, attacking in waves to disorient and overwhelm. Let's go!"

A collective growl rippled through the assembled creatures as the alpha's eyes scanned his troops, meeting each gaze with a nod of approval. They were ready, as ready as they'd ever be. And it was time.

With a swift leap, the alpha led the charge, his pack spreading out behind him in a deadly formation. Lizards skittered along the flanks, their natural armor glistening in the patchy moonlight. The alpha's heightened senses took over as they closed the distance to Dunbar. Every scent was magnified, every sound amplified, as his body prepared for the battle to come.

The moonlight hit him, and he began to charge his special skill. He felt his muscles tense and bulge, his eyes dilate, and his claws grow larger.

Just as they reached the edge of the forest and onto the outskirts of the town, a guttural roar reverberated through the night sky, followed by four more. The Alpha saw the dragons swooping toward the city, bellies glowing a bright blue color. They swooped down from above like avenging angels. Horns sounded in the distance, alerting the city of the impending attack.

The battle for Dunbar had begun.

Chapter 24

The Fifth Battle of Dunbar

I LOOKED INTO THE FOREST AS I SAW ICE-BLUE DRAGONS shoot out of them and soar over our city. I stumbled back, momentarily stunned by their appearance. They were even bigger than Mara described them from her scrying trips. My eyes darted to Mara who gave me a squeeze on the arm in confidence.

It was time.

"Mara, get to the air mages! Coordinate the energy flow to the Tesla coils!" I shouted, snapping back into action. Ice and snow rained down on us as the dragons made a pass, dropping the temperature at least fifty degrees.

"On it," Mara replied, her eyes already a distant silver as she focused her magical senses. I could tell she was communicating with Kyle telepathically, just as we had prepared.

Typh ran over to me, flanked by my best warriors and platoon leaders. "Shall we begin ballistics?" he asked.

Another one of the dragons roared, then flew from the gulf side of the settlement, blasting the city with ice and snow. The palace became a wintery wonderland as hunters and warriors ran to their positions on the dirt below to wait for the lizardmen.

675

It made walking around the settlement much more difficult. However, it seemed as though the dragons were going with non-lethal attacks at the moment, which was good news for us.

"Yes, initiate ballistics," I commanded. "Target the ground forces first as they cross the first moat. Let's thin their numbers before they reach the walls as they go over the moat. Use large ammo for the dragons. Aim for their wings. The coils should be up soon! But I will need them to get close first. We may have to take a few ice blasts before engaging. I want the dragons to get comfortable attacking before we roast them."

"Understood," Typh nodded, then turned to relay the orders. A flurry of activity erupted along the wall as archers nocked their arrows and ballistae were loaded with massive bolts, each one enchanted to carry an explosive payload.

Another dragon swooped down toward the moat, blasting it with ice. The water began icing over from the edges, crackling with energy. Another dragon flew over behind it, the icy blast the same as the first dragon. One more followed behind, and the water finished freezing, making the drawbridge completely irrelevant. I cursed loudly. In a span of fifteen seconds, a city defense was made irrelevant.

The Shadowalker army came out of the trees at full speed. There was no howling or barking this time as the hairless dogs shot out of the trees as if they came out of a cannon. Unlike last time, the lizards stayed on the surface until they were over the frozen water.

So I was right. They couldn't burrow through the water. I wish I had more time to erect a proper defense against them coming under my walls.

The first volley of arrows and bolts shot through the air from my hunter class Feka who were the first troops to get to the walls. The large ballista let out a thunderous twang as a large missile missed a nearby dragon and hit a tree.

My mages formed up behind me, fire wands at the ready. My tattoo seemed to itch on my right arm—a sensory reminder that the city of Dunbar, now a 'Fortified Bastion,' was being put to its first real test. The air mages slogged through the snow toward the coils. It was now or never.

Let them come, I thought. Dunbar is ready. And as the next wave of attackers advanced, I steeled myself for the battle that would define us all.

From the vantage of a small hill at the forest's edge, the alpha watched as his dragons unleashed torrents of ice over the city. The watery barrier in front of them was frosted over within moments, a bridge of ice forming to allow passage for his ground forces.

"Ladders!" he roared, his voice piercing through the clamor of the impending battle. "Attach them to the walls! Quickly! The snow in their settlement will slow them down from gaining a defensive position!"

On cue, squads of hyenas hastened forward with ladders clamped between their jaws. Arrows from Dunbar's archers began raining down; each aimed to kill. Yet the hyenas moved with agility, their keen senses dodging the majority of the projectiles.

"Lizards- shields up!" the alpha commanded as he spotted the humans preparing to unleash those damned fire attacks.

Giant lizard warriors, carrying large, leafy green wooden shields, emerged from the ranks. They positioned themselves in front of the advancing troops, their shields forming a wall that absorbed the brunt of the magical fire attacks.

A grim smile spread across the alpha's muzzle. He had to hand it to the humans; they were resourceful. Their new barriers were more formidable than he had anticipated. It stopped the lizards

677

from burrowing, which removed their surprise. But he had adapted, too, and he still had tricks up his furry sleeves.

As the first wave of Shadowalkers and lizards reached the iced-over water and scrambled over it, slipping and sliding, the alpha continued feeling uncertain. He looked again at the gleaming devices on the wall, waiting for them.

He shook his head. The next few moments would determine not just the outcome of this battle but perhaps the fate of his pack and all the territories they had conquered. He had no time for doubt. He had employed the most powerful beasts in the land and couldn't lose.

His eyes narrowed as he watched the scene unfold, every muscle in his body taut, ready to spring into action. He was calculating, waiting for just the right moment to unleash his Stalker generals into the fray. Now wasn't the time for the Stalker generals, his most elite warriors—yet. They were his trump card, the shadowy assassins capable of sowing chaos and disarray deep within enemy lines. But they were also few in number and not to be spent frivolously. Timing was crucial.

Fireballs started launching toward his troops, mixing with the arrows from the cats shooting down from the walls. Just as a dragon swooped down, its mouth glowing with the telltale light of a charged ice attack, the alpha felt a shift in the air, an almost palpable vibration. His eyes darted to the strange human-made device on Dunbar's wall with the other one mounted to their palace structure, their cores humming with a frequency that resonated with the air itself.

The next moment unfolded like a nightmare.

With a deafening crack, bolts of electricity lanced from both of the large coils, converging on the descending dragon almost as if they were connected. The creature had no time to veer off or unleash its attack; it was enveloped in a storm of electrical energy, its shriek of surprise and agony piercing through the night.

The dragon tumbled out of the sky, its body smashing into the stone wall and spasming uncontrollably as it crashed into the ground, landing with a horrific thud among the alpha's ground troops as they loaded ladders against the walls. The soldiers that escaped being crushed, but still closest to the impact were thrown off their feet, their cries of shock and confusion adding to the disarray as a nearby ladder exploded from the weight of the dragon's dead body.

For a moment, the alpha was paralyzed, his eyes locked on the fallen dragon, its scales still sparking with residual electricity. This was a catastrophe, a blow to not only his forces but also to the morale of all who followed him.

Another dragon swooped in low, apparently not seeing his comrade fall in such a horrific fashion as it came at the settlement from the jungle.

"No!" The alpha's scream tore through the night, desperate for the dragon to pull back, but it was too late. The strange towers came to life again, with an even more powerful discharge. Lightning arced from the devices, fanning out in an intricate web of electrical energy that met the dragon mid-flight. The night sky lit up as if it were day, casting an eerie, unnatural light over the entire battlefield. The dragon's shrieks were swallowed by the booming crackle of thunder, its body spasming in the air like its brother before plummeting into the upper reaches of Dunbar.

The sight was horrific, even for a seasoned warrior like the alpha. Not one, but two dragons—symbols of raw power and invincibility—had fallen tonight. The air was thick with the smell of burnt scales and ozone, a nauseating cocktail that seemed to hang like a shroud over his retreating troops.

This time the other three dragons saw their fellow fall, having circled the city for another pass. They let out loud, agonizing roars into the night sky.

His forces were in disarray, scrambling back to the cover of the trees. The howls and cries of wounded or disoriented Shadowalkers mixed with the acrid scent of magical discharge and the unsettling vibrations still resonated from those accursed devices. The dragons wheeled in the sky, letting out one more roar before retreating back toward the north.

He reluctantly followed suit and let out a roar, signaling his army to retreat. It was hard for him to believe what had happened, but knew better than push and lose his army.

As he retreated, the alpha couldn't help but cast another glance back at Dunbar, its walls still standing, its devices still humming. His rage was so pronounced that the moonlight fed into it, casting him into a horrible sight to behold. But another emotion surfaced that he couldn't quite identify—was it respect for a worthy adversary? Or perhaps it was doubt, creeping in from the furthest corners of his mind.

He just couldn't beat this place.

The alpha's ears twitched at the sound of cheers and celebration emanating from the walls of Dunbar. Each jubilant shout felt like a dagger to his pride, each triumphant Fekan roar mocking his failed assault.

He looked up just in time to see the human boy, the one responsible for those damnable devices, standing on the upper level of the city's walls. If only the Overlord wouldn't have let him get away. If only they had just killed him instead of putting him to work in their mines. That selfish human bastard had ruined everything for him.

Rage boiled within the alpha, hot and corrosive. Yet, even in the throes of his anger, he couldn't completely discount the ingenuity and resilience the humans had shown. They had taken his measure, matched his force with cunning, and emerged victorious.

His eyes locked onto the boy for a long moment. The young human had changed the rules of the game tonight, and though it galled him to admit it, the alpha recognized that he had underestimated his foe once more. He knew magic that had never graced this world, and for that, he had to bow down to him, for the moment at least.

As he turned away, slinking back into the dark embrace of the forest, the alpha felt the reluctant respect. Dunbar had repelled him tonight, as it always had. The boy had sent him a clear message, and it was one he fully intended to answer.

Even from this distance, the Alpha could make out the triumphant pump of his fist, followed by a crude gesture involving the boy's middle finger.

Interlude II

POMIUS LAY ASLEEP, THE NIGHTMARES COMING TO HIM LIKE always. It had been two years since he had killed Eldric the creator. He had slipped away without anyone noticing, so Eldric just disappeared, never to be seen again. But he knew what had really happened that day.

Since then, the hunger had only grown. His void mage class remained an enigma to him with no answers and no usage. He was level 1, and no closer to gaining experience using his skill than he was all those nights ago.

He had tried looking for an answer, but had found none. Dreams were the only times that he received glimpses of his true power, and they were broken fragments at best. He never knew what to make of them, only a robed figure seemed central to each of them.

But this time, the dream was different. He could feel it. A hooded figure came to him, and with it, the feeling of rot, decay, and death. The being felt...stronger somehow.

The figure moved with an eerie grace, like a shadow melding seamlessly with the darkness. Every step it took resonated with a deep, foreboding echo, the sound a combination of whispers and screams.

As the hooded figure approached, Pomius could see nothing of its face, save for two pale, luminescent eyes that seemed to pierce through the very fabric of his soul. Those eyes held lifetimes of torment and a sadness that was profound, yet they also bore a malevolence that sent shivers down his spine.

In the dream, Pomius tried to move, to scream, to do anything, but his body felt anchored, weighed down by an oppressive force that kept him rooted to the spot. The very air around him grew cold, every breath he took stinging his lungs.

The figure stopped inches away from him, its ragged breaths mixing with the chilling wind, filling the silence with a palpable tension. Then, with a voice that sounded like the rustling of dead leaves, it spoke, *"Why do you resist, Pomius? You heeded my voice so readily when you first unlocked your gift. Why do you run from your destiny?"*

Pomius wanted to retort, to deny whatever this being was insinuating, but words failed him. His throat felt constricted, his voice a mere whisper as he managed to say, *"Who are you?"*

The figure leaned in, the air growing colder, the scent of decay stronger. *"I am your master. I am the void. I am the hunger. I am the price that magic pays."*

The hooded being reached out, its fingers skeletal, the touch cold and lifeless. As it made contact with Pomius's forehead, a rush of memories flooded his mind. He saw glimpses into other worlds, where magic did not exist. In those worlds, the mana was absorbed into this creature. It grew strong.

The teenager gasped as the being took his finger away. *"What do you want?"* Pomius asked, panting.

"To show you. You must find a creator, and get it to use the void. You must grow your skills."

Pomius shivered. *"Are you real?"*

"What is real? A dream is just a void of human consciousness. And I am the master of the void. Are you not still real elsewhere?"

The creature's voice resonated in his mind, an echo that rumbled through every corner of his thoughts. His eyes darted around, attempting to find some semblance of sense in this dreamlike reality.

He didn't have a response to the creature's reasoning. *"You speak of creators and the void. Why me? Why show me this?"* Pomius demanded, his voice shaky yet defiant.

The hooded being seemed to ponder for a moment, the eerie silence stretching on. *"Because you, Pomius, are my void mage apprentice. You are on the cusp of understanding true power. The realms you see in my memories; they are mine now. I am the true power. The mana gets absorbed, leading to a world devoid of the very essence of magic. And in their place, I grow stronger. There is no resistance to my power."*

Pomius tried to make sense of the creature's words. *"Are you saying that in these worlds, you... consume the mana?"*

"The void consumes, but it also creates. It's a cycle, one that's been going on for eons. But it is now out of balance here. There is a tree, and it has granted power against me. You must stop them. You must help me defeat the guardian. And in return, I will make you the ultimate ruler of this world."

Pomius felt an inexplicable chill at the words, as if a dark cloud had descended upon him. *"Why should I trust you? What is this tree you speak of?"*

The hooded being hesitated for a moment, its hollow eyes staring into the distance. *"The World Tree. A cosmic entity that has maintained the balance of mana in this realm. It's the very core of this world's existence. But its guardians, they have tapped into its power, using it to combat the natural flow of the void. This world is on the brink, teetering between creation and destruction."*

Pomius tried to comprehend the scale of what he was hearing. *"And what role do I play in all of this?"*

The figure looked him over again, pausing. *"There has not been a void mage in this world for some time. I have finally grown strong enough to visit you in your dream state. I will come to you with more instructions, apprentice. For now, know that we must bring another creator here. He must be forced to make you what you desire."*

His dream started turning fuzzy, and the hooded creature seemed to narrow his eyes. *"But remember, the sands of time are running out. Make your choice soon."*

Pomius woke up from his dream and shot upright, sweat pooling on his bed around him. A dark mark remained where the creature had touched his forehead.

Chapter 25

Levels

I JUMPED DOWN FROM THE WALL, STILL FEELING THE tingling electricity in the air. The coils were still charged even though they had discharged a ton of their stored energy into the dragons.

"Everyone back from that thing!" I said, but I didn't need to tell people twice. I could see the Feka, their feline eyes wide and alert, watching the devices with awe and a bit of fear. Their gazes shifted to me, seeking reassurance. A bolt of lightning from the palace coil shot off into the sky with a *buzz,* and we all jumped in surprise.

"It's alright," I called out, moving towards the nearest group. My steps felt light, unburdened by the weight of defeat and doom we had all feared. "They did their job. Now we need to make sure they're safely discharged."

With a weary sigh, I approached the remains of the fallen dragons. One had fallen on the upper level of Dunbar, exploding a nearby fountain. The other was below in the dirt. Their ethereal blue scales shined, painting a delicate mosaic in the soft embrace of the moonlight. A gust of wind gently brushed against the fallen beasts, their once majestic forms now silent and still.

As I drew closer to the dragon on the upper level, it dissolved into a vaporous mist, leaving behind only what I assumed to be an extremely high-level ingredient.

A large patch of scales now lay before me, and as I knelt beside the remains, my hand gently grazed the surface of the scales. They were cold to the touch, their lustrous sheen belying the hardened resilience that had once armored the majestic beasts. I picked it up, inspecting it hastily.

[DRAGON SCALES - LEVEL 10 INGREDIENT]

I whistled. I didn't even know what a level 10 ingredient could do. These were potent ingredients, remnants of beings of power and majesty. It made me think of that level 8 stalker pelt I still had stored in the secret basement.

Suddenly, I looked up from the ingredients and noticed the cheering had stopped as both Feka and humans gathered around me. They had been watching as I picked up the scales. I nodded to the scene, then walked down the ramp to the location of the other dragon.

There, the body had left a huge icy claw. I gathered the claw, feeling the weight of it in my hands. The whispers of the night swirled around me, the cold air a strange feeling in the usually hot jungles. My breath misted before me as I slung the claw over my shoulder.

I looked back towards Dunbar, the city standing resilient under the celestial gaze of the stars. The Tesla coils stood silent now, their purpose fulfilled, their energy spent. The city had stood against the tide once again, against the wrath of dragons, lizards, and wolves. And in the aftermath, amidst the silence and the stars, Dunbar stood triumphant, a beacon of light in the embrace of the night.

During the death of the dragons, I had felt myself level up, which wasn't surprising.

What was surprising was that I actually gained two whole levels during the battle.

[NOAH]
[Lv 17 - BLACKSMITH JOURNEYMAN]

[BONDED]

[HEALTH 135/135]
[MANA 45/160]

 -L6

-L6

-Passive

-L2

-L9

 -L2

[UNSELECTED SKILLS - NONE]

690

I walked back towards the city, feeling the drag of tired muscles and the ache of a hard-won battle. My tattoos burned as they changed, but the numbers there told me what I already felt in my bones: I was worn out, but my skills were sharper for it. 'MANUFACTURE' and 'ENGINEERING' had both jumped up two whole levels, a nice payoff for all the effort and brainpower I'd sunk into the Tesla coils. And 'PATRON' edged up a level, too, probably thanks to those mages blasting dragons out of the sky. I could inspect them and get more information, but would do that in the morning.

I felt completely drained. My mana pool was down to a mere [45/160], a dim, flickering light compared to its usual bright blaze. My head throbbed from the mana poisoning, taking effect now as the bracer had worn out earlier in the day.

As I walked back up the ramp into the upper levels of Dunbar, I just wanted to crash. I was longing for a warm bed and some solid sleep to wipe away the night's chaos and bring some kind of peace to my rattled brain.

But even as I thought of rest, I couldn't forget my mages. They'd been right in the thick of it, channeling lightning and saving us. I was glad for them. They had gotten redemption from the first battle where they were utterly ineffective. I wished I could check on them, use my party skill, but with my mana as low as it was, I knew I wouldn't be casting anything else tonight.

Mara rushed up to me, embracing me in a kiss. When she pulled away, her forehead settled against my chest, her breath warm against my skin.

"I was so scared," she whispered, her voice shaky. "Those dragons, and the lightning... it was terrifying. They were trying to bury us in the snow so we would be sitting ducks for the Shadowalkers. But you did it, Noah, you really did it."

I held her tighter, feeling her heartbeat against mine, steady and sure. Her presence grounded me and pushed away the lingering pain and exhaustion. "*We* did it," I corrected gently. "Couldn't have done it without you, or the mages, or Romas and the others."

Her laugh was soft, a gentle hum against my chest. "Always so modest," she murmured, but I could hear the smile in her voice. "Come on, let's go get some rest. You look like you could use it."

I didn't argue, letting her lead me through the now quiet streets of Dunbar. It appeared everyone had retreated, just in case the enemy made another pass at the city. The night was still, the earlier chaos a distant memory as we walked hand in hand, the city's peace wrapping around us like a warm cloak. The battles would come again, the struggles and the fear, but for now, we were together, and all was right in our small corner of the world.

The following day the sun was shining, but the air still had a crisp chill to it. I walked around the city, checking how things were holding up after that crazy night. The Tesla coils stood tall, looking just as solid as before. The city walls had some ice damage here and there. Some places were slick with melted snow and ice as well as some damage where the dragon hit the wall, but otherwise, everything looked good.

I looked up at the coils still not believing they had worked as well as they had. The large metallic structures were silent now, but memories of the battle paraded around in my mind. I was proud of them, but also pretty terrified of the power they produced.

The silvery metal from the wall coil shined bright in the sunlight and caused me to squint and cover the tops of my eyes. I could almost feel the leftover energy buzzing around them.

Walking along the city walls, I could see spots where the stones were wet and dark, dripping water down into the muddy ground below. Patches of ice and snow from the dragons' attack had all melted away, leaving everything soaked and dripping. The ground would be mushy and soft for a while, but that was a small price to pay for having survived an attack by water dragons and a whole pack of werewolves.

I continued my rounds, feeling more and more relieved with each step. Sure, we had a lot of cleaning up and repairing to do, but that was fine. A mine cart zipped by me puffing steam merrily into the air. Apparently, the miners were back to work already.

Making my way back to the smithy, I passed by folks already out and about, starting the cleanup process. Everyone was working together to get the city back in shape. There were smiles and laughter; a shared relief that we had made it through the night.

Inside the smithy, the familiar scent of metal and fire welcomed me. Romas was already at work, his hammer ringing as he shaped a piece of metal on the anvil. He had been able to grab a few ingredients of his own and it looked like he was making some new armor. He looked up as I entered, a grin spreading across his face.

"Well, if it isn't the hero of Dunbar!" he boomed, his voice echoing through the smithy.

I rolled my eyes but couldn't help the smile that tugged at my lips. "It was a group effort! You know that," I said, but I felt a warm glow inside at the praise.

Romas just laughed, his eyes crinkling at the corners. "Always so humble, boy. But you deserve the credit. Those Tesla coils? Genius idea. Should call them Noah coils here, since this *Tesla* character you keep talking about is from your world! You've got a good head on your shoulders, Noah. Don't ever forget that."

I plunked myself down on a stool next to Romas, my head buzzing with all the new stuff I'd racked up. "Noah coils. I like that. So, got a question for you," I said, leaning towards the big panther.

Romas set his hammer down, wiped his paw on a rag, and turned to me. "Shoot."

I took a deep breath. "What the heck do I do with all these high-level ingredients? I mean, I've got level 8 and level 10 stuff now!" I exclaimed, my eyes wide as I thought about the dragon scales and claw I had snagged.

Romas scratched his furry chin thoughtfully. "Well, that's some pretty hefty loot," he said. "Could make some killer gear with that. Armor, weapons, you name it. Or, maybe you could sell them to the capital smithy in Fayport. I bet you'd fetch a pretty penny for dragon materials. We haven't seen a dead dragon in...well, I don't know if we've ever even killed one before."

My mind started spinning with the possibilities. "Armor would be amazing," I muttered, picturing myself decked out in shiny dragon-scale armor.

"But you gotta remember," Romas cut in, "working with something like dragon materials isn't easy. It's gonna take some serious skills and the right tools and facilities. We don't have that here, even with the workbenches downstairs. You're talking about something that might cost around 1000 mana and need skills you don't even have yet to make something with them."

My head drooped a bit, but I nodded, taking it all in. It was a lot to think about, and I didn't want to make any hasty decisions. "Thanks, Romas," I said, slapping the panther on the back.

Now that the threat had been dealt with, I had to figure out what I wanted to do next. The Overlord was still out there with his high-level steel weaponry, the Shadowalkers were always a threat, and I imagined that the dragons would be furious that I had killed a couple of them.

I thought about Mara and her ability to find people and talk to them telepathically. Maybe it was time for a sit-down with the alpha werewolf.

Chapter 26

Summons

THE SUN WAS SETTING BY THE TIME I DROPPED THE LAST piece of debris onto the cleanup pile. I was exhausted, but it felt good to help put the town back together. Suddenly, through the settling dust and the noise of repairs, I heard my name.

I looked up, wiping sweat off my forehead with the back of my hand. A cheetah-looking messenger in the bright red colors of the Monarch was hurrying towards me. He stopped, panting slightly, and handed me a rolled-up parchment sealed with wax.

"Baron Noah, the Monarch requests your presence in the capital," he said formally. His eyes darted around at the rebuilding efforts as he took in the damage. "She would like to discuss the battle and all upcoming plans for the city of Dunbar."

I raised my eyebrows, surprised. "Oh, uh, sure. Thanks." I said, breaking the seal and quickly scanning the official message. It was true. The Monarch had heard about the attack and wanted to see me as soon as possible.

My heart started to race with excitement. This was big. I'd never been to the capital before and didn't quite know what to expect. "Tell her I'll leave first thing in the morning."

"Yes, Baron," he said, bowing slightly before turning and heading back the way he had come.

I watched him go, then looked around at Dunbar. The town was battered, but the Tesla coils, or Noah coils as I would call them now, still stood tall against the darkening sky as a beacon of our resilience. I felt a surge of pride and determination. I was ready to represent my town and tell the Monarch about what happened here.

I thought about the implications. The Monarch, with her farseeing powers, must have known about the attack, but the city would have been shrouded from the anti-scrying device. *Had she left me to fend for myself to see how I would do? Did she see my victory play out? What did she see next for us?*

I had so many questions. Typh walked over, looking on as the cheetah dashed off into the southern part of the settlement. "What did he want?"

I turned to see Typh's curious face as he approached. The sunlight had almost completely disappeared beyond the horizon, painting the sky with hues of pink and orange. The temperature had returned to the normal, sweltering heat.

"Hey, Typh," I greeted him, still clutching the rolled-up parchment in my hand. "The Monarch's called me to the capital. Wants to talk about the battle and the dragons, I guess." I shrugged, trying to appear calm, but the anxiety bubbled inside me.

Typh raised his eyebrows, impressed. "Well, well. It appears your stature continues to climb, Noah," he said as a smile tugged at the corner of his mouth. "Your absence will be felt here, though. There remains much to be accomplished."

I nodded, my eyes following his gaze. "I know, Typh. I trust you all to keep things moving here. And I'll be back as soon as I can."

Typh frowned. "You think you're going alone? I will be coming, of course. You will need your guard to escort you."

I laughed, shaking my head at Typh's stern, protective demeanor. "Always so ready to jump into the fray, huh? Alright, big guy, I'd be glad to have you by my side."

He shook his head, most likely at me calling him *big guy*. "Besides, I can't wait to see how you react to the...political landscape in our people's capital. They aren't like the Feka here."

I laughed. "I'm sure I'll love it."

Together, we started back towards the palace. The night was settling in, a blanket of stars beginning to unveil themselves above. Despite the darkness, the town still abuzz with activity. Fires glowed in intervals as they cast moving shadows on my workers and city residents.

Typh told me he had a few things left to do and rounds to make, so he bid me farewell. Music played at a nearby establishment as Feka and humans alike stumbled around. It appeared the ale was flowing. "Not too much, you fools!" Typh shouted. "In case there is another attack!"

His voice was drowned out by grumbles and paw waves, the warriors calling Typh a whole slew of names.

We had discussed plans and preparations for the journey, deciding to leave at first light. Once we reached the capital, there would be a lot to manage and navigate. Mara and Romas would oversee the city while I was away. Mara and I had talked about the plan last night in my room.

Well, that, and a few other activities.

As we left the palace, I saw Typh standing there, back straight. "Good morning, Baron." He looked between Mara and me. "We have a long day ahead. I surely hope you got some rest last night."

Mara blushed, then lightly punched the leopard on the furry arm. "Watch it, Typh!" Mara said, her cheeks still flushed as she tried to suppress a smile. I couldn't help but laugh, my nerves for the day's journey slightly eased by their banter.

"Good morning to you too, Typh," I said, clapping him on the shoulder. His massive frame barely moved at my gesture. "Ready to hit the road?"

Typh nodded, adjusting the sword strapped to his side. His eyes were serious and alert, already scanning the horizon beyond the city gates. "Always ready, Baron. Let's get moving."

Mara bid me farewell, and the two of us set out as the sun just began to rise. The city was quiet, most of its inhabitants still in the grasp of sleep. The echo of our footsteps against the cobbled path seemed to resonate louder as we walked toward the small path leading to the road to Fayport. We had to pass the docks first to access the rear of the settlement.

The gulf was to our right, and I saw ships as they bobbed gently, their sails lowered, as fishermen prepared their vessels for a day at sea. I saw my modified fish-smashing devices gleaming in the sunlight and couldn't help but smile at them. I thought back to my experience with them when Typh dropped me off for the day to *harden* me up a bit.

Up ahead, trees lined both sides, blocking out much of the sun. The air felt cooler here, the shade of the towering trees providing a pleasant relief from the gradually intensifying sun. The path was almost a straight shot to the capital, worn smooth by the passage of countless travelers over the years. Birds chirped and flitted overhead, their shadows dancing on the path in front of us.

This is where I had previously captured the city's Baron when he tried to escape. The thought of my transfer of power came back to me in a rush and I closed my eyes as I bowed my head for a moment.

Typh's footsteps were silent on the soft earth, a testament to his agility and grace. My boots thudded rhythmically as we made our way under the leafy canopy.

As we walked, I noticed the light changing, the sun moving higher, and the shadows shortening. The scent of the forest, earthy and rich, filled my nostrils. The occasional rabbit darted across our path, and I could see the fluttering of butterfly wings among the wildflowers that lined the road.

From the maps I had seen, the capital was about a 15-mile walk. If we kept this pace up, we would be there by sunset. My stamina had improved over the last few months, and my increased health and levels were doing wonders for my general well-being.

I heard a sound and looked up. Hunter class Feka dotted trees here and there, watching the road for danger. They nodded to us as we passed, eyes constantly scanning. Most were similar to Dee in appearance, their smaller feline frames perfect for climbing the trees.

About four hours in, we reached a clearing where the trees parted, giving way to a sprawling vista to the northeast of rolling hills and fields of wildflowers, their colors a vibrant mosaic under the azure sky. In the distance to the south, the spires and towers of the capital rose, silhouetted against the horizon.

We stood for a moment, taking in the sight before us.

"Beautiful, isn't it?" Typh asked me.

"Yeah, it really is," I answered, my eyes drinking in the landscape before us.

I could feel the calmness of the nature around me seeping into my veins, soothing the lingering anxiety from the recent battle and the anticipation of the upcoming meeting with the Monarch. The world felt still here, peaceful and untouched by the chaos that had unfolded back in the city.

Typh's voice pulled me back from my thoughts. "It's easy to forget about places like this when you're always in the thick of things, dealing with politics, battles, and dragons. It's good to remind ourselves that places of peace and beauty still exist."

I nodded, a small smile playing on my lips. "You've been there for all the battles, Typh. I appreciate it."

He gave me another one of those small Typh smiles, his gaze still on the vibrant view ahead. "Anytime, Noah. Let's finish this so you can return to Dunbar and make something else for us."

Chapter 27

Fayport

I walked up to the gates of Fayport as the enormous walls greeted us. Two huge rhino guards stood at the gate with their weapons crossed. Typh walked over to them, addressing the one on the right.

"We're here to see the Monarch," he said, puffing his chest out slightly.

I nodded at the two creatures. The rhino guards eyed us up and down, their expressions stoic and unyielding. The fading sunlight glinted off their polished armor, and their massive horns looked as sharp as blades. After a tense moment, the one on the right spoke in a deep, resonant voice. "State your names and titles."

Typh growled slightly, stepping forward toward the guards. "I am Typh, and you know me. I am the Marshall of Dunbar. Do not waste our time."

I stepped forward, feeling the weight of the guards' scrutiny as I put my hand on Typh to calm him. "I am Baron Noah, called upon by the Monarch herself."

The guards looked at each other, communicating in a silent language of nods and glances. Finally, the guards uncrossed their massive weapons, stepping aside to allow us entry.

"Proceed," the right guard intoned, his voice as heavy as his appearance. "The Monarch is expecting you. Follow the blue path. It will lead you directly to the palace."

We thanked them, and as we walked through the massive gate. "If we were expected, why did we have to state our names," I murmured to Typh. He didn't respond, but I saw the smile tug at his lips again.

The city inside was even more majestic than it appeared from the outside, bustling with activity and alive with a diverse array of creatures, from small cats darting agilely through the streets to elegant lions in royal attire. The buildings were grand, adorned with intricate designs and shimmering in various hues under the evening light.

We followed the blue path as instructed, a bright line painted on the cobbled streets that guided us through the thrumming heart of the city. Red and green lines followed next to the blue, then darted off in various directions. It led us through various sectors of the city before turning to the main road to the palace, its spires piercing the sky and its walls adorned with shimmering gems that reflected the sunlight in a dazzling dance of colors.

We walked down the road and were again questioned by guards outside the doors of the magnificent structure.

As we stepped inside, the bustling noise of the city was immediately muted, replaced by the soft rustling of leaves and the gentle babble of flowing water. The palace's interior was like stepping into another world, a perfect harmony of nature and architecture. The hallway stretched before us, the ceiling high above adorned with luminous jewels that replicated the sky outside, bathing the corridor in a soft, natural light.

Tall, sturdy trees soared, their branches arching overhead, interweaving to form a living canopy. Vines trailed down the walls, lush and green, and vibrant flowers peeked out from unexpected corners, splashing the space with bursts of color. The air was fresh and fragrant with the scent of blossoms and earth.

A clear, sparkling river flowed gracefully through the center of the hallway, its course unhurried as it weaved and wound its way deeper into the palace. Small, beautifully designed ornate bridges arched over the water at intervals. I saw fish swimming below, their scales glinting as they moved through the crystal clear waters.

Our footsteps were softened by the mossy path that led us along the river's edge, each step like a whisper on the earth. The environment was calming and I felt a weight lift from my shoulders as we walked, the serenity of the space seeping into my soul.

As we ventured further, we arrived at a wider, circular space, where the river pooled into a pond, lily pads floating on its surface. The trees here fanned out, and their leaves filtered the light, casting dappled shadows on the ground.

In the center of the space, sitting on a high, T-shaped chair, was a small, black furred Feka. It observed us with bright, intelligent eyes as we approached.

"Greetings, Baron Noah and Marshall Typh," the cat said in a clear, high-pitched voice, its tone polite and formal. Its tail flicked back and forth gently as it surveyed us from its elevated position. The cat's eyes scanned me before landing on my boots. A disgusted expression crossed its face. "Please, if you would be so kind..."

I startled. "Oh, no shoes? Sorry about that."

The cat nodded as I kicked the boots off, my socks landing softly on the moss. "You are expected. Please, follow me."

It descended gracefully from its chair and led us along another pathway. The landscape within the palace continued to unfold, revealing more wonders and beauty. Exotic birds with vibrant plumage flitted between the trees, and butterflies danced in the air, their wings delicate and colorful. I didn't see any openings in the palace's ceiling for the birds to come and go, and the architecture amazed me.

We took a few turns down various hallways, following the small cat, and then got to a large stairwell. "Please take the stairs and wait in the council chambers to your right. The Monarch will be with you shortly."

"Thank you," I replied with a nod, my voice soft in the serene environment. The small cat bowed its head and swiftly turned, disappearing down a corridor lined with ferns and flowering plants.

Typh and I ascended the grand stairwell. It was carved from what looked like a seamless piece of polished stone, the steps cool and smooth underfoot. The banister was intertwined with more green vines, blossoms blooming along its length, and it felt sturdy in my grip.

At the top, we arrived at a landing with several arched doorways. The one to the right stood open, leading into a chamber with high ceilings adorned with more of the brilliant gems that cast soft light below. The air here was still, yet it carried the subtle fragrance of pine and lavender.

We entered the council chambers, a grand room with a round table at its center, made of polished wood and surrounded by more T-shaped plush chairs. The walls were made of a smooth, light stone and lined with ancient tapestries depicting various scenes from the city's history. I noticed a picture of a human and a royal-looking Feka, but didn't ask anything about it.

I was tired from the journey and hoped we wouldn't have too much talking to do tonight. I didn't know where we would be staying, but I wanted a warm bed and some food. We had been ushered straight here, much to the dismay of my rumbling stomach. All we had to eat today were some road rations.

Typh and I took a seat, and the silence enveloped us, a comforting blanket in the grandeur of the chamber. We waited in the calm; our minds eased by the surrounding beauty as we prepared to meet the Monarch.

The door opened, and another cat entered, this one slightly larger than the other attendant. The feline wore shiny jewels in its hair that gleamed in the light as it walked.

"I present our Highness, the Monarch."

The announcement echoed through the chamber as the cat bowed deeply, its eyes respectfully lowered. Behind it, the grand double doors opened wider, and a familiar figure stepped through.

The Monarch was an elegant creature, a tall, graceful lynx Feka with a thick, lush coat patterned with marbled swirls of cream and silver. Her eyes were an arresting shade of silver, just like Mara's, and they swept the room with a calm, assured gaze. Around her neck, a few delicate gold necklaces rested, inlaid with brilliant sapphires that echoed the cool tones of the palace. She had gained a few necklaces since I last saw her.

She had also gained a few scars. I wondered where they came from.

She moved with a silent, languid grace as she approached the table. The murmurs of the attendants and guards in the room quieted to utter silence in her presence. The only sound was the soft rustle of the leaves outside the arched windows, their branches swaying gently in the breeze.

I rose and bowed deeply in respect, Typh doing the same by my side. "Your Highness," I responded, formality in my tone. "We are excited to be here."

"Please," she said, paw in the air. She waved to her attendants, who hurried out of the room. "We have much to discuss," the Monarch said, signaling for us to take our seats.

Chapter 28

Impressing the Boss

As we sat down, the Monarch's intense silver eyes studied me, then shifted to Typh, taking in every detail, every nuance of our expressions. The room, bathed in the soft golden light filtering through the lush green foliage outside the window, seemed to hold its breath, waiting for her to speak again.

"Tell me everything," she said softly, leaning forward, her poise regal yet inviting. "I see you're still wearing that belt that keeps this conversation private. Good. I want to know about these dragons, the battle, and especially these devices you've engineered. My sight is obscured by your anti-scrying device, much like when the Fulgarians were blocking me. But I saw them approach from the north."

Though softly spoken, her words echoed in the silence, underscoring the gravity of the situation. I nodded, clearing my throat as I recounted the harrowing night of the attack.

I spoke of the dragons, their unexpected assault, their icy breath, and their fearsome appearance, and then I explained the creation and operation of the Noah coils. I talked about the collaboration with my air mages and the successful discharge of their lightning spells that had brought down the dragons, leaving behind only their high-level ingredients.

Typh added details where necessary, his concise words painting a clear, complementary picture to my narrative. The Monarch listened intently, her sharp eyes never leaving our faces as we spoke. She nodded occasionally, her expression thoughtful, absorbing every piece of the story, considering the implications of this new threat, and the innovative defense we had mounted.

"And the aftermath?" she inquired as I concluded the tale. "What are the losses? How far away did they retreat? And what do you intend to do with these ingredients?"

I shared the state of our settlement post-battle, mentioning the minor damage and no serious casualties. Typh interjected that his scouts did not see any signs of them in the swamps and that he assumed they had retreated toward Niridge.

I expressed my uncertainty about the dragon scales and claw – potent materials I had no experience with, especially at the high levels.

The Monarch's gaze softened. "You have done remarkably well, Baron Noah of Dunbar," she said warmly. "Your ingenuity and leadership have saved many lives. As for the ingredients, keep them safe. You will need them later on."

I didn't know what she meant, but I didn't push it. She was right, of course. I had no idea what to do with such high-level ingredients. I couldn't even use the pelt yet.

Or could I? I would have to go into the basement and see, now that my engineering was level 6.

She continued, "Tell me of the cave trolls."

My eyebrow raised at that. I had no idea how she knew about them. I hesitated, studying the Monarch's face. Her expression remained calm and expectant, giving away nothing of her thoughts or how she had come by this information.

Taking a deep breath, I decided to trust her, not knowing if she would be pleased or not with my dealings with another race. "Your

Highness," I began, choosing my words carefully, "We struck a deal with the cave trolls. They are now our allies. They helped us transport the silver ore from the mines to the city for building the anti-scrying box," I explained the tentative nature of our alliance with the trolls, their unpredictability, and their invaluable assistance.

"I believe that the silver ore could be very valuable to us. In my culture back home, silver has extremely effective properties against werewolves." I paused, assessing her reaction, and continued, "With your permission and guidance, I would like to start manufacturing silvered weapons. It could be a game-changer for us when the Shadowalkers attack next."

The Monarch's eyes lit up with interest at this new information. "Intriguing..." she murmured. She pondered for a moment, her fingers tapping gently on the armrest of her throne. "Silvered weapons, you say? That is a worthy endeavor. I give my consent and support for this project, Baron Noah. However, maintain caution with these trolls. Trolls can be fickle allies. And they are not so easily slain."

I remembered the fight with just the scout troll and shuddered. If it wasn't for my huge explosive earth bomb, I doubted we would have made it out of there.

"Hopefully, they will respect my earth mages," I replied, but wasn't so sure myself. I made a mental note to make sure I prepared a few more earth bombs, just in case.

She nodded, her gaze firm yet kind. "You surely have grown powerful during your stay on Prixa. And now, about your next steps. You'll need more than Noah coils and alliances to safeguard your city and strengthen its defenses. The enemy is determined to win the jungle lands and will stop at nothing to gain them."

Typh and I nodded, listening to what she had to say. She smiled a warm, reassuring smile that spread a glow in the opulent chamber as she continued. "We stand united against our enemies, Baron Noah. Your victory is our victory, and your security ensures the safety of the entire region. My foresight...it is not what it once was."

She stood and began pacing around the small room, a faraway look in her eyes. As she paced, her tail gently swayed in rhythm with her steps. The jewels in her hair shimmered with each movement, casting delicate reflections upon the ornate walls of the council chamber. "We have a darkness clouding this glorious land. One that we must destroy. I look to you, Noah. You have been the torch to light the way. However, be careful in the darkness. For the void comes. And Fulgar awakens."

I had no idea what she was talking about, but I let her keep talking, hoping there was a point soon. I heard my stomach rumble again and really wished I could eat something.

The Monarch stopped, turning to me, almost as if she heard my stomach. "But we will discuss my plans more tomorrow. You are invited to the special council session that I am hosting tomorrow. For now, go to your rooms and rest. Your meals have been prepared there and are the freshest fish that Fayport has to offer you. Please make yourselves comfortable so that we can reconvene in the morning."

The doors flew open, and attendants stood at the ready, almost looking like little cat butlers. Behind me, the Monarch dismissed us, and the small cats nodded, leading the way out of the room. Typh and I pushed ourselves up from the table and bid the Monarch goodnight, heading out into the hallway.

I sighed in relief as I walked out and followed the cat down the winding hallways. The cat stopped and opened another door, this time leading to a suite in the palace. The inside was beautiful, and a tray of food sat in the middle of a table. "I'll see you tomorrow!" I said to Typh and rushed into the room, closing the door behind me.

I leaned against the closed door for a moment, taking in the suite's beauty. The room was spacious, with tall, vaulted ceilings. The walls were adorned with intricate tapestries depicting scenes of lush forests, mighty creatures, and elegant felines in majestic poses. A large, plush bed sat against the far wall, covered with pillows and a luxurious velvet blanket.

The central table, made of rich, dark wood, held a tray filled with various delectable foods. There were freshly baked bread rolls, a steaming pot of stew, a plate of assorted cheeses, and a decanter of what appeared to be wine.

My stomach growled again, reminding me of the long, eventful day and the journey that had led me here. I walked over to the table and sat down, eagerly reaching for the food. The meal was delicious, each bite a mix of rich flavors and satisfying warmth. The wine was a perfect complement to the food. Its robust flavor exploded in my mouth with cherries and vanilla.

As I ate, I couldn't help but reflect on the events that had unfolded. I didn't know what the council meeting was about, but I was getting a weird vibe for some reason. But for now, in this peaceful moment, I allowed myself to relax and enjoy the tranquility and comfort of the palace suite.

With my hunger sated, I stretched and made my way to the inviting bed. The soft mattress and plush pillows cradled me as I sank into their embrace. Exhaustion soon washed over me, and I closed my eyes, eventually falling into the gentle lull of deep sleep.

The Monarch entered her sitting room and shut the door quietly behind her, the cougar staring back at her from the dark room as his eyes glittered off the moonlight from the window. "I'm afraid, Konna. He is growing more and more powerful every day. And his humans can kill dragons now. Dragons! If he turns on us..."

The words hung heavily in the silent chamber. Konna stepped from the shadows, his golden eyes now reflecting the single lantern flickering on the wall. His voice was soft but filled with the strength that had guided the Monarch through many a dire situation. "Your Highness, you have always led with wisdom and courage. Your fears are not unfounded, but remember the bond that has been formed, the trust that has been given and received."

The Monarch sighed, her shoulders heavy with the burden of her crown and the fate of her kingdom. "His power grows, and with it, the balance shifts. The ancient pacts that have held for centuries now tremble under the weight of new forces. I can feel it. The Fulgarians changed everything bringing him here. And I have reason to believe a Fulgarian spy was following them on their trip to see the trolls. If he found the right ingredients in the darkness..."

Konna moved closer, his graceful stride silent on the cold stone floor. "Then we adapt, my Queen, as we have always done. We watch, we learn, and we guide where we can. Should the tide turn against us, we will stand, as we have always stood, unbroken and united. The darkness will always follow the light."

The Monarch nodded. "The meeting tomorrow will be a diffi-cult one. All the Fekan eyes will be on Noah. He may not leave here alive if he does not persuade them that he is no threat to the Feka."

The Monarch's eyes darkened at the thought. She knew the harshness that could reside in the hearts of her kind, the fierce protection they held for their lands and their own. The council was not known for their leniency, and with the rising tensions and fear, they might indeed see the young human as a threat rather than an ally, especially after she bestowed the Barony upon him.

Her heart ached at the prospect; she had seen the fire in his eyes, the genuine desire to aid and protect. He had shown respect and understanding, qualities that were often overlooked in the heat of suspicion and paranoia. And after the last Baron she had appointed, he was a breath of fresh air for the kingdom, for none could have turned away an enemy force filled with dragons and lizardmen. But that strength was also what made him so threatening.

"Konna," the Monarch said quietly, her voice firm with resolution, "ensure that Noah has a fair chance to speak before the council. Let no harm befall him within these walls. If we are to stand strong against the shadow that creeps upon our lands, we must not let fear blind us to potential allies."

Konna bowed his head in acknowledgment. "Your will shall be done, Your Highness."

The Monarch returned to her window, watching as the moon bathed the palace gardens in a gentle, silver glow. The world was changing; new forces and powers emerged from the shadows, and the path ahead was uncertain. Tomorrow's meeting would indeed be a test, a pivotal moment in Noah's path.

Should he fail to impress, she feared what would happen.

She turned away from the window and slid into the soft sheets, Konna climbing in behind her.

Chapter 29

The Meeting of the Minds

I heard a knock at my door as sunlight streamed into the room, but couldn't help but have a slight panic attack that I was back in Fulgar. A quick look around the affluent suite reminded me that I was actually in Fayport with allies. With my *liege* as my city codex said.

I took a deep breath, trying to steady my racing heart. The rich, detailed tapestries hanging on the walls and the luxurious, plush bed I was sitting on were a far cry from the bleak, cold setting of Fulgar. Still, it took a moment for my mind to shake the gripping dread that had momentarily taken hold.

Another knock echoed through the room, more persistent this time.

"Yes, come in," I called, getting up and slipping on my clothes.

The door creaked open, revealing a human man dressed in plain clothes with a downcast look. He held a tray with a steaming pot of tea and a plate of assorted pastries.

"Good morning, Baron Noah. I hope you slept well. The Monarch sends her regards and this small breakfast," the man said as he entered the room, placing the tray on a small table by the window.

"Thank you," I murmured, my stomach growling at the sight and smell of food. I sipped the tea, the warm liquid calming my nerves as I bit into a pastry.

The man cleared his throat. "The council meeting is scheduled in an hour, Baron. If you allow, I can lead you to the council chambers once ready."

I nodded, my mind now focused on the impending meeting. Despite the opulence surrounding me, a heavy sense of responsibility and trepidation weighed on my chest. The human's servile demeanor reminded me of the imbalance here, the subservience I so strongly opposed.

"Thank you..." I trailed off, hoping the man would say his name.

"Tim, sir," he replied.

"Thank you, Tim," I said with a warm smile, aiming to project some semblance of equality in our exchange. The name, so common in my old world, felt slightly out of place here amidst the Feka and the sprawling forests and majestic creatures, but it provided a subtle comfort.

Tim gave a modest nod, his eyes still downcast. "You're welcome, Baron. Is there anything else I can assist you with this morning?"

I glanced around the room, taking in the elegance and precision with which everything was arranged. "No need to be so formal, Tim. Calling me Noah is fine." His eyes shot open, but he hid his surprise well. I continued, "I'll get ready for the meeting. Could you please return in about half an hour to lead me to the council chambers?"

"Of course, Baron, er, Noah," Tim responded, turning to leave the room. I watched him go, and a pang of sadness hit me for the clear division between our stations. Back home, Tim would just be another guy, someone I might pass on the street and exchange a nod with, equals in the grand tapestry of life.

I had worked so hard in Dunbar to get humans on equal footing to the Feka, and here, just a mere fifteen miles away, that hadn't set in yet.

Shaking my head to dispel the gloomy thoughts, I prepared for the meeting.

Tim moved silently ahead of me, his gait steady and sure through the ornate corridors of the palace. The hallway was a marvel itself, the walls lined with intricate murals depicting historic Feka battles and serene landscapes. Tall, arched windows punctuated the expanse, allowing slivers of the early morning light to bathe the corridor in a soft, golden glow.

I walked behind Tim, my steps echoing softly on the polished stone floor. Each footfall felt like a disruption to the peaceful aura that enveloped the palace interiors. Vibrant tapestries hung from the ceiling to the floor, their rich hues of blue, red, and gold painting stories of harmony and prosperity.

In one corner, a small fountain tinkled softly, a delicate sculpture of a frolicking fox in its center. The water caught the light, sending tiny rainbows scattering across the adjacent walls.

We passed by a few other human servants, their heads bowed, eyes averted, a mirror image of Tim's own demeanor. Despite the beauty surrounding me, a heaviness settled in my chest. The palace was a world away from the chaos and danger beyond its walls, a place where beauty and artistry flourished, but at the distraction from the issue of human freedom.

Tim stopped before a grand set of double doors, adorned with gold and pearls. "The council chambers, Baron Noah, sir," he announced softly.

I took a deep breath, steadying myself. I didn't comment on him calling me Baron, since I thought that was proper in view of any nearby high-ranking Feka. "Thank you, Tim."

I stepped forward, pushing the doors open to face the assembly of Fekan leaders, my heart thudding in my chest. It appeared that most of the council was present already, with all the chairs full except a few.

A giant tiger stood when I entered and pointed with his paw to the head of the table. Typh was seated to the right. When he saw me enter, he stood and bowed, causing the other Feka to frown slightly.

This was going to be a lovely morning, I thought grimly.

The massive table was carved from a single piece of dark wood, polished to a mirror shine, and around it sat the various Fekan leaders. They represented every species and rank within the Fekan society, from the burly tigers to elegant lions with furry manes. Their expressions ranged from curiously intrigued to outright hostile, the latter no doubt unhappy with my presence in this esteemed assembly.

I moved to the head of the table, my footsteps echoing in the sudden silence that had fallen over the chamber. I felt their eyes on me, assessing, judging, weighing my worth and the words I would speak. I took my place, giving Typh a brief nod of acknowledgment. His loyalty was a beacon of comfort in this sea of uncertainty.

Before I could gather my thoughts, the double doors behind me swung open with a dramatic flourish. A swift breeze followed, causing the towering banners hanging from the ceiling to ripple and sway.

In walked the Monarch, her presence a calming balm to the charged atmosphere. Her lustrous coat was meticulously groomed, the rich browns and blacks contrasting strikingly with the bright jewels adorning her neck. Behind her trailed two smaller felines carrying a majestic train that fanned out in hues of deep blue and emerald green, embroidered with intricate gold patterns. I hadn't seen her wear this intricate of a getup before but assumed it had to do with the meeting.

The council members, who had been whispering amongst themselves, fell into immediate silence at her entrance. The

Monarch moved towards the head of the table, her eyes scanning the room, acknowledging the gathered assembly with a subtle nod. Her gaze rested on me for a heartbeat longer, a silent communication of reassurance or perhaps a plea for understanding.

I certainly didn't like that look. It was the same look she gave me before she had named me the head of Dunbar.

She reached her place, the feline attendants gently placing her train in a neat arrangement behind her as she sat, bringing a regal air to the head of the long table.

"We are all here today to discuss the happenings at Dunbar," she began. "Many of you have raised concerns over the growing power of the human populace in our outlying town and my appointing of a human leader. I have invited the Baron of the town here to respond to any concerns you may have."

What the hell?? I thought in a panic.

All eyes snapped to me. I saw distrustful glances, eyes narrowed, and teeth bared softly in apprehension. I realized this was more than a mere assembly; this was a test, a critical assessment of not just me but humanity's place among the Feka.

The Monarch's voice, clear and steady, sliced through my racing mind. "We shall begin the council. Baron Noah, the floor is yours."

With a deep breath to steady my nerves, I stood up, feeling dozens of eyes upon me, their gazes like physical weights. Bile rose in my throat, as always. I wanted nothing more than to curl up in the corner and give up the Barony to someone else.

But I thought about what had happened at Dunbar and how we had stopped a threat of creatures far above our station and grew confident. I had earned a place at this table. I was a Creator.

My voice initially shook as I spoke. "Honorable council members, I stand before you, not as a symbol of threat but as a representation of unity between our races."

A great start! I thought to myself, pausing to think through what I would say to these creatures. I made eye contact with various members of the table. No one moved.

"I am aware of the historic tension between our kind and yours. I understand that we are the weaker species and that your protection is required here in this dangerous land. But the humans of Dunbar have worked hand in hand with the Feka, contributing to the defenses, the prosperity, and the welfare of the town. We have built structures that defend us, mined resources to improve us, and grown and caught supplies to feed us."

A few Feka looked at each other, some unspoken debate warring between them. My heart beat like a drum against my chest, echoing in my ears.

A sizable lion spoke up, his voice like a deep growl, "And what of these devices, these contraptions used to fell the dragons? What guarantee do we have that they will not be turned upon us? Our kind has *never* killed such a beast, and yours has killed two! In the same attack!"

Growls sounded out around the table. I knew this question would arise but never thought it would be in this setting.

"I can assure you," I began, my voice steady despite the nerves dancing in my stomach, "that these devices, created for defense, will always serve that purpose. They were born from necessity, to protect Dunbar from those who would see it fall."

"How do you plan to police it? To police your mages?" asked a snow leopard from the other end of the table. "I cannot believe that you can control all of your human mages. As we know from our dealings in Fulgar, they are unpredictable. Unstable, even!"

More growls. This was not going as I hoped.

Another lion, this one a female, spoke up over the growling. "The Monarch has informed the council of an alliance with trolls now. What do you have to say about that? You're telling us that you will control them, too, *almighty human Creator?*"

The stinging sarcasm of her words hung in the air, and a murmur spread across the room, a wave of unrest. The Monarch held her paw up, and the room calmed. "Give the Baron a chance to speak."

The lion who had just spoken growled but nodded.

"No," I said, meeting her eyes, trying to convey my sincerity. "I do not control them. It is a partnership, one born of mutual respect and necessity. The trolls know the mines, their strength, and the skills they contribute. In return, they gain the protection and resources they need. It's a cooperative effort, not domination."

I paused, letting my words sink in, "This is not about control, but collaboration. Working together strengthens us all, and unity is our greatest ally."

"Until it isn't," another councilor said.

I took a deep breath. "The Shadowalker threat *will* return. They keep trying to take the city. I believe they want to control the jungle and see our town as the last thing to conquer before that happens. They would have taken it, too, if not for our work there. My human mages are formidable, yes. But so are the Feka. There is a balance there. We can live in harmony."

A slow, quiet murmur of agreement began to ripple through the council chambers. The Monarch, her posture calm and composed, watched the interaction unfold, a silent overseer of the fragile bridge being built.

"Thank you, Baron. We will discuss your words. Please return to your room."

I looked around one last time, the faces still looking back at me with distrust. I nodded, showing my respect to the Monarch and the council.

"Thank you for allowing me to speak," I said calmly, my voice steady despite the thudding of my heart against my chest.

With a final glance at Typh, who gave a subtle nod of encouragement, I turned and exited the council chambers. The massive doors closed behind me with a resounding thud, leaving me in the silence of the hallway. My footsteps echoed through the empty corridor as I returned to my suite. I couldn't help but replay the meeting in my head, analyzing the expressions, the whispers, and the subtle gestures exchanged between the Fekan leaders.

Back in my suite, I sank into the plush chair and looked out the window at the sprawling capital city. Birds flew outside the window in a V-formation. The city was alive outside the window with sights and sounds. I found myself just watching and letting my mind wander. But one thought remained.

I hoped the Feka would let me leave.

Chapter 30

Striking a Bargain

EVENTUALLY THE CALMNESS OF THE OUTSIDE WORLD WORE off, and I paced the length of the lavish suite, the ornate rugs muffling the sound of my footsteps. Minutes passed like days. I stopped pacing and gazed at my reflection in the ornate mirror on the wall. My face looked worn; my eyes burdened with my time here on Prixa. But I had lost about all of my fat and was well chiseled.

I thought about my family again. I had no idea how anyone was doing back on Earth. The possibility of this all being a dream was a distant fantasy, and I had come to terms with that realization long ago. Still, I thought about what it would be like if I just woke up one day, perhaps in some kind of coma this whole time.

My mind snapped back to the present, however, and the Monarch's words, and the council's reaction to my statements. Questions lingered unanswered, fueling the engine of my anxiety. *What would the future hold for Dunbar? For the humans and the Feka?*

A sudden knock on the door shattered the silence, sending my heart leaping into my throat. I quickly composed myself, straightening my attire and taking a deep, steadying breath.

"Come in," I called, my voice steadier than I felt.

The door creaked open, revealing the diminutive form of a feline servant. "The Monarch will see you now," she announced in a crisp, respectful tone.

I nodded, a rush of adrenaline surging through my veins. "Thank you."

The walk to the Monarch's chambers was a blur, my feet mechanically following the servant as my mind raced, preparing and discarding speeches, apologies, explanations, and arguments. My eyes kept darting around the dim corridors, looking for threats that would jump out at me in a moment's notice, like when the old Baron had tried to have me killed. But we eventually made it to the Monarch's chambers.

I took a deep breath as the doors opened, stepping into the ornate room. The Monarch sat on her throne, an air of solemnity about her. My heart hammered as I approached, ready to face whatever lay ahead.

"Thank you, Gila. You may leave us." The Monarch's voice, soft yet commanding, echoed through the spacious chamber as she dismissed the servant with a graceful wave of her paw.

Gila bowed deeply, her head nearly touching the polished stone floor before she retreated, the heavy doors closing behind her with a resounding thud. The sound reverberated through the silence, leaving me there with the lynx.

The Monarch's eyes met mine. "Baron Noah," she began, "you've walked a difficult path today, one that many would falter upon. For that, I congratulate you."

I frowned. "Thanks?"

"The council has deliberated. Many do not wish for you to be Baron any longer, and even more wish for your mages to be stripped of their magical items and taken out of our realm."

I gasped. "What! But.."

She held up a paw. "But I am not one of them. Those same members are beginning to understand that Fayport most likely would have fallen if only the five dragons had attacked. The balance of power has shifted, and the Feka alone don't have the strength to stand alone. We must adapt. I was able to talk my fellow Feka into another means of keeping the peace."

I was unsure where this was going, but she had that smile on her face again. The one where I would have to trust her.

"I have stated that you will utilize your new army to conquer the Shadowalkers to the north."

She paused, letting her words sink in, her gaze never leaving mine. The flicker of the candle flames danced in her eyes, casting shadows upon her majestic visage.

I stared at her, open-mouthed. "I..." I stammered, my mind a whirl of emotions and thoughts. This was a daunting task, even with the newly formed alliance with the trolls and the potent powers of the mages.

The Shadowalkers were a force of enigmatic and deadly power, their lands shrouded in darkness, their ways unknown. To my knowledge, no one had even been to their city. It was located through brutal swamps and into the mountains. And now that the lizardmen were allied with them, there were even more enemies standing between us. It still amazed me that the were-wolf creatures had made the trip to invade Dunbar as many times as they had.

The Monarch's usually commanding voice softened. "I believe in your strength, Baron Noah, and the might of unity between our kinds. You have shown us the power of ingenuity, resilience, and collaboration. The path will be arduous, strewn with trials that will test our bonds, our valor, and our resolve. But it is a path we must tread to secure the future for both Feka and human alike. There is a darkness that we must watch out for. One that threatens to destroy us all. We must strike the werewolves from this world while we have the chance. Otherwise, it would appear that you are gaining power and alliances to rise against Fayport and the Feka."

"But, your Highness..." I began, my voice a mere whisper amidst the grandeur of the chamber, "I'm not a general. I don't know how to lead an army all the way through a swamp and into enemy territory!"

The Monarch stared at me, her eyes filled with stern resolve. "Baron Noah, in times of peace, you may not be a general, but in times of war, you must become what the people need. I see the strength within you, the strength to unite, to lead, and to overcome."

She paused, her eyes softening a bit. "Plus, you will not be alone. You will have Typh. He will be of great assistance to you. And the trolls, if they will fight with you, which I doubt. And you can ask for assistance from across the ocean."

A knowing look showed on her face, but I didn't say anything about the Trial Moon mages. She continued, "You will learn, as all great leaders do. I do not expect you to become a master tactician overnight, but to grow into the role as you face these challenges head on. Trust in those around you, trust in yourself, and you will find a way."

I closed my eyes, feeling the weight of her words. "This is the only way?"

The Monarch nodded. "If you can do this, then your power and influence will be looked at as a benefit, not as a threat. It is how my people think."

And if me and my mages die in the process, all the better. Got it.

I opened my eyes, meeting the Monarch's steady gaze, feeling the fragile ember of resolve kindle within the depths of my being, a nascent flame striving against the gale of doubt.

"And if I do this? What then? If the council is worried about how much power I have now, won't they be more upset if I can conquer a whole city?"

The Monarch took a moment, her eyes reflecting the maelstrom of thoughts whirling within. "Your concern is valid, Baron

Noah. Power is a delicate balance, a shifting scale that can tip into turmoil with but a breath."

She stepped closer, her voice a hushed murmur amidst the silence of the chamber. "The council fears the unknown, the surge of change that accompanies triumph and growth. Yet within the cauldron of challenge, true alliances are forged, unity strengthened, and the chaff of distrust burnt away in the blaze of shared victory."

Her gaze was unwavering. "Conquering the enemy city is not an end, but a beginning. A test of loyalty, resolve, and unity. It is a crucible to burn away the shroud of suspicion, to illuminate the bonds that bind us together, transcending species and realms. We must eliminate these threats to our people, and in doing so, will gain the peace you spoke of."

She moved away, her tail softly brushing against the rich tapestry adorning the chamber's walls. "After the battle, after the city is reclaimed from the grasp of shadows, the real task begins. The council, the people of Dunbar, the trolls, and you, together will shape the future, build bridges of trust, and lay the foundations of lasting peace. For if we succeed, we needn't have towers of lightning guarding our cities."

It all made sense now. Eliminate the enemy, and we had no need for powerful Tesla coils, mages, or troll warriors. I still didn't believe that this would be the end of the Fekan mistrust, but didn't feel like I had much other choice.

"And if I don't agree to the quest?"

She frowned. "Then we will strip your titles, remove your mages, and deal with the Shadowalkers in our own way when they return."

I sighed and shook my head. These cats were so stubborn. I certainly didn't want to see the city get wiped out, nor did I want to give up my position. As stressful as this all was, I enjoyed running the city.

I came to a decision. "I will do my best, your Highness."

Her nod was slow and deliberate, a seal of approval and commitment. "Your best is all anyone can ask for, Baron Noah. Go now, prepare your people, and when you are ready, march forth to meet the shadows in the north. May the stars guide your path, and may the *winds* of fortune be ever at your back."

There that look was again. And the way she emphasized *winds* certainly wasn't lost on me.

It appeared that I would need Mara's help when I returned to Dunbar. I bid the Monarch farewell and walked toward the doors to leave the palace.

Chapter 31

Back to it

THE CITY OF FAYPORT GRADUALLY SHRANK BEHIND US AS we made our way down the well-trodden path, our steps syncopated with the sounds of birds chirping in the treetops along the path.

Typh and I had left the city around lunchtime, but to get back to Dunbar in time before nightfall our pace had to be really quick. But that was fine with me. I had a ton of nervous energy to use up.

We jogged side by side for around two miles, both lost in our thoughts, the gentle hills working our leg muscles.

"Baron Noah..." Typh's voice broke the silence like a pebble cast upon a tranquil lake, the ripples of sound gently brushing against the veil of quietude that enveloped us. His gaze was affixed upon the horizon, where the sun began dropping toward the treeline. "I know the burden upon your shoulders is heavy; the path uncertain and fraught with peril. Remember, you do not bear this weight alone. I stand by your side, as do many others."

I glanced at him, wiping sweat from my brow. I was breathing pretty heavily at this point, unlike the leopard gracefully jogging next to me. The Monarch had briefed the Marshall of Dunbar on the quest the council had given, and he had bristled at the task.

"Your support means more than you know. I'm scared... but maybe we can do this."

Typh stopped jogging, a gentle smile breaking the solemnity of his expression. He looked me right in the eye. "Fear is but the herald of triumph, Baron. It sharpens the blade, steels the heart, and in its crucible, the seeds of greatness are sown. Let it not be your shackle but your spur. Together, we will face the shadows."

"Wow," I said, smiling. "Where did you hear that one?"

The smile vanished. "Hear what one?"

"That saying. Expression. Whatever you just spit out. What was that?"

Typh rolled his eyes and started jogging again, this time noticeably faster.

"I'm just saying! It was impressive, and if it hasn't been written down, it should be," I called out.

He glanced back over his shoulder, a smirk playing on his lips. "You talk too much, Baron. Try keeping up instead."

I huffed, lengthening my stride to catch up to him. "Oh, come on! We were having a moment there!"

He chuckled, his laughter echoing through the tree-lined road, turning our earlier solemn mood on its head. "Moments are well and good, but we've got ground to cover. And at this rate, the Shadowalkers will have tea ready for us by the time we arrive."

I groaned, realizing the challenge he'd subtly thrown my way. "Alright, alright! Let's pick up the pace."

The two of us pushed on, a friendly competition spurring our steps.

The soft light in the room brushed against everything, making the silk curtains glow as they moved in the breeze. Mara sat near the window; her eyes glued to the horizon. The beautiful colors of the sunset were gone now, leaving behind a sky full of stars. The moons, climbing up in the sky, gently lit up the world, making shadows dance around. The largest moon was almost full, so there was plenty of light for Noah to return. But she was worried. He was only supposed to be gone for two days.

Mara was a bundle of nerves. She stood up, pacing around, her steps quiet on the stone floor. She couldn't stop thinking about Noah, hoping he was okay.

She stopped moving, looking back out at the horizon. She thought about heading out into the astral planes to go looking for him, but the mages of Fulgar still patrolled near the city outside of the anti-scrying box's influence.

She took a deep, centering breath through her nose and released it out of her mouth. She knew Noah was capable. And Typh was with him. But she still didn't trust these cat creatures. They were territorial, and Noah was undoubtedly taking some territory for his own, whether he meant to or not.

With a resigned sigh, she sank into a plush chair, her fingers absently stroking the soft fabric. She tried to focus her mind, but her eyes kept darting to the window. She sighed again, got up, and walked back to the window, taking up her position on the window once more.

She had really started falling for him. He was kind and gentle, yet fierce and determined. He seemed to care for her as well, but neither had said the 'L' word yet. She was thinking about dropping an *I love you* soon because, in this dangerous world of the Feka, she didn't take any day for granted. She wanted to express how she felt and take the relationship to the next level.

Mara's eyes widened through the dim light as she spotted the two figures darting toward the settlement. The robust form of Typh, the leopard, led the way, his long legs making swift strides, his eyes intent and forward-facing. Close behind, Noah's now-muscular frame followed, his movement nimble yet strained as if they had been running for a while.

Mara's heartbeat synced with the pounding of their feet against the ground. Relief flooded her as she dashed out, the wooden door slamming behind her as she ran down the palace hallways toward the entrance. As she blasted out into the night sky, the crisp night air brushed against her face, but she paid it no mind.

As they met, Typh slowed, allowing Noah to catch up, both breathing heavily from the run. Mara's eyes searched Noah's, a flurry of unspoken questions swirling within her. She noticed the unease in his posture, the tension in his gaze, as he tried to steady his breathing. He punched Typh in the furry shoulder playfully, but she could tell he was anxious.

"What happened?" she managed to ask, her voice filled with concern. Her hands reached out to grasp Noah's, seeking to offer comfort and stability in the midst of the uncertainty that loomed over them.

Typh's deep voice responded, "We should go inside. There's much to discuss."

They returned to the palace and walked quickly into the council chambers. Dee stepped into the central area of the palace from a side hallway, then saw them and smiled. "You guys are back!"

"Yeah, we're back, Dee," Noah replied, his voice carrying a weight of weariness and concern.

Dee's jovial smile faltered a bit at the timbre of Noah's voice. She followed closely as they moved towards the center of the room, her paws plodding along behind to keep pace with Noah and Typh's long strides. "What's going on? You both look like you've seen a ghost. Did it not go very well in Fayport?"

Typh glanced over, his eyes serious, "It's a long story, Dee. Let's find a place to sit down and talk."

"I haven't heard yet either. Let's get some tea and talk about what happened," Mara said to the group.

They moved toward a secluded corner of the council chambers, a plush, rounded seat offering a space for them to gather and talk.

Moments later, with steaming cups of tea, Noah took a deep breath and told everyone what happened.

Chapter 32

What is Love

THE OVERLORD WOKE UP FROM HIS DREAMLIKE STATE, writing down the information from the encounter with the Void Master. He had learned that if he didn't write these things down that he would lose them from memory.

The creature had been coming to him more and more regularly now. He had been made aware of Mara's trip across the ocean and Noah's trip into the caves. After he returned to Dunbar, his scrying mages became blocked. It didn't take a genius to realize what he had found down there.

Now, he waited for his spymaster to come back from his long journey to the north.

The Overlord's chamber, a vast expanse filled with shadows and the dim light of braziers, was a quiet place. The distant sound of his city celebrating midweek echoed outside of his open windows. The walls, made of blackened stones, held various relics and symbols from the conquered to the west.

The Overlord contemplated what would happen when he touched the voidbloom. He hoped it would advance his powers, but wasn't sure.

When he watched Noah create during his brief time in Fulgar, he had learned a lot. He never thought the boy would escape, however. He would regret that for a long time. But without him, he would have to grow his powers in a different way.

Had he handled the situation incorrectly? Perhaps. But there was no use looking back.

There was a soft knock on the chamber's heavy doors. Pomius dropped his book and leaned forward toward the door, his heart beating faster.

"Enter," the Overlord commanded.

The doors creaked open, revealing a cloaked figure. The Spymaster. He gracefully moved towards the Overlord, his movements silent, his face hidden beneath the hood of his cloak. Only his piercing eyes, always observant, always calculating, were visible.

"You've returned. Report," the Overlord said, not wasting any time on pleasantries.

The Spymaster paused for a moment before speaking, "I have followed Noah and his group into the cavern and remained undetected. I discovered where they went. They made an alliance with a city of trolls. And I found this!"

He set a package on the table, the aura undeniable, then backed hurriedly away.

The Overlord jumped from his seat and reached across the desk, quickly snatching the package and drawing it closer to him. He reached out to unwrap it but then hesitated, his fingers inches away.

He didn't know what would happen when he touched it, and certainly didn't want another to see. He wrapped the paper back up. "I will study this flower. What else?"

The spymaster cleared his throat. "The trolls of the underworld appear to have an odd alliance with Noah and his group. With their help, Noah will be able to devise a strategy to attack the Shadowalkers and eventually take over their city. He is resourceful and will see the path through the mountains, just as you or I."

"Good," the Overlord responded. He couldn't help but look down at the package again. "Dismissed!"

The spymaster paused but then bowed and walked from the room.

The Overlord waited for a moment, ensuring he was truly alone before his fingers reached out to unwrap the package. The room seemed to grow colder, the ambient energy shifting. As he slowly unfurled the paper, the voidbloom was revealed, its dark colors glistening with an otherworldly sheen.

Hesitating only for a moment, the Overlord extended a finger to touch the flower. Instantly, a rush of cold darkness spread up his arm, filling his veins with a chilling power. His vision blurred momentarily, and when it cleared, he was no longer in his chamber.

He stood on a vast, barren plain, the sky overhead a swirling mass of dark clouds with occasional flashes of purple lightning. A sense of overwhelming emptiness pressed down on him. Before him stood the hooded figure from his dreams, its cloak billowing in a wind that he couldn't feel.

"You've touched the bloom," the figure whispered, its voice echoing in the vastness of the void. "Good. You have unlocked your first skill. It is called 'FEED' and will satiate the hunger."

He felt the change as a tattoo burned onto his left arm below the symbol of the void. It was the symbol of an open mouth, its teeth cut in large fangs.

The being spoke again, purple lightning sparking in the darkness behind him. "The Shadowalkers have a similar powerset. In order to truly rule this world, they must be eliminated. Let the human destroy them when he attacks without any warning from you."

The Overlord squinted at the Void Master. "Noah? He's going to attack them?"

"Focus on developing your power. Use this newfound ability wisely. And remember, the void is neither friend nor foe. It simply is. Now go, apprentice. Strengthen yourself so we may take this world."

With a flash of purple lightning, the Overlord was transported back to his chambers.

The next morning dawned, but the sky was heavy with dark, brooding clouds. Rain hammered against the stone facade of the palace, a rhythmic sound that echoed through the empty corridors. The wind howled, carrying whispers of the storm that raged above as lightning forked across the sky, followed by the resonant boom of thunder.

I stood on the balcony of my chamber, the rain pelting my face as I gazed out at the blurred landscape stretched below. The gardens, usually vibrant and lively, now lay battered under the onslaught of the storm, their beauty shrouded by the gray veil of rain.

The meeting from the previous day replayed in my head over and over. I couldn't shake the looks the Fekan councilors had been giving me. The expectation to lead an army north to face the Shadowalkers loomed like the dark clouds above.

A sudden gust of wind blew the balcony doors wide open, and a hand reached out to pull me inside. I turned to see Mara, her hair sticking to her face, raindrops clinging to her lashes. "Come inside," she urged.

I nodded, then followed her in, the warmth of the chamber a stark contrast to the surprising chill of the storm outside.

"You haven't slept, have you?" she asked, her eyes filled with concern, the ambient light of the chamber casting a soft glow on her beautiful face. Her hair was wild from sleep, and she quickly threw it up into a ponytail.

I shook my head, water dripping from my hair onto the stone floor. "No. I keep trying to design things in my head, and my list of things to do is so long, and..."

Mara moved closer, her presence a comforting shelter in the storm raging both outside and within my mind. "We've got this," she assured me, her voice unwavering amidst the clamor of the storm. "All of us. You are not alone in this."

"Yeah, you're the second person to say that to me," I said.

"That's probably because you need to hear it," she said. She got closer and rested her face on my chest. Her voice came out a bit muffled. "You gave me some time to think yesterday, and with you gone, I realized something. Something that kind of scared me."

I pulled my head back. "Yeah? Uh oh. That doesn't sound good."

She looked at me, locking eyes with me. "I realized I'm falling in love with you."

My eyes widened in surprise. A girl had never said that to me, and while I felt like we were getting pretty close, I didn't think she would say it this quickly.

I blinked, the words hanging in the air like the charged particles of the storm outside. Everything seemed to pause in that moment. My palms became instantly clammy holding onto her back.

Her eyes, earnest and a little anxious, searched mine for a reaction. The warm golden hues of the chamber lights cast a delicate glow on her face, highlighting her freckles and making her eyes sparkle. In this suspended moment, she had never looked more beautiful. The moment burned into my brain, stored away forever.

"I... Mara..." I stuttered, grappling with my feelings amidst the whirlwind of responsibility and uncertainty that swirled within me. My heart hammered against my chest, a common occurrence these last few days.

I cupped her face with my hand, feeling the cool dampness of her skin. "I am falling in love with you, too," I whispered, my words a soft murmur against the noise of the tempest outside. "But I'm a mess. I don't want you worrying about me and if I survive, and..."

Her eyes softened, relief and affection melting the tension that had held her. She wrapped her arms around me, her head nestling back into its normal spot against my chest. We stood enveloped in the warmth of our embrace, the world outside forgotten, if just for a moment.

"I don't care about any of that. I'm here for it. All of it." She spoke softly.

I smiled, then lay back on the bed, pulling her with me. The bed, soft and welcoming, cradled us as we continued to hold each other, if just for a few more moments before we tackled the quest ahead of us.

As I walked into the smithy, I still smiled like a fool. The shop was abuzz with the sound of metal clanging against metal, and the fiery furnaces cast a warm, orange glow over everything.

Jasper looked up from his breakfast, a huge grin plastered all over his face. "So she said it, then? How did it feel?"

My face jerked back in surprise. "What the hell? How do you know?"

Jasper looked at Romas, and even the cat grinned back. "They're roommates, ya dummy. If you don't think girls gossip about this..." he tailed off, then shook his head, laughing again. "Come on then. Out with it. How did it go?"

"Wait, who? Jamie? How did you hear about this from Jamie?"

Jasper's grin got comically large now. "Yeah, that's right. We've started going out."

I nodded appreciatively. "Nice, man! When did this all start?"

Romas barked out a laugh. "Well, *Baron,* you've been a bit preoccupied these days. But life isn't just going on adventures and making tower monstrosities. Sometimes people need more than that."

Jasper cut in. "Out with it, then! Stop changing the subject!"

I hesitated but decided there was no harm. "Alright, alright," I conceded, laughing. "Mara, she... she said she loves me."

"Ha! I knew it!" Jasper *whooped* in a loud cheer, his voice echoing throughout the smithy as he pumped his fist. "The way she's been looking at you? Like you're a freshly forged sword, all shiny and new. Jamie knew it was only a matter of time! I told her it would be you who cracked first. Guess I'm buying dinner."

My cheeks went a bright red, but the warm glow inside me didn't dim. "Yeah, well... we'll see how it goes. It's no big deal."

The two shared another sideways glance, but I sighed. "Guy's, let's get to it. We have a lot of planning to do to get this attack off. I want to head out in the next week to minimize the enemy's chance to get back together after their defeat. It was a quick fight, and they didn't spend too many troops. I need to find new mages for earth and water mana, figure out how to traverse a jungle with an army, and get Mara to try and negotiate with the monks across a whole damn ocean."

Jasper's laughter slowly died down, and he looked at me with serious eyes. "You're right. Let's get down to business."

"We will gather everyone this afternoon to do the selection. We have an earth mana item with that ring of yours, but what about water? What ingredients do you have?"

"I have the troll eye from when we killed that scout troll in the caves. I haven't even given it any thought." I paused, thinking. "You know, I remember I tried to make a healing wand but required water mana. I wonder if I could make that now. Healing would be awesome to have on our team of mages."

Jasper and Romas nodded as I continued. "And I don't know if mana regeneration is possible, but if so, we would be almost unstoppable. The main problem with my mages is their tiny mana pools. And if we have a fight between here and Niridge, then forget it. We will be screwed."

Jasper stroked his scruffy blond beard thoughtfully, and I almost laughed watching him. "Sounds like we have a basic plan together, though. I'll head into the jungle with the fire mages to gather other ingredients for the alchemists. Romas will need to figure out a way for us to travel through the jungle and swamp without moving at a slow pace. Mara needs to talk to the astral mages across the ocean. And Noah needs to make all kinds of items."

"Yeah, and I will also need Mara to try and contact the trolls. We are going to need them, I think. Those Stalkers are tough fighters. We won't be able to take them down without a ton of Fekan warriors with us."

Jasper and Romas nodded in agreement. "So the Monarch won't send many of the troops with us, then?" Romas asked.

"Didn't sound like it. I bet Typh will bring some, but it won't be many."

A silence broke out as each of us were lost in our own thoughts.

I sighed. "We've got a long week ahead; let's make every moment count."

I turned and headed into the basement to get to work.

Chapter 33

Water Mages

I FIGURED I ONLY NEEDED AN HOUR OR SO TO DESIGN A simple water mana item as Jasper ran out to gather the no-classers at the settlement for magic trials. I made my way into the basement with the troll eye in my pocket, ready to craft something to unlock some water mages. I sat down at the design table and fired up my magical HUD.

I pulled out the troll eye, setting it gently on the table. It gleamed under the light, its depths swirling with unknown potentials. I studied it for a moment, appreciating its raw beauty and power, before the world slowed to a crawl.

I brought up designs for amulets, each detailed with various properties that the eye could produce. It seemed as though the trolls were ice-based, so an amulet with this ingredient would produce something that would lean in that direction.

After finalizing the design, I prepared the necessary materials and tools. I chose a silver chain for its high magical affinity. The trolls used it, and perhaps unknowingly, it was a perfect conductor of water magic.

I snapped off the skill and headed over to the anvil to create the object. I didn't use a free item because it was only five mana. As I concentrated, the silver, the last piece I had, stretched out into a fine chain, forming an amulet at the base. The eye spun and hovered as the metal flowed like liquid around the troll eye, enveloping it in a delicate embrace, intertwining with the smooth surface to hold it securely in place.

The entire amulet glowed with a soft, azure light, emanating a tranquil and potent energy that filled the air around me. I inspected the object.

[TROLL EYE AMULET - LEVEL 1 - WATER MANA - ICE AFFINITY]

Easy enough, I thought. I was pleased that I got additional information about items when I inspected them. I didn't know if that was from my engineering skill or just my overall level. Since I was over level 15 now, I didn't know if that came with added benefits.

There was still so much about this world that I didn't understand.

I held the necklace to the light one last time before nodding, slipping it into my pocket, and walking back up the stairs.

The smithy was empty as I walked through; both Jasper and Romas were off in the settlement by now. I took a few moments in the quiet to center myself. Then, I walked through the door and out into the city's upper level.

The group of no-classers was gathered in the courtyard, the sound of anxious conversations filling my ears as I walked toward them. They saw me coming and the talking died down.

The other mages gathered near the ramp, looking on at the scene. I'm sure they hadn't forgotten what it was like to become unlocked. To become a classed.

I took a deep breath, my hand in my pocket, feeling the cool metal of the amulet. I knew how much was riding on my mages. There were only three earth mages so far in Dunbar, so I was praying that many of the thirty or so people standing here had water mana deep within them.

I glanced at the anxious faces before me, many filled with hope while others reflected the uncertainty that echoed within my own mind.

"Good morning," I began, my voice strong and clear, carrying across the courtyard. "I know many of you are nervous about the days to come. I share that nervousness with you. Before you agree to participate in the Unlocking, know that we stand on the brink of a journey, the outcome of which we cannot foresee."

Confused glances between both the mages and the people standing in the courtyard. "Our Monarch has tasked me with invading the Shadowalkers to the north and eliminating them."

The announcement sent a shockwave of disbelief through the crowd, and the whispers turned to stunned silence. Nearby Feka let out surprised growls, and humans audibly gasped.

I held up my hands, signaling for calm, but the restless energy continued to buzz through the crowd. I knew this task seemed impossible, and the fear was palpable among us.

"Listen to me!" I called, my voice cutting through the noise. The crowd gradually quieted down, their eyes filled with uncertainty and expectation. "I know it sounds impossible. I know the journey will be dangerous, and we may face losses. But we've been given an opportunity to prove ourselves, to show our strength and courage. The Monarch believes we can do this, and I believe in every one of you."

I looked around the courtyard, locking eyes with as many people as possible. "We have faced adversity before. We have stood together and triumphed over the odds. And we will do it again. The Shadowalkers will never expect an attack from us. We have the element of surprise, and we can succeed with careful planning and coordination."

The crowd remained silent, digesting my words, weighing the risks and the rewards in their minds. I knew I was asking a lot from them, and I knew that not everyone would join this mission.

"And so, before you take this amulet in your hands, ask yourself if you are ready to come with me on this mission. If you are, please line up before me to see if you have the final affinity."

I stepped back and stopped, letting the silence stretch on for a moment longer. A tall boy squared his shoulders and stood in front of me. Then another. Then another. Until everyone in the courtyard stood in line.

I couldn't help but finally snap on my 'PATRON' skill to see what I was working with.

And to my surprise, almost everyone in line glowed two shades of blue before me.

I slipped the necklace around the final person in line, and she, like 24 others before her, went through a transition into becoming a classed. Considering the location of the settlement, I supposed that it wasn't surprising that many of the humans here at Dunbar had water affinities. Still, it surprised me how many mages I now had under my control.

The girl's eyes went wide as the cold metal of the necklace touched her skin. A blue glow emanated from the troll's eye amulet, wrapping her in a soft luminescence. The energy swirled, creating intricate patterns in the air as it danced around her.

She spoke her name out loud, locking in her class. A tattoo with stats burned into her arm, but I didn't need to look. She was the same light blue as the others, most likely a healing class.

I knew that I had a lot of equipment to make for these mages, but didn't have the materials. I would have to figure out what I could mass produce to fill the needs of these mages. I hoped my

'MANUFACTURE' skill would help with that, as the name indicated.

I looked at the five people who had not been selected and walked over to them. "Don't worry, guys. There may be other magic that I haven't unlocked yet. But for now, keep your heads up. Mara over there didn't have an affinity until she picked up a powerful ingredient. There are other things that we can try."

Their expressions, which had turned glum as they watched their peers unlock classes, brightened slightly at my words. They exchanged uncertain glances before focusing on me, hope rekindling in their eyes.

I continued, "Each one of you has talents and skills that are invaluable to us. With or without magic, you are essential to our mission and our community. Magic is not the only form of strength or path to success. And remember, our journey is far from over. There's a world full of undiscovered possibilities out there, and each day brings new opportunities."

The group nodded, gratitude and appreciation reflected in their smiles as they thanked me.

"Alright, everyone, come show me your tattoos. I need to see what we unlocked here."

A warmth spread across my chest, but this felt different, almost like when I had leveled up to 10.

I looked down at my arm and saw a new tattoo burning where the 'PATRON' skill was before.

Chapter 34

Echo Through Time

I SAW THE NEW PICTURE FINISH, ROUNDING OUT MY SKILLS.
The voice lady announced the change in my mind.

[YOUR **PATRON** SKILL HAS BEEN UPGRADED TO **ANCESTRAL ECHO**]

I felt a rush of energy, a slight tingle that radiated from the center of my being to the tips of my fingers and toes. A connection to something ancient and vast hummed in the background of my consciousness.

I took a breath, looking down at my arm.

[NOAH]
[Lv 18 - BLACKSMITH JOURNEYMAN]

[BONDED]

[HEALTH 140/140]
[MANA 142/162]

-L6

-L6

-Passive

-L2

-L9

-L2

[UNSELECTED SKILLS - NONE]

. . .

I closed my eyes, taking a moment to let this newfound ability settle within me. I could sense whispers at the edge of my perception, the murmur of many voices speaking words I couldn't yet understand. It was as though a vast sea of experience and wisdom had opened up before me, waiting to be navigated.

I inspected the new skill and got a whole bunch of new information.

[ANCESTRAL ECHO - COST 2 MANA / SECOND -
SECONDARY SKILL - PARTY INTERFACE]
[*With this skill, gain the ability to invoke the wisdom and knowledge of other Creators. For a short duration, receive guidance from the echoes of your ancestors, enhancing your decision-making, insight into your patrons, and strategic planning abilities. The echoes provide counsel based on the accumulated experiences and wisdom of those who have come before, offering a unique perspective on challenges and situations*]
[NOTE: THE GUIDANCE RECEIVED IS SPECTRAL
AND SYMBOLIC AND UTILIZES YOUR **ASTRAL**
MANA AFFINITY. IT IS UP TO THE USER TO
INTERPRET AND APPLY THE INSIGHTS PROVIDED]

What the hell? I thought quickly. *Up to me to do what now? Since when did I get a tutorial on new skills?*

This was indeed a first. I blinked at the HUD, rereading the description of 'ANCESTRAL ECHO' to ensure I hadn't missed anything. The words remained the same, offering spectral and symbolic guidance from the echoes of ancestors.

"But how?" I muttered to myself, pacing back and forth in the empty courtyard. I wasn't prepared for this type of magic, not in the least.

The idea of communicating, even in a symbolic way, with those long gone was intriguing, yet it filled me with a certain trepidation. There were so many questions and so many unknown variables. *Would these ancestors understand our current world? Would their advice, possibly outdated, do more harm than good? Could they understand the nuances of our present situation?*

Despite the uncertainty swirling in my mind, I felt an odd comfort. In the journey that lay ahead, filled with shadows and unknown threats, the whispers of those who had navigated their own darknesses might prove to be the guiding light I needed.

I decided to activate the skill.

A shimmering, silvery mist seemed to fill the air around me as mana began pouring out of my tattoo. It was almost as though I was seeing into another plane like Mara did when she activated her scrying.

I looked at one of my new mages, and a new voice began speaking to me, as if sitting on my shoulder. It was deep and male, almost like an elderly man reading a story to a kid.

[*Ice mages are fickle in most situations. They flourish in environments where they can use the elements to their advantage, turning the very atmosphere into a weapon. But beware in arid, hot climates, where their powers are significantly diminished. Coordinate with them to use their abilities strategically, freezing enemies in place or creating barriers of ice to block attacks.*]

The whispering voice, clear and calm, filled my ears. It felt ancient and wise, its tones imbued with the weight of experience. I glanced again at the ice mage, a young woman named Eira, and she looked at me uncertainly.

"Yes?" she asked.

"Oh, nothing," I said through the silver mist.

[*I would advise holding training sessions,*] the voice continued. [*Allow your new mages to practice their abilities, learn the limits and potential of their powers, and collaborate with one another to create synergized attacks]*

Synergized attacks? I mentally asked the voice. I looked at my arm, almost like looking at a watch. 56 mana had drained away already. But I kept the skill going. This sounded like something I desperately needed to learn.

[Yes. It is like your Tesla coil attack, young Creator. Which, I must say, was quite ingenious. Quite ingenious indeed. If you take a fine mist created by an ice mage and place lightning through it, you can electrify it and create a massive storm. If you combine wind and fire, you can create a whirlwind of flames, a devastating attack that can engulf multiple enemies at once. Similarly, earth and water can work together to create a quagmire, trapping foes and leaving them vulnerable to attacks. Understanding the elements and how they interact is crucial for maximizing the effectiveness of your mages in battle]

Holy crap, man. The possibilities swirled in my mind, visions of elemental forces combining to create unstoppable forces on the battlefield. It was daunting, but also thrilling. The voice continued, offering more insight and guidance since I hadn't cut off the skill yet.

[Remember...do not rely on one tactic too heavily, for a wise enemy will adapt. Change your strategies, keep the enemy guessing, and use the terrain to your advantage. Practice these synergized attacks with your mages, let them experiment, and learn to coordinate their powers effectively. Your enemies will be formidable, but with strategy, coordination, and the guidance of the ancestors, you will prevail.]

I nodded, more to myself than to the voice. "Thank you," I murmured, unsure if the ancestors could hear my gratitude.

[You're welcome, descendant. Remember, the echoes of the past are here to guide you. Trust in them, and trust in yourself]

Another look at my arm saw my mana at [30/165]. *Holy shit, that drained a lot of mana!* I cut the skill off quickly and my head instantly started pounding. But I felt a new confidence blossoming within me. My biggest complaint about my skills was that I rarely knew how the hell to use them.

But if I could get a training manual and ask a few questions, even if it burned through mana like fire through tinder, that would be an enormous help for me.

I approached the mages, ready to share the insights I had received and begin the process of experimentation.

After a few hours with the various leaders of the mage groups, I went to go find Mara to see how her interactions with the trolls had gone. I didn't know if she could project her astral being to them or not, but if she could, I was afraid we would freak the poor bastards out.

I found her in one of the serene gardens of the palace. It was a place of peace, where lush greenery thrived, and vibrant flowers bloomed amidst ancient statues of Feka heroes and deities. She sat on a stone bench, her eyes closed, and an aura of calm enveloped her. I hesitated to disturb her, but the anticipation and curiosity bubbled within me. I found her mediating more and more these days...advice from the Monarch.

I gently approached her, my steps quiet on the moss-covered path. "Mara," I whispered.

Her eyes fluttered open, a soft smile greeting me as her ethereal gaze met mine. "Noah," she responded sweetly, beaming up at me.

"How did it go?" I asked, my voice filled with eager curiosity.

Mara's eyes glittered as she began to recount her experience. "It was incredible. I even unlocked a new skill called Astral Projection. Now I can choose between scouting with my scrying skill, mentally talking with my telekinesis skill, or full-on projecting myself, like the mage did across the ocean!"

I smiled, "That's cool! What did they say?"

She continued, "The trolls are gentle souls, their spirits deeply intertwined with the earth through their cave systems. They were startled when they saw me, but also intrigued. We communicated not through words but through emotions and images. It's hard to explain. I could feel their connection to the jungle, their desires for peace, and their fears of the encroaching Shadowalkers. They interact with a different part of the jungle than the Feka do, and want the same thing we do in this war. That's why you were able to get an alliance with them."

"And will they help us?"

"They will, in their own way," she answered, her voice carrying a melody of hope and warmth. "They will not fight since they feel that they don't have enough warriors to lend, but they will lend us their knowledge of the land, the paths through the swamp, and the secrets of the Shadowalkers' territory. We could get almost halfway to Niridge through the caves."

I let out a sigh of relief, the weight of uncertainty lifting. That was certainly one issue out of the way. I would need to bring them lots of gifts if we were to take one hundred fifty mages through their cave system.

"Great job. Well, you look beat. Did that take all your mana?" I said, looking her over.

"Yeah. And you don't look too great yourself. How did it go out there?"

I let out a huge grin. "Wait until you hear what happened!"

Chapter 35

Garnierite

THE NEXT DAY, I NEEDED TO DESIGN WATER MANA equipment, and Mara needed to talk to the air mages. We said we would meet up later in the afternoon for dinner and to debrief. I bid her farewell after some quick breakfast and went back into the basement to consult with my design table.

I was careful not to tap into my new skill despite desperately wanting to. The allure of utilizing the new skill was powerful, but patience was a steadfast companion in the journey of creation. The depth of that newfound ability was a realm to explore with caution. Plus, I needed all the mana I could get for today.

I needed to create something that complimented my mages and their abilities. I thought about what I had already. Jasper and his team had fireballs; some even unlocked the firewall skill. The alchemists could make any range of smoke and firebombs. My air mages were front-line defenders and the others could shoot lightning. Finally, my three earth mages could move earth, and one of them could move stealthily within it.

I had noticed something else during my training session yesterday. The mages with opposite mana types didn't seem to get along, even personality-wise. My air and fire mages continuously bickered, as did Liza with the new water mages.

I leaned back in the wooden chair at the table, the backrest creaking slightly under the shift in weight. My gaze fell upon the intricate patterns etched into the table's surface as my mind furiously worked. I allowed my thoughts to drift, a free flow of imagination and strategy mingling in the vast expanse of my mind.

As of yesterday's event, I had fifteen ice mages, called Hayle Mages, and ten mages that I assumed produced water, called Hydroxi. They had a simple tattoo of a water drop, while the Hayales had a picture of what appeared to be a glacier.

I designed a simple water wand similar to the other mana starter wands that I could mass produce. I wasn't sure yet about what the Hydroxi would need. They seemed to be specialized mages, similar to the Zephrys and Alchemists, so I would handle them second.

The two ingredients came up, and I mentally sighed. I needed a mangrove branch and garnierite, whatever the hell that was. I inspected the two ingredients to see what information I could get.

[MANGROVE BRANCH - *Obtained from mangrove trees, which typically grow along coastlines in tropical regions. Best harvested at high tide for maximum water mana properties. Advisable to use a silver or enchanted blade for the cutting to maintain the branch's potency. Found in your local region near large bodies of water.*]

I knew that the Feka understood how to harvest magical lumber since they grew all sorts around Dunbar. I continued to the ore.

[GARNIERITE ORE - *A green, nickel ore mineral, often found within weathered areas of ultramafic rocks and nickel-rich deposits. Harnesses a mild magnetism and capable of drawing in and enhancing water-based magical energies. Must be extracted from nickel-rich ore deposits, typically found in geologically*

ancient regions. Best handled with gloves, as the nickel content
may cause skin irritation for some individuals.]*

Best handled with gloves? I thought as I laughed out loud with a
snort. I didn't know where these prompts were coming from, but
they were starting to get either very snarky or protective of me.
Even the mysterious forces behind my creation abilities seemed
to have a sense of humor. Maybe they knew I needed a bit of
lightness in this moment, and I was grateful for that.

I assumed the mangrove branch would be easier to procure; it
was just a matter of sending a team of water mages to the gulf to
start exploring, much like I made my fire and air mages do when
they first got their powers.

But I needed garnierite, a nickel ore, so I had to venture into the
mines. I left the smithy to go and find the water mages to give
them instructions for finding the trees. An hour or so had passed,
and the sun was nearing high noon. I realized that I was hungry
and stopped to get some lunch first.

I paused in my journey and made a detour to the bustling
market square. The sun hung high, casting short shadows as it
poured its light onto the vibrant array of stalls. The air was filled
with the aroma of spices, baked goods, and the enticing scent of
various dishes being cooked at food stalls.

I headed to my favorite vendor, an elderly Fekan merchant with
white and black fur who made the most delicious fish pies. "Ah,
Baron!" the old Feka greeted me warmly as he handed over a
freshly baked pie, still warm from the oven. "On the house for
you, my boy. Good luck today!"

I thanked him, savoring the flaky crust and the fresh filling as I
continued my walk to find the water mages. Once there, I gathered them together and explained the task. Many were fishermen or worked on the boats near the docks.

"We need a mangrove branch from a tree within this area, most
likely near swampy areas near the gulf," I detailed. "I'll be
venturing into the mines to retrieve garnierite for the wands, but

I need you all to work as a team to retrieve the branches. Stay together, and use these basic weapons should you run into trouble. I will also send a few Zephyrs with you."

I nodded to Kyle, who nodded back. The water mages smiled and looked at each other, but I could see the nervousness on their faces. I bid them good luck and left them to prepare for their mission.

Then, it was time for me to embark on my own mission. Equipped with my pickaxe, a sturdy mushroom light lantern, and a map of the known mine tunnels, I headed toward the jungle.

Taking a deep breath, I stepped over the threshold into the gloom of the mine. The mushroom light lantern emitted a soft, ethereal glow, piercing the darkness and revealing the rocky, narrow paths that wound further into the cave system. I passed by the miners who swung steel pickaxes at the cave walls in search of iron ore and kept walking, this time going right in the fork.

Hours passed as I explored the tunnels, looking for various new shades of ore from my mining skill in search of garnierite. The dim, purple light of the mushroom lantern illuminated the walls, painting them in shades of eerie azure and cobalt. I had to switch the mushrooms out a few times as they ran out of light.

I noticed a vein of greenish-blue ore embedded in the rock face in one of the chambers. My heart raced as I recognized it as something I hadn't seen before. It was pretty deep, but not as deep as some of the ores I had mined.

I always got excited when I unlocked new mana types. It was like the world unlocked further before my very eyes.

I stuck my hand on the wall and activated my Manufacture skill as the mining subskill went to work, sucking all nearby ores out of the wall like a high-powered vacuum. Green ore shot out of the wall along with black ore that I recognized as iron. As the ores were extracted, they swirled around me like a metallic maelstrom, their cold, hard surfaces catching the lantern's glow.

I cut the skill off, sending the pieces to the dirt path, and hastily picked up the nearest piece, inspecting it.

[GARNIERITE ORE - LEVEL 1 INGREDIENT]

I cheered and stashed the pieces into my fanny pack that hung from my belt. I had four pieces now and figured I had around fifteen wands to create. This ore was almost as prevalent as the iron ore was in these caves, and I thanked my lucky stars.

Suddenly, I paused, thinking about my situation.

I had a magical class with a quest to beat evil monsters by building an army and making items for them, and now I was off in a cave scouring the walls for rare ingredients to craft items. This was starting to feel more and more like a video game as my skills advanced. I chuckled, the noise echoing off the walls.

Shaking my head, I set off further into the darkness.

Chapter 36

Tail Between Legs

THROUGH THE DENSE FOLIAGE AND UNDER THE SHADOWED canopies, the alpha moved with a grace that belied his hulking frame. Yet as he journeyed back to Niridge, the air was thick with a dread he had never before carried in his mighty chest. He was the alpha, the untamed and unyielding leader of the Shadowalkers, and fear was a stranger to his indomitable spirit until now.

The image of the unassuming and seemingly weak human haunted his thoughts. The sound of his lightning machine killing those dragons echoed in the chambers of his mind, a chilling cadence that spoke of strength hidden behind a mask of frailty. The strange and potent artifacts, devices infused with magic, unfamiliar and fearsome, added to the enigma that the human presented.

The three remaining dragons had flown back into the mountains without another word. He feared what that would mean for his pack, but tried releasing those thoughts from his mind. For he had enough to worry about.

As he entered the borders of Niridge, the familiar terrain dotted with the homes of his brethren, his heart tightened within the armored cage of his chest. The energy of the Shadowalkers

763

vibrated through the earth beneath his feet as they moved about, taking on various responsibilities throughout the city. They would know of his defeat, and they would look to him for answers, for direction in the face of this unprecedented threat. The human, a Creator with forces that continuously surprised him, had ignited a flame of uncertainty within the alpha, casting shadows upon his path and sowing seeds of doubt in the fertile soil of his resolve.

For not even the mighty dragons could take Dunbar.

The massive gate of Niridge, intricately woven with roots and vines, shuddered open to allow the weary Shadowalkers entry into the sanctity of their den. The alpha stood to one side, his towering form cast in the dappled light that filtered through the interlaced foliage above.

To his right, he saw a shadowy figure leaned against a tree, waiting for him. It was one of those human teleporting mages. They all gave him the creeps, and that was saying something.

He turned and walked over to the man.

"The Overlord sends his regards." A mocking smile crossed the man's hooded face, and it was everything he could do not to rip him limb from limb.

"I'm sure he heard about our defeat," Annos responded, baring his teeth slightly.

"He has. He recommends that you stay put and recover for a while in your city. We have been watching the boy and believe he has no reason to improve his settlement further or make any additional moves. You will be able to attack him when you are full strength. The Overlord will use his influence to have the human called to Fayport soon, so you can attack while he is gone."

The wolf growled. "It will be a while before we are ready again. The cold season is coming, and I will have to figure something else out for feeding my pack."

The man nodded. "Very well. We will return if anything changes."

With that, he vanished.

Odd creatures, those mages.

His gaze tracked each warrior as they shuffled past, none looking at the angry werewolf. The alpha watched his troops shuffle through the gate into the city, their tails between their legs, just like his. He felt it in his bones, that prickle of fear and uncertainty. They weren't used to this, being unsure, being scared. They had always been the dominant force here.

"What did they have to say?" Rhykar, his new beta, mumbled, walking up beside him.

"Nothing good," the alpha growled back.

A moment passed between the two wolves as they watched the last few troops enter the city. "They're looking to you. For what to do next," Riz said, still avoiding his gaze.

He knew that, and it disturbed him even more. What was he supposed to tell them? He didn't know how to fight this human and his strange magic, his powerful devices that could summon the elements at will. His mages, with their fire and lightning.

"I know," he finally growled back to Riz. He cleared his throat, squaring his shoulders, trying to push down the uncertainty that twisted his insides. "Gather them in the square. I'll speak to them."

Riz nodded and went off, barking orders. It was time to face them, time to figure out what their next move would be. He had to bring back the confidence, not just in himself but in his pack.

Otherwise, they would kill him and find another who would.

———

The vast expanse of the ocean lay beneath Mara, its deep blue surface sparkling under the sun's kiss. Her astral form soared over the waters, unburdened by the physical constraints of her human body, left miles and miles away. She relished these moments, feeling a oneness with the universe that eluded her in her grounded, everyday life.

There were more dark shapes. They seemed to follow her as she traveled, but disappeared when she looked at them long enough.

Her mana had grown over the last week, and she felt much more powerful. She loved her new skills, and the ability to project herself was immensely helpful. Scrying alone wouldn't let people see her.

Well, unless you were powerful Astral mages who lived next to an ancient tree.

Mara's ethereal form descended gracefully onto the ornate bridge leading to the temple. The monks, draped in robes of moonlight silver, moved about. Most of them couldn't see her outside of the temple, but they stirred, feeling her presence.

She moved to the temple's inner sanctum, where the high monk would be meditating. Mara called out with her soul's voice to the abbot whose inner eye flashed open, seeing her. [Ah, if it isn't the astral princess from the western lands!]

Mara smiled, now used to people calling her that. Mara's form shimmered, a spectral reflection in the monk's tranquil gaze. [I come bearing the weight of an impending conflict, seeking guidance and the wisdom of the stars to navigate the treacherous path that lies ahead.]

She chuckled. The way these monks spoke was rubbing off on her.

The High Monk's inner eye cast a gentle light upon her, bathing her astral form in a celestial glow. [Fear not the gathering storm, child of the cosmos. Even amidst the tempest's fury, the stars above retain their steady gaze, guiding the wayward back to the path of light.]

Mara didn't know what this guy was talking about most of the time, but she continued. [We need your help. Our Monarch has tasked us with ridding the world of the shadows to the north. We are to destroy the Shadowalkers once and for all. But I fear we do not have enough power to do so. Can we call on your people to help? Is there even a way for you to cross the ocean?]

[Ah, the call to arms echoes even in the silence of the cosmos,] he uttered softly. His form unfolded, revealing a magic view of the vast world, a tapestry woven with the threads of countless destinies intertwined. Mara looked on with awe. [The Shadowalkers walk the path shrouded in darkness, yet within them, the spark of the cosmos still flickers, yearning for the embrace of light.]

He guided Mara's gaze across the astral world to the northern realms where shadows held dominion, their dark embrace veiling the land in obscurity. Amidst the darkness, the faint flickers of light, ensnared and dimmed, called out for liberation.

[The cosmic dance transcends the boundaries of land and sea, child of the astral realms. The ocean's vast expanse is but a single step in the boundless waltz of the stars,] the monk thought, his words weaving ethereal bridges across the astral expanse.

[The Trial Moon Sect, guardians of celestial equilibrium, shall lend their energies to your endeavor. Yet remember, even in the quest to conquer the darkness, the light must seek harmony, not domination. In the shadows' embrace, uncover the ensnared sparks, and guide them back to the cosmic dance.]

She chewed on that for a moment. [So...you will lend us mana for our fight? Is that what you're saying?]

He smiled up at her. [Yes, child of the astral. This is the way that we can push your people forward. With our energies intertwined, let the cosmic dance weave patterns of harmony and liberation across the world's vast expanse. Now go, for you have much to still prepare.]

With a warm smile of gratitude, Mara's astral form began to recede from the cosmic expanse. [Thank you,] she said. [My people will be in your debt.]

She left the temple and cut off her scrying, then opened her physical eyes to the sun's gentle caress. She was on the hidden top layer of Dunbar, surrounded below by trees and fountains. She found that her powers worked even better, the earthly air filling her lungs as the astral echoes reverberated within her soul.

Nodding, she walked over to Konna. He had arrived this morning from Fayport to help her, mumbling something about saving her energy. She took his arm, and the two teleported down to go find Noah.

Chapter 37

Final Preparations

THE DAYS MELTED INTO A BLUR OF PREPARATION AND planning. My mind was a whirlwind of strategy meetings, equipment checks, and training sessions. The faces of the new mages, now under my responsibility, flashed before my eyes in quiet moments. I couldn't help but wonder if I was leading them to their doom.

The mine had yielded enough garnierite for the wands, and I eventually finished the final water wand the next day. The mages continued practicing with their new weapons; each Hayle mage had unlocked 'ICE SHARD,' which was basically the water version of fireball.

Similar to the alchemists, the Hydroxi mages loved being near the water and in the jungle. They found plants and even teamed up with their fire counterparts to search for things in the woods. No one told me what they were doing, but I didn't press them.

I made each of them wands, too, but all they could do was make a rain cloud with it, which didn't seem all that threatening. I quickly used my new skill on them to find out that it was a healing rain that would wash away most afflictions. It appeared that they were a healing class, after all.

Mara returned from her astral voyage with promises of aid from the Trial Moon Sect monks. A boost to our mana would be most welcome, but I didn't really understand how they would pull that off. She continued trying to get a glimpse into Niridge without much success. The Fulgarian mages must be hiding their ally's city.

Unknown variables weighed heavy on my mind, the shadow of Niridge casting a long, ominous darkness over my thoughts. Mara's inability to penetrate a shadow that hung over the city told me there was more than met the eye there.

My thoughts turned to the alpha, defeated and fearful, retreating to the enigma of Niridge. To the dragons, who most likely would be back for their revenge. And to the Overlord, whom I had not heard from in some time. I wondered what he was up to.

Each night, as the world darkened and the stars stretched across the vast sky, I would find quiet moments amidst the chaos. I would sit within the confines of my chambers, maps and parchments strewn around, as Mara sat with me. I planned out my mage formations, their uses, and the strategies I would employ. I planned out the attack on the city and what I wanted to do.

Mara liked the plan but thought it was a bit simple. It involved a lot of water mages to start with, and since they were new to my squad, she worried that they wouldn't be able to do what I was asking.

I hoped she was wrong. "I understand what you're saying," I said, nodding. "They're new, untested in real battle scenarios, and we are asking a lot from them. But they've got this."

She paced the floor, her movements graceful and fluid, like the ebb and flow of ocean tides. "What if we integrate them more with the other mages? Let the experienced ones guide them and create a mentor-mentee relationship. That way, they're not thrust into the chaos alone."

I thought back to the voice that had explained everything to me. I liked the idea of environmental attacks. "I'm trying something from my Echo skill. It shouldn't split everyone up," I said.

She nodded, "I remember. I'm just saying, chaos reigns once everyone is in the middle of a battle. If you don't have experienced people mixed in with new people, I'm just afraid of what would happen."

I thought about that for a moment. "I mean, I can see what you're saying. Okay. Let's form squadrons then, and the head of each one will report to you. During the battle, I will need you to telepathically issue commands so that we work as a hive mind."

So, we set to work, reshaping the army's structure into squadrons. Each elemental group was formed into its own respective teams, led by the most powerful among them and with a few Fekan warriors sprinkled in for melee support.

We completed a few more lists of things to keep Dunbar moving forward for Romas and Typh, who weren't allowed to come, and I packed.

And then, just like that, I couldn't think of anything else to do to prepare.

It was time.

Early the next morning before the sun had brightened the sky, Konna delivered a message from the Monarch. Mara told me he had visited a few times during the previous days to assist her teleport up to the secret top level of Dunbar, where she could be alone and use her powers.

The royal seal was stamped at the bottom of the parchment, its intricate design matching the flag of the capital city. It said:

To Baron Noah,

As you stand on the threshold of an endeavor monumental and treacherous, let these words echo in the hearts and minds of you and your noble force. Know that you march with the blessing and the strength of the throne behind you. In your quest to quell the shadows that stain our world, let your stride be unyielding, your resolve unshakable.

Your apprehensions may cloud the path ahead, but remember that even in the densest obscurity, a single spark can illuminate the way. Your assembly of diverse elements is that spark, a beacon to pierce the veil of darkness and light the path to victory.

As you embark on this journey to the north, let courage be your compass, unity your shield, and conviction your blade. The unwavering faith of the Monarch travels with you, a silent sentinel to guard and guide your way.

Emerge triumphant, and let the dawn of a new era rise from the ashes of the obliterated shadows, an epoch where light reigns unchallenged and the harmonious hum of peace resonates through the expanse of our world.

With unyielding support and boundless esteem,

Your Monarch

I handed it to Mara, who read it over as well.

"Laying it on a little thick, don't you think?" she said, pursing her lips.

I snorted. "I think she feels a bit guilty about all of this. But she's right. If we can bring peace to the land, then I can expand the city, trade with the trolls, and maybe even make peace with the dragons. And then our ports could be pointed across the ocean to trade with the monks!"

Mara held up a hand. "Woah, there. Let's just come out of this alive first, alright?"

I let out a chuckle, the tension easing from my shoulders at Mara's pragmatic words. "I know," I said with a slight nod. "One step at a time."

We sat in the stillness of the still dark morning sky, the stars still hanging above us like a sprawling tapestry of light, each one a distant beacon in the vast expanse of the cosmos. I could feel the pulse of the world beneath us, the gentle hum of the elements intertwined in a cosmic dance, their energies ebbing and flowing in a harmonious rhythm. It felt like the earth itself was whispering words of encouragement, its voice a soft murmur on the breeze.

Mara's hand gently touched my arm, her presence a grounding force amidst the swirl of anticipation. "We've got this, Noah. We've prepared as much as we can, and we have each other, and a formidable force of mages, soldiers, and allies. Whatever lies ahead, we'll face it together."

I looked into her eyes, finding a reflection of my own resolve mirrored in her gaze. I drew in a deep breath, filling my lungs with the crisp night air, and exhaled slowly, the monarch's message still echoing in the chambers of my mind.

"Yes," I murmured, my voice steadfast. "Together. Let's go address the troops!"

Chapter 38

Return to Rock Town

I CLEARED MY THROAT, MY HEART THUMPING AGAINST MY chest so hard that I feared everyone could hear it. "Friends," I began, my voice slightly shaky, "Today, we embark on a journey to rid the north of the Shadows that have plagued these lands."

I looked at my mages, their faces focused on mine. "We have trained, prepared, and banded together. We are creators, mages, warriors. We come from different paths, different stories, even different worlds. But today, we stand united as one force against the darkness," I continued, my voice growing steadier and stronger with each word.

I pointed northward towards the shadowed lands beyond the jungle. "Beyond these peaceful walls, evil lurks, poisoning the earth and the air, bringing terror and death. They have tried to bring that here, but we have repelled them each and every time. The Shadows have no regard for life, for beauty, for the harmony of the world. They seek only to destroy, to conquer, to *consume.*"

I took a breath, really rolling now. I channeled my inner Brave-heart and continued. "Let us march forward, friends, as bearers of light, as warriors of hope, into the north, into the shadows, and let us bring peace to these hallowed lands once and for all!"

As my words faded into the cool morning air, a resounding cheer erupted from the crowd, their voices melding into a harmonious cry.

I grinned like a fool as I observed the response from the army. There were almost three hundred of us, Feka and humans combined. I tried to think of the movie Braveheart while I was speaking, and thought I had done a pretty damn good job.

The group started forward, backpacks rattling as we walked toward the mines. The first leg of our trip would be underground to meet up with the trolls.

The shadows of the subterranean world enveloped us as we ventured through the mines. Every step echoed in the vast chambers, filled with veins of countless ores, glinting in the luminescence. A few soft conversations broke out here and there, but overall, no one spoke. The cave floor was uneven, so everyone was paying attention to where they walked.

It was cool seeing a three hundred person army journey through a cavern if I was being honest with myself. Even if the logistics had almost broken me over the past few days.

We took a break in the high-ceiling cavern where we had fought those spitting creatures weeks ago, as mostly everyone could fit in the wide room. Snacks and water were passed around as I walked among the groups. We still had a little way to go to get to the troll city. Mara took a little break to project herself to them, warning the trolls of our coming arrival.

We were going at a much slower pace than we had the first time going to the troll kingdom. The difference was the lack of fighting from small creatures. There was always an uncanny awareness from monsters when the threat around them was too large.

The room buzzed with the muted conversation of my mages and Fekan soldiers. The haunting echoes of the caverns seemed less intimidating now, filled with the warmth of comradeship and shared purpose. People began to relax a bit more, but a few hunter-class Feka patrolled the outer edges of the group, looking for threats. With this large of a group, however, I wasn't worried.

Mara sat in a quiet corner of the cavern, her body limp as her spirit journeyed further into the cavern. Her duty was to scout ahead, but also communicate with the trolls to tell them of our imminent arrival. Her quiet whispers filled the space around her, the words a gentle murmur, unintelligible but filled with the resonance of her astral might.

Amid this respite, my mind pondered the path ahead. My hand subconsciously brushed against the hilt of my pickaxe, the cool metal pulsing back at me through my bond with it.

As the break drew to a close, Mara's form stirred, her astral journey completed. She stood and moved towards me, her gait steady and her expression calm. But she looked tired from the mental journey.

"The trolls are aware of our approach," she conveyed softly, serenely. "They seemed pretty nervous, though. We had better be cautious. Hurbnurr is waiting for you."

I nodded. "Alright, everyone! Let's keep moving! We have around another four hours of walking through the caves before we get to the troll city, where we will stop for the night!"

People began getting up and gathering their things as we moved out. I just hoped we wouldn't have a fight on our hands when we made it to the outside of Rock Town.

As we resumed our march, the winding passages of the mines became a rhythmic blur of stomping boots and grunts. Traffic jams formed as tunnels tightened to one or two person max, conversations passing the time. There was a stretch of about an hour where the paths we traversed were all narrow and cramped, making the going much slower than normal.

Despite the looming walls and the press of darkness, the spirits of my comrades held firm, their faces marked by determination and the gleam of anticipation. I kept reminding myself that these people were mostly in servitude before serving as a mage, and this was their chance to be truly free.

We continued navigating through the depths with the guidance of my map and the flickering luminescence of our lanterns, their light casting eerie patterns upon the rough-hewn walls. Time became a nebulous concept in the embrace of the dark world, marked only by the steady pace of our march and the gradual fatigue that whispered at the edges of our endurance. We had no idea what time it was down here.

Hours passed in a seamless stretch of movement, breaks, and muted conversation. Our goal was to get to the troll town in one day of solid marching.

Finally, the narrow corridors widened, and the oppressive ceiling rose into a towering cavern. The transition was subtle, the creeping growth of space barely noticeable until we found ourselves in the massive expanse of the trolls' domain. The walls receded into the distance as we walked up onto the ledge that looked down into their town.

I remember this spot from when we battled the scout troll. Many of the mages gasped at the sight of a whole town deep within the earth. The welcome seemed warm as the trolls approached, their towering forms lumbering along the ground toward us.

"Everyone wait here for a moment while I talk to them," I said to the group.

"I'll come with you," Mara said.

I nodded to her, then started down the dirt path. Mara and I walked side by side, the noise of our group fading as we moved down the path toward the meeting place, where Hurbnurr and a few other trolls were waiting for us. They waited a moment, then walked toward us.

Here we go, I thought, taking a steadying breath.

"Good to see you again, human," Hurbnurr's voice echoed, deep and resonant like the hum of the earth itself. He didn't seem worried to have nearly three hundred people outside of his gates.

"And you, Hurbnurr," I responded, offering a respectful nod. "Thank you for allowing us to pass through your land. It sure beats traveling by swamp to the north!"

His massive head tilted, a slow and deliberate movement. "You no like Shadowalker, we no like Shadowalker. We friends, we together," Hurbnurr said in a simple, earnest manner, his words heavy but filled with sincerity.

"I come bearing gifts, Hurbnurr! Just like I said I would."

His eyes grew big as he walked closer. "What you bring Hurbnurr?"

I dug a few things out of the bag I had packed especially for this occasion, and handed them over. There were various silvered swords and clubs with spikes, all shining in the lights from the town. The troll looked them over with awe in his eyes. "Oooh, they are made of silver like our rocks?"

"No, Hurbnurr. Those are different. Those are something called *steel*. They're very sturdy weapons that I made for you."

He nodded, then handed it to the warriors next to him. In the troll's hands, the swords almost looked like daggers.

"Do you mind if we stay here? I assume it's night outside these walls, and we have journeyed far today," I asked the huge troll.

Hurbnurr scratched his large, rough head, considering the request. "Hmm... you stay, yes. Night outside, dark and cold. You tired, you rest here. We keep watch, you safe. Then, in morning, I show you to the jungle."

His voice echoed through the cavernous space. I gave a tired but grateful smile, "Thank you, Hurbnurr. Your hospitality is much appreciated."

The giant troll nodded, the movement slow and deliberate, his face expressionless and his eyes still locked on the weapons I had given him.

I waved to Jasper, who got everyone moving down the hill to the cavern to start setting up for the night.

Chapter 39

The Road Less Traveled

THE NIGHT STARTED A BIT TENUOUS BUT THEN OPENED UP as more trolls joined us. Pretty soon, laughter filled the air as the races mingled. I stayed on the outskirts, worry still taking up most of my thoughts.

Despite the warmth of companionship blossoming around, a chill of concern threaded through my thoughts. The laughter seemed distant as I observed my newly minted water mages interacting with the colossal figures of the trolls. It seemed that their affinities had drawn them together, their gestures wide and welcoming.

Could the mages, just beginning to grasp their newfound abilities, harness their power in time to face the looming threat? I looked over to Mara, her ethereal presence a calming beacon amid the lively bustle. She caught my eye and offered a gentle smile.

I knew I needed sleep but doubted it would come. I moved away from the merriment, slipping up the slope and into the shadows where the golden glow of the bonfires couldn't reach. Here, in the darkness, I had time to think. With my back settled against the rough-hewn rock, I reviewed the plan again. I stared upwards, where the cavern's ceiling arched like a cathedral of ancient stone, stalactites hanging like nature's chandeliers.

I also took a moment to make a small...*adjustment* to my pickaxe.

The muffled laughter and exchanges from the gathering beyond played a lulling, distant melody, and I almost dozed off into sleep. It was hard to fall into a regular sleep pattern down here without a sun or moon. I wondered how the trolls did it.

Eventually, after a few minutes to myself, I returned to the group, most of whom were lying down to rest. I did the same, but my eyes stared up at the ceiling.

I woke up with one of those *where was I* feelings, the cave floor hard on my back. Blinking the sleep from my eyes, I stared up but only saw darkness. It took a moment for the blurry shapes to coalesce into the familiar roughness of the cavern ceiling. I shifted, stretching my aching back. The echoes of laughter and conversation had quieted to the soft hum of slumbering breaths and the occasional rustle of movement.

The quiet dark, broken only by the embers of the dying bonfires, provided the only light as Rock Town was also dark. I lit a lantern and looked around again. I figured it was right around dawn on the surface judging by the coals around me.

I pushed myself up to go and find Hurbnurr, the slight stiffness in my joints protesting the abrupt change. The slumbering forms of trolls and my fellow humans scattered in peaceful disarray around me. Apparently, some of the trolls stayed out with us.

Moving quietly, I navigated the sea of sleeping figures, seeking the city's gates. As I approached, the gates swung open, and Hurbnurr emerged. He was holding one of the new steel swords and greeted me with a grunt. His eyes glinted in the dim light from the torches that lined the pathway to the gates.

"Mmm, was just coming to find you!" he rumbled, his voice as coarse as gravel. I nodded, and his large hand gestured for me to follow him. "Me take you up. Quiet. Many still sleeping."

We moved through the twisting paths of the troll city, his heavy footsteps surprisingly soft on the stony ground. I couldn't help but admire the construction of the city again as we passed through it. It was carved straight from the mountain itself, the stone structures mixed with silver stone accents.

As we ascended, I could feel the gradient of the path increasing, and the air began to warm further. The guard led me through another set of gates, these smaller but heavily fortified, and out onto a rough-hewn path that zigzagged toward a light. The climb was steep and challenging, but the troll moved with a sure-footed grace that didn't match his massive size.

After a considerable climb, we reached a hole in the side of a large hill. It looked down on the swamplands below, the warm air blowing softly in my face.

I took a deep breath, filling my lungs with the cold, pure mountain air. Hurbnurr pointed to the north with his new sword. The landscape was bathed in the light of countless stars, apparently not quite morning yet.

"Shadowalker land," he said, his voice low. The horizon was filled with jagged mountains to our north, their peaks like the teeth of some colossal beast. Crickets chirped below us, filling in the sounds of the jungle swamps. More mountains shot up from the ground to the east to form one huge valley.

"Thank you," I said, my voice a whisper in the immense silence of the early morning. I took a moment to absorb the view, committing the lay of the land to memory. I knew that once we were down in the trees I had the chance to get turned around.

He nodded, his expression grave. He pointed to a crude map scratched into the cave wall. "We here. Werewolf here."

He pointed to a spot on the map, a small circle etched into the stone. His finger trailed along a winding path that led north towards another marked area. The second area was represented with jagged lines, reminiscent of a beast's maw, indicating the land of the Shadowalkers.

"You go through here, valley. Swamps. Dangerous, full of shadow and mean creatures," he grumbled, his finger tapping the path repeatedly. "They scout. They see you come. Make loud wolf noises. No good, everyone dead."

He moved his grubby fingers to the west. The route skirted around towering mountains, crossed over a blue line, most likely a river, and led straight into the enemy's lair from the rear.

"This way, better. Sneaky. Less Shadowalkers and monsters. But river fast, dangerous," he said with a hint of concern. "And dragons sometimes near."

I certainly didn't want to run into any dragons, especially after what we had done to them. And without my Tesla coils, I doubted we had a chance against even one of them.

I looked closely at the western route, noting the advantages of bypassing the main territories of the Shadowalkers. Approaching from the rear could indeed give us the element of surprise, but the river... it could be a challenge for our group.

"Do you have any way to cross the river?" I inquired, hoping the trolls might have a secret or two up their sleeves.

He scratched his chin for a moment, thinking, then nodded. "We have old bridges, but not strong. Need to be careful. Or... water mages can help?"

"Yes, we have several mages skilled with water. They might be able to help us control the flow, or even create a temporary path across." My mind was working a hundred miles an hour.

He nodded with understanding. "Good, good. This way, less fight, more surprise. But be quick. Shadowalkers have no scouts on that side of mountain, but if they see you, they know something coming. It lead to here."

He pointed to the edge of the mountain. It looked like a strategically great place to attack the city from. This was everything I could have hoped for.

"Thank you, Hurbnurr! You have been an enormous help." I held out my hand, and he clasped it, then turned to head back into the caves.

With the map and the troll's advice fresh in my mind, I returned to the group.

———

We gathered in a semi-circle, everyone's face illuminated by the glow of our mushroom lanterns. I described the map that was scratched on the cave wall and explained our plan of action, sharing the troll's advice. Everyone listened attentively.

Mara was at my side, her presence a calming beacon. "We can use the ice mages to help cross the river. They will practice on smaller streams to make sure we can make it across safely," I said, my voice carrying confidence.

The group murmured in agreement, their faces filled with determination. It felt good to have a solid plan in place. The element of surprise and our diverse set of skills would be our biggest assets, and this was the part that was keeping me up all night. But with the water mages assisting in crossing the river, and the other mages prepared for combat, we had a fighting chance.

We packed up our things and walked through the troll town. The massive figures of the trolls leaned over, their hands raised in warm farewell, their rough voices wishing us luck and victory.

The blue-skinned children peeked from behind their parent's legs, their eyes wide with curiosity and wonder at the Feka and human procession. It felt like walking through a forest of living ice, their bodies towering and solid, providing a sense of strength and stability. I couldn't help but smile at their goodwill and the unexpected friendship between our races.

We passed the rear gate that I had seen before, then the trolls left us at the last juncture, their large hands patting our backs with words of encouragement. They pointed us in the direction of the final path that would lead to the surface, even though I knew the way now.

And then we were on our own, navigating the narrowing tunnel until we finally emerged onto the surface of the rock face. The light of day was bright; more time passed than I would have liked. The sun tried to shine on the swamp below, but it seemed to absorb the light into its bleak, shadowy darkness.

We moved with heightened alertness, conscious of every sound in the vibrant wilderness surrounding us. The scent of pine and earth filled the air, a natural balm to the nervous anticipation that tingled through our group as we descended the cliff face.

I sent scouts sent ahead to ensure the path was clear as the mages prepared to wield their powers immediately, and warriors gripped their weapons with ready resolve. Each step was a step closer to the conflict, and it weighed on the group now, the fun from yesterday's troll encounter now officially worn off.

Ahead, the turbulent river that the trolls had described to us roared, its white-capped waves crashing against the rugged stones that lined its banks.

I had no clue how we were supposed to cross this thing and make it the six miles or so to the Shadowalkers lands.

But I had to figure it out. And quickly.

Chapter 40

Weather Forecast

THE COOL WIND TUGGED AT THE TATTERED EDGES OF THE scout's dark fur as he stood atop the city walls, eyes scanning the horizon. For the Shadowalker, this part of the wall was the least liked among his peers because it faced the treacherous mountains and the chilling river. But he had learned to appreciate the solitude it offered, away from the constant chatter and clamor of the city below.

However, today, there was an unsettling weight in the air. The winds whispered secrets they hadn't before, the distant trees seemed to be rustling with more than just the breeze, and the mountains, always majestic, felt oppressive. The sun was rising, the light showing early morning mist that rose lazily from the grassy plains at the foothills.

His eyes, accustomed to the dim lights and the deep shades of the night, flicked to a small disturbance in the terrain. Just for a moment, it looked like the top of a human head, an unfamiliar sight in these lands. But it was gone as quickly as it appeared, melting back into the earth.

The scout blinked, trying to dispel the oddity from his sight. *Could it be a trick of the light? An illusion from the weariness of the long shift?* He rubbed his eyes and took a deep breath, trying to push the feeling of unease to the back of his mind.

"They're working us too hard," he growled out, taking a moment to stretch his limbs. Maybe the weariness was playing tricks on his senses. Yet, a part of him, deep inside, tingled with an alertness he hadn't felt in years. As if to make him even more uncertain, he thought he felt some tremors below the wall. He planted his four paws firmly on the wall, looking around with wide eyes.

But no one had reacted in the settlement, so he decided to shake it off, reasoning with himself that he was just being overly cautious. But as he resumed his patrol, every shadow, every rustle, and every whisper of the wind made him more alert, his instincts telling him that the long quiet that had blanketed their city might soon be disrupted.

He just needed to get through the shift. Then it was someone else's problem.

Then, a new scent filled his nose. Something he had never smelled before. *What was that?* Something was definitely wrong. The scout paced, nose high in over the walls.

Curiosity piqued, the scout paused and took a long, deep inhale. The smell was odd, out of place in the familiar backdrop of earth, moss, and the damp coolness of the surrounding forest. This was... fresher, like an open field after a summer rain, combined with something metallic, like cold steel. *And maybe leather?*

He tried to place the scent in his vast memory of smells, but it eluded him. The Shadowalkers, for all their prowess, relied heavily on their sense of smell just as much as their sight and hearing. Each scent told a story, and this one was a mystery. He strained his ears, but heard nothing out of the ordinary.

Furrowing his brow, he tried to discern where the smell was coming from. The wind carried it from the direction of the mountains and the river. *Was it possible that someone had come from that direction?* The very thought sent a chill down his spine. That route was deemed inaccessible, especially from the river's side.

Deciding it was best to report this unfamiliar scent to his superiors, the scout returned to the city before the shift horn rang. He hoped that he was wrong, that it was just some natural occurrence he hadn't encountered before. But deep down, an alarming sense of dread began to root.

Rubbing my temples, I took a moment to gather myself amidst the elemental chaos, my eyes darting to the earth mage who was making his way toward me. He was muddy, with sweat streaming down his brow. He seemed drained, like he had poured every ounce of his energy into the task I gave him.

It had been a stressful few hours as we made our way down the last part of the river, crossing at certain points with ice and earth bridges as the rapids roared around us. My team was exhausted and needed to rest while I put the fire and water mages to work.

"Report, Eldrin," I called out, motioning for him to come over. I fired up my party interface to monitor everyone's mana usage.

Wiping the mud off his hands, he gave me a weary nod, "The inner walls have weak points, especially near the western gate. The rumbling did more than we hoped. I've created fissures deep enough to exploit. Making the quicksand there from that location should do it."

I nodded, thinking about the steam cannon I had brought. "Nice. What did you see?"

He took a moment to catch his breath, his eyes drifting to where our fire mages worked closely with the water mages. With synchronized movements, fireballs were being thrown into the water, sending thick clouds of steam into the air. The water mages, showing impressive skill, were bending and shaping these clouds, moving them strategically over the mountain pass toward the city. The ice mages waited for their turn, relaxing near the river.

The sight was mesmerizing. The steam clouds hung heavily, becoming a curtain that would soon envelop the city, obscuring their vision and dampening their senses.

"Guard patrols are still frequent, but their numbers seem... off. I couldn't spot many on the walls, which was surprising. I heard noises from the inner parts of the city, but not as many as I would have thought. If they're beasts of the night, maybe they're going to sleep."

I nodded. "They probably don't get attacked very often up here, if ever," I said, more to myself than anyone listening.

He sighed, looking toward the mages working on the clouds. "Whatever we're doing, we should do it fast. Those clouds won't last forever."

I agreed. "Once the clouds blanket the city, it will be game time."

Mara wiped some water from her brow. "They're doing good. It's getting pretty cloudy in here. We should be in for a show once the ice mages cool it."

"You ready? I need you to keep these guys in the right positions out there! I don't have any other way to communicate with everyone."

Mara nodded. "I'm ready. I can feel the presence of the monks. They're here, waiting for us. At least three spirits and a lot of mana."

I gave her a kiss and one last look. "Let's get our squads in position."

I clapped my hands together, trying to rally everyone's spirits. I jumped on a nearby ledge, and everyone looked up at me. "Alright, team, this is it. We have one shot at this, and we need to make it count. Let's get into position and wait for the signal. The moment those clouds cover Niridge, we strike."

Chapter 41

The Battle of Niridge

ANNOS RAISED HIS HAND, CATCHING THE GENTLE snowflakes, watching as they melted against the warmth of his skin. Snow, in this season? Impossible. It defied the natural order of things. Yet here it was, steadily accumulating on the ground, rooftops, and tree branches, painting the city in a shroud of white.

Around him, the city's inhabitants stirred, looking up in wonder, pointing to the sky. Pups ran out of their dens, barking and trying to catch the snowflakes with their tongues, their innocence undeterred by the oddity of the situation. But the adults exchanged glances, the unease evident in their eyes. Snow had just barely started topping the mountains this time of year...but down here? It was unheard of.

As more and more clouds formed overhead, the snowfall intensified. Soon, visibility decreased, making it harder to see even a few feet ahead. Annos moved quickly, barking orders to his subordinates. "Light the torches along the walls. Ensure the pathways remain clear. And get me every soldier we have. I think we're under attack."

That blasted human lied to me, the alpha thought with an angry growl. *They knew!*

791

He thought back to what that scout had said, and worry began coiling around his mind like a snake. As the city scrambled to adapt to this sudden change, Annos's instincts screamed at him. In all of his time at Niridge, no one had dared attack them. The walls were up to keep out the beasts of the forest, not to keep an enemy out.

But if mages were attacking him...his thoughts turned bleakly to that cursed human from Dunbar. *Had he made the trip through the swamps to come find him? How?!? He had hunting parties everywhere! There was no way he would have made it past them.*

The winds started really whipping now as the storm grew in severity, and the Shadowalkers inside the city began taking shelter. Many were heading to sleep as it was.

From every corner of the city, the howling wind carried a clamor of sounds: doors slamming shut, windows being boarded, and the distant cries of those caught off guard. Stiff, cold winds were common around here, so the residents of the city knew what to do. But they were still surprising at this time of year.

The streets quickly emptied as everyone sought refuge from the increasingly intense snowstorm.

Shadowalker merchants frantically pulled down their shop awnings, trying to salvage what goods they could. Parents clutched their pups close, hurrying them inside dens. Guards on patrol scrambled for cover, their usual composed demeanor replaced with alarm.

From his vantage point atop the city's central tower, Annos watched as the town transformed before him. The streets were now blanketed in a thick layer of white, only the glow of lanterns and torches providing some semblance of warmth against the cold backdrop.

His beta rushed up beside him, looking up at the ongoing blizzard. "Sire, what's happening?"

The realization hit him like a cold slap to the face. The defenses, the guards, the walls – all of it would mean nothing if everyone was off hiding in their dens.

"This is a trap! We need to prepare for a siege!" he barked, feeling the urgency build. The city was in danger, and it was up to him to lead them through this literal and metaphorical storm.

———

From my vantage point on the rocky outcrop, the Shadowalker city below appeared surreal, almost like a shadowy snow globe. The heavy clouds, fed by our water mages, hung like a shroud over the city, and snow began to blanket the world below as the ice mages got involved in cooling the air.

From our experimentation and talking to my ancestors, they believed that a spell was one thing, but the actual work of controlling the element you had an affinity for was another, just like I could control ore bodies by sucking them out of the wall or morph ingredients into weapons. I was controlling my affinity for creation.

That small piece of information changed everything for me.

I felt my anticipation bubble over as I turned to the air mages. "Let's give them a light show they won't forget," I said, watching as their eyes closed in deep concentration and wands directed lightning into the sky to join the heavy snow clouds.

A few bolts missed the clouds and shot off into the darkened sky, since the mage-created storm was moving further and further away.

Crackling sounds echoed in the air, building the tension. From what I could make out in the flashes of lightning, I saw the alpha werewolf atop a tower. I could imagine the rage and desperation in his eyes as I saw him roar an order, pointing in our direction before the snow blocked him out entirely.

To my side, one of the earth mages nudged me, "Once the light-ning does its job, we're ready to move everyone out."

I only nodded, my focus on the scene below. When the first bolt of lightning struck, it was blinding. The city below lit up, with walls, towers, and streets eerily illuminated by the successive bolts that followed. Each crash of thunder reverberated through my chest, and I could see small fires breaking out where lightning struck wood. The snow, combined with the sudden assault, sowed confusion amongst the Shadowalkers.

"Move onto phase two! Let's go, everyone!" I screamed as the entire army took off running down the embankment. I stayed and watched from here with Mara as the Feka took off, roaring and sprinting through the trees on all fours as their swords bounced on their backs with the mages right behind them.

Liza and the other earth mage ran in front of my human army, clearing a path through the foliage as they ran. Pretty soon, they disappeared into the jungle.

Back in Niridge, the storm had taken on a mind of its own, with lightning blasting down by its own free will. Smoke billowed out here and there as structures caught on fire, but most likely couldn't catch and just smoldered from the dense snow. We heard more barking and howling as lightning continued thrashing wildly from the supercharged clouds.

"Mara, tell Kyle to add more lightning. We need more attacking power. Then, head to Jasper. He's going to need to get up to a tree or something with his Tinder mages and launch fireballs down into the city," I yelled to Mara over the booming thunder.

"I know, I know!" Mara yelled back, closing her eyes.

The gate opened as troops began pouring out of the city in our general direction. There was about one hundred feet of clear land before the jungle, similar to how Dunbar was set up. The Shadowalkers melee troops, a group of the pitbull creatures and the hairless dogs, were covered in snow, their dark fur splotched with white, making them look oddly spectral against the stormy backdrop. But even with their hindrances, their movements were fast and deliberate.

I looked at the amount of troops still remaining and realized that a frontal assault would be catastrophic for my small army. We needed to thin their numbers and divert their focus.

"Jasper and his team are in position. They're ready," Mara said. "And the mana from the monks is going to start flowing to keep our mages topped up! Not sure how long that will last, though!"

I nodded, watching eagerly as the fire started raining down on the city and the dogs that stood outside the walls.

The Shadowalkers, though strong and fast, were caught off-guard by the combined elements. Fire danced around them, sending steam up into the sky and sending them yelping away or catching ablaze. And every time they tried to regroup or push forward, another torrent of flames sent them scattering. The sound of the fire, combined with the booming thunder and the muffled screams of the city occupants, was almost deafening.

"We have to keep up the pressure!" I stated, watching as the melee Feka joined the battle.

With the aid of the monks, our mages looked invigorated. Their spells were more potent, and more lightning and fire joined the battle. At this point, lightning was flying everywhere from the blizzard clouds, blowing up structures throughout the city.

"Begin phase three!" I yelled as Mara nodded, then closed her eyes, communicating with the squadron leaders. More Shadowalkers escaped the death trap of a city, fleeing the walls. I took off running down the hill to join my troops since the last of the plan was in motion. I wanted to join my friends in this battle to see this to the end.

I watched the final series of coordinated movements begin before I disappeared into the trees. The water mages summoned torrents of water with their wands, directing it to the ground in front of the city gates, where the three earth mages quickly fashioned channels and trenches. Within moments, the land between our army and the city became a muddled quagmire, impeding the Shadowalkers' movement and rendering their lightning speed ineffective.

The Zephyrs amplified the force of the storm, directing the fierce gales towards the city. The wind carried the fire from Jasper's mages, turning it into a searing, heated tempest that singed and disoriented the enemy with smoke. Fire tornados kicked up, fierce funnel clouds of pure destruction as they churned through the canine troops.

A group of stealth Fekan hunters I had reserved for this very moment, including Dee, emerged from our left flank, moving quickly and silently. Their aim was to infiltrate the rear of the city and create internal havoc, cutting off any reinforcements or escape routes.

And through all of that, I ran. I ran faster than I had ever run before. I heard Mara's voice echoing in my mind as she sent me a telepathic message.

You've got this. I love you. We have them all confused, and they haven't been able to group up and attack yet!

I smiled and kept going, my pickaxe swinging back and forth on my back. The sound of battle reached my ears, and I heard a howl. It was long and guttural, piercing through my brain and causing me to stop in my tracks. I felt fear unlike anything I had ever experienced before. More howls called out over the thunder, seemingly answering the alpha's call.

Shaking off the initial paralysis, I refocused, calling on every bit of training I had received with Dee and the bond I shared with Mara. Each step became more determined as I pushed forward, breaking through the treeline and into the fight, my pickaxe glowing with an ethereal light. It was made to fight the darkness, and the weapon knew it.

The world around me was a blur. All I could focus on was finding Annos, the alpha werewolf. I needed to end this, not just for Dunbar, but for everyone threatened by the Shadowalker existence. While I knew we had them scattered and broken right now, it wouldn't take much for them to regroup and take out the couple hundred of us.

I finally saw him, engaged in combat with several of our best warriors; his swift movements were barely perceptible. The Feka fought back, but I could tell he was burning through whatever strength propelled him. He swiped a few Feka to the side, and they lay there, unmoving.

Even though he was a better fighter than me, there was no moon to fuel his fighting this time. This was my chance. I needed to strike before he regained his stamina.

With a roar, I charged at him, pickaxe raised. As I neared him, our eyes locked, and I could sense his surprise. From behind me, Zephyrs joined me, four of them running alongside, their wind pushing me forward. More lightning struck what was left of Niridge behind me.

The alpha had murder in his dark eyes as he charged us. He raised his paw and swung at me with all his might, but it was like it happened in slow motion as the wind blew around me. My pickaxe met his powerful claws, silver against dark matter, creating sparks and shearing off a few of his claws. He howled in pain and we circled each other, looking for an opening.

He held back, striking at me again as his Stalker generals joined the fight with my Zephyrs. They had sensed their alpha's danger and had come to his aid. Fireballs rained down on the back lines near their walls, killing more troops. My party interface showed mana depleted across my mages even with the help from the monks..

More dogs rushed in around me as my people fought and died, and elemental attacks continued. I needed to finish this and quickly. I was running out of Zephyrs and Feka to defend us.

The mana from the monks ran out! Mara's voice called in my mind, alerting me to what I already knew.

I channeled all my energy and lunged again at a beast I had no business fighting. The snowy, wet ground beneath us cracked and shifted, but neither of us paid it any mind. Annos swung with an unmatched speed and power. I dodged to the left, narrowly missing his claws which grazed the side of my armor, leaving deep scratches.

My pickaxe found its mark several times, but the alpha was built tough. Each blow was met with a guttural growl and a retaliatory strike that was even more ferocious. The silver at the tip of my pickaxe sizzled against his hide, but he seemed to shrug off the pain.

And so, we danced, matching each other's movements. Every time I thought I had him, he would counter, his claws coming within inches of my face. The taste of blood filled my mouth as a stray swipe caught my cheek. Pain flared, but I used it, fueling my determination. I didn't even bother looking at my health bar, but I knew it was working hard to keep me alive.

Drawing upon the last of my strength, I baited him into a lunge, swinging my pickaxe down in a vertical arc. At the last possible second, I sidestepped, and the silver-tipped pickaxe embedded itself deep into Annos's shoulder. He howled in pain, a deep, agonizing sound that echoed throughout the snowy landscape.

But I didn't let up. I swung again, aiming for his legs, trying to knock him off balance. Annos, though in pain, was not defeated. He swiped at me, catching my side and sending me sprawling.

The world spun. For a moment, I thought I was done for. But as Annos loomed over me, preparing for the final blow, my hand grasped the handle of my pickaxe one last time. With a desperate heave, I thrust it upward, piercing the underside of Annos's jaw. The silver glowed bright, and a flash of energy surged through the weapon, as if absorbing the darkness.

The alpha werewolf's eyes widened in shock and pain. He staggered backward, taking the pickaxe with him. as the weapon protruded gruesomely from beneath his chin. With his immense strength, he tried to pull the pickaxe free, his claws scraping at the handle, but the silver seemed to paralyze him further with every touch.

Black blood oozed down his chin as his hands feebly tried to grasp the pickaxe handle. His legs faltered, and he went down on one knee, gasping for air.

Around us, the battle seemed to slow. Both sides took notice of their respective leader's engagement, and for a brief moment, there was a pause in the chaos. I slowly rose to my feet, clutching my side where Annos had landed a blow, feeling the warmth of my blood against my fingers.

The giant werewolf's gaze locked onto mine, his eyes showing rage, pain, and, surprisingly, respect. His deep black eyes, which once held the ferocity of a wild animal, now reflected a hint of sadness and acceptance.

With a final, struggling effort, Annos tried to pull the pickaxe out, but the strength had left him. He let out a raspy, labored breath and crumpled to the snowy ground, the darkness in his eyes dimming.

Chapter 42

A New World Order

My boots splashed in the still snowy settlement as I walked around inside the walls, observing the strange canine architecture as my warriors rounded up the Shadowalkers who hadn't fled into the woods. The city, built with a mix of rough-hewn stone and carved wood, had an organic flow to its design. Buildings seemed to grow out of the ground, with their walls flowing with the rolling hills that made up the landscape this far north.

Dee came and found me, asking if I was okay. I told her that I was, and asked how she was doing. She was rounding up any last stragglers with the other hunters that I had sent around the back of the settlement before the attack. I let her run back off and join her fellow hunters as I continued my stroll.

In the heart of the city stood a large, intimidating structure that I assumed was the main hall or perhaps the residence of the alpha. It was grander and more elaborately decorated than the surrounding buildings, with intricate carvings depicting battles, hunts, and what I assumed were legendary tales of the Shadowalkers.

I occasionally spotted small tokens and talismans hanging from doorways or staked into the ground. They seemed to be wards or charms, possibly for protection or good luck. Their designs varied, but most contained symbols of the moon and stars, hinting at a deep connection to the night and celestial bodies. Many were made from a bright white stone that I couldn't place, but I felt power radiating from the items.

Some of the Shadowalkers, young pups mostly, watched us warily from a distance, reminding me of dogs from Earth looking at something with a tilted head and a floppy ear. It struck me how different their world must have been just days ago. They were creatures of the night, rulers of their domain, and in a blink, their world had been turned upside down.

A soft whimper drew my attention to a young Shadowalker pup, separated from its family, hiding behind a barrel. Its fur was matted with snow and mud, and its eyes darted around, looking for a way to escape. It was missing an ear and blood flowed freely down its furry face.

Crouching down slowly, I tried to offer a reassuring smile. "It's okay. We won't hurt you," I murmured softly, reaching into my pocket to pull out a piece of dried meat.

A few Stalker generals came around the corner, held firmly by Fekan warriors. The hatred in their eyes snapped me back to reality. But I couldn't help looking back into those sad eyes and feeling remorse for killing these creatures.

I realized there was more to do than just secure the city. We needed to heal, rebuild trust, and find a way to coexist. This wasn't just a victory for us, but an opportunity to foster a new beginning for both our races.

All around me, a darkness pulled at me. It felt like I was standing near the void box or something.

I watched as the generals were marched into an open courtyard area. The proud and fierce expressions on their faces belied their captured status. The animosity in their eyes was unmistakable. They were warriors who had fought for their people and city, and now, they had been defeated.

For a moment, I locked eyes with one of the generals; a tall, sleek, black-furred Shadowalker with scars marring his snout. In his gaze, I saw a deep, seething rage but also a hint of acknowledgment. He was one of the Stalkers that I had seen back from when Dee and I were attacked all those long months ago.

We have to find a way to make amends, I thought grimly. Once again, I found myself outside of my comfort zone.

"Let me go," the Shadowalker growled, squirming under the grips of the Feka. "I wish to speak to your warlord."

The Feka looked at me, and I nodded. The Feka warriors released the Shadowalker, who cautiously straightened up but did not immediately move towards me. There was a wariness in his eyes that he couldn't shake off.

"You have defeated us," he began, his voice resonant and carrying a heavy weight as he addressed the group of us. "But we do not wish for our kind to be exterminated. We are a proud race, and even in defeat, we hold our heads high."

I looked at him, noting the deep-set pride that blazed in his eyes. Fires continued blazing behind him, and a structure collapsed nearby.

"I have no intention of exterminating your kind," I replied. "War is a brutal thing, and decisions made in the heat of battle are not always the right ones. But now that the battle is over, we must find a way to coexist."

The Shadowalker seemed taken aback by my words. "You would not enslave us?"

Why is it always about servitude and slavery with these creatures on Prixa?

"No," I said firmly. "But there needs to be a new order, a way for us to coexist without constant threats and warfare. Your city will be protected, and your people will not be harmed as long as there is no further threat from the Shadowalkers."

He looked thoughtful for a moment. "We need to rebuild. We are running out of jungle space and food is an issue for us. That's why we have attacked your people. Plus, our city has been damaged, and our people are scared. We need assurance that we will not be attacked again."

"And you will have that assurance," I said. "I will figure out a way to feed your pack. In return, I ask for peace. A lasting peace between our people."

The Shadowalker nodded slowly. "It will take time. Time for wounds to heal, for trust to be rebuilt. But perhaps it is a start."

I extended my hand towards him. "A start is all we need. My name is Noah. And yours?"

He looked at my hand in fear, almost like it would cast more magic at him. I smiled, my expression soft toward the creature.

The Stalker took a long moment, looking between his people and my hand. But I held it there, unmoving. Finally, he sighed. "My name is Rhykar, and I am the beta of this city. The title of alpha has always been one of leadership. With the fall of our leader, you have inadvertently taken that mantle. Whether by fate or by force, you are the alpha of the Shadowalkers now."

My head jerked back at that, startled. The responsibility, the weight of it all, was something I hadn't expected. But I saw the respect and the plea in Rhykar's eyes. He wasn't asking me to become one of them, but to guide them, to give them a chance at peace and prosperity.

"We will help rebuild," I promised him. "And together, we can forge a new path, one where both our people can coexist harmoniously."

The werewolf stared at me as if assessing my words. No one moved for a long moment.

Finally, he started howling into the cloudy sky, a long, slow howl. It was joined by the other Stalkers, then other dogs in the settlement. I watched as the sound carried outwards, echoing off the mountains and resonating off the walls in a haunting harmony. Each howl seemed to carry with it the acceptance of its people.

The Feka warriors, and even my own human comrades, looked around, many in confusion, some with wonder. The symphony of howls was unlike anything any of us had ever heard. It was as if the very soul of the Shadowalkers was being laid bare, a collective release of emotions that had been pent up for too long.

Mara walked up next to me, grabbing my hand. The howling began to die down, the final echoes fading away, leaving behind a stillness that seemed almost sacred. I felt the weight of countless eyes on me, watching, waiting, and hoping. The burden of leadership, the mantle of the alpha, lay heavy on my shoulders.

"Then accept this gift, Alpha Noah. Take what has been rightfully won in battle."

He walked over to my side as the Feka bristled, but I held up my hand. He knelt and picked up a large wolf head that sat on the ground. It was the alpha. "May it bring us prosperity in the moons to come."

I walked over and accepted the head, inspecting it quickly.

[ALPHA WEREWOLF HEAD - LEVEL 15 INGREDIENT]

Epilogue

Five years later

I INSPECTED THE BOAT, MARVELING AT ITS SLEEK DESIGN and sturdy construction. The flag of Dunbar was painted on its sides - a pickaxe and a flame, signifying the union of mining and magic that had transformed our city over the past decade. But now, the emblem had an additional symbol - a silhouette of a howling Shadowalker.

I had finally passed the level 20 wall in 'MANUFACTURING' and was able to pick a subclass. I chose 'TRADE' and all kinds of designs for ships, carts, and air vehicles opened up, with their costs and stats all listed. It was an incredible opportunity for me to expand my reach and trade partners. I was level 18 in engineering and couldn't wait to see what I could choose for a subclass in that field. I hoped it was something to do with mining. I really enjoyed spending time in the ever-expanding mines of Dunbar.

Dunbar had not only flourished but had become a beacon of unity and progress. The integration of the Shadowalkers into our society had brought about remarkable advancements, as had the expanded trade between my city and Fayport. The Shadowalkers taught us new techniques in hunting, stealth, and survival while we introduced them to the wonders of agriculture, engineering, and trade.

We even had a fledgling academy, where the residents from Fayport and Dunbar could study engineering, trade, and all kinds of useful things. But the Feka had never believed in writing their knowledge down, so it was going to be an uphill battle. But the academy was a promising start.

I had not heard from the Overlord in a long time, and any scrying we tried to do, even as Mara advanced her levels, was met with a blockade from their mages. She even tried to see what was to the southwest of them beyond Fulgar, but the whole area was shrouded from our view for some reason.

But they seemed to leave us alone now, and the fogs of their power had left our cities. Mara could use her powers freely now, even without the scrying device.

But with his silence came a sense of dread. I had no idea what he was up to down there, and hoped I wouldn't find out for some time. Darkness still followed her everywhere she went, and she tried explaining the shadows that lurked in the world's astral planes.

I looked down at my newly formed necklace, **Alpha's Crest**. I finally used the level 15 head to make the amulet under the full moon. I could call on the necklace once per full moon and summon the spectral werewolf to fight alongside me. I felt it was a fitting memory to the alpha.

I had given the other high level ingredients to Fayport as a token of goodwill, so to speak. Romas had moved into Fayport full time now and was helping implement some of the things he had learned while with me. When he left, he told me to take good care of his anvil, which I of course promised I would. He told me it was his gift to me for how I was treated before, which was unnecessary, but I appreciated nonetheless.

Children ran along the docks, their laughter echoing in the air. Among them were a few Shadowalker pups and small Feka, playing together without a care in the world. The generations that followed would only know the stories of the great battle and not the prejudices that had led up to it. One of the kids hit another with a bolt of lighting, scorching the other boy's garment.

"Hey! No magic!" Kyle said, chasing the little boy down the dock as the dogs barked enthusiastically. I had started seeing more and more of the canines come down here, even though most of the other Shadowalkers liked the colder northern climate.

Mara approached, her hair now streaked with strands of silver from her advanced levels. Holding her hand was a little girl, our daughter, who had her mother's fiery spirit and my stubborn determination. The three-year-old looked up at the boat with wide-eyed wonder.

"Well, well," Mara said, her voice filled with pride. "The first trade vessel to set sail towards the Trial Moon."

One of the air mages fired up the bottom cylinders and the boat hovered a few inches off the water. Cheers broke out among the dockworkers before it splashed back into the water.

I nodded, wrapping an arm around her waist. "We've come a long way, haven't we?"

She leaned into me. "Yes, we have. And there's still so much more to explore and learn."

Our daughter tugged at Mara's hand, pointing excitedly at the boat. "Can we go on it, Mama?"

Mara chuckled, "Maybe one day, little one. Let father get the kinks out first." She winked at me as I laughed.

"Go play with Owen and Caleb," I said, pointing to Jasper's sons. Jamie waved at me, then gave me a thumbs up at the boat. I smiled as Bria ran over, giggles sounding through the dock's noise.

"I have a surprise for our wedding anniversary," Mara whispered in my ear, a mischievous grin spreading on her face.

"Wait, I thought we weren't doing gifts??" I said, raising my hand to my mouth in mock horror as she punched me playfully in the arm.

"I haven't told you, but I've turned level 10 in Astral projection. And you know what that means!"

I rolled my eyes. "I could check with my skill, but how about I just let you tell me."

"It means the skill has been upgraded. And the new skill is called "Celestial Projection."

I looked at her, confused. "Wait, what does it do?"

The humor dropped from her expression. "I can bring you with me. I've done the calculations, and with the help from the Trial Moon, we can go see your mother. All three of us. She can meet her granddaughter. You can finally tell her you're okay."

"My..." A lump formed in my throat, memories of my mother flooding back. The thought of seeing her again was overwhelming. My eyes darted to our daughter, playing with the two boys and some Shadowalker pups nearby, her laughter echoing with pure joy. The thought of her meeting my mother, even in the celestial realm...

I swallowed hard, trying to find the right words. "Are... are you sure? How does that even work?"

Mara took a deep breath. "I've been practicing my projections with the abbot of Trial Moon. But when I leveled up, the monks explained it. With Celestial Projection, we can find her together. They can guide us. They said your soul has an odd marker on it that will match the people of your planet. But your soul will match hers. I can find her, Noah. Like the mages in Fulgar found you when they brought you here."

That mage. Voice lady. She spoke to me through my headphones all those years ago. I've never met her!

Our daughter ran up to us, her eyes filled with excitement. "Mama, can we do the star thingy now?"

I scoffed. "Oh, so she already knew about this?"

Mara knelt down, brushing a strand of hair behind our daughter's ear. "Soon, love. Let's go home first."

As we returned to our house, I couldn't help but wonder about the experience. Seeing my mother again, after all these years, felt like a dream. A chance to introduce her to her granddaughter, to tell her about all the adventures and challenges we had faced, was a gift beyond any I could have imagined.

That night, as the stars twinkled overhead, Mara began the process. She chanted and swayed, her hands weaving intricate patterns in the air. Our daughter and I sat cross-legged opposite her, waiting. The smell of mana filled around me as the world around us started to blur and shimmer, and then, in the blink of an eye, we were somewhere else.

[*Take my hand,*] Mara said in my mind.

My daughter, the fearless warrior she was, giggled, the sound echoing around in the cosmic space.

A vast, shimmering expanse stretched out in every direction. Stars, galaxies, and nebulae surrounded us, creating a breathtaking tapestry of lights and colors.

I felt another power surge as the astral mages filled Mara with energy, and we sped off. We seemed to zoom through the darkness for a long time until, finally, I saw it.

I saw my old planet. It sat in front of me, just like I remembered it. Mara concentrated further; then we sped down to the surface. I saw the United States, then New York, then the boroughs.

Finally, we landed in the streets of Brooklyn. It felt like a dream, or more accurately, a memory. The place looked exactly how I remembered it, from the old brick buildings to the street vendors selling hot dogs and pretzels. People bustled around, caught up in the rhythms of city life, seemingly unaware of our ethereal presence.

Mara looked at me, curiosity shining in her eyes. [*Is this it? Your old home? It looks so strange!*]

I nodded, suddenly overwhelmed by a rush of memories. The fire hydrant where my friends and I would cool off during sweltering summers, the bodega on the corner where I'd buy candy after school, and the graffiti-tagged walls that had the same swear words on them.

Tears formed in my eyes. *I never thought I'd see this place again,* I thought, taking in the familiar sounds of car horns, distant music, and children laughing. We were like ghosts, watching things unfold. Without the interference of magic, there was no haze, like when Mara traveled on Prixa.

Mara held my spectral hand. [*Just remember, this is a visit, a glimpse. We can't stay for long. My mana is starting to get low, even with the help we're getting.*]

[*I know,*] I said.

We blinked, and suddenly, we were inside the apartment. My apartment. My mother sat at the table, scribbling in a crossword puzzle. On her lap sat Dingo, the fat lard himself. He looked old and grey, a relaxed look on his face. Suddenly, he felt the disturbance and shot off my mother's lap, hissing on the table. I heard a pitbull barking in the distance.

"Dingo!!" My mother looked up, startled by the cat. "What's gotten into you, old boy?" she murmured, reaching out to calm him.

Mara slowly reached out, gently cradling my mother's face. She gasped, feeling the bond. She looked around, her eyes wild. Her pupils turned a bright silver, and she looked at me.

Confusion crossed her features, then tears welled up in her eyes, making them shine even brighter with the reflected silver.

[*Noah?*] she whispered, her voice trembling through our connection.

[*It's me, Mom,*] I replied, feeling a lump in my throat. [*I've missed you.*]

She stood up slowly, reaching out to touch my face. [*What is this? How is this possible?*] she asked, looking between me and Mara.

[*It's a long story,*] I chuckled.

I watched as my mother's eyes roamed over my form, taking in the man I had become in such a short time. She looked at Mara, then at my daughter, whose astral form hid behind my leg shyly. [*I don't understand. Is this...?*]

[*Mother, I would like you to meet Mara. My wife. She's the one who is doing this. I'm on another world right now. And this is our daughter,*] I said, my voice breaking. [*Your granddaughter, Bria.*]

A sob escaped her lips, and she touched the child's astral cheek. [*She's beautiful,*] she whispered, tears streaming down her face. [*Is this real?*]

We spent the next few minutes talking, laughing, crying, and catching up. All the while, Dingo kept meowing and circling us, somehow knowing we were there. I kept my stories short, but explained how I was taken to Prixa, about the Feka, and the world of magic.

I didn't know if she believed that this was anything other than a dream. But it was better than nothing.

Mara didn't speak. She just watched the whole thing with a happy yet strained expression. Tears were streaming down her face.

[*Time's up,*] she said. [*I'm sorry, but we have to go. It was great meeting you!*]

I looked at my mother one last time. [*I love you, Mom,*] I whispered.

She sobbed. [*I love you too, baby.*]

With a final wave, Mara cut off the connection, leaving my old home behind and returning me to Prixa.

END OF BOOK 3

About the Author

With a background in mining engineering, Matt brings a unique perspective to his writing, infusing his work with a blend of technical expertise and imaginative storytelling. Matt's goal is to take complex feats of engineering in our world and transport them into his fantasy stories. He loves LitRPG, but does not believe that normal, everyday people would become overpowered mega-characters and believes in slow, steady character growth. Beyond his writing endeavors, Matt is a loving husband and father of three children. Additionally, Matt shares his home with a mischievous feline companion named Sergio, whose playful antics often provided inspiration for his story.

About the Publisher

Royal Guard Publishing was established in 2020 and is audiobook & ebook publisher ran by authors.

We primarily focus on LitRPG, GameLit, Progression Fantasy, Harem Lit and Cultivation Fantasy.

We hope to provide an escape and adventure for our listeners and readers.

We aim to provide a more authentic, transparent and personal experience for our authors.

We are always happy to hear from you!

Website- https://royalguardpublishing.com/

Facebook- https://www.facebook.com/RoyalGuard2020

Email - publisher@royalguardpublishing.com

TikTok- https://www.tiktok.com/@royalguardpublishing

Reddit- https://www.reddit.com/user/RoyalGuard2020

Insta- https://www.instagram.com/royalguardpublishing/

Email - publisher@royalguardpublishing.com

For more LitRPG check out the following:

https://www.facebook.com/groups/LitRPG.books

https://www.facebook.com/groups/litrpgforum

https://www.facebook.com/groups/LitRPGReleases

https://www.reddit.com/r/litrpg/

https://www.facebook.com/groups/LitRPGsociety

Made in United States
Orlando, FL
14 December 2024

55599345R00447